KNOT *all* IS RUINED

INTERNATIONAL Bestselling Author
ELIZABETH KNIGHT

Knight, Elizabeth
Knot All Is Ruined: Complete Duet
Editing: Swish Editing & Design
Cover artist: Emily Wittig Designs
Formatting: Creative Wonder Publishing

Dear Readers,
Knot All Is Ruined is a book that contains subject matter that could be triggering to some people. If you feel like this could be a problem for you, please protect yourself. No work of fiction is worth your mental health.
The full detailed list of content warnings is available on my website.
https://geni.us/omegaverseCW

Contents

CHAPTER 1
Danella

They told us we'd be helping our country, that through our efforts we'd be preventing war. It was all one big fucking lie. A lie we believed—until it was too late, and our fates were sealed.

The quiet sheltered lives we Omegas had been living in the Care Centers left us woefully unprepared for what was about to come. I'd been taken to the center when I was seventeen, which was older than most. My family held a prominent place in our society and tried everything they could to keep me at home. My mother had been unwilling to hand me over to the government for them to handle my education. They somehow managed to hold them off for a year, but that ended the day a black van showed up with soldiers to escort me to the Care Center.

It was clear they didn't give a shit about whether or not I wanted to join them. Causing my mother to collapse in the entryway of our home, unable to bear the shock of it all. My mother's heart had never been strong, and it almost killed her to have me. She used to tell me that what kept her going was the fact she refused to leave me motherless. In fact, she called me her ray of sunshine, a reason to live and fight day after day. Seeing her like that, I tried to go to her, but the soldiers used the chaos to snatch me up and hauled me out to the van. Screaming and thrashing in their grasp, I tried to get back to my mother—but it was no use.

Once in the van, a Care Center attendant drugged me, muttering that everything would be just fine. To this day, I still have no idea if my mother is alive because once we enter the Center, we're cut off from everything involving the outside world. For our well-being, of course—what a load of bullshit. Due to my charming attitude upon arrival, I was kept in isolation for a week as they performed their medical tests on me.

The Care Center's purpose and reason for why we were sent here was to ensure that any women born with the designation of Omega were healthy and fit to bear children for the pack they were to be matched to. Our world revolved around a person's designation, meaning you were either an Alpha, Beta, or Omega. Alphas are men and women who have a built-in sense of leadership and command of others. They're at the top of the food chain and are those who become CEOs, world leaders, high-powered lawyers, and anything that gives them the fulfillment of leading others. Betas make the world turn. Without them being the worker bees who do the bulk of the lifting, nothing would get done. They also happen to make up the majority of our population. It's also customary for people to gather into family units or packs, as many refer to them.

While some might choose only to have a single partner, it's much more likely to have a community mindset. Many packs are polyamorous, meaning they are in relationships with each other emotionally and physically. While other packs are formed with a group of people who find combining their lives and resources advantageous for advancement in social status or business. Things nowadays are more strategic when building a pack since Omegas have become scarcer. An Omega is a female who is the center of a pack, and a deep emotional bond can be created through them. When the Alpha members of the pack bond with the Omega, a connection is formed unlike anything you can have in a standard partnership, which makes them so desirable.

Once upon a time, there used to be a plentiful amount of Omegas. Only after a terrorist attack by a group of Betas called

Equality for Betas, or EQ, a whole generation of mothers and babies were killed due to tainting a drug that helped to manipulate the chances of a baby being an Omega to a higher percentage. Compound this with the fact that an Alpha must be the mother or the father of the child if there's a chance it will be born an Omega. This is why Omegas are considered rare, and when an Omega is partnered with an Alpha, the possibility of it being an Omega offspring is far greater.

After the attack, the government overreacted and started these facilities called Care Centers. Anyone who presented as an Omega at sixteen must be surrendered to the Center. Through the Center, the Omega would be paired with a pack that met the proper qualifications needed. Those being: financially stable, a secure home, and having private security to protect their Omega. With the current economic decline, packs found it increasingly harder to meet these rigorous standards to the government's satisfaction. This was when they began the Omega Goodwill Program.

Those picked for the OGP would be sent to one of the neighboring countries in an effort to support their population crisis. Seems that in our world, Oscad—my home country, one of the three most powerful nations, has the largest population of Omegas. Four times a year, they would send at least ten Omegas to either Asturg to the west or Shearia to the East. Each time they claimed there was a random selection, but I didn't think it was that random. There always seemed to be a particular type of Omega that just so happened to be picked for Shearia. Those who ended up being sent to Asturg weren't desirable in looks or education. Many also had stubborn dispositions.

This is how I ended up being drugged one night and waking up to find myself on a bus crossing over the border to Asturg.

"What the fuck," I blurted as I looked out the window watching the border guards wave the bus through the break in the massive metal wall with the Asturg flag painted on it.

In our time at the Center, a large part of our education was learning about the different countries and our own. They ensured we were well versed in things that would be common for an Omega to know in Shearia as well as Asturg. We knew there was a chance we could be sent to either of these countries if we didn't get picked for a pack in Oscad. Over the four and a half years I was at the Center, only three Omegas were paired with local packs while the rest of us bided our time.

Now here I was, being shipped off to one of the worst war-torn countries that have ever existed. Asturg was an enormous country that was divided into two sections. North Asturg was controlled by General Rasvan, who in my personal opinion, was deemed a ruthless tyrant who didn't care about anything but winning. Of course, that sort of talk and free thinking was not welcome in the Care Center. No, General Rasvan was a prominent leader who did what he thought was best for his people with the situation handed down to him.

As for the Southern leader, President Dragomire, there wasn't much known about him, for sure. He was reclusive, but his military was better equipped and educated in warfare. They also had a far smaller population than the North. This meant they had to use their skill with tactics instead of throwing bodies into battle as the North did. Which is why the Northern country, as a whole, needed us Omegas to help produce more children for them to raise, train, and lose to this pointless war.

Women were looked at as nothing more than breeding stock or cannon fodder for the enemy. Betas were given a choice to either become a breeder in one of the breeding houses or become a soldier. Omegas were not given that choice since we either produced another Omega or an Alpha. Both were valuable to them in their own way, but the whole concept made me sick.

Shifting in my seat, I found Violet's blonde head slumped against me, still knocked out from the drug. My heart broke at the thought they chose this sweet, gentle Omega to be sent here just because she was born with a cleft lip. The damn thing had been repaired as a baby, leaving her with a less traditional appearance. These bastards decided it was better to send her to a country that wouldn't care what she looked like as long as she could pop out babies. Violet was quiet, smart, and had just turned twenty a month ago. Sending her to Asturg was a death sentence in the making.

Looking at the other seats, I realized there were more of us than usual. This bus was almost full when the last few groups sent off were of about ten women. I was betting there were at least thirty of us this time around, and this trip was earlier than it should've been. The last busload was sent off only two months ago to Shearia. Scanning the faces, I knew every single one of these women. Some had only arrived a few weeks ago, barely getting any of the promised education. Typically, they waited until we were at least twenty-one to send us. Then my gaze landed on Tori, the youngest girl in the Care Center at seventeen.

What the fuck was she doing here?

Carefully I maneuvered Violet so I could get up and move her over so she rested against the wall of the bus. Carefully I made my way as the bus was moving along at a relatively quick pace down a road that was apparently riddled with potholes. This made my journey challenging as it bounced and rattled trying to knock me off my feet. Finally, I made it to Tori and crouched beside her seat.

Why was I the only one awake?

Granted, this wasn't the first time I'd been drugged into being more manageable, though it hadn't been that many times I was getting a resistance to it...right?

"Tori," I whispered, shaking her lightly. "Come on, Tori-bear, wake up for me."

She groaned and lifted a hand to rub the sleep out of her eyes. "Dani?"

"Hey," I greeted with a smile. "You okay?"

"Where are we? Oh my god, are we on a bus right now?" she gasped once her brain took in the reality of where we were. "No, no, this can't be happening." Tori pleaded, starting to sob.

"Shh, we don't want to draw attention from the driver. I'm not sure what might happen," I warned, glancing up to the front where a gate cut us off from leaving. "Do you remember anything about last night? Everything is a bit fuzzy for me."

Tori frowned, rubbed her forehead, and then stopped and

looked at me. "There was a visitor at dinner. You wouldn't know since you got sent to your room—again. He was an older man dressed in a nice suit talking with the Head Caretaker. It almost seemed like that man was picking out girls like they do when we are paired with a local pack. When he left, four women were sent to their rooms to pack."

"Did you hear them say anything about sending us so early? There was supposed to be another two months before we were shipped off," I pressed.

"Dani, I'm sorry, but the girls around me were chatting away about some romance book they were reading, and Sybble kept asking me for help with her math homework. There was no formal announcement like they normally do when it's time for those picked to be relocated." Tori looked at me helplessly, and I didn't have the heart to press her for more information.

Tori had been turned over to the Care Center the moment her designation was revealed. She'd mentioned before that her father had been laid off at the factory and they were barely scraping by. I'm sure her mother made the choice to give her up, so she'd have a better life than they could give her. Being at the Center meant Tori got three meals a day, education, clean clothes, and a roof over her head until she was paired. I didn't blame her mother, Tori had a brilliant mind for numbers and it surprised me she'd been chosen for Asturg. She was much more suited for Shearia, all but because she was clumsy as hell. Broke more dishes than anyone I'd ever seen tripping over her own feet.

"Wait," Tori gasped, grabbing my arm. "They passed out hot chocolate and cookies to everyone that night to take up to our rooms. Do you think they drugged us with that? It's a super long drive to the border and, looking at the sun, it's got to be close to noon. We would have needed to leave super early in the morning. Plus, we're all dressed and not in our nightgowns."

It wasn't until she said it I looked down at the stupid uniform they made us wear at the Care Center. Button-down, long-sleeve white shirts with drab calf-length navy skirts. Let's not forget the uncomfortable navy flats to go with it. They told us it was a way to keep us all equal with each other by having a uniform. No one knew, based on appearance, who was rich or poor, all in the hopes of creating a supportive community as we lived together. The whole thing made me want to scream since it didn't matter in the long run. The rich girls couldn't be stripped of the entitlement they were raised to have, and the poor girls were made of grit and steel, never backing down.

Somehow I, one of the richest and highest Omegas on the social ladder, seemed to fit better with the girls who had some grit to them. They were authentic, and as a woman who spoke her mind constantly, they got me. The richies turned up their noses and wanted nothing to do with me, which suited me just fine.

"That's good, Tori, real good," I praised, giving her hand a squeeze. "I left Violet to come to check on you, so I'm going back to check on her. Don't worry, I'm not far and we'll get through this together, alright?"

Tori nodded but didn't let go of me as I stood. "Dani, we're in Asturg, aren't we?"

"Yeah, we are," I answered, never willing to lie to myself or others about the reality of a situation. "I promise you, Tori. If I can get us out of here, I will, no matter how long it takes. No one deserves the fate of being an Omega here."

A tear spilled out of the corner of one of Tori's blue eyes, but she brushed it away and released my arm. "I believe you, Dani. You never make a promise you can't keep."

God, I really fucking hope I can keep this one.

THE DRIVE SEEMED to take hours, and the scenery left much to be desired. It almost seemed that the land was at war with itself, as the people were. Brown tufts of what I assume used to be grass littered the barren rolling plains. Small trees with no leaves looked stark against the bright blue sky and I felt sweat rolling down between my shoulders.

Oscad had a mild climate that veered on the side of being cooler than warmer, making this weather, while not extreme, uncomfortable with the heavy clothes I was wearing. We passed through some abandoned cities, buildings destroyed and crumbling from the war that's ravaged this place for centuries. Black scorch marks were left on cement walls where fires had raged as the town was laid to waste.

I had a feeling those images were going to haunt me for a long time, having never imagined anything like that was possible. Oscad had its own problems, but it never resorted to war in such a ruthless manner. None of our history books had pictures of either of our neighboring countries leaving us clueless as to its true nature. I knew they'd been in the longest drought they'd ever experienced here in the north. What had once been an agricultural mecca has now been reduced to cracked ground and dust blowing on the wind.

The sun set as the driver turned down another road. This seemed to have once been a highway but was just as riddled with potholes and crumbling asphalt. Because of that, the bus driver couldn't drive that fast, or we'd end up with a wheel stuck in a hole. As we got closer, I spotted a city rising in the distance through the chain-link gate blocking us from the driver. All the girls were awake at this point. There had been wailing hysterics from many while others just sat in stunned silence.

At one point, the driver had to stop and march back here to give a few girls another dose of whatever they used to knock us out. Seeing the consequences, everyone else shut up and stayed seated, heads down until he returned to his seat. Violet gripped my hand so tightly I thought I was going to lose circulation but I wouldn't tell her to let go. If I could help her in some small way by letting her hold my hand then that was what I was going to do.

I must have dozed off since I was shaken awake by Violet. "Danella, look."

Groaning at the awkward angle I'd ended up in, I straightened. Taking a moment to rub the back of my neck even though I knew it was pointless. It was now dark, but it was easy to see what Violet had woken me for. There, glowing in the pitch-black darkness, was a beacon of a city. It reminded me of Oscad with its tall buildings clustered together, but it seemed that only part of the buildings were lit up. The top halves were shrouded in darkness.

People were all over the streets as we pulled into the city limits. Many were dressed in military uniforms with rifles slung over their shoulders. At the same time, others were in worn clothes that seemed to have been patched and patched again. Vendors had stalls set up selling food, clothing, and other goods, and many of the stalls had a guard standing watch to prevent thieves, or that was my assumption.

This was our new home.

The war-torn remnants of a world that used to be one of the biggest producers of all things agricultural. Now the North has turned to mining so they could continue to make weapons to further their war. It was apparent they still had up-to-date technology, but it seemed to clash with how minimal everything else was. Almost as if it didn't further their efforts in the war, there was no need to change it.

Finally, the bus stopped in front of a small three-story building with two guards outside its door. I wasn't sure why they were needed when this end of town seemed far quieter, with only a few people wandering by.

The bus driver rose and unlocked the gate giving us all an irritated look.

"Listen up, *breeders*." He barked. "You will line up, single file, without protest or lollygagging. When that door opens, you will proceed straight into the building and wait in the lobby until everyone is off the bus. Then a group of doctors will come to look you over. If they clear you, you'll be placed at your location starting tomorrow based on the needs of our great nation. Say your good-byes to each other now, there's no telling if you'll ever see one another again."

Rage flared in my stomach, and I had to fist my hands as I forced my body to stand perfectly still. Lashing out at this asshole wouldn't do anyone any good. Better to wait and see what happens once we are in the building.

"Now march," he ordered, pointing a finger to the door.

CHAPTER 2

Danella

The outside of the building was shabby and deteriorating, as was the rest of the city. Inside was mildly better, but other than making sure the structure was sound they weren't going above and beyond. The lobby was a simple tiled room with plastic folding chairs along the outer edge of the wall. Fluorescent lights lit up the space in that harsh, cool tone that did no one any favors.

Did the Council of Four, our leading government for Oscad, know what the conditions were like here? I suppose the better question would be, did they even care? Clearly, they felt it was important enough to ship us off to another country without even letting us know. Why would they care how we were treated? We were no longer their problem.

It didn't take long for us all to make our way into the building and have the front door slammed closed behind the last girl. This must have signaled the doctors because two older men came into the room moments later. Both of them had on graying lab coats that I assume used to be white at one point. One had on glasses, and the other had a scraggly beard that made him look unkempt.

"Welcome to your new home in the Northern faction of Asturg. We will take two of you at a time to examine and ensure that you're fit for breeding. This is the first and foremost important duty of

Omegas in our country. Without good breeders, we don't have the soldiers to keep fighting to reclaim our lands from the bastard Southerners," Glasses informed us. "Now, I would like you to line up in the order of oldest to youngest, please."

Only one other girl was older than me in this group, so we both stepped to the front of the line. It ended with Tori and then Violet, a few girls up from her. Many of those they sent this time were in a range of twenty to twenty-three. I had just turned twenty-two a few weeks earlier and feared something like this would happen. Having children was harder the older you got, and no one over the age of twenty-two had been paired with a local pack.

"You two come with us. The rest of you sit in the chairs in this order. We will come and call you back, two at a time, when we are ready," Creepy Beard instructed.

Pushing through a set of swinging double doors, we entered an exam room. It was basic, with two exam tables for us to climb up on, a long counter that had drawers and cabinets, and two rolling chairs for the doctors to use.

"Please strip down to your undergarments and take a seat on the exam tables," Glasses ordered.

I looked over at Samantha and was greeted with a look of terror that I'm sure matched my own. We'd had medical exams before. It was standard once a year, sometimes twice if there were any issues. I'd been one of the lucky ones who had to go twice a year since I had yet to experience my first heat. There were some late bloomers, if you will, but never past the age of twenty-one. Yet every time I was examined, there was no medical reason it should be happening.

"Do it now," Creepy Beard barked, making both of us jump and whine at the Alpha order.

An Alpha bark to an Omega was like a slap to the face. Instinctively our need to please and follow the Alphas' wishes was set into overdrive when an Alpha bark was given. Instantly Samantha was undoing her skirt, but I gritted my teeth fighting against the need to do as I was told until I physically couldn't anymore. I'd rarely experienced a bark yet the rage that flooded my body when it was used somehow lessened the power of it. Not enough to disregard it, but enough to refrain from automatically giving in.

With a soft growl of irritation, I started to unbutton my shirt—as slowly as possible. I was doing as requested, but I wasn't going above and beyond. Of course, they made sure the doctors, or at least one of them, was an Alpha to ensure they could control us. It wouldn't do for a military country such as Asturg to have unruly *breeders*. Fuck, I hated that word so much.

Taking my time to neatly fold all my clothes and set them off to the side, I then sat on the exam table. It was cold, uncomfortable, and the look on Creepy Beard's face when he skimmed his eyes over me made me want to vomit. Not to mention this close, I could catch his scent. It was an overpowering aroma of vinegar with a bite of pepper, making me crinkle my nose in distaste. In all our education, we were told that the scent of an Alpha who would have the highest chance of breeding successfully with an Omega had to have an appealing scent. It was obvious to me that this crusty old Alpha wouldn't be getting it up anytime soon.

He tucked the stethoscope in his ears and listened to my heart and lungs. This was standard, and I knew what was expected. Then came a blood pressure check and looking in my nose, ears, and at my eyes.

"Do you need to wear glasses?" he asked.

"Wouldn't I be wearing them if I did?" I retorted before I could even think about what I was saying.

Creepy Beard narrowed his eyes at me. "I'll give you one warning, *breeder*. You're not in Oscad anymore. Here we don't tolerate those of lower stations talking back when asked a yes or no question. Do it again, and you'll quickly learn the punishments used around here."

When I had nothing to say about his threat or didn't appear at all daunted by it, I saw his jaw muscle twitch. *Yeah, sorry, asshole, I have that effect on people I don't like.*

"Now, I'll ask you again, do you wear glasses?" Creepy Beard repeated slower than before, like I was stupid or something.

"What were my choices again? Oh, right, yes or no," I muttered to myself. "Do I wear glasses? No, I'm pretty sure I don't."

A hand whipped out and connected with my cheek so hard that it had my head jerking to the side and I could taste blood in my mouth. Seems my own teeth had cut the inside of my cheek with the force of the blow.

"I warned you," he snarled. "Keep that shit up, and breeder or not, we'll put you on the front line with no weapon. You'll last all of three seconds before you're riddled with bullets."

"Somehow, I doubt that threat is real. You're in need of Omegas so desperately that you have them shipped in from another country. There's no way your leader would let you do something so stupid as to kill one of us like that," I challenged.

Glasses stepped away from Samantha and grabbed Creepy Beard's arm. "I'll finish up with her. You do the last part of the exam on the other."

Creepy yanked out of his hold and glared at me before walking over to Samantha and snappingthe curtain closed between the exam tables.

"Open," Glasses ordered, gesturing to my mouth.

I did as he asked, letting him use the tongue depressor to check the bleeding cheek. When he was finished, he just gave a nod, and I closed my mouth. Moving around me, he poked here and there, checking a few things before pressing me to lie on my back. I heard a bottle being squirted, but I didn't really think anything of it until he pulled aside my underwear. Shooting up into a sitting position, I yanked my knees close to my body, cracking him in the jaw as I did so.

"Mother fucker," Glasses swore as his glasses clattered to the floor.

Creepy was back shoving the curtain out of his way. "What the hell is going on here?"

He spotted his fellow doctor clearly in pain and searching for his glasses on the floor. "You little bitch, you attacked him, didn't you? Now I can see why Oscad was so keen to get rid of such a feral

Omega. They're too soft to handle the likes of you, but here in Asturg, we know just what to do."

Before I could fight back, Creepy grabbed my arm and yanked me off the table, slamming my body to the floor. Tile wasn't a forgiving substance in any way shape or form, so when my head bounced off of it, I had a moment to see them coming at me with a syringe before I lost consciousness.

Groaning, I lifted a hand to touch my head that felt like someone had dropped a car on it. Only something prevented me from being able to do that. Cracking open an eye, I started to panic when I couldn't see anything. Had I lost my eyesight? What had they done to me? My panic eased when I saw a faint outline of what might be a door. The room I was in had no windows, or it was still possibly nighttime.

Carefully I shifted and realized I had been propped up against a wall and my right arm seemed to be shackled while my left was free. Gingerly I felt along my head and hissed when I found the lump on the back side of my head where it hit the floor. *Fuck those assholes.* How dare they think they can just stick their fingers wherever they like? Not even at the Care Center has a male ever ventured near my vagina.

Wait? Is that what they were going to do to all of us? Violet? Tori? Fuck, why can't I ever think before I act? Now I'm locked up here when I could be figuring out how to get us the hell out of here.

My mental tirade was cut short as the door opened, and the room was flooded with light. Room might have been a little too strong of a word, it was more like a closet now that I could see how large it was.

"So, breeder, are you ready to let us finish your exam?" Creepy asked with a challenge in his tone.

He wanted me to say no. The bastard liked to handle those of us too feral, as he called it. It gave him the excuse to exert what little power he had here in this building. Now that I'd had my time out and got my head right, I knew I couldn't fight him. I had to be with the others. It was the only way I could protect them—they needed me.

"Yes, sir," I said, even though the words tasted like acid in my mouth. "I'm sorry for my actions earlier."

His whole body seemed to deflate at my submissive behavior. Seems I'd been right about him wanting me to fight back.

"Fine then, but I'm going to finish it here where you're restrained for my safety," he informed me.

My answer was to give a simple nod.

Humiliation burned in me almost as hot as my rage when he didn't even bother to put on a pair of gloves. No, I was being punished, and he wanted me to react so badly that he didn't even use any lube before he jammed a finger up inside me to poke around for far longer than was needed.

"You're untouched," he said, almost as if he was surprised. "Someone of your age, I would think, has been on her back for others already. Oscad makes no sense, they have all these Omegas and they just collect them to give away to others. Imagine the army you could provide for them if they filled your belly with a child as soon as you started your heats."

"They have us on suppressors," I said. "Some packs want their Omegas untouched."

It was a lie, but he didn't know that. Omegas were given an option when they reached their heat if they wanted to use medication, replacements, or one of the alpha staff members to relieve the symptoms of heat. Since I hadn't had my first heat yet, there was no need to consider any of those options.

Creepy grumbled under his breath as he pulled out a needle and jammed it into my vein to take a blood sample. "You'll remain here for the rest of the night. Can't trust you to be in the room with the other girls. No telling what nonsense you might fill their heads with."

I bit my lip so hard I made it bleed with the effort not to attack this fucking shitstain of a man. He wanted me to react, fight, curse him out, or do anything that gave him the grounds to discipline me. Sorry, dickhead, I wasn't going to give you what you wanted, but I'm sure I've already marked myself as trouble, and it was going to land me in hell.

~

SLEEPING with my arm chained to a wall was nearly impossible. I couldn't even lie down. Turning to my right I and leaned against the wall pulling my knees to my chest and trying to keep what little body heat I could. The tile floor seemed to suck all the warmth right out of my ass, and the cinderblock wall didn't help either. I must have dozed off at some point because I was awoken when the closet door crashed open.

Startled, I floundered about trying to remember where I was and why my whole body hurt. When I looked at the door, I instantly shrank away from the hulking beast of a man whose sharp green eyes examined me.

"This is the breeder who caused you so much trouble, Flavius?" the man asked, his deep voice sounding like gravel.

Creepy peered past the man's arm to look at me. "Trust me, General, she's got a smart mouth and a nasty attitude. Attacked Bortolami when he tried to do her exam, kneed him right in the nose."

Hearing this, the man sneered though I think it might have been an attempt at smiling. "So she's got spirit for a breeder."

"If that's what you want to call it," Creepy said with a sniff.

"Send her and the two others untouched to Qita, where Lucian and his men are. I think I might have finally found something that might get his cock hard," General Boulder said, but who he was talking to, I wasn't sure. "One damn son abandoned me. Let's hope his half-brother didn't inherit that bitch's ideals like Savo did. Lucian just needs to provide his own heir, and I'll be able to get a little more rest at night. If the line of succession is lost, then all hell breaks loose, and that's just what President Dragomire wants."

Stepping out of the doorway, there were two other men standing behind him. While they weren't the same bulk as the General, they were muscled to the max. Both of them tried to enter the room, but it was too small for both to fit so one unchained me while the other tossed a pair of pants and a shirt at me.

"Get dressed, breeder." One of them ordered. "We're taking you to your new home, got to look presentable."

Examining the clothes, I doubted that's what they would accomplish—worn jeans that had random holes in them and a pale blue shirt with a weird black stain. Almost like someone had spilled ink on it and it never washed out. The jeans were too big and hung off my hips but they managed not to fall all the way off. Slipping the shirt over my head, I discovered it was a pretty snug fit that showed off my chest. A chest that I'd been overly blessed with, in my opinion. No matter how hard I tugged at it, I couldn't get it to cover my stomach, leaving me with a hand-width gap from my belly button to the top of the jeans.

I wasn't a prude by any means, and I was thrilled to be out of the overly modest Care Center clothes, but this just made me feel vulnerable. I caught the way those two men leered at me as they dragged me out of the closet and down the hall. What did they care? I was a breeder to them. Only fit for laying on my back and getting pregnant to make them more soldiers. *Barf.*

When we made it down two flights of stairs back to that lobby area, I found Violet and Tori waiting there. Tori looked as though she'd been crying all night, and Violet's eyes seemed hollow, as if she'd already given up hope. They perked up a little when they saw me but didn't move from where they stood. They'd also been given different clothes that didn't fit them though thankfully they were oversized since they were both short and rather thin.

Tori opened her mouth to say something, but I shook my head no. Now was not the time to speak, and I didn't want these gorillas to know they were important to me. Her jaw snapped shut and she lifted her hand to her mouth to start chewing at her nails, a terrible habit they'd been attempting to train her out of.

These men didn't seem to care either way as they gave their orders. "Let's get a move on it. We're the last ones to leave for our assignment, so get in the back of the truck and don't give us any trouble, or you won't be enjoying this long ride to Qita."

One kept his hold on my arm as he practically dragged me to the beat-up truck. Dropping the tailgate, he grabbed my hips and chucked me in. I stumbled forward and caught myself on the back of the cab.

"Put the cuffs on," he ordered.

Laying there were metal cuffs that had short chains attached to the side of the truck bed. Clearly, they've had people jump out of here before and used this to deter them from making that leap. When I hesitated, he pulled out a device and pushed the button sending an arc of electricity between two points.

"Do as you're told, or I'll tase your ass, breeder. The doc might like to use his hands but one zap from this, and you'll be wishing it was him instead of me," he threatened.

While I might be stubborn, smart-mouthed, and confrontational, I wasn't stupid. Dropping to my knees, I locked the thick metal cuffs in place. The chain was about two feet long so even if I jumped out, I would just be dragged along the side of the vehicle. The method was crude but effective. Tori was tossed in next with Violet right behind her. Clearly, I was the one they were worried about since those two didn't question the order to lock themselves in this truck.

The other guard handed us all bandanas. "You're gonna want those, the road can get real dusty back here. With all the fighting and weapons that have been used over the years, you never know what might be in the ground. Wouldn't want you breeders getting sick on us before we have the chance to get you pregnant."

I wanted to scream and yell at them for being so vile and degrading. Didn't they know Omegas can only get pregnant when they are in heat? That happens once, sometimes twice a year. What the hell kind of excuse did they use to justify every other time they felt the need to make another soldier?

Oh god, don't tell me they might have the drug that Oscad created years ago, which the EQ contaminated, killing all those Omegas. That was the only thing I'd ever heard of that increased the chances of the baby being an Omega and *increased the number of heats in a year.*

With that cheerful thought, the truck rumbled to life and took off out of the city.

CHAPTER 3

Danella

The outside of the building was shabby and deteriorating, as was the rest of the city. Inside was mildly better, but other than making sure the structure was sound they weren't going above and beyond. The lobby was a simple tiled room with plastic folding chairs along the outer edge of the wall. Fluorescent lights lit up the space in that harsh, cool tone that did no one any favors.

Did the Council of Four, our leading government for Oscad, know what the conditions were like here? I suppose the better question would be, did they even care? Clearly, they felt it was important enough to ship us off to another country without even letting us know. Why would they care how we were treated? We were no longer their problem.

It didn't take long for us all to make our way into the building and have the front door slammed closed behind the last girl. This must have signaled the doctors because two older men came into the room moments later. Both of them had on graying lab coats that I assume used to be white at one point. One had on glasses, and the other had a scraggly beard that made him look unkempt.

"Welcome to your new home in the Northern faction of Asturg. We will take two of you at a time to examine and ensure that you're fit for breeding. This is the first and foremost important duty of

Omegas in our country. Without good breeders, we don't have the soldiers to keep fighting to reclaim our lands from the bastard Southerners," Glasses informed us. "Now, I would like you to line up in the order of oldest to youngest, please."

Only one other girl was older than me in this group, so we both stepped to the front of the line. It ended with Tori and then Violet, a few girls up from her. Many of those they sent this time were in a range of twenty to twenty-three. I had just turned twenty-two a few weeks earlier and feared something like this would happen. Having children was harder the older you got, and no one over the age of twenty-two had been paired with a local pack.

"You two come with us. The rest of you sit in the chairs in this order. We will come and call you back, two at a time, when we are ready," Creepy Beard instructed.

Pushing through a set of swinging double doors, we entered an exam room. It was basic, with two exam tables for us to climb up on, a long counter that had drawers and cabinets, and two rolling chairs for the doctors to use.

"Please strip down to your undergarments and take a seat on the exam tables," Glasses ordered.

I looked over at Samantha and was greeted with a look of terror that I'm sure matched my own. We'd had medical exams before. It was standard once a year, sometimes twice if there were any issues. I'd been one of the lucky ones who had to go twice a year since I had yet to experience my first heat. There were some late bloomers, if you will, but never past the age of twenty-one. Yet every time I was examined, there was no medical reason it should be happening.

"Do it now," Creepy Beard barked, making both of us jump and whine at the Alpha order.

An Alpha bark to an Omega was like a slap to the face. Instinctively our need to please and follow the Alphas' wishes was set into overdrive when an Alpha bark was given. Instantly Samantha was undoing her skirt, but I gritted my teeth fighting against the need to do as I was told until I physically couldn't anymore. I'd rarely experienced a bark yet the rage that flooded my body when it was used somehow lessened the power of it. Not enough to disregard it, but enough to refrain from automatically giving in.

With a soft growl of irritation, I started to unbutton my shirt—as slowly as possible. I was doing as requested, but I wasn't going above and beyond. Of course, they made sure the doctors, or at least one of them, was an Alpha to ensure they could control us. It wouldn't do for a military country such as Asturg to have unruly *breeders*. Fuck, I hated that word so much.

Taking my time to neatly fold all my clothes and set them off to the side, I then sat on the exam table. It was cold, uncomfortable, and the look on Creepy Beard's face when he skimmed his eyes over me made me want to vomit. Not to mention this close, I could catch his scent. It was an overpowering aroma of vinegar with a bite of pepper, making me crinkle my nose in distaste. In all our education, we were told that the scent of an Alpha who would have the highest chance of breeding successfully with an Omega had to have an appealing scent. It was obvious to me that this crusty old Alpha wouldn't be getting it up anytime soon.

He tucked the stethoscope in his ears and listened to my heart and lungs. This was standard, and I knew what was expected. Then came a blood pressure check and looking in my nose, ears, and at my eyes.

"Do you need to wear glasses?" he asked.

"Wouldn't I be wearing them if I did?" I retorted before I could even think about what I was saying.

Creepy Beard narrowed his eyes at me. "I'll give you one warning, *breeder*. You're not in Oscad anymore. Here we don't tolerate those of lower stations talking back when asked a yes or no question. Do it again, and you'll quickly learn the punishments used around here."

When I had nothing to say about his threat or didn't appear at all daunted by it, I saw his jaw muscle twitch. *Yeah, sorry, asshole, I have that effect on people I don't like.*

"Now, I'll ask you again, do you wear glasses?" Creepy Beard repeated slower than before, like I was stupid or something.

"What were my choices again? Oh, right, yes or no," I muttered to myself. "Do I wear glasses? No, I'm pretty sure I don't."

A hand whipped out and connected with my cheek so hard that it had my head jerking to the side and I could taste blood in my mouth. Seems my own teeth had cut the inside of my cheek with the force of the blow.

"I warned you," he snarled. "Keep that shit up, and breeder or not, we'll put you on the front line with no weapon. You'll last all of three seconds before you're riddled with bullets."

"Somehow, I doubt that threat is real. You're in need of Omegas so desperately that you have them shipped in from another country. There's no way your leader would let you do something so stupid as to kill one of us like that," I challenged.

Glasses stepped away from Samantha and grabbed Creepy Beard's arm. "I'll finish up with her. You do the last part of the exam on the other."

Creepy yanked out of his hold and glared at me before walking over to Samantha and snappingthe curtain closed between the exam tables.

"Open," Glasses ordered, gesturing to my mouth.

I did as he asked, letting him use the tongue depressor to check the bleeding cheek. When he was finished, he just gave a nod, and I closed my mouth. Moving around me, he poked here and there, checking a few things before pressing me to lie on my back. I heard a bottle being squirted, but I didn't really think anything of it until he pulled aside my underwear. Shooting up into a sitting position, I yanked my knees close to my body, cracking him in the jaw as I did so.

"Mother fucker," Glasses swore as his glasses clattered to the floor.

Creepy was back shoving the curtain out of his way. "What the hell is going on here?"

He spotted his fellow doctor clearly in pain and searching for his glasses on the floor. "You little bitch, you attacked him, didn't you? Now I can see why Oscad was so keen to get rid of such a feral

Omega. They're too soft to handle the likes of you, but here in Asturg, we know just what to do."

Before I could fight back, Creepy grabbed my arm and yanked me off the table, slamming my body to the floor. Tile wasn't a forgiving substance in any way shape or form, so when my head bounced off of it, I had a moment to see them coming at me with a syringe before I lost consciousness.

Groaning, I lifted a hand to touch my head that felt like someone had dropped a car on it. Only something prevented me from being able to do that. Cracking open an eye, I started to panic when I couldn't see anything. Had I lost my eyesight? What had they done to me? My panic eased when I saw a faint outline of what might be a door. The room I was in had no windows, or it was still possibly nighttime.

Carefully I shifted and realized I had been propped up against a wall and my right arm seemed to be shackled while my left was free. Gingerly I felt along my head and hissed when I found the lump on the back side of my head where it hit the floor. *Fuck those assholes.* How dare they think they can just stick their fingers wherever they like? Not even at the Care Center has a male ever ventured near my vagina.

Wait? Is that what they were going to do to all of us? Violet? Tori? Fuck, why can't I ever think before I act? Now I'm locked up here when I could be figuring out how to get us the hell out of here.

My mental tirade was cut short as the door opened, and the room was flooded with light. Room might have been a little too strong of a word, it was more like a closet now that I could see how large it was.

"So, breeder, are you ready to let us finish your exam?" Creepy asked with a challenge in his tone.

He wanted me to say no. The bastard liked to handle those of us too feral, as he called it. It gave him the excuse to exert what little power he had here in this building. Now that I'd had my time out and got my head right, I knew I couldn't fight him. I had to be with the others. It was the only way I could protect them—they needed me.

"Yes, sir," I said, even though the words tasted like acid in my mouth. "I'm sorry for my actions earlier."

His whole body seemed to deflate at my submissive behavior. Seems I'd been right about him wanting me to fight back.

"Fine then, but I'm going to finish it here where you're restrained for my safety," he informed me.

My answer was to give a simple nod.

Humiliation burned in me almost as hot as my rage when he didn't even bother to put on a pair of gloves. No, I was being punished, and he wanted me to react so badly that he didn't even use any lube before he jammed a finger up inside me to poke around for far longer than was needed.

"You're untouched," he said, almost as if he was surprised. "Someone of your age, I would think, has been on her back for others already. Oscad makes no sense, they have all these Omegas and they just collect them to give away to others. Imagine the army you could provide for them if they filled your belly with a child as soon as you started your heats."

"They have us on suppressors," I said. "Some packs want their Omegas untouched."

It was a lie, but he didn't know that. Omegas were given an option when they reached their heat if they wanted to use medication, replacements, or one of the alpha staff members to relieve the symptoms of heat. Since I hadn't had my first heat yet, there was no need to consider any of those options.

Creepy grumbled under his breath as he pulled out a needle and jammed it into my vein to take a blood sample. "You'll remain here for the rest of the night. Can't trust you to be in the room with the other girls. No telling what nonsense you might fill their heads with."

I bit my lip so hard I made it bleed with the effort not to attack this fucking shitstain of a man. He wanted me to react, fight, curse him out, or do anything that gave him the grounds to discipline me. Sorry, dickhead, I wasn't going to give you what you wanted, but I'm sure I've already marked myself as trouble, and it was going to land me in hell.

~

SLEEPING with my arm chained to a wall was nearly impossible. I couldn't even lie down. Turning to my right I and leaned against the wall pulling my knees to my chest and trying to keep what little body heat I could. The tile floor seemed to suck all the warmth right out of my ass, and the cinderblock wall didn't help either. I must have dozed off at some point because I was awoken when the closet door crashed open.

Startled, I floundered about trying to remember where I was and why my whole body hurt. When I looked at the door, I instantly shrank away from the hulking beast of a man whose sharp green eyes examined me.

"This is the breeder who caused you so much trouble, Flavius?" the man asked, his deep voice sounding like gravel.

Creepy peered past the man's arm to look at me. "Trust me, General, she's got a smart mouth and a nasty attitude. Attacked Bortolami when he tried to do her exam, kneed him right in the nose."

Hearing this, the man sneered though I think it might have been an attempt at smiling. "So she's got spirit for a breeder."

"If that's what you want to call it," Creepy said with a sniff.

"Send her and the two others untouched to Qita, where Lucian and his men are. I think I might have finally found something that might get his cock hard," General Boulder said, but who he was talking to, I wasn't sure. "One damn son abandoned me. Let's hope his half-brother didn't inherit that bitch's ideals like Savo did. Lucian just needs to provide his own heir, and I'll be able to get a little more rest at night. If the line of succession is lost, then all hell breaks loose, and that's just what President Dragomire wants."

Stepping out of the doorway, there were two other men standing behind him. While they weren't the same bulk as the General, they were muscled to the max. Both of them tried to enter the room, but it was too small for both to fit so one unchained me while the other tossed a pair of pants and a shirt at me.

"Get dressed, breeder." One of them ordered. "We're taking you to your new home, got to look presentable."

Examining the clothes, I doubted that's what they would accomplish—worn jeans that had random holes in them and a pale blue shirt with a weird black stain. Almost like someone had spilled ink on it and it never washed out. The jeans were too big and hung off my hips but they managed not to fall all the way off. Slipping the shirt over my head, I discovered it was a pretty snug fit that showed off my chest. A chest that I'd been overly blessed with, in my opinion. No matter how hard I tugged at it, I couldn't get it to cover my stomach, leaving me with a hand-width gap from my belly button to the top of the jeans.

I wasn't a prude by any means, and I was thrilled to be out of the overly modest Care Center clothes, but this just made me feel vulnerable. I caught the way those two men leered at me as they dragged me out of the closet and down the hall. What did they care? I was a breeder to them. Only fit for laying on my back and getting pregnant to make them more soldiers. *Barf*.

When we made it down two flights of stairs back to that lobby area, I found Violet and Tori waiting there. Tori looked as though she'd been crying all night, and Violet's eyes seemed hollow, as if she'd already given up hope. They perked up a little when they saw me but didn't move from where they stood. They'd also been given different clothes that didn't fit them though thankfully they were oversized since they were both short and rather thin.

Tori opened her mouth to say something, but I shook my head no. Now was not the time to speak, and I didn't want these gorillas to know they were important to me. Her jaw snapped shut and she lifted her hand to her mouth to start chewing at her nails, a terrible habit they'd been attempting to train her out of.

These men didn't seem to care either way as they gave their orders. "Let's get a move on it. We're the last ones to leave for our assignment, so get in the back of the truck and don't give us any trouble, or you won't be enjoying this long ride to Qita."

One kept his hold on my arm as he practically dragged me to the beat-up truck. Dropping the tailgate, he grabbed my hips and chucked me in. I stumbled forward and caught myself on the back of the cab.

"Put the cuffs on," he ordered.

Laying there were metal cuffs that had short chains attached to the side of the truck bed. Clearly, they've had people jump out of here before and used this to deter them from making that leap. When I hesitated, he pulled out a device and pushed the button sending an arc of electricity between two points.

"Do as you're told, or I'll tase your ass, breeder. The doc might like to use his hands but one zap from this, and you'll be wishing it was him instead of me," he threatened.

While I might be stubborn, smart-mouthed, and confrontational, I wasn't stupid. Dropping to my knees, I locked the thick metal cuffs in place. The chain was about two feet long so even if I jumped out, I would just be dragged along the side of the vehicle. The method was crude but effective. Tori was tossed in next with Violet right behind her. Clearly, I was the one they were worried about since those two didn't question the order to lock themselves in this truck.

The other guard handed us all bandanas. "You're gonna want those, the road can get real dusty back here. With all the fighting and weapons that have been used over the years, you never know what might be in the ground. Wouldn't want you breeders getting sick on us before we have the chance to get you pregnant."

I wanted to scream and yell at them for being so vile and degrading. Didn't they know Omegas can only get pregnant when they are in heat? That happens once, sometimes twice a year. What the hell kind of excuse did they use to justify every other time they felt the need to make another soldier?

Oh god, don't tell me they might have the drug that Oscad created years ago, which the EQ contaminated, killing all those Omegas. That was the only thing I'd ever heard of that increased the chances of the baby being an Omega and increased the number of heats in a year.

With that cheerful thought, the truck rumbled to life and took off out of the city.

CHAPTER 4

Lucian

I'd been away from Qita for three weeks as I took my small infiltration team and crossed into the South territory. It was a four-day journey just to get to the border, but it was the safest way for us to move without leaving a trace. Plus, we used river access and anything motorized would have never worked. While we had numbers, they used technology to make up for their lack of soldiers. That meant along the border, they had sensors that would pick up on noise above a certain level adding another reason why we had to hoof it.

There had been rumors that they were building a power generator on the river further into their lands. If that was true, then it was our top priority to take out since it would bring power closer to the front lines. While we in the North were far more skilled in battle, we lacked the minds they had in creating weapons that could take out massive amounts of us at once.

Drawing out time in the South, we didn't see any signs of something being built although that didn't mean it wasn't in the works. They still had rainfall which is the only reason the river still had water flowing. The Stern River was one of two rivers in our country that flowed north instead of south. One of the primary reasons we needed to push them back away from it. Our biggest fear is that they would find a way to cut off the flow before it got to us but from what we hear, any attempts to do so resulted in flooding the moment it rained.

Just one of the many things we feared from the South, driving us to protect what little we had left of our way of life. I didn't know what held back the South from just dropping a bomb on us and ending it in one fell swoop. My father, the general, would have done it without hesitation being the cold, ruthless man he was. I didn't think it was possible for him to become even more callus but I was proved wrong when Savo turned his back on us. Father never told Savo about his half-siblings after seeing how he was with his little sister. The Alpha was a disgrace, and there was no room for being that soft when we had to fight tooth and nail for all we had.

"Commander," one of my men called.

I shook myself out of my mental musings to meet his gaze. "What is it, Ján?"

"We're coming up on camp," he said.

Grunting, I grabbed the flare gun, loaded a shell, then lifted it straight up over my head and pulled the trigger. The flare shot out of the weapon and whistled into the sky with a pop releasing a bright orange-colored bloom. This let the guards at the gate know that we were Northern soldiers and not to shoot on sight. Shooting off a flare didn't change the fact that there were land mines around the perimeter or that the fence was charged, it simply gave us a chance to get to the gate without getting killed. Once they could verify who we were, then we'd be allowed entrance.

I don't care how well-trained you are or what shape you're in, walking for three weeks is exhausting. My feet were begging me to rest, but that might be because my boots were slightly too small. We hadn't had a shipment of uniform supplies in almost six months. Supposedly we'd worked out a deal with Oscad to supply us with things we needed, but so far, all I've seen is fucking timid Omegas who pissed themselves at the sight of me. Who wanted to fuck something that might die of fright if you got too close? While the General seemed to believe that Omegas were at the top of the list of things we needed to continue the line of soldiers, it didn't help to keep the soldiers alive that we already had.

Our people were starving, barely could find decent clothes to wear, and all our towns were crumbling since there weren't any supplies to fix them. What good was winning a war if you destroyed everything in the process? While I didn't agree with Savo for leaving and forcing me to take his place, I couldn't blame him for not wanting to see the demise of our people. Passing through the gate, I looked at the small town we used as a military outpost. Men were drinking in the bar that never seemed to run out of beer except when you looked in the windows of the supply depot, there was hardly anything left on the shelves.

Growling under my breath, I turned to face the four men who'd come with me. "As of this moment, you're on leave for the next three days. Good work, men, enjoy the time as you please."

They all grinned and slapped each other on the back as they headed for their barracks. My place was over the armory. Being the commander and top military officer of this outpost, I got my own apartment. It wasn't much, but it gave me a place to think and plan without interruption unless it was necessary. Clomping up the steps at the back of the building, I shoved open my door. I'd never felt the need to lock it, knowing that if I caught anyone's scent in here I would slit their throats for entering my private space.

Toeing off my boots, I dropped my pack on the small table in the kitchen area. It had a wood-burning stove, sink, and fridge that I didn't really ever keep anything in. While we had electricity here, it was unreliable so you never knew how long it would be out and any food left there would be spoiled. Filling a bucket with water, I used it to wash my face and hands to start. I'd get to the rest of it later but what I wanted right now was to strip out of these clothes I'd been in for three weeks and get some fucking sleep on a real bed.

Peeling off my shirt, I kicked open my bedroom door which had been left ajar and came to an abrupt halt. I was smacked in the face with the gentle scent of something floral that had a bright, spicy twist. My cock grew rock-hard as I closed my eyes and took a deep inhale of the scent that coated my room. It was soft, feminine yet had an undercurrent of something sharp and unyielding. When I opened my eyes, I searched the room for where the intoxicating scent came from until I landed on the sight of a woman in my bed.

The way her scent permeated the room, she'd had to have been up here for quite some time. On the floor, I saw a tray with bread and gruel that had been untouched. There was also a bucket that I assumed would be what she'd been using for needs since she was clearly chained to the back wall of my room. A growl started to trickle out of my mouth at the thought of someone touching her, let alone chaining her to a fucking wall.

Seconds after I realized what I'd just thought, I was disgusted at the fact that I would ever think such things about a breeder that I didn't even know. I was the commander of my father's army, second in power only to him. To hold that position I'd learned any sort of emotions or tenderness toward others was a luxury I could never afford. When I was much younger and being looked after by an older Alpha female with the rest of my various half-siblings, I'd grown attached to her. Father caught wind of this and beat the hell out of me saying it was to toughen me up. At any moment I'd dared to show weakness, he'd be there with his whip and fists to remind me there was no place in this world for bullshit like that.

As a daily reminder of those lessons, I carried their marks on my body. Each time I looked in the mirror, I was shown the result of allowing kindness of any sort to take root in me. Rewarding soldiers who deserved the praise was one thing; it would make them fight harder, push further, and give all they had to their leader. This is where my efforts should be put, not baseless feelings about some Omega bitch they'd tried to force on me once more.

Spinning on my heel, I slammed the bedroom door closed and heard a gasp behind me—but I pushed it out of my mind. Not bothering to put a shirt back on, I stormed out of my apartment and right up to the doors of the breeder house. Entering the dim building, I headed for Babaka's sitting room. The ancient woman spent most of her time there when she wasn't dealing with the breeders. At this time of day, I'm sure most, if not all the breeders would be fulfilling their purpose.

The moment I entered her sitting room, I found the woman in her favorite overstuffed chair knitting. She didn't even bother to look up from her work. Babaka just smirked. "Welcome back, Commander Lucian," she said in our native tongue. While Babaka could manage in the common tongue this was her first language.

"Why the fuck is there a breeder in my bed?" I demanded, keeping to our language as well. "I leave for three weeks and come back to find a strange woman chained up in my room with no warning?"

"General sent her for you, it wasn't a request I could ignore. He wants you to produce an heir and he's not taking no for an answer this time. I'm supposed to monitor your use of her and send word back to General Rasvan who will deal with you and the breeder personally," Babaka explained, finally lifting her gaze to mine. "Your refusal to use breeders has now garnered his attention, and he fears you'll be another failure like Savo. He won't allow it. I believe he'd rather kill you than let you make a fool of him."

"Fuck," I swore, running a hand over my hair which had gotten too long for my liking.

Babka chucked. "I believe that's the idea. Look, you don't need to knot the breeder until she's in heat, but she's untouched. You have the next three days to fix that and allow me to confirm, then send word to the general you're doing as you're told."

Everything about this made me want to push back even more. I didn't want an heir. Who would want a child to grow up in a world like this? My father was a bastard and I followed my general's orders when I believed they were in the best interest of our people, but this wasn't. It's not like he was going to die since he'd taken a step back from the front lines after his recent injury making it difficult for him to fight. Not that anyone but those closest to him would know how hurt he really was. Now that he saw his mortality firsthand, he was forcing his fears on me. Fuck, there were enough of my siblings that I could make one of them my heir instead of breeding one of my own. Our country couldn't support the people we had now, but no matter what, Father swore that more soldiers were what we needed to win.

Growling in frustration, I turned to leave but paused. "What happens to her if I don't?"

"I believe she will be fed to the wolves, although if she's as much of a fighter as I've seen then she won't last long before pissing someone off to the point they kill her," Babaka answered. "That one's got spirit the likes I haven't seen since your mother."

I flinched at the mention of my mother. Father had cared for her, I think, from how people talked. However, she wasn't an Omega that accepted her place. She'd pushed my father too far, and he'd killed her publicly when she made a scene in front of other officers disagreeing with his choice. One reason he'd been the general for as long as he had is the fact people were scared shitless of him. No one vocalized their disagreement, a lesson I didn't need to be taught after watching him kill my own mother at the age of ten.

"Let's hope she doesn't end up with her same fate," I muttered.

"You're the only one who can see that she doesn't," Babaka called after me as I left the breeder house.

Trudging back to my place, I sighed as I stood at the bottom of the stairs, almost dreading going back up there. The reaction that I had to her scent alone made me wary of what might happen if I talked to her. No matter what, I could never allow myself to care for her. She was a breeder, a vessel to produce an heir and keep my father off my back. She couldn't be anything more than that because it would absolutely get her killed, and it would be my fault. Some lessons I didn't need to learn from experience. I knew it would be devastating if I let someone in and then became the reason they died —it would kill me and turn me into a man like my father. Which was the last thing our people and country needed.

Clenching my hands into fists, I clomped up the stairs wanting to make sure she heard me coming. I assumed she was awake since I'd startled her with the slamming door when I left. Now she was going to get the first look at the man who was forced to be her Alpha and breed her until she had a child. *No, it was better she hated me.* If she never softened her feelings toward me, then it would make it easier to ignore what my Alpha instincts were telling me.

Asturg didn't do packs. There were no family units, so to speak.

Women were breeders, nannies, and soldiers, while the men went off to training camp as soon as they turned fifteen. Men served until they were killed or too injured to fight, then were sent back to the major towns to retire. Many worked or ran stores if they were able-bodied enough or just spent the rest of their days in the dorms. Many who ended up with that fate took their own lives, seeing no point in living if they couldn't be useful. This was no place to become attached to anyone because they could be gone in a blink of an eye.

Once more in my living area of the apartment, I glanced down and grimaced at my grimy appearance. Half tempted to wash up before meeting this breeder who had been forced upon me, I took a step toward the bucket of water. Then I stopped myself. What's the point? I wanted her to hate me, to find me repulsive. The scars on my face and body alone would do the trick. Most women shied away from me based on my appearance before they found out who I was. Gritting my teeth, I walked to the bedroom door and grasped the handle hating the way I fucking loved her scent that was seeping out of the door.

Definitely going to need to open the windows and air out the room if I plan on getting any sort of rest. Maybe it would be better to just sleep on the lumpy couch, even if half my body would hang off the damn thing. *Fuck,* I just wanted to come home and rest. Why the hell had this happened to me? Twisting the knob, I shoved the door open and stood in the doorway as I found the woman clutching my pillow back against the wall in the furthest corner of the room she could get to.

Her green eyes were wide as she took me in, and I'm sure in the dim light I looked even more terrifying than normal. Moving over to the desk, I switched on the light, half expecting it not to work, but it seemed the fates decided we'd be able to see each other more clearly. Pulling out my desk chair, I took a seat diagonal to her and rested my elbows on my knees as I contemplated her. With the added light, I could tell her eyes weren't just green but had flecks of gold, making them far more interesting to gaze into. It was clear she was afraid of me but yet I saw her jaw clench as she refused to break the connection.

Her hair was a mass of curls that seemed to have a life of their own in a tarnished gold color. The color made her eyes stand out even more as I forced myself to take in the rest of her. She seemed of average height, even though it was hard to tell with her all balled up. Seeing how lush and filled-out her body was in all the right places to drive a man wild, I knew she had to be from Oscad. None of the women here has the luxury of eating enough to have that particular softness. Soon enough, neither would she, especially if she chose not to eat what we offered her. That was one thing I wouldn't allow. Too many people were starving for this breeder to turn up her nose at the food.

When my gaze snagged on her neck, my stomach dropped upon seeing my personal mark on her. Babaka was right, Father was done with me playing games and ignoring my duty. That mark sentenced her to a life tied to me forever. If she did give me an heir, she'd be allowed to raise the child instead of handing it over to the nannies who looked after all the children born of breeders. The other thing it meant was that my failures and subsequent punishment would also be inflicted upon her. It was the closest thing you'd ever see to an Alpha, Omega bonding in Asturg. Never had a breeder been marked with my brand before, it was one of the reasons I refused to claim one. It was a barbaric old custom that should have died with the old king that created it.

There was nothing I could do. She was mine whether I liked it or not. "I'm Commander Lucian, your Alpha."

CHAPTER 5

Danella

The man who claimed to be my Alpha sat there staring at me with gray-blue eyes that were cold as steel. He was just as muscular as the guards who brought me here two weeks ago. Seeing him there without a shirt on gave me a clear view of his physical condition. His hair was dark and cut short on the sides, but the top was long and pulled back into a short ponytail. The hairstyle seemed to enhance the appearance of the scar that started at his eyebrow and curved along the side of his head disappearing behind his ear. Another scar on the same side of his face made his upper lip twist just slightly so he looked like he was sneering all the time. It was thicker and reached to the swell of his cheekbone.

Sitting here locked in a staring contest with the Alpha, I realized he smelled like melt-in-your-mouth chocolate with the added spice of cinnamon. This was his home, and I'd been spending all my time in his fucking bed. He better not get any ideas because I'd been goddamn chained to the damn thing. Grinding my teeth, I tried to hold back anything to say to his announcement after all the stories all the men who brought me food delighted in sharing with me. If there was remotely any truth to what they said, Commander Lucian was a tyrant.

"Are you mute?" Lucian demanded.

I debated telling him just how well I could speak but decided he didn't deserve to hear my voice. He hadn't asked me a question before, just made a statement. What was I supposed to say to that? Oh, joy, you seem to be such a swell guy. Let me fawn all over you. Nah, fuck that. He was gonna get an answer, just not a verbal one.

My answer to that stupid question was a shake of my head without breaking our visual connection. He'd come in here earlier as I pretended to still be asleep and watched him storm out of the room. If I were a betting woman, I'd say he had a chat with Babaka, who'd visit me every day to make sure I took a suppressant. Apparently, I wasn't allowed to go into heat when he wasn't around. That suited me just fine, it gave me cover for the fact I'd never had a heat yet.

"Breeder, I asked you a question, and I expect a verbal answer in return," Lucian ordered like the commander he was.

Who knew how much I could come to hate that fucking word in such a short amount of time—*breeder*.

There was silence as he waited for me to fulfill the demand he'd put before me, but I was more than happy to wait him out. I'd seen this shit before; the Alphas huffed and puffed, demanding their way like it would get them my respect. Well, assuming they want my respect—probably not. Breeders just follow orders like good little Omegas do, bending over and taking it, and thanking them when they are finished. Fuck that noise.

"You are mine, breeder. I can do as I see fit with my own property, and no one will say a word otherwise. That brand on your neck is just as powerful as a bonding mark here in Asturg. Play whatever game you want, but soon you'll figure out that being stubborn will only get you killed," Lucian pointed out.

Good to know if I said fuck it, I can't do this anymore. That I could probably provoke him into just ending it all for me. Babaka had taken every opportunity to tell me that I *had* to produce a child for this man, or I'd be beaten and killed. Thing is, part of me didn't believe that to be true. They needed Omegas from another country. Would they really just snuff out one because she was trouble? Then the rational part of my brain would cut in and remind me just how little value they put into the sanctity of life in general.

Letting out a growl, Lucian stood and stripped out of the rest of his clothes. I nearly swallowed my tongue at this man's sculpted body, even if it was littered with scars. Never did I think an ass would look as sexy as his did and it just made me mad that I was even thinking that. It was obvious that Lucian was a warrior and had survived many battles. Even without being the general's son, I feel like he'd be someone important all on his own merit.

When he turned around, I got a clear view of his cock that hung heavy between his legs. It was semi-hard, but under my gaze it started to stiffen. Yanking my eyes up to his face, he gave me a smirk and fisted his cock stroking it slowly as if to show me what I had to look forward to. Pausing, he pulled open a drawer and grabbed a jar, scooped out a small amount of what was inside, and spread it on his cock.

"Figured you should know what my cock looks like since you won't see it while it's buried deep in your untouched pussy," he shared as he continued to stroke himself.

Yes, it was true that I'd never had sex, but that didn't mean I'd never seen a penis before. To be fair, it had only been in books, so seeing it in person was a much different experience. As much as I wanted to look away, it was as if my body refused to let me dismiss this moment. His scent was heavy in the air as he started to hasten up his movements and liquid glistened at the tip of his penis. As if in answer to his actions, my pussy began to weep with slick, and a burn started low in my stomach that made me want to rub my legs together. Fighting against the urge, I licked my lips which had his gaze zeroing in on them, his hand speeding up.

"Would you look at that, is the little Omega getting turned-on?" Lucian growled out, his breath becoming more labored. "Fuck, your perfume is pouring off you and choking me with your desire."

His words had me snapping out of whatever trance I'd been in, breaking the hold his actions had on me. The bastard was right, I was fucking perfuming for this man. It didn't matter that I had zero interest in him. Being an Omega, when an Alpha presented himself as Lucian was doing, biology seemed not to give a flying fuck what I thought.

"Don't worry, I'll make sure to take care of that soon enough for you," Lucian said, his voice breathy as he was getting close.

With a grunt, he had to grab the back of the chair he was standing next to as he reached the tipping point. My eyes widened as I saw his knot swelling at the base. Lucian gave up standing and dropped onto the chair and squeezed his knot as he continued to stroke his angry red cock. With a roar, he came, his cum shooting out in my direction but it fell short of hitting me. As if torturing himself, he continued to rub out every last drop of his seed onto the floor.

"If I have to deal with sleeping on a bed covered in your scent, then you can sleep on a floor covered in mine," Lucian stated as he used his discarded clothing to clean off his hands and his cock, then shut off the light and fell into bed without another word.

Stunned by the whole interaction, I just sat there staring at the evidence that I hadn't been dreaming. Lucian had indeed just jacked off in front of me and gone to bed like it was perfectly normal. My body was hot, and shivers skated along my skin as my mind replayed the look on his face as he came. That contorted look of pure pleasure forced his whole body to contract as he exploded. In a purely analytical moment of thought, I'd been amazed at how much cum had ended up on the floor. For some reason, I'd thought it wouldn't be all that much, but clearly, I was mistaken.

Rattling snores started from the bed, making me jump at the sudden and deafening sound. In the Care Center, a few of the girls snored yet it was nothing like this bone-vibrating noise. How the hell was I going to sleep? Maybe it would stop after a while and then I'd manage. Curling up in the corner, I clutched the pillow and wondered if it would be better to just smother myself with it. Instead, I decided to wrap it around my head to act as a barrier to the noise in the hope that I could sleep.

My hopes went unheard as time ticked on, and he was *still* snoring so fucking loudly. Groaning, I flopped on my back to look up at the skylight in hopes that counting the stars might help me fall asleep. As I counted, I kept losing track each time I caught a trace of his scent causing my body to hum. Even though I'd never gone through a heat, I'd gotten horny before, which gave me some I wasn't completely broken. The other girls who'd gone through heat talked about how insatiable they were for weeks after, and the only option was to deal with it themselves. Some talked about using their fingers, while others asked for dildos or similar options to accomplish the same need.

Slowly I slid my hand down my stomach to the top of my jeans. They were loose enough that I could have slipped my hand in them without undoing the button, but I'd get a better angle if I did. By the sound of the even bouts of snoring, it was clear Lucian was fast asleep. The sound of the zipper seemed so loud in my ears yet there wasn't even a hint of change in Lucian's breathing. I wriggled around so I could stretch out, then shoved my jeans and underwear down onto my thighs.

Closing my eyes, I took a deep breath letting Lucian's scent curl around me. Gliding my hand between my legs, I felt how wet I was and used it as my finger slid over my opening and then up to my clit. Unbidden, my mind pictured his body in the soft lamplight and how the shadows it cast emphasized all his muscles. His gray-blue eyes pinned me in place as he stroked himself, heat glowing in them. I timed my movement to his using two fingers to swirl over my nub sending jolts of pleasure through my body. As he moved faster, the need I had wasn't getting met with what I was doing, so I let a finger sink inside me.

Fuck I needed more.

Adding a second finger was better, but I couldn't seem to get the right spot. Frustrated, I let out a small growl and kicked off my pants, pulling my knees up. When I reinserted my fingers I was able to find that sweet spot that made my body shake when I came. Lucian's scent got stronger the faster my fingers moved, and it was almost as if I could feel his hot breath on my body ratcheting up my desire. Damn, who knew all I needed was to watch some Alpha porn to get myself in the mood.

Arching my back, I felt my orgasm building so I slid my free hand under my shirt and palmed my breast. My nipples were so hard and erect, that they ached as I rolled them between my fingers. God, I'd never been this sensitive before. A moan escaped my mouth before I could stop it, although I was too far gone to care. Instead, I bit my bottom lip keeping my mouth shut as I imploded. Euphoric pleasure flooded my body unlike anything I'd ever felt before making me sigh.

"It seems you were more affected by my little show than you let on," Lucian said, his voice was thick with need and sounding like it was right in front of me.

Snapping my eyes open, I lifted my head and there between my legs, his face inches away from my pussy, was Lucian. I started to say something, but he closed the distance and locked his mouth on my pussy. The feel of his tongue laving over my sensitive clit made me shout and buck my hips. He growled against me, which had me moaning with the vibrations of the sound. Placing his hands on the back of my thighs, he pressed my legs to my chest and speared his tongue into my pussy.

"Oh my god," I cried as sensations I'd never felt before flooded my body.

Never had I experienced something like this when I touched myself. It was like every movement and touch was charged with electricity. My hands groped for something to hold on to and finally settled on his forearms as I dug my nails into his skin. He paused to hiss, but it didn't slow him down for long as he dove right back in.

Licking, nipping, and sucking every inch of my pussy Lucian brought me to tears as another orgasm ripped through my body. This one made my eyes see stars, and my whole body shook as I screamed long and loud. Just when I thought he had to be finished with me, he caught my ankles together and held them both in one hand. He pulled them to the side, shifting my lower half so he could pin my legs to the floor. Struggling to figure out what he was doing, I tensed as I felt a finger slide into me.

That finger stroked my innermost parts, and it was amazing and terrifying all at the same time. The roughness of his finger just added to the sensations, and I groaned when he pulled out, craving for him to put it back in. Fighting the urge to beg him to do just that, I bit my bottom lip hard enough that it hurt attempting to clear the lust-filled fog in my brain. I shouldn't have worried because Lucian had only pulled his one finger out so he could replace it with two. The fullness I was feeling was what I could achieve with three fingers telling me just how thick his hands were. They were the hands of a man, a warrior, and the man who planned on fucking me until I gave him a child.

"Get you're fucking hands off me, you bastard," I snarled and tried to wriggle out of his hold, only for a stinging crack to land on my asscheek.

"Lay still, breeder," Lucian ordered. "You are mine to use as I like, be glad that I'm willing to warm you up so shoving my cock in you won't be as surprising."

While my lower body was pinned to the floor, my upper body was still free, so I shoved up on my arm to glare at him. "Don't you dare pretend you are doing anything with my care in mind. It's been made perfectly clear to me how you view your *breeders*." I spat that last word hating every syllable. "I said get your fucking hands off me. Don't you know the meaning of the word *no*? Or did that privilege get revoked once I crossed the border into Asturg?"

"Watch your mouth," he warned with a growl rumbling in his voice. "You are an Omega, and I am an Alpha. Your Alpha, whose mark you bear clearly on display for all to see."

Grabbing the pillow behind me, I hurled it at him but, at the same time threw myself off balance and thudded to the ground. "You're a beast, an animal, all of you are. Who the hell brands people? It's barbaric."

"You have a lot to say for a slutty Omega who was just stroking herself and moaning loud enough to wake me from a dead sleep." Running his finger through the lips of my pussy and showing me his glistening fingers. "Your body doesn't seem to be complaining about this one bit.   It would appear it doesn't mind at all that I'm more animal than man."

Rage and fear collided inside me as I realized it didn't matter what I wanted or how much I fought. I'd never be able to stop him if he decided to do what he wanted with me. Tears rolled down my cheeks as I stared him down.

"Do what you want, *Alpha*. It's not like it matters if I care or what trauma I'll have after you're finished with me. Just know I'll never give you what you want. This body won't ever produce a child for you," I announced, giving him a smirk as tears still leaked from my eyes. "Guess it sucks you got stuck with the one Omega who doesn't go into heat."

It was probably stupid of me to have told him that, but right now I was too fucking pissed to care.

Lucian jerked back from me as if my words had actually slapped him. Sitting there on his heels, he regarded me with a wary eye. "What do you mean you can't have children?"

"I'm sure even you know this, but the only time an Omega can get pregnant is when they are in heat. Well, I don't have heats." I tossed at him as I moved away and put my back to the wall with my knees hugged to my chest.

To my absolute and utter shock, Lucian let out a sigh as his whole body relaxed. "Thank fuck."

Totally fucking confused, I just sat there silently watching him and curious to see if he would explain *that* reaction. Every single person I'd interacted with since coming here had been shoving it down my throat that I needed to have a child. Now here was the goddamn commander looking like I just gave him the best present ever at not being able to do that.

Lucian walked over to a dresser, pulled out a pair of boxers, tossed them at me, and then put a pair on himself. "This conversation needs clothes."

Not looking a gift horse in the mouth, I hurried to pull them on, though I didn't move from the corner. Lucian pulled the chair so he sat in front of me but made sure there was enough space between us.

"Now that you're talking to me, even though I think I enjoyed you more when you didn't speak, will you tell me your name?" Lucian asked.

Narrowing my eyes, I considered if I should tell him the truth or not. Then again, what good would it do for me to lie and tell him something fake? If using my name got him to stop calling me breeder, then it was a no-brainer.

"I'll tell you what it is if you promise to stop calling me breeder. It's disgusting," I challenged.

Lucian cocked his head, and I couldn't tell if he was actually trying to smother a smile or if it was the way the scar tugged his lip. "I can only offer that when we are in private. If I did that where others could hear, it would draw too much attention, and trust me when I tell you that's the last thing you want."

I considered that offer, lifting my hand to chew on the skin around my thumb. It was a bad habit I developed in the Care Center when I got super stressed out. The pain helped me focus and keep my mind on what was important rather than letting it spiral into darker thoughts.

"Guess I don't have much to bargain with, do I?" I grumbled. "It's Danella, Danella Holdstad."

His gaze seemed to warm for a split second before it was gone, almost as if I'd imagined it. "Danella, I have a proposition for you that I think might work out the best for both of us."

Dropping my legs so I was sitting cross-legged, I leaned forward to give him my full attention. "You finally realized that I'm going to be the biggest pain in the ass so you're going to take me out to the middle of nowhere and drop me off?"

That actually got a harsh bark of laughter out of him that he smothered instantly. "You might not believe me, but that is a far worse option than staying here with me. There are those who have decided to hide in the mountains so they don't have to serve in the military. They've turned feral and would attack you in a heartbeat. Rumors say they would even eat those who dare to trespass on their land."

Even though I didn't know if I believed him or not, nothing about that sounded like I wanted to chance it. "Alright then, what's your proposition?"

He sobered and his body became more rigid as if he'd caught himself relaxing as he talked to me and snapped back into his commander persona. It was almost as if he couldn't allow himself to be anything except harsh and domineering.

"I don't want an heir, I don't ever want to bring a child into this world. The reason things have been done the way they have with you is because I refused all other Omegas they've tried to get me to be with," Lucian said, dropping a bomb I didn't see coming. "The fact you don't go into heat is perfectly fine with me, but you'll need my help to keep that secret. If you can't produce a child, then to Asturg you're useless and we don't need extra mouths to feed."

"Well, this is comforting," I muttered.

"It's not supposed to be comforting," Lucian snapped. "Nothing about this world you've been dumped into will give one shit about your feelings or comforts. It is a harsh, cruel place where only the strongest survive and that's exactly how they want it."

"That has been making itself perfectly clear to me at every turn," I answered bitterly. "So what do you want in exchange for keeping my secret?"

"Letting me fuck you at least once a week. The first time must happen in the next two days before I return to duty," Lucian said flatly.

If my jaw could have hit the floor, it would've. The absolute blasé manner that he just used to make that demand had me reeling. Honestly though, in the incredibly short amount of time I've interacted with him, Lucian had been blunt, matter-of-fact, and crass in his words. While I respected that I knew where I stood, I wasn't sure I enjoyed the brutal honesty.

"So instead of stooping to the level of raping me, you're just going to blackmail me into sleeping with you? Wow, that is just what I should expect from a man from Asturg, only caring about himself and his needs." I bit out, my anger licking at me like a warm, comforting flame. "How can you just sit there and ask me that like it's not a totally fucked up request?"

"Danella, enough," Lucian barked, making me flinch, and my mouth shut with a click of teeth. "There is no possible way for us to manage staying alive without it involving me fucking you. Babaka is coming to check you in three days to make sure I've used you. If she finds that you are still untouched, she will tell my father, General Rasvan. There is no telling what he will do when he learns I've defied him but I do know it will mean taking out his anger on you. Trust me, I know from personal experience what that looks like. I barely survived it, which tells me he'd break you like a twig."

"So, death might be better than living this life," I yelled at him, refusing to submit to the idea that I had no way out of this.

Lucian let out a dark chuckle. "He won't let you die, especially if you look like that's what you want. No, he'd used whatever he could to find your worst fear and used that to manipulate and torture you. If he knew being raped was your trigger, he'd put you in stocks and let any soldier who wanted take their turn with you. Death would be something you begged for and never would get."

CHAPTER 6

Danella

A shiver went through my body at his description of what my fate would be at the hands of his father. Lucian was right, that sounded worse than death and wasn't something I would ever want to experience. Still, the thought of giving up my body just to survive didn't seem like a much better situation.

"So my options are, let you fuck me in order to keep from getting noticed by your father. Or if I don't let you do that, then I'm going to be tortured and beg for death and never get it? Did I get that right?" I asked, the disgust clear in my tone. "Really, I feel like this is a win-lose situation for you and a lose-lose worse situation for me. How can a girl choose which shitty fate she'd like to have for the rest of her existence?"

"Does it give you any comfort to know that the moment my father is dead and I take over I'll set you free?" Lucian offered. "The way he is doing things now won't sustain us in the long run, however he's too powerful for me to do anything about now. He can't live forever, but I can keep you safe until that time."

Groaning, I dropped my head into my hands trying to figure out what I'd done wrong in my life to ever deserve to end up like this. Even if I wanted to stand my ground and tell him and his cock to kick rocks, I couldn't. Staying alive here in this shitty town meant

I might find a way to get the three of us   out of here. A defeat now didn't mean it was the end of my options, it just meant I had to suffer for a little longer.

"Fine," I bit out. "But I have rules."

Lucian's brows went up, surprised and intrigued. "They are?"

"You will not kiss me," I ordered. "Do not cuddle me or in any way make me believe that this is anything more than a deal to keep us both alive. I will allow one night a week. Whatever night you choose is fine, but you will only get your dick wet once every seven days. Of course, if something comes up, it can be altered as long as it keeps me alive. We will need to fake a heat once a year, but you won't get a free pass for that time unless they plan to see how well you did your job. Bottom line, I'm not *your* Omega, you are not my Alpha, and we are making a business transaction. I give you sex, and you give me protection until the time comes and your father dies then I'm released from this contract."

Lucian sat back in his chair, giving me a rather impressed look. "I can see why my father felt you would be of interest to me. A sharp mind along with a sharp tongue can be a deadly combination when they have a body like yours to go along with it."

"Oh, don't even with the flattery," I huffed, rolling my eyes. "Do you agree or not?"

Rubbing his chin with a hand, he seemed to consider my offer. "I agree, but I want to clarify when you say one night a week does that mean I get you all night? Or just once during that night? I'm not a fan of the latter if I'm only going to get relief once a week."

"Really? That's your one complaint: how many times can you get off?" I asked incredulously.

"What, I'm a man, and just so we're clear, this means you get off more than once as well. While this is a transaction between us, I think it's only fair you get something out of it too. You seemed pretty happy with the sampling I gave you a few minutes ago," Lucian rebutted. "The next question is do you want me to finish what I started and get it over with now or give yourself some time?"

While my libido was more than happy with the idea of him

making me see stars again, I felt it was better to think about this after some sleep. "I'd rather have some time to adjust."

"Fair enough, now get on the bed," he ordered as he stood.

"What?" I blurted. "I just said no."

"I'm not going to do anything to you, but you need to sleep next to me so that my scent is on you. If any other Alpha had an Omega at his disposal as I do you, there's no way they wouldn't be indulging in that gift as often as they could. If someone shows up here and you don't have a shred of my scent on you, it will make it glaringly obvious I'm not doing what I should. With you sleeping next to me, it will solve that problem. Unless you really love sleeping on the floor?" Lucian questioned with a tilt of his head.

With an angry growl, I shoved up on my feet and climbed up on the bed putting my back firmly against the wall and crossing my arms over my chest as if that would ward him off. He just shook his head at me, then slipped under the covers and put his back to me. The bed itself wasn't really meant for an Alpha his size to share with anyone, but if the goal was to have his scent on me that would be accomplished.

This time as I drifted off to sleep, I noticed that he wasn't snoring in the slightest. Had that all been a ruse to see what I would do while he was asleep? God, just when I didn't think I could find him more irritating or underhanded, he proved me wrong. Thankfully I was so worn out from the stress of the last few hours I fell asleep quickly. My dreams were filled with visions of me sitting by a warm fire sipping hot chocolate far, far away from here. One day...   one day I would make that dream a reality with Tori and Violet right there with me.

～

WAKING UP, I felt so comfortable and warm almost as if I had a heated blanket wrapped around me. It was my favorite part of the cooler weather when we got to add those to our beds. I'd get in trouble for being late and not getting down to classes on time, but those extra five minutes were so worth it. Shifting, I tried to pull the blanket up to my chin, but instead of a blanket I found an arm nestled between my breasts with a hand gently holding my throat. Reality came crashing down on me, and I froze.

It would seem that sometime in the night, Lucian rolled over and tugged me to his chest. My head was resting on his other arm, his large hand splayed open as if it was waiting to catch something. While I knew he couldn't help what happened when we were sleeping, this was exactly why I'd told him no cuddling. No matter what, I couldn't allow myself to have feelings for this man. It would be a terrible fate to develop hope and dreams about someone who would never see you as anything more than something to fuck and keep his father off his back.

I deserved more than that, not only as an Omega but as a person. No one should be in a loveless relationship. That might be naive of me, and quite possibly I've read too many romance novels which might possibly have skewed my expectations. Nevertheless, was it so wrong to dream of being loved?

Carefully I gripped his wrist and started to pull it away from my neck, not trusting him to have access to such a vulnerable spot. As I moved his arm, I thought I was in the clear when his arm tensed and the next thing I knew, I was being slammed against the wall. The hold on my neck had me pinned as I clawed at this arm to loosen his grip so I could breathe. Lucian's scarred face loomed before me, a snarl on his lips before he finally seemed to register who I was.

Instantly he released me and threw himself off the bed, falling to the floor with a *thud*. Coughing as I sucked air into my lungs as tears burned in my eyes at the adrenaline that was coursing through my body. I'd cried in front of him last night, and that was going to be the last time I'd ever let that happen. Whatever might grow between us wouldn't involve me showing my feelings and allowing him to use them against me.

"Danella, I'm so sorry," Lucian said emphatically as he picked himself up off the floor. "I... I didn't realize it was you. No one's ever shared my bed with me before. *Fuck*," he swore, running a hand through his hair that had come undone from its tiny ponytail.

He reached out to me, but I flinched and curled away from him.

His hand pulled back then balled into a fist as if he was actually mad at himself for what he'd done. With a heavy sigh, he turned away from me and grabbed a few things out of his dresser.

"I'm going to clean up and see what I can make for breakfast." With that announcement, he left the room, closing the door behind him.

Relaxing slightly, I let out a sob I'd been fighting back yet forced myself to focus on my breathing to help calm me down. Everything about Lucian had me utterly confused. One minute he was the commander of the Northern Asturg army, then the next he was an insecure Alpha who seemed to be fucking everything up. The way he held me when I woke up was as if he was shielding me from whatever dangers there might be.

Once I felt calm enough, I got up from the bed, pulled up the covers, and replaced the pillow in its spot. While I'd been stuck up here for two weeks waiting for whoever lived here to return, I'd made routines to give me something to do with my time. Now it seems to have become a habit. Since Lucian hadn't felt the need to unchain me from the wall, I used my bucket toilet. I'd gotten over the humiliation since my other alternative was to piss myself, which would only make this experience worse. Besides, Lucian was the one who'd have to empty it out since I couldn't.

Another routine I'd made for myself was doing simple exercises so I wouldn't get stiff or weak. It was hard to run for your life if you'd become so weak you couldn't even make a run for it. We'd had physical fitness classes at the Care Center twice a week to help keep our bodies healthy. So I just picked from the exercises I could remember and made up some others that were modifications of ones I couldn't do in my confines.

Typically I would finish all of this by the time the guard would come up and drop off a canteen of water and a tray of food. Sometimes they would leave me edible food, while other days they would do things to it, making it impossible to eat. When they discovered that I didn't eat it, they threatened to beat me or tell Lucian when he got back so he would discipline me for wasting food. The previous day they'd mixed sand in with my gruel, and I hadn't figured it out until I'd shoved a spoonful in my mouth, *bastards.*

Granted that didn't start until after I spat in that one Beta's face when he pinned me against the wall and groped my boobs. "Don't worry, little Omega, I'm just getting a sample of what I'll get to play with once Lucian tosses you aside, regardless of wearing his mark."

It had been one of those moments where my gut reaction had been the wrong choice. When that wad of spit landed on his face, the rage that contorted his features had me truly fearing I might not live much longer. Thankfully there had been another man with him, and he pulled the Beta off me before he could do more than slam my head against the wall. Since then, more often than not, my food was fucked with; a way they could retaliate and not get in trouble for it.

The bedroom door opened, and Lucian walked in with his hair damp, smelling much cleaner, and in a fresh pair of black pants and a black t-shirt. In his hands were a large glass of water and something that looked like a biscuit with a delicious smell of egg wafting over to me. The growl that came from my stomach had me blushing and looking away from him.

"Come sit at the desk and eat," Lucian instructed.

"I can't," I said, pointing to my ankle. "The chain won't go that far."

Almost as if he'd forgotten about that minor detail, he headed back out of the room but didn't bother closing the door. I could see him walking into the kitchen area and pulling open a drawer, grabbing something, and coming back to kneel before me.

"Know that if you run from me, Danella," he started, then looked me in the eyes. "I will find you, no matter how far you run. I'm one of the best trackers this military has, so just forget the idea. I've promised to free you once my father is gone, but until then you're mine to be responsible for."

I didn't respond, knowing that no matter what he said I was going to find a way to get the fuck out of here. All he'd done was help me by letting me know he was their best tracker. Now I just needed to learn what other skills people around here had, so when I found my chance I knew what I was up against. The feeling of having the metal cuff off my ankle was almost like getting some hope back. If he left me free to roam around his home, it would give me many more options.

"Sit," he ordered, pointing at the desk. "It's not much, but it seems we got a shipment of food a few days ago. Enjoy the biscuit and eggs. They're a treat, so savor them. It will be back to gruel tomorrow."

Even though I wanted to do just as he said and eat this slowly, I was so hungry I couldn't hold myself back from shoving it in my face. Out of the corner of my eye, I saw him picking up the tray and scowling down at the bowl while poking at it with the spoon.

"Danella, did you put the sand in your food?" he asked, the warning clear in his tone. If my answer was yes, I would have been in massive amounts of trouble.

"No," I stated.

His gaze locked with mine, but I didn't back down—I'd done nothing wrong. "I see. Finish your food and drink all the water. It helps with the hunger. Unfortunately, that's a feeling you'll have to get used to. Food is one thing we don't have an abundance of."

Nodding, I shoved another bite of the biscuit and egg sandwich into my mouth. It wasn't a good biscuit either, it was grainy and hardly had any flavor. Thankfully, the salty eggs made up for what the biscuit lacked, making this meal worth eating. As much as I hated thinking about it, I knew Lucian was right, I'd have to adjust to the reality of living in a war-torn country. From my education at the Care Center, I knew part of the South's plan was to weaken the North by starving them. While the North was experiencing the worst drought ever seen, the South was still getting rainfall regularly.

After I'd finished my food, Lucian returned with a bucket, a bar of soap, and a rag. It didn't take much to put two and two together and assume he wanted me to bathe. What surprised me was when he dropped to his knees, tugged the chair away from the desk, and gingerly gripped my ankle where the cuff had been. The skin under it was raw, and now that I'd acknowledged its existence, it started to burn.

"This needs to be cleaned, and I'll put some ointment on it. If there are any other scrapes, cuts, or abrasions, you need to tell me so I can keep an eye on them. There isn't much in the way of medical help outside of the larger cities. We have field doctors, but it's more the supplies we come up short on. Antibiotics are too valuable and only given out sparingly and when needed. I'll ask the same of you if there is something I can't attend to myself," Lucian instructed as he got the rag when and wet down my leg before soaping it up.

"That's the only thing to worry about," I said, trying to pull my leg back. "I can wash myself."

"No," Lucian snapped, then closed his eyes and took a deep breath. "You need to get comfortable with me touching you. I felt this was a neutral way for you to get used to my touch so not every experience you have with me is contingent on sex."

I blinked at him in surprise. "Why?"

"While I agree that us forming any attachment to each other is not wise or what either of us wants..." Pausing, he looked up at me. "...I don't really want you to be repulsed by me or my touch. I know what I look like, and I've seen that fear and disgust in too many females' eyes that I don't particularly relish the idea of you doing the same thing. I can take your hate and rage, I deserve that. It's the fear I truly loathe to see."

Utter shock at his words had me speechless. Not waiting for me to come up with something to say, he continued with his efforts to bathe me. *What the fuck was I supposed to do with that?* One second he's threatening me with a life worse than death if I don't sleep with him, then he comes at me with shit like that. Yes, his face and body were scarred, but I didn't think it made him terrifying. His presence did that more than anything. The way his gaze could make me shake with fear knowing he would absolutely do what he said or threatened to do, was far more fear-inducing than his features.

"Stand," he ordered.

Rolling my eyes, I did as he demanded, trying to remind myself he was a *military* commander and used to giving orders. "Is it possible to get the occasional *please*?" I inquired, the bite in my words obvious.

Lucian hesitated at my request then gave a sharp nod of his head without any further acknowledgment. When he reached up and yanked the boxers off me, letting them fall to my ankles, I yelped and tried to pull away. My feet got caught in the fabric, and I started to tip backward, but a hand snaked around my wrist and pulled me forward instead. Collapsing against Lucian's chest, I stayed there a moment with my heart in my throat, adrenaline coursing through my veins.

Once I regained my composure, I shoved off his chest and ended up on my knees in front of him. "What the fuck do you think you're doing?"

"Did you expect me to bathe you with your clothes on?" he asked with a cocked brow. "I don't think that's how you wash, no matter where you're from."

I let out an incredulous huff of laughter as I tried to come up with some sort of comeback, but he had me there. "Yes, but typically when I wash I do it by myself, in a shower."

"Hmm, see, we don't have those. Not having enough water to go around, we use buckets and rags. Also, I believe I explained the purpose of doing this was so that you'd get used to me touching you. Fairly soon, you and I will be rather intimately entwined." Lucian countered as he grabbed my hips and hoisted me back to my feet. The boxers were still hooked around one ankle, which he removed while keeping me steady. "Now, let's try this again."

To my mortification, he had me spread my legs apart so that he could make sure every inch of me was washed. The one thing I had to hand to him was the fact he kept it purely business. There weren't lingering touches or sly tricks to get his fingers back in my pussy like he'd done last night.

"Arms up," he directed. When I glowered at him, he let out a heavy sigh as he stood. "Danella, will you *please* put your arms up."

While I didn't appreciate the tone, I knew I couldn't fight him when he'd done exactly what I'd asked. Lifting them, he made quick work of removing my shirt and I tried not to instantly cover myself. Having some clothing kept me from wanting to melt into a puddle of embarrassment now I was stripped bare to him. I felt his eyes roving over my body, yet his touch was still purposeful. He impressed me when he tied my hair up in a high pony to get it out of the way as he started on my back.

Even though I hated why this was happening and wasn't all that thrilled about who was doing it, I had to admit that he'd had a point when he said doing this would get me used to his touch. When he got to my brand, he cleaned it well enough that it had me hissing in pain as the flesh was still tender and not all the scabs had fallen off it. The first few days they gave me an ointment to put on it but it burned like a bitch. Once he was finished, he spread a cooling cream over that spot and my ankle.

I knew the moment the mood in the room changed as he lifted his gaze to meet mine, setting   aside the cream. This time when he brushed his hand up my leg, I could see the want in his eyes. "I promise to make sure you enjoy this, Danella, although the longer we wait the more time you have to destroy yourself further in struggling to make the choice. I will respect the requests you have made and I will give you one of my own. Please...don't fight me."

CHAPTER 7

Lucian

The worry and fear in her bright green eyes had me gritting my teeth. I *knew* this was the right choice, and it would keep us both alive to see another day. The second I had the power to do something about how Omegas were treated in this world, I would. Until then, I needed to do what was best for my people as a whole, and staying alive to make those changes was my top priority. I raged at the fact that Father put me in this position and forced me to make myself even more of a monster than I already was.

Danella was vibrant, intelligent, and her sharp tongue was something that kept me on my toes. I never knew what was going to come out of her mouth. One moment I wanted to kiss the hell out of her, and the next I wanted to tape it closed so she couldn't say the words I always thought in my head. She was gorgeous, and the sight of her body had my cock throbbing with need. However, as I told her, I wouldn't do anything to make her look at me the way so many had before.

Oh, I'd earned myself some looks already when I pushed her or she fought back. The difference was the look of terror at my appearance or reputation had never been one of them. That alone would have had me on my knees begging her to let me show her my gratitude in a way only an Alpha could to an Omega. Now everything was fucked-up and twisted, leaving me once more to be the villain in this story.

"Danella," I said, my hands gripping her lush thighs as I fought back the urge to bury my face in her pussy again. Feasting on it last night had me almost coming at the taste alone. She tasted as good as she smelled, which was decadent.

Her body trembled in my grip, but I could see the moment she came to her decision to let me have the gift of her body. "Okay," she whispered, then tore her gaze away from mine to look anywhere but at me.

I would let her do whatever she needed to make herself feel more comfortable, but I hoped that I could get her lost in the passion of how this was supposed to be. Previous to Danella, there had been one other woman, a Beta that I'd met in training camp. We'd fallen into lust with each other and found any occasion to indulge in that until it came time for us to be sent out into the battlefield.

She'd been placed in a different unit than I was, and I didn't hear from her after that. Soon after the first encounter with the Southern forces, I got a list of all those who'd fallen and her name was on there. It was a reality that everyone faced, and while I'd tried not to get too attached to her, being so young and inexperienced with matters of the heart, how could I not? This time would be different; I would do everything I could to protect Danella. It wasn't her fault that her life had been tied to mine, but a cruel twist of fate that no one deserved.

Leaning in, I pressed a kiss to her stomach and inched lower, placing gentle kisses as I went until I reached her pussy. Hitching one leg over my shoulder, I grabbed her ass, holding her in place as I let my tongue slide from entrance to clit. This time when her body shivered, I knew it wasn't from fear, and that had me growling with triumph. I swirled my tongue around her clit, sucking it into my mouth and letting my teeth ever so lightly scrape over it. Her shout of pleasure had me searching for what exactly I'd just done that made her so vocal. Releasing her clit I lapped at her entrance, and the slick that was starting to leak out of her reassured me that she was feeling good.

Throwing my tongue up into her, I kneaded her ass at the same time as getting her to roll her hips and ride my face like she'd soon be riding my cock. I knew that as an Omega she was built to take my cock and knot, but I wanted her good and slick before trying to introduce anything other than my fingers.

"Oh fuck," she moaned as I hooked my thumb up inside her and returned to her clit. A hand fisted my hair as her hips started to buck when I removed my thumb and replaced it with two fingers.

I slowly worked them in and out of her, wanting to draw out the build of her climax. She'd come so easily for me last night I knew I could get her to come twice before laying her down on my bed and fucked her into another. My plan was she'd always come first before I ever entered her. No matter what, sex should be something that's enjoyed, not this forced regiment I see in the breeding house. She clenched around my fingers as she exploded, tossing her head back and her legs trembling, threatening to collapse under her. I caught her against my body when they did give out on her, and then I picked her up to set her on the bed.

"How would you like to do this?" I asked. "Or would it be easier if I make that choice?"

She gulped, but after a moment's hesitation, she rolled onto her stomach and clutched the pillow. "I don't want to watch."

Rage at this situation roared through me, and I clenched my hands. This isn't how it should be. I knew what they promised them at the Care Centers before they shipped them over to us. It was all lies and then they were blindsided when they arrived and were forced into a meaningless life of becoming a breeder.

Having managed to find a sense of calm, I sat on the edge of the bed and ran a hand up and down her back. I massaged her tense muscles and stayed silent as I worked a futile effort to help make her more comfortable. It helped some, but she tensed again when I moved lower, so I continued to do the massage down her legs. I snagged the towel I'd used to dry her off and rolled it up to place it under her hips. Letting my hand slide between her legs, I slid two fingers into her again and slowly thrust into her as I settled myself behind her.

Even though I wanted to give into my urge to make her scream again, I chose to keep the movements languid, simply giving pleasure. Finally, she relaxed into my touch and let out little moans of enjoyment as I swirled a finger around her clit. Her slick was soaking my sheets except I didn't give a fuck, it was just further proof that I'd done as requested. As I felt her starting to clench, I removed my fingers making her whimper with need.

Using the slick on my hand, I coated my cock with it then nudged the tip to her entrance. Just as I had hoped, her body was begging for the climax that it was teetering on and accepted me readily. I didn't thrust all the way in, instead, I did shallow pumps to get her used to the feeling. Clearly unsatisfied with what I was giving her, she started to push back on me. That was the signal I'd been looking for, the green light to tell me that she was allowing herself to find enjoyment in this, even if it was under shitty circumstances.

Caging her in with my body, I slid my whole cock into her in one easy motion. Her cries of pleasure were music to my ears and eased my own worries that she was gritting her teeth through this whole thing. Knowing this was her first time, I waited a moment for her to adjust and kissed down her spine. She'd told me no kissing on the lips, but that didn't mean I couldn't kiss other places. I wanted so badly to bury my face in her neck, to see if she tasted as sweet as she smelled, but I refrained. When her breathing eased up a bit and wasn't quite so frantic, I started to move.

Easing back, I started with small strokes, and as her slick made my movements smoother I shifted to fuck her deeper. Having gone so long only using my own hand for relief, I had to force myself to take it slow. Once she'd had her first experience, then I could see just what she liked or how far I could push her. Everything about this was ass backwards, but I couldn't think about that right now, not with how my cock throbbed in her warm wet pussy.

Once I felt like I could move freely, I sat back and grabbed her hips, lifting them so she was head down, ass up. She didn't want to watch fine, but I was going to fuck her good letting her experience the pleasure of sex. Now I had access to her breasts and her clit, experimenting with what would get those satisfying little cries of pleasure. I watched as she fisted the sheets holding on as I thrust into her, the sound of slapping skin accenting my growls of enjoyment.

"See, Danella, I told you I would make this as good for you as it would be for me," I said as I draped myself over her back with one hand bracing me and the other rolling her nipple between my fingers. "Is it like what you imagined when you played with yourself?"

She opened her mouth to answer, but I shifted my hips to hit that spot every woman had that made them scream. I grinned and hugged her around the waist and pulled her up, so she was sitting in my lap. Hooking her legs over mine, it opened her up for me to start playing with her clit. I wanted her to get one more orgasm before I couldn't hold on any longer. I could feel my knot starting to swell, and I had the urge to back out enough that it wouldn't lock me to her. Then I thought better of it. Babak would be checking her, and I'm betting she'll want to ensure I seeded her good and deep to prove I was following orders.

Usually when an Omega isn't in heat, they aren't allowed to be knotted. It's too risky with danger being so close at hand. Just the thought of knowing you were attached to an Omega when a raid or something else could happen at any moment was a nightmare. When one of the breeders went into heat, three chosen soldiers would be sequestered with the Omega. They would be in a designated section of the breeder house and locked in for the next five days. They would not be counted on to do anything other than deal with the heat. It was the best solution we'd come up with and it was less than ideal.

With a few more strokes of my fingers over her wonderfully sensitive nub, Danella shattered in my arms. The way her body tensed, squeezing me so tightly as if trying to milk me dry, had me losing my battle with my knot. I could feel it begin to swell, and I couldn't fight it anymore. So I didn't. Instead, I hugged her tightly and thrusted deep into her, pressing her down so my knot locked her to me as I roared my release.

Having only been with a Beta who'd never really been able to take my knot, this was a whole new experience. For the first time in my life, I understood what was so addictive about Omegas for Alphas. The way it felt to claim her body and to feel her gripping me just as tightly in return made me feel so possessive of her. She was *mine,* I was her Alpha, and one day she would bear my child as a result of me marking her inside and out. The urge to mark her, to smother her in my scent, rode me as my mouth found its way to her neck.

"No," Danella gasped. "Lucian, please don't. Don't claim me. Come back to your senses, please, please, please."

Her words registered, and I jerked back from her, all but forgetting that I was literally attached to her. She cried out as my knot tugged sharply inside her, making me freeze. "Fuck," I swore, wrapping my arms around her again to keep her close to me. "I'm sorry, I lost myself for a minute but I'm thinking straight again. I didn't mean to scare you, I promise," I murmured against her back where I hid my face.

Goddamn, I'd never felt instinct like that so strongly before. It was almost as if it took over my whole brain, bringing me down to a baser need like an animal. Oh fuck, was I going into rut? Babaka had warned me about that with how long I'd been putting off 'taking care of my needs' as she called it. That was the last thing I needed right now was to turn into a sex-crazed Alpha with an Omega who hated him.

"I get it," she whispered. "It's easy to lose yourself in how good everything feels."

Carefully as I could, I maneuvered us so we were laying on our sides, legs intertwined and my arms still holding her. She'd said no cuddling, but there wasn't another way to hold her that would be comfortable for either of us. Granted, other than today, I didn't plan on knotting her so that should deter it from happening again.

"How are you feeling?" I asked. "I didn't hurt you did I?"

She shook her head, hands tucked up close while hiding her face from me. The Alpha in me wanted to demand what was wrong and fix whatever it was, but I knew that wasn't my place. She was an Omega—just not *my* Omega. Just like I was an Alpha—but not *her* Alpha. Damn, it was going to be a lot fucking harder not to get attached to Danella than I thought. The way she fit so perfectly in my arms, how soft and warm she was, and God, her scent was like a drug I never wanted to give up. How the hell was I going to keep us alive when I wasn't sure I could keep from falling for her?

When I noticed her breathing even out and soft little sighs escaped from her as she drifted off to sleep. Even though I knew it was dangerous, I let myself dream and imagine a world where Danella might actually fall for me. I would give myself today and only today to indulge in that fairy tale knowing it would never come true.

I let her sleep for a few hours then woke her up with me feasting on her pussy until she was writhing in pleasure. Then I flipped her over and fucked her again with possessive abandonment I knew proved I was indeed in the throes of rut. A rut that lasted for two days where I wouldn't let Danella out of my sight and fucked her at the slightest whiff of her getting turned on. I don't know if Omegas can go into rut as well, but at some point Dani stopped trying to divert my attention and began inviting my advances. It seemed we were both allowing ourselves to forget for the moment that it wasn't going to stay like this. But fuck if I wasn't going to revel in every goddamn second of it.

When my rut subsided and Babaka came to check on us, the woman didn't even enter my home before smiling and patting me on the arm. "Told you waiting so long wasn't smart, but I'll tell your father you used your time off wisely. Now do your breeder a favor and air this place out, it reeks of sex. If you need new bedding, I have some stashed away if the store is out, but I doubt you'll be able to get what you've got clean enough to use again."

Unable to say anything to her, I simply nodded while she cackled her way down the stairs and back to the breeder house. Shutting the door, I opened the windows in the main area before stepping back into my room. Danella was sprawled out on the bed, the sheet just covering her ass leaving the rest of her naked body visible with her blonde curls laying wildly around her head. She looked tired, thoroughly fucked, and stunningly gorgeous, but now it was time to end the fantasy. Tomorrow I was back on duty and the commander of the Northern army couldn't be mooning over a pretty Omega. I had to set the tone for the rest of our time together until I could set her free—even if it might kill me to let her go.

CHAPTER 8

Danella

How is it that so much time has passed, but nothing about the world I live in has changed? Looking up from the clothes I was patching for the various soldiers who dropped them off at the breeding house, I caught Violet's gaze and smiled at her. It took her a few tries, but she finally returned my smile, only for it to fall as a tear rolled down her cheek. The poor thing had carried a baby to term and held it in her arms for all of an hour as she fed the little guy before he was taken from her. It had broken my heart to hear her wailing from the secluded room they used for birthing. She was then given two weeks where she wouldn't be expected to fulfill her breeding duties which wasn't much at all if you asked me.

Tori had already given birth last year, but even though we'd seen it repeatedly happen throughout the year, it was never easy. All of us would do what we could for the grieving mother knowing they would never see their child again, although what else would truly help other than to put an end to this?

Lucian and I fought again after they took Violet's son from her, only the prick had nothing helpful to say. He towed the company line saying it was just how things were here in Asturg. *Fuck that*. He could do something if he really wanted to. I'd seen him move mountains to ensure his men got the medical help they needed or the supplies we'd run out of. The Alpha just wasn't willing to extend the effort for an Omega. Especially since he never had to worry about that particular problem with me.

Even now, three years later, I still haven't had my first heat. Oh, the whole outpost genuinely believed that I'd gone into heat twice, yet those three days locked in the apartment with Lucian were hell. He'd get his one day of sex and, like always, used it to his full advantage even if he gave as much as he got. The other two days however were him sleeping in, working on reports, and other things he needed to catch up on while I climbed the walls from boredom.

It had taken Lucian a week to figure out that I needed a purpose and that I couldn't be trapped in his home all the time. Thankfully there was always work to be done, and most of it was put in the hands of the breeders. It makes sense we're the ones who have nothing better to do if we're not getting plowed by various males. Each day Lucian would escort me to the breeder house where I would help with chores such as mending, laundry, and helping to prepare for the evening meal that all the soldiers had together three times a week. It didn't make sense to me, though Lucian said it was to build morale and create a stronger unit.

The only saving grace is that Lucian was sent out on missions for weeks at a time, and I would bunk at the breeder house in Babaka's private area. How she lived her life listening to the sound of men grunting and fucking all night long, I'll never understand. I had to make earplugs out of old foam from a pillow; it helped but didn't change the fact that it was happening. The self-loathing I felt from knowing I only had Lucian to deal with while Tori and Violet were free to be used by whoever wanted them had turned me so jaded.

Gone was the woman who had dreams of any sort of future. I couldn't let myself dream, realizing the chances of it ever happening were slim to none. I'd spent the first year trying to find a way to escape from here, yet every chance was thwarted by the fact Lucian had everyone watching me. It's like he knew I would rather risk death than be stuck in this life forever. While I wasn't actively creating a plan to get the fuck out of here, I was always keeping my eyes and ears open for news. The only news I got consistently was how the war was going, and how things seemed worse than ever.

The Southern Military was steadily recovering from losing the powerplant they'd built on the river. That had been the biggest victory a year and a half ago, with a party in the streets and a special food delivery from the General. All that victory had done was pour gasoline on the Southerners' anger, making them double down on their efforts. Rumors had been flying around that specialized task forces had been pulled from the front lines. Apparently, they'd been dealing with the General's army further north along the border and were coming after us.

"Did you see they're doubling the patrol teams?" Sarah whispered, not lifting her eyes from her work.

Babaka didn't mind if we talked as long as we kept working, but she didn't tolerate any trash-talking of Asturg. The second she caught wind of it, we'd be lashed with her cane, and for an old woman she was fairly strong.

"So you think the rumors are true about them coming after us?" Tori asked, her voice quivering with fear.

I'd never done well with being around a whole bunch of women, and these women were all scared as fuck, even if they'd been born and raised here. This outpost was known to be one that you didn't want to get sent to, being so close to the Southern border. Actually many years ago, before Lucian was sent here, there'd been a massacre. Lucian admitted to me that he'd been sent here to prove that if the General was willing to send his heir here, everyone else needed to suck it up.

"Ladies," I cut in, knowing that letting this go on would cause panic. "Let's keep in mind that the South is always after us. We are at war with them, so it stands to reason that we would be their number one enemy. We should be happy about the fact that they are putting extra people on patrol, not scared."

"Really, Danella, and why is that?" Coral asked, her tone all snark and sass. "Is there something the commander whispered to you while he was fucking you before he left?"

Coral hated me. She'd had her eyes on winning Lucian's affection, being the Omega who was sent to him before me. He'd dismissed her right to the breeder house without even a second glance. Coral was stunning with large boobs, shiny brunette hair, and a heart-shaped face with pouty lips. The crowning trait was the fact that she was a raging bitch and made everyone's life hell. She was born and raised here in Asturg, which added to why she hated those brought in from Oscad.

"Seriously?" I said with a scoff. "It's simple, but I'll break it down for you since you seem at a loss. More guards mean more eyes. More eyes mean better chances of spotting an attack. Put it all together, and we're left with the knowledge that the Commander isn't taking any chances. Make more sense now, Coral?"

Scrunching up her face in disgust, she sniffed and turned away from me to pluck another sock to yarn. She was so bad at mending that Babaka would only risk giving her socks to work on after she sewed a pair of pants together inside out.

"Whatever, there's no way that the Northern army would ever let Southerners get that far over the border without getting spotted. We are the superior half of the nation, after all," Coral added, flicking her hair out of her face. "Too bad the bitch who's supposed to produce an heir can't seem to entice our Commander into knotting her. It's just so tragic."

"Says the bitch he took one look at and sent to the breeding house because his dick couldn't even get hard," I muttered under my breath.

Unfortunately, I hadn't said it quiet enough, and the next thing I knew, Coral launched herself at me. She grabbed my hair and yanked hard enough to make me hiss as I rounded on her slamming my fist into her face. The collective gasp that could be heard from the others didn't surprise me. If any other Omega acted the way I was right now, they would be disciplined harshly and swiftly by the guards who were always watching us in the breeder house.

Strong arms wrapped around me and started to drag me off Coral but not before she got a swipe at my face with her long nails. My cheek stung even though it was worth seeing the skin around her eye already swelling. The black eye I'd just given her would last for weeks, and every time she looked at it she'd remember not to fuck with me.

"Enough," Babaka barked, her Alpha command slicing through the tension in the room. "Take Danella into my rooms and send for the doctor."

I didn't fight the guards, my beef wasn't with them, and out of the two of us I wasn't the one who started it—this time. In the past year, I'd become far more confrontational and had zero qualms about using my fists to make a point. One thing that Asturg did right was realizing that women can fight just as well as men. So Lucian took time to teach me some basic skills in case something ever happened, and no one was around to help me, I'd be able to at least getaway. Those lessons promptly stopped happening once I started using those skills to settle scores as I'd done with Coral.

"That was foolish," one of the guards muttered as he shoved me ahead of him. "Lucian isn't here, and he won't be back for another week at the earliest. That's more than enough time for you to be punished and all signs of it heal before he gets back."

Yanking my arm out of his hold, I turned to face him. Branko was one of four Betas assigned to guard the breeder house so he'd become a familiar face in my days. He'd also been the one who was teaching me their native language. I was pretty fluent at this point, only stumbling on more uncommon words or terms. The Beta had a kind spirit, something that he tried to hide. However, in the evenings, when it was just Babaka and me in the common rooms, he relaxed. I think it's one reason Babaka chose him to keep a close eye on me. I was willing to at least listen to what he had to say, even if I didn't follow his commands often.

"You watched the whole thing happen. I was defending myself from her attack," I shot back.

Branko looked at me with a raised brow. "So it wasn't your sharp tongue that spurred her need to attack you?"

"Hey, I can't control what that bitch does. She should learn to have more self-control and watch her mouth before she says that kind of thing in front of the wrong person," I countered.

"Danella," Branko chidded. "You and Coral have had a personal war since the day you met. If you keep causing a problem, the one who will be removed from here is you, not her. I know you don't want to be trapped in the Commander's home, but that's what's going to happen if the other breeders are in danger from you."

That gave me pause. Lucian had been sent out on missions more frequently over the last few months. Even though I'd told the girls not to worry about the increase in patrol, I knew it wasn't a good sign. Lucian left two days ago, and he'd taken the whole day to keep me in bed with him, almost as if he was afraid he'd never come back. He'd given me this look that held too many emotions I didn't want to acknowledge. While I didn't loathe him, and we'd found a more amicable way in sharing space and a bed after the past few years, the look in his blue-gray eyes before he walked out the door had me questioning things.

Could Lucian care more than he let on? Other than when we were naked and in the throes of sex, when neither of us could deny how good it felt, he was so detached and distant. Almost as if I was an afterthought that he needed to make sure was fed, clothed, and monitored. On the last mission, he'd been gone a whole month. That night, he'd held me so tight, not even interested in sex, just tucking his face in my neck with his body wrapped around me.

I'd given up on the no-cuddling rule, the bed was too small and I wasn't going to be the one who slept on the lumpy couch. The only comfortable way to sleep was for us to spoon or for him to lay half on me, which was oddly comforting. While the nights might prove that he still had a heart and a remote sense of care, the moment the sun was up, the cold commander was firmly in place. I'd given up trying to figure him out, and he didn't try to learn more about me than was necessary to keep up our act.

"You make a good point," I admitted flopping into the chair I always used when staying here and peering up at the Beta. "If I asked you why there's an increase in patrol, would you tell me?"

"Are you asking?" he challenged. "Because I'm pretty sure I heard you explain to the others exactly what I would tell you. We don't discuss military matters, Danella, no matter how much I like you."

"No, I'm not asking," I sighed, rubbing my forehead. "Just curious what the possible response would be when it comes to breeders if there was an attack. Are we left for dead, smuggled out, killed, or told to run for our lives northward?"

"There has been one other attack on an outpost town like this, and in that situation, all the breeders were evacuated by the guards assigned to the breeding house. Our purpose is to keep an eye on breeders and ensure you're where you should be," Branko answered without giving me an honest answer.

Nodding, I turned away to look out the window at the clear blue sky. The nights in this country were typically cool but we were now in the season where the sun scorched the earth, making it clear why everything looked like it was a shriveled husk of itself. There had been rain only ten times in the three years I'd been here, and the ground was so thirsty it sucked up every drop. It wasn't nearly enough to fix how barren the land was now.

"I'll come back when the doctor gets here to look at your cheek," Branko said before leaving the room and locking the door behind him.

At the reminder of my battle wound, I touched a finger to where my cheek burned and bit back a yelp of pain. Fucking crazy bitch managed to get me good, but it was never going to happen again. The next time she came at me, I would beat the shit out of her to the point she'd never dare to touch me. My ability to let go of situations and things to rise above the petty reaction had vanished. Out here, it was an eye for an eye, survival of the fittest philosophy and it was easy to see why people became the unfeeling monsters they were. I wouldn't allow myself to fall to their level, but I wasn't going to be the Omega doormat they wanted, either. It wasn't how I was wired, and I had zero plans to change anytime soon.

The doctor, Jan, was a middle-aged Beta who'd been injured in battle and walked with a limp. Jan told me he'd been a field medic, but after his injury they put him at an outpost so he could still serve his country. Medics, the good ones, were far too valuable to lose when soldiers dropped like flies on the battlefield. Many had been trucked over for him to work on since he was the best medic in our area.

Not long after Branko left me, there was a knock on the door and Jan walked in with his medic bag. His gaze landed on my face and his brows knit together. The biggest fear here on the front lines was getting an infection. Medication was in short supply and would only be used on those desperately needing it. Sometimes they waited too long, and the person died because of it. I'd helped out Jan when there was a surge in soldiers being brought in.

I actually enjoyed the work and learned a lot, it was nice to feel like I had a purpose. Of course, I was only allowed to work with the women since they wouldn't risk something happening to me. When men were in pain, they were unpredictable, tending to lash out at those around them. Either way, it got me out of the breeding house, and even if I was just boiling bandages, it was peaceful.

"Dani," Jan said with an exasperated tone. "How many times have I told you to stop using your fists to settle fights? You're worse than the young Alphas in training who believe they're hot shit."

"Didn't Branko tell you? This time I didn't start it, Coral attacked me and I was left with no choice but to defend myself," I countered, smirking at the doc.

His expression told me he didn't believe a word I'd said. "Let's have a look at you."

Standing from my seat, I walked over to the dining table and pulled out one of the wooden chairs. I sat so the sunlight was right on my face giving him plenty of light to work with. Setting his bag on the table, he grabbed a cloth and a bottle of cleaning solution and scrubbed at my cheek. It burned like he'd poured acid on my face, but I knew it would kill anything that might have gotten in the wound. For something small like this, it was better to clean it to death than use the natural antiseptic cream they made from plants that grew in the river. The salve smelled like shit, but it did the job.

"Maybe you should grow out your nails so you both look like you got into a catfight," Jan commented as he worked. "Although that right hook of yours is pretty lethal. I wouldn't be surprised if you fractured her orbital bone with that much force."

I snorted at his catfight dig. Only I couldn't help but feel a little proud of the blow I'd landed on the bitch. "It's pointless to have longer nails. They break and snag on everything. Besides, who do I have to impress?"

"You realize Branko and I are the only two who find you funny, right?" Jan muttered as he finished doctoring my face.

"That's why you two are my favorite and make such a cute couple," I teased.

Jan froze then looked at me, eyes wide. "What did you just say?"

"You mean about you and Branko? Was I not supposed to know?" I asked, now slightly worried I'd made a mistake.

Over the past three years, I'd seen the two of them together, sharing intimate moments when they thought no one was paying attention. I understood not wanting to make a big deal out of it since it didn't seem as common of an occurrence as it was in Oscad. While Oscad was far more open-minded, some still didn't fully support those who loved someone of the same sex, but I didn't see any reason why you can't love who you want to.

"No, it's..." Jan started then let out a breath. "It's fine, Dani, you're right Branko and I are lovers although we just don't like to give the higher-ups any reason to think we aren't doing our duty as well. It was at my request to keep it quiet. You just surprised me, is all. I didn't think we were that noticeable."

"You're not, I'm just observant and actually pay attention to others around me. Besides the two girls I came here with, I'd consider you and Branko my friends. Both of you have been good to me even if I don't make it all that easy," I admitted. "If you want to keep what you two have to yourselves, that's fine. I have zero interest in controlling other people's lives."

Jan smiled at me and gave my shoulder a squeeze. "Thank you, it's not forbidden for us to be together as long as we still do our duty if we're picked for when an Omega is in heat. However, I'm never going to get picked since they can't afford to have me locked away in a room for three to five days. Most won't take a chance and fall for someone since they can be killed in the blink of an eye and you're left with heartache."

I gave him a small smile. "You're both lucky. Branko would only be sent out to fight if something happened here since he's assigned to us troublesome Omegas."

"Ha," Jan laughed. "The only one who is trouble around here is you." Flicking my nose playfully with his finger, he packed up his bag. "Now you know what to do. If you need more ointment, let Branko know, and I'll make sure you get it. Let's just hope this won't scar so I don't have to deal with a furious Lucian when he sees it."

Rolling my eyes, I stood. "Like he would really care? Once he finds out it was another Omega and not one of his men messing with his favorite toy, he'll get over it."

"If you want to believe that, I can't stop you," Jan said with a shrug. "You don't give that man enough credit. He does truly care for you. The only reason you don't see the signs is because you don't want to."

"We're not having this conversation again, Jan. I like you, really I do. If you keep pushing this matter, I'm going to show you just how good my right hook is," I warned.

Jan put up his hands in surrender. "Okay, okay, I'll drop it. But, Dani, I'll warn you, the longer things go without you getting pregnant and the Commander being gone more... it's not going to be the outcome you want. He's all that's standing between you and being chained to a bed upstairs, and I don't want that for you."

"I know, you don't want that for any of us. Yet here we are," I pointed out. "Thank you for the warning. I'll keep it in mind."

Jan reached out and gave my arm a reassuring squeeze then left the room. The snick of the lock told me I was being put in time-out for the rest of the day. Oh goodie.

CHAPTER 9

Danella

Babaka banished me to work alone in her rooms for the remainder of the day and only allowed me to join the others for dinner. Coral and I were placed on opposite sides of the room to ensure neither of us incurred any more damage. Tori sat next to me, and Violet was across from us, absently picking at her food. My heart broke for her. I wanted to rage, fight, and scream about how all of this was pointless. What good did it do to take the child away from its mother?

Was this why everyone in this country was so cold and heartless? They never knew the love of a mother or what it felt like to be held and cherished. The General wanted them strong and fearless, so he'd rather train them from the moment they took their first breath to when they took their last on the battlefield. It was senseless, and I don't know why I was the only one who saw it.

"Dani, are you okay?" Tori asked in a low voice. "Those scratches look like they hurt."

I gave her a warm smile and squeezed her hand. "I'm fine, nothing to worry about. The doc looked at it, made sure it was good and clean, then warned against scratching so I didn't get a scar."

Tori nodded and returned to her bland, tasteless soup that had been made for dinner. The food shortage this time was the worst it's ever been. Normally we'd have enough to make it through before we ended up at the point we are now. We were down to grinding up beans and potatoes to make this weak, watery soup that we added essential vitamins and minerals to so we didn't get sick. The shipment was supposed to arrive two weeks ago, and I know Lucian had been talking with the general about it. From the stormy looks on his face when he ended his phone calls with his father it wasn't an answer any of us wanted to hear.

The soldiers were given the better food, such as dried jerky and hard-tack biscuits that never seemed to go bad. You needed to soak them in water to gnaw on them, but it was better than this gruel we had. Last year we tried to make a garden, saving the seeds from the vegetables, but nothing survived other than the potatoes and onions. It also used up more of our water supply than was worth it. We kept up with the potatoes and onions, which is what was saving us right now.

When Lucian warned me about learning to get used to being hungry, I'd thought he'd been using it as a scare tactic. Now I understood he was telling the truth. When the clawing pain stopped, I lost all body fat, and one meal a day could last me until the next I fully understood what he'd been trying to say. There was no way to prepare for that though, when all you've known is having enough. The three of us chatted, talking about Oscad and a few others who had been sent before us adding in.

"Remember that one teacher who had to clear his throat every five minutes? It used to drive me up the wall," Erica said with a groan. "What did he teach? I can't remember, it was hard to pay attention."

"Oh that was Mr. Otterbe, he taught health and wellness I think," Violet answered, joining in the conversation after just listening to us talk. "He used to say it was because he was allergic to milk and that we never had soy milk or lactose-free for him to use in his coffee."

"God, he had the worst coffee breath ever," Tori blurted. "He'd lean over my shoulder to look over my work and his breath was just deadly."

Everyone laughed at that, making the Asturg women glare at us. They never got an education, there was no reason for them to learn anything other than to read and write. It amazed me how limited their knowledge was of the outside world and what was happening around them. They didn't even know there was another country until the first wave of Omegas started to get sent to Oscad. I tried not to pity them, but the fact the general was using his peoples' ignorance to keep them stuck here was just fucked up.

"Would you all shut the fuck up?" Coral snarled. "No one wants to hear about your past life. Clearly, your country didn't want you, so they shipped you off here where nothing you learned is ever going to be of use to you. Unless you plan to bore the men fucking you so they finish faster."

Tori slammed her spoon on the table. "Why do you have to be such a bitch, Coral? None of us asked for this. We were drugged and put on a bus without our knowledge. Now we're stuck here in hell."

"You better watch your fucking mouth," Coral sneered, shoving up from her seat. "Don't you dare speak like that about this country."

"Really, why is that? What's it ever done for me, or you for that matter?" Tori shot back.

After losing her baby, the sweet shy Tori had vanished and she reminded me of me. No longer was she going to let people walk all over her. She was standing her ground, and it was heartwarming to see.

"You don't know what you're talking about. This country has done everything to take care of me," Coral argued. "Without them fighting and protecting the border, the Southerners would have taken over and slaughtered all of us."

Violet let out a huff of laughter. "You have to be fucking kidding me? Is that what you believe? Your own fucking general is doing that already while you just line up and beg to be picked for battle. Besides, your country chose to do everything for you since they never allowed your mother to care for you. They ripped you out of her arms and stole you away." Violet was yelling as she said the last part, her hand gripping so tightly around her spoon that her hand turned white.

Reaching out for her, she jerked away and knocked her bowl off the table where it shattered on the floor. Tears streamed down her face as she hurled the spoon at the wall and stormed up the stairs to where their rooms were. Generally after dinner, the men would start arriving, and Babaka would have stormed after Violet to deal with her. Luckily, Lucian had ordered the breeding house closed to soldiers while he was gone. He'd taken half the unit with him on this mission telling me it was a big deal. With so many gone, It would be too dangerous to have men distracted with getting their dick wet when there was less of them to cover for each other.

"You Oscad bitches are fucking crazy," Coral muttered as she took her seat and resumed eating.

"She's not wrong, though," I shot back, standing up and taking my bowl with me as I joined Violet upstairs. Tori was also hot on my heels with the remainder of her meal. We couldn't let Violet not eat so soon after having a baby, it could get her sick.

Violet was in the bunk room where the rows of beds were set up. This was where they slept, and no males were allowed in here. There were other rooms that they used for fucking since not all the girls would be available all at once. Apparently, they found even for Omegas that our vaginas needed a break every so often. Even face down in her pillow, I could hear her sobs and it was like someone had reached in and grabbed my heart squeezed tightly. The rage that simmered under my skin fought to break free seeing my friend so broken.

Setting the bowl on the nightstand between the beds, I climbed in behind her and cuddled her to my chest. Wrapping my arm around her, she clung to me as she cried. Tori joined us on the other side, so we cocooned Violet in between us doing all we could to protect her from the world. I sang softly to her, knowing she'd told me that her mother used to do that for her if she had a nightmare. While I didn't have the world's best singing voice I was passable, and right now, I was willing to do whatever it took to help her. I was surprised that Babaka hadn't come to yell at us for leaving the table and the scene that Violet caused, but something told me she knew the first child was the hardest to recover from. The old bat might be a hard-ass Alpha when she needed to be, but the more I got to know her, I discovered she actually had a heart.

At some point, the three of us fell asleep after Violet finally calmed down, only to be awoken by screaming. Shooting upright, I rubbed my eyes to clear the sleep out of them and looked around the room. It was dark, and the girls had all come up to bed but, like me, were now waking up at the sound. Just when I thought I might have been hearing coyotes or something the sound of gunshots were heard followed by more screams.

We were under attack.

Rolling out of bed, I grabbed Violet and yanked her up, then reached for Tori. "We need to move." I snapped.

"What—"

"No," I cut Tori off. "No questions, just run. Get downstairs, we need to get the fuck out of this building."

Violet stood there frozen, eyes wide as more gunshots sounded. Tugging on her arm, I tried to get her moving, but she wasn't budging. Doing the only thing I could, I put my shoulder in her stomach and grabbed her legs as I hoisted her up. She was heavier than I expected but it didn't matter I needed to get us the fuck out of here before they stormed in and shot us like fish in a barrel. While I didn't believe they were the monsters that Coral and the others said, this was war. You never knew who was going to be a risk, so I'd undoubtedly shoot first. Why wouldn't they?

Tori raced down ahead of me while the other girls panicked, screaming and crying. The war in my heart about getting all of them to safety raged in my chest, yet Tori and Violet were my priority. I'd promised them that I would make sure we survived this, and I would keep my promise. In the common room, I found Branko and the other guard weapons at the ready stationed at the windows. Even Babaka had a gun in her hands, standing on a table and peering out the window. None of them turned to look at us, fixated on what was happening outside.

Everyone believed there was only one entrance to the breeding house however I knew that having stayed in Babaka's room for so long there was a backdoor in her suite. I put a finger over my lips to keep Tori quiet as I waved her to follow me. Violet was starting to come out of her shock and wiggling in my grip, I just needed her to hold on until we got out of the main room.

Once in Babaka's sitting room, I sat her down and grabbed her face with my hands. "Violet, I need you to hear me and listen well. Can you do that?" I asked.

"Yes," she breathed, panic making her eyes wide as she watched me.

"We're getting out of this place. Once we step foot outside of the breeder house, we're going to make a run for it. I won't stick around to see if the Southern army is going to murder us all or not. I've studied maps that Lucian left in his room so I know where to go. What I need from you is to be quiet, don't look back, and no matter what... don't stop running." Glancing over my shoulder at Tori, who was watching the door and I pinned her with a look. "Same goes for you."

"Lead the way, Dani, I trust you," Tori said, making my eyes burn with tears at her trust.

Clearing my throat, I looked at Violet. "Can you do this for me, Vi?"

She didn't speak, just nodded her head as her whole body shook. Taking her hand in mine, I squeezed it before towing her after me. When we came to the wall hanging, I grabbed it and ripped it off the wall revealing the door. It was secured by a deadbolt so I just needed to undo that and we were out of here. Looking around the space once more to ensure I didn't miss anything useful, I took a deep breath.

"No turning back," I whispered to myself as I tossed open the bolt and yanked open the door revealing the night beyond. "*Run.*"

To the girls' credit, they didn't hesitate as we shot out into the darkness. Purposely the outpost was barren of all trees, shrubs, or anything else the enemy could use to hide behind. While this was good for us running in the dark, it also meant there was nowhere to duck for cover if shots started up. Right now, it sounded like the fight was going on behind us, which made sense since Lucian had built everything to make it look like the most accessible place to enter so they went through the minefield. I probably wasn't supposed to know any of this, but Lucian liked to talk as he got ready for bed to wind down from the day. Since there wasn't much for him to talk about besides the war, I just sat and listened, taking in every bit of information.

Of course, he'd never guess that I was still planning to run after three years, but I'd never given up hope. If there was ever a chance, I would take it no matter what. So here we were, running across the back half of the outpost to the northwest corner. The fence there was being upgraded and they had men working on it day and night. I hoped that their supplies and trucks were still there so we could use them to get the fuck out of here.

The first explosion echoed through the air with a flash of bright light and screaming. Half the landmines had been removed and went with Lucian on their mission. Another thing the supply shipment that hadn't come yet was supposed to have. Not only was food becoming scarce, so were ammo and other weapons. It was almost like the General was hoping something like this would happen and set us up for failure.

"Dani, where are we running to?" Tori asked, her breathing labored.

The breeders didn't leave the breeder house, so it was inevitable that the girls would be out of shape. Another tactic was to make sure they couldn't run, but I hadn't let that happen, doing all that I could to keep myself as fit as possible.

"We need to get to the section of fence they are repairing," I answered, but I didn't give much more instruction since I wasn't sure what would happen after that.

Yelling and gunshots sounded closer to us, along with the thudding of feet running. "Don't look. Just keep running," I ordered, even though I wanted to know what or who was coming after us.

In the distance, I saw piles of fencing stacked on the ground. A beat-up work truck that didn't have doors, and the bed was full of tools and other supplies. The lights they'd been using to work by had been knocked over and two bodies were on the ground, blood pooling around them.

Stupid, stupid, stupid, Dani. I berated myself, realizing that anyone with a speck of military training would know to hit more than one spot when attacking. This was a weak point; if they'd been watching the outpost, they would know that to work on a section, they diverted the electrical current when they fitted in the new panels. There were also far fewer land mines scattered, having removed them to keep the soldiers safe as they worked and replaced the ones missing from the funnel they created.

"Oh my god, are they dead?" Violet gasped as we got closer.

My answer was cut off as the *ting* of a bullet hitting the old truck had me shoving Violet then Tori to the ground. "Quick, we need to crawl under the truck. With the lights down, we're in the shadows so move fast."

I urged them ahead of me, needing to make sure they were going to be okay. Then I spotted another soldier dead, slumped in the cab of the truck. I saw his handgun still in the holster on his hip. Biting my lip, I peered over my shoulder and saw the shadows of people moving, the flash of guns firing, followed quickly by sounds of pain and thuds to the ground. Kneeling, I reached up and grabbed the soldier's pants and yanked with all my might sending him crashing to the dirt. Quickly I searched his body finding a knife, gun, and what I think was what you put in the gun for more bullets when it ran out. Slipping them into my back pocket, I shoved the knife in its sheath down the front of my hip and kept the gun in hand.

"Dani, where are you?" Violet called, her voice bordering on hysterical.

I checked the soldier's pockets once more, praying the keys might be there. No such luck. With a last-second glance up in the cab, I saw them dangling from the steering column. The soldier had been trying to drive away but only got as far as the keys in the ignition.

"Get in the truck," I whisper-shouted, as I pulled myself off the ground and into the cab.

Violet was shoved in with Tori behind her as I fumbled to grab the keys and turn them. The gun in my left hand made things awkward only I wasn't letting go of it. My father had just started to teach me how to drive before I was taken away, so I knew the basics except a dozen lessons didn't make me an expert.

"Do you know what you're doing?" Violet challenged.

Twisting the key, the engine roared to life sounding deafening in the quiet. "Guess we're going to find out."

I didn't know if there were headlights or if they even worked but I didn't bother. All I needed was to get us far enough away to give us a head start. We'd be heading to the north part of Oscad that curved around Asturg. Neither section of the country was very populated but that's exactly what we needed. The fewer people we had to deal with, the fewer problems we'd have. Wrapping my hand around the gear shifter, I pushed in the clutch and prayed to god I wouldn't stall it out.

The truck lurched into a jerking motion wildly tossing us around. When the engine started screaming, I shifted again and things smoothed out a little. Thank fuck, my father always felt it was best to learn on the most challenging version of something, otherwise, I'm not sure if I'd ever know what to do with a manual vehicle.

"Hey, stop that truck!" someone shouted. "We can't let anyone get away! Call for backup!"

The hailstorm of bullets flying our way had my heart in my throat as I hunched down as far as I could while still being able to see. "You two get on the floor, hide in the footwell," I ordered as I shifted into third picking up speed as I aimed right for the fence.

A panel had been cut which allowed the intruders entry, but I was about to see who was going to win in a fight between fence and truck. Gunning it into fourth then shifting it to fifth gear, we made contact with the fence. I shut my eyes and braced. The sound of metal slamming into metal was thunderous and the truck jolted and rattled yet still managed to keep going. The impact had slowed us down some so I had to downshift to get us moving faster.

The engine groaned and spluttered, not at all pleased with the abuse it was going through but as long as it kept moving I didn't care. The sound of shouting and gunfire grew more faint but all that changed the moment I realized I drove over a landmine.

CHAPTER 10

Danella

Everything was chaos. The world was spinning as I was slammed around the inside of the vehicle, only to be tossed out. Landing in the dirt was a welcomed pain since it meant I'd come to a stop. My ears rang, vision blurred, but I knew I couldn't stop moving. Feeling like a newborn trying to learn how to crawl, I got on my hands and knees, floundering as my vision cleared enough for me to see the truck on fire.

"*No*," I screamed, shoving to my feet and stumbling toward it.

There was a sudden second explosion that knocked me flat on my ass and took the wind right out of my lungs. Looking up at the stars as I gasped for air as tears pooled in my eyes at the pain I was experiencing. The mere thought that Violet and Tori might still be in the truck felt like a knife thrust into my chest. How had I failed them so badly? We'd finally gotten our chance and I'd fucked it up by getting them killed. Then unexpectedly, Tori's dirt and blood-covered face appeared over mine. She was yelling at me, shaking my arm, then pulling as if trying to get me to my feet.

"—you need to get up," Tori begged, as my hearing finally seemed to snap back on. "Please, you need to help me. I can't lift you on my own and Violet's hurt."

That had me fighting to pull my shit together as I helped Tori get me to my feet. Taking quick stock of myself, I didn't see any major injuries, just cuts, scrapes, and the pounding in my head that I prayed wasn't a concussion.

"Where is she?" I managed to get out, my voice rough and raspy.

"Over here, I think she broke her arm," Tori shared as she led the way.

Violet was leaning against a thin three that didn't look like it should have the strength to hold her up. She cradled her arm against her chest as tears streamed down her face making tracks in the dirt and grime that covered it.

"Let me have a look, okay?" I said, giving her what I hoped was a reassuring smile.

Taking hold of her arms, I gently squeezed to see if there was anything broken. When I got to her shoulder, I let out a sigh of relief— she'd only dislocated it. This often happened with soldiers when they were training or during battles, so I'd seen Jan fix them a dozen times. I'd never personally done it, but he always talked his patient through what was happening as he did it to keep them calm.

"Good news, nothing's broken," I assured Violet. "I'm going to work as fast as I can to get us out of here. Try to keep as still as you can. Tori, grab her other hand so she has something to hold onto."

Wasting no time, I began to shift the arm into the position I needed as I tried to remember everything Jan had said. Traction, slow movements, keep the patient calm and relaxed... that wasn't going to happen, but I'd do the best I could. With the arm at ninety degrees, I rotated it outward slowly, and when I felt it shifting, I started to pull the arm straight and lift it up. Watching the shape of her shoulder, I saw when it finally slipped back into place and breathed out a sigh. Thank god that had gone perfectly, or I'm not sure what I would have done next. Yanking off the belt from my pants, I wrapped it around her to make a sling of sorts.

"You need to keep your arm close to your chest for a little while. It will also help with any pain you might have. We can't stay here much longer. The fire from the truck is going to attract attention, and that's the last thing we want," I explained, as Tori and I got Violet to her feet.

Looking around at the ground, I prayed we'd made it past the last of the land mines. I was betting we had since shrubs, weeds, and other undergrowth that refused to shrivel up and die littered the ground. I spotted the hills that we needed to head toward as well. When we got closer to them, we'd have to head north, but cutting up too soon would land us near another large city, and I couldn't risk that. On the other hand, getting too close to the mountains would take us far too close to the wild people who'd abandoned civilization and become feral versions of themselves.

"We ready?" I asked, trying not to push them too hard after the crash, but time wasn't a luxury we had.

Swiftly as we could move, we guided Violet who still wasn't fully back to her senses, though we managed. The sound of shouting had me urging the girls to move faster—they found the truck. The beam of flashlights told me how close the soldiers were and that there were more of them than I wanted to deal with.

"I can't keep up at this pace," Violet whimpered, an Omega whine leaking into her words.

Slapping a hand to her mouth, I cut off the whine in exchange for a gasp. "Don't you dare let out a whine. Even the faintest echo of that will have Alphas crawling up our asses. That is the last thing we need."

Violet's eyes filled with tears at my harsh words, nevertheless I couldn't feel bad about it. I was going to keep us alive no matter what.

"Dani, give her a break," Tori bit out, glaring at me.

Growling in frustration, I turned my back to her. "Climb on. If you can't walk, then I guess I'm going to have to carry you."

"No, I'm just—"

"Violet," I snapped, cutting her off. "I promised you I would get us the fuck out of here. Now let me do that because leaving you behind isn't an option. So, get the fuck on my back."

Wordlessly she nodded and wrapped her good arm around my neck as Tori helped to boost her up so I could catch her legs. Holding onto her as tightly as I could, I started to jog even if it might cause Violet's arm to hurt. She'd thank me once this was over and we were back safe and sound in Oscad. Better to live in the countryside of a place we wouldn't have to sell our bodies to survive.

The shouting and footsteps didn't stop coming after us as I thought they would. Could it be that others were running from the camp, or were they trying to ensure we were all dead? No witnesses to tell what happened that night. Probably didn't matter that we had no idea or that we knew nothing about the Northern army. Okay, that wasn't totally true in my case. I knew a lot more than I'd ever let Lucian realize. When I saw an outcropping of rocks, I switched directions and headed right for them. The three of us needed to get out of sight. If we couldn't outrun them, then we needed to hide until they left and we'd be able to keep moving.

What looked like an outcropping was actually the edge of a cliff. The bottom wasn't all that far down. The drop down was more angled than sheer, meaning we had a chance to slide our way down. It would be noisy and draw attention, yet below was far more cover for us, with lots of slopes and buttes to hide in. It looked like a giant had dug its fingers into the dirt and left it that way. It seemed like the perfect place to get lost and never be found— or that was the plan, anyway.

"No, no, Dani, we are not doing what I think you're thinking," Violet whispered harshly into my ear. "The plan is to live through this, right? How is this a good idea?"

"Because if we don't find a way to get out of sight, then we'll be shot or dragged back to the breeder house. All of us will be locked away forever, and I'll be killed for trying to escape when I'm the property of the general's son," I seethed. "For me, I'd rather die on my own terms, and fighting for freedom is one hell of a way to go."

Before Violet could fight my hold, I stepped off the cliff and dug my heels in and settled our weight back so I landed once more on my ass. Violet swore in my ear as we started to skid, sending rock and loose soil down ahead of us. Another oomph and more swearing behind us told me that Tori had taken the leap as well.

"Over here," someone shouted above us. "We've got three runners."

Shit, shit, shit! Now we were sitting ducks until we reached the bottom.

"Don't waste your bullets. If they make it to the bottom alive, we'll find them easily enough in the badlands," another voice that seemed cold as ice answered.

Peering over my shoulder, I caught sight of a hulking man with a face so cruel I prayed I'd never run into him again. If I did, I had no doubt he'd kill me without a second thought and spit on my body for causing him the trouble.

"Dani, watch out," Violet shrieked.

Whipping my head forward, I saw the boulder ahead of us and had to make a split-second decision. Twisting, I grabbed Violet and rolled over and over again, but I hadn't made it completely out of the way. My hip slammed into the boulder knocking loose my grasp on Violet, who screamed and tumbled away from me. The last thing I remember before blacking out was that at least I made it to the bottom and saw Violet and Tori there coughing, battered, and bruised—but they were alive.

PAIN. I was in so much pain.

What the fuck had happened to me that I was hurting so bad? None of the soldiers would have dared to touch me for fear of what Lucian would do in return.

"Look, I think she's waking up," Tori whispered.

What was Tori doing here? Was I in the breeder house? Did something happen?

"That gash on her head must have happened when we got tossed out of the car. There's no telling how much blood she's lost," Violet said, panic clear in her voice. "How could she not know her head was bleeding?"

"Shh, Vi, it's going to be all right. Dani's too stubborn to die, not when we're so close to getting out of this whole mess." Tori soothed.

"That man said they would hunt us here in the badlands. My

arm's fucked up, the bruise on her hip is massive, and we don't know how badly she's really hurt," Violet sobbed. "What's the point of surviving if we don't all make it out of this?"

Was I that bad for Violet to believe I was going to die?

"Hey, don't write me off yet," I croaked.

A hand quickly caught mine and hugged it to their chest. "Dani, I'm sorry. You know me always panicking and worrying about things I shouldn't be." Violet sniffled.

Taking a few deep breaths, I opened my eyes and found that we were in some sort of cave. Or at least that was my guess from seeing all the stones surrounding us. "Where are we?"

"The two of us managed to carry you away from the cliff and into the badlands. Both of us tried to go as far as we could, but we're just not as strong as you right now. Then we found this overhang that would keep us out of the elements and keep us hidden from sight," Tori explained, her round eyes observing me. "Did we do good?"

I managed a smile since nodding my head was out of the question. "You did great, exactly what I would have said to do."

"You've been asleep a long time. We were worried you might not wake up. The sun's already halfway up in the sky," Violet added.

Fuck, we'd been here far too long, but with me unconscious, I get it. There's not much to do when your leader is out for the count and left to make the best choice. Now the question was, do we stay here until dark or risk making a break for it when we could see better? Both had their drawbacks, and there was only one way to find out if I could even move at this point.

"Here, help me sit up," I said, reaching out my other hand to Tori.

"Are you sure? That seems rather risky right now, doesn't it?" Violet argued.

Letting out a sigh, I tried not to get upset with her, since she was just looking out for me. "Vi, the only way I'm going to know if I can make it is if you help me up. I need to see how bad things are. If it's too much I'll have you put me right back down."

She gave me a speculative look, and I couldn't blame her. I

was never one to tell the truth about being in pain or not. Eventually, she gave in, and they pulled me up into a sitting position. I gritted my teeth to keep the whimper from slipping out of my lips. Everything hurt, my vision swam, and I felt so nauseous that whatever meager remnants of my dinner might make an appearance.

"Dani," Tori warned as she stopped pulling me up. "I think you need to lay back down."

"No," I bit out. "Just get me up against the wall, and I'll be fine."

Neither of them seemed to agree with that choice, yet they helped me anyways. Once up and not trying to move any part of my body, the pain subsided to a dull throb from my head to the tips of my toes.

"Dani, you look white as a ghost," Violet fretted. "There's no way we can leave here now. You have to rest."

"What if resting gets us killed? You heard that man, he's going to come after us, and I have zero doubt he'll shoot us dead," I argued.

"So stumbling around in the middle of the day is a better choice?" Tori retorted. "Yeah, why not give the asshole a way better chance of shooting us in the head, so at least it's not painful."

"Don't talk like that," I growled out. "We are going to make it out of this together. I promised you both I would get us back home, and that's what I intend to do."

Tori snorted and shook her head. "Right, and the second we make it back home, the only thing keeping you alive will be gone. You'll drop dead right on the border. Sounds like a much better plan, don't you think, Vi?"

I cracked open an eye to look at Tori, surprised by her words. "Since when did you become so cynical?"

"Takes one to know one," she muttered. "Look, just close your eyes and rest. I know you want to keep going, but right now, that will kill us faster. Vi and I can't lug your heavy ass around, so just sit tight and store up all that energy."

With extreme effort, I lifted my hand and flipped her off.

"Glad to see taking on a boulder hasn't ruined your humor," Tori sassed.

I let out a huff of laughter which had me hissing in pain. *Fucking hell, why does everything have to hurt so goddam much?* A body pressed up against me and a head rested on my shoulder, and I knew by the soft powdery scent it was Violet. She'd always been one to need physical reassurance when she was scared or stressed—right now, I'm sure she was both. Her body kept me warm, which I appreciated since I couldn't stop shivering. Tori cuddled in on my other side and I drifted back into the darkness where the pain wasn't quite so bad.

CHAPTER 11

Danella

The next time I woke, it was to the feel of a blade on my throat. Snapping my eyes open, I was greeted with the face of the man who threatened to kill us on the cliff. Now that I could see him up close he had the face of a killer. Dull gray eyes studied me as I studied him in return. His face was void of emotion, but I got the feeling he was waiting for something. If he thought he would get a reaction out of me, he was going to be sorely disappointed. The fact that we were still here in Asturg meant I failed. Death would be a more welcome ending to this than having to continue living life as something these people considered to be lower than dirt.

"Did you chicken out, or do you prefer your victims to know they're about to die before you slit their throats?" I asked, my tone board.

He blinked once as if mildly surprised at my comeback. "What makes you think I'm going to kill you?"

"Pretty sure you mentioned it last night. You know if we survived making it down the cliff." I raised my arms slightly as if to gesture to the surroundings. "Here we are, some more alive than others, but we made it. Plus, the blade at my throat isn't helping your case if murder wasn't what you were going for."

He let out a scoff of laughter. "How are you still alive with a smart fucking mouth like that living in Northern Austurg?"

"Wonders never cease," I drawled.

"I suppose they do, seeing as I'm not going to kill you. At the time, I didn't know you three were Omegas. They are rare around these parts," he informed me.

I rolled my eyes. "You don't say, so rare, in fact, they ship them in from another country."

"Ah, guess you wouldn't know, but that ended three years ago. Seems Oscad's government was overthrown and new leaders were put in place. As a matter of fact, there's a rumor going around that they're sneaking into Northern territory and stealing Omegas back. That makes you even more rare than you thought, doesn't it?"

"Yippee," I cheered, twirling a finger. "So, since you're so well informed of the outside world, I'm going to take a wild guess and assume you're not a Northerner."

"Sassy and smart, maybe I won't hand you over to the elites and keep you for myself," he sneered, letting his eyes drift over my body in a way that made me feel so gross.

"Yeah... been there and done that. I think I'll let you slice my throat instead," I said, tilting my chin up to give him better access.

He gripped my jaw in a painful grasp, making me wince. "See, it's no fun killing someone who isn't afraid of death. The panic in their eyes, how fast their breathing gets. Oh, and who could forget about the tears. Yes, those delicious tears streaming down their faces. You...are going to give me none of that. Your friends, however, those two will fulfill all my needs so beautifully," He told me almost wistfully.

Ignoring how much it hurt to move, I yanked my face out of his hold and slammed my elbow into his nose which appeared to have been broken many times before. "Don't you dare lay a finger on them."

"*Fuck*," the man swore, jerking away from me to clutch his nose.

Even as my vision swam from moving so much, I looked everywhere for the other two. Deciding that getting the fuck out of here while Dead Eyes was still dealing with his nose, which was gushing blood, I used the rock wall to steady myself as I stood. Once on my feet, the whole world heaved and bucked like I was on a boat. I closed my eyes and took some deep breaths trying to ground my senses. When I opened them again, it still felt like I was looking at the world from underwater, but I could manage.

Following the wall to the entrance, I made it to the opening where I saw Tori and Violet tied up with five men standing guard with guns. They seemed unhurt even if they were bound and gagged. I'd known it'd been too quiet when I first woke up, though my brain isn't firing on all cylinders right now to be that observant. Tori saw me, and her eyes went wide, telling me that Dead Eyes was coming up behind me. I dropped to my knees as the wind and the whistling sound of a knife flew over my head.

"Draza," an Alpha barked, telling me that Dead Eyes was a fucking Beta. No wonder the asshole had such a big chip on his shoulder. "I told you that I wanted them alive."

"The bitch broke my nose," Draza muttered.

A man entered my vision and knelt in front of me. Tucking a finger under my chin, he forced me to raise my gaze. "Half dead and foolishly fearless, you take on an elite assassin. Maybe I should give you the job instead."

His voice was soothing in a way that made no sense as he studied me with rich brown eyes. His head was shaved bald, and the only hair he had was a beard that was kept short and neat. It was hard to miss the fact he was a well-trained soldier. I mean, his muscles had muscles, for Christ's sake. Then the light evening breeze wafted his eucalyptus and wintergreen scent right into my face. Taking a deep breath seemed to energize me and clear my head a little more to fully take in what was happening.

Southern soldiers had found us, and it sounded like they didn't have any intention of killing us or leaving us behind. I was trading being enslaved by one half of Asturg for the other. I seriously can not catch a break.

The Alpha and I continued to stare each other down like we were locked in our own battle of wills. As an Omega, I was supposed to be submissive, let my eyes fall, and listen to whatever the Alpha told me to do. Yeah, well, this Omega was fucking sick of rolling over and taking orders. I'd gone from one prison to another, each one becoming worse than the last. If this asshole was hoping for me to be as sweet and demure as the Northerners demanded, I was all out of fucks to give on that one.

"How could one so fierce survive so long?" the Alpha murmured. "They must be desperate if they are willing to overlook the defiant fire that burns bright in your eyes, little Omega."

"Oh, and you're going to be so different? Aren't all of you cut from the same cloth?" I demanded.

His brows rose, and the curiosity grew in his gaze. "I suppose in the beginning, before the country fractured, we shared more of the same ideals. Not so much now. Although you'll be able to learn that for yourself once we get you across the border."

"Yeah, I'll pass and let Dead Eyes over here kill me. I feel like it will be a much better choice," I informed him.

"I can see why you would think that, except I'm afraid that wasn't really supposed to be taken as a take it or leave it option. You and your friends will be coming with us back to the South, where you will receive medical attention and food, and then we'll discuss where your placement will be," he explained. "It's also clear to me that you are dead on your feet, so our medic Cristofor will keep an eye on you."

The Alpha pointed to a man with sandy blond hair, bright blue eyes, and a kind smile. Walking over, he kneeled next to the Alpha and started to grab a few things out of his medic bag. He seemed younger, less affected by the war than the others on his team. I was impressed they already had a medic for a group this small, but I had doubts with how young he was if he'd be any help at all.

"I'm going to take a look at your head wound first. They tend to bleed a lot, making it seem worse than it is. So you might get off lucky with just a gash and nothing more," Cristofor shared as he shuffled on his knees to get closer to my head.

When he reached out, I jerked away, not wanting to have him touch me. The last thing in the world I wanted to deal with right now was a stranger putting his hands on me. I knew it wasn't just a cut with how rattled my brain was feeling, and having him poking around it would just make it hurt even more.

"It's not just a cut," I snapped. "If it's not actively bleeding, then just leave it be. There's nothing you can do about it so don't waste your meager supplies."

"Meager…" Cristofor blinked at me a few times. "What makes you think I wouldn't have medical supplies to treat you? Never mind." He waved off the question. "The bleeding has stopped, but I'd like to see how bad the damage is. Are you having trouble with your vision? Nauseous? Any memory lapses?"

"God, listening to you is making it worse. I told you, just leave it alone. I don't want anyone touching me," I grumbled.

The Alpha wasn't pleased with my response and turned his attention to Cristofor. "I believe it might be best to help our patient rest while we travel. Staying here longer isn't wise, and we need to hoof it back to the river."

I didn't catch his meaning until Cristofor poured a liquid onto a gauze pad. The second I realized it was to knock me out, I tried to pull away, only that damn muscled Alpha grabbed hold of my shoulders. He was so strong and my body was in so much pain I didn't have the energy to fight. I'd used it all up against Dead Eyes and fleeing out of the cave. Tori had been right, I was far worse off than I thought.

The gauze covered my mouth and nose, and even as I tried not to breathe, I couldn't take it any longer and gasped. The sickly sweet smell coated the inside of my nose and tongue. My nails dug into the Alpha's arms, needing to leave some proof that I'd not gone willingly. Soon the world started to fade and I slumped into his arms, my head resting on his shoulder. Still, I fought to stay conscious but ultimately lost.

Fucking assholes.

CHAPTER 12

Cristofor

I couldn't help but snicker as this little firecracker of an Omega called us assholes under her breath. Really, I couldn't blame her, especially if she'd lived in the North. It made sense they weren't known for their caring ways. Not that we Southerners were a soft bunch, but we didn't rape a whole designation of women to produce children for us. Omegas were placed in situations to give the best chances of breeding, but it wasn't their sole purpose of existence. In fact, we trained them to be soldiers alongside us Betas if they met the standards. Something told me this woman would absolutely be accepted into training.

"Cris, I still want you to look at her head, but we've hung around far too long looking for them," Sorin stated as he gathered the Omega in his arms with a smirk on his face as he peered down at her. "I suppose I should be impressed that they gave us a run for our money without any training."

I spotted the marks on his arms where she'd clawed him as I knocked her out. Grabbing an alcohol wipe, I cleaned them and put on some ointment knowing he'd never let me put a bandage on them. "That amount of sedative should have been able to take out Victor within a few minutes. Just how stubborn does a person have to be to fight that hard?"

"Trust me, Cris, if she's that wild and managed to keep her tongue inside her mouth, then she's one hell of a fighter," Petru interjected as he looked down at the other two. "Now, what of you two? Are you going to come with us without any trouble, or do we need to toss you over our shoulders?" Both shook their heads, not at all interested in that option.

Petru, our gun specialist, squatted and pulled the gag off the pretty Omega who'd clearly had surgery performed on her upper lip. That wasn't something that could be done in the North, so she must be one of the Omegas from Oscad. God, I could only imagine what hell that must have been to be taken from your family and sent here of all places. While she'd remained silent, her friend, on the other hand, took the opportunity to share her thoughts with us.

"You touch us, and it won't go well for you when Dani wakes up," she spat. "Do you even know whose Omega she is?"

That had us all surprised. As far as any of us knew, the North didn't have packs or create bonds with each other for some crazy fucked up reason. While you couldn't have an official pack without an Omega in the mix, those of us in units like ours were a pack. We all lived, trained, ate, and fought together—trusting the other would have your back no matter what. Except for Draza, who'd gotten separated from his team, this was my pack. My family and I would have the same loyalty to them that these three women seemed to have for each other.

Victor yanked Petru out of the way and glared down at the two making them cower. Victor, the unit's explosives expert, wasn't the most friendly-looking guy. His dark brown hair was cut close to his head, while his full beard grew wild. I'd tried to get him to maintain it, but that was a losing battle so I finally gave up. The look in his hazel eyes was intense, and with his size and bulk, he came across as one scary fucker. It probably also had to do with the fact that I don't think I've ever seen the asshole smile before. He was the picture of friendliness, that one, but once you had his loyalty, there wasn't a person he wouldn't kill to keep you safe.

"Who?" Victor bit out.

The younger one just crossed her arms and glared, not willing to make it that easy. I snorted, it would seem this little firecracker had rubbed off on her friends. Victor took a menacing step forward and the other cracked, bursting into sobs, which was the reaction Victor got most of the time dealing with women.

"Please, please don't hurt us," she begged, clasping her tied-up hands. "We'll do as you ask, I promise. Just don't beat us."

Victor's lip curled in a snarl at the way this Omega pleaded. I caught Petru's gaze and gave a small jerk of my head knowing that Victor and weak women weren't a good mix. Petru rolled his deep green eyes at me, running a hand through his coppery red hair before stepping in.

"Vic," Petru warned, grabbing his arm. "We need to get moving, and once we get past the river, you can ask them all your questions. The outpost is destroyed. Whoever they're worried about is gone, so this conversation is pointless."

Victor yanked his arm out of Petru's hold, shouldered his pack, and stomped off. Groaning, I turned to Sorin but he hadn't been paying any attention to us. Instead, I found him seated on a boulder trying to wash out the wound on the woman's head. Sorin was our leader and head Alpha, if you will. However, he wasn't a man who felt the need to flex that muscle. Instead, we worked as equals, which being the only Beta in a pack of Alphas was unheard of. Most units like ours could only have two Alphas at the most. We had four plus myself, and that led to moments like this where tempers flared, but they always cooled in the end.

"Sorin," I called to him, causing his head to snap up like he'd been caught doing something he shouldn't. "I should take her so I can monitor her breathing and pulse as we go."

"The wound looks pretty nasty, but it's not bleeding anymore," he told me as he stood, handing her over. "We need to get her to the Med Center sooner rather than later."

Her weight settled into my arms as her head fit perfectly on my shoulder, forehead resting on my neck. The scent of her caught my attention so much that I found my nose in her hair before I even realized it. A rich earthy spice wrapped around me that had a bite to it yet was softened by a sweet floral scent of magnolias. They'd been my mother's favorite flower and reminded me of the warmth of home. I hummed with delight as I cuddled her closer to me.

When someone aggressively cleared their throat, I opened my eyes to find Toma smirking at me. "Been that long since you've held a woman? What, are the two of us not enough to satisfy you?"

Toma was all hard lines and bronze skin that made him sexy as fuck. His black hair, similar to ours except for Sorin's, was cut short as the military required. On him, though, it just showed off his features making him that masculine beauty that instantly makes me hard. The shimmer of humor in his eyes that were so dark brown they looked almost black, only expressed to me he wasn't being serious.

Was it uncommon for the Betas in the unit to develop sexual relationships with the Alphas? No, not at all. There wasn't a whole lot of time to find relief elsewhere. Did it matter that I was one man who had been fucked by them all? Not one fucking bit. While I didn't sleep with all of them anymore, we'd all been open to the idea. I cared for them all and loved each in their own way, even though my heart belonged to two of the four Alphas. As for which two, that would be Toma and Petru. They might both be Alphas, but they'd been friends since childhood and fell in love. It was uncommon for Alphas to develop relationships like that, but those two were meant for each other. I was part of that now, and the three of us just fit together like puzzle pieces.

"She certainly smells a lot better than you lot," I teased. "And way more cuddlier without all those hard muscles. Sometimes I swear my cheek goes numb from sleeping on your pec muscle."

Toma tossed his head back and laughed, flipping me off as he grabbed his stuff. "For that, you can sleep in the tent with Draza tonight."

"If I didn't have a patient who I was responsible for, then that might truly be a threat," I countered.

"Hey," Draza snarled. "Fuck you all. I didn't ask to be part of your group, and the second I get the chance, I'll be out of your hair."

I had to bite my lip to keep from laughing as he spoke, sounding like a petulant child with a stopped-up nose. He had the gauze I'd given him hanging out of his nose like an idiot, but at least it stopped bleeding.

"Nah," Toma said, slapping the Beta's back. "We have Cris for that. Thanks for the offer, though."

Petru shook his head and crouched in front of the Omegas again. "Alright, ladies, we need you to keep quiet so we don't have to gag you again. If you follow the orders given, everything will be fine and we'll get you somewhere safe. Just know that if you make trouble for us, you'll be tossed over Victor's shoulder like a sack of potatoes. Trust me when I say, no one wants that."

With surprising willingness, they let him help them to their feet and stood there waiting for instruction. Sorin took the lead with Toma, then Petru and I boxed in the girls, leaving Victor and Draza to watch our backs. Things were slow moving since the girls didn't have shoes and this land was pretty rocky, but they didn't complain. The sun was quickly starting to fall, however we needed the cover of night to make this crossing without drawing too much attention. We had people waiting for us on the other side who would make getting back to base much faster.

We'd been walking for a few hours when Dani started to stir in my arms. "Hold up, guys, I need to administer the sedative."

Now that she wasn't going to fight me, I decided to mix a cocktail of painkillers and sedatives. It would keep her under longer and provide more relief. I'd been worried about her head injury, but at this point, we needed to keep her calm and quiet. Until we got her to the Med Center to have her examined, it would be best not to have her fight us and fight she would.

Holding my small flashlight with my teeth, I grabbed a syringe out of my pack and drew from the small vials. When I brushed aside her wild curly hair to inject it into her vein, I paused. My mouth went dry as I saw the large brand that had been burned into her skin. I had no clue what the symbol meant. Nonetheless, it was barbaric to even consider doing that to a person. No wonder she hadn't wanted me to touch her. She'd had more than enough pain at the hands of soldiers. Shaking myself out of my anger, I administered the medication. She flinched, but after a few moments, her whole body relaxed and she even breathed a sigh of relief. Just how much pain had she been in?

"Sorin," I said, pulling the flashlight from my mouth.

My tone clearly indicated that it was something he needed to see, so he approached quickly. When I shone the light on her neck, he hissed as if, like me, he imagined the pain she must have been in. His face clouded with anger as his hands were fisted so tightly his knuckles turned white.

"Those fucking monsters," he growled. "How could they do something so savage? I knew they didn't give a fuck about their Omegas, but I would never have thought they'd stoop to this level to make them feel like livestock."

Shoving to his feet, he turned to the two other girls. "Did they do this to you too?" he demanded.

They shook their heads frantically, sensing his anger. In a world of designations, not every Alpha was created equal, and Sorin was Alpha to the extreme. When he got upset, it was hard to ignore the dominance that pulsed off of him like now.

"Who, who did that to her?" he pressed.

They'd refused to speak about it before, and I had little doubt they would answer him now.

"It's a mark to show she belongs to the Commander," the blonde-haired woman said, her voice barely above a whisper. "She wasn't in the breeding house like us. Dani lived with him unless he was on a mission."

There was only one man who was labeled the 'Commander of the Northern Army', and that was Lucian Bakal, General Rasvan's heir. Holy fucking shit, we had the Commander's personal breeder right here in front of us. Eyes wide, I looked up at Sorin wondering if he understood what this meant, only he refused to look back for me to see his expression. The Commander is who we'd been after when we attacked, but no one could find him. So Sorin made the call to deal with who was there since it would be a blow to them, regardless. We'd had one team who was to gather the Omegas and bring them back, and it seems these three had made a break for it in hopes of making it back home to Oscad.

My eyes fell to the woman who lay before me, beaten, battered, and branded but full of more fight than I'd ever seen. Where all the other Omegas had cowered in the corner, Dani had grabbed her friends and made a break for it. Could she be the one who took the truck through the fence? We'd picked up their trail at the site of the burning truck, which is why we thought they were soldiers. The second we found them curled up in the cave, it was clear they were no Northern soldiers. I lightly brushed my fingers over the brand, my heart aching for her and how old this wound felt.

Maybe she would help us get revenge on them and finally aid us in ending this pointless war. So many lives have been lost on both sides. There had to be another option, and just maybe we had it right here in the least expected of places. Now there was no other option except to make sure we saved her. This could mean there was hope; hope for a new beginning. Maybe not all was as hopeless as we thought.

CHAPTER 13

Danella

Soft voices murmured around me, accompanied by the sound of beeping. It was a soft, steady sound that seemed to happen in time with my heartbeat. My body still hurt, but it wasn't nearly as bad as the last time I came to. Flashes of memories of blue eyes and blond hair with a soothing tone reassured me I was alright. Then there was the feeling of someone cradling me to them, the scent of fresh spruce trees and the heady aroma of patchouli.

Where was I that this combination of sensations and smell would be combined? Searching my memory, I tried to figure out what the last thing I remembered was. Gunshots, screaming, pain, Violet's tear-streaked face, and Tori screaming at me to get up. My heart started to race, and the beeping increased right along with it. Where were they? Had we been taken? Did Lucian find me again like he always promised he would?

"Easy there," a gentle female voice soothed, cutting into my mental spiral. "You're at the Med Center in our main military outpost. You've been through a lot and have been unconscious for three days."

Three days!? How could I have been out for that long? What of Tori and Violet? Fuck, I had to get out of here. I had to find them.

"Dani, I know you're anxious, but I need you to try and stay calm. You lost a lot of blood, fractured your skull, and suffered a severe concussion. We kept you under for this long to try and allow your body to heal. We thought we might have to do surgery, but it seems you're a lot stronger than you look," she shared, making me pause. "Now, can you try and open your eyes for me?"

My eyes weren't open already? Shit, why hadn't I done that already? What the fuck was wrong with me?

Shoving that panic aside, I took a deep breath. Well, as deep as I could without my body protesting. Focusing on the few muscles I needed to open my eyes, I put all my energy into that effort. Slowly they lifted then I slammed them shut when the brightest fucking light I'd ever seen stabbed into my brain.

"Shoot, sorry about that. Wait one moment for me to turn off the overhead lights. That should help," the woman said as I listened to her footsteps moving around the room. "Okay, the room is as dark as I can make it."

It made all the difference. This time when I managed to crack my eyes open, I wasn't assaulted by light. The room was cast in a dim glow by the medical equipment placed in various areas around the bed. It reminded me of Oscad with how current and updated everything was. Instead of the shabby ruins I'd been living in for the past three years, I was back in the modern era.

A woman's face entered my eyesight. She was older, probably in her late forties with a gentle smile and kind, honey-brown eyes. Her brunette hair was pulled back in a ponytail and she was wearing scrubs. "Hello, Dani. It's nice to finally meet you. I'm Bethany, the nurse who's been looking after you the past few days."

I just gave her a long slow blink as my brain tried to absorb all the information I was receiving.

"Do you feel up to answering a few questions for me?" Bethany asked.

Licking my lips, I opened my mouth to speak, but my throat was so dry I just emitted a croak.

"Hold on, I'm gonna get you some water," she explained as she stepped away from my bed.

The door opened, and light filtered in along with the

sounds of people talking, footsteps, and the general hustle and bustle of a busy area. When the door closed, the room was quiet once more and I relaxed slightly to take stock of myself. Shifting, I tried to sit up except when I went to move my left arm, it came to an abrupt halt due to the metal cuff anchoring me to the bed.

Did they honestly think I was going to run away?

"It's just a precaution. However, if you prove to us that you're not going to make a break for it, then I might be persuaded to remove it," a man said to my right.

Snapping my head in the direction of his voice, I found a soldier sitting in a chair out of the way in the corner of the room. I groaned and pressed my right hand to my temple as the pounding in my skull started at the sudden movement.

"Whoa, easy now," the man said, getting up to walk over to me. "I didn't mean to scare you, I thought you knew I was here." He tried to reach out to touch me, but I flinched away, feeling far too vulnerable to trust anything at this point.

Backing off, he lifted his hands in surrender, then slipped them into his pockets. "Hey, I'm not here to hurt you. If we were going to do that, then we wouldn't have gone through the effort of healing you."

He had a point, although I still wasn't going to let him touch me. Thankfully the nurse returned and paused for a moment seeing the man next to my bed. "Toma, is there a problem?"

"No Beth, no problem. I just unfortunately scared her since I didn't realize she had no idea I was here," Toma explained. "Thought for sure she would have sensed an Alpha in the room."

"How exactly was she supposed to realize that when she's been in a medically-induced coma and had her brain rattled around so hard it started to swell? Would you be on the top of your game if something like that happened?" Bethany demanded, glaring at the man I now could undoubtedly tell was an Alpha.

"B—"

"Nope, I don't want to hear it. I allowed you and the others to stay in here to keep an eye on her as long as you stayed out of my way. Now go back to your chair, and don't move unless there is something wrong," Bethany ordered.

Shocking the hell out of me, Toma hung his head and did as he was told. I could tell that Bethany wasn't an Alpha, so how in the world did she have the right to order him about like that? It was becoming more apparent to me that the South definitely had a different way of dealing with things. Pretty sure if I'd tried to do that while helping Jan I would have ended up in a medical bed for the beating I got.

Bethany must have seen my expression as she used the remote to bring up the bed so I could sit up, then held out the water with the straw in it. "Small sips, I don't want you choking on it. Coughing is not your friend right now, so go...slow. Oh, and just ignore my little brother, he's a pain in the ass."

I'd just started to take a sip when I stopped and looked up at her, surprised. For a family to have more than one child was amazing but to have one be a Beta and the second child be an Alpha was even more exceptional. When she didn't add anything further, I just worked on drinking the water and ignored the feel of eyes from the corner. Bethany told me to ignore him, so ignore him I shall.

"I'm going to stop you there. Too much, and you might make yourself sick," Bethany warned, pulling the water away from me. "Let's start with the basics. Can you tell me your name?"

I hesitated at the question. *Did it matter if I told them my real name? It's not like they were going to go after my family if they found out we were rich. They were in Oscad and probably forgot all about me at this point.*

"Danella Holstand," I answered, my voice husky from disuse.

Setting aside the water she grabbed a clipboard and started writing down information. "How old are you, Danella... or do you prefer Dani? That's the name your two friends gave us."

"Danella. Only my friends call me Dani," I told her.

Not at all bothered by my attitude, she just continued on, "How old?"

"I'm not really sure, we never had access to dates or anything. So I'm guessing twenty-four or twenty-five," I answered.

"That's fine, Danella. What's your birthdate and then I can figure that out," Bethany assured me.

I rattled it off, and she added that in my chart and did some quick math. "You're twenty-five, almost twenty-six, and your birthday is next month."

Rather than making me feel better having that information, it only made me realize how much time I'd lost. How in the world did all this start when I was twenty-one, and now suddenly, I'm almost twenty-six?

"Do you have any allergies to foods or medication?" she inquired, trying to keep us moving. I simply shook my head and started picking at the blanket with my free hand. "What about children? Have you given birth?"

While I knew that was a practical question to ask, everything in me raged at her digging into my life. "No." I bit out.

"When was your last heat?"

"Why? So you know when best to stick me in a room with strange men to rape and breed me?" I snarled. "Fuck you and your questions. I'm not answering any more of them. If you think that just because this place isn't a shit hole like it was in the North, I'm going to be more willing to spread my legs for your men. You've got another thing coming. I'd rather bite my own tongue and drown in the blood than be treated like a fucking piece of meat to shove a dick into."

My rage burned under my skin as hot tears rolled down my cheeks. Bethany, for her credit, didn't react, allowing me to spew my angry words at her. On the other hand, Toma wasn't quite so willing to let me get away with that as he shoved himself out of his chair and marched up to the bed.

"You think you can fucking talk like that to my sister? All she's done is help you," he snapped.

"Toma," Bethany cut in. "Don't. She has every right to feel this way. We know how the North views Omegas. How does she know that we are any different? Sit down, *please*, and let me handle this," Bethany begged her brother, giving him a look that told him she wasn't really asking.

Toma glared at her, but when his dark brown, almost black eyes landed on me I could see the pity, and that made me even more upset.

"Don't you dare pity me," I warned. "Not from the likes of you who just a second ago was furious at me for speaking the truth of the life I've had to live. Do you know what I would have given to have someone stand up for me like that? Instead, all I could do was choose between a torturous death or allowing a man to use my body to stay alive. Until you know how to choose from one version of hell over another, don't you fucking dare pity me."

I hadn't meant to be so cruel or allow myself to get this worked up. However, to be treated like an actual human for the first time in a long time seemed to break me. Using my free hand, I wiped away my tears, furious that I was crying in front of them. I'd given up on wasting tears over the shit situation my life had become. Why were they appearing all of a sudden now?

"Toma, I think it might be best if you gave us a little space. She's awake now, so didn't Team Leader Sorin ask for an update when that happened?" Bethany said, obviously understanding he was doing more harm than good being here.

He frowned at his sister but gave her a curt nod, then spared me another glance, but there wasn't any pity this time. It was quite the opposite. I might actually call that look—respect. He stepped out into the hall, closing the door behind him and leaving me alone with Bethany. She turned to take down some notes from readings she found on the various machines giving me a chance to collect myself.

"He's not all that bad, you know," Bethany commented as she set down the clipboard to take my blood pressure. "Like all men, he has no idea how to deal with women or say the right thing when we're feeling particularly vulnerable. Life here in the South isn't easy by any means, but it's not the hell you've lived through. Everyone carries scars, some aren't as old as others, and we tend to forget what it feels like to have such fresh wounds."

I couldn't argue with that. I'd seen it on the other Omegas who'd either grown up in Asturg or had been there longer. They'd hardened, callused themselves to the reality of their situation so it wouldn't hurt so bad. Truthfully, I thought I'd been one of those people, only the way I'd just reacted to Toma made it clear that wasn't the case.

"Where are you from, Danella?" Bethany asked after a moment. "I suppose I should ask, more specifically, where you were born. I'm not sure how it works in other countries or if you've been shuffled around to more than one in your lifetime."

While they seemed to be far more informed here than in the North, I still got the sense they didn't know much about places outside of Asturg. "I was born in Oscad, near the capital city. My parents were influential people since our ancestors were part of the government before the terrorist attack. I lived with my parents until I was seventeen, then I was removed from their home to live in a Care Center. It's a facility they have to keep us Omegas safe and ensure we are educated in the right manner. I lived there without any contact with the outside world until I was drugged and loaded on a bus with about ten other girls to be driven off to Asturg."

Bethany pulled the stethoscope out of her ears, slowly looping the item around her neck. "Why would they need to drug you to send you here?"

"I have no idea, but the Omegas they chose to send to Asturg were typically the troublemakers. Or those they couldn't send to Shearia because of their looks, intelligence, or personality," I explained. "Normally, we were given a warning that we were being sent off, except there was never a choice in the matter. They said go, and we went."

Contemplating everything I told her, she sat on the edge of my bed searching my face. "Danella, you are an amazing woman to have lived so few years and gone through so much. I can't tell you that things will be better now that you're here, but I can promise they will teach you how to fight. No one with the heart of a warrior like you is overlooked just because of your designation. Let me help you get better, so you can learn to never be a victim again."

God, her words sounded like a dream. How could I trust that what she was saying was true? Why the fuck would they want to teach me to fight when I was found in the clutches of the enemy? Then, on the other hand, how could I refuse such an offer? To never be a victim and have the ability to protect myself? Fuck, I wanted that more than anything. The real question was...could I trust Bethany to be telling me the truth?

As if sensing my apprehension, Bethany reached into her pocket and pulled out a small key showing it to me. "Promise me you will cooperate as you heal, and I will see that you're never cuffed to this bed again. That should be a good starting point toward proving I'm a woman of my word."

I couldn't help but grin at her. Bethany was quickly growing on me and I didn't like many people—especially women. Yet here she was willing to put her actions where her mouth was to prove herself.

"I have two requests," I countered.

Bethany smirked and nodded her head for me to go on.

"No men touch me without my permission. I don't care if I'm dying or unconscious, they can keep their fucking paws off me. I've had enough people feel like my body was their god-given right to touch, and that's not happening anymore." I stated.

"Alright, I can work with that. We have enough women on staff so I don't see this as an issue. What the second?" she inquired.

Sitting up a little straighter and jutting my chin, I held her gaze intently. "I want to be put on suppressants."

Even though I hated the arrangement with Lucian, it had kept me alive, and that was something I wanted to continue doing. While I didn't know what the Southern view on breed might be, I wasn't going to be one of their livestock.

"Deal, we like to have all new Omegas on them for the first few months while they acclimate. The last thing we want is a new Omega such as yourself dealing with many changes and then getting thrown into heat. I will warn you though, if you get assigned to an Elite Unit and go on a mission you won't be getting the bi-weekly shots. An Omega's self-preservation often keeps them from going into heat in high-stress situations, although I can't make any promises," Bethany warned.

The suppressant being a shot was new, but the fact that it would only have to be given twice a month instead of a daily pill was totally fine with me. "Thank you for being honest with me."

"Danella, one thing *I* will never do is lie to you. Of course, I can't speak for others, but you won't get anything but full honesty from me," she assured me as she unlocked the cuff from my wrist. "Now I'm going to lie you back down so you can get some rest. When you wake up next, we'll get some food into you."

As if her words seemed to trigger something in me, I let out a yawn so wide it made my jaw crack. Now that my wrist was free, I curled up on my side trying to get comfortable and fell asleep instantly.

CHAPTER 14

Toma

The guys and I had been switching off who was staying at the hospital while Dani—sorry, Danella—slept. I'd been around more just because we made sure she was put with Bethany making it easier to get away with shit. Now that she was awake, it was clear to me that things weren't going to go as smoothly as we thought. Knowing Beth wouldn't let anything happen to her, I left the hospital and pulled out my phone to call Sorin. Now that we were back in the central city we could use all our technology. The closer we got to the Northern border, it was like returning to the dark ages.

"She awake?" Sorin asked when he picked up.

"You could say that," I muttered. "That woman might be an Omega by designation, but she's got the attitude of an Alpha."

Sorin actually chuckled, which shocked the hell out of me. "Come back to the barracks. I got a rather interesting call today from an old friend."

"Seeing as I got kicked out of the room by Beth, I don't foresee being allowed back in anytime soon," I shared with a sigh. "Give me five minutes and I'll be there."

Not feeling the need to say anything more, Sorin hung up, which was far more typical than a man who chuckled. I sent a text to Beth letting her know I had to head back to the barracks and to text me if she needed anything. Then I spotted a private driving one of the military hum-vees and waved him down.

"Yes, Sergeant, what can I do for you?" the private asked when he stopped in front of me.

"I need to get to Alpha Blue barracks," I informed him as I hopped in.

The private nodded and took off, not even questioning my orders. Such was the luxury of not only being a ranking officer but the fact that people knew I was part of the most respected Elite Alpha Unit in our military. Sorin, being the President's son, was part of it, but we earned the titles on our own. It was an honor to serve and protect our country, and if it just happened to be alongside the men I respected and called family, all the better.

It didn't take long to get from the Med Center to our building that houses the apartment we shared as a unit. Unlike the lower-ranking soldiers, we had our own space with a common room in the middle and three rooms that broke off from there. I shared a room with Cristofor, Victor, and Petru, while Sorin got a room to himself as our leader as well as being ranked as a Major. We'd been together for ten years and moved as a well-oiled machine with the most successful mission rate out of all the Elite Units.

Walking down the hall of the barracks, the other soldiers got out of my way, nodding their respect as I passed. I'd never been one to need or want that kind of shit from people. Growing up just like all of them with humble beginnings, I didn't feel it was right to get that kind of response from people. Just because I happened to be a technology wiz and could handle anything computer related that was thrown at me didn't make me better than them. It was something I struggled with a lot, but Petru kept telling me just to let people do what they wanted and accept their feelings on the matter. He and I had been best friends since we were toddlers and grew into something more as we got older. While it wasn't common for Alphas to end up in a physical relationship with each other, I don't think it could have happened any other way for us. We'd loved each other forever, it seemed. Designations, be damned. Then Cristofor joined our unit, and he seemed to fit perfectly into the relationship Petru and I had.

I knew Cris had slept with all the guys when he first joined, and it didn't matter. Who was I to judge who he shared his body with? In the end though, Cris chose to become our third exclusively. I knew Sorin cared for him deeply, even if it hadn't manifested into love. Victor shared his affection by being overprotective of Cris. He ensured none of the other units or soldiers messed with our caring and happy-go-lucky Beta. I'm not sure Victor could love anyone, but he certainly had a soft spot for the Beta he'd never admit to.

Swiping my keycard for the lock to our room, I watched the green light blink a few times before the chirp sounded, meaning the door was open. Shoving the door open, I entered our common space which had a couch, armchair, TV, and coffee table. Off to the side was a small kitchenette that provided us with a sink, microwave, fridge, and cabinets to store basic food or snacks. This was our home when we were out on a mission, which seemed like always these past few months. I couldn't remember us staying here longer than a few days before we got our next order. Petru and Cristofor were already there with Cris sprawled on the couch, head in Petru's lap, eyes half closed as Petru absently stroked fingers through his hair.

They both turned to look at my entrance, and Cris smiled wide. "Look what the cat dragged in. I didn't think we'd get you to leave that room the way you've been so vigilant."

"Yeah, well, she's awake if Sorin didn't tell you that already," I shared as I grabbed his legs, lifting them so I could sit. "That woman's got a mouth on her, that's for damn sure. Ended up with Beth kicking me the fuck out of the room because I was upsetting her."

Cris snickered and Petru just smiled, shaking his head. "You mean to tell me there's a woman out there immune to your smooth manner?"

I flipped Petru off since he knew I had never tried to attract the attention of the women who swarmed around me. I had Cris and

Petru for lovers; the other two were brothers and family—why would I need anyone else?

Sorin walked out of his room reading something on his phone with an odd expression on his face. Almost as if he was conflicted about something. The front door opened, and Victor walked in with two duffle bags that he carried right into his bedroom. We've learned over the years not to bother asking what he might be bringing back with him because it was always harder to sleep when you knew he had liquid TNT stashed away under his bed. He was the best there was when it came to shit like that, so we trusted him not to get us all killed—most of the time.

A moment later, he returned and flopped down in the armchair watching Sorin expectantly. "So, what's the big deal you had to pull me from the workshop for?"

Sorin didn't respond right away instead he held up a finger telling us to give him a moment as he responded to something. Finished, he tucked his phone into his pocket, crossed his arms, and put his feet in a wide stable stance. This was our Major's biggest tell when he had something to tell us that we might not like. It's as if he was stabilizing himself for us to be upset and take it out on him.

"I had a rather interesting phone call today," Sorin started, his tone neutral so we couldn't tell if he was upset about this or not. "An old friend, who I honestly never expected to hear from, reached out. He needed a favor, and it just so happened that I'm in a position to help him out if and only if the rest of my team agreed."

The frown I felt deepening on my face matched the other's expression. Cris slid his feet off my lap and sat up as we waited for Sorin to give us the terms of the request. None of us had ever heard him talk about a childhood friend before, or even someone outside of his cousin who was like a brother to him.

"God damn it, boss, just tell us what the hell he asked," Victor blurted when the silence seemed to just linger uncomfortably.

"The three Omegas we just found and brought back with us... he wants me to help smuggle them out and return them to Oscad," Sorin announced.

My jaw dropped, not at all expecting something like that to have been the request. "How the fuck does this person know about them?" I demanded. "Is there a mole in our midst? It was Draza, wasn't it? That bastard doesn't know how to keep his mouth shut no matter what we threaten him with."

"Boss, you can't be serious. That Omega we've been watching over for the past few days is the key to crushing the Northerners. There's no way you could let someone that valuable go," Victor challenged.

Petru stood and started to pace. He was a man who couldn't think unless he was on his feet moving about. He even started to rub his hand through his hair which told me how stressed he was about this request. We all knew what it meant to have someone like Danella in our grasp, and now someone was telling us to give her back to Oscad? Nah, that didn't seem right to me. Why would Oscad care if they were the ones who shipped them out here to Asturg in the first place? I knew about the government change, but why would they extend the effort to worry about this when I'm sure there were other things to manage?

"Is this person reliable?" Cris asked, reaching out to place a hand on my bouncing leg. He hated it when I started doing that, and having his touch always seemed to help take the edge off my anxiety.

Sorin seemed to contemplate that question a moment before he nodded. "I don't see any reason why he would have another motive than to bring the girls home and return them to their families. A lot has changed in their government and how they care for their Omegas. I also learned that no one knew the old leaders were selling out their own country. None of the families had any idea their daughters were being shipped off to Asturg and Shearia. Knowing that, I could completely understand why they would want to reunite them with whatever family they have left."

"What if we send back the other two and keep the sassy one," Victor interjected. "Really, she's the only one we need. Those other two are like fragile little flowers that will get ground into the dirt if they can't toughen up."

"Pretty sure what they've already survived should have made

them rougher and tougher. If that isn't the case, they need to leave," Petru reasoned. "They won't be accepted into training and sending them to the city would be more work than we need. The placement test for non-military jobs is ridiculous, and since we found them we have to make sure they don't cause trouble or run away."

I knew Petru didn't mean to sound as cold as he was, although growing up, he took care of his little brother and his cousins until he was old enough to enlist. None of those four kids would make it as a soldier, so he had to start their training from a young age by learning a skill that could be useful. Everyone in the South worked, pulled their weight, and helped the war effort in whatever way possible. All kids went to school to learn how to read, write, cook, and basically test their skills. If they had a gift for something, they would be fast-tracked into learning all there was about that specific skill so that they could be placed in the best position to further the cause when they were old enough.

We in the South fought smarter, not harder, using technology and our talents to build and produce weapons that could wipe out the North. Problem was, if we wiped it out it could ruin what was left of the drought-stricken land. With proper care and skill, it would be easy enough to bring back the North to the glory our ancestors tell us about. Taking adults who haven't been raised the way we have and finding a place for them in the massive cog that runs the wheel of productivity in the South would be a lot of fucking work.

"I agree with all of you, which is why I didn't say yes right away. What I'd like to do is offer our new friend Dani a deal. One where we get her friends out of here back to Oscad, and in return, she helps us with the North. If she's willing to tell us all she knows about Commander Lucian, the army, how bad things really are, and what it would take to ruin them... we send her friends back home to Oscad," Sorin explained.

The way I'd seen her protecting those two, I figured it would be an easy sell. What I wasn't sure about was if the two would leave her.

"What do we do if she wants to go back with them?" Cris asked.

Sorin scratched at his beard a moment, then seemed to come to a conclusion. "I would tell her that once we've used the information she's given us to take out whatever locations she can tell us about, she can go back too."

"Just like that?" Petru challenged. "She helps us win this war, and we just send her on her way?"

"Would there be another reason to keep hold of her?" Sorin challenged.

Petru stopped his pacing to face Sorin head-on. "She's our Omega. What more reason do we need other than that?"

Just when I didn't think I could be more surprised by this conversation than I already was, the man I thought I knew best just blew my mind.

"When did she become ours?" Victor demanded, shooting to his feet. "I don't remember laying claim to her. Wait, did we lay claim to her?" He backtracked, looking at all of us.

Since none of us seemed to have an answer for that question, we just turned to look at Petru hoping he would. Evidently, there was something that all of us missed if he was out here making those kinds of announcements.

Petru just growled and ran his hands through his hair again making it stand up on end. He looked as frazzled and frustrated as we all felt. "Seriously, you guys can't truly be sitting there and telling me we didn't pick her after spending the past few days at her bedside. Sorin, I saw the way you reacted to her when we discovered what she was. Hell, Cris almost didn't let the Med Center staff take her from him. Obviously, all of us are feeling rather attached to her, even if you don't want to admit it."

I burst out laughing at this, her words running through my mind. "Yeah, even if I believed for a moment that you were right, there is no fucking way that woman is going to stick around. She's properly ready to tell all of us to fuck right off for being male and Alphas. The moment Beth asked her about kids and heats, she flipped and started going on this rant about how she's not a fucking breeder and everyone can fuck off. If you tell her she can go back, that will be her first priority."

Both Cris and Petru looked at me disapprovingly, like it was my fault that she felt this way. Victor, who was still standing, his hands flexing in agitation, just glared at Sorin like he was waiting for the so-called *boss* to tell us his take on things. Ignoring my two lovers, I kept my attention on Sorin as well. It didn't matter what the rest of us thought, if he told us we were keeping her, then that's what we were damn well doing. No one went against Sorin's orders. It was the one thing all of us were trained to do—never second guess your commanding officer.

"I think we take it one step at a time. We offer Dani—"

"Danella," I cut in. "She made it incredibly clear that only her friends could call her Dani, which we are not."

Sorin held my gaze for a moment, letting me know with that look he didn't appreciate getting interrupted. Our leader was a fair man, but the one thing he hated most was to be interrupted. Usually Victor was the one to make that mistake though it seemed today was my day to fuck all the shit up.

"We offer Danella the proposal about her friends and see where that leads us. If she's willing to agree and make it happen, then we'll deal with what comes next at that point. Even with the position I'm in, I'm not sure I can acquire an Omega outright and not send her through basic training," Sorin warned. "If that's what happens, even fast-tracked with us all helping, it will take three to four weeks before they'll let her go on a mission."

That was the rub of it all for me. We couldn't just take Danella at her word. She'd need to prove to us that the information she shared was accurate. In order to do that, she'd have to be granted mission status that required basic training just like any other soldier. *How the fuck are we going to survive that long here on base?* It had been years since we'd had a whole month to spend inactive. Of course, I'm sure there is plenty we could do in that time. I'd been in sore need of updating some of my equipment to the relevant information.

"You're the one doing the talking, right?" Victor asked Sorin. "Because there's no fucking way I'm going to be able to make any of it sound enticing. Hell, Toma got kicked out of the fucking room, and he's the most charming out of us all."

I growled out a *fuck you* and flipped the man. He just smiled and took his seat, blowing me a kiss that turned into him returning the middle finger. Victor was an asshole ninety percent of the time —but he was our asshole.

Sorin rolled his eyes at our antics, then shoved his hand into his pockets, telling me he was no longer worried about our reaction. "Of course, I'll be the one to talk to her. Fuck, right now I think the only person who might be able to talk to her without causing more problems for us is Cris. She didn't seem to be quite as hostile to him before."

"Not sure that will apply anymore since I'm the one who fucking drugged her," Cris pointed out. "She might hold a grudge against that as well."

"All the more reason to leave it to me. I know how to talk to her, and I have all the information on getting her friends out of here. It won't be easy, seeing as we need to get them closer to the Northern border for their people to grab them. However, as I said, we'll cross that bridge when we get to it," Sorin admitted.

A thought crossed my mind that I hadn't quite considered before. "What happens if Lucian wants her back and comes looking for her? We know he wasn't there at the Outpost, so he's supposedly still out there. It could come to bite us in the ass," I warned.

Sorin just nodded briefly then spoke. "The man would have to view her as more than property to come after her, and we know no Northerner could ever manage to pull that off. That's one of the last things I'm worried about now that I know she's not trying to get back to him. I'd been slightly afraid she might think the devil she knew would be better than the devil she didn't. If all of us are in agreement, then I'll talk to her about our plans when Beth feels she's up to it."

We all gave our consent just as the bell signaling dinner chimed down the hall. Now it was going to be a waiting game to see if this fiery little Omega was going to be reasonable or not.

CHAPTER 15

Danella

Two more days passed, and I made good on my promise to Bethany. I let her do what she needed to help me get better, and I was blown away by their medical advancement. I'd always believed that Oscad was on top of its game when it came to advancements. While that was true for industry and economics, I'd say the Southerners of Asturg were far beyond what Oscad could provide. The medications and treatments they had took an injury as severe as mine and cut the recovery time in half.

I no longer had a fractured skull, bruised brain, or concussion. I still struggled with headaches, and bright lights shining directly in my eyes hurt like hell, but overall, I was feeling human again. Bethany had forced me out of my room today and made me join the other recovering soldiers for lunch. They'd given me clothes to wear, black tactical pants along with a black T-shirt, and simple slip-on shoes—also black. It seemed to be the only color worn outside the Med Center staff. Why this seemed to be the color of choice I have not a fucking clue.

Walking through the buffet line, I filled my plate with all the delicious-smelling food. Oddly enough, I went for all the fresh veggies and things I'd been without the past three years. Having fluffy bread with butter along with a salad made my mouth water.

What I couldn't get over was the abundance of strawberries. They were my favorite fruit, and I swear, I could eat an entire plate full of them—or maybe I already had and learned the hard way I'd make myself sick doing it. Now I only took a few and saved them for the end of my meal. There was also plenty of meat, but when you have grass for animals to graze on, it made all the difference in the world.

Humming with delight, I mixed all my salad ingredients together before stabbing my fork into the mass of food. Just as I shoved the bite into my mouth, someone sat across from me. I'd picked a table in the corner out of the way so I didn't have to share the table with anyone. There were plenty of other places for them to sit. Why the hell did they need to pick me?

"Hello, Danella, it's nice to see you up and about looking far better than the last time we met," the massive bald man said.

Hearing his voice, I stopped chewing and looked up at him full-on instead of the quick glance I'd done when he sat. Seeing those deep brown eyes once more and the invigorating scent of wintergreen and eucalyptus connected the dots—Sorin, his name was Sorin. I swallowed and grabbed my water to give myself another moment before responding. He just watched me with relaxed interest, waiting for me to say something.

What the hell did he expect me to say? Thanks for kidnapping me as I was running for my life? You should have let me die back there, so I didn't have to continue living this life. Maybe I should just sit here and not answer at all, what would he do then?

Choosing to take that course of action, I took another fork full of food and continued to eat. There was a glimmer of humor in his gaze that told me he seemed to be amused by my choice. Still not saying anything, he just rested his elbow on the table and plopped his chin on his hand. *Was he just going to watch me eat?* It would seem that he was because I didn't stop eating to ask and he just continued to wait me out. Once my plate was empty and all my water was gone, he took my tray and slid it over leaving nothing for me to use as a buffer.

"Now that you've gotten to eat, I'd like to discuss your future, as well as your friends', here in South Asturg. I'm well aware of how things work up north, and I hope the short time you've been here you can see that we're incredibly different. No breeder houses, no food shortage, and we try to treat every one of every designation equally as we can," Sorin pointed out.

Even though I could tell he wasn't trying to corner me or threaten me outright, I knew that this conversation wasn't going to be about my needs or those of Violet or Tori. It was clear he wanted something, and I was the one he expected to get it from. The question was... would I be willing to give it?

"What would you say if a member of Oscad's new government reached out to me because he knew about the three of you?" Sorin asked, leaving that morsel to dangle before me.

Fucking asshole knew I wouldn't be able to leave that question alone. God, I fucking hate Alphas. They always seemed to have this ability to manipulate people.

"Why the fuck would they give a shit when they're the ones who sold our asses to Asturg in the first place?" I shot back bitterly.

He scratched his chin for a moment as if contemplating my question. Fucker was trying real hard to make me believe he was actually making an effort. "Of course, I'm not the right person to give you this answer, but I'll tell you what I do know. Oscad has changed immensely in the past few years you've been gone. All the old leaders save one have been removed, killed, or retired from their title of Council of Four. Now they have a different type of leader who is trying to turn things around from what the old council fucked up. Their biggest priority is returning Omegas, who'd been sent to other countries, back to their families. They have been sending smugglers into Shearia and Asturg looking for all the women they sold," Sorin informed me. "The only reason I got a phone call is because you crossed into Southern territory, and it's far more difficult to sneak around our lands with the drones patrolling all the time."

That had me blinking in surprise. He'd just let that nugget of information fall like I wasn't going to notice. Not only had he told me there were drones, he'd also crushed any hope of trying to run once I was able to. This bastard was clever. I'd give him that, but this show of not hiding information from me made me wonder what else might be lurking in the shadows.

"What reason would you have to give up Omegas when you need them as badly as any other country?" I challenged, trying to get him to lead with the catch.

"It's true that, like all countries, we lack Omegas. Although, unlike the North, we don't put as high of a price on them. Of course, we do all we can to support Omegas through their heat, ensuring there is the best chance for a child to be produced. The difference is that we don't want it to be at the sacrifice of the woman's health, mentally or physically. When an Omega is happy, healthy, and feels safe, that's when the best chance of a full-term pregnancy happens," Sorin explained almost as if he was an infomercial for reasons why you should live in South Asturg.

"Why bother telling me all that when you just said Oscad wants us back?" I countered.

"Because I want to make a deal with you," Sorin stated as he folded his hands and met my gaze.

About fucking time he admitted it.

Leaning back in my chair, I crossed my arms giving Sorin a once over and trying to gauge what the hell he could possibly want from me. I wasn't getting the feeling he wanted anything physical. It was clear from how people were watching him, even as he sat here with me, that he'd have no trouble in that department. That meant something else had him sitting here across from me acting all chummy. Whatever that something was, it clearly wasn't something he felt he could get another way.

"You have my attention," I offered with a raised brow. "Just know I'm not feeling much in the way of generosity."

A smile tugged at his lips, but he refused to let it play across his face. Something told me if he ever let himself smile it would transform his whole demeanor. "Noted, and thanks for the warning, Danella. I'll make sure to keep that in mind."

He got up and that had me sitting up in surprise. "Aren't you going to ask me?"

Sorin paused and looked over his shoulder at me. "You pretty much just told me you weren't in the mood to be helpful so I figured it would be smarter for me to come back another time. Unless you'd care to join me for a walk about the base?"

My brows knit together. "You want to go on a walk with me?"

"You've been cooped up here in the Med Center, so I thought it might be a nice change for you to get a little fresh air. I've already talked to Beth, and she said it would be fine. In fact, she encouraged the idea." Sorin reasoned.

Everything screamed at me that this was a trap, only on the other hand, getting out of this fucking place sounded like a dream. While I hadn't wanted to leave my room and be forced to interact with strangers, if Sorin was with me I had a feeling most people would leave us alone. It was clear people wanted his attention but weren't going to butt in and demand it. He had far more pins and shit on his uniform and a fancy design on his shoulder that I would guess marked him as a specific rank. No matter what country you were from, all military came with ranks; it was just the easiest way to keep order in the world.

"Do we have to talk?" I asked.

"No, we can walk in silence if you wish. However, if you ask a question and I can answer it, then I get to do the same in return," Sorin countered.

Fuck, this man was a sneaky bastard.

"Hope you enjoy quiet walks," I muttered as I got to my feet.

Sorin let out something that sounded like a chuckle and reached to place a hand on my elbow but I jerked away. "I'd rather you didn't touch me." I bit out through clenched teeth.

He froze for a second, took a step back, and nodded. "My apologies. Toma mentioned you didn't care for being touched and it slipped my mind. Most Omegas find comfort in such actions, yet I can understand why you might not feel the same."

The image of Bethany's little brother flashed before my eyes at the mention of his name. His bright orange and earthy basil scent came to mind, along with those dark eyes filled with sadness. He hadn't been back since the day his sister threw him out, which surprised me a little. The man didn't seem the type to take being scolded well by me or his sister. I'd thought for sure he'd be back to threaten me or tell me I was going to get in trouble for sassing him the way I had. I opened my mouth to ask Sorin about it but snapped it shut knowing the rules he'd put into play.

"If you'll follow me, I'll show you the way out of the Med Center," Sorin instructed. "Right now, you're at the largest military base, the Mraz Command Outpost, where we train our soldiers. It's not too far from the capital city of Couver, where the President resides. You'll notice that we are technologically more advanced in many ways than the North, and we like to keep it that way. It's our one advantage over them while they have the numbers we lack."

Why the hell was he telling me all this? How stupid could he be to share all this information when Oscad was looking for me? Granted, as far as I knew, Oscad had no beef with Asturg North or South, so it might not be that big of a deal. Who would believe the word of an Omega, right?

When we exited the Med Center, I was hit with the sun's bright rays making me hiss and throw an arm over my eyes. As much as I've recovered this was one area I still struggled with a lot and right now it was revealing itself right in front of a man I really shouldn't be taking my eyes off of.

"Here, these should help," Sorin offered as he gently pulled my arm away from my eyes to slide something on my face. He also plopped what I would guess was a hat on my head before I trusted to even crack one eye open to see what he'd done.

It was a black cap with the bill blocking most of the sun's rays along with the sunglasses he's settled on my face, kept anything else from being an issue. Looking up, I could see a reflection of myself in his own glasses and I looked like any other soldier wandering around this place.

"Beth warned me the sun might still be too much. Nanotechnology is amazing and has been instrumental in dealing with many injuries we thought were too far gone. There are just some areas where it lacks the ability to heal or, in some cases, can make things worse. The eyes are one body part it can't do anything with to heal. So while the brain is fine, any damage to the optic nerve or surrounding tissue is still healing like normal," Sorin explained, even though pretty much all the science of it flew over my head. Not my best subject, even if I like the medical aspect of it.

Obviously, this was his game— getting me to ask a question so he could do the same in return. Fucker was clever, and it had almost worked a few times yet I wasn't going to let him manipulate me so easily. This was going to be a game of which cat was going to corner the other first.

Once my eyes had adjusted to the sunlight, I took in my surroundings and all but gasped at the sight of lush green grass. Even the trees had leaves that waved in the breeze and cast shadows over the ground. It had been so long since I could be outside with nature that I stood there stunned, taking in the rolling mountains in the distance that had signs of green life on them as well. The breeze was light and clean, not caked with the dust of a land that had given up long ago, surrendering to the harsh sun's light. Here it was like I'd entered a different world instead of just crossing over a river.

"It's all so green," I commented, ensuring nothing I said could be taken as a question.

"Yes, we are incredibly blessed to have the rains and the river to keep our land so fertile. It's probably the biggest advantage we have over the North," Sorin murmured as he gestured for me to follow him. "Let me show you some of the greenhouses we have on base. We like to ensure none of the military takes from the farms and other sources that feed into the cities."

My skin itched with the desire to ask questions. The more I looked around, the more I wanted to know but I bit my tongue to keep quiet. All the buildings were made of brick or concrete, telling me this outpost didn't move with the fight and had been here for an incredibly long time. None of the buildings were labeled with any kind of information I could use to even guess their purpose. Like everything else I've seen so far, everything about this place was uniform and systematic. If I wasn't careful to keep an eye on Sorin I could get lost and have no clue how to find my way back to the Med Center.

"Major Sorin," a man called out, causing us to pause. The man jogged up to Sorin, paused, saluted—which Sorin returned—then just waited there watching Sorin expectantly.

My gaze flicked between the men utterly confused at what was happening. Clearly, this man had something to say, and Sorin had stopped to listen so why didn't he just spit it out already? Sorin clasped his hands behind his back and just stared at the man, whose brow started to bead with sweat. My guess is that he wasn't used to bearing the weight of his superiors' attention in such a way. Irritation began to grow as I could see how uncomfortable this poor man was and Sorin was just standing there playing power games.

"Stop being such a prick and ask the man what he needs," I snapped. "God, what is it with you fucking Alphas?"

Sorin flicked his gaze to me and flashed me a bright smile so fast I thought I might have been mistaken except for the fact it was emblazoned on my mind. I'd been right, that fucking smile transformed him from this hard military man into someone who I found far too enticing for my own good. "Thank you for sharing your thoughts, Danella. Allow me to deal with this private's needs, then I'll be happy to answer that question," Sorin said with a smugness that made me want to slap him.

Bastard had mother fucking managed to outsmart me once. Now that I knew he'd done this whole thing on purpose, I wouldn't lose again. If he was going to involve others in this situation, then two could play that game. He might be the one making the rules here but nothing was saying I couldn't do the same thing.

"Yes, Private Ambroz?" Sorin asked, his voice much more clipped and gruffer than I've heard.

"I'm sorry to interrupt, sir, but a letter has just been wired in from the State House for you," Private Ambroz stated.

"Was it marked urgent?" Sorin questioned.

"No, sir, but it was marked, *your eyes only,* or I would have brought it with me," Ambroz answered.

Sorin nodded and waved the other man off. "Thank you for letting me know. I'll stop by later to get the letter."

As if a string had pulled the man upright and together, he

snapped his heels and saluted once more before turning in place and heading back the way he came.

"Don't you need to deal with that? It sounded important." The words were out of my mouth before I knew what was happening and I wanted to kick myself. *Fuck!*

Sorin let out a sigh and shook his head. "The letter is from my father, and he makes them seem vastly important so I make the effort to read them on the off chance it might *actually* be important. While I'm his sole heir, he wasn't at all pleased with the fact I went for the military instead of politics like him."

To be honest, I was shocked he told me so much. I'd been expecting a brush-off on the matter but got far more information about him than I think he realized. Or maybe he didn't care... Could it be that he genuinely wasn't looking to hide things from me? Perhaps he believed if he showed a little of himself, then I would give up more in the false sense that we had some bond growing between us—ha. Asshole was going to need to try harder than *my dad disapproves of me* bullshit for us to connect.

We started walking again, but he didn't try to push me for answers to the two questions he now could ask in return. Granted, he'd only answered one of mine, so I wasn't going to count the other until he'd given me some insight into his need to be a dominant asshole. Who knows, I might actually learn something helpful with that one. All those worries flew out of my head as we entered an open area with men and women of all designations training. From what I could see, there was hand-to-hand fighting, people running laps, a shooting range, and an obstacle course. I'm sure there was more going on. The massive space captivated me, so I was rooted in place. I couldn't get over seeing women facing off with the men and holding their own. It would seem that my time with the Northerners had done more to twist my mind than I thought to find this so amazing.

All that aside, I knew I wanted it. I wanted to be one of those women learning to fight and protect myself and those I loved. Now I just needed to figure out how the fuck to make that happen and not get trapped here forever.

CHAPTER 16
Sorin

All I could think as I watched her observing the training grounds was—*gotcha*. I'd seen her fighting spirit when we found them in the badlands, but to see the wonder fill her gaze as she watched the soldiers training told me all I needed to know. We had a shot. There was a chance she would work with us if I pulled this off the right way. It would never work if I didn't find a way to make it *her* idea. Through the short time I'd just spent with her, I could tell how smart and calculating she was to the world around her.

Hell, she'd caught onto my plan seconds after I laid out the rules. I'm also pretty sure if she wasn't coming to that private's aid, she'd have held out a lot longer. Abuse of power seemed to be a trigger and I couldn't blame her after all she's been through. Yet to see her going toe to toe with me, not flinching even once, was a sight. She was something special, and though I disagreed with Petru on her being destined for our pack, I could see why he'd think so. He was a man of faith, believing that the universe put people in our paths and they couldn't be ignored. Whether or not this stubborn Omega was part of our destiny, I had a feeling she was going to be leaving an impression on us one way or another.

"Come on, the greenhouses are back this way," I called, pulling her attention back to me. Her bright green eyes were hidden by the sunglasses, but I vividly remembered them from when she stared me down at the lunch table.

Reluctantly she followed as we walked along the outer edge of the running track. Men and women jogged by as we walked on the other side of the fence towards the open fields of our crops. Many crops could be grown in the soil without any assistance. Then, other more delicate plants, needed shade from direct sunlight to survive. Seeing Danella drink in all the life that grew around us had my chest swelling with pride that we were so visually different from the North. There was no way for her to mistake where she was. Now we just needed to prove that we in the South didn't share the views of the North when it came to Omegas.

"Do you have a favorite fruit or vegetable?" I asked, using up one of the questions I'd managed to sneak out of her. There was no hurry since I knew she wasn't yet cleared to leave the Med Center. A key part of all this working is if she truly believed that we had her and her friends' best intentions in mind.

I could feel her gaze on me as I opened the door to the first greenhouse and waved her in. The light inside was far more manageable and the need to have her remove the sunglasses so I could study her expression was heady. Never had I needed to convince a total stranger to trust me. I was the son of the President and a decorated Major in the military. People didn't question my intentions the way this woman was. Lucky for her, I loved a good challenge.

"That would be using up your only question," she pointed out, her green gaze flicking up to meet mine. "You still haven't answered the other question I asked so it doesn't count."

Oh, would you look at that, the sneaky Omega just boxed me in with my own rules.

"You make a valid point," I conceded. "I still stand behind my question, and I have every intention of answering the first question. Personally, I felt it was best to do it in private since I would normally never allow a subordinate to speak to me in such a manner."

I held up a hand to stop her from speaking as the outrage on her face spoke volumes. "I'm fully aware you are not part of the military or under my command. Nevertheless, as the person who brought you on base, I am responsible for your actions while you're here. Which is why I didn't address the offense in front of the private."

Crossing her arms, she let out a little huff of indignation at my words. *Fuck, why did everything about this woman just want to make me smile?* It's like she had no idea she was the mouse in this situation and I wasn't just a cat—I was a lion.

"Strawberries," she stated flatly. When I just stared at her questioningly, she sighed and elaborated. "They're my favorite fruit."

"You're in luck, this is the season for them. We have strawberries coming out of our ears. Would you like to pick some to snack on?" I questioned as I led the way through the rows of plants. "This whole greenhouse is just for fruit, and the strawberries have taken over half the place. We had a bad crop last year so we grew as many as we could to save the seeds."

Grabbing a small white bucket, I handed it back to her and swept my arm towards my left to show off the rows of plants hanging from the rafters of the greenhouse. We'd had to get creative to cultivate so many hanging them from floor to ceiling seemed to be the best solution. Danella stared at the sight, but it took her all of a second before she was heading for the first plant.

"This is amazing," she murmured as she picked a ripe berry and bit into it.

The hum of delight as the juice of the fruit rolled down the corner of her mouth and down her neck had my cock hardening. Never had I wanted to lick the trail of juice off of someone as badly as I did her. Stunned at my feral response to her, I shook my head and forced myself to look away. Everything in my body ached to act on the attraction I had to this Omega and her sweet, spicy scent.

Pull it the fuck together. The last thing she needs is you losing yourself to rut and using her as all the other Alphas had. For fucks sake, you're better than this.

The scolding did little to calm my raging hard-on, but I managed to get my emotions under control. Maybe Petru was right about her? Why the hell else would I have such a visceral response to this woman I barely knew? *Enough,* I growled to myself. There was too much to do and not as much time as I would like to make it happen. If we were going to get her friends out of Asturg the fewer people who knew they were even here, the better.

"Before you asked me what it was with us Alphas," I said, breaking the silence between us. "Am I to assume you had an issue with me making Private Ambroz wait until I was ready to hear what he had to say?" She gave me a sideways glance and then only nodded her head, giving me a response without actually speaking.

God damn, why was it so attractive to see her finding all the loopholes in our game?

"Since I know you won't hold a conversation for fear of asking a question, you're going to have to forgive me if you know this information already," I stated before taking a seat on a pallet of bagged potting soil. "The first thing we teach each and every recruit in the military is how to take orders without question. Doing so can be the difference between life and death. Most are here at this base because they are either newbies training, soldiers recovering from wounds, or elites like myself and my team taking RnR between missions. Those of us who are senior military are expected to train and teach anyone of a lower station. You never know what situation you might find yourself in so every moment is a learning moment.

"That private had no idea who I was with, and if he'd just come right out and blurted his message it could have been detrimental to our mission. Yes, we are on base and that means there's a ninety percent chance that no one will use the information against us. Except as proven with you being here, it's never a hundred percent. By asking him to wait, hold his tongue, and trust that I would tell him when it was safe for him to speak, he is learning to be a better soldier," I explained. "You might see it as a power play, and I'll admit I wanted to see if it would bother you. Since you don't seem all that keen on talking to me, I have little choice but to gather what information I can other ways."

She paused in her picking and turned to face me, brows knit together as she processed what I said. "Are you telling me—" She stopped mid-sentence and ground her teeth together before she could finish that question.

Taking a breath, she tried again. "I don't see the point in talking to you when you've already told me my country has asked for me back. There is nothing I have to say that you will want to hear, and I just want to go back home where it's safe. I'm allowed to have a life and an opinion."

"Freedom is everything to you," I stated without questioning the truth of that for a second. "What would you do to give that same freedom to more than just your friends?"

It was a risk to use that as my second question since she might just blow off the whole thing and not bother answering it. While I'd set up this game to keep her on her toes, there was no reason for her to answer, but fuck, if I didn't pray she would.

"Freedom is something I believe everyone should have and that might seem naive to you, but speaking as someone who's had little of it... Yes, It's everything to me," she answered in a soft voice that didn't match the fire flickering in her eyes. "As for your question, when it comes to my friends, there is nothing I wouldn't do to give them back the life they deserve. None of us asked to be sent here, hell none of us asked to be torn away from our families and sent to a Care Center. Right now, I would say fuck packs, fuck being an Omega, and fuck designations for trapping us in these roles. What makes an Omega so weak in everyone's eyes? How is it that we've been told since day one that we can't protect ourselves so others have to do it for us? Tell me, Sorin, where in the history of our world did an entire designation get demoted to being fucking breeders? Huh?"

It would seem my question had lit a match to tinder I didn't know was there. The courage and authority she had right now with her back straight, head high, and eyes boring into mine, had me eternally glad I'd chosen to sit down. This woman was an explosion waiting to happen, and I abso-fucking-lutly wanted to be there when she finally went off. It would be a sight to see, that's for damn sure.

"Will you help me change it?" I asked, ignoring the fact she just asked me multiple questions I had no clue how to fucking answer.

This seemed to stun her into silence as her bucket slipped from her fingers and landed on the floor. "Change what, the world?" she asked with a bitter laugh. "You really believe I'm going to fall for some bullshit like that? Let me guess. You're going to tell me that if I help you then my friends and I can go back home, no problem. However if I don't, then we're fucked. Is that it? Was that what you wanted, to find my weakness and exploit it? Does anyone really even know we're here, or was that a lie too? God, to think I even entertained the idea there might be a decent male out there in the world."

The speed at which this whole thing derailed before my eyes had me reeling. What the hell just happened? How could one innocent question have just flipped the switch on the situation? It was as if she connected all the dots in the blink of an eye but twisted them into a skewed sense of reality.

What had the world done to this woman to make her so jaded?

"Damn, and here I was thinking I had the corner market on being the cynical bastard but fuck if you didn't just slap our Major's hopes to pieces," a deep raspy voice I knew well interjected.

I knew the fucker wouldn't let me talk to her alone. He, out of all my men, hated the unknown and any new people, especially since she was a woman. Turning to my left, I watched as Victor ambled over to us, hands in his pocket with licorice root in his mouth. He'd quit smoking but took up the nasty habit of chewing on those instead. Out of the two, it was the lesser evil, and not having to deal with him if he ran out of smokes was well worth it.

Victor and I were the same height, and we both spent far too much time in the gym bulking up. Only I didn't have the fuck around and find out energy that oozed out of him. He was a prick, but there was no one I trusted more to have my back when shit hit the fan than Victor. His hazel eyes never wavered from Danella's, and she planted her feet, much as she had with me, not backing down. Fuck, I hadn't considered these two either might end up either killing each other or fucking for life the way the sparks flew between them.

"What hopes would that be?" Danella challenged. "The crafty Alpha hasn't told me shit."

Victor looked over at me, a little surprised. "Shit, she got that pissed at you and you still haven't actually told her what you wanted? Yeah, I don't think this plan of yours is gonna work, boss. Better to just tell Oscad sorry we don't know which Omegas you're talking about at this point. She's not gonna barter."

It took me a second to figure out what the hell Victor was doing but I caught up quickly enough. "She did say she'd be willing to do anything for her friends. I'm just not sure she really means it."

This play was risky, yet Victor might have the right idea. If it took her getting mad and the need to protect her friends to push her over the edge, I'd do it. While I wanted to be the better Alpha for her, I still had a whole country to think about. If she could just see her way to helping us, it could change everything, and that's what I needed to focus on. Not the fact that I didn't want to hurt this Omega I barely knew.

"For fucks sake, just tell me what you want. I'm sick and tired of the games so just tell it to me straight," Danella said with a sigh, her shoulders sagging some of the fire in her dimming.

Was she playing games with us now, or is she really over all of it? Not waiting for me to take the lead, Victor stepped up to square-off with her, a smirk on his face. I'd seen this side of Victor where he liked to push people to their limits to figure them out. It didn't come out often since there was rarely anyone who seemed to pique his interest.

"You want it rough and raw, alright I'll give it to you just as you asked," Victor assured her. "We know you were the personal fuck toy to the Commander named Lucian, the general's heir. Seeing that you were living with him, and I'm sure you've heard more than your share of things over time with him, we want you to tell us how to take down the North. You give us all the information you know, come with us to make sure it's not bullshit, and we send your friends back to the comforts of Oscad. After we win the war, I don't see a reason we'd need to keep you with us, so you can go back home too."

Holding my breath, I waited to see how Danella reacted to Victor's explanation. She cocked her head and just stared at Vic like she was trying to ascertain if he was telling her the truth or playing more games. If she decided to help us out, she'd learn that Victor didn't play those kinds of games. He would never lie or manipulate someone after the trauma he'd gone through with his past lover. Oh, he'd undoubtedly have no problem laying out the truth and pissing you off with his inability to sugarcoat anything. But, the thing with Victor is you always knew where you stood; that was a gift in our world.

"What makes you think that I know things?" Danella challenged.

"You saying you don't? If that's the case, why should we risk sneaking your friends over the border to the North so they can be rescued? We don't run a charity around here. If you hadn't noticed, we're at war and everyone needs to pull their weight. If you can't help with information, we'll just have to put all three of you to work," Victor challenged.

Her gaze shifted to me. "Is that the way of things? If I want my friends' freedom, then I have to stay here and be your walking-talking insight to the North?"

"Yes, that's the root of things. Personally, I feel like it's a fair deal since your friends get to go free before you fulfill your end of the bargain," I pointed out. "If we were trying to screw you over, we'd make your friends wait until you'd given us the information we needed."

"Hypothetically, if I said I have information and would agree to your terms, then what?" she questioned.

Standing, I tucked my hands in my pockets and approached. "You'd tell us what you know, if it's enough for us to act on, then you'd be put into training. You wouldn't be able to complete the full six weeks, but we'd make sure you knew how to handle a gun, the basics of defense, and how teams like ours work to help you blend into the unit. That roughly would be two-ish weeks before we act on whatever it is you share with us. I'd hold your friends for the two weeks, then I'd have a trusted team take them to the meeting point to hand them over to Oscad. Then once the war is over and we rule the North, it will be a simple matter to get you back home as well."

"Just to be crystal clear, your only stipulation is the knowledge I have, nothing else," she demanded.

"Danella, I know you don't have a reason to trust when I say this, but the South does not force Omegas into breeding. To us, you are an equal member of the unit and deserve the same respect as any other member. If anyone so much as touches you without your permission, tell me and I will handle it. We need your mind and insight into the North, not your body. If you choose to indulge in physical pleasure with someone, that's between you and that person, no one else," I stated emphatically.

I knew this would be the hardest thing for her to understand and trust, but I wasn't sure how much clearer on the subject I could be.

"Alright then," Danella said with a sharp nod. "I know things."

CHAPTER 17

Danella

It was clear that I only had one thing to bargain with, and that was precisely what they wanted. Violet and Tori couldn't survive living in Asturg for much longer, and I knew that. They were already so broken and bruised from the past three years I feared what any more time might do to them. Now I just needed to make sure what I had to share with them would be enough information to make the risk worth it.

"So, does that mean you'll agree to the terms I laid out?" Sorin asked.

My attention flicked back to the other Alpha who was doing everything in his power to intimidate me. His whole energy and stance were aggressive, using his bulk to try and tower over me. His spicy ginger and clove scent made my nose tingle and my hair stand on end with how vibrant it was, adding to his dominating presence. Thing was, other than the girls, I didn't have much to fear in losing. I'd been staring down men like him every day for the past three years. None of the other males at the outpost liked me, always telling me my day of reckoning was coming the moment Lucian tossed me away.

"Is he part of your unit?" I inquired, feeling like I should remember him from when they found us, but I'd been so hazy it was hard to be sure.

The Alpha just gave me a toothy grin and a mock bow. "Victor Hosdue, explosives and hand-to-hand combat expert, at your service."

Oh, goodie, a guy who could break my neck or blow me up without a care in the world. Aren't I just so fortunate.

Returning my attention to Sorin, I asked the truly important question. "Do I get protection while I'm with your unit? Meaning, am I considered a captive to be killed if things don't go well sleeping with one eye open or as a valuable asset to keep alive?"

Shock flared in his eye for a moment before he frowned. "You think I would go to all this effort to try and get you to work with us then turn around and kill you?"

"Why not? As you've both made abundantly clear, you're at war and deadweight won't be tolerated," I reasoned.

"Fuck, you genuinely are one jaded Omega, aren't you? Even I wouldn't have thought that dark about the situation, even if you make a valid argument," Victor commented with a bark of laughter. "Well, I can only speak for myself, but if you're really going to help us put an end to this fight, I'll make sure you live to see your home again."

"To be clear, you would be added to our unit as an official member. The only people who would know what's really going on would be my team. This is too important for this kind of information to be given to anyone else. As a member of my unit, you will be given all the same assurances of safety as the others. We will have your back, and we'd expect the same from you in return. Unlike the North, we see every person as someone who can fight, which applies to you. Even if we can only do two weeks of training here, we will continue it as we act on your information," Sorin informed me, laying it all out there almost as if he was offended that I would even ask that.

"So now what?" I asked, looking between them both.

Sorin ran a hand over his bald head then let out a breath of air. "Do you feel up to talking with the rest of my team now? If not, we can do it tomorrow, I know you haven't been out of the Med Center and I don't want to push your recovery."

"Meaning you don't want to get in trouble with Beth," Victor commented with a snicker. "Did she tell you how long she could be gone?"

"An hour, but this changes things," Sorin argued.

There was something pleasing to know that both men were scared of Bethany. It went a long way to show they weren't just saying things I wanted to hear. As for how I was feeling, as much as I didn't want to admit it, my body felt like it was ten pounds heavier than normal, and how badly I wanted a nap.

"I think this has been enough excitement for one day," I shared. "If you two are this exhausting, I can't imagine what three more of you will be like. Do they enjoy playing mind games as much as you two?"

"Hey," Victor snapped, leaning in to glare at me. "I don't play no fucking mind games, you hear me?"

"Right, and acting like a prick and using your size to intimidate me isn't a mind game? You just keep telling yourself that if it helps you sleep at night. Trust me when I say I've experienced more of this..." I motioned to him with a wave of my hand. "... than I've ever cared to endure. If you want to get under my skin, try a new tactic."

Victor gaped at me, and I had to dig deep to keep from laughing at the sight. One point for Dani, zero for Victor. It was nice to see that I could play his game just as well, if not better than he could. Let's see who can get under whose skin first.

"Fair enough, let's get you back to Beth and I'll tell her I'll come to get you after breakfast tomorrow," Sorin said then stooped to pick up the bucket of strawberries. "How about I take them with me, and you can have them when you join us tomorrow?"

"More bribery? Well, I suppose there could be worse ways for you to manipulate me. Food these days is always going to be a sure win," I admitted hating how skinny I was. Just another reminder of the hell I'd been living through.

Both men paused as they led the way out of the greenhouse to look back at me. I could tell Sorin wanted to say something, but he didn't. He just pulled open the door and let Victor and me out. Both Alphas fell in step on either side of me as if to act like a barrier to anyone who might dare to talk to me or stop us. I kept feeling like I should be afraid of them. Both these men were massive, highly trained soldiers, and my captors. Yeah, they were nice enough and treated me with more respect, but even if they told me I was going to be part of their unit I knew that wasn't the way of things. I'd be the outsider kept at a distance to only be used for milking information from, which I was totally fine with. Once this was all over, I'd be going back to Oscad, and I just prayed my father would still be alive. I'd already accepted that my mother probably passed the day I was taken and no one ever bothered to tell me.

It didn't take us as long to get back to the Med Center, making me question what way Sorin had chosen the first time. Bethany was there at the front desk, arms crossed and fingers tapping in irritation.

"I told you that you could have lunch with her," Bethany snapped. "The rules were that you had to make sure that she ate and didn't bother her until her meal was done. At no point did I say you could remove her from the Med Center. I don't care who your father is or what rank you have, Sorin. You don't mess with my patients."

Victor was no longer at my side, and when I looked back I found him by the entrance. He'd left his leader to deal with Bethany all on his own. Some team they had, can't even handle a scolding together. Yeah, that boded well for me.

"Beth—"

"Nope, I don't want to hear it. Dani, come on, darling, let's get you to your room. You look exhausted," Bethany said, reaching out for me. "At least he had the decency to give you sunglasses. Taking you out in the middle of the afternoon, what was he thinking?"

Sorin cleared his throat and cut Bethany off before she could get to the door that took us back to the medical area. "Beth, I know you're mad, but there's more going on than you realize. Danella has offered to help us and I need to meet with her tomorrow after breakfast. I'd like to take her to our rooms where I know it's safe and we won't be overheard."

"The hell you will," Beth berated. "If you want to speak with her privately, I can make that happen here. How could you even consider bringing her into the barracks when she doesn't know any of you? Good god, use your brain, will you?"

Sorin opened his mouth to answer then closed it, rubbing his head a moment. "Fine, if you can guarantee there is a place where we can talk that no one will overhear what we have to say, then that's what we'll do."

"Damn straight you will. Have a good day, and I'll see you and the boys tomorrow. Not a moment sooner," Bethany ordered and hurried me away to my room, where she fussed over me before leaving me to nap

IT WOULD SEEM that I underestimated how tired I was since I slept through dinner and woke up in the middle of the night. Glancing at the clock, I groaned at seeing it was three in the morning. My stomach rumbled, voicing its irritation for missing a meal when we didn't have to. Thankfully Bethany had left me a covered tray of food. Lifting the lid, I found a simple sandwich and vegetables to munch on. She thought I was so strange for loving to eat raw vegetables, but I'd just missed the taste of fresh. Cooking them down would make them like the weak soup or gruel we'd eaten—a taste I wanted to avoid at all costs.

I quickly ate the sandwich, and as I snacked on the chunks of carrot, I mulled over what information I might have to give Sorin. Doing so had me remembering the days we'd be together in the house, pretending like we were fucking like bunnies. Oh, the one day he would get that's exactly what happened. We would only take a break to eat or hydrate, but Lucian was a man of stamina. He wouldn't knot me until the end when we'd fall asleep stuck to each other. I knew being able to knot in an Omega was a superior feeling for an Alpha, so only doing it once was for my benefit.

After hearing the other Omegas talk when I stayed at the breeder house, it was glaringly obvious that Lucian was treating me well. Many of the other women never got an orgasm since the men were more concerned with their own needs, getting in and getting off. That was never the case for me. It was almost as if Lucian liked to give me as much pleasure as he got from sex. On the days that he wasn't in a hurry or before leaving on a mission, he would spend half the time just making me come in various ways.

The feel of his hands on me was always gentle and caring, never harsh or abusive in any way. While I hated that we had to make this agreement, I could never say he wasn't treating my body with whatever respect he could give it and me. There were moments I wondered if he might have feelings for me as he stared into my eyes as we fucked. Once we were out of the bed and back in the real world, it was like we were awkward roommates. A strange friendship of sorts had built between us, but there were limits to how far that would extend.

He'd be telling me about a mission he just came back from or was going on, and then he would realize he was saying too much and shut down. Not to mention how careless he was, leaving papers, maps, and other information around the apartment. Of course, he was used to the fact that most Omegas couldn't read since no one felt it was vital for them to learn. I'd always kept an open ear and watchful eye on things keeping my escape in mind.

Babaka knew more than most as well, so being around her and in her quarters gave me insight into a different side of the military. She was always in the loop about supplies and things for the outpost. Not to mention if they were sending new Omegas places. I'd come to learn that she was the head of the breeding houses, and if the General didn't give orders for new Omegas she would decide where they went. Through her, I learned how many outposts there were and how large they were based on the amount of Omegas they had. We were a smaller outpost even though we had many of the elite soldiers stationed here. It was also the closest to the border, making it easier for them to infiltrate.

Now that I was taking stock in what I knew about the Northern army, I was impressed. So much of the knowledge I had I'd discounted since it didn't get me out of there, but in my current situation, I had plenty to offer. If they were telling the truth about letting Tori and Violet go back to Oscad, then staying and seeing the North fall, thanks to my knowledge, would be an amazing act of revenge. That smug tyrant of a General deserved to have his world crumble at the hands of an Omega. He'd never see it coming, and I would take great pleasure in making sure he knew it was *me*. The Omega he handpicked to send to his son, and who wanted nothing more than to change everything his father was doing.

Too bad the bastard was too stubborn to die on the battlefield as I'd hoped, but now he hid away in the capitol city only giving orders from afar. That's fine, there was another asshole of an Alpha I needed to settle a score with when we got there. Hopefully, that bastard of a doctor would still be alive for me to wring his fucking neck. I'd show him what it felt like to be knocked around for no reason other than just not liking him.

Diving back into those first days had my blood boiling to the point I needed to get out of this room. I didn't care if I had to walk the halls, but I couldn't be trapped in this space. Everything felt like it was closing in around me and I just wanted to feel the fresh air on my face. I didn't know if I could sneak out of the Med Center, although getting out to at least walk would help some. Slipping on my shoes, I pulled open the door to my room and stepped out. They'd placed me in the wing of the Center where the long-term recovering patients stayed while they did physical therapy or whatever else they needed. The rooms were nice, clean, and simple but the best part was that I got it all to myself.

I refused to admit that it was hard to sleep without the sound of someone nearby or strong arms wrapped around me. Lucian had been gone more than ever the past few months, leaving me to deal with Babaka's snoring. Never would I confess I slept the best when Lucian was wrapped around me, and that was the main reason I didn't leave to sleep on the couch or enforce my no-cuddling rule. There was something about the sound of a heartbeat at my back and his soft even breathing that lulled me to sleep. These days I slept because my body gave me no choice, but I knew sleeping now would be impossible.

Everything was quiet in the early morning hours. Only the echoes of others that snored could be heard as I walked past their room. The low overhead light gave me plenty to see, yet it didn't take away my night vision. I found my way to the cafeteria, and the room felt even larger with no one in it and the soft glow of moonlight through the windows casting shadows. The dark never scared me, because the day held far more dangers. Making my way down the center of the room, I stopped at the double doors that led out to a patio. I had no idea if there was an alarm or if they were even unlocked, but I was willing to take the risk just for a little bit of fresh air.

Holding my breath, I pushed the handle down and it gave easily under the pressure. No siren went off as I stood still for a heartbeat or two, waiting to make sure. Slipping off a shoe, I stuck it in the doorway to ensure I wasn't locked out. The last thing I needed was to be stranded out here until someone from the kitchen arrived. Who knows what trouble I would get in for being caught outside the Med Center. I wasn't one of their soldiers. No, I was worse. I was a stranger who'd been with the enemy and might turn on them just as they were asking me to betray the North. It was all laughable, in any case. I'm not sure why anyone would want to protect the people of the North after the way they treated each and every one of their citizens. Then my thoughts drifted to Coral and how she believed with all her soul that the North was the superior nation. Goes to show that you can get anyone to believe anything if you start training them from birth.

The night air was cool compared to the warmth of the day, and it seemed to quell the heat of my anger. The patio had tables and chairs, but past that was an open grassy area. There was a large fence around the whole space to ensure we didn't leave or anyone trespassed, I suppose. The Med Center was, as the name stated, at the center of the whole encampment. At least that's what I've gathered listening to those talking around me. After being out with Sorin, it was easy to confirm that I was deep in the base's territory. Outside that fence was another world of military men and women training and doing their duties. Soon I would be joining that world and, for the first time, not be viewed as an Omega that needed to be safeguarded.

Lucian had already started teaching me to protect myself. Of course, he wasn't happy with me for using it against his men or other Omegas, but hey, a girl's gotta do what a girl's gotta do. Kicking off my other shoe, I let my bare feet sink into the grass as I breathed a sigh of relief at the familiar feeling. How long had it been since I was free to just be? Even in the Care Center, we never ventured outside. There was a small garden, even though it was more like a conservatory with paved floors and plants in flower beds. Right now, toes wiggling in the grass was the freest I'd been since I was seventeen.

Tipping my head up to the moon, I took a long, slow, deep breath then let the breath out just as slowly, trying to purge the past from my body. Having been on strict bed rest and in recovery, I hadn't had a chance to do any of the stretches or exercises I'd done daily. I might have lost weight, been malnourished, and been trapped most of the time indoors, but I never gave up the dream of running. It's probably what saved us, to be honest. I'm not sure if all three of us were that weak if we'd have been able to pull it off.

"Why the hell are they making us transfer these Omegas so goddamn early?" a voice grumbled on the other side of the fence.

"They were found running from the outpost Major Sorin and Bravo team took down a week ago. The two were placed in quarantine to make sure they weren't sick or pregnant per procedure. Now it's time to start integration by having them stay with a host mother," another man answered.

"Why save them at all? Everyone knows you can never trust Northern bitches," the first man spat. "That's the real reason we have to move them off base in the middle of the night. If anyone found out we had them here, they'd be dead."

"Rumor is they're from Oscad, some of the Omegas that were sold off to fatten some politician's pocket," a woman cut in. "That's the real reason they were saved. If we can barter them back to Oscad, we might get the new leaders to help us win this war, once and for all."

"Keep dreaming, Sal, no way those snooty Oscadians will help us out. They had plenty of time to side with the right half of Asturg, and from what I can see, they picked the North. Fuck them. We don't need their pity bitches." Grumpy guy scoffed.

My heart sank knowing they were talking about Tori and Violet. *How could they be leaving the base? Didn't Sorin say he was going to send them back after we spoke? Was this all a lie?*

Resentment burned in my chest at having for one second believed they might be telling me the truth. Why the fuck would they care about a few Omegas that got dumped at the feet of the Northern army? That's it, I wasn't going to stand by while they took my friends someplace I would never be able to find them again. All they wanted was the information I had, but I wasn't going to so blindly believe them anymore.

Running across the grass, I vaulted myself at the fence managing to grab the top. Bare feet scrabbling against the wood, I managed to heave myself up to get my chest over the top. Pausing, I looked around the area and spotted the trio walking ahead of where I was but no one else. Right now, I was thankful for the black clothes, even if my blonde hair was noticeable in the moonlight. Carefully and quietly as I could, I lowered myself as far as possible down the other side and dropped the last few feet. The impact made my feet burn, but shoving that aside, I hurried after the three people who would lead me to my friends.

Thankfully they were so deep in conversation they didn't notice me. One thing I learned from living in a military town is they always believed they were safe there. Many let down their guard or didn't keep as careful of an eye out for dangers right under their noses. That same belief was working in my favor as I trailed after them ducking into the shadows of buildings as I went. While this place was confusing and massive, there were tons of buildings to hide behind. Then they stopped in front of one and let the woman enter with a code that made the door buzz and open for them. If what they'd said was true, they'd be coming out with my friends. When they did, I planned to remind them why they should always watch their back.

Standing, I stepped out from behind the dumpster and started to cross the road. Seconds later, a hand grabbed my arm then yanked me back as another hand covered my mouth so I couldn't scream.

Fuck, how had I not watched my own back?

CHAPTER 18

Petru

Sorin returned with the news that the feisty Omega we found was willing to help us take down the North. I wasn't surprised at this information, since I'd known all along that she was going to give in eventually. Sorin had made the right call taking the time for her to get to know him a little with their lunch interaction. What I was surprised about is that Victor seemed rather interested in the surly little minx, as he called her. After the hell he went through with the last woman he'd been in a relationship with, I was shocked at how relaxed he was about this.

"You really think she has information we can use?" Toma asked.

Victor kicked his feet up on the coffee table and grinned. "Oh, she's got plenty to spill. She wouldn't risk her friends by telling us she's got intel and not have any. Pretty sure the only thing she cares about is those two Omegas."

"Now what?" Cristofor asked.

"First, we must get her friends off base and to a secure location until Danella is trained. I told her it would take two weeks for her to get the basics down, although seeing the look on her face as she watched those other women training, it may be faster. I'll have to see what Beth says about her recovery. The last thing we need is to rush it and delay us even more," Sorin explained.

"Why the rush?" Cristofor inquired. I loved that Beta with all my heart, but no one would ever say he was a strategist. He took the world at face value, living in the moment, not worrying about what was to come.

Sorin didn't scold him for not seeing it. Instead, he just answered the question. "I'm worried that a good portion of the men stationed at the outpost were missing. I'd hoped it would take longer for news to get back to General Rasvan, but I don't think it will happen. Those men will return, find the slaughter we left behind and run straight to the General. Question is, will he do something this time or just brush it under the rug like last time."

"He should know that we won't let outposts that close to the border. That town slipped past us since it's in such a desolate place. Did you see the state of it all?" Toma demanded. "How could anyone live like that? Not to mention surviving after we took out the supply run heading for their camp that would leave them with nothing."

"It was hard to miss," Sorin agreed. "Beth told me that Danella only asks for fresh fruits and vegetables with her meals, nothing cooked other than her meat. Imagine being so starved for real food you want to snack on raw beets and cucumbers. I managed to learn one thing about Danella, though... Strawberries are her favorite. So no one touches the bucket I brought back with me."

I tried not to smile, only I couldn't help it. Just the sound of our tough, fearless leader defending a pail of strawberries for a woman he barely knew was proof I was right. This Omega we watched throw herself down a cliff to get away from us and keep her friends safe, was ours. It would take the others time to see it, but I knew they'd come to understand the longer we interacted with her and broke through her justified walls of protection. As a unit, we'd ventured as far as we could together, and we were ready for the next level. She would be the person to make it happen—the final piece of the puzzle for us to see the whole picture.

"Duly noted, but that doesn't explain why we need to get the other two off base?" Toma stated.

While I'd expected one of us to resist what was happening, I hadn't at all expected it to be Toma. He was the one I knew the best and loved the longest on our team. This show of stubbornness didn't really make sense to me. He wasn't like this when Cristofor joined the unit. Hell, he was the third in our relationship filling a void I never saw was there. How could Toma not see that Danella would be the same? However, unlike our Beta, the place she was going to fill was glaringly obvious to me.

We were a pack with roots that ran deep through years of shared experience and trust. The thing that we lacked was an anchor, or center, if you will. At first glance, you might believe that Cristofor filled that role, and even though he tried, it wasn't his place. I knew Victor and Sorin loved Cristofor and shared intimate moments, but it wasn't like how things were with Toma and me. To us, Cristofor was a lover, part of my soul, and Toma felt the same. The other two Alphas needed something *more, something* that only an Omega could give them. Each of them desperately needed a person to protect, cherish, and fulfill that primal need dominant males had to bond. Toma and I were both Alphas, but as much as I wished to mark Cristofor as mine to gain that bond that would connect us on a deeper level, it didn't detract from what we had. Those two craved it even if they didn't realize it, and this Omega would give them a run for their money.

"The fewer people interact with or notice them, the easier it will be to smuggle them back to Oscad when the time comes. I'll reach out to Savo once we know Danella is making good on her end of the deal. Then between the two of us, we'll make plans to get them back where they belong. After that, Danella can join them when it's all over," Sorin informed us.

Instantly I frowned. "She can't leave."

Sorin let out a sigh and rubbed his head showing his uncertainty. "I know your feelings on the matter, Tru, but after the hell she's already been through I'm not sure I can force her to stay if she doesn't want to. How does that make us any better than fucking Commander Lucian and his father, the great, all-powerful general?"

"I have faith that when the time comes, she won't ask to leave," I answered. "One must put their intention out into the world if they expect to get the same result in return."

Toma reached up from where he was sitting to take my hand, pulling my attention to him. "Tru, you know I love and respect your ideology. It's what makes you... you. I think what all of us are struggling with is not wanting to trap her in a life she doesn't want. From what Beth has said and what little I've heard, Danella hasn't had a say in her future. Ever. The last thing I want is for us to do that to her as well."

I took a moment to mull over his words in my mind. It was hard for me to relate when I knew with certainty things would turn out as I saw them. Fate didn't make mistakes, and it wasn't making one here with her. Our determined little wildflower needed us as much as we needed her. She'd been fighting for so long it was time for her to learn she could count on others to take care of her. Yet I had to accept that if she looked me in the eyes and told me she was going back to Oscad, I wasn't sure I could stop her. Toma was right, if she were to be who I believed she was to us, I'd have to trust there was a reason she'd need to leave. Nevertheless, I'm pretty sure I'd always be waiting for her to come back.

"I suppose we can cross that bridge when we get to it, although while you all choose to live in uncertainty, I will trust in the fates," I announced.

Toma pulled my hand to his lips and pressed a kiss to it. "As you should. They've always led you in the right direction."

"Now that we've settled that whole pointless discussion, when are we moving the other two Omegas? Do we even have a place to put them?" Victor cut in. He hated believing anything controlled his life other than him.

"Cris, you think your mother will look after them?" Sorin asked.

Cristofor scratched his chin then nodded. "I think if I explain what's going on, she'll agree with what we're doing. Plus, it isn't all that different from working with women we bring back from the North who we're trying to acclimate to the Southern way of thinking."

"Does she have any women she's working with now?" Sorin questioned. "I don't want to add more to her plate even though I think the Omegas will be easy to care for."

"When I talked to her a few days ago, she was taking time off since my father was supposed to be coming back for leave. Since he changed plans at the last minute, she's at the back of the list for placement," Cristofor shared.

Anger flickered in my chest as, once again, I heard how his father, a complete bastard, was jerking his mother around being careless of her feelings. Klarisa was an angel who opened her home and heart to the battered women we rescued from the North. She worked with them on learning to read, write, and have their own opinions and thoughts. The woman who stayed with her left transformed into someone who could live in our society. It was a gift, yet Lino found it disgusting that she would allow a Northerner into their home, so he found any and all excuses never to be there.

"Bastard," I snarled.

Toma squeezed my hand in warning, it was one of the only topics Cristofor refused to see reason on. I understood no one wanted to see their parents in a bad light, except he didn't deserve Cristofor's adoration, either.

Sorin gave me a disapproving look before continuing, "If you could call your mother and ask her if she'd help I'd appreciate it."

"I'll ask, but we all know her answer is going to be yes," Cristofor pointed out. We all chuckled at that knowing he was right, but he pulled his phone out and left the common room.

"Now all we need to decide on is who's supervising the transfer, discreetly?" Sorin asked.

Victor snorted and shoved out of his chair. "That means I'm out of the running. Looks like it's one of you two idiots."

I knew Toma had been working late the past few nights on a new military program, and tonight he didn't have to go in. "I'll do it, besides I only need four hours of sleep to be functional. The benefits of sniper training include sleeping as little as possible to keep your scope on the target."

"Then that settles it. Once we get the go-ahead from Cris' mom,

I'll assign a few low-grade soldiers who owe me a favor to make it happen. All I need you to do is make sure they don't fuck it up and only intervene if there's no other option. I don't want anyone thinking we have a special attachment to these women," Sorin instructed.

Nodding, I headed back to my room planning to get a nap now, that way I knew for sure I'd be up and alert for the job. Being able to sleep anywhere at any time was a skill most soldiers picked up. You never know what could happen next, so better to be well-rested when shit hits the fan.

~

THE VIBRATION of my phone from under my pillow was all I needed to get me up and moving. Shutting off the alarm, I tugged on my boots and headed out to the common room. Cristofor had woken me up for dinner, where Sorin gave me the final details of how this was supposed to go down.

In the silence of the apartment, I grabbed my gun out of the safe and secured it to my hip. There was no reason to think I would need to use it on base, but in my years of being in the military, one thing I learned was to never get too comfortable. Once you let down your guard, it was easier to have your life snuffed out in the blink of an eye. Our base here was secure, though not every person was cut out to be a soldier and that caused some to crack under the pressure.

Taking another look around the room, I ensured I had everything I needed and headed out. It wasn't uncommon for people to be up and around at this hour, but we'd done this to keep a low profile. Our unit was held under a microscope with having the President's son as our leader. Sorin never wanted the fame or recognition that his father did, which is why the military was such a better fit for him. Later on, when President Dragomire needed to retire, his one and only son would be expected to take his place. That was an issue for another day. However, no one was looking to buy trouble flaunting the fact that we were helping to smuggle these two Omegas out of the country.

Exiting the barracks, I took a deep breath of the crisp night air, grounding myself in the moment and pushing aside all other thoughts. This was a simple task of keeping an eye on a team of three soldiers, but I was now on duty, and I took my role in this seriously. If we wanted Danella to trust in us, then we needed to prove that we could keep our word, and this was a good start. Moving swiftly and silently through the base, I found the barracks the soldiers were stationed in and waited.

They didn't keep me waiting long, except they weren't overtly worried about being quiet either, that's for sure. The three talked readily as they made their way to the quarantine section we used for our holding area. The North didn't provide the same vaccinations we did, which had led to a few outbreaks of illnesses that had been absent for many years. Now protocol was to keep them in isolation for a week before bringing them into the population. Danella had been an exception due to her medical needs, yet she'd still been kept apart from the others for the most part.

Rounding the Med Center, I wondered how our little wild Daisy was doing. Was she sleeping well? Did she have nightmares? I knew her life had been hard so it wasn't uncommon to struggle with those memories when you were at your most vulnerable. Realizing that my attention was drifting from my mission, I shook myself back to the present situation. The trio had moved on a head far enough that I couldn't make out their words. Before I could move to catch up, I was brought to a halt when I heard the sound of someone climbing the Med Center fence. Slipping back into the shadows, I waited to see what or who might be making their appearance.

A grin split across my face as I saw a mass of curly blonde hair and bright green eyes that glowed in the moonlight. In an impressive feat, she hoisted herself over the edge and lowered herself down the other side to land with a soft *thud*. My grin quickly turned to a scowl as I saw she didn't have any shoes on. How had that landing not hurt? The packed dirt that made up the roads on the base was far from forgiving. As much as I wanted to ask her right away, I was beyond curious to see what she was up to.

Had she lied about knowing things and was now trying to run away?

No, that couldn't be it. There must be another reason. Watching her take a quick look around, she spotted the trio and darted off after them. My brows rocketed up at my surprise at seeing her quite intentionally tailing the group. Did she know that they were going to her friends?

Damn, I should have been listening to what they'd been saying. If she'd been in the garden, it wouldn't have been hard for her to hear what they were talking about with how loud they were. It would also seem that now I would have to keep an eye on her as well as the others. For a person not trained in how to trail someone covertly, she was doing a damn good job of it. Sticking to the shadows, not getting too close, her bare feet were silent as a whisper. When the soldiers finally reached the quarantine building, I hurried to catch up to Danella. Just as she was about to dart across the road, I grabbed her arm and snatched her back against my chest. Covering her mouth with a hand, I dragged her back into the shadows before whispering in her ear.

"Easy, Danella, I'm not going to hurt you," I soothed.

She, of course, didn't believe a word I said and started thrashing in my hold, kicking and clawing at me. I grunted when her nails dug into the back of my hand, although I didn't let go. The last thing we needed was her screaming and alerting everyone to what was happening. I needed to convince her to settle down before I dared to release her.

"Danella, my name is Petru, and I'm one of Sorin's pack. I was sent to follow these soldiers and ensure they took your friends to the safe house we set up for them. We need to get them off base if we want to smuggle them out later. There was no way to wait longer when they'd be expected to transfer to the city and start the integration process," I explained, praying to the fates she would believe me and settle down. "Please, I need you to settle and not draw attention to us. If you do, I'll bring you along so you can see where we are having them stay."

That got her attention, slowing her assault on me until she

finally stood still. Letting out the breath I'd been holding, I rested my head against the back of hers, breathing in her scent for a moment. The sweet scent of magnolia combined with the spice of coriander was the perfect blend to match this woman's energy.

"I'm going to lower my hand, but if you try to scream or call out, I will put it right back," I warned, then waited for a heartbeat before letting it fall from her mouth.

Thanking the fates, I slowly turned her to face me and was met with a glare that Victor would be proud of. She was not at all pleased with my interference, and while she agreed to my request I had no delusions that could change in an instant.

"Hello there," I said with a small smile. "This wasn't how I planned our first official meeting to go, yet something tells me I should get used to that with you around."

"Where are they taking them?" Danella demanded.

Alright, it would seem that small talk wasn't going to happen right now.

"They are moving your two friends to the home of a woman we trust. Her job is to help women freed from the North get their footing before integration occurs. She is aware that we plan to send them to Oscad and need a place to hide them out of sight until we can make that happen. Keeping them with her means the best chance of there being no issues getting them out," I assured her.

Her eyes narrowed as she held my gaze. "They said you were going to use them to barter favor with Oscad. Is that true? Are you getting something out of them too, for sending my friends back? What about the fact that those soldiers would rather see any North-erner dead regardless of whether they are a soldier or not? Are Omegas now a target, a strategy to kill them off so there won't be soldiers left to fight?"

The anger, hurt, and betrayal dripping from her made me almost want to take a step back. Encountering the brunt of her ire wasn't something I'd expected to deal with. Toma's reaction now made far more sense. To force her into anything she didn't choose for herself would be heartless of us. It seemed there was far more ice to chisel through than I expected, but on the other hand, I couldn't wait to see the person she would blossom into once given a chance to thrive.

"Would you believe me if I told you, no, we weren't bartering with Oscad for your friends?" I countered.

She opened her mouth then shut it again as she crossed her arms in irritation.

"I believe that actions speak louder than words. My job tonight was to follow these soldiers and ensure they did as they were ordered. If you can keep as silent as you were moments ago following them, I'll take you along. You can even talk to your friends if you like once we get them safely to the other location," I offered.

Sorin would lose his shit if he found out I allowed this, but I wasn't going to waste any chance of showing Danella why she should choose us. This was a crucial moment that would either get her to acknowledge we were holding up our end of the deal or shatter the whole arrangement into pieces before it got a chance to begin.

CHAPTER 19

Danella

Staring down a man in a dark alley between buildings, who was a fair bit taller than me with a shock of red hair and eyes a deeper shade of green than my own, was a new experience. I wasn't afraid of him even though I could visibly see he was armed. There was something about the way he spoke and the relaxed body language that kept me from wanting to bolt. As I studied him, there was no indication he was lying to me about taking me along to follow my friends. Could it be that there was actually an Alpha who wasn't playing games with me?

The soft evening breeze swirled his scent of bergamot and thyme around me. It was equal parts manly and strong yet earthy and real—grounded. He didn't try to rush me for my answer but patiently waited for me to speak in my own time. If he was really going to let me talk to them and I could see where they'd be staying, it would make things easier if I needed to run. They wanted to get the information from me, but would they continue to treat me like this once I no longer had the same value to them? Better to be prepared for the worst than blindly trusting and ending up in hell.

"You have a deal. I'll keep quiet and won't cause any trouble as long as I get to speak to my friends once it's safe. If I feel like everything you just said is a lie, then I will scream bloody murder and deal with whatever fallout happens from that point," I warned.

There was a flicker of something I would almost call pride in his emerald gaze as he nodded. "I'm sure they will appreciate getting to see you as well. They've been in isolation for about a week, and I'm not certain anyone's told them how you're doing. Klarisa is a good woman, so I have no doubt you will agree once you've met her."

I was about to share my feelings on that but snapped my mouth shut at the sound of the door opening and voices. Spinning on my heel, I watched as the two men dragged Tori and Violet along. They looked alright except for being gagged. They were in clean, fresh clothes and hair combed back into ponytails. Tori was glaring daggers at one of them, trying to free her arm, but he just yanked her off balance so she had to stumble to keep up. Hands balling into fists, I took a step forward when a hand rested on my shoulder, warning me to stay where I was.

"God, Jozef, no need to drag the poor thing around," the woman, Sal, snapped. "We said yes to this job because we need to gain some favor with the Elites, don't make things worse."

Jozef just sneered at Sal, which made him the angry soldier, the one who felt all Northern bitches should be put down. "Mind your own business, Sal, can't have you going all female on us and getting soft."

"Fuck you," Sal bit out, shouldering past the guy. "Let's just get this done so I can get a few more hours of sleep."

"Damn it, Jo, you know you're on your last strike, don't you? If they catch wind of what you truly think about women in the military, you'll be in some serious fucking trouble," the third of the group muttered as they walked past our hiding spot.

My gaze flicked up to Petru to see how he felt about this tidbit of information, and the stormy look I saw didn't bode well for Jozef. Maybe this Alpha was right about actions speaking louder than words. If he had that kind of reaction to how a man in the North felt he had the right to speak about a woman, then it might be possible the South did do things differently. We tailed the group until they loaded up into a covered truck and Sal got into the driver's seat.

"How are we supposed to follow them if they're driving off?" I whispered.

"We aren't. I know where they're going, so I plan to beat them there. I just want to see them get in and drive off before we take the road less traveled," Petru explained. "With Sal driving, I know they won't be making any unexpected stops. Your friends will be safe."

I wasn't sure I believed that, for a lot could happen in the back of a truck. It wouldn't be the first time a man got his jolly's in however he could. If either of my girls came out of that truck looking like they'd gotten bent over a bench, I'd fucking lose it. The vehicle rumbled to life and slowly rolled away through a pair of chain-link fence gates. Once it turned the corner, we lost our line of sight, but before I could panic, a hand clasped mine and pulled me to follow. Usually I would struggle and demand he removes his hand, only there was something different about his touch.

It was warm and gentle. I knew I could pull free if I wanted to. He wasn't trying to keep me, just guiding me wherever we were going. It turned out to be a dirt bike covered with a tarp and a lock around it. Petru deftly entered the numbers needed and the lock snicked open, freeing the tarp. Together we pulled it off and folded it up, stashing it in a wooden storage box nearby.

"Ever ridden on a bike before?" Petru asked as he swung his leg over.

Shaking my head, I eyed the two-wheeled machine with caution. I'd seen people riding on them yet never felt the desire to face death at such a high speed. People might see me as reckless but it was a thought-out risk, not impulsiveness.

"Climb on, we don't want them getting too much of a head start," Petru encouraged, reaching out a hand to me.

Thinking it over once more, I groaned and hurried forward to take his hand and pull me up behind him. Once there, I didn't know where to put my hands. There was no handle or strap to grab, only... him.

"You have two options, either wrap your arms around my waist or grab the belt loops at my hips. Just avoid the gun," he instructed.

Taking a second to consider, I decided on the belt loops. I jumped when the bike growled to life at how loud it was in the silence of the night. There were small pegs for me to place my feet giving me more stability as Petru took a few steps forward before revving the throttle. Shooting off like a rocket, I squealed and threw my arms around his body. *Holy fuck, I might actually die tonight.*

Heading in the opposite direction than the truck, another gate appeared and was being opened for us. Shutting my eyes, I held my breath waiting for us to crash into the fence with how fast we were going and how slow it was opening. When the moment never came, I lifted my head and found myself outside the base grounds. A large open field lay before us with rolling hills like you'd see in a magazine. The moon gave us plenty of light as Petru raced over the empty stretch of land.

The wind buffeted me, tussling my hair in all different directions and causing the back of my shirt to ride up. None of that mattered, however. This had to be the most freeing moment of my life. No walls around me, the wind chilling my cheeks, and the moon above shining down. This was the freedom I'd been craving. The feeling that no one could stop me or trap me in a life I didn't want. I could go anywhere and do anything just because I wanted to. My heart soared with elation only made more enticing with Petru's scent and warm body so close. Before I realized it, I found myself nuzzling into the space between his shoulders as I hugged him tightly.

All too soon, the moment was over as we slowed, entering a neighborhood of simple two-story houses. They were spaced relatively wide apart, with lush yards surrounding them. It reminded me of Oscad in some ways, but the city would never have been able to afford that much land with how many people needed to be housed.

Petru pulled into a driveway and killed the engine. "Here we are, figured we'll head inside and greet them when they arrive. That gives you a chance to meet Klarisa and see where they'll be living until we get them back to Oscad."

The vibrations of the bike had made my legs numb, and I almost ate concrete as I hopped off. Thankfully Petru had quick reflexes and managed to snatch me to his chest. This was becoming a common occurrence between us. I also noticed that my reaction to his physical contact didn't make me instantly want to pull away as it did with most men. Lucian was the only other person I felt this comfortable with, but I figured that was because I'd grown used to it over the years. Either way, it was something to be aware of since it was so opposite to the normal.

Petru didn't bother hiding the bike or moving it out of the driveway, he simply left it in plain sight. "Are we not hiding from the other soldiers anymore?" I questioned.

He shrugged and motioned for me to follow. "My job was to make sure they did their job. As long as they show up here with both women unharmed, their work is done. It's not their place to question why we had them do this job. Part of the training is learning to trust when a superior officer gives you an order, you do it."

"Seriously, you expect everyone to do as they're told without question? What if your orders are wrong or they ask you to do something bad? How could you even begin to trust someone so blindly?" I asked, my mind reeling with situations that could go so awry.

Knocking on the front door, Petru studied me with a curious expression. "I get the feeling you're not one for taking orders. As for your questions, let's deal with this situation first and then come back to it. None of your concerns have simple answers, and I have a feeling I'm going to need the others to chime in on this matter."

He was right. I didn't much like taking orders or accepting that things just were, because someone said so. Yet I saw the reason and logic for saving this conversation for another time and place. Right now, I needed to be focused on Tori and Violet. I could deal with the other problems once I knew they would be safe. The front door opened to reveal a woman who was probably around my mother's age if she was still alive.

Her blonde hair was going white at her temples, only noticeable because it was pulled back. Kind blue eyes greeted me with a gentle smile on her lips. Everything about this woman radiated warmth, safety, and love. It was like she was the perfect embodiment of what every person dreamt of their mother to be. She was closer to my height, which was nice for a change with all these giant soldiers marching around.

"Good morning, Petru. I didn't realize plans had changed, weren't there supposed to be two ladies I was going to look after?" Klarisa asked, her voice sweet and light, setting you at ease.

To my shock, Petru stepped up to the woman and wrapped her in a tight hug before answering. "Good morning, mom," he murmured, then released her. "Thanks so much for helping us out and I'm sorry Lino is acting like a bastard. No, plans haven't changed. The two you're going to care for should be here shortly. This is Danella, she's incredibly close to the other two. In fact, we rescued them all together, but Danella got hurt and hasn't been released by Beth yet."

"I see, so how is it that she found herself on the back of your bike to show up at my home in the early morning hours? Something I doubt Beth would allow if she knew it was happening," Klarisa challenged.

Petru looked slightly chastised but glanced at me almost as if to check if I was okay with him telling her what had happened. Rolling my eyes, I decided to speak up for myself. "I gave him little choice in the matter. Tori, Violet, and I have known each other for a long time, and I refused to let them go somewhere I couldn't find or know if they were okay. When Sorin and the others found us, we had been fleeing from a Northern outpost."

Klarisa reached out to stroke my arm as she made a distressed noise at my words. That's the moment I realized she was an Omega. This woman was living on her own, helping other mistreated women, and no one seemed to be batting an eyelash about it. I'm not sure even Oscad would allow that. They'd demand that she'd at least have protection.

"I'm sorry if this is rude but how are you able here, alone, in a home with no Alpha or pack?" I blurted.

She smiled and ushered me inside to a living room that was welcoming and inviting. If her scent and mannerisms hadn't given away the fact she was an Omega, this room would've. Everything about this space was worthy of being in a nest; soft blankets, fluffy pillows, an overstuffed couch that looked like you could practically sink into it. The urge to find out was so overwhelming, but I didn't want to intrude in her personal space. Many Omegas were particularly fussy about things like that.

"Please make yourself comfortable, and I'll try to explain things," Klarisa urged.

At her approval, I headed right for the couch, snatched up a pillow, and snuggled into the corner letting out a sigh. There were some things we couldn't escape from our designations, and when it came to Omegas, comfort was a *need* more than a want. Some instinct drove us to crave safety, comfort, and physical touch from our pack. Not having had any of that for most of my life, this was like a balm to a wound I never realized had gotten so bad. Sitting here, it was like the world fell away and all that mattered was how fucking fluffy this pillow was.

The sound of Klarisa's chuckle had my eyes snapping back open to find them both watching me with amused smiles. "I had to custom order that couch, but it's been the best thing for starved Omegas such as yourself. No one truly realizes how important things like a soft bed, warm blankets, and the feeling of being cuddled are to an Omega. All the women who come to stay with me end up living on that couch for at least a day or two before they can bear to leave its security."

"So the fact I legitimately couldn't help myself is normal?" I questioned.

Klarisa nodded as she shoved Petru forward toward me. "Go on, sit beside her. Having you close will also help with you being an Alpha and all."

I eyed him, skeptically, not wanting what she said to be true, but I felt I was going to lose this fight after what I noticed on the ride over here. To his credit, Petru took a seat but didn't crowd me. Only Klarisa had other thoughts on that.

"No, you need to be touching her," she ordered. "Scooch over until at least your legs are touching. I promise I'm not just being bossy, this is what I do for a living. It will help more than either of you understand."

Doing as he was told, the Alpha slid up next to me melding the side of his body to mine. Instantly I tensed, feeling the need to pull away. He was too close and now I was trapped, and with how squishy this couch was, it would be nearly impossible to get away quickly. Then a purr started to rumble out of him as he slowly draped an arm around my shoulder and drew me to him. The deep soothing sound chased away all my fears and had me turning into putty. Before I knew it, I was curled against him, my hand fisting his shirt as I nuzzled his neck. Bright sparks of thyme and the heady bergamot lulled me into closing my eyes and drinking up the feel of his warm body against mine.

How could this feel so right? Images of that first night with Lucian flickered through my mind. I'd felt this way with him too at first, then we'd both closed ourselves off from each other and the feeling faded. *Was this how it should be with an Alpha? Or was I so starved that any Alpha showing me kindness was enough to bring this out in me?* The fear of being manipulated by my baser needs had me beginning to pull back except Petru wasn't having it. Instead, he hauled up and maneuvered me so I was straddling his lap as he purred and stroked my back soothingly. He nuzzled into my hair, taking a deep breath as if he enjoyed my scent as much as I did his.

"Easy, Little Wildflower, you have nothing to fear from me," Petru whispered into my ear.

God, I wanted to believe him, but we'd just met. How could anyone trust they were safe when they barely knew the person? It was just foolish to assume people would look out for you, the world had taught me that many times over.

The sound of the truck pulling up to the house had me sitting up and on alert. Klarisa motioned for us to stay put. "It's fine, I'll go out and meet them. Stay right where you are, Danella. You have no idea how important this moment is for you and your well-being. Trust an Omega that's been where you are and nearly lost her life due to lack of affection."

Her words had me blinking in surprise—what could she possibly mean by that?

A hand cupped the back of my head and gently applied pressure trying to get me to place my head back on his shoulder. "Listen to her, Wildflower. There is a reason we picked her to protect and look after your friends. It's not my story to tell though maybe one day she'll feel comfortable enough to tell you herself. Now, relax and snuggle with me."

The absurdity of those words had me smiling even as the will to keep fighting what my body was screaming for was a losing battle. It almost reminded me of when I first learned what it felt like to be truly hungry. The way every cell of my body begged for me to feed it, the hollowness of my stomach as water sloshed around in it. When I reached the point I knew my stomach shrunk so small because finishing a bowl of gruel was sometimes too much to handle. Now here I was, having been starved for the *right* kind of physical contact and attempting to consume my fill when I was unsure how much I could manage.

Had telling Lucian we couldn't cuddle been the right call? Was protecting myself from him and the pull I felt that first night worth the damage I'd done? No, I couldn't think like that. The risk of falling for Lucian was too high if I'd let him use me as he saw fit. If I'd given in and become his Omega, would I have been able to run, or would I have been trapped in a life that would never see me as more than a breeder?

"I don't know what you're thinking about right now, but whatever it is, has got you starting to panic," Petru commented as a hand slid into my hair and fingers massaged my scalp. "Take a slow deep breath for me. Come on, I'll do it with you."

His chest started to rise as he took a deep breath and I followed suit. When my lungs couldn't hold any more, I stopped and waited for him to release his. Together we exhaled and the anxiety that had been clawing at me seemed to dissipate.

"Good, that's good, Little Wildflower," Petru praised. "Now I'm going to move you to sit beside me because I have a feeling you won't like the others seeing you so vulnerable."

The relief and appreciation I had for this man right now was immense. For him to recognize that worry and care enough to do something about it had me fighting back tears of all things. Something inside me had cracked with the affection and comfort I'd just been given. I couldn't put my finger on what it was exactly, although Klarisa had been right, something changed. Question was should it have changed?

CHAPTER 20

Danella

Now back in the corner of the couch where I'd started when I sat down, Petru shifted just enough to give me space but not too far. The fact that I wanted to reach out and cling to his shirt to make sure he didn't move any farther had me panicking slightly. While I didn't want to be 'starved' as Klarisa called it, becoming dependent on someone was also not what I inevitably wanted.

"Come on in, ladies. There's someone here I think you'll be happy to see," Klarisa greeted as she held the front door open.

Tossing the pillow aside, I struggled to get to my feet. Seeing what I was attempting, Petru placed a hand on my back and gave a good shove to help me up. The second Violet's eyes landed on me, I flew across the room and hugged her. Instantly her arms were around me and a sob broke out of her. Holding her close, I kept telling her I was okay and rubbing her back.

"Dani!" Tori yelled, slamming into us and wrapping her short arms around both of us. "Oh my god, I can't believe you're here. We've been so worried about you. No one would tell us if you were okay or if they'd taken you."

Releasing one arm from Violet, I used it to tug Tori closer. "I'm fine. They've been taking good care of me, I promise. That tumble down the cliff really fucked me up, but they put me back together again."

The three of us clung to each other for a moment longer before I released them both so I could look them over. I cupped Violet's face in my hands and searched her expression, and other than the shadows of loss, she seemed fine. "You good? They didn't hurt you or try to touch you in any way?"

She shook her head, more tears falling to land on my hands. "No, I'm okay, better than okay now that I know you're safe and healthy."

Shifting, I faced Tori who threw herself at me for another hug. "Dani, don't you dare do something like that again. I thought we'd lost you for sure when they wouldn't tell us if you were alright. How could you be so reckless it doesn't do us any good if we don't make it through this together, alive."

Sometimes I forgot just how much younger Tori was than myself. I'd been looking after her since the moment she walked into the Care Center. She'd been so scared that I couldn't stand by and watch as the mean girls went after her. These two had been the reason I kept fighting; they'd needed me to keep them safe and sane. Now I was making a deal to ensure they returned home even if I couldn't join them immediately. It was better to know they were safe, happy, and free so I didn't have to worry about them as I helped take down the North. There was sure to be danger and fighting along the way, since we were in the middle of a war. Knowing I had them to keep watch over would split my attention, and that surely would get me hurt or killed.

Goodbyes wouldn't happen now, but they would happen sooner than any of us would like. After meeting Klarisa, I trusted they would be well looked after. Maybe she could chase some of the shadows out of Violet's eyes, and help Tori to remember what it was like not to be so angry. Most of all, I just hoped they wouldn't hate me when it came time to tell them what was really going on.

"I'm so, so sorry, Tori," I whispered, hugging her tight before pulling her back. Looking into her gaze, the relief and trust I saw made my heart squeeze at the thought of them being angry with me.

But I would do what I'd always done, take care of them first. "You're right, I was being reckless, and I took you guys with me. But I am glad to see you're not hurt."

"We had some scrapes and bruises, though nothing like you," Violet shared. "You took the brunt of the fall, protecting me."

I smiled and took her hand. "Didn't I promise you I'd get you through this?" Violet nodded as she clenched tightly on my hand. "Then don't you dare blame yourself for me getting hurt. You didn't choose to jump, I did. Of course, I would protect you. What the hell kind of friend would I be if I didn't?"

"A batshit crazy one," Tori said with a snort. "Anyway, did they tell you why we were brought here?"

I glanced at Petru, standing next to Klarisa, unsure of how to answer. "Not really..."

Klarisa is the one who took the lead walking over to us with her soft smile. "My home is what I like to call a transition stop. A place to recover, adjust to life away from the North, and hopefully get you back on your feet living a normal happy life. I've helped many Omegas over the years who spent time in the North and managed to escape or were rescued by Southern soldiers. My role is just to help you acclimate back into society."

This seemed to stun the girls as they came to the same realization that Klarisa was an Omega herself. Once they got over the shock, they both seemed to relax. When they were instructed to take a seat on the couch, I got to witness firsthand how I'd looked. The blissful look on their faces had me smiling as they curled up into balls letting out little sighs of contentment. Violet tugged a blanket off the back and wrapped herself up in it until you could only see her eyes. Tori, like myself, clutched a pillow as she rested her head against the back of the couch, her eyelids drooping, betraying how tired she must be.

When a hand slid to grip the back of my neck, massaging the tight muscles, I jumped then relaxed into the touch while groaning at how good it felt. "We should go," Petru informed me. "As Klarisa said, they won't be moving from those spots for some time."

Wistfully I watched them, envious that I couldn't join them, but I had to keep my part of the deal to get them back home. Nodding, I let him guide me back to the front door Klarisa held open for us.

"Danella, you're welcome to come by anytime. I know they would love to have you stay here too," she remarked, holding my gaze as if telling me all I had to do was ask, and she'd make it happen.

"Thank you, truly. I appreciate you looking after them and making sure they're safe. I've not been cleared from the Med Center yet, and there's something else I need to do before that could happen," I explained. "But I would like to come by after a few days to see how they are."

"Don't let them push you into something you don't want, Danella. Things here in the South are different, and you have the right to say no," she warned, as her attention shifted to Petru. "You might be my son's lover and an Alpha I respect, but I won't stand by and watch anyone be manipulated for selfish reasons."

Just when I didn't think this woman could keep surprising me, she went and called out an Alpha to his face.

"I hear you, Klarisa, and if you ever think that's what's happening, I expect you to call me or the others on it. Our agreement with Danella is far from selfish, and I believe we can come to fair terms that won't be perceived as manipulation," Petru informed her before giving her a quick hug and a kiss on the cheek. "I'll tell Cris you said hello."

"Look after him, Petru, and your new friend as well," Klarisa added as she waved goodbye and headed back into the house.

Hand on the small of my back, he guided me back to the bike. However, there was no sign of the truck that brought the girls over. "They just left?"

"Once they handed them over to Klarisa, their job was done," Petru reminded me. "If they'd dared to step foot in her home, the mama bear side of Klarisa would have come out. No one but people she trusts and approves of is allowed in her safe haven. Her husband is a bigwig in the military, and no one wants to piss his wife off."

Huh, well, that made sense why she was home alone all the time and why she would feel safe to live by herself. It also explained why she had such a heart for taking care of others, it kept her from getting too lonely along the way.

"Now what? You planning on dropping me back off at the Med Center, or am I in trouble now that all is said and done?" I questioned, facing off with the Alpha. There was no way I was getting on that bike without some assurances that I wasn't going to be locked up.

Petru just grinned and mirrored my stance while crossing his arms. "Why do you think you're in trouble?"

"Seriously? I snuck out of the Med Center, was going to attack those soldiers for taking my friends, and probably ran off into the night with them," I pointed out.

"I see," he mused, stroking his chin. "Now, as far as I witnessed, you happened to be out for an evening stroll, saw something suspicious happening, and went to investigate. When you came to a higher-ranking officer, you stopped and informed him of your concerns allowing him to handle the matter. None of that would constitute you getting in trouble by our rules, at least. Is there another gauge I should take into consideration?"

Frowning, I cocked my head. "Why are you doing this? There is no reason for you to be nice to me or trust that I'm not going to cause trouble or stab you in the back. I could easily snatch your gun while on the bike and kill you so I can get away."

"That is all true. However, you won't do any of that, because you won't want to put your friends in danger. Also, I think even though you've built up this hard exterior to keep yourself safe after all you've been through, taking a life wouldn't be that easy for you," Petru reasoned. "Now, my plan is for us to head back to base, and you join me and my unit for breakfast. You had questions, and I promised you answers when we were done with this. So what do you say?"

My fingers dug into my arms as I considered his offer. He was offering me information with nothing in exchange, and he let me see Tori and Violet. Knowing they were safe and with Klarisa eased a weight off my shoulders I hadn't known was so heavy.

"I'll come back with you," I answered.

Instantly his face burst into a smile and he relaxed his posture. "Excellent. Do you want to go back the way we came or take the proper roads?"

"How fast can we go on the road?" I countered.

Petru gave a nod and a wink. "Back the way we came, it is. I knew you were having fun. Riding the bike is one of my favorite things. Nothing beats the freedom you feel with the wind in your face. Now hop on."

I had to agree with him as we tore through the fields once more, and this time I didn't hesitate to wrap my arms around him. After what Klarisa told me, I thought it was wise to soak up all the comfort I could while his hands and attention were elsewhere. While that might make me sound paranoid, I just couldn't give up the years of knowing I'd been left with little choice in what to do with my body or life.

All too soon, we were back at the base slowing for the back gate to open. Petru didn't take the bike back to where we'd picked it up. Instead he slowly drove through the quiet roads until we stopped at a building. It was three stories high and more deep than wide but, all in all, was fairly nondescript. He helped me off, this time holding my arm until I had my feet under me, then dismounted.

"Welcome to our home sweet home, the Alpha barracks. The dwelling for all elite units in the Southern military. Our apartment is on the third floor so I hope you don't mind walking up a few stairs," Petru shared as he swiped a keycard to open the main door.

Silently I followed after him, and he hadn't been kidding about the stairs. By the time we reached the third floor, I was a little out of breath and my cheeks felt hot. Damn, I'd lost a lot of stamina. That had to change if I was going to keep up with these guys because I wasn't going to be left in the dust. Petru led the way down the long hall to the end, where he used his keycard again to unlock the door. It was odd seeing so much technology used so casually after the past few years in the dark ages. The apartment was simple, not much of a personal touch to it. In fact, it didn't really look like anyone lived here. It was clean, even if it smelled slightly of men, but that was to be expected.

"Make yourself at home. They might still be sleeping, though most of us are up by five. I'm going to make some coffee. Would you like some?" Petru asked as he stepped into the simple kitchenette.

"I'm sorry, did you just say coffee?" I asked, perking up at the prospect.

In answer, he grabbed a bag of it out of the cabinet and waved it at me. "Sure did, and I'm gonna take that response as a yes."

"Yes, that's definitely a yes. I can't remember the last time I had coffee," I said as I drifted closer to him. "Could I... would you mind if I just smelled it?"

His brows shot up in surprise, but he gave me a soft smile and handed the package over to me. Holding it with two hands, I took a deep breath letting the familiar smell engulf my senses. Letting out a moaning sigh, I all but cuddled the coffee to my chest with how excited I was about this simple pleasure.

"Ah..." A voice I didn't recognize said.

In my hurry to not look like I was a complete and total freak, I thrust the coffee back at Petru. He almost didn't catch it, completely caught off guard by my reaction, but thankfully he managed to get a hold of it and no coffee grounds were lost.

"Sorry," the shirtless man said, rubbing the back of his head. "I didn't mean to startle you. Just surprised to find we had a guest so early in the morning."

Taking in his blond hair and blue eyes, I relaxed as I remembered him. He was the Beta and medic on their team. I couldn't remember his name for the life of me, although I'm impressed I remembered anything at all from that time. My head was so rattled, and the pain had been so intense I couldn't believe I'd been able to stand. Now here I was, barefoot, my hair was probably a wild mess from the bike ride, and snorting coffee in a stranger's mini kitchen.

"He said I could be here," I blurted, pointing a finger at Petru.

The Alpha chuckled and closed the space between him and the Beta to press a kiss to the man's lips. "Good morning, Cris. I just so happened to run into Danella while dealing with other matters and invited her for breakfast."

"You better be making a full pot, I have a feeling some of the others are going to need it," Cris said with a smile, then reached out a hand to me. "Cristofor Ungur, it's nice to actually meet you, Danella. I'm glad to see you looking so much better. It's truly impressive how fast you've recovered."

Taking his hand, he clasped mine gently but with confidence. "Thank you for looking after me until I could make it to the Med Center. Bethany tells me it could have been far worse if it wasn't for you."

The man started to blush at my words, shocking me. In a way though, it was probably the most adorable thing I'd ever seen. He dropped his gaze and cleared his throat before speaking, making me like him even more.

"No need to thank me. I'm a medic, that's what we do," he said, slightly stumbling over his words. He turned to leave then paused to gaze at me again. "I'll be right back. I'm just gonna grab a shirt and make sure Toma doesn't walk out here in just his boxers. None of us want you to feel uncomfortable being here." With a charming smile, he ducked his head and left just as silently as he appeared.

Blinking a few times while still trying to absorb the whole inter-action, I looked over to Petru. "Did I make him nervous?"

Clicking the 'on' button, the coffee maker started to gurgle and steam rose out of the basket holding the grounds. After finishing that task, Petru grasped my hand and led me back to the couch where he sat, then tried to tug me onto his lap. Glaring at him, I resisted. If he thought I was going to cuddle him all the time now, he'd have another thing coming. This wasn't neutral ground like Klarisa's, this was his home with his pack. I was at a disadvantage here.

"Please, little wildflower, come sit with me," Petru encouraged. "I promise you nothing is going to happen other than you taking comfort from me, as I enjoy being able to hold you."

"Really and how would your lover feel when he comes back out here and sees me sitting on your lap? No, I'd rather not be the woman who causes problems in other people's relationships," I argued.

"I see. Well then, let me put you at ease. Neither Toma nor Cris will take issue with us cuddling. Moreover, I'm fairly certain Cris would encourage it and come to sit right next to me so he can offer you more reassuring comfort. Being here is stressing you out and I'm only trying to alleviate that emotion," Petru explained. "Now, what other arguments do you still have so I can dissuade those too."

The cocky confidence that every Alpha seemed to have was peeking its head out where Petru was concerned. So far, he'd been reasonable in his requests and given me a valid explanation for why he was doing something. This situation right here was a power play, and I didn't like it one bit.

"There is only one argument going on here, and it has nothing to do with providing comfort," I stated, yanking my hand out of his hold.

"By all means, oh feisty one. Share with the class, we'd like to know what Tru's up to," a raspy voice said into my ear.

Spinning to face the person, I found Victor in a pair of low-slung sweats watching me with an intense gaze. The Alpha was jacked, not quite as much as Sorin but without a shirt on it was clear to see how chiseled his chest and arms were. If this man wanted to snap me in half, he could with ease. His beard was wild having just woken up which only added to his wild intensity. Squaring up my shoulders, I balled my hands and faced off with the man. I was done keeping silent, playing the submissive role and letting things happen to me without a fight. No more. I'd never been weak, but I'd been silent, and that was just as severe of an offense to myself as well as my designation.

It was time to show these Alphas I wasn't going to be so easily manipulated.

CHAPTER 21

Victor

Imagine my surprise when I wake to the smell of coffee and walk out to find Petru, of all people, in a standoff with Danella. *What the hell was going on? How had she even gotten in here? Did Tru bring her? Had something gone wrong with the plan?* Fuck. Too many questions and no coffee, not a great way to start the day.

"There is only one argument going on here, and it has nothing to do with giving comfort." Danella all but snarled, yanking her arm back.

The concern and worry in Tru's eyes told me this was not going how he'd expected. Petru didn't do much without knowing how the other person would react. For him to have made a miscalculation this big had me curious. Unable to keep from inserting myself into the situation, needing to see what would happen if I pushed her further, I snuck up behind the Omega.

Leaning down, I was caught in her sweet, spicy scent as I lit the match to the fuse. You could learn so much about a person by how they respond to intense or dangerous situations. It was time to see if this little firecracker would send sparks flying or fizzle out like a dud.

"By all means, oh feisty one. Share with the class, we'd like to know what Tru's up to," I taunted.

Whirling to face me, panic written all over her face, I feared that her fire was just for show. Standing up at my full height, I crossed my arms knowing it made me look bigger than I was. *Don't disappoint me, little firecracker. I want to see you shine.* Almost as if she heard what I was thinking, she transformed before my eyes, squaring up to face me head-on. Shoulders back, head held high, green eyes flickering with her anger making the gold in them stand out. She thrust her chin out at me and gave me exactly what I was looking for.

"You really want to know what's pissing me off? Hmm? I'm sure you're thinking, oh look, the poor, weak, timid Omega is having a tantrum. Well, you asked for this, so it's too late to change your mind because I'm happy to tell you what's on my mind," Danella said, ending that rant practically shouting.

If Sorin had still been asleep, he wouldn't be now. I gave the boss to the count of three to come out here and see what the hell was going on. One...two... oh look, there he is now. Good thing he thought to put pants on before coming out and not just in his towel from showering. He started to say something, and then when he spotted the feisty little Omega standing off with me, he shut up. Smart man, he could probably guess I started this, and I didn't need him to get me out of this mess. I was seeing it all the way through, even if I got singed along the way— it would be worth it.

"For too long, I've stayed silent in the belief that nothing I said would make a goddamn difference, but I'm fucking sick of being quiet. Who decided that Omegas couldn't make choices for themselves? Where in the hell did they get the idea we were weak, timid women who couldn't fight for themselves? Yes, I understand we require certain things to remain healthy and of sound mind but doesn't everyone? Hell, if an Alpha couldn't be in control they'd lose their shit and demand to be given a role that fit their skills. No one seems to think it's a problem allowing them to have the right to dictate what I can do with my life because I'm the only thing they can fucking knot. So really, it's not Alphas who make the rules, it's their cocks."

Taking a second to catch her breath, I flicked my gaze around to see everyone was here to witness this moment. I had to fight back the urge to smile hearing her decide it was our cocks making the calls because, in many ways, she wasn't wrong. Once Alphas had found that Omegas could take everything we had to give and crave it, god, that's like a fucking drug.

"So Petru asked if he could knot you?" I poked, not wanting her to lose steam when I felt like she had more to get off her chest.

Eyes flashing with rage, she stalked up to me prodding me with her pointer finger. "That would be the first thing you think of, isn't it? Always thinking with the lower brain than the one in your head, which is astoundingly more useful. Give it a try some time, you might surprise yourself with what you think up."

Oh fuck, I hope she couldn't see how hard I was getting from the way she was challenging me. God, I'm seriously one fucked up bastard if having a woman right up in my face, pissed as a demon spat from hell, had me wanting to beg on my knees to fuck her fury out of her.

"As for the situation that you happened to walk in on between Petru and me. That had everything to do with him thinking he could take advantage of a moment that occurred on neutral ground and use it to make me submit to his wishes on his turf." Turning so she could see the others without entirely giving me her back, she leveled them all with a disdainful look. "I'm the one who controls what happens with my body, no one else. For most of my life, I've had no say in what to eat, wear, learn, live, or fuck, and that ends now. You keep telling me that you're different from the North, that I have choices, but from what I see, the South is just better at hiding the fact I have no choice with pretty words and illusions. What would have happened if I didn't have anything to share about the North? Would you have let me leave with my friends? No, of course not, because at that point none of us would be leaving the South. Everyone desperately needs Omegas, so why the hell would you let three of them walk away? So that's what I have on my mind. Oh, and before you jackasses decide to toss out the whole deal we made and lock me up somewhere, I'm getting a fucking cup of coffee."

Which is precisely what the little firecracker did, slamming the cabinets until she found a mug and filled the thing to the brim. The respect I had for that woman right now was more than I think I'd had for any female. She took the bull by the horns and spoke her mind. Consequences, be damned. Honestly, though, these assholes should be thanking me for that outburst. It told us pretty much everything we needed to know about her that was important. She didn't trust anyone but her two friends. She had an independent streak wider than the badlands, and no one should touch her without her permission. This is where I'm assuming Petru missed the mark in the earlier situation. I'm not sure why he thought he could get away with that, but he wouldn't have tried unless it was something he'd thought she'd welcome.

Feeling like my work was done, I headed to get a coffee myself. Not bothering to move our little badass out of the way, I just reached over her head and grabbed a mug. She'd planted herself right in front of the coffee maker as if to stake her claim on it. As cute as I thought she was, it wasn't enough to keep me from my coffee.

"Just so we're clear, I'm going to get some coffee. It's up to you if I do this going around you, which guarantees I will make contact, or you scooch over a step. As you said, you make the choices on who touches you. I'm just laying out the facts," I informed her.

She narrowed her eyes at me even when I didn't budge from where I stood. She made her choice with us having only an inch of space between us. Taking half a step over gave me enough room to shift sideways if I didn't want to come into contact with her arm. Oh, this girl was wicked clever, and I don't think she even realized what she did. Now both of us had to give to get what we wanted, making the fight for dominance completely null. That, and the fact I wanted to show her the respect she'd just demanded, told me more about myself than I cared to admit. Had fucking Tru been right? Was this ball-busting Omega meant to be ours? God, I fucking hoped so, because I'm not sure I could handle someone else trying to make a move on her.

Armed with my coffee, I took a long gulp before I made my next move. "Okay, Firecracker, we've heard what you had to say. Now you're going to sit your feisty ass down and listen to us."

Raising a hand, I stopped her from speaking. "Nope, you've had your time to tell us all that we're just a bunch of Alpha assholes, which in my case, is one hundred percent true. Now that we know your issues with us and the world at large, we can have a real, honest to god, raw conversation. We will happily take off the kid gloves for you and tell it like it is, though I don't want to hear shit if you don't like how this goes after you just handed us our asses."

Hiding behind sipping a drink of her coffee Danella studied me. When she pulled the mug from her mouth, she quirked a brow at me, almost as if asking if she could talk now. I motioned for her to go right ahead. It was odd being able to read someone so clearly who wasn't one of my unit mates. Granted, I usually didn't give a shit about other people and didn't pay that much attention. Still, she intrigued me in a way only explosives had.

"Trust me when I say a raw, call-it-like-it-is conversation is exactly what I want. I even promise to listen to your opening argument before commenting," she offered.

I snorted while taking another sip. "Yeah, I fucking doubt that. My bet is the second one of us says something you don't like, you'll be jumping down our throats. Doesn't bother me at all, but you'll have to take it easy on the others. They're more sensitive than they look."

"Vic," Sorin said in a warning tone.

"Yeah, yeah, boss," I commented so he knew I heard the warning. Bossy bastard should know when I'm saying shit just to be an ass and not get so easily offended. "Let's go, sassy pants, take a seat where you like and get comfortable. I have a feeling this conversation's gonna be a long one."

With no further motivation required, Danella pushed off the counter and headed over to the others. She, of course, picked the chair I always sat in. However, it put your back to a corner and gave you a view of the whole room, so it was a wise choice. One, I couldn't begrudge her, for it was a tactical advantage when in a room with five men who she didn't really know or trust. Plus, we had home turf advantage, as she previously pointed out. Even still I wanted her to feel comfortable here in our space for some godforsaken reason.

"I did the hard work. Now one of you has to do the talking," I told the others, flapping a hand for them to do something.

Sorin took the lead, as I expected, but he didn't start on the subject I thought he would. "Can I ask how it is that you ended up in our apartment at five a.m.?"

"I happened to be out on the back patio and heard a commotion, so I decided to investigate it. As I looked around, I saw three suspicious-looking people so when I found Petru, a higher-ranking soldier, I alerted him to the issue, and he addressed it," she explained rather unconvincingly.

None of us believed a word she'd just said, so we all turned to Petru who I knew wouldn't lie.

He ran a hand through his hair and sighed. "I told her to say that if she was asked. The truth of the matter is she overheard the privates we asked to make the transfer, and she was worried about her friends. I stopped her before she tried to attack the privates, and we came to an agreement that she wouldn't interfere if I took her to where they'd be staying."

Cris shifted forward on the couch to look past Toma. "You took her to see my mother?"

"She says hello, by the way," Petru said as an answer.

Cris then shifted his attention to Danella. "Did she let you sit on the couch?"

What the hell kind of question is that?!

"God, that couch was like a little bit of heaven," Danella said with a sigh. "I'm a little jealous of Tori and Violet right now, they just get to sit there for as long as they like."

"Do you mind if I ask you a personal question?" Cris ventured.

Danella considered that a second before nodding. "You can ask, but I might not answer."

"That's fair. I'm just curious because Tru isn't someone who's forward or pushy when it comes to people he doesn't know. Did my mother make you two sit together on the couch?" Cris asked.

Seriously was he really talking about a couch, or was this slang for something else? How could a couch be that special?

"Yes, she did," Danella answered simply.

Cris tugged at his lower lip as he nodded absently, mulling that over before looking back at Tru. "The situation that sparked the argument, did you try to recreate that scenario here?"

"Yes, I could tell she was stressed out being here in our space and wanted to give her that comfort and assurance she seemed to need." He shifted his gaze to Danella as he said this next part. "In no way was I trying to force you to do something you didn't want to do. I was trying to understand why it was okay such a short time ago, and now it seems to be so awful. Danella, I sincerely apologize if you felt I was doing it for ulterior motives. In full transparency, I've never courted a woman before, and it seems I've made a rather massive mistake."

Welp, we said this was going to be a raw and transparent conversation. Leave it to Petru to take that to heart and lay it out there. Not sure now was the best time to tell her that fate brought her to us, and he believed she would be *our* Omega, but what the hell. Let's just throw that in the pot and see if the fates can take the heat.

CHAPTER 22

Danella

Did he just say courting? Could he possibly mean what I think he's saying? Was this pack under the impression they were going to court me to be their Omega? My mind whirled a million miles an hour, trying to catch up to how on earth he got to that idea in his head.

"Danella," Cristofor interjected. "Please forgive Petru's misstep. He's not familiar with being around Omegas or those who have survived what you have. Truly, he meant well, but he didn't really consider that you're at a disadvantage here in our space. These idiots have only known life with Alpha men around being an elite team. They don't see things such as how you would feel the need to protect yourself from them. With you being at my mother's house, she was there to keep an eye on things and it wasn't a space claimed by either of you. Am I close?"

It would seem that growing up with a mother like Klarisa would make him far more aware of things than most. He'd hit the problem right on the nose. "I'd say you were right on the money. That, and I know he's in a relationship with you as well as Toma. I respect committed couples and I would never want to be the reason there is trouble. In the North, no one had loyalty to anyone. Even if they wanted to, there was an expected duty to ensure more soldiers could be born. For you to have a triad that clearly loves each other, that is something rare and to be treasured. To ask me to put a relationship like that to the test is the last thing I want."

Cristofor gave me a sweet smile and looked at his two Alphas. "I am lucky to have them, and we do love each other." They returned his smile, and Toma rested a hand on his leg, giving it a squeeze. Returning his attention to me, he continued, "You grew up in Oscad, correct?"

I nodded, unsure of what that had to do with anything.

"If you were to have been placed with a pack that had a dynamic like ours, would you feel like you were intruding or causing others to cheat on their partners?" Cristofor challenged.

Opening my mouth, I was about to argue then stopped and thought through his question for a moment longer. Any pack approved for the program by the CoF would be aware that the Omega would become a vital part of that pack. The hope was that all members bonded with the Omega creating that special connection only an Omega could provide. If a relationship was already established, it would be expected they'd be open to the Omega joining that dynamic as well.

"No, but it's understood if they are granted an Omega, they attempt to have the Omega bond with all members. There is no way for me to know or understand the expectations in a group like yours. This is a military base, and you were all brought together for the purpose that you work well together. That has nothing to do with being a real pack," I reasoned.

This seemed to stun all of them into silence.

"Hold on," Toma finally spoke, shifting so he was sitting on the edge of his seat, leaning forward to get as close to me as he could without getting up. "Are you telling me you think the five of us are just soldiers who got paired up together by some general after training, based on our scores?"

"I take it that you're not," I guessed based on his incredulity.

All of them looked over at Sorin, who was watching me with a clarity that made me nervous. It's as if he'd finally figured something out about me that had been bothering him. When he still didn't speak, I decided to hide my nerves by sipping on my coffee. Not sure caffeine was the best choice right now after having gone so long without it, but what the hell, you only live once, right?

"Let's back this whole conversation up," Sorin said as he wandered over to the coffee maker and poured himself a mug. When he returned, he perched on the arm of the couch and took a swig. "Allow me to introduce myself. I'm Sorin Dragomire, son of President Dragomire who controls the South. This is my team which I hand-picked myself to work with after observing them in training or on other operations when they were part of a different unit. My last name gives me certain privileges even when I wish it didn't. The only one I've taken advantage of is collecting this pack of men who are family to me. We are one hundred percent a pack. And when I say that, I mean the old world thinking of a pack.

Meaning we knew if there was an Omega that we matched well with, we'd be more than happy to bring them on the team. I'm not saying that's what's happening here with you, but I want to be crystal clear that we've always intended to have an Omega as part of our family. It would be our dream to find that one person who fit and built a relationship with our unit as a whole. Now that I said all that, I want you to know that wasn't our thinking when we found you. As soldiers of the South, our duty is to rescue and help all who flee from the North. The knowledge you were Commander Lucian's Omega didn't become a factor until your friends told us that bit of information when we saw your brand. That was when the hope you might have insight into the North came into play," Sorin shared, laying it all out there for me to absorb.

Taking a few gulps of coffee, he rested the mug on his knee and continued, "You asked what would have happened to you and your friends if you didn't have anything to share with us. I would have questioned you about what you did know, everything you saw, heard, or experienced while living in that outpost. After being as positive as I could be, I would have sent all three of you back to Oscad. While our leader might not agree with my choice, I have no right to hold you here when your country knows about your presence within our borders and has requested you back."

"You would give us back just like that? Without a second thought of going against your own father? I find that hard to believe," I challenged.

"Is it genuinely that hard to believe a father and son have differing opinions?" Sorin countered. "Just because my father does what he thinks is best for our country and people, doesn't mean I feel the same way. In fact, there are many things I would change, like finding a solution to end this war for good instead of how to destroy the North once and for all."

"The North would never give up the fight. They've been brainwashed since birth to believe they are in the right and everyone else is wrong. It's terrifying, if I'm being honest," I admitted. "We Omegas give birth, and they rip them away from us the second they can to place them in a group home where they teach them lies. None of them have a chance to make their own choice on the subject, and if they try, they're put on the front lines and slaughtered."

"Fucking barbaric," Victor muttered, as the others murmured their agreement on that sentiment as well.

"So tell me, Danella, knowing what you do about the North, what would be the first step in making changes?" Sorin asked.

Frowning, I leaned back in my chair and pulled my feet up, hugging my legs to my chest. The people up North were desperate for food, water, clothes, a roof over their heads, electricity, and medicine. If life wasn't a struggle and their misfortunes weren't blamed on the South, it would be easier to convince them of a change. Their only hope is to win the war, and maybe life would be just a little easier. That and the only thing that unified them was the one goal since having relationships with others wasn't possible.

"Resources," I answered. "Many don't fear dying on the battlefield, but they live in terror of getting sick and suffering slowly without medication. It's a horrible thing to witness, and the way they beg you to just kill them is the thing of nightmares. If there was food, good food, that wasn't rationed down to the last grain it would be life-changing. One of the first things I was told when I was placed in that outpost was to be prepared to know what true hunger was and to appreciate whatever I could get. I didn't believe them at first. Then, it wasn't long before I experienced the truth of their words."

"So the general is using the shortages to fuel the anger people have towards the South," Petru interjected. "It's crude and primitive, but clearly, it's been used as a well-honed weapon to keep his people fighting even in the worst situation."

"I don't know if it's you guys controlling things but getting the power to make anything work is a joke. It's like living in the dark ages. Everything is manual or only of use for short periods of time. It really hinders everything and stops any sort of growth from happening. It's like those books you read about when the world ends, and we're brought back to surviving off the land," I shared. "The North is dying, not just the people but the land itself. It doesn't make sense to me, how can one half of a country just shrivel up and die while the South and Oscad thrive?"

Petru ran a hand through his hair, making it all stick up before flattening it back down with another brush of his hand. "There are those of us who believe the fates have cursed the land. That it will only be restored once the fighting has stopped. General Rasvan might be a cruel warlord, but he isn't the first of their kind to control the North. It seems that they just become more and more violent as the generations go on."

"You can't seriously believe that an unknown force is controlling the weather and punishing a group of people, do you?" I questioned.

Petru shrugged. "No one really has an answer, and this is the one I choose to accept. I'm sure if you spoke to a man of science, he would have a different opinion. Since I'm a man who believes in the fates, this gives me comfort and something to hold on to. The other truth is that the North isn't doing anything to fix it. There are ways they could harness the river to water the land and create crops to feed their people, only they've chose to throw out any logic that won't help win them the war."

"Now that reasoning makes sense to me," I shared. "So what

else do you need to know? I'm not sure what information I've picked up along the way will be useful to you."

Sorin picked up the lead once more, turning to Cristofor. "Can you get paper and pen so we can write all this down? I have a feeling there's going to be lots of information we might not be able to use right away but will later on."

The Beta stood and left the common room to return with a notebook. He sat at the coffee table and clicked the pen, signaling he was ready. So for the next hour or so they asked me question after question, picking up on the littlest thing I might have noticed. Shipment times, how many men guarded them. Did I know how many towns or outposts there were in the country? Had I met the General? Then they asked a lot about Lucian, and those were harder to answer. It was almost as if they were trying to make me tell them that he was like his father when he was anything but. The strangest part was how I wanted to defend him, that he'd protected me but telling them why I needed protection wasn't a topic I wanted to cover with them.

Finally, Toma called for a break. "I don't know about you guys but I'm starving. Coffee is great, however it doesn't fill an empty stomach, so I say we head down to eat then start again if we need to."

The guys agreed and left to get dressed for the day, leaving me alone. Part of me wondered if I should stay or just head back to the Med Center. Bethany must have been out of her mind when she discovered I was missing. Of course, I hadn't planned on all this happening when I left to get some air, although if they found my shoes it could look like someone kidnapped me. That decided it for me, I'd go back to the Med Center and check in with Bethany. I could get some shoes, eat, then figure out if the guys still had more questions or if I was done for the day.

Placing my cup in the sink, I headed for the door. When I turned the handle and started to pull it open, a hand appeared overhead and slammed it shut. Gasping, I jerked back and into the chest of whoever was behind me. They wrapped an arm around my waist to keep me from falling forward and the fragrant scent of orange and basil told me it was Toma.

"Where do you think you're going, Danella?" Toma asked, his voice calm and curious when I'd expected it to be angry.

Twisting to look up at him, I found his dark eyes watching me intently. "I... I was going back to the Med Center. Bethany must be worried that I wasn't in my room and I also left my shoes behind. She's been so good to me that I don't want her thinking I ran away or was kidnapped."

Toma released me and took a half step back so we could look at each other more easily. "You don't have to worry about that. I sent her a text to let her know you were with us. She wasn't happy about it, but Beth gets a little overprotective over people she's in charge of taking care of. However, she did make me promise that you would eat breakfast no matter how much you complained about it."

"That was before I realized what you guys consider breakfast," I countered. "I'd been living off bland, gritty gruel for years, and it's made me hate anything close to that texture. That first morning she gave me oatmeal, and I refused to eat it, so she returned with a plate of eggs and bacon. Who would say no to that?"

A smile tugged at his lips. "Yeah, I'm not sure I would have been thrilled about oatmeal, no matter what fancy stuff they put in it to make it taste better. Although if you're stuck in a pinch and on a mission with that being your only option, peanut butter is pretty awesome mixed in it. As for the matter of shoes, I think Cris will be the best option since he has the smallest feet out of all of us. I'm pretty sure he's got some sandals that would work."

He lightly put a hand on my back as if testing the waters on how I would respond to his touch. When I didn't flinch or tell him off, he used it to guide me to one of the bedrooms and entered without even knocking. The sound of water running told me someone was showering in the ensuite bathroom with the door open. Toma directed me to sit on one of the two beds, which had been neatly made with crisp precision. There was a trunk at the foot of each bed and two dressers lined the far wall. Except everything about this room was blank, as if no one really lived here.

"Petru said this is your home, but it doesn't feel like anyone actually lives here," I commented. "There's not even a trace of something personal lying around."

Toma's head popped up over the open trunk's lid. "That's probably because until recently, we never stayed here for more than a day or two between missions. We are one of the elite units they send out to deal with things when all else has failed. Most of the time, we either travel on foot or use all-terrain vehicles to get as far as we can. Either way, we travel light and only take what's needed. Living like that doesn't give you much opportunity to collect personal knickknacks."

"Why is this time different?" I asked, even though I had a feeling I knew the answer.

Just as Toma was going to say something, a moan trickled its way out of the bathroom. My eyes grew wide as they snapped to Toma, who just smirked and shook his head, returning to whatever he was doing. The moans became louder and more frequent, the sound of wet flesh slapping adding to the soundtrack of their lovemaking.

"Oh god," Cristofor's voice cried out. "Just like that, please don't stop, Tru. I'm so close."

I was no stranger to sex or hearing it throughout the night when staying at the breeder house. Yet somehow, this was different. Petru and Cristofor loved each other, and this intimate moment was happening because they clearly couldn't keep their hands to themselves for the length of a shower. It almost felt wrong to listen since they didn't know I was here. Even though I couldn't see anything, it wasn't hard to imagine the two men in the throes of passion.

As if that one thought of picturing Cristofor pressed up against the wall of the shower with Petru fucking him from behind had opened the floodgates, I was soon lost in my imagination. Their bodies wet and glistening as muscles rippled under their skin as they moved together. Cristofor's innocent looking face pressed to the tile wall with an expression of bliss as Petru's hand gripped his hair to keep him in place. The Alpha's ass clenched as he trapped his Beta with his body thrusting deep into Cristofor's ass. I could picture

Petru whispering his approval in his lover's ear praising him for how well he was taking his cock.

Then Toma appeared, slowly stripping out of his clothes to join them. No longer able to withstand hearing their pleasure through the door. Grasping Cristofor's face he'd kiss him deeply stroking his Beta's hard dick that was already leaking, unable to contain how good he was feeling. The hitching gasp that burst from Cristofor spurred both Alphas on needing their Beta to come.

"Danella?"

Toma's voice had me snapping out of my daydream, and I found all three of them standing in a semicircle around me. Petru and Cristofor had towels wrapped around their waists yet looked as if they'd been in a hurry to dry off. My mouth was dry, and my body was hot making me shiver, which made no sense.

"Yes," I managed to squeak out.

"Please don't take this the wrong way, but you are perfuming like crazy," Cristofor informed me. "You aren't close to going into heat, are you?"

That question was like a bucket of ice being doused over my head. "No, in fact, I'm on a suppressant. Bethany said it's supposed to last two weeks, so there's no way I could be."

Cristofor squatted down in front of me, his hands resting on my knees. "This is going to be an incredibly awkward question, but I promise it has a purpose. How often did you have sex before ending up here with us?"

I wanted to curl up and die at the fact he was asking me this. "Only about once a week, he was busy coming and going on missions. When we did have sex though, it would practically be the whole day if he could manage it. Why does that matter?"

"Once Omegas start becoming sexually active, they tend to have an incredibly high sex drive. This means if you're used to getting a certain amount of sex, going without for long periods of time can make you... um... let's say needy," Cristofor explained, stumbling over the last part.

My jaw dropped at this nugget of information he'd just dropped in my lap. "Are you telling me that because I've gone almost two weeks without sex, I'm now craving it? That hearing you and Petru in the shower flipped some switch and made me start perfuming so I could get someone to fuck me?"

"Dani, take a deep breath for me," Cristofor instructed. "We see this all the time with Omegas from the North. You were lucky it was only once a week or so. Imagine what the other women are going through who were open breeders. In some ways, it's like dealing with an addict going through withdrawal, you just have to help them through the process. Your situation is incredibly different though I should have expected this, since it's incredibly common."

"Fuck," Toma swore, kicking the trunk. "I should have known better than to put her in this position. There's no way you two can take a shower together and not fuck around. I'm so sorry, Danella, it's my fault for not taking your needs into consideration. I selfishly wanted you in our space to help you feel more comfortable being here."

None of this was making sense. Why would he want me in his space? Also, why would it matter if I was comfortable being here or not?

"Hey, where's Dan—" Sorin started to say as he walked into the room, then stopped dead in his tracks.

His eyes closed, and he took a deep breath which was followed by a rumbling sound deep in his chest. When he opened his chocolate brown eyes, they connected with mine, and I could see a look of heat and need within them. It was an expression I saw on Lucian's face from time to time when he was lost in the moment. Without saying a word, he turned on his heel and left the room, slamming the door behind him.

CHAPTER 23

Danella

Shame and confusion flooded through me at Sorin's reaction, which just pissed me off because why the fuck should I care what he thinks. I stoked that anger letting it burn brighter, knowing it would drown out the hormones that had been taking over moments before. Shoving to my feet, I almost knocked Cristofor over, who was still kneeling before me. Toma grabbed his arm and hauled him up but then this caused the towel to slip from his body, leaving me with a perfect view of his hard cock.

I yanked my gaze away from the clearly eager man sausage bobbing in excitement at being noticed. Fuck, I needed to get out of this room before I lost complete control of my body and gave in to the aching feeling between my legs. Sex didn't need to be part of my life until I was good and ready to let someone that close again. It certainly wasn't going to happen here or now because of a dirty dream I'd had listening to two men fucking in the shower. Storming out of the room, I headed for the front door, jerked it open and raced down the hallway.

I couldn't do this. There's no way I could be around so many men when dealing with this withdrawal, as Cristofor called it. What I needed was to locate Bethany and find out if there was something she could do or give to help me manage this situation. If it was typical for Omegas from the North to deal with this, why didn't anyone say something? Or is that why Bethany had been so cautious to have me around this team of Alphas? Rushing headlong down the stairs, lost in my panic and anger, I didn't see the man walking up until I collided into him. Bouncing off his chest, I crashed to the stairs swearing under my breath.

"Fuck, I'm sorry I wasn't looking where I was going," I muttered as I picked myself up and faced the man I'd run into.

The disgust on his face had me frozen in place before I realized it was Draza—the Beta whose nose I'd broken back in the cave. Back then, he'd made it clear he had no qualms about making me pay for what I'd done to him. Only Sorin had stopped him. Well, Sorin wasn't here to call him off, but this time I wasn't half dead so I liked my chances.

"If it isn't the Northern Omega whore," Draza sneered, grabbing my arm in a crushing grip. "The fates must be smiling on me for us to run into each other like this. Tell me, breeder, whose bed were you warming last night? I feel like I should check to make sure they're still alive with how fast you were running away."

"Get your hands off me," I spat, trying to jerk my arm free.

"Now, is that any way for you to speak to a superior officer?" he taunted. "Those of lower or no rank should learn their place."

"Yeah, and where exactly should we be because it seems you're a little lost yourself," I said, cocking a brow, hoping it would piss him off enough for me to make a move.

"You bitch," Draza snarled, yanking me forward, which is exactly what I'd hoped he'd do.

Pushing off the step, I added to the momentum as my knee came up slamming right into his dick. A groan with a slight whimper told me I'd landed my mark. It was hard to tell, with how small he was to judge by feel. Together we fell a few steps before he slammed into the wall of the landing, eliciting a hiss of pain from him as I watched his head bounce off the concrete. He still refused to let go of my arm so I wound up and punched him right in the throat. I missed the spot I was aiming for right in the front, but either way, I'm sure it hurt like hell.

Finally, Draza released me and I threw myself back, bracing for the impact of landing on the stairs. Only that never happened. Instead, someone caught me and hugged my body to theirs.

"What the fuck is going on," Victor roared at the stunned Beta.

Draza tried to shake his head clear, but I knew how hard he'd hit it and I didn't think the few marbles he had left would help him any. "She fucking attacked me!" he blurted, a hand pressed to his head. "That's the second time that bitch has laid hands on a soldier of the South. She needs to be put down like the rest of her kind."

Victor tucked me behind him as he charged forward and grabbed the man by the throat, slamming him to the wall, and lifting until his feet barely touched the ground. "What did you just say?"

Unable to speak, the Beta let out a garbled noise as he wrapped his hands around Victor's wrist trying to get the Alpha off him. It was futile since Victor was twice his size and had way more muscle packed on him. The rage that blanketed Victor's face would have made any man piss himself and made me pray he never found a reason to be that angry at me.

"I will say this once, so you better listen up good," Victor ordered, his tone full of loathing and fury. "If you ever speak, look, or touch this Omega *ever* again, I will remove your head from your body. She is under my protection, and no one will ever show her that kind of disrespect again."

Finished with what he had to say, Victor tossed the Beta down the stairs to crash into the next landing. "Spread the word. There won't be another warning, just blood and missing body parts."

Draza struggled to pick himself up but only managed to get into a sitting position as he coughed and struggled to get his breath. Stunned at what just happened, I didn't notice Victor stalking up to me before scooping me up with one arm under my ass. Instinctively I wrapped an arm around his neck as he carried me down the rest of the stairs, through a hall full of soldiers, into the cafeteria. The shocked faces of the men and women watching me being hauled around by this intimidating man had me struggling not to laugh. I could just imagine the picture we made.

Arriving at a table with six chairs, Victor put me down and pointed to a chair. "Sit."

The order instantly had me bristling. "No."

"Yes," he responded, crossing his arms.

I matched his look, and I jutted my chin out. If I had to look up at him, I was going to make it clear he didn't scare me... much. The fucking Alphas and their bossy tendencies always thinking they know what's best. Would it kill them to say *please*?

"Danella, sit down." He bit out through clenched teeth.

"Vicky, say please," I countered.

His brows crashed together. "That nickname isn't happening, Little Spark. Now, *please*, for the love of all that is holy, sit down."

"Thank you for saying please," I said, taking a seat. "Although I'm absolutely going to call you Vicky now, seeing how much you enjoy it," I added with a flash of a smile.

Glaring at me, he turned but paused and stabbed a finger at me. "Don't. Move."

Cocking my head, I lifted a hand to my ear. "I'm sorry, what was that?"

"*Please*," Victor all but growled.

"Oh, sure thing." I grinned, leaning back in the chair, and gave him a thumbs-up.

"Fucking Omega, she's lucky she's cute when she's being sassy," Victor muttered as he shook his head and walked away.

That had me snorting and covering my mouth so I didn't laugh and draw more attention from the others eating. Glancing around the room, I noticed it was rather full and the food smelled amazing. With a loud rumble, my stomach agreed, excited to be fed. It didn't take long for the other four to enter the cafeteria and make their way over to the table. This must be their usual table since it wasn't easy to spot being in the back corner.

"Danella, why is everyone saying that Victor hauled you in here over his shoulder, kicking and screaming?" Sorin asked as he came to stand in front of me.

That's when I finally lost it and fell into a fit of laughter. This had Sorin's eyes growing wide as his brows shot up. It had been so long since I'd laughed. Really laughed, the kind that makes your cheeks hurt and your eyes water. The situation wasn't that funny, but everything about this day so far had been one curve ball after the other and I just couldn't stop it once it started. The man in question returned with a tray that had two plates loaded with food.

"What did you do?" Victor snapped, slamming the tray on the table. "Why is she crying?"

My laughter subsided to mere chuckles as I wiped at my eyes. "I'm fine, Vicky, just had a good laugh, is all. Oh man, I can't remember the last time that happened."

Toma pulled out a chair and sank into it next to me. "Vicky?"

Within seconds a dinner knife was being held against his throat. "No. Wipe it from your memory because it's not happening," Victor threatened as he dropped the knife and shifted his glare from his friend to me. "Not happening, Little Spark."

I just gave him a toothy smile and flipped him the bird. The others laughed at that response and headed off to get food. Slapping Victor on the back as they passed resulting in him telling them to fuck off. None of them seemed bothered by his irritation so I took that as a sign I hadn't truly made him mad.

"Here," Victor said as he slid over a plate and slapped silverware next to it. "Didn't know what you liked, so I got a bit of everything. Eat what you want and what's left over, I'll take care of."

The overflowing plate of food had my mouth watering. Scrambled eggs with cheese mixed in, bacon, sausage, two pancakes covered in syrup, and seasoned potatoes. Diving into the food, I took a bite of everything just to sample the taste and decide what I wanted to be sure to eat before my stomach was too full. Over the past few days of eating three meals, my stomach had gotten bigger though I would be lucky to eat half of what was on the plate. The pancake was fluffy and the syrup was divine so I started on that. Unable to keep still as I ate, my excitement over the yummy food had me rocking side to side as I hummed.

"Is she dancing?" Petru questioned as he took his seat.

Freezing, I swallowed the food I'd been chewing and grabbed the glass of water Sorin set in front of me before I choked.

"It's adorable," Cristofor said, sitting next to me, and then leaned in to whisper, "Ignore them. They've never really had women around to know it's a completely normal occurrence. Especially for Omegas."

Nodding, I took another sip of water trying to get the image of him naked out of my mind before I made a fool out of myself again.

"Also, I wanted to say I'm sorry for what happened back at the apartment. I shouldn't have dropped all that on you like that. Sometimes all the knowledge I know from my mom just comes tumbling out before I make sure it's the right time to bring it up. You've had a lot thrown at you the last few days, you didn't need more put on your plate," Cristofor apologized, resting a hand lightly on my arm as if he needed to make sure I knew he was being sincere.

Meeting his gaze, I saw the worry in his eyes, and something about that expression had the crack in my walls growing bigger. "Thank you for apologizing, but I don't think I handled things well, either. It seems when fighting isn't an option for me, my flight skills are pretty intense."

Cris let out a huff of laughter, his eyes shining with mirth. "You should have seen how fast you moved. It was pretty impressive."

Feeling much more relaxed, I returned to my food as the guys started to shovel their breakfast into their mouths. It was like watching a black hole sucking in whatever got too close. Only Cris seemed to eat with any kind of civility. Sorin paused after a few minutes and waved his fork at Victor. "You know why Draza's walking around talking shit about you?"

"Yup," he answered simply.

Sorin let out a sigh and set his fork down. "Care to elaborate?"

"Not really."

"Am I going to have to order you to tell me?" Sorin warned.

Victor slammed his fork down and locked eyes with Sorin as flashes of anger and irritation only Alphas could give off pickled along my skin. "The prick forgot his place and touched what's under my protection. Now he and everyone else knows better. That a good enough explanation for you, boss?"

"Don't get pissy with me, Vic. I need to know these things to keep you out of trouble. You have every right to put a lower-ranking soldier in their place, but Draza is your equal in rank. This wouldn't be a problem if you'd let me promote you like I want to," Sorin pointed out.

"Yeah, but that means I'll have more bullshit to deal with and I just want to do my job," Victor muttered. "This really gonna cause me problems?"

"Depends on what happened," Sorin countered as the muscle in his jaw started to twitch. This clearly wasn't the first time they'd had this argument.

Shoving my chair back, I stood. "It's my fault."

"Sit the fuck back down and eat your food," Victor ordered.

I leveled him a flat look before facing Sorin. "I got freaked out and needed to get out of the apartment. I planned to head back to the Med Center, and in my rush, I ran into Draza. He was still pissed at me for breaking his nose and decided to teach me a lesson. I defended myself as best I could when Victor stepped in to end the situation. Draza is an asshole and deserved what he got."

Sorin searched my face for a moment before scratching his jaw and leaning back. "What did Draza say to you?"

"The normal shit," I brushed off, taking my seat, and poked at the food left. "I'm a whore. I should know my place. I'm a no-good Northern breeder who doesn't deserve to be rescued. He was going to beat me, maybe rape me, definitely spit in my face and leave me to die like the trash I am. That man made no effort to hide his disdain for my existence."

"You said you defended yourself?" Petru inquired, his tone holding something dangerous in it.

Looking up, I glanced at all of them and various levels of rage were written across their faces. "Ah..."

"It's alright, Danella, you're not in trouble. You had every right to protect yourself when faced with that sort of attack," Sorin assured me.

Licking my lips, I decided to trust him on that. Not like I would have done anything differently if I had the chance to do it over. In fact, I'd have tried to find another way to break his nose again. Then he'd remember what happens when you fuck with me since he seemed to forget the first time.

"I kneed him in the balls, slammed him into the wall, and punched him in the throat. I missed the sweet spot but I knew it still fucking hurt," I answered.

Victor gave me a wicked grin. "Should have seen her, she wasn't backing down for shit."

"Seems what training you picked up has served you well, but I think it's time to see if we can start your training sooner than later," Sorin decided. "I'll talk to Beth and your doctors to see what we can agree on. In the meantime, we can start with gun basics, weak points in the body, and how to handle a knife. None of those should be too much for her and will get the ball rolling on her foundation."

They all nodded in agreement as I was left to gawk at them. "Wait, what? You're going to teach me how to fire a gun?"

"It would be stupid to have them all over the place without you knowing the basics. Besides, in the South, every person has the right to learn to defend themselves if they so choose," Petru answered. "This is always what we meant when talking about training. If you're going to be around our unit and possibly going on a mission, then you need to know these things. We'll also need to cover traveling basics like how to build a fire, set up a tent, read a map, use a compass, and things like that."

If only they'd known that leading with this part of the deal would have had me saying yes in a heartbeat. These were skills and resources I could use for the rest of my life. I'd expected some hand-to-hand training and maybe a few other skills, but this was far beyond what I dreamed.

"There's one thing I need to make clear before we move forward," Sorin interjected. His face and tone had me on alert with how serious he'd gotten. "If you accept the offer, you will do so with the knowledge that you're training to be part of *our* unit. This means you will train, eat, and live with us for the duration to build a connection as a team."

Well shit.

CHAPTER 24

Sorin

It was risky to lay it out for her, but I wasn't going to chance her saying we didn't lay everything out on the table. Since the moment I got out of the shower and heard her yelling in our home, I knew I wasn't going to get another chance to make this happen. She'd faced off with Victor, stood her ground, and won the bastard over where many had failed before her. I'm not talking about any sort of romantic dynamic. She'd gained his respect which is what he needed to give before he would ever chance something more with a person, male or female.

Hearing that he'd come to her rescue and seeing him smile more than once this morning told me all I needed to know. Petru was already of the mind that she was ours, and it was clear that Cris also seemed to agree. Toma was a little hard to read, yet while the man drew a lot of attention with his looks and charming personality, he was off his game with her. I enjoyed seeing it and watching him work for it for a change if that's what he wanted.

As for myself...

Something about the fire inside her drew me to her. I wanted to know what she would do next, test that sharp mind of hers, see what she could be once we gave her the skills to stand alongside us. That's where I wanted her. If she was going to be part of our unit, it would be on equal footing. The one thing she pounded home in all her outbursts was needing to feel she could make choices, have a voice, and stand on her own two feet. I also wanted that for her with us at her back to offer support if she needed it. There was so much hiding under the surface that I hadn't had a chance to be nurtured. It was the same thing I saw in all the men I brought into my unit.

"You want me to live with you?" she questioned, finally breaking the silence that had fallen over the table.

I could feel it in the tension of the men around me. They wanted her to say yes, to us, to staying, to building trust, and something more. People say that instinct can only get you so far, but I believe with everything I am, this gut need to keep her close was the right call to make. Even with how little I knew about her—she fit. Our unit was made up of many strong males, including myself, but she didn't seem to notice, going toe-to-toe with any of us if she felt like we were abusing our power. We needed that, a person to challenge and ground us when things got heated as it tends to do with any family. Cris was a good man, but he was a peacekeeper, not the person to call us on our shit and defend ourselves.

"Yes," I answered, but held up a hand when I saw her starting to shut down. "Let me give you the details before you reject the deal."

The wariness in her expression and how apprehensive she'd become, ready to bolt at any second, had me begging the fates to let her hear me. If they truly planned for this woman to be ours, then I would need all the help I could to make it happen. She'd been shown time after time that people only wanted to use her, and I admit when I came up with the idea to get information from her, I fell into that category. Yet she was like a thorn in my foot, burying herself deeper into my mind so that I couldn't stop thinking about her. She was fire, passion, a warrior at heart, desperate to change the world. That was something I couldn't agree with her more on.

"Training normally takes up to six weeks, but we don't have that time. We're going to cut it in half to make it three weeks. I would prefer two, but you're still recovering and I don't want to cause any setbacks. Furthermore, in a show of good faith, I'm going to reach out to my contact in Oscad and let him know that two of the girls are ready to be extracted. Your friends will no longer be a pawn in anyone's game. You all deserve better than that," I shared, having already decided this when I moved them off base. "My request is that you give us three weeks. Learn from us, train, and give us a chance to show you not all Alphas feel the need to put Omegas in a protective box. Allow us those three weeks to see if this is the right fit for us all, because I believe it is. We need someone like you in our pack as much as you need us, even if you don't want to admit it. The only rules are you have to live with us, keep an open mind, and train to the best of your ability. No holding back."

She didn't answer immediately, and I took that as a good sign. "Explain to me the living together aspect."

"Currently, I'm the only one who doesn't share a room with someone. We'll have a bed, trunk, and dresser brought in just like all the others have. As a unit, we train together for part of the day, then each of us has work to do in our specialty areas. It could be teaching new recruits or working on a project for the military. When it comes to meals we all eat together, that would also apply to you. You will have the same rules as all the members of my unit, and while we all might be of varying rank, we treat each other as equals," I pointed out, wanting to drive that fact home. "That would include you as well. You won't be an Omega or trainee to us, you'll be our teammate."

"So sex isn't involved in any way," she asked bluntly.

"That is up to you," I answered without thinking. "Full transparency because we don't keep secrets in this unit. When Cris first joined, he slept with us all on occasion, and after some time, feelings evolved to love and others remained affectionate. There were no hard feelings or bitterness when Cris chose to be with just Tru and Toma. Anyone with eyes could see the bond they share. Everyone was honest, upfront, and didn't hide things from each other, making the shift in dynamic simple. No one got their feelings hurt, and our unit became stronger for it. All that to say, we have no problem sharing or understanding if stronger connections build between some but not all. Just don't be sneaky about your intentions and ask for what you need from us. As a family, we support each other any way we can."

"You're telling me that if I say no sex ever, you'd be fine with that? Or if I just picked one of you and not the others, it wouldn't cause the rest of you to be jealous?" Danella challenged, like she was trying to corner me into telling her what I'd said was all bullshit.

Turning to the guys, I waved for them to answer feeling like she wouldn't take my word for it. Let her hear it from the horse's mouth. Maybe then she'd actually listen to what we were saying.

Petru spoke first, which didn't surprise me at all. "Danella, I'm more than willing to court you and see if something more comes of it, physical or otherwise. That being said, if you told me that there was too much trauma for it to ever lead to sex, then I would happily abide by that for you. I care more about your understanding that I'll respect and care for you than anything else. I have two other lovers who can tend to that need, so why would I force you into that situation?"

"Same," Toma added. "What kind of pack would we be if we put our own physical needs ahead of your well-being?"

Cris nodded his head and shifted to face Danella. "I've seen first-hand the after-effects of what you've been through many, many times. There's no way I could ever be that cruel or selfish to force you to give something you don't want to willingly. That isn't caring for someone, and that's certainly not what I want for any of my family."

I waited, curious to see what Vic would say on this matter. He's the only one of us that had a relationship outside the pack that became fairly serious until he found she'd cheated on him with three other men in her own unit. She'd just used Vic and his connections to get the job placement she wanted, allowing her to never have to see combat. It happened shortly after he joined our unit, and it changed him into this callus bastard who refused to let people in. Vic was one of the most loyal men I'd ever served with, and to have that kind of betrayal, it hurt him to the core.

"Little Spark, I threatened to rip off a man's head if he dared to look at you. How the fuck could you think I'd ever stoop so low as to force something from you that you don't want to give? Cris's story alone should answer your other concern. Do any of us seem the least bit bothered that he chose those two?" Vic asked, jerking his thumb at the two Alphas. "Nah, you love who you love, end of story."

To me, that pretty much summed up the sentiment of everyone at the table. The question was, would she believe us?

"So when does this start?" she asked, pushing her plate towards Vic, who placed it on top of his empty one to finish it off.

"I'll go back with you to the Med Center and talk to Beth along with your doctor. For today I think you've had enough happen that it's best you relax at the Med Center. I'm sure Beth will want to do a full workup to see if you're ready for this," I shared. "Does that mean you agree to the terms I've set before you?"

She pulled a leg up to hug to her chest, something I noticed she did when she was deep in thought or talking about something uncomfortable. Like she needed the added comfort it gave her and covered the vulnerable parts of her body.

"I will agree to the three weeks." Danella decided.

Reaching out a hand to her, she paused for a heartbeat then leaned forward to grab it. I held her hand firmly and locked eyes with her. "Then it's official. For the next three weeks, you're part of our unit."

CHAPTER 25

Danella

True to his word, Sorin brought me back to the Med Center and was instantly set upon by Bethany. "What in the world were you thinking taking her out of here without alerting anyone and without shoes, for fucks sake."

"Beth, I believe this is a conversation not meant for the halls of the facility. Get Danella settled, and then I'd like to speak with you and Doc Rosen, where I would be happy to address all your concerns," Sorin instructed with a firm yet gentle tone.

Bethany seemed none too pleased with his orders, but she wrapped an arm around my shoulders guiding me down the hall, muttering under her breath. "Damn Alphas always thinking they know better, not here, not in my house."

Feeling it was in my best interest not to tell her I ran off, I remained silent. Arriving at my room, I found a clean pair of clothes on the bed and the shoes I'd abandoned in the garden.

"Dani, please tell me they fed you breakfast?" Bethany asked as she collected my shower caddy and towel, handing them to me.

The rooms didn't have attached bathrooms, instead, we all shared a community shower area and I was used to this. Although it wasn't as nice as the one in the Care Center, it still provided the basic necessities.

"Yes, Vicky got me a massive plate of food," I assured her.

Frowning, she settled my clothes on top of the pile in my arms. "Vicky? Since when do they have a woman hanging around them?"

"Sorry, Victor," I corrected. "Victor made sure I ate."

Her mouth dropped open for a second before she recovered and collected herself. "Victor, the man with the beard, muscles, and permanent scowl on his face like he's ready to kill you? That Victor?"

Grinning, I nodded. "That's the one."

"He let you call him Vicky?" Bethany pressed.

"Let would be a strong word, he keeps telling me it's not going to stick and I remind him that he has no choice in the matter. Though your brother tried to use it and almost got gutted with a table knife," I shared.

Tossing back her head, laughter bubbled out of her. "Oh that sounds like Vic, alright. Now, I want you to shower, change, and be in this room resting when I come back to check on you. Don't think for one second I don't know you snuck out of here. I'm not going to ask why or how you ended up with Toma and the others at the crack of dawn. Being here recovering can make you stir crazy, but this is your one pass. Don't ever try it again, or you'll find out how easy it is for me to take away your privileges. You're under my care, and I'll be damned if I let anything happen to you. Have I made myself clear?"

Biting my lip, I nodded. "I'm sorry, Bethany, I didn't intend to leave the premises like that."

"For the tenth time, call me Beth. I feel like we know each other well enough not to be so formal. Run along, and stay out of trouble for a little while at least, please," Beth pleaded, then squeezed my arm reassuringly and left to meet with Sorin.

"That went better than expected," I mumbled to myself as I headed for the showers.

One thing I will never take for granted again is hot water that I can let run for as long as I like. Not feeling completely safe here in the showers, I never took long, except today I decided to indulge myself. That, and it took forever to get the tangles out of my curly hair from the bike ride. I refused to look at the mirrors when I came in, not willing to see how bad it was. Letting the conditioner sit was an excellent excuse for lingering in the steamy shower. Allowing myself to just be while sitting on the pulldown bench was magical. Until I wasn't alone in the shower room anymore.

"Did you see that Sorin is back again today? I don't think I've seen him at the Med Center so often before," a woman said.

"Rumor is that he brought back an Omega from the North and has taken a shine to her," another woman added.

There was a scoff, and the sound of the shower curtain to my left was pulled back. "Seriously? What, no woman from the South is good enough for him and his pack that they have to pluck one from the dirt of the North? Maybe it's because she's a breeder and doesn't expect anything from life but to be fucked."

"Mora," her friend scolded. "How could you think that of the President's son? Besides, they have that baby-faced Beta male they all fuck around with. Why would they need another whore when they have one ready to bend over and take it from any of them?"

An image of Cris' kind smile flashed before my eyes, followed by a wave of anger that they would dare talk like that about him. Out of all the men, he'd been nothing but sweet, kind, and gentle. How could they even think of him like that? Obviously, they were jealous they would choose to sleep with a man rather than them, but it was clear why that was. Who would want a snake in their bed? Needing to get the hell out of here before they finished with their showers, I started to rinse the conditioner from my hair, not caring if it still had tangles.

"They can all have the Beta, I just want Sorin. Furthermore, who else would want to sleep with that monster Victor? You know he killed two of the men in his last unit, don't you? It makes me question why he was allowed to live after killing two of our own. Maybe he's working with the North and this breeder is an informant. It wouldn't be the first time they tried something like that, which is why we need to make sure Sorin only surrounds himself with people he can trust." Mora reasoned.

Her friend laughed. "Oh, and I bet you think you're the right person to keep him safe and out of the clutches of some bitch with a hidden motive?"

"Of course," Mora said, her self-grandeur dripping off her words. "Who better than a woman whose father is on the board of advisors to the President? It's like I was born to support the next man to be our leader. Then I can cut away all the useless baggage holding him back from greatness. It's like he feels the need to take in the outcasts no one else would want, taking pity on them. Seriously, it's just disgusting to think of that riffraff sullying his reputation."

That. Was. It. I'd had enough. I couldn't take it anymore. I might not know those men, but from what I'd seen they were a family who cared and looked after each other. How dare this woman think to strip him from the pack he built himself? Did no one understand the sacred bond a pack has to each other?

"What about Petru? I hear his father was a traitor, which is why he was executed, and his mother killed herself. The poor thing was left to take care of his little brother and his cousins, those his mother took in. He can't be all that bad if he did all that," Mora's friend commented.

The water turned off next to me, allowing me to hear her hollow laugh. "You can't honestly believe that a traitor's son would be any better, do you? He might be the worst of them all. How can you trust someone whose family has already betrayed the South? His father's actions caused the lives of a whole village to be lost. The whole family should have been put to death to ensure the poison was cleansed from the population."

The last strand of control I had snapped hearing how callus she was about the matter. Ripping back the shower curtain, I saw the woman walk out of the stall turning away from me as she dried her hair with a towel. Using that to my advantage, I tackled the bitch slamming her to the tiled floor with a screech. She was pretty with dark brown hair, blue eyes, a tiny nose, and full lips. I fucking hated her.

"What the hell, you psycho, get the fuck off me," Mora yelled, batting at me with her hands in a lame attempt to attack me.

I punched her right in the mouth making her scream and thrash under me. "You should learn to watch your fucking mouth, you entitled cunt," I spat.

"Vela, get help," Mora cried out as I slammed my other fist into her face.

Mora was now trying to fight back in earnest and landed a blow to my chin, but I shook it off and kept pummeling her. She tried to hook her leg around me to get me off her, only I grabbed her hair and yanked her head back so she couldn't see me making it harder to fight back.

Leaning down, I whispered in her ear, "Seems you might be wrong about the breeder bitch from the North. Thing is, that life makes us feral, more prone to violence. So I'd watch yourself and what you say, especially regarding my unit. I won't let you destroy them, and if I have to, I'll take a page from Victor's book... dead cunts don't cause trouble."

"You crazy bitch, do you know who I am?" She spluttered, thrashing under me.

"Nope, and I don't plan to," I shared, letting go of her hair to grab her throat. I then smashed my fist into her cute little nose, liking the idea that it wouldn't be so perfect after this. "But you'll remember me, that's for damn sure."

"Dani, stop," Sorin barked.

My body froze at the Alpha command, fist primed and ready to greet her face one more time. I looked up from my prey to find not only Sorin but Toma standing there with him along with Beth. Sorin stalked forward grabbing a towel, looped an arm around my waist, and hauled me off Mora. Setting me on my feet, he wrapped the towel around me, picked me up like a toddler, and settled me on his hip.

He glared at me then looked down at Mora. "I'm sorry, Ms. Korda. I'll get to the bottom of this and ensure the matter is settled appropriately. Allow Nurse Bethany to look after you in the meantime."

That made me lose my shit all over again. "You're taking that cunt's side without even knowing what happened? Of course, why would you believe the Northern breeder? We're just wild animals picked out of the dirt."

Sorin's brows knitted together. "That's not what I'm doing, and no matter who's at fault, Ms. Korda will need medical attention. You, on the other hand, seem unharmed or I would have requested the same for you."

Beth stepped forward and knelt beside Mora to examine her face then met mine with such a profound look of disappointment. "Come, Ms. Korda, let's get you dried off and cleaned up."

Toma reached down to help, and I practically hissed at the action. "Sure, help the witch but know that you'll be helping a woman who bitched about Petru being a traitor. Who she believes should be killed because of association. Not to mention her view on Cris being nothing except a man whore for the unit. Or the fact that Victor is a monster who killed members of his old unit and should be put to death himself. Yeah, I might be the one who bloodied her face, but she's the one who keeps saying people should be killed. Go right ahead, help the woman who wants to prune the dead weight from her precious Sorin once she lures him into being her lover."

That got everyone's attention, and Sorin turned to set me on the counter to box me in with his arms. "Dani-girl, I need you to know that what you're accusing her of is a serious offense. What you said about Petru and Victor are part of sealed records that no one is supposed to know about. Are you one hundred percent positive that this woman, Mora Korda, is the one who said those things?"

Leaning in so our noses almost touched and I could feel his breath on my face, I answered. "That's the bitch I beat up, isn't it?"

Sorin searched my expression then nodded and turned to face the rest of our little gathering. "The perpetrator has been identified by a witness. This identification has been corroborated by myself, Staff Sergeant Dalca, as well as Senior Nurse Dalca. Staff Sergeant, if you could please see that the accused is clothed and handed off to the MPs while I file the paperwork."

Toma stood to attention and lifted his left hand, placing two fingers near his eye, and flicked them out in a salute. "Right away, Major."

Reaching down, Toma grabbed her arm and yanked her to her feet. "You won't get away with this," Mora snapped. "Do you know how many people know about your unit of misfits and soldiers who should have never been allowed the positions they hold? It's disgraceful to see our President's son surrounding himself with such filth. My father will not stand for this. He'll have you all discharged and thrown in jail, especially that Northern whore of an Omega."

Lunging at her, I was thwarted when Sorin scooped me up again, holding me with both arms around my waist. "Joke's on you bitch, I'm from Oscad."

"Toma," Sorin ordered.

Knowing exactly what his leader wanted, Toma snagged the towel from Beth, wrapped it around Mora, then tossed the furious woman over his shoulder to march out of the showers. I caught a glimpse of Victor blocking the way into the bathroom. He spared a glance over his shoulder and winked at me. Bet the crazy bastard heard everything we'd said in here since I hadn't really kept my voice down.

"Can I put you down now, or do you plan on exacting more justice on our unit's behalf?" Sorin asked, his voice back to its calm, smooth tone.

"I couldn't take it anymore," I muttered as I was once more placed on my feet. "You should have heard the bullshit that was spewing from her mouth. Someone needed to shut her up."

The towel had slid down to my hips so I pulled it up and secured it before facing Sorin. Clearly, everyone in this room had gotten a free look at me, though I hated how all it showed was the years of starvation I'd lived through. I'd never been vain about my physical appearance, but no one finds half-starved attractive.

"I'm sorry you had to hear all that from someone else and not from us. Everything that was said is true to a point. No one but myself, the person directly involved, and a judge has all the facts where Victor is concerned. You already know the truth about Cris, and Petru... Well, that's not my story to tell. All I will say is that his father was executed for treason, and his mother killed herself soon after. The why behind all of it, will be up to him to share," Sorin explained as he reached out and rested his hands on my shoulders. "Dani-girl, you need to know these men have all been through hell in their own way but came out of it stronger. When they give you their loyalty, nothing could make them give it up or turn their back on that person. What just happened here shows me you're exactly the same way."

Leaning down, he pressed a soft kiss to my forehead letting his lips linger there for a moment. "Thank you," he whispered before stepping around me and heading for the door. "Get dressed Dani-girl. I think it's better if we move you in right away. Seems leaving you on your own gets you into trouble."

Well, I couldn't argue with him there.

Letting out a sigh, I noticed the knuckles on my right hand were split and were bleeding a little though it wasn't anything I was too worried about. Grabbing my shower caddy from the stall, I plucked out the wide tooth comb and started working on my hair. Once it was tangle-free, I dried off and slipped into the clean uniform. For once in my life, I'd love to be able to wear something I chose, but it seems that day would be far off by the looks of it. Giving my hair one last scrunch with the towel, I headed out of the bathroom to find that Victor was still waiting for me.

"You're like my fricken shadow, always popping up in places," I commented as I headed down the hall to my room.

He snorted. "More like public protection detail. Can't let you wander off and attack more unsuspecting shit-talkers. If I did, there might not be anyone left to fight the good fight."

That made me laugh because he was probably right. "What can I say, I don't like it when people get too full of themselves or speak out of turn. Life is hard enough without people sticking their noses in places they don't belong."

"How the hell did you survive living in the North?" Victor asked, shaking his head.

"Because I was owned by the man whose mark I bear. If not for his protection, I would have been beaten and killed long before this. In fact, many were waiting for the chance to do just that when he got tired of me," I shared as we entered my room. "So, Sorin said you're pulling me out of here."

Victor didn't answer immediately. He just stared at me like I'd done something odd, or odder than usual. "You're not going to argue about that, demand you get the time we promised you? Or, I don't know, grumble about it in some manner? I feel like this is a trick that you're being so willing about it right now."

I shrugged my shoulders. "Look, I get that I'm a pain in the ass and that I have authority issues, but I'm not stupid. That woman I just beat the shit out of mentioned who her father is. I tried to hold back, except she just wouldn't stop parading all your faults and flaws to that friend of hers. You mean to tell me a woman that vicious doesn't have her own dirty laundry hiding in the closet? Either way I look at it, being officially part of your unit gives me more protection than fighting against it. I didn't survive this long without learning to make a deal with the lesser of two evils."

"Huh," Victor grunted. "Smart, sassy, and clearly has a mean right hook. Not at all what I would have expected from an Omega. I think I'll enjoy learning what other surprises you have in store for us, Little Spark."

CHAPTER 26

Danella

The move didn't take long since I had nothing to my name except the things Beth had given me. Victor and Sorin took me to the supply depot and got me three changes of clothes, combat boots, socks, undergarments, and any personal grooming essentials. It was all neatly packed into a duffle and handed to me to carry. We didn't go back to the barracks right away, there was one more stop to meet with the enlistment office to get my paperwork filed. Finished with that, I had my very own keycard that would allow me into the barracks and the other training buildings I would need access to.

"That key will open any area you are allowed to be in. If it doesn't work, then you shouldn't be there," the enlisting officer warned. "There are logs of every swipe of a card. We expect the occasional new recruit to end up in a place they don't belong, although just know we are well aware of any and all attempts made."

"Understood, sir," I answered.

He looked at me over his glasses like he didn't believe me but grunted and turned back to his computer. "Your chart says you're on the injections to keep you from going into heat. This is your responsibility to maintain, no one else's. Any other medical information we need to know?"

"No, sir, not that I'm aware of."

"Good, everything looks in order. You will be on probation for six weeks. If at all during that time you choose this isn't the life for you or your unit leader comes to that conclusion, you will be dismissed with no blemish on your record. If those six weeks pass and you flunk out, or your unit leader dismisses you, there will be a discharge record. This can affect your ability to get a higher-level job leaving you stuck with the more menial labor. So I suggest you make up your mind quickly on the matter." The warning look I got from him told me he didn't think I would make it six weeks.

Too bad for him, I loved proving people wrong.

"Thank you, Lieutenant Colonel Harvo. I'll manage the rest from here," Sorin assured the older man.

"See that you do. It's not like you to pick such an inexperienced person to join your unit," Harvo pointed out.

"True, but I've always known what my unit needs to be successful, and Danella is the right woman for the job. Good afternoon, sir," Sorin said with a quick salute and motioned for me to head out of the room.

Outside I took a better look at the card. It was white with my name and barrack number written on it, simple and to the point. I could get behind that. In fact, I'd noticed that the South didn't really have symbols, crests, or flags on anything. Even the uniforms just displayed your rank and what kind of unit you were a part of, but nothing about the country itself. Grabbing my duffle from where I'd left it with Victor, I tossed it over my shoulder and shoved the card into my pocket.

"Now what?" I asked.

"That's it for the official stuff," Sorin answered. "Why don't we head back to the apartment, have you drop off your stuff, and I'll take you to the training areas. This way, if you ever need to meet one of us there for some reason, you know the way."

"You sure you'd trust me to be alone that long?" I teased.

Sorin reached out and tugged on my ponytail. "My hope is that giving you a way to release all that pent-up anger will keep you from picking fights."

"Yeah, about that," I muttered, kicking a stone in the road. "Lucian thought that too, but I just ended up using what he taught me to get even with those who tried to mess with me. That's when the lessons stopped."

"Let's see if the second time's the charm. Plus, we'll be back on the road once we're confident enough in your ability not to get yourself killed if a fight breaks out. I've already gotten pushback from us taking time, but now that we officially have a new recruit on our roster, they can't do a damn thing about it," Sorin explained.

When we got to the barracks, both Alphas turned to me expectantly. Grinning, I whipped out my keycard and swiped it. Seconds later it buzzed allowing me to open the door. The reality that I'd been given a key allowing me to come and go as I please hit me like a ton of bricks. Since the day I was taken from my childhood home, that privilege had been stripped from me. Now, here of all places, I was given that right back. I no longer believed I was locked away like a prisoner in a cage. I might still have guards keeping an eye on me, but I didn't fear they would hurt me and god, did that make all the difference in the world.

"Little Spark, you coming?" Victor called from ahead.

Snapping out of my melancholy, I jogged after them. "Sorry, I just got a little lost in thought there."

The burly man just nodded, not at all interested in prying, which I was thankful for. Sorin held the apartment door open for us, and a second realization hit me. This was now going to be my home for the next three weeks, at least. It was hard even to think that far ahead with how fast things had been changing.

Cris walked out of the far room and grinned at me. "Care to see your space?"

Swallowing my emotions, I nodded and walked over to him and peeked my head into the room. It looked exactly like Toma and Cris's room but for the fact that Sorin had a slightly bigger bed which was now pushed to one side. A simple single-person bed was on the left side of the room closer to the bathroom, with a trunk at the end of the bed and a dresser on the wall, just as promised. Cautiously I stepped into the space and was overwhelmed by the wintergreen and eucalyptus scent that was Sorin. It was like taking a deep breath on a winter morning after a fresh snowfall; clean, crisp, and invigorating.

"There is space in the bathroom for you to put your things there, and the towel on the right hook is mine. Laundry is switched out once a week. We're responsible for putting it all in a bag for them to take and making the beds when they drop off a clean set," Sorin shared when he saw me peeking around the space. "I know it will take you a little time to adjust to being here, but we will do our best to make it easy on you. None of us have spent much time around a woman in roughly ten years, so you'll have to forgive us if we do something to offend you. Our rule is if you have a problem you voice it during our weekly check-in. Unless there is something that needs to be handled right away then share it with me first and I'll make the call on next steps."

Setting my duffle on the bed that was now mine, I tuned and sat, dropping my head into my hands. I'd thought I had a handle on things, but the sense of being overwhelmed just hit me out of nowhere. The bed dipped as someone sat next to me and the distinct smell of patchouli and spruce told me it was Cris.

He slowly put his arm around my shoulders, giving me a gentle half-hug. "It's okay to be overwhelmed, Dani. So much has changed, and none of it you were prepared for. You thought you were finally running to your freedom, only to end up in yet another new country with different laws and rules. Some are better, some might be the same, but none of it is what you wanted."

His words hit how I was feeling dead center on the target. The need for his comfort had me sinking into his side, resting my head on his shoulder as he ran his hand up and down my arm. He didn't speak, just let me soak up the peace he was freely offering without trying to take advantage of the situation. The sensation wasn't the same as it had been with Petru, but that didn't mean it was less, just different. It reminded me more of times when Violet or Tori needed this from me and I just held them. Could it be that all of us were so starved for affection we tried to find it amongst ourselves during our time in the Care Center?

I took a deep breath, and the contented sigh I exhaled said more than I could have imagined. What would happen if I got attached to these men, but at the end of three weeks they didn't want me? That was absurd. Why would I choose to stay rather than go home? Yet the thought nagged at me until I lifted my head to meet Cris's warm, inviting blue eyes.

"I need you to be honest with me, Cris," I said, pausing to lick my lips. "Is your pack really looking to add an Omega, or is that something you thought of to make me feel better about staying?"

The Beta shifted and pulled my legs over his so I could look at him more head-on. He lightly cupped my face in his hands searching my expression before he answered me. "Before you fell into our laps, not once had any of us talked about adding an Omega to our unit. None of us opposed the idea, but it wasn't something we were actively seeking. Then you showed up and made us sit up and take notice. Every time one of them interacted with you, the subject came up more and more. Petru is a man who believes in fate to the point he is absolutely certain that the fates brought you to us. That we were meant to be off course trying to save Draza when he got separated from his team just for the purpose of stumbling upon you and your friends. If we'd gone back the way we came, we'd never have run into you, and who knows, maybe you'd be back in Oscad." Cris whispered, leaning forward and resting his forehead on mine, letting that thought set in.

"Yet that's not what happened," I said softly.

"You're right, it's not," Cris agreed. "Our unit is the one you ran into that night, and that set things in motion. When you stumbled out of the cave, face covered in blood, dead on your feet, but fearlessly ready to take us on to save your friends. That's when Sorin changed his mind on what he would do with you. Then when I held you in my arms the whole way back to base taking stock of all the injuries you suffered told me what kind of person you are, Dani. Strong, fearless, a leader, and someone who will never turn her back on the people she loves. It made me insanely jealous of your two friends, because I wanted to know what it felt like to experience that kind of fierce love. We all feel that way about you, even if some of us don't realize it ourselves yet. That's why we asked you to be part of our unit, Danella. It's no trick or ploy, just a desperate attempt to make you give us a chance. That's the truth none of them are willing to tell you, yet I think you need to know how we feel."

Slowly, oh so slowly, giving me every moment to pull away, Cris lowered his lips to mine in a kiss so light and soft I almost didn't believe it happened. I ached for more but he pulled back and instead pressed a kiss firmly to my forehead, letting his lips linger as he still held my face. When he sat back up, the warmth and hope in his expression made me want to wrap my arms around him just as much as it terrified me.

"Take a nap, Dani. I think you're more worn out than you realize," Cris urged as he stood, letting his hands fall away.

The loss of contact almost had me whining in desperation to make him stay, but I swallowed the urge down. He must be right, I was just tired and it was making me feel this way. Once I got some sleep I'd feel more like myself and this moment could be dismissed as an act of delirium.

"I think you're right," I agreed. "Are you sure it will be alright if I rest? Sorin wanted to take me to the training grounds."

"He can do that later. You weren't supposed to start training until tomorrow, anyways. I'll tell him, as the unit's medic, you need rest and he won't argue with me." Cris assured me.

I kicked off my shoes and grabbed my pillow that smelled just like Sorin, and curled around it. It didn't take me long to drift off to sleep showing me just how tired I really was. Then again, I'd been up since three in the morning. What a busy, busy day it's been.

CHAPTER 27

Danella

Someone was chasing me. I don't know how I knew, but I could feel their eyes on me as the hair on the back of my neck rose. Everywhere I looked, there was no place to hide, no cover, just dried, cracked dirt for as far as the eye could see. My heart pounded in my chest as I kept running, pushing harder. If I just ran fast enough, I might be able to get away. No matter what, I couldn't go back there. I couldn't go back to that life. We'd made it out, not the way we planned on it, but Tori and Violet were going to be safe, and I was going to learn how to fight. Things were finally starting to work out for the better.

Hands grabbed me and pulled me against their body. I screamed, fighting with all that I had, using every trick in the book I remembered. I wasn't going to be silent, no more holding back. I would fight until the end if I had to. I wasn't a weakling needing to be locked away for my own good.

No more. No. More.

I wasn't going to be a victim; they wouldn't break me. I was stronger than they realized, and I wasn't going to let them see my fear. No matter what, I would fight. They couldn't make me weak, I wouldn't let them. They didn't deserve that power and I wasn't going to give it to them.

They'll see, I'll show them. Omegas can be lambs on the outside but when you look beneath the surface, we have a lion's heart. One that will never stop fighting for what's right and just, until the world sees us for who we truly are.

"Dani-girl, you need to wake up. You're dreaming. Everything's okay, you're safe here with me. Come on, my fierce little fighter, I've got you. It's time to wake up now."

Sorin's voice cut through the panic and fear. I clung to it like it was a lifeline knowing whatever was chasing me was getting closer. Something in my gut knew he would protect me, and as much as I wanted to fight right now, I couldn't. As I'd told Victor, I didn't survive this long by being stupid. Soon, soon enough, I would be ready to fight on my own. These men would help me get there, and I'll never have to be afraid again. I would be armed with the power to protect myself and those I care around me, never to be a victim again. Instead, I would be the rescuer.

"Please, Dani-girl, I need you to wake up," Sorin pleaded, desperation in his voice.

My eyes snapped open and I gasped for air. Now I realized in my panicked state I'd seized up and stopped breathing, causing Sorin's panic.

"Oh, thank fuck," Sorin exhaled in relief, dropping his head to my shoulder. "Don't you ever scare me like that again. Holy shit, I'm so glad I came to check on you when I did, or I don't know what would have happened."

The feel of his arms wrapped so tightly around me should have been too much after a dream like that. Instead, it made me feel completely and utterly safe at knowing nothing could touch me right now. It was an odd, unfamiliar feeling yet one I relished as I wrapped my arms around his neck. His lips brushed the skin of my neck, making me inhale sharply at the sensation. When I didn't pull away, he kissed his way up my neck to my jaw, where he pulled back to look me in the eye. There was a question in his gaze, and I don't know if it was the battle I had just waged in my own mind, but I didn't want to be afraid anymore. If I wasn't a victim and I was going to stand up for what I wanted, then it's time to stop acting in fear. Instead, I was going to make a choice based on the simple fact that I wanted this. I wanted to kiss Sorin, to feel how real this moment was all the way down to the tip of my toes.

"Yes," I croaked out, needing to say it out loud. To start claiming back things that had been forced from me, regardless of whether it was for survival or not.

Sorin regarded me for a second before his lips melded to mine. The jolt of pleasure and rightness that shot through me at this simple touch only confirmed my choice. This was exactly what I wanted. What I needed. No stranger to sex, kissing was a whole other matter. Lucian had stuck to my request, never kissing me, so I was a little at a loss for what to do. Sorin didn't seem to see this as a problem and took control as he kissed, sucked, and nipped at my lips. Needing to feel me closer, he pulled me onto his lap so I was straddling him. I gasped as he pressed me against his erection with a hand cupping my ass.

"Fuck," Sorin whispered against my lips. "You taste as good as you smell, Dani-girl."

I groaned at his words, and he used the opportunity to sweep his tongue into my mouth. At first, I was shocked and didn't quite know how to handle the intrusion, but Sorin just blazed ahead. He sucked on my tongue making me squirm in his lap, rubbing up against him. My body blazed with a heat I'd never felt before, it was like I craved him on a level I'd never craved anyone. His hand on my ass squeezed while the other slipped under my shirt and came up to palm my breast. I used to have much more in that area before coming to Asturg. In fact, I'd wished for the day I didn't have to fight to keep my shirts from gaping or needing to have them squashed down in a bra. Now they were half the size and barely an entire handful.

Sorin didn't seem to care about that one bit as his fingers found my nipple and twisted it between two fingers. "Is it normal for you not to wear a bra?" Sorin asked, his voice strained with his obvious need.

I cried out as he gave a slight tug making me grind into him more. "Beth forgot to give me underclothes when she hurried me to the showers."

The Alpha froze and pulled back to see my face more clearly. "Are you telling me you're not wearing underwear either right now?"

Pulling my lower lip between my teeth, I nodded and gave a little wiggle for shits and giggles. Sorin swore and muttered something about being the death of him under his breath. Then his hand moved from my ass to the back of my head, where he fisted my hair and held me as he feasted on my mouth. It was like kissing me was the only thing that would keep him alive, and I reveled in it. I was divided in the thought of how I'd gone so long without this feeling and glad that I'd waited for a moment that it was *my* choice to give this to a person I wanted to. The kiss was rough and hungry as his hand kept playing with my breasts driving my need higher and higher.

Breaking our kiss, Sorin rested his head on my shoulder breathing like he'd been running for miles. I let my hand caress the back of his neck and the smooth skin of his scalp, making him shudder. "Dani-girl, you keep touching me like that, and this will go farther than I think you're ready for."

"Why don't you let me be the judge of that," I countered, leaning in to nip at the tip of his ear.

With a growl, Sorin had me on my back with him looming over me, eyes burning with hunger. "You're playing with fire, Dani-girl."

"Haven't you figured out yet that I'm not very good at following the rules? My teachers used to say I had a problem with authority," I teased.

He reached up and caressed my face letting his hand drift down to my neck where he gripped it firmly, but I wasn't worried he would harm me. "We'll have to work on that, won't we? What if I told you that good little Omegas get rewards? Does that make you feel more inclined to listen?"

"Depends on what the reward is..." I challenged him.

He smirked and leaned in brushing our noses along each other in a sweet and surprisingly intimate caress. "I guess you're just going to have to be good and find out for yourself." He punctuated his words with a quick kiss before sitting up.

This had me instantly pouting that he wasn't going to do more. I wanted to strip him and explore every inch of his body as he did the same for me. Craving the feeling you could only get from skin-to-skin contact. My body was revved up and ready to go, slick weeping out of me until it soaked into my pants. I'm sure he could scent it, but the black was awfully handy at disguising the dampness.

"I came to check on you and let you know we were heading down to dinner," Sorin informed me. "Only when I tried to wake you it seemed to send you into a panic attack which is when you stopped breathing. Does that happen to you often?"

Well, that topic change was a major buzz kill.

Sighing, I brushed my hands over my face as I sat up against the headboard. "I do get nightmares, but I haven't had bad ones in a long time. I'm finding that sleeping alone is part of the problem. Lucian only had one bed in his home, so we shared it. Then when he was gone on missions, I would stay with the woman who ran the breeding house. We didn't share a bed, but she was in the same room with me. Now that I've been here alone in the Med Center it's gotten much worse."

Nodding more to himself, he stood and reached out a hand to me. "Then it's a good thing you're going to have a roommate again. Come on, you need to change your pants, put on some goddamn underwear, and we'll head down for dinner."

"That bit of information making it hard for you to not be... hard?" I goaded, letting him pull me to my feet.

He switched his grip on my wrist and pulled me right up against his body as his other hand slipped around the back of my neck. "Trust me when I tell you that if the others catch a whiff of your scent right now, it will throw the whole unit into rut. It's a damn miracle that I managed to keep my head with your begging pussy rubbing on me with the knowledge there was one layer of fabric keeping me from eating you for dinner instead."

The heat in those words and the grip on my neck had me shivering with anticipation. "If you're trying to calm me down, saying shit like that isn't helping."

"You're not the only one who can be trouble, Dani-girl. Now go clean yourself up," Sorin ordered a command covering his words, but the full force of his bark wasn't behind it. More like a warning that he would use it if I didn't behave.

Grabbing my duffle that I hadn't unpacked yet, I headed for the bathroom, shut the door, and locked it. Dropping my bag, I walked to the sink and turned it on, splashing water on my face to cool my body down. *Holy hell, what had gotten into me?* Drying off with a hand towel I'd found on the top of a fresh set that had been placed on the toilet for me, I assumed. Stripping off my pants, I paused when feeling the slick on my legs, echoing the ache of my pussy from being teased and left wanting. Glancing at myself in the mirror, I saw how swollen my lips were from Sorin's kisses and enjoyed the look it gave me. It added a flush to my cheeks and brightness to my eyes I hadn't seen in a long time.

Leaning back against the wall, I spread my legs a little wider and slipped my finger inside letting my palm rub against my clit. Biting back a groan, I tossed my head back and arched into the touch. *Fuck,* I was beyond horny right now, but helping myself out would take the edge off it— or so I hoped. My fingers moved easily with how wet I was, pumping in and out, hitting that one spot at the right angle causing my climax to roar up on me. I didn't have time for a long self-care session, but, holy fuck, I wasn't sure one orgasm would be enough. When it slammed into me, my legs almost gave out. They were shaking like a leaf struggling to hold onto the branch as I milked every second of the euphoric feeling. My whole body tingled as I panted to keep my whimpers silent as I kneaded my breast, trying to ease the desperate feeling for them to be plucked and sucked.

As the high started to fade, the door to the bathroom burst open and Sorin was charging for me. Grabbing my hips, he lifted me until my pussy was right at face level, legs over his shoulders, and back pinned to the bathroom wall. There were no words, no communication of any kind, before he buried his face in my pussy and speared me with his tongue. The shriek that burst from me was all he needed to hear as he adjusted his grip to cup my ass so he could get deeper. The feel of his teeth gently scraping over my clit had my eyes rolling back in my head. Desperate, my hands sought out something to hold onto as my body exploded into another orgasm. Finally, I found purchase on his sleeves, clinging to him as he lapped up the slick he'd encouraged to pour out of me.

It was clear he wasn't done as he continued to suck, lick, and nip at my pussy. He was determined to get everything he could out of me. A hand shifted under me as a finger gathered up some slick and started to massage it into my ass. That was an area that hadn't been broached, but the feel of his touch had me relaxing into it instead of voicing my concerns. With a harsh suck on my clit he pressed the tip of his finger in, just past the tight ring of my entrance.

The barrage of sensation had my body bucking, and a scream tore out of my throat. "Fuck *yes.*"

Sorin started to purr causing his whole body to vibrate, including his tongue, which he thrust inside me. As his tongue worked my pussy, his finger slowly made shallow thrusts opposite his efforts upfront. Just when I didn't think my body could handle any more, he worked in a second finger, pushing me right off the cliff he'd left me teetering on. The orgasm that imploded within me had me going rigid as I exploded not only internally but externally as well. To my horror, I thought I was peeing myself, however, Sorin didn't react other than to latch on gulping down whatever was happening down there.

Slowly he licked me clean as my body twitched and convulsed at the lightest touch. Never in my life had I felt as spent as I had right now. My whole body was a puddle of jello, unable to control any of my limbs if I wanted to. Sorin slowly lowered me until I could flop my arms around his neck and rest my head against his. The purring never stopped as he cradled me in his arms and held me for a moment before heading back out to the bedroom. Victor was leaning against the wall near the door to the bedroom, a grin plastered on his face. I was too high off my orgasms to care that he'd undoubtedly heard what just happened and the fact I didn't have any pants on.

Sorin set me down on his bed, kissed my forehead, and headed back to the bathroom. He returned with my bag and two towels. In an act sweeter than any I'd experienced before, he took a wet towel and cleaned me up, then dried me off and slipped on my underwear. Lifting my hips to help him once I realized what he was doing got me a soft kiss on my stomach before he did the same with my pants. Tears welled up in my eyes. No matter how hard I tried to prevent those damn things from escaping, I could feel them rolling down my cheeks. Throwing an arm over my face, I attempted to hide them, although I should have known better.

A hand gently tugged my arm away, but instead of it being Sorin, Victor's face appeared before me. "Little Spark, you tell me right now. Did Sorin force you into doing something you didn't want to?" The anger coating his words made me sit up, realizing what he must be assuming.

"No," I blurted, my voice raw and rough. "It wasn't like that at all."

Brushing a hand along my cheek, he caught a tear that slipped out. "Then you shouldn't be crying. It's okay to tell me the truth, Danella. It doesn't matter who they are, what rank they have, or what role their fathers have in our world. No one," Victor bit out, grabbing my jaw and forcing me to look him in the eyes. "I mean, not one goddamn human, is allowed to take advantage of you after I've given you my protection."

This just had the tears coming faster as I reached out my arms to him. Surprised, he hesitated a moment before I clung to him and sobbed into his neck. His arms wrapped around me like a vice as he picked me up and carried me somewhere where he chose to sit and hold me as tightly as he could without cutting off my ability to breathe. The purr that started deep in his chest was rough, like an engine sitting idle for too long. It had a few false starts, but once it got warmed up, it was so strong I could feel it in my bones.

How? How had I managed to survive for so long without this?

The respect, care, and comfort both of these Alphas had instinctively given to me when I needed it most was overwhelming, to say the least. It was like someone turned on the lights in a room and I could finally see everything I'd been missing. Things I didn't even know I needed were showered upon me, making the life I'd lived up until now seem ten times more wretched and heartbreaking. No wonder the Omegas never fought against it; they didn't have any concept of what they were missing. If that discovery ever got out, there's no way Omegas would allow themselves to be treated that way anymore.

"Little Spark, talk to me," Victor pleaded after a bit. "I need to know what's wrong so I can fix it or kill it."

That got a tearful laugh out of me as I pushed back to look him in the face. "That's just the thing, there's nothing wrong."

He frowned at me, clearly confused by my words and previous reaction.

"This is going to be the stupidest thing that's ever come out of my mouth, but I'm crying because things are good. Well… better than good, I suppose." Pulling down my sleeve, I used it to wipe my eyes and snot from my face.

Then a tissue appeared, and I looked up to find Sorin hovering with a box of tissues in one hand and a worried expression on his face. Victor snapped his head to the side and growled at his leader. Sorin shot him an angry look but took a step back, nonetheless. That's when it hit me. Victor thought I was crying because of what just happened between Sorin and me. My mind had been so overwhelmed with emotion I hadn't connected the dots.

Grabbing Victor's face, I forced him to look away from Sorin and meet my gaze. "Stop, Sorin did nothing wrong. Everything you heard happening in the bathroom was one hundred percent consensual. Hell, that was one of the most amazing moments of foreplay that I've ever had."

"Then why are you crying?" Victor demanded.

I gave him a watery smile and rested my forehead against his, unable to admit this while holding his intense gaze. "Because he gave a shit, Vicky. He gave me two mind-blowing orgasms, asked for nothing in return, then the crazy bastard cleaned me up and dressed me like I meant something to him. That, that level of respect and care the like of which I haven't received since my own fucking mother gave it to me, is what made me cry. Then you had to go and get all protective, telling me you'd kill anyone who dared to take liberties, even if it was Sorin, a man you consider family."

Victor cupped my head in his hands and pulled me back. "If they were the type to force themselves on a woman, they wouldn't be my family any longer. No woman deserves to fear the people who are supposed to keep them safe. That's the reason I killed those two men that bitch was talking about. We stayed the night at a small town on our way to a mission, and two of our team had trouble understanding the word 'no'. It was the middle of the night, and a young woman barely over seventeen came stumbling into the bar for help. When I tried to offer my assistance, she screamed and started to ramble that I was just like them, that I was going to rape her too.

Once, one of the other women in the bar got her to calm down enough to figure out what had happened. That's when I learned those two men had taken her to the woods and had their way with her. So I hunted them down, dragged them to the woods, and made sure no one else would ever live with the fear that soldiers wouldn't keep them safe. It is an honor to fight for our country and keep our people safe. To commit such a vile act deserves an equal or greater punishment, don't you think?" Victor asked.

Pulling out of his hold, I pressed my lips to his, enjoying the feeling of his beard tickling my skin. He gave a small moan but didn't try to hold me to him, when I sat back. "If I were in your shoes, I would have done the same thing. People need to know there are consequences for their actions so others can learn from them. Don't ever doubt that you did the right thing. They wouldn't have stopped otherwise."

Lifting my head, I looked over to Sorin, who still seemed a bit worried. "Thank you, Sorin, thank you for proving that actions indeed speak louder than words."

My stomach took that moment to interrupt the conversation,

making me laugh, and Victor pushed to his feet to set me down. "Come on, Little Spark, let's get some food in you. Training starts tomorrow, and I wouldn't count on any of us taking it easy on you just because you're a woman or an Omega."

"Good, just the way I wanted it," I agreed, giving them both a bright smile. "Bring it on."

CHAPTER 28

Lucian

Two weeks.

Two weeks in hell.

Fourteen days since the outpost was attacked, the majority of my men were slaughtered, and Danella was taken by the South. I finally found her after a week of searching the Southern lands and have been watching her for another week even though it felt like years instead of days. It was incredibly risky to be this close to their main base of operations, but I couldn't force myself to be any farther from her.

When I arrived back at the outpost the following morning after the attack and saw the ruins left smoldering in the morning light, a panic unlike anything I'd known before took hold of me. Without a second thought, I tore through what used to be my home for the past few years and headed right for the breeder house. That building was the only one left standing, untouched by the enemy. Crashing through the door, I searched the place from top to bottom, but it was empty. There were two guards, one on the stairs leading to the room the Omegas slept in and the other in the main space. It was clear they tried but were overwhelmed and never stood a chance.

The door to Babaka's room was shut and I had to kick it down. The woman had blockaded the door the best she could, but she didn't have the strength she once had. I found her barely alive, sitting on the floor with a shotgun in her hands and bleeding from two bullet wounds in her chest. Blood leaked out of her mouth as she tried to speak when she caught sight of me. Dropping to my knees, I shifted the woman so her head was resting in my lap. The old battle axe didn't have long to live but I wasn't going to leave her alone. She'd always been on my side, watching my back when it came to my father's demands.

"I've got you, Babaka," I soothed, as she coughed and groaned as more blood leaked out of her mouth.

She tried to lift a hand, so I reached out and took it, leaning closer to hear what she was trying to tell me. "Your girl...she...she escaped."

Hope flooded through me at this. "Dani got out?"

"Friends...too," she whispered before another coughing fit took over. She tried to gasp for air, but all I could hear was her coking on the blood filling her lungs.

I squeezed her hand and smoothed a hand down her arm. "Okay, that's enough talking. I'm going to ask you some yes or no questions. Grip my hand once if yes, twice for no, got it?"

She squeezed once.

"Did they take the other Omegas?"

One squeeze.

"Okay, so if she ends up getting found, chances are they won't kill her. Was it the South?"

Yes.

"Damn them," I seethed. "If I had gotten back sooner, we would have had a fighting chance."

No.

I frowned at the woman. "What do you mean no? I had all the best people with me. If they'd been here, it wouldn't have been a slaughter."

"You..." she gasped. "They wanted you."

"Me? They did all this because they knew this was the base I controlled?" I pressed.

None of this made sense. Why the hell would they come after

me personally? Could they know I was the one who led the attack on the power station?

"Traitor..."

"Meaning they had help in breaching security."

This would make sense how they knew but didn't explain why they attacked when I wasn't here. If they were after me and someone inside knew about it, they wouldn't have picked a time when I was gone.

"Sorin," Babaka gasped, gripping my hand fiercely as she struggled to breathe. "General...he...knows..."

"Babaka, please, you're only making things worse trying to talk," I tried to reason with her, but the expression on her face told me it was pointless.

"No, the first...first time...common enemy... they fight," she pushed out. "Kill a few...save the many." Coughing wracked her body as she groaned in pain, although she wasn't finished. "He... did this... again. You have. Stop him. Be better. Save us..."

With those final words, she took her last breath and her body fell limp in my arms. People might have seen the cold exterior of Babaka, the female Alpha who ran the breeding house. I'd on the other hand had the honor to know her differently and knew she did her best to protect the women she housed. Especially when it came to Dani and all the trouble she caused. While people might fear and respect me, they lived in terror of Babaka coming after them. Thanks to her, I'd always felt better about leaving Dani for so long. Even now, with her dying breath, she was trying to do her best for her people.

I didn't know what all she meant, but I knew it was important. My first mission was to get Dani back, and then I could figure out what she'd meant about my father and a traitor in our ranks. Cradling the old woman's body in my arms, I carried her out and placed her among the others we would have a ceremonial fire for. The ground was too hard, and there were too many for us to bury them all. We would show them honor this way and not let wild beasts feed on them; it was the least we could do.

"*Commander*," someone yelled.

Turning away from the bodies of our fallen, I spotted two of my men dragging someone between them. Striding over, I recognized the all-black uniform and patches that were on his shoulder—Southerner. It looked as if he'd been shot in the leg and shoulder but otherwise in decent shape. They dropped him at my feet, letting him fall face-first into the dirt. The Southern soldier didn't even try to stop the fall, making me second-guess my assessment. I kicked him over by using my boot so he was on his back and saw the foam bubbling out of his mouth.

"The fucker's poisoned himself," I growled, kneeling beside the man and grabbing his jaw to shove a finger in his mouth. Sure enough, there was the shell of a pill he'd bitten through. He wasn't dead yet, and I planned to get some answers.

"Where are they taking the prisoner?" I demanded, slapping him sharply. "What was your purpose in attacking this outpost? How did you know we were here?"

The man just let out a spluttering laugh. "Fuck you, Northern scum. You'll never get anything out of me before I die."

Rage flooded me, and I slammed my fist into his face, but he wouldn't stop laughing. Standing, I pulled my gun from its holster and shot the man right between the eyes just to make him stop laughing. He was right. There was no way to force him to tell me what he knew, not when death was already imminent.

"Search his body. Make sure he doesn't have anything left on him we can use," I ordered before walking away.

I didn't know where I would go, since everything but the breeding house was just husks of what used to be a town. The acrid scent of smoke burned in my nose as I took in the wreckage. This is the truth of war, nowhere was safe, and everything could be taken from you. When we'd gotten word of the attack, it had been too late to do anything. If we'd had better technology that we could count on to transmit properly, things might have been different. I know Babaka said it wouldn't have mattered, only I couldn't live with that answer. It was my duty as their commander and heir to the Northern Territory to do all that was in my power to protect my people.

"Commander Lucian, I have a message from the General for you," a soldier called out.

Pausing, I turned on my heel. "The General already knows?" I questioned.

That shouldn't be possible. If the attack happened as suddenly as it appeared, there's no way they could send out a message to me, or the general. Our telecommunications equipment was spotty at best along with the power to run the damn thing. We'd gotten the news just before dawn well after everything was said and done.

"That's what his message said," the soldier informed me with a shrug. "I managed to get our portable system hooked up to the town's power. Now that there isn't much being drawn from it, the connection seems to be more stable. Meaning we can send and receive more quickly than before."

I held my hand out for the message, but he just simply shook his head. "Sorry, Commander, but there's no paper to write on. You'll have to read it off the screen."

"Of course," I muttered. "Lead the way."

Set up behind what used to be the supply depot was a tent that had been erected and turned into our communications command. This was typical for us when we made camp before a battle, so I wasn't surprised that my soldiers had taken the initiative. Both soldiers left the tent, allowing me to read the communication privately and respond.

Attention Commander Lucian—
News has reached me about the Southern military's vicious attack on the Qita. I'm recalling all personnel who remain, to be reassigned where they can be most useful. I'm ordering you back to the Capital so I can be debriefed on how you could let this happen. We cannot let this attack on our land and people stand. The South is becoming far too bold if they dare to destroy an outpost run by my own son. It calls into question the priorities

highest on the list, one being if you are the right man to take over once I'm gone. Furthermore, you've been unable to produce an heir of your own, which has always been a requirement.

Our people cannot win this war if their leaders are not ruthless in their mission to destroy the South and all they stand for. That being said, I expect you to stand before me and explain your actions in three days' time.

General Rasvan.

I read the letter three times before I deleted it and stood. If he wanted the soldiers to be sent back to the Capital, fine, but I wasn't going with them. Over the many years of observing my father and learning to survive him, I knew what that letter was. It was my death sentence. One I planned to ignore fully in favor of going to find my Omega. She was all that mattered now. Once I rescued her from the South, I would then decide what to do about my father. It was clear that he was no longer fit to rule our people because the only way he could have known about what happened here was if he knew it had been coming.

Had this been what Babaka was talking about? Using the attack here to remove me and rally our people who were losing hope each passing day about ever seeing victory? If that's the case, I needed to know how he managed to communicate with the Southern military to make these horrific blitz attacks happen. My time of laying low and waiting for the bastard to die was over. There had to be a better way, a way that didn't involve my country dying at the hand of a crazed power-hungry man.

What I needed was *her*.

The fiery Omega that had stolen my heart that first night we met and tightened her grip on it each passing day. Being with her was such a bittersweet feeling, but I couldn't stay away even though I knew it would be better for us both if I did. My sweet, stubborn, combative Dani had no idea how I felt or how she'd slowly changed me in ways I never knew possible. Her view of the world was so different from anything I could even fathom. If I had her with me, I know we could find a way to save the North before it's too late. The actual question was— would she help me?

Had I destroyed any hope of convincing her that I was in love with her? That she was my true north, leading me in the direction I needed to go even if I refused to see it. Did she have any clue how hard it was each and every time I had to leave her? That I made sure men I trusted to look after her were left at the outpost. God, how do I even begin to beg her forgiveness and ask for a second chance to be together? Not because we needed to survive, or that she was an Omega and I was an Alpha, but because I fucking loved her. There were moments over the years when I'd seen a look in her eyes that told me she had feelings for me, and that was a hope that I clung to like it was the rope that would save my life.

I knew I didn't deserve her or her love, and if I wanted Dani to even give me a second glance, I would need to prove I was sincere. Along with groveling... lots of groveling. Everything about the start of our connection was fucked up and twisted, making it nearly impossible to see her even considering giving me a second chance. Despite all of that, I had to try. It was time for me to stand up and fight after allowing myself to be controlled for so long. What better thing to fight for than a woman who deserved everything good in this world; I wanted to give her that.

This is how I landed myself skulking in the forest, watching Dani through a pair of binoculars for the past week. Every time I saw her, she was with two or more men at all times as she moved about the base. It didn't seem like they were keeping her captive, but noticeably, she wasn't free to go places without an escort. What I found odd and didn't make any sense whatsoever was the fact they were training her. I'd seen them out in the practice yard working on her hand-to-hand skills that I'd started teaching her. They'd also spent a fair amount of time in the shooting range, but the way it was set up, I couldn't see more than her entering and leaving. Nothing about this was making sense.

As the week progressed, she smiled more. Her cheeks were

filling out now that she was getting regular meals. I hadn't seen her look this way before. The carefree way she walked, no longer watching for threats that could pop out at any second. She even laughed so hard she doubled over, clinging to her stomach with her face flushed with life. What I couldn't stand to watch was how all these men with her observed her with the same expression I had when she wasn't looking. The simple touches they gave her that I never could, and the chaste kiss she placed on one of their cheeks nearly had me going mad with envy.

Danella was *mine*. She bore my mark on her proving my claim. Those Southern bastards had no right to touch something that didn't belong to them. This needed to end. I wasn't going to be able to get to her on base, so I needed to get them outside those protective walls.

Dropping from the tree I'd been watching from, I headed over to the cave I'd been living in. It was also where I kept my new friend who'd been more than willing to share lots of information about these men. Seems he had a grudge of his own towards the men who were keeping my Omega from me.

"Draza, wake up," I snapped, throwing water in the Beta's face. "I need your help."

He spluttered awake and glared at me, shaking the water off since his hands were tied behind his back. "What the hell, man, haven't I done enough for you to untie me?"

I raised a brow at him. "If our roles were reversed, would you untie me?"

"No, I suppose not," he admitted.

"You're right, there's no way for me to get on base and do what needs to be done. So I need you to tell me what kind of emergency would force your military to pull them from what they're doing in order to deal with the problem?" I questioned, squatting before the man.

"Sorin's team is the best of the best, which means they go after the worst of the worst. You need something no other team could be trusted to do," Draza explained. "I'm assuming you know about our power plants?"

I nodded and motioned for him to continue.

"There is one they just finished building farther south. It's bigger than any they've built before and is supposed to be able to power the entire capital city. This would allow the other power plants to be used for other purposes since they won't be bogged down with keeping the Capital running. From what I hear, computers run the new system they used so it doesn't need to be manned by a whole crew. They believe it will be safer there since it's farther south, nowhere near the battle line. If you can figure out a way to disable the system, they will absolutely send Sorin's team to deal with the problem. One of his guys, Toma, helped create the computer program that runs it," Draza informed me.

"How far is it from here?"

"On foot, three days. If you get your hands on a vehicle, cut that travel time in half. I might even be able to do that for you, get you a vehicle, I mean," he offered. "Look, I've only been missing for three days? I could easily make up a story they'll believe, and I pull shit like this all the time."

I didn't trust this man for shit, but if he was going to be helpful, then who was I to look a gift horse in the mouth. His hate for Sorin's team was strong enough that I trusted he would do whatever it took to get his revenge. Which is what he thought I wanted after I told him I was a soldier from the outpost they destroyed. What he didn't realize is that I also held him personally responsible for what happened since he'd shared with me that he'd been there.

"Alright," I said, leaning forward and cutting the bindings on his hands. "You have yourself a deal."

CHAPTER 29

Danella

I had no idea how utterly out of shape I was. The first two days of training were hell on my body, although I'd never felt better. Muscles I didn't even know I had cried for mercy at the end of the day. I could barely stay awake for dinner, and I knew all of them were taking it easy on me even if they didn't draw attention to it. Thankfully with how tired I was, there were no issues with nightmares. It might also be because I knew Sorin was just on the other side of the room, but I wasn't going to focus on that.

Sorin didn't mention that he'd given me some of the best orgasms of my life that day, nor did Victor mention I sobbed all over his shoulder to the others. It seems that while they told each other everything, some things they didn't volunteer. Which I was perfectly alright with. That day had been full of turbulent emotions and one of the worst nightmares I'd had. So I was going to call it a fluke of a fucking day and move forward. The only thing that changed was the fact I was trying to be more open to getting to know the guys better. None of them were pushy unless it came to training, then I wanted to punch them all in the face.

The morning started at the crack of dawn, with breakfast, conditioning in the gym, and hand-to-hand combat training with Sorin and Victor. After that, I got an hour's break to work with Cris as he assessed what I knew from working with the doc back at the outpost. I quickly realized just how archaic the tools and supplies we'd had to use were compared to what was standard for the South. It was fun to learn again, and Cris was an excellent teacher finding ways to tweak what I knew to be more effective. When my time with Cris was over, I went with Petru to the shooting range and learned the name of every gun, ammo, and tool we carried with us on missions. It was three days before I even started the process of learning how to shoot.

"Dani, you need to know the basic knowledge so I know you won't hurt yourself in the midst of panic," Petru informed me. "These things need to be second nature, and if we don't start with a proper foundation, then everything we build off of it will crumble."

"Who knew there could be so much to a simple weapon," I grumbled.

Petru caught my chin, forcing me to meet his gaze. "No weapon is simple, not when it has the ability to take a life. Yes, we are at war; if we don't kill them, we will end up dead ourselves. You must maintain a certain respect for the choice you make the second that gun is in your hands. With the ease of pulling one bit of metal, you can end the life of another. Self-defense or not, those deaths will be a weight on your shoulders. How much a person can handle varies, so not adding unnecessarily is always a wise choice."

"How heavy is your burden?" I asked before realizing just how cruel that question was. "I'm sorry, that was thoughtless of me to ask," I hurried, resting my hand on his wrist as he continued his hold on me.

Instead of irritation or anger at my words, his eyes grew soft, almost sad. "The weight I bear changes. Some days I feel like it's crushing me, reminding me of all the lives I've taken. Then we have a mission where we get to save some lives or protect innocents who would have been crushed without thought. Those days it's like there's no weight at all and I'm reminded why I chose to do this job. Each day I see you smile or hear you laugh, it keeps me from being overwhelmed. But if I'm to teach you the skills to kill, knowing the price you'll pay with that knowledge, I'm not letting you do so blindly."

Leaning forward, I pressed a quick kiss to his lips. "Thank you for teaching me how to protect myself from all forms of enemies."

"It is my honor, Wildflower. Now let's get back to the training," Petru instructed.

When my time with Petru ended, it was time for lunch. Victor always had me sit and wait at the table as he got both our meals. He was forever filling my plate with everything available and telling me to eat what I wanted then he'd clean up. At first, I thought it was because he couldn't go back for seconds and knew I'd only eat a quarter, maybe half, of the food. That reasoning fell through when I observed others going back for more.

"You know I can handle getting my own food. I know what most of it is now and how the whole routine works," I argued one day.

Victor just glared at me. "No, you will wait here."

"Vicky," I snapped, shooting to my feet. "This is silly. There is no reason I can't go with you and get my own meal for fucks sake."

The hulking Alpha set both hands on the table and leaned down so our faces were mere inches apart. "I said no, Little Spark. Soldiers are assholes when it comes to chow time, and if one of them so much as bumps into you, I'm going to rip their arm off."

That answer had me blinking at him in surprise. "Oh…"

"Yeah, oh, now sit the fuck down and be good so I don't have to create more work for the janitors and get locked up in jail before we've had a chance to eat." With that declaration, I sat and he marched off to get in line.

This time as I watched, no one dared to get near him. He had a good bubble of about two-feet at all times. It made me smile to think he did all that so no one would mess with me. It was adorable in a sick kind of way since I was not bothered by the fact that when he said he'd rip off a limb, I believed him.

Making it safely through lunch with no incidents, I left with Toma. He was teaching me about all the computer equipment they had. There were the standard radios for short-distance communications, but each team had a laptop connected to satellites, allowing us to use it anywhere we went. There were various programs to be used for contacting bases, towns, and even some of the generator plants they had scattered all over the South. We also worked on navigation with only a compass and the stars. Then we upgraded to using a map which sped things along since I knew how to read one.

As Toma and I worked together, he also had maps of the North, and I was marking down everything I knew or heard of. I amazed myself at what I picked up over the three years and with my information, Toma had even sent out drones to check out a few places. They had to be located near the border since communication with the drones could only go so far. There had been missions to set up more relay antennas at one point. However, the North caught on to what they were and destroyed them. This explained to me, at least, why they had such sparse knowledge of what life there was really like.

"Have you guys ever thought about sending someone undercover to find out stuff like this? Soldiers get transferred all over the place at random times for no reason. It seems like it would be easy for you to pull off," I asked as I worked on translating our pretend location into the formula the computer system needed.

"I'm not sure," Toma said, pausing whatever he was typing to give me his full attention.

That was something I noticed he did a lot when I initiated a conversation. It's almost as if he never wanted me to think he didn't have time for the multitude of questions I asked. As he taught me about the South and how they lived life, I couldn't help but compare and contrast the two halves of the same whole. Thinking of this having been all one nation just seemed mind-blowing to me. Goes to show that leadership can make or break whatever they are put in charge of.

"While on the surface that sounds logical. Yet I'm sure you've noticed how Northern people blindly follow whatever they're told. No one questions anything, ever, from what you tell me. Just picture a Southern person put in that equation. They'd blow it within the first day," Toma reasoned. "I suppose if a person was rescued, flipped, and sent back to gather intel, that might work. Then again, if there's no way for them to travel from place to place freely and get information back to us, is it any help? If we can't count on getting what we need when we need it, the purpose of the whole plan gets called into question."

The man had a point. It would be almost impossible to have an average soldier gathering intel. The only people who could come and go would be higher-ranking officers, and which of them would ever turn on their country? Falling back into a comfortable silence with only the sound of computer keys filling the air, I peeked over the screen to observe Toma. When he was here in the computer lab working on some project for the military, he changed. His passion for this was clear and showed in how people regarded his feedback. It was unusual for us to be alone here. Usually at least three or four others were working on various projects, but Toma mentioned they were testing something so they'd be gone for the day.

"Did you want to be in the military?" I blurted. "It's just that you seem to love this part of what you do and I feel like that's something they'd let you do outside the base. Like the person they brought in for this project that they're testing. She isn't part of the military."

"That's true, I could probably work anywhere I wanted to at this point with the skill level I have with computer coding. The thing with that is I wouldn't be this good without the military. When I showed promise for it in training, they sent me to extra classes and built on that skill. If I had chosen to live a civilian life, I would have gotten my standard education until I was seventeen, then gone through the testing process. I might have shown the same skill but sucking me into loving this was the strategy behind it. Here they give you a problem and a limited amount of supplies, and you have to make do. It's the pressure of knowing you could be the only thing that stands in the way of your team dying or getting your location to the support team who would then send for reinforcements. It's hard to explain, but the rush that gives you is unlike anything you'd find in a civilian job," Toma shared, then smiled and shook his head.

"That and Petru was enlisting. No way was he going to leave me behind, plus it was the only way he could support his family. When you enlist, they look after your family. So they found a place for his brother and cousins to live and be looked after while serving his country. Those kids wanted for nothing until they could support themselves, and I respect the hell out of that. It's things like that which made it impossible for me not to fall in love with him. He is everything good and pure in the world. There was no way I wouldn't be right by his side, watching his back and keeping him selfishly alive," he admitted with a laugh. "God, I don't think I've ever admitted that to anyone before. I joined the military because the man I love was putting himself in danger, and I wasn't going to let him do that alone. Talk about a melodrama."

Grinning, I laughed along with him because he was right, it sounded like something out of a book. "I don't think I've ever seen three people love and care for each other the way you guys do. To be honest, I thought a love like that was lost to the world. So much of the time it's about strategy, what you can get out of someone, rather than what you can create with them."

"I doubted for a long time myself if we could make this happen with the world we live in, but the three of us decided that we would fight for our happiness. Once we made that choice, it gave us all the reassurance we needed to keep forging forward," Toma said, a distant look on his face like he was remembering that moment.

The peace of our day was shattered when an alarm went off in the room and the warning lights flashed. Having no clue what was going on, I stayed where I was as Toma raced over to one of the computer terminals. He'd told me earlier that week that this room was used to monitor all the power stations so they could be alerted if there was any trouble after one got blown up. I did not share that I knew all about that situation since Lucian and his men were the ones who blew it up.

"Fuck," Toma swore and grabbed a radio. "Base command, this is Staff Sergeant Dalca, I have an SOS coming from power plant number eight."

"Understood. Head back to your barracks, we'll be rolling your unit out immediately," the man on the other side of the radio ordered.

"Command, please be aware that whoever's messing with the plant has disabled all remote access. I'll have to hardwire into it manually to make sure the pressure doesn't build and blow the whole place up," Toma said, running his hand through his hair looking genuinely worried. He caught my eye and signaled for me to pack everything up.

Quick as I could, I stuffed everything we brought back into the pack, strapping things tight to keep them safe as we traveled. I tuned out whatever Toma was saying to command as I focused on my task. Searching the space, I ensured I didn't forget anything as I slipped the pack over my shoulders and headed for the door.

"Dani." Spinning on my heels, I faced Toma.

"Head for the barracks. The others will be there already. I need to grab a few things to fix this problem, so I'll meet you there. Don't stop for anything," Toma ordered.

"Got it," I called as I pulled the door open and bolted into the hall.

Doing just as he asked, I ran the whole way back to the dorms. Skidding to a halt, I unlocked the front door then took the stairs two at a time, making it to the top floor without falling on my face. Taking a second to catch my breath quickly, I dashed down the hall and found our door ajar. I hesitated a moment before it was yanked open and Victor almost bowled me over.

"Fuck, Little Spark, I nearly trampled you. What are you doing lurking in the hall?" he demanded.

"The door was open and I didn't know who was inside. You all tell me time and time again not to rush into things, so I was waiting to hear who was in our place," I answered, hands on my hips, not appreciating his snark.

Grabbing the strap to my pack, he pulled me forward and planted a fierce kiss on my lips. "Look at my Little Spark already using her training. Good thing too, because it seems a week is all you're going to get." In a move I didn't understand or comprehend, he pulled the pack off my back and shoved me into the apartment.

"Go put the rest of the things in your go-bag we set up the other day. We're leaving in fifteen, so let's see how fast that cute ass of yours can move."

I spared a second to flip him off as I headed for my room. "Don't be a jackass, Vicky."

The bastard just grinned at me, far too pleased with my reaction. In the bedroom, I found Sorin packing the last of his things while my pack was on the foot of my bed, zipped and ready to go.

"Dani-girl, you're gonna need to put on the full uniform for this," Sorin instructed.

There was a small closet in the bathroom that held the two uniform jackets that I'd been given, along with Sorin's. It was made out of a thick material, had a long sleeve, and was velcroed down the front rather than buttons. There were places for someone to put patches on their shoulders, but I didn't have any so mine was blank. When training, I hadn't needed to be in full uniform, but it made sense since we were going on a mission. Taking my hair out of the low pony, I pulled it up higher and wrapped it into a tight bun so it would be covered when I put the cap on. They'd stressed time and time again that if I was on a mission, I kept my gender as neutral as possible. The enemy might let women fight, but they always saw us as weaker so they were trained to target them first. This was a fact I was well aware of, yet I understood their desire to keep me safe and I appreciated it.

Tugging on the simple black cloth cap with a brim that shadowed my face, I grabbed my go-bag and headed out to the common room. Sorin caught my arm and turned me to face him, tucking a finger under my chin, urging me to look him in the eye.

"Danella, I need you to understand the second we leave this room that I am not only your commanding officer but the leader of this unit. I wish we had more time to prepare you, a week is hardly any time, but you're smart and pick up on things faster than most. Be alert, remember what we've taught you, and most importantly, obey my orders. I know this is going to be the hardest part for you, regardless of how much training you have. You don't like blind trust, and while I understand that and in any other situation would respect it, I can't," Sorin stated as he searched my face waiting for my reaction.

"I will do my best," I offered.

"No," Sorin bit out. "That's not good enough."

"What do you want me to say? I'm not going to lie to you," I countered.

"Danella, do you believe I want to keep you safe? That I would do everything in my power to make sure you come back from whatever this might be so you can see your friends off?" Sorin asked.

When he put it like that, I did believe he would do those things. "Yes."

"Then I'm begging you to allow me to make that possible. If I can't trust you will do as I say, then I won't be doing everything within my power to keep you safe. I've been leading this group of men for ten years and have been in the military for eighteen. The knowledge I have is through experience and instinct, things I can't explain in the moment where I have two seconds to make a call that will impact us all. I've seen my unit through hell and come out the other side. Please, Dani-girl, don't let me fail you or them," Sorin pleaded.

"Okay, I'll trust you. For this mission, you have my promise to trust what orders you give me. But know that if I find you've used me or betrayed me with those orders, I will never listen to you again," I warned.

Sorin reached up and pulled the cap off my head before sweeping in to steal my breath away with a kiss. Dropping my bag, I reached for him, fisting his jacket in my hand as I opened for him. The kiss was full of so much emotion I couldn't tell which one of us needed the assurance of it more. A faint whimper spilled from my lips when he pulled away.

"Thank you, Dani-girl," Sorin whispered against my lips. "I will keep you safe and will never betray you. That's a promise I plan to keep forever, no matter where you end up in life. I'll always find you when you need me."

With one more toe-curling kiss, he stepped back and placed the cap back on my head. Taking a deep breath, I saw the kind, patient

Alpha I'd grown to know shift into the commanding leader of one of the best elite units of the Southern Military. Snatching his bag, he gave me a nod and headed into the common room. Rushing, I grabbed mine and was hot on his heels to find the other four ready and waiting for us.

"Let's move," Sorin ordered.

CHAPTER 30

Danella

When the Southern Military moves into action, they don't skimp on anything. Where the Northern Army was lucky to have vehicles that still worked and hadn't broken down, I was sitting pretty in a military Humvee. The space was cramped for all of us to fit in, because all the men in my unit were muscled giants, but we made do. Since I was obviously the smallest, I was put in the jump seat. When I say *seat,* that might give too much credit for the padded four-by-four square my ass sat on that pulled down from the wall. The seatbelt I latched on was a shoulder harness so I felt like I was going to be ejected from the car or go into space.

While maintained and in perfect condition, the Humvee left a lot to be desired in its smoothness. After a few hours, I'd become grateful for the harness. It kept me from being tossed around the vehicle like a rag doll. We'd started out on paved roads that were used often, then that changed to dirt roads that had clearly been created in a hurry. The number of rocks, potholes, and roots that littered the way told me that no one came this way unless they needed to.

What I found interesting is that no one spoke. The second Sorin gave his order to move out, it's like a switch had been flipped and everyone turned into men I'd never met. Their expressions were determined and, in a way, blank, like they were resigning themselves to whatever might be happening. Since I was in the room when Toma said what was going on, I had an inkling of what we might be heading into but did the others know? I'm positive the base command told Sorin the situation yet since I arrived at the apartment, no one has mentioned the power plant. Could it be that they're worried about talking in front of me? That if I leave after three weeks, they don't want me knowing things? None of it made sense to me but I kept my mouth shut until I could figure out what the fuck happened to the team of men I was getting to know.

It had been late afternoon when we left the base, and now we'd been driving in the dark for some time. The area we were traveling through was hilly and full of prairie lands so there weren't many trees to worry about running into. Even with the headlights, it was becoming difficult to see the dirt track Victor considered a road to follow. Sorin, acting as co-pilot, was tracking our progress on a map with the route marked in red. From my vantage point in the back I couldn't see much of the map so it was hard to tell where our intended destination was. When it got to the point I was so tired I was nodding off, I knew we'd been driving for a long time.

"Vic, pull off here to the left," Sorin instructed. "There's lodging for the construction crew that we can rest at."

Rubbing the sleep from my eyes, I saw the simple building Sorin had been referring to. There was a gravel area for parking and nothing else. Once we parked, the guys poured out of the vehicle with practiced ease. It took me a second to figure out how to get out of the harness though I managed. Free and out of the Humvee, I grabbed my bag from the rack on the back we'd strapped them down on.

An arm wrapped around my shoulders and I flinched until I caught that tell-tale scent of patchouli. "Hang in there a little longer, and you can get some sleep," Cris encouraged. "This place marks that we're only a few hours away from our destination. When they built this power plant, they had teams working round the clock so the off team would sleep and eat here then rotate when it was their time."

Lights flicked on in the building and it was as bare bones as you could make it. Rows of bunk beds took up half of the space, and then there was a kitchen along with tables and chairs. The beds didn't have any mattresses, just metal frames and springs. The kitchen wasn't so much a kitchen anymore since all the appliances were missing. It's like they just left what they didn't want or couldn't use and abandoned the place.

"Why build it so far from the plant? Wouldn't it make sense to keep them closer?" I asked, stifling a yawn.

"It was set up this way so if there was an accident or the plant blew up, it wouldn't kill everyone," Toma answered. "The energy plant we're going to is the first of its kind, and the power generated is more than anything we've ever accomplished. Honestly, the whole project was experimental so the powers-that-be decided to prepare for the worst. At least it gives us a place to get a few hours of sleep before hitting the road again."

I didn't even want to ask how much sleep we'd actually be getting since I knew this was a time-sensitive matter. What I cared about though, is whoever was going to drive got as much sleep as possible. Wouldn't want us driving off a cliff or something before we even got to our destination.

"I want a watch set up, changing every hour. Petru, you take the first watch, then myself, Cris, Toma, and Victor goes last," Sorin instructed. "Danella, you'll be sleeping next to Victor."

The guys grunted their acknowledgement, pulled their sleeping bags out of their packs, and arranged them on the floor. Victor grabbed my bag and set my sleeping bag behind his, so he'd be blocking me if anything happened. I wanted to argue but bit my tongue, knowing I promised I would listen. Petru grabbed a chair and placed it near the front door by one of the windows. Looking around the space, I realized that there were only windows placed at the front of the building to let in light. I guess it made sense since this wasn't supposed to be anything special, just a place to sleep and eat.

Making my way over to my spot, I noticed that Toma had done the same thing for Cris, putting himself in front. It made me smile to see such a simple act showing how much he cared. Looking at it from that perspective, I scolded myself for thinking the worst when Victor was doing the same thing for me. Sliding into my bed for the night, I was surprised at how warm it was for being so thin. I'm sure they made it to be light and not take up space for soldiers. As warm as it was, it certainly didn't do much for padding, only right now I was so tired none of that mattered.

It was odd not to have a pillow to sleep on, and I kept shifting trying to find the best way to sleep. Flopping over on my stomach, I crossed my arms to see if that would work better. Then turned to one side and then the other when they started to lose circulation. Letting out a grumble, I wriggled around to my side to see if that was better to rest my arm on. That lasted all of a few minutes before my arm started to tingle. Just as I planned to roll to the other side, an arm grabbed me around the waist and pulled me back against a giant warm body. Victor adjusted me against him until I was now sleeping on his shoulder as he sprawled out on his back.

"Sleep, Little Spark, the call to move out will come much sooner than any of us would like," Victor muttered and started to absently stroke my back. Hearing his steady heartbeat and feeling his soothing touch lulled me to sleep within seconds.

"Up and at 'em," Sorin called, snapping me out of my sleep.

Pushing myself up, I looked around to find Victor and I were the last ones to wake up. Rubbing the sleep from my eyes, I crawled out of my sleeping bag, yawning. It felt like I'd just fallen asleep, but the morning sun told me that wasn't the case. It was low in the sky yet bright enough to light up the whole inside of the building. Not much changed about it in the daylight other than maybe it looked even more abandoned than it had in the dark.

Kneeling, I rolled up my sleeping bag and shoved it into its designated pocket in my pack. After zipping everything up and getting my boots on, a hand reached out to me. Glancing up, I found it was Toma looking far more rested than he should. Grabbing his hand, he pulled me to my feet.

"Here, it's not fancy, but it will stick with you," Toma offered, handing me a power bar and a bottle of water. "I would say you get used to sleeping in odd places after a while, but I'd be lying to you. What you learn is how to fall asleep fast so your brain doesn't tell you how uncomfortable you are. Then again, I'm pretty sure any of us would be happy to be used as your pillow."

I have no idea why that comment about being my pillow made me blush, but it did. The heat in my cheeks and the smile that bloomed on Toma's face were all I needed to confirm I was indeed fucking blushing. Ducking my head, I concentrated on getting the power bar open as I got my face under control.

"You should do that more often," Toma whispered in my ear, his breath causing the loose hairs on my neck to tickle my skin. "It makes you look rather adorable when you blush like that."

His words had my face burning to which he just chuckled and brushed a soft kiss to my cheeks. "Come on, they're almost packed up and we need to get a move on."

Grabbing my bag, I tugged on my cap and hurried after Toma, the power bar hanging from my mouth. Tossing my pack up on the stack, I helped Cris tighten the straps before clambering into the Humvee. Back in my jumpseat, I stuffed the bar in my mouth and gulped down the water knowing I'd never be able to eat on this wild ride. Loaded and ready, Victor started up the vehicle and we were off.

This time I got to see where we were going, and I was stunned to see the mountains in the distance. Clouds clung to their peaks hiding them from view, but I thought I spotted snow near the tops. Oscad didn't have mountains; I'd seen some in Northern Asturg, but these were massive. The further towards them we went, the larger they got and the more detail I got to see on them.

"Are those mountains part of Asturg?" I was unable to keep my question to myself as I broke the silence of the ride.

"Part of them are," Petru answered. "They are the border between us and another country that no one's ventured into. Oscad,

Asturg, and Shearia are the largest and most established countries that span our continent. No one has really ever decided to venture past the mountain since it's such a treacherous journey. There was a story once about a man who'd made it across and stumbled into one of our smaller farming towns. He spoke a different language and had strange, tattooed markings on his face. Then again, it could all be made up since the story is so old and passed from town-to-town."

The whole idea of there being an undiscovered world beyond the mountains made me so curious. Although looking at what you'd have to cross to get there had me thinking better of the idea. I could easily see how one could lose their life taking the wrong step, not to mention if it was cold and you weren't prepared for it. Just the thought alone had me shivering.

Soon we turned away from the mountains and headed for the lush open fields with trees sprinkling the land. It was as if this place hadn't been touched by human hands leaving nature to take its course. Deer darted through sections of the tall grass, making me realize I hadn't seen a wild animal in decades. My thirst for knowledge and adventure had me so absorbed in watching the nature around me I didn't realize we were almost to our destination until I saw the massive building appear on the horizon. The whole thing stuck out like a sore thumb, an abrupt halt against the landscape. Without even needing an order, Victor pulled off the road and drove into the small grove of trees.

"Everyone out, we're hoofing it from here," Sorin ordered as he shoved open his door. "Cris, grab the covering. I want to ensure we hide the Humvee enough that you can't see it from a distance."

Cris tapped my foot and opened a compartment I had no idea was even there. He grabbed an odd-looking green mesh tarp with cutouts that mimicked leaves in a way. Once everyone was out, and we'd gotten what we needed from the vehicle, they draped the netting over it. Up close, you could clearly see something was there, but it was hard to distinguish what exactly it was.

Sorin spread out the map over a large rock and motioned us over. "We have no information about what's happening in the plant other than someone took the systems offline. As a failsafe, a code gets implemented that will keep the plant running as it should for a day. We're about twenty hours into that timeframe so we need to get in, secure the building, and find the problem for Toma to fix. I need to clarify that we only have an hour and a half to make all that happen. If it can't be solved in that amount of time, we are out of there and getting as far away from here as fucking possible. I won't lose my whole team in a plant explosion, so when I give the order to evacuate, you better fucking drop what you're doing and run."

"Understood," Petru agreed with a sharp nod.

"Yes, sir," Cris answered.

Toma gave a thumbs up. "Got it."

"I'm not planning on dying today," Victor muttered.

"Yeah, not gonna question that order," I said, shivering at the thought of being blown up.

"I want to split up into three teams. Victor, with Toma, we need to make sure he gets to the control room no matter what. Petru, I want you with Dani coming in from the east side of the building. Tru, you should be able to work your way through the tall grass and scope the place out before crossing the open land to the plant operations building. Cris and I will come at it from the west. Once Tru and I give the signal that the coast is clear, Victor, you and Toma make your move, and we'll cover you if anything happens," Sorin instructed, laying out the plan with practiced ease. "Gear up, stay sharp, and watch each other's backs."

CHAPTER 31

Danella

With that final order, the guys instantly started on their routine. Guns were checked to ensure their ammo was full, knives strapped to the hip, comms placed on our ears, and emergency packs strapped to their belts. Cris and Toma double-checked their specialty kits before shouldering their backpacks and clipping them tight to their body. Petru walked over and threaded a belt with a holster on for me and tugged the thigh strap so it was snug but didn't hinder movement.

We'd just started working on how to pull a gun from a thigh holster in training. I knew the feel but it was still odd. This holster also had a place for a knife as well. The blade was wicked sharp and I'd only ever handled a wooden one so I would know how not to slice myself open when having it on me. I was beginning to see how much I still had to learn and how little I knew.

"Do your own equipment check for me," Petru instructed, as he passed me the handgun I'd been assigned.

This part I was confident in. The number of times Petru had me do this during all our sessions made it reflexive. Now I understood what he meant about needing a solid foundation to build off of. Understanding one part made it easier to flow into another and add on as my skills grew. Finished with my check, I placed it in the holster and continued making sure I had the two extra magazines of ammo in the pouch. Normally there would be a few other things, but since we hadn't covered grenades and flashbangs, I wasn't allowed to carry those. Which I didn't argue about.

"Equipment checked and ready," I announced.

"Nicely done, Wildflower," Petru praised as he shouldered his sniper rifle. "Stay behind me and be as quiet as you can. I'll be using hand signals to communicate. If you see something or need to get my attention, tap on my arm twice."

"Understood," I said, having learned to always give a verbal affirmative when given an order or instruction.

Petru smiled and squeezed my shoulder before giving the signal to move out and taking off at a steady jog. All the men in this unit had irritatingly long legs, and while I wasn't short, I didn't cover the same amount of ground they could. So a simple, easy jog for Petru was more like a run for me, but thankfully, all the daily conditioning and runs helped immensely. We were able to stay in the grove of trees for a bit, then he called a halt as we came to a chunk of open space before heading into the tall prairie grass. Both of us pulled out our binoculars and searched the area for any signs of movement or someone having passed through here.

This was one area I was still incredibly novice in. I understood the theory of the matter, but noticing if grass had been trampled or branches had been snapped from such a distance wasn't easy to spot. Petru and Victor were the best at this in the unit, so while I doubted my skills, I trusted his. After a few minutes, there was a tap on my shoulder and we were on the move. I thought being in the tall grass would be helpful and keep us hidden from view. What I didn't count on was the fact you couldn't fucking see anything. Crouched low and moving like a little gremlin, I had no way of knowing if we were even heading in the right direction. The sound of the rushing river grew much louder and that's when I realized what Petru was doing. Using the sound and keeping it on his right as we moved forward would lead us right where we needed to be.

"West is clear," Sorin whispered over the comms, nearly making me jump out of my skin.

I'd all but forgotten the damn thing was in my ear. Petru, on the other hand, didn't even flinch as he kept his sure steady pace forward. I drifted after him, walking in the path he made in the grass, remembering it helped to disguise the number of people in the group. Being so focused on my surroundings and keeping up, I almost ran into the man when he came to a sudden halt. Backing up a step I dropped to my knee and rested a hand on my gun, glancing in the direction the Alpha was. Petru motioned for me to stay where I was as he took his rifle in hand, looking at something through the scope. A growl caught my attention and I realized it was coming from Petru.

Lowering the gun, he tapped on his comm. "Guys, I'm seeing a Southern military vehicle stashed behind some rocks. It's one of those all-terrain two-seaters."

"Do you see any sign of someone around it?" Sorin asked.

"Negative, but if you want me to check it out, I can. It's not too far off course," Petru offered.

"Stick to the original plan. We need to get Toma in that control room. Once the coast is clear and he's inside with Victor, double back and check it out," Sorin ordered. "At least we know there might be two people to watch out for."

"Roger that," Petru acknowledged and silenced his comm.

With a flick of his fingers, we were on the move as he shouldered his weapon once more. It was only another few minutes before we came to another halt. Only, this time I could see the plant building right in front of us. Shifting to catch my eye, Petru instructed me to go left, closer to the river, and scout while he went right. He tapped his ear twice, telling me to signal with it if I found anything. I signaled my understanding and headed off to do my part. With the river blocking anyone from sneaking up on us from that direction, it made sense he would have to check it out. The grass became shorter and didn't offer as much coverage the closer I got to the water. When I was on the edge of being fully exposed, I dropped to a knee and lifted my binoculars.

This was my first look at the river I'd been listening to this whole time. It wasn't at all what I thought of when I pictured a river. The water was moving so fast that it had white caps and the roar was deafening this close even as I was still ten feet from the edge. I could see why they wanted to build the power station here since I could only imagine how much energy was created with its speed. The fact that the river was also a good two miles wide made it impossible for anyone to use as a way to get access to the plant itself, so if attacked, it could only happen from the direction we came. Not seeing anything that would cause me to believe anyone was lying in wait or another vehicle had driven through, I headed back.

Keeping an eye that the building was where it should be, I retraced my path through the grass. The sound of something rustling to my right had me freezing in place. Dropping low, I undid the strap holding my gun securely in the holster and listened. Closing my eyes, I tried to focus on the sounds other than the roar of the river. The sound of a stone being kicked came from ahead, another rustle to my right, and then the sound of a foot scuffing softly on the dirt behind me.

Fuck, I was surrounded. My only hope was that the person ahead of me was Petru, who would be close enough to help. Reaching up to my comm, I taped it twice then followed it up with the signal that I was in danger. Seconds later, someone leapt out at me from the grass, slamming me to the ground. Trying to make sense of what was happening, I thrust out with my knee and connected with the person making them grunt. Thrashing, I managed to get an arm free and smashed it into the closest body part I could. It happened to be their chest and while it didn't do much, it would leave one hell of a bruise and got them to loosen their hold on me.

Scrabbling back, I caught sight of who it was. "Draza."

"Hello, little Omega bitch," he sneered, pulling out his knife. "Looks like there's no one to save you from me this time. I think it's time you and I had a little fun as I pay you back for everything you've done to me."

Twisting, I reached for my gun and aimed it at the crazed man before me. My hand started to shake as he advanced upon me making it hard to hold the damn thing steady.

"Aww, looks like you're not as brave as you keep pretending to be. See, that's the thing about bitches, you can never trust them to follow through when it comes to the dirty work. They just don't have the stomach for it," Draza taunted.

Gritting my teeth, I pushed myself up to stand, both hands on my gun. Now was not the time to lose my nerve and let fear overtake me. This bastard was going to kill me, of that, I had no doubt. So why hadn't I pulled the trigger yet?

The sadistic Beta took a step closer, flipping his knife as if he didn't have a worry in the world. "Come on, you stupid whore, shoot me. If you don't, then I'm going to fuck you good and hard before I slit your throat and cum all over your dead, bleeding body. It's the only fate you Northern cunts deserve."

I caught movement out of the corner of my eye, and I assumed it was Petru—but it wasn't. The last person I ever expected to find here rose from out of the grass, grabbed my arm, yanked me to his chest, then wrapped his hand around mine still holding the gun, and squeezed the trigger twice in quick succession. Draza's face showed his shock as he dropped to his knees, blood trickling out of the bullet hole between his eyes. Before I could stop him, the gun was ripped from my hand and tossed away, quickly followed by my comm.

I tried to jerk out of his hold, but he was just as strong as I remembered. His other hand gripped my throat, forcing me to look into his gray-blue eyes as I was enveloped in the familiar scent of chocolate and cinnamon.

"Lucian," I rasped.

"I told you I would find you no matter where you ran," he reminded me, his voice deep and commanding as ever. He dropped his head as he pulled me to him and fused his lips to mine. The kiss was commanding, dominant, and full of desperation. "You're mine, my fierce, sweet Omega. I won't let them have you."

My heart thundered in my ears as my brain realized what he was saying. It was as if my body was at war with itself. Elation at seeing him again and feeling his body pressed against mine, my lips burned from a kiss I'd been aching for but would never admit. Yet I knew it could never be like what Sorin and the others were building with me. They wanted me to be part of their team, a family, and I would never find that with Lucian, alone fearing death in the North.

"No, please, Lucian, don't do this," I pleaded. "Don't make me go back to a life where I mean nothing and fear death every day. I can't survive like that. If you care about me at all, just let me go. Tell your father I died in the raid, and you can choose another Omega to take my place."

The anger written all over Lucian's face told me I didn't have a chance in hell of him letting me go. "There is no other Omega for me. You are all that I want. I tried, Dani, I tried not letting you take over my heart as we agreed, but I failed miserably. You are everything to me, and I don't intend for us to go back to the life we had. I'm going to change everything, no matter what it takes. I will make my world safe for you to be by my side. Without you there challenging me to be more, I'll fail because nothing matters more to me than you."

Everything he was saying was so opposite to everything I understood about our dynamic that I didn't know how to process it. "How? How can you possibly change things for that to happen? Your entire world is built on the foundation that Omegas are breeders and nothing matters more than winning the war."

Lucian shifted his grip to cup my face tenderly in his hands. "Don't you understand? For you, my heart, I will burn it all down to ensure you're safe. The first step will be killing my father and taking my place as leader of the North. That's how I'm going to change things."

Stunned by what he'd just said, all I could do was gawk at him. Where had the man who was biding his time for his father to die gone? What had changed his mind? I refused to believe it was just losing me. There had to be something else to it.

"You have two seconds to let her go before I blow your head off," Petru threatened from behind me.

I tried to twist to see him, but Lucian held a tight grip on my face forcing me to keep looking only at him. "Listen to him, please. He's one of the best marksmen the South has. He won't miss, especially not this close. Go back North. Do what you said, change the world and then maybe we can talk."

"So you're willing to fight with them but not with me?" Lucian challenged. "Have they poisoned your mind against the North, turned you against me?"

"They didn't have to turn me against the North. Your father did a good enough job all on his own to make me despise what he's created," I pointed out. "As for the team I've been training with, they've been teaching me how to fight, shoot, and protect myself so I'll never be a victim ever again. They view me as an equal, someone they trust to watch their back in battle. These five men are a family, a pack, something I've ached to have all my life."

The hurt and pain in Lucian's eyes tore at me. I didn't want to hurt him, for he'd suffered as much as I had through life. Neither of us had the chance to be our own person until now. If he was ready to break free from his father's hold, it would be the best thing for him. We might have had a chance to be something more if we hadn't ended up living in such different worlds. I reached up, stroking his scarred cheek making him flinch at the touch.

"Lucian," I whispered his name, begging for him to understand.

"You're Lucian," Petru snarled. "I should shoot you dead right here for all you've done. Come to blow up another power plant?"

This time when I whirled around to face Petru, Lucian was too distracted to stop me. "Wait, Petru, please, he came for me. He's trying to rescue me but didn't realize I was staying willingly."

"It doesn't matter, Wildflower," Petru argued, stepping forward, causing Lucian to grab me once more and retreat a step. "That man will become just like his father the moment he takes over. Only he will be more deadly having managed to infiltrate our border and even turned one of our own against us."

Lucian scoffed. "That man is the reason I'm here. He got the vehicle and told me how to disable the plant to make your team specifically come here. The man you claim to be one of your own wanted nothing more than to kill you and the rest of your unit. In fact, I had to step in and take him out before he tried to kill Dani.

He evidently didn't need my influence to act on his hatred of your unit."

"None of that makes any difference," Petru stated, raising his handgun. "I still can't let you leave here alive. Let her go. I won't ask again."

Lucian grabbed my bun, telling me I'd lost my cap at some point in the struggle. Using it, he tilted my head to the side exposing his bran on my neck. "Do you see this? It's my mark on her. You can't take what's mine. Whether in life or death, she'll always be mine."

"Your brand is barbaric and means nothing here, you hold no claim on her whatsoever," Petru shot back, taking a step closer. "Just know that I won't be the one carrying the burden of your death. She will. The memory of this moment will live on in her mind forever and, for that alone, I loathe you for making me do this."

"No more than I, for you making me do this," Lucian murmured. "Danella, I hope one day I will earn your forgiveness, but I will never let them take you away from me."

Not understanding what he was talking about, I gasped as his teeth pierced my flesh in the same spot his brand was on my neck.

"NO, you fucking bastard!" Petru bellowed.

Just as suddenly as the bite started, it was over. Quickly followed by a flash of light exploding in front of me, blinding me momentarily as smoke filled the air. The next thing I knew, Lucian hauled me over his shoulder and was running. I tried to fight, to wriggle out of his hold but the sting of a needle piercing the skin of my leg told me he'd come prepared. In my last lucid moments, I watched Petru appear out of the smoke, lift his rifle, and take aim. No shot was fired, though, because the last thing I remember was how fucking cold the river was.

To be completed in Knot All Is Ruined Part: 2

PART TWO

CHAPTER 32

Danella

The world seemed to pass by me in a blur of sensations and glimpses of reality. Whatever drug Lucian had dosed me with didn't knock me out entirely, but it certainly kept me compliant. The water from the river was fucking cold. I don't know how we didn't drown when I couldn't swim and it felt like my clothes were weighing me down. The sound of Petru yelling after us tugged at my heart, which was an odd feeling in and of itself. I don't know how long we were in the river or how far downstream we were taken with how fast the water was moving. Eventually, I remember getting dragged out of the water and up onto dry land.

"Dani, My Heart, this is not how I wanted things to go," Lucian murmured as he brushed my hair out of my face. "Why did you have to be with them willingly? Doesn't matter, you're back with me now, and I'll keep you safe, starting with getting you dry and warm."

I felt him pick me up, but other than that, I have no idea how we ended up in a cave with a small fire burning. Odder still, I was naked, with Lucian wrapped around me and a blanket covering us. Where the hell had the blanket come from? Had he stashed supplies away in anticipation of this? Wait, was he the one who damaged the power plant drawing my unit out to investigate?

No matter how much I wanted to demand answers from Lucian, the drug still had a hold on me. Deciding it was better just to rest and let the meds wear off, I closed my eyes. Sorin and the others would find me. Besides, Victor wouldn't allow them to just abandon me. No, what I needed to do was rest so I could have a clear head about things in the morning. If I could talk Lucian into leaving me behind as he went off to do all that, he said it would be the best option for all of us.

Could he really be serious about killing his father, the general of the Northern Asturg army? A cruel and vicious man who'd left me with the choice of becoming his son's personal breeder or death. I'd met the bastard once when I was first shipped to Asturg from my home country, Oscad, three years ago. They'd lied to us at the Care Center, pretending to do their best for the country, protecting us from war and all that bullshit. The reality was that they sold us off to keep General Rasvan from attacking us when he realized he couldn't win against the South.

So many Omegas had been sent to our bordering countries, never seeing their families again. Each of us had been raised hoping to be part of a pack with the love and comfort that came with it. Instead, I'd learned what it felt like to feel *real* hunger and to fear for my life every day. No longer was I regarded as a woman with her own mind and feelings about things. In Asturg, I was a breeder, something to fill with a baby and steal away to raise in a group setting. Their entire purpose being to grow up and fight in this centuries-old war that no one truly understood.

How do you win a war when you're not sure why it started in the first place?

After an attack on the outpost I'd been living at with Lucian for the past three years, I managed to make a run for it. Unwilling to leave two of my best friends behind, I also got them out. Only it didn't go quite as we planned, seeing as we got caught by the Southern Asturg military. The escape had been brutal, and I suffered some massive injuries yet hung in there long enough for the advanced medical team to heal me. That's when I met Sorin and the others. The men who, in all honesty, saved my life. They also happen to be the top unit of the Southern military's Elite Units. Those five men quickly became the center of my world as we struck a bargain. I gave them information on the North, and they trained me to be a fighter. Giving me the ability to fight and protect myself so I no longer lived in fear of being a victim.

I'd managed to complete a week out of the three they wanted me to have before we got the call to deal with a situation at the power plant. We moved out instantly, unsure of what we'd land ourselves in. However, if what I'm piecing together is right, then that was an elaborate scheme for Lucian to have the opportunity to rescue me—or at least in his mind. While I'd given my unit hell when we first met, I was swiftly discovering they might mean more to me than I realized. Faced with the choice of staying or leaving, I would have told you I'd leave hands down to return to Oscad. Now having been ripped away from them, I honestly don't know what my answer would be.

"Sleep, Dani," Lucian grumbled as he tugged me closer and buried his nose in my hair. "I can hear your beautiful mind whirling, trying to figure out what's going on. It can wait till morning, so rest. We have a long trek ahead of us to get to the Northern capital city."

When I tried to speak, I realized I couldn't get my mouth to work, so I resorted to a distinctly unhappy grunt.

"Don't be mad. Please, My Heart, I can't handle you being upset with me," Lucian said as he sat up and rolled me on my back to look up at him. "I'm sorry, I'm so sorry your life with me had to start the way it did. Still, if I had the chance to go back in time and do it all over, I'm not sure I would change a thing other than not hiding how I felt about you. While living in the north is harsh and cruel, the best thing it ever did for me was to bless me with you."

His lips caressed my neck, and the sensation blazed through my body, making me gasp. How had I forgotten that he'd claimed me? The bastard fucking bit me right where his brand marked my skin for all to see. Now that I remembered that tiny detail, I could *feel* Lucian and how desperate he was not to lose me. Unwilling to deal with this now, when I couldn't talk or yell at him, I just forced myself to sleep. Hopefully, when I woke up, I would regain control of my body.

~

WAKING, I lifted my arm to block the sun's rays searing into my eyes. Rolling on my side, I groaned at how sore I was. It seemed our river adventure had taken its toll on me, no matter how relaxed I was. Pushing up, I looked around the cave that Lucian had brought us to and was impressed. It was large enough for the Alpha to stand in and not worry about his head hitting. The cave was wide enough for us to fit along with maybe one other person before it became too claustrophobic.

Sitting up fully, the blanket that had been covering me fell away, and I saw the bruises on my arms and legs from being battered in the river. Now being sore made sense. I was alone in the cave, but I could feel Lucian wasn't far and he knew that I was awake. Having this connection to him was strange, like having a GPS and a mood tracker all in one within a person. Was this what it would have been like to be bonded to the others? How would that have worked with Cristofor being a Beta? Why was I even thinking about that?

Tossing off the blanket, I stood looking for my clothes that must be around here somewhere. Not finding them in the cave, I peeked out the opening and spotted them hanging from a tree branch. I paused to listen, feeling confident that there was no one else around but Lucian, who might see me running out of the cave naked. Darting over, I yanked down the shirt and bra, but the underwear got caught on a smaller branch. Not having the height to get to it, I tried to pull on it harder, but then the sound of ripping fabric stopped me.

"You've got to be fucking kidding me," I grumbled. "First, I get drugged, marked, tossed into a river, and now my fucking under-wear is being held hostage by a goddamn tree."

When an arm wrapped around my waist, I yelped. He lifted me up to the point where I could easily get the rest of my clothes. "Someone seems to have woken up on the wrong side of the bed,"

Lucian commented, kissing my neck before setting me back down. "I would have gotten those for you, My Heart."

Spinning in his arms, my hand whipped out, cracking across his cheek. The sound was so loud it echoed in the woods around us. "You fucking asshole," I yelled, shoving him as hard as I could. The man barely moved with how solidly he was made of muscle. That just pissed me off even more.

"How could you do this to me?" I screamed, using my whole body to express my feelings, hands balled into fists. "We had an agreement. It was to never get attached to each other and when this was all over, we'd go our separate ways. I was finally *free,* for once in my life. You could've easily told your father that I died in the fight ending this, *but no*, you had to track me down."

Lucian didn't say a word, just watched me with his solemn gray-blue eyes. The scars on his face seemed more pronounced at the moment as a pained expression was shown on his features. My rage poured out of me as I used all my strength and slammed my fists against his chest repeatedly. Right now, all I wanted to do was scream, cry, and use his face as a punching bag.

Running out of steam a sobbed tore out of me as I slumped against him. "You marked me Lucian, *again*. Only this time it's forever. Why, *why* do all the choices for my future keep getting taken away from me? What did I do in this life to deserve that?" My sob had now become full on ugly crying as I clawed his shirt.

"How?" I demanded, my voice raspy with emotion. "How can you call me your heart, when you constantly break mine?"

Slowly, ever so slowly, he wrapped his arms around me. They hugged me tightly, almost as if he was worried I was going to shatter. I didn't want to cry anymore. Yet the pain of having seen a future— one I finally thought I'd be able to choose—was once again ripped away from me. As my body shook with my sobs Lucian hoisted me up, cradled me in his arms, stooped to pick up my clothes, and carried me back to the cave. He draped a blanket over my back as he cuddled me against his chest and began to purr.

He'd only done that once before, the first night we were together. I'd never forgot how fucking calming it was, almost like an automatic off switch to my anxiety and panic. It could lull me into blissful peace, no matter how hard I wanted to fight it.

He nuzzled the side of my neck where his marks were, pressing soft kisses along the brand. "I will never be able to express how sorry I am, Danella," he murmured. "Just know that I plan to spend the rest of my life making up for everything that's happened. I get you have no reason to trust me or my words. Which is why I'll work that much harder to put actions behind them and prove myself to you."

He fell silent for a moment just letting his hand stroke up and down my spine as I calmed down. Resting his head on top of mine I felt the cool dampness of a tear hit my scalp. "We will find a way to be happy, I *know* it. The reason why I'm so sure, is because the only life worth living is one where we're together. Without that, for me life is meaningless."

The gentleness of his words had me clinging to him because not only did I hear it, I *felt* it. Every word was coated in longing, love, and regret with an echo of hope. This mighty warrior was willing to do whatever it took to get me to forgive him. I didn't know if it was possible, but for both our sakes, I hoped it would be. Our fates were sealed together forever, because once a bond is created between an Alpha and an Omega—it can never be taken back.

In fact, those from the country of Shearia, believe the bond lasts even after a partner dies, making it impossible for them to ever have another pack in that lifetime. If that were true, then it means I would never have a chance with the others, even if they did find me. Putting that thought aside, I didn't want to dwell on that possibility right now. Things were hard enough already without making that wound bigger and more painful than it was.

"Dani," Lucian started in a hesitant voice. "Could it be that you really cared for them? Those Southern soldiers?"

"I don't want to talk about it right now." I bit out. "It doesn't matter. You and I have bonded, so that's that."

"It matters greatly to me, My Heart," Lucian argued. "If you had feelings for these men, then not only am I working against all that's gone wrong between us but the challenge of your heart being given to them as well."

"They didn't have my heart." I scoffed, sitting up and pushing away from him. "I was using them to learn how to fight and protect myself, something I've sorely needed in this life. Why would I allow myself to get attached when I was finally free?"

Lucian caught my chin with his hand, forcing me to look at him. "Dani, I thought we'd gotten to the point where we didn't lie to each other."

"Like you're one to fucking talk. You've been lying this whole time about how you felt about me," I shot back, poking his chest with a finger—*hard*.

"Alright, then tell me this. If I'd come to you and told you that I was in love with you and wanted an *actual* relationship, would I have even had a chance?" Lucian challenged.

I opened my mouth to answer, then shut it when I realized I had no clue. Was it possible that I'd never consider there being something more between us? He already knew about the fact I didn't go into heat, which didn't seem to bother him at all. Yet, that had been when he didn't want to have a child fearing what his father would do to said child. Would that change now that we were bonded and he planned to kill his father?

"Do you still not want to have kids?" I blurted, the need to know the answer driving my actions.

He blinked at me slowly, as if trying to hide his surprise at my question. "Has something changed for you in that area?"

"No..." I hedged, wringing my hands. "...it's just you were okay with that when you didn't want a kid, a relationship, or an Omega, and that's all changed."

With a sigh Lucian shook his head. "Dani, what's changed is that I realized I was a fucking idiot who didn't see the gift I'd been given in you from that first moment I laid eyes on you."

That had me frowning, but he just smiled and tucked my hair behind my ear.

"The moment I caught your scent and saw you sleeping on my bed, I knew I wanted you physically," he admitted. "What I hadn't counted on was that I'd never want to let you go, and having you with me made me a better person. It showed me I wasn't living, I was surviving, and if I wanted to change things for my people, then I couldn't hide anymore," Lucian explained as he lovingly grasped my face in his firm hands. "You deserve a world where you're seen for the incredible, sassy, smart woman that you are. Not a fucking breeder. Having you by my side, I know I'll be able to change the world, because I won't allow a danger to exist that could harm you. If I have the ability to remove that threat, you bet your perfect ass I'll do it."

Reaching up, I let my fingers glide over the scars that marred the right side of his face. How he felt like he'd just been surviving when he gained those wounds at the hands of his father, and this fucking war wasn't how I saw it. Like me, he'd been forced into a life he couldn't avoid. For fuck's sake, he's seen his mother murdered before his eyes when she tried to speak against his father. The General had seen to it that Lucian never forgot who held his leash and the fate that would befall him if he didn't follow orders.

I might be fucking pissed, and justly so, but I agreed to our deal in the first place because I saw something of myself in him. We both got dealt shit hands in life, but I chose to rebel and speak my mind on matters. Meanwhile, he became the strong, resilient mastermind waiting for the time to act. Then as time went on and we got to know each other, I think deep down, it came to the point I struggled with the thought of leaving him to survive on his own.

Just like Tori and Violet, this compassionate warrior had become mine in an odd way. The more Sorin, Petru, Toma, Victor, and Cris chipped at the walls around my heart, it also revealed something I didn't expect. I did care for Lucian—not to say I was *in love* with him—but he was important to me. That was why I couldn't let Petru shoot him when he had the chance.

"When you say you want to remove the threat against me, are you talking about your father?" I questioned.

"Yes," he murmured, turning to kiss my palm. "He is the biggest threat to us both. If he were to remain alive, then we'd spend the rest of our lives watching our backs, which isn't the life I want for us. Seeing what the South is like this deep into their country, I can't help but wish this for my people. They've been struggling enough, fighting a war that will never end, and will ultimately cost us every-thing. The only way to change anything is to cut the head off the snake."

"Is that the plan? Leave here and head for Stalhold City, where your father is?" I asked, giving in to the need to be held by him.

He tugged the blanket up so I was covered before securing his arms around me. "Right now, we just need to get out of Southern territory without getting caught. Once we return to Northern land, I'll need to find the resistance hiding in the mountains. If I'm going to overthrow my father, then I'm going to need an army of my own. Having one that hates him as much as I do will certainly help."

"Are we leaving right away?"

"Tonight, when it's dark, we'll head out. So rest, My Heart, it's going to be a hard journey on foot," Lucian shared as he started to purr again, coaxing me into sleep.

CHAPTER 33

Danella

Lucian shifting me out of his lap woke me. I didn't know how long I'd been asleep, but the sun was still bright so it couldn't have been that long.

"Is something wrong?" I questioned, seeing his intense expression.

He lifted a hand to his lips and crawled to the front of the cave, drawing a knife from the sheath on his leg. Clutching the blanket to myself, I didn't know if I should yell for help or keep silent. If it was one of the guys, I couldn't let Lucian kill them. Even if they wanted nothing to do with me now that I was bonded to their enemy, I refused to let them be harmed. If I was going to help them, I needed to get close enough to Lucian to stop him, so I let the blanket fall away and crawled to the entrance.

Lucian had slipped out and headed to the left so that's what I did as well. Keeping low, I paused to listen just as the guys had taught me. The key to tracking was using all your senses and being aware of your surroundings. When I heard the rustling of leaves and the snap of twigs, it was off to the right. Just as I turned to look, a pig-like animal with large sharp looking tusks darted out of the underbrush. Clenching my jaw tight, it took everything in me not to scream as I moved back further into the cave, hoping it didn't see me.

No longer in its eyesight, I stood and looked around the small cave for where my weapons might be. I'd gone into the river with a knife, handgun, and extra ammo. The fact that everything was black didn't help matters. Even with the sunlight still filtering in, I managed to find them tucked between some rocks. It was almost as if Lucian didn't want to give them up but didn't want me to have them, either. Guess I couldn't blame him when he didn't know how mad I was going to be with him. The sound of the animal's snuffling grew louder as it got closer to the cave.

Darting to the weapons, I grabbed the gun but found it empty of ammo when I checked it. "Fuck."

Tossing it aside, I snatched up the knife and yanked off the sheath. A shrill squeal filled the cave, alerting me to the fact that the creature had discovered I was in here. Spinning around, I brandished the knife just like Victor and Sorin had been teaching me. We hadn't spent much time on this skill other than how not to cut myself with the damn thing. I had seconds before the animal was charging at me to make my choice of how to deal with this.

Most animals function on dominance, right? What would be a more dominant display, standing my ground or charging? Fuck it, I was meeting this asshole head-on.

Letting out a battle cry, I ran right at the scary bastard with only my knife and leapt over the damn thing. It let out an enraged squeal and scrambled to turn around before bolting toward me again. This time I felt more confident with more space. When it was almost upon me, I grabbed one of those mean-looking tusks and dropped to the ground forcing the animal's head to twist, knocking it off balance. My heart pounded in my chest as I tried to figure out what the fuck I was going to do now that I was face-to-face with the animal. Its legs thrashed as it tried to get to its feet while fighting against my hold. Not knowing what else to do, I just started stabbing into the creature as it hollered and bellowed with each blow. I felt awful for causing it so much pain. However, I also knew if I didn't do something, it would wound or even kill me, given the chance.

"Danella," Lucian roared as he appeared, grabbing the beast like it weighed nothing and tossing it away from me. Pulling out his gun, two shots sounded followed by another pain-filled squeal before the forest around us fell silent.

Within seconds Lucian was hovering over me, running his hands over my body. "Dani, are you hurt? Is this blood yours? What the hell were you thinking?"

"I'm fine. I don't think it got me," I panted. "Pretty sure the blood is from the pig thing, not me."

"Do you have any idea how dangerous boars are? Grown men have died from being gutted by them, and you decided to wrestle with it?" Lucian growled as he hoisted me up. "Foolish, foolish Omega."

"Where the fuck were you?" I yelled. "I crawled after you, but then you vanished when the damn boar or whatever the fuck it's called showed up. If you'd left me the bullet from my gun, I wouldn't have been in any danger."

"Forgive me for not waiting to get shot in my sleep with how furious you were with me," Lucian shot back. "I told you to stay in the cave. If you'd listened, the boar wouldn't have caught your scent and charged after you. With those things, you need to come at them from behind, keep your scent upwind so they don't know you're coming."

"Well, how was I supposed to know all that? Maybe next time, use your words instead of thinking I can just read your goddamn mind," I grumbled.

The next thing I knew, I was being dropped into a pond, the cool water shocking me as it enveloped me. Spluttering, I flailed, panicking that I would drown until my feet hit the bottom and I could stand. "Are you out of your goddamn mind?" I screamed. "I don't know how to mother fucking swim."

"Good thing I dropped you in somewhere you don't have to," Lucian muttered as he stripped out of his pants and waded in. "You were covered in boar's blood and wouldn't stop yelling at me, so I thought this was the quickest way to deal with both."

"Fucking Alphas, always needing to do things the brutish way," I snarled, turning away from him.

Lucian caught my arm and dragged me back, slamming his lips to mine. Stunned, I didn't pull away, allowing him to slide his hand into my hair, gripping it securely as he devoured me. Resting a hand on his chest, I groaned at his taste, not realizing how intense it would be to truly kiss him. For the past three years, not once had his lips touched mine until yesterday and again now. The bond between us hummed with delight as he deepened the kiss, his hand on my ass pressing me tightly to him.

I could feel his cock hard and ready, trapped against my stomach, making it incredibly clear how much my Alpha wanted me. Struggling with the desire to give in, knowing how good he would make me feel, coupled with how needy my body had been, clashed with the part of my brain that told me he didn't deserve to fuck me after what he'd done. When he finally broke the kiss, we were both panting and looking at each other with need.

"Don't take risks like that, My Heart," Lucian murmured, resting his forehead against mine. "If anything happened to you, I'm not sure I'd survive it. Losing you for the past few weeks has been hell, but the knowledge that I would find you kept me from going insane."

"I'm not helpless, Lucian. If you truly want things to work out between us, you're going to need to accept that," I argued. "We're bonded, which means a connection for life no matter what I want. There's no walking away from this, although if you think I'm going to be the same woman who's kept her head down to survive, you've got another thing coming," I warned.

Cupping my face in his hands, he pressed a kiss to my lips. "The only Omega I could fall in love with is one who has her own mind. Dani, you are a warrior, a protector of those you hold dear. This makes you unlike any woman I've ever met and exactly what I've been searching for. I'll admit it will take time and your help to find a balance between the Alpha I've been raised to be and the Omega you were born to be. Keep challenging me, pushing me to the edge, and forcing me to see the world through a different lens so I can grow.

We'll fight, and I have no doubt that I'll say the wrong thing, pissing you off, but I want to be what you need. All I ask is that you understand the one thing that will never change is my overwhelming desire to protect you. You, Danella, are my whole world now. There is nothing I won't do for you. Just let me keep you safe." Lucian pleaded.

Letting out a heavy sigh, I nodded. "You can't be the only one trying to make this work, or it will never happen. I'll try, except following rules has never been something I'm good at."

"Really?" Lucian chuckled. "How could I have missed that fact about you after three years?"

"Oh fuck off," I muttered, splashing water at him.

Lucian grabbed my hips and lifted me so the tip of his cock nudged at my entrance. "Was that an invitation? Because my answer will always be yes to fucking you, My Heart."

All reservations went out the window at the tantalizing feel of him teasing me. Rolling my hips, I moaned at the sensation of that warm, rounded head gliding through my slick pumping against my clit. "Yes," I whined. "Please, Alpha, will you fuck me?"

In an agonizingly slow motion, he lowered me onto his cock until he was seated so deep inside me that my clit rubbed against his skin. Tossing my head back, I let out a moan of ecstasy, finally getting what I'd been craving for days and only been teased with.

"Fuck, Dani, you feel so good," Lucian mumbled against my shoulder. "I love the way you can take everything I have to give you in that perfect pussy. Now I'm not going to fuck you like normal."

This had me whimpering and whining as I rocked into him, not at all happy about this plan. "Shh, My Heart, I'll take care of your needs. This time I will make love to you how I've always wanted to."

Moving out of the water, he settled me on the ground without pulling out of me onto a large patch of soft moss. With his body covering mine, he showered my face in kisses as he slowly pulled out, only to press back in just as slow. Letting his kisses travel to my neck, he wrapped his lips around the spot he marked, caressing it with his tongue making me keen with pleasure. Every stroke of his tongue felt as if he was between my legs doing the same thing as he tortured me with his slow thrusts.

"Please, Lucian, I need more," I begged.

A finger started to circle my nipple causing me to arch into his touch. "What kind of more do you need, my sweet Omega?"

"Faster, fuck me faster," I gasped as his teeth scraped over the nipple. I dug my fingers into his arms and legs, tightening around his waist and forcing him deeper.

Taking me seriously, he picked up the speed keeping his thrusts just as deep as I cried out in pleasure. "Yes, god yes, just like that."

"Fuck, you're clamping down on me so tight," Lucian grunted. "Are you looking for my knot? Is that what you need to be fuck and knotted, owned by your Alpha good and proper?"

"Please, Alpha, I want to be knotted, filled with you until I can't take anymore," I pleaded, my mind utterly lost in the pleasure of what was happening. Not since the first day together had our sex been like this, all-consuming with need and ecstasy.

I yelped as Lucian flipped us over, putting me on top, hands splayed on his broad chest. Gray-blue eyes captivated me as they seemed to stare into my soul, full of lust and overwhelming love. "Ride me, My Heart. Take what you need from your Alpha. I will give it all to you happily."

Having never been in this position before, I felt a little intimidated, though I did start to rock at the urging of his hands. Shifting my legs so they were in a better position to support me, I sat up tall trusting his hold on me to keep me safe. Tossing my head back to look up through the trees at the sky, I did just what he said and took my own pleasure from him. Instead of moving up and down, I swirled my hips, rolling them back and forth so my clit was receiving friction as well as the rest of my pussy.

The building orgasm had me falling forward grabbing his face and tongue fucking his mouth as I rocked with urgency. His hands gripped my ass and started to thrust up into me, matching the speed I was going, sending me over the edge. Screaming into his mouth, I came so hard my body started to convulse. It only intensified as he followed right behind me, his knot expanding into place. Soon we were locked together and could only manage the barest of movements, yet those movements hit all the right fucking spots making me come again stronger than the first. Breaking our kiss, I tucked my head into the crook of his shoulder, shuddering and whimpering as he stroked his hands gently up and down my back.

"I love you so fucking much, Danella, and one day I hope you'll feel the same about me," Lucian whispered in my ear as he nuzzled against my hair. "I'll earn those words from you. That's a fucking promise."

Unable to respond even if I knew how to, I simply clung to him while breathing in his sweet, spicy scent of chocolate and cinnamon. It made me want to lick him from head to toe, checking to see if he tasted as good as he smelled. While he'd given me plenty of oral pleasure, that wasn't something I'd done for him. Anything I could do that would cut down the intimacy of these acts I did. Being on your knees for a man giving them an experience that gave you no absolute pleasure, was exceedingly intimate in my mind. Now, though, I was thinking that might be something to explore.

"We'll head out once the sun's gone down," Lucian shared. "It's easier to avoid the drones they have flying over the open lands between the main city and the border."

I'd forgotten about that. Sorin had mentioned there were drones that monitored the Southern territory, freeing soldiers to be used elsewhere. He'd told me that, so I would think twice about making a run for it.

"How did you manage to avoid them?" I asked, sitting up enough to look him in the face.

"There are lots of little tricks you can use if they stumble upon you, nonetheless they cover so much space it's easy to avoid them altogether if you wait. Once a drone passes an area, it takes hours for it to come back and check it again. By then, we'll be long gone. The challenge is they change the pattern the drones use every other day, so you can't predict where it will be or where it will go," Lucian informed me as he rolled us to the side, making it easier to look at each other. "Danella, I need to know... if they come for you, will you let them take you from me?"

Closing my eyes, I struggled with how to answer that and didn't want to look him in the face as I did. "Would you accept an answer of, I don't know? Petru saw you mark me, and they knew who you were. What I'd be asking is if they will let me go if they find us. In their eyes, I'm no longer the Omega they rescued from the North. I'm bonded to the heir of the Northern Army. If they were smart, I could see them using me against you, taking whatever advantage they could get to end this war."

"Do you honestly believe that?" Lucian asked, his tone surprised, drawing me to look at him. "I recognized the look in that Alpha's eyes because it's the way I look at you. There isn't a chance in hell that they would let you go that easily. If I were them, I'd kill me and then that would be the end of it. The heir to the Northern Army would be dead and they'd have their Omega back free of attachment."

"That would never be the end of it for me," I whispered. "There's no way I could let them kill you or allow you to kill them. As for going with them..." I paused, rubbing my face with my hands, growling in frustration. "Lucian, you and I are bonded. There's no way I could leave you. I realize you don't understand much about this side of Omegas, but once a bond is established, that connection is unlike anything else. Can't you feel it between us?"

"Of course I can feel it," Lucian snapped. "You are the literal representation of my heart living and breathing outside my body. I can feel your pain and uncertainty about this whole situation. You want them, that isn't a question. Your heart is tied to them just as your body is tied to mine, but what I *need* to know is if you ever see them again will you run to them or away with me."

Tears pricked at my eyes. "I don't know. Lucian, I don't know. Honestly, I have no idea what I'll do at that moment. There isn't a choice that doesn't leave me devastated one way or the other," I sobbed.

"Shh, Dani, it's okay," Lucian soothed, hugging me. "I'm sorry I pushed. You were being honest with me and I let my fear press you harder than was needed. We'll figure this out together if the time comes. Who knows, they may never find us."

Shaking my head, I sniffed. "No, if they're looking, nothing will stop them from getting to me. They are the best of the best and they promised to keep me safe."

"I guess we'll just have to wait and see then, but for now, we stick to my plan and head for the North. No matter what, my father needs to be removed before he kills everyone over a meaningless war," Lucian admitted.

Snuggling close, I pressed a kiss to Lucian's heart. For better or worse, I was his now, but that also made him mine, and I took that sort of thing seriously. Saving the North from General Rasvan's control was a mission I could support Lucian in. So that's what I planned to focus on, not the hollow space in my heart that six certain men seemed to fill unbeknownst to me.

Sorin

Standing on the banks of the Corpar River, I looked downstream where Danella had been swept away in the current moments ago. Petru had called for help the second he realized there was trouble, but it had been too late. The Northern bastard had used our Omega as a shield, making it impossible for Petru to get a shot off. Then he had the balls to fucking bite her, bonding them together. The rage that churned in me was of the likes I'd never experienced before. I wanted to rip off the Alpha's head with my bare hands for daring to touch Danella, let alone mark her.

How had things gone so wrong? Danella was supposed to be safe with us. There had been no indication that Commander Lucian would come looking for her. He'd been summoned back to Stalhold City to answer for the attack on the outpost. We'd purposely left enough power intact for them to use for communications which we cloned to gather once they left the outpost. I'd gotten word about a week ago about the assholes' orders.

So why hadn't he followed them? Could it be that this whole situation at the plant was simply to draw us out?

"Sorin," Petru called. "There's another body you should look at."

Turning to face my fellow teammate who'd been in charge of looking after our Omega. Petru was known for being even-tempered, hard to upset, and overly logical. The man I was looking at right now was anything but that. The fury I saw in his dark green eyes set them alight as if a fire was burning behind them, fueled by his anger. A muscle in his jaw ticked at the strain it was under being clenched so hard, just another tell of how badly he was blaming himself.

Reaching the spot he called me to, I found the body of a Southern soldier I knew well, Draza.

"What the fuck was he thinking?" Petru snarled. "Why would he turn against the South like this, and why pick this place? He doesn't know the first thing about power plants."

"You're right, but at one point, he'd been stationed here as a punishment while they were building," I shared. "If anyone would know of a situation that would draw us out into the open, this sack of shit would."

Petru's head snapped up to look at me. "Are you saying he helped that Northern prick set this all in motion? I assumed it was just bullshit to get me angry and give him an opening to run."

"That might be what Lucian told Draza, only the Commander didn't want us," I pointed out.

"Danella," Petru whispered. "All this was to get us out here so he could get to Danella. It makes sense. On base, she didn't go anywhere without one of us. Not to mention it was too highly guarded for a Northerner to sneak in, let alone sneak someone out. That's why he had the sedative. He knew and was prepared for her to resist."

"He drugged her?" I demanded, turning to look at the river again. "Fucking idiot, why choose the river if she was unable to help herself? Goddamn bastard is going to get her killed, and I'm going to rip him into pieces when I find him."

"She wasn't going to let him take her," Petru explained. "She also wouldn't let me shoot him, either."

Whipping my head back to look at him. "What?"

"She was begging him to let her go and just leave, that if he just left, I wouldn't shoot him. In fact, she stood in my way pleading for me to just let Lucian go," Petru shared. "Kept saying that Lucian was going to kill his father and end the war."

"Well, I guess we should ask him about that when we find them," I growled. "Let's head in. Clearly, these two were the only ones out here, so we just need Toma to fix the plant, and we can start the hunt."

"Where is Cris?" Petru asked as he trudged through the tall grass towards the plant.

"Should be just up here. I didn't want anyone sneaking up on us," I said before lifting two fingers and letting out a shrill whistle.

Seconds later, Cris' blond head popped up before he stood to see us approaching him. "What happened? Where's Dani?"

As our medic, I tried to keep him away from the action if I could, since he was invaluable to us. Not that he couldn't hold his own in a fight. He was as well trained as the rest of the unit. The difference was that no one could do his job if something happened to him.

"Seems we've been set up," I announced. "I'll explain once we know the plant isn't going to blow up and I can cover this once."

"Sorin," Cris snapped, shocking the shit out of me. "What the fuck happened to Dani?"

Petru walked over to his lover and gripped the Beta by the back of the neck and shook him slightly. "You don't ever speak to a superior officer like that. I don't care if we're family or not. We're on a mission, and that is not fucking acceptable. If he tells you he'll explain when we get to the others, then that's what he's gonna do. Now, let's go."

I wasn't sure if it was the fact Cris had never seen Petru like this or if he realized how badly he'd just fucked up just now. Either way, he gritted his teeth, jerked away from Petru, and headed for the plant.

"Tru, it's going to be easier to get her back if the team isn't pissed at each other," I commented. "I understand you feel responsible, but don't fucking take it out on the others just because they love you."

Petru glanced at me out of the corner of his eye and gave a sharp nod but didn't say anything. Guess it's better to say nothing at all than to rip someone a new asshole as he'd just done to Cris. We headed inside the power plant, walking along the metal gangplanks that spanned over the generators chugging away under us. The machinery drowned out the roar of the river and it unsettled me to be around so many things that could blow up if Toma wasn't as good at his job as he was. Cris beat us to the control room. He was sulking in the corner, arms crossed, refusing to look at Petru or me. There weren't many moments Cris showed he was the youngest of the unit; it had only happened twice before now.

While I respected the man's choice to be upset about the scolding he got, Petru hadn't been wrong. As I told Dani when I asked her to follow my commands, it was the difference between life and death. Soldiers didn't second-guess their commanding officer. If they did, their chances of living through the situation dropped immensely.

"Hey, where's my little firecracker?" Victor asked, peering past me for Dani.

"Is the plant secure?" I questioned.

"Two more seconds. It looks like they just disabled some of the security protocol," Toma called from the computer station he was working at. "Vic, I need you to flip that switch labeled auxiliary unit."

Victor turned to the control panel that was littered with buttons and switches. It took him a minute, but he found it. "You want me to flip it now?"

"Nooot, yeett," Toma said, drawing out the words as his fingers flew over the keyboard. "Okay, now."

Once the switch was flipped, everything inside the plant paused for a second then resumed like nothing had happened. Twirling in the station chair, Toma looked at the rest of us with a pleased smile clapping his hands. "Hey, now we're not gonna blow up."

"Good, now we have a bigger problem to deal with," I shared, causing the smile to drop from Toma's face as he stood. "Danella was taken."

Vic charged up to me, grabbed my jacket, and snarled in my face. "What did you just say?"

"Vic, I will give you two seconds to unhand me before I deal with the matter," I warned.

He let out an angry snarl and backed off. "My apologies, Major, but I thought you said our Omega was taken."

"That's correct," I said, tugging my jacket straight. "It would seem this whole situation was a ruse to get us off base and out here where she could be stolen right out from under our noses."

"How the fuck are you so calm?" Toma yelled as he chucked a flashlight across the space. "Why are you just standing there so calmly when we should be charging out of here after them? The plant's fine. We can go right this second, they couldn't have gotten far."

I glared at my unit, gritting my teeth, trying to keep from doing what I'd just admonished Petru for. "Do *not* mistake my calm exterior. I am livid that not only was Danella taken from us, but it was by none other than the fucking Commander Lucian."

At that information, I had all three of them harassing me with questions, demanding action, and accusing me of letting this happen. Turning on my heel, I walked calmly away, down the stairs and back out to the open land with my unit hot on my trail.

"What the hell, Sorin, you're just going to drop that on us and walk away?" Cris demanded.

Letting out a roar of my built-up frustration and anger, I turned to face them. "*Enough.*"

This had them all falling into silence.

"Since when has this been a democracy? Tell me. Have I suddenly been demoted, and I'm no longer the leader of this unit? Have you all lost your goddamn minds acting like this? No wonder we haven't won the war when losing an Omega seems to cripple one of the top elite units of the Southern Military," I raged. "If all of you will give me a fucking chance to explain things, then you might have answers to some of your questions."

The five men before me seemed properly cowed at my outburst

and I felt guilty as shit. This wasn't how I wanted to handle this, but they'd left me no choice except to put them in their place.

"The only way we're going to get Danella back, and we fucking will, is if we do this with a level head," I explained. "We're not dealing with an average Northern soldier here. No, this is the Commander himself who led the attack on the power plant. If we don't think this through and plan our attack, he will slip through our fingers."

Victor nodded and crossed his arms. "Okay, you made your fucking point. Now, will you tell us what the hell happened, Major?"

Coming from Vic, that was about as much respect as anyone hoped to get, so I took it as the win that it was. "I believe Petru is the better one to inform us of what happened since he was there."

Now the angry, judgmental eyes were turned on him, and he seemed to enjoy that about as much as I had.

"As we were searching our section, I sent Dani off toward the river knowing the chance of anyone hiding out there was slim. They wouldn't want to be trapped with the building in front and the river to the side. She was to radio me if there was any trouble," Petru shared in a tone as detached from the events as I'd ever heard him.

"I was on my way back from clearing my section when she signaled for help, and I hightailed it over. I wasn't fast enough, and I heard gunshots. When I came upon them, Lucian had Danella in his grasp using her as a shield and trying to get her to come with him. She wasn't in favor of that idea and tried to convince him to let her go and run. We exchanged words to no avail, and when he finally determined that Danella would not leave with him, he bit her, bonding them. I was so shocked I didn't know how to respond. He used that moment to set off a flashbang, disorienting me enough for him to jump into the river with Danella. It's my fault this happened. If there's anyone you should be mad at, it's me, not Sorin," Petru said, his whole body tense and ready to take whatever they threw at him.

"I'm sorry. Did you say he bonded her?" Toma questioned. "As in marked her for real as only an Alpha can with an Omega, that kind of bond?"

"Yes," Petru whispered.

No one spoke for a moment, digesting what that meant, until Victor broke the silence. "You said she tried to get him to leave…"

"Not like that," Petru cut in. "She wasn't turning on us, although she was unwilling to let me kill him. Kept saying that Lucian wanted to go back North and kill his father so he could take over the North and end the war."

"She believed him?" Victor spat. "No one should believe a word that lying sack of shit says."

Clearing my throat loudly, they all turned their attention to me. "You're missing something in all this. Danella spent three years living with this man, and in all our conversations with her, I've never heard her say he was cruel or mean to her. Yes, she was forced to sleep with him, but she told me they had rules. I wouldn't count it out of the realm of possibilities that she feels protective of him. You've seen the way she is with her two Omega friends. Danella is loyal to those she feels have earned it."

"So we don't kill him?" Cris asked, scratching his head. "Can we do that?"

"All I'm trying to say is that we need to be prepared for the fact that she might not let us kill him. If given a chance to come back to us, I believe she'd say yes. It didn't sound like she wanted to go with him at all. The major problem is they're now bonded," I reminded them.

Cris dropped to his knees, looking absolutely dejected. "Then there's nothing we can do. The law is clear on this. If she's bonded to him, then he is her pack and we can't claim her as long as he's still alive. Danella, as jaded and fierce as she is, won't let us kill him to free her. Guys, we've lost her."

"No, I refuse to believe that," Petru growled. "The fates gave her to us. She's ours, I know she is. Even just the week she spent with us felt like she belonged in our family and was the missing piece to the unit we've always been looking for. She can't be lost to us."

"The law—" Cris started.

"Fuck the goddamn law," Victor blurted. "When we get to her and give her the chance to choose for herself what she wants, then we'll figure out what to do. No one but the five of us knows about Lucian bonding to her. If the fucker will leave us the hell alone and kill off his old man, then I say more power to him. With the fucking war over no one's gonna give two shits about what happens with our Omega."

"What if she doesn't come back?" Toma murmured. "What if she chooses him? A connection like theirs, forged through the fires of survival, is strong, and now if they are bonded for real it will only make that connection even stronger."

Victor slammed his fist into Toma's shoulder, almost knocking the man off his feet. "I'm gonna need you to keep shit like that to yourself, fucker. You can think it all you want, but don't you utter a goddamn word of it where the fates or whoever fucking else can hear you. There is no way I'm gonna let anything keep me from getting to my Little Spark."

"Damn it, Vic, you don't need to break my fucking arm," Toma groaned, rubbing the spot he was hit. "How helpful will I be if I only have one arm to use?" Victor just grunted at the man and flipped him off.

"So what's the plan?" Petru asked. "That river runs fast. There's no telling how far they were swept downriver."

"My bet is Lucian will drag her out in the shallows a few miles down the way where it slows down. There's also a pretty dense forest in that area as well making for good coverage," I said, pulling the map out of my pack and kneeling to spread it on the ground. "The bad part of all this is the forest is fairly extensive and runs for miles."

"I could get some drones to cover the area," Toma offered.

Glancing up at him, I quirked a brow. "What exactly would you tell the drone team you're looking for?"

"Ah fuck," he swore, kicking a rock into the field. "Forgot we need to do this off-grid. If the brass finds out Lucian mother fucking Bakal is here, then they'll send out a whole strike team of men."

"Not that they would have a chance hunting them down. We're the only ones who can pull it off as it is," Victor pointed out. "Let's just tell the drone team we think someone from the attack on the plant might have snuck off into the forest and we could use some backup. This way, there are eyes on the area but nothing too suspicious. They'll also tell us first."

"That's a better plan, but I really want to keep this just between us," I countered. "The more people who know there's trouble, the more we need to lie or dodge questions. I don't want there to be more for us to combat with once we get back to base. Think long-term, men, because the moment that Omega is back in our care, I don't plan on her ever fucking leaving again."

Everyone mutters their agreement, nodding their heads at that.

"Do we take the Humvee?" Petru asked. "They'll be able to track our movements with that."

That had me thinking we needed the speed to catch up, but on the other hand, I certainly didn't want the higher-ups to know what was going on. "I say we go on foot. We know this land like the back of our hands and once we hit the forest we won't be able to use it. My plan is to call in and let them know the plant is safe and no longer in danger. However, we feel that the attack might be to test out our response time for another attack, and it might be wise to let us camp out at a distance to ensure nothing comes of it. That will give us a few days before we have more questions to answer about what's taking so long."

"What if Lucian is telling the truth and he wants to kill his father," Cris interjected. The guys glared at him like he was being a fool to believe anything that was said, but he ignored them to hold his gaze on me. "It's something we should consider, Major. If there is even the smallest glimmer of a chance this war could end with his help, I think it should at least be discussed."

The Beta made a fair point. If Lucian were indeed planning to take out his father, it would be worth a conversation. "I will make a call on that matter once I get a better handle on the situation as a whole. Danella comes first, then whatever else must be dealt with happens afterward."

Cristofor nodded, letting the matter drop as I folded the map and stood. "Alright, let's head back to the Humvee, get the supplies we need, and get a move on it. They already have a head start on us, so let's not waste daylight. We'll rest for the night and hit it hard at first light since we aren't equipped with gear for a night search."

Everyone fell in line as we jogged back to the Humvee, which took half the time since we didn't need to worry about stealth. With the ease of practice, we gathered what we could use, packed up, and headed out to find our Omega and bring her back home.

CHAPTER 35

Danella

Lucian didn't wait for full dark before we headed out. I got the sense that he felt like we had people on our heels, and waiting longer would put them closer to us. He packed up everything in silence and shouldered his pack before turning to me.

"Ready?" he asked.

"It's not like I had much to worry about," I commented. "Thanks for letting me have my knife and gun with ammo in it."

"You've proven that you obviously need them to keep out of trouble. I'm also fairly confident you won't shoot me now," Lucian reasoned as we headed out of the cave. "I'm gonna push us to cover a good bit of ground while we still have some light, but I'll try not to push you too hard."

Tying my hair back, I rolled my eyes. "Set whatever pace you want, Lucian. I'll keep up just fine."

Turning, he gripped my chin and caught my gaze. "This isn't a sprint, Dani. We will be on the move for days, and I don't want to burn either of us out. Reaching Northern territory means we'll be able to travel at a slower pace, but we're plotting a rebellion. Once word gets out about it, and it will, then we'll be on the run until this is over and done."

"I understand, Lucian. Believe me, I do. What I'm trying to tell you is I've been leading a rebellion against any authority trying to oppress Omegas since the day I learned I was one. Throw whatever you want at me, and I'll hold my own like I always have," I explained.

His gaze softened and his grip turned gentle as he leaned down to kiss me. "You're not fighting alone anymore, My Heart. I'll be right here by your side for as long as I'm alive."

Goddamn, could this man be a real smooth talker when he wanted to. This made it so much harder to hold any kind of grudge against him.

"Okay, enough with the mushy stuff," I said, ducking out of his hold. "Let's get going, we have a rebellion to start."

Lucian chuckled as he swiftly pressed a kiss to my cheek and jogged into the forest. I fought with the need to leave something here on the off chance the guys were coming for me. Giving in, I dropped my cap on the dirt and shifted it, so the bill pointed in our direction. Guilt and hope warred in my chest as I took off after Lucian, terrified if they actually found us and what might happen if they did.

Soon that worry fell away as Lucian hadn't been kidding about the pace he would set. My breathing was labored, and for a time, I could only focus on one foot in front of the other as it got darker. However, the difference in this daring escape was how much better equipped I was. The boots on my feet offered protection from the ground. The clothes kept me from getting scratched and cut up by tree branches, and the weapons hanging from my belt provided security. By the time it was fully dark, we'd traveled quite some distance and Lucian slackened to a quick walk. For me, it was almost a jog, but I kept up just like I promised I would. Finally, we stopped, and I slumped against a tree to gulp down water from the canteen he passed to me.

"How far are we trying to get tonight?" I asked between gulps.

"I'd like to keep pushing until we have to stop and rest for the day," Lucian answered as he stepped into my space, causing me to look up at him. Taking a moment to search my face, he tucked a loose bit of hair behind my ear, letting his hand smooth down my neck over the brand. Even his touch over his mark could make my pussy clench and my eyes flutter closed with the pleasure of it. "You've proven you can keep up, Dani, although I need to know if it's something you can sustain?"

That was the real question, wasn't it? Could I keep up at this pace for an unknown amount of time and distance, sleep and do it again, and again, and again...

"The only way I'll get stronger and for this to become easier isn't to back off. If I keep going, pushing myself a little more than I'm able, then my body will adjust. That's how training works, right? When I started training with the guys, everything hurt and I wanted nothing more than to just sleep. Each day I got up and did it again. Things got better, and the pain began to dissipate. This will be no different," I reasoned, packing away the canteen. "We have no idea how long it will take to get enough people to back you taking over the North. You vowed to make this world safe for me. Well, I vow to never slow you down or hold you back. I won't be a stumbling block to you."

Startling me, Lucian grabbed my throat and pushed me against the tree I was leaning on. "I don't ever want to hear you say shit like that about yourself ever again. Do you hear me?"

Shocked, I didn't speak, just stared at him with an open mouth.

"Answer me, Danella," Lucian barked out, the command forcing me into action.

I let out a squeak but answered. "Yes, I understand."

"My Heart, don't you realize that you're the one making all this happen? You could never make me stumble, because until I met you, I couldn't stand tall on my own. Cowed by fear of my father. If it weren't for you pushing me, forcing me to see outside my own small world, then I'd never have found the balls to do what needed to be done," Lucian stated, expression full of the emotions I was feeling through our bond.

His love and admiration for me were overwhelming, making me

utterly stunned I didn't see it before now. "You give me too much credit," I whispered. "I'm just a troublemaker who doesn't know how to keep her mouth shut or her opinions to herself."

"No, you're more than that," Lucian whispered against my lips. "You're a fucking queen, and I plan to put you on the throne next to me when this is all finished."

Grabbing his face, I closed the hairsbreadth of space between us and kissed him with all the passion I was receiving from him. All his emotions poured into me and at this point I couldn't tell who was feeling what. All I knew was I couldn't get enough of it. Dropping my hands, I scrambled to undo his pants, pulling a growl from him as I grasped his hard cock. Pre-cum was already leaking out of him as I smeared it over the head, giving me some lube to work with as I stroked him.

"My Heart, it isn't safe to do that here," he mumbled, his breath coming in quick pants.

"I have total faith you'll keep me safe," I whispered, dropping to my knees. "Let your Omega do as she wishes."

"Da—"

His words were cut off as I wrapped my mouth around him, taking him as deep as I could manage. With one hand on his thigh to keep me steady and the other holding the base of him, I got to work. Using everything I remembered the other Omegas talking about as we mended socks, I reveled in the sounds of pleasure coming from my Alpha. He reached a hand out to steady himself on the tree as I took his balls in hand, rolling them gently as I swirled my tongue around the head of his cock.

"Holy fuck," Lucian gasped. "Dani, if you keep doing that, I'm going to come."

Letting my mouth pop off him, I grinned as I peered up. "I believe that's the idea here."

"Please, let me make you feel good. Let me come inside you," Lucian pleaded.

"No, we don't have time for that," I teased, before swallowing him down once more.

The feral snarl that I elicited from him was everything, and I wanted to see if I could do it again. Sure enough, the same move had him shouting his pleasure to the world as his knot started to swell. Grasping it in both hands, I squeezed as hard as I could as he came shooting his cum into my mouth, which I easily swallowed down. I took satisfaction in knowing it occurred because of my doing, that I'd made him come. Taking a moment to tuck him back in his pants, I then wiped my mouth with the back of my sleeve.

Lucian pulled me to my feet and kissed me thoroughly. "My Heart, you did not need to do that for me. Every time I receive pleasure I want you to experience it as well."

"Believe me, Lucian, I enjoyed the hell out of that," I shared, giving him a swift kiss. "I have to be honest, I wasn't sure it was going to be all that enjoyable after hearing the others talk about it, but it was quite satisfying."

"If you didn't think you'd like doing that for me, then why did you do it?" he asked, perplexed.

I shrugged. "I wanted to see what it would be like when I decided to do it and how I wanted to. It's rather amazing how different things are when you call the shots."

Lucian let out a huff of laughter. "Dani, if that's you calling the shots, then by all means, My Heart. Call as many shots as you like because that was amazing."

Giving him a wink and another quick kiss, I pushed him back. "Shall we keep pushing on?"

"I'm not sure I have the strength after you sucked it right out of me," Lucian said dramatically as he swung the pack onto his back. "But as any good soldier, I'll press on."

"What a martyr you are," I commented as I followed after him. "At least we have a decent amount of light from the moon to see by."

"We're lucky it's not closer to the new moon. It would have made getting through the woods ten times harder. Once we're back in the Northern territory, it will be easier. I know that terrain like the back of my hand," Lucian said as we trudged on.

My feet ached, and my calf muscles burned as we entered a more hilly area. There was a slight glow on the horizon making the promise that the night was soon to be over and the sun was making its journey. I hated to admit it, but I might have pushed myself too hard to keep up when I should have just asked to slow down. Even though I'd tried to hide my discomfort from Lucian through our bond, I could tell he knew. Especially with the way he kept casting glances at me, along with how much slower he was moving.

"I don't see any caves for us to hide in for the day, but there is some dense brush over here we should be able to make a nest of sorts in. It will keep us hidden enough and cover our scent so as to not alarm the animals. The less we can disturb the area, the less attention we draw," he explained after I gave him a questioning look.

At this point, I didn't care; I only wanted a place to curl up and pass out. There was a gap in the bushes like an animal had also thought of the same idea. Lucian ventured in first, army crawling his way in, then whistled for me to join him. Shoving the pack ahead of me, I slithered along the ground and was pleased to find an animal had made a hollow of sorts for us to rest in. Lucian shoved the pack off to the side and pulled me to lay on him as if he were my bed.

"Sleep. I'll keep watch," Lucian whispered.

Nuzzling into his neck, I let out a sigh. "Wake me in a few hours so you can sleep."

"I'll be fine, My Heart. We soldiers have learned to live off little sleep and are used to taking quick naps where possible. So don't worry your pretty head about it," Lucian instructed.

I wanted to argue to tell him that I would stand watch, but the second he pulled my hair loose and started to massage my head, I lost the will to fight. Letting out a contented little moan, I was out before I even realized it.

~

"Dani, we need to move. Now," Lucian said urgently, snapping me out of the dreamless sleep I'd been in.

My eyes sprang open, and it took me a moment to figure out

what was going on and where I was. Seeing the branches of the leafy bush surrounding us, it all came flooding back. Not bothering to hide our exit, Lucian grabbed me around the waist with an arm and surged out of the brush. Fighting to get free from the twigs and thorns stalled him, but the second he was clear, he hauled ass and ran. I figured he would put me down but that wasn't the case. He just adjusted me so I could cling to him on his back like a monkey and held on.

Having no idea what set this reaction into motion, I looked around the forest but couldn't hear a damn thing with how loud Lucian was. As much as I wanted to ask him what the hell had set him off, I didn't want to speak if we needed to be quiet. The sun was halfway up in the sky so I'd managed to get a few hours of sleep. Still, we were nowhere close to it being nightfall. Not that I wasn't awake and alert with the adrenaline pumping through my veins right.

Then the crack of a gun and a bullet whizzing by us, smacked into a tree causing a burst of bark as to where it landed, It immediately had me ducking. Lucian shifted, heading to the left, weaving through the dense grove of trees to give us cover. My gaze searched the forest to figure out who the fuck was shooting at us because it wouldn't be my guys... at least, I hoped to god it wasn't. Whoever it was had skill hiding, but when the next shot came, I caught a glimpse of the muzzle flash.

"You better not be my unit, or I'm gonna get in so much trouble," I muttered as I grabbed the gun out of Lucian's holster and aimed. Letting off two shots, one where I saw the flash and another slightly more to the right just in case they'd started to move to follow us.

There was a crash like something, or someone had fallen, making Lucian duck behind a large tree and kneel. Snatching the gun out of my hand, he motioned for me to stay put and remain quiet. Nodding, I pulled my own gun free and sat with my back pressed to the trees trying to calm my breaths and listen. There was never just one soldier. The South functioned in units of six to ten soldiers per group, if not more. Either we were dealing with a rogue gunman or more people were lurking in the woods.

Peeking around the tree, I attempted to see if I could track Lucian except the forest fell silent. *So the man could move through the woods without sounding like an elephant.* A twig snapped off to the left, followed by the sound of shifting soil to the right. Either Lucian was closing in, or I was trapped between two people I did not want to find me. Looking up, I spotted a branch hanging low enough that I should be able to grab onto it. Shoving my gun back in the holster, I stood, took a few steps back and ran at the tree. Making it partway up the trunk got me close enough to grab the branch.

Using all my tired arms could give me, I managed to pull myself up, wiggling until I got my foot hooked to provide me with more stability. Once fully seated, I climbed up higher into the branches letting the leaves shield me from sight. I wasn't totally hidden, but I remembered something Lucian had told me once. He'd trained all his men to always glance up because nine times out of ten, that was something the average person never did. Letting people slip by. Holding my breath, I retrieved my gun once more and waited. Sure enough, two men appeared from either side dressed in Northern colors, not Southern like I'd suspected.

"Where the fuck did he go?" one asked in a harsh whisper.

"What I want to know is who that woman with him was," the other countered. "We were told he'd be alone, so he'd be easy to take down on enemy territory."

"Whoever she is, she's one hell of a shot hitting Havel like that with a handgun," the first soldier muttered. "Do you think that's why he turned on his own people, a woman?"

"What fuck does it matter? A traitor is a traitor, and if we can use his corpse here in Southern territory to spur our soldiers to victory, then what does it matter who the bitch is?" the second man spat.

The more these two idiots kept talking, the deeper my frown grew. *Why the hell would they think Lucian turned on his people?* I'd never met a person more committed to the North. Well, maybe that twat Omega Coral from the breeder house could give him a run for his money. Regardless, Lucian would never be the one to betray his own.

"He couldn't have gotten far, not with a woman weighing him down. Let's circle back and see if we can trap him before those Southern soldiers who've been tracking us catch up."

The fact they had soldiers tracking them didn't bode well for us, since they'd clearly been following us. This needed to be handled, and fast, before it turned into something worse like getting us caught or killed. Shifting my position, I took a deep calming breath and ran through everything Petru had taught me. There was a lot we still needed to cover, but I was a decent shot with a still-standing target like these two. What kept playing through my head was hearing him tell me that to pull the trigger was to take a life.

Was I willing to bear that burden for the rest of my life? Yes.

Is this the only answer to this problem? No, but it was the simplest one that would keep it from biting us in the ass later.

With one more deep breath in, I took aim and just as they started to walk away, I shot the man on the right. Then I instantly shifted to do the same for the man on the left. I waited for the feeling of regret, shame, or sadness at taking their lives, yet nothing happened. Another shot reverberated through the quiet, which I assumed was Lucian taking out the third man they'd said I'd wounded. If they'd been honest, which having no reason to lie, I assumed they were. The danger was now passed. Save for the matter of the Southern soldiers heading this way.

"Dani," a voice whispered.

Cocking my head, I stayed silent until I saw Lucian appear kneeling by the men to check to see if they were alive or not.

"Dani, it's safe. You can come out now," Lucian reassured.

At the sound of my climbing down, his head snapped up, spotting me with surprise on his face. Getting to the last branch, I crouched and dropped to the ground, lessening the impact on my feet.

"Did you deal with these two?" he asked, keeping his voice low as he started to search their bodies.

"Why would they think you deserted the North?" I questioned.

Lucian froze for a second, then took the extra ammo and a few other supplies we needed. The second man had a pack, so I yanked that off him and grabbed whatever I could off his body as well.

"My father ordered me home right after the massacre at the outpost. He wanted to hold me responsible for it, and I decided to ignore the summons to find you," Lucian informed me. "It's been about a week, and I still haven't followed that direct order."

"Why would your father blame you for what happened?" I demanded, my voice growing louder with my irritation. "You had nothing to do with it. Fuck, you weren't even there."

"There might be a few reasons for that, one being that he's a sadistic bastard who hasn't had the opportunity to beat up and threaten his son in a while. It's been years since I've seen him, and he probably fears that I might forget who holds the end of my leash," Lucian answered bitterly. "He's right to be worried, although the problem is he's realized it too late. That and it's been mentioned that these attacks on our border outposts might not be as random as they'd like us to think they are."

That last comment had me reeling back. "I'm sorry, what?"

"Babaka said with her dying breath that I needed to look at this differently, and my father might be working with someone in the South," Lucian explained, rising to his feet. "The more I think about it and see what's happened, it makes sense. Whenever we think we're going to lose the battle and there's no reason to keep fighting, something stokes that anger back into an inferno."

"Do you know what that will do if anyone else realizes that theory?" I snapped. "Lucian, he just sent people to kill you because you didn't follow an order. The hell that will break loose when he discovers that you not only are turning against him but plan to overthrow him will be monumental."

Shouldering his pack, Lucian took a deep breath. "Yes, I'm incredibly aware of how incredibly fucking pissed my father will be. This won't be the last time we see a hit squad out for me, either. The biggest blessing is he has no idea about you, and with these men dead, he won't for a while longer."

"That's not all we have to worry about..." I shared, pausing to look him in the eye. "Southern soldiers were tracking these three, and they mentioned they weren't far behind them."

"Fuck, we won't be able to rest any longer. We need to be on the move," Lucian announced, telling me what I had already assumed.

Nodding, I adjusted the pack and motioned for him to lead the way. "Then let's get the hell outta here."

CHAPTER 36

Victor

We'd assumed Lucian was working alone, but that was until we stumbled upon a group of Northern soldiers. Sorin decided that instead of killing them, we would follow the men. Keep out of sight, until we could determine if they were working with Lucian or possibly had another mission. After we'd seen them catch the trail of Lucian and Dani, we figured they were working together but must have gotten separated. The three men seemed to have a good handle on tracking the pair, so we let them do the hard work while maintaining our distance.

Sometime in the night, they must have figured out they were being followed since they'd given us the slip. Realizing we couldn't catch up since we needed to rest for a short time gave them a bit of a lead. These lunkheads, though, weren't as good at covering their tracks as the other two, so we weren't worried about picking up their trail again. Tracking anything in the dark was hard, but these guys were like a herd of cattle paving the way for us.

"I think it would be wise to take another quick break to eat and drink before we catch up with them. Seems they're also gaining on Lucian and Dani, so I want us to be ready for anything," Sorin instructed as we came upon a small river.

We dropped in a heap on the ground, happy to rest for a few

minutes. Last night I think I'd managed about three hours of sleep before the call to move out. Grabbing my water and a power bar out of my pack, I shoved the whole thing in my mouth, using the water to soften it.

"How is Lucian moving so fast?" Toma questioned. "There's no way he could be this familiar with our territory."

"I wouldn't be so sure," Petru countered. "He knew it well enough to get all the way to that power plant undetected."

"Yeah, but he had help," Toma reasoned.

Cris settled next to Toma and grabbed his water bottle out of the Alpha's hands. "He doesn't now, and he's moving through these woods like he's been in them hundreds of times. Dani wouldn't be able to tell him where to go, so it's him leading the charge."

"Whose side are you on?" Toma muttered, grabbing back his water.

"Look, I can dislike the guy and still be impressed with his skills," Cris answered with a shrug. "Just like you can admire a deadly weapon, I see his value as a soldier. Honestly, I'm glad to see he's a worthy opponent, which means we didn't fail her as badly as we all believe we did."

"When you put it that way..." Toma grumbled but didn't finish the sentence.

Flopping on my back, I looked up at the sky through the trees, watching the wisps of clouds pass by. As much as I wanted to charge forward and snatch our Omega out of his grasp, we weren't just dealing with one guy now. If three were looking to meet up with them, there's bound to be others. We needed to find a way to take the men out and get Dani without her being in the middle. Last thing we needed was for her to get hurt during the rescue. What kind of message would that send to my Little Spark?

Gunshots echoed through the forest, and I was on my feet faster than the others. Not bothering to shoulder my pack since all I needed was my gun in hand. If those bastards laid a finger on her, I would rip it off and shove it down their throat. No one fucked with what was mine, and that sassy Omega was *ours*. Branches whipped me in the face, but it didn't slow me down as I ran. What did slow me down was the dead body hidden under a bush I tripped over. It sent me spluttering into the dirt as leaves flew into my face.

Shoving to my feet, I turned and found the body of a Northern soldier with a shoulder wound and a headshot. It looked as if someone tagged him in the shoulder and then circled back to finish him off. Taking a closer look, I found that the body had been searched. Anything that had been in his pack or pockets was now gone. *Maybe Lucian wasn't working with these thugs after all.* The only reason I would take shit off a dead body is because I wasn't sure when I'd be able to restock. That or it could just be what the Northerners do since they're so poor. Either way, I was beginning to look at this a little differently.

"Two bodies over here," Sorin called.

Grabbing my gun, I hurried off in the direction of his voice. "I've found another one back there as well." I shared when I approached the others.

"Seems like we might've read the situation wrong," Petru interjected from where he squatted next to the bodies. "These shots were made from above with the intent to kill."

Looking up at the giant oak tree they were lying under, I guessed who might have done the deed. If my Little Spark killed these men, then there must have been a damn good reason for it. I know how Petru taught the soldiers he trained, and he wouldn't have encouraged taking a life unless it was necessary.

"So now the question is...why the fuck are they hunting Lucian?" I murmured.

"Last we'd intercepted was that the commander had been summoned back to Stalhold City to report to the general," Sorin shared. "Clearly, he didn't do that if he's here looking for Dani, and that makes me think maybe General Rasvan might consider that to be treason."

"So he'd just kill Lucian?" Cris asked.

The Beta always seemed to find a way to keep seeing the world as a place where people acted rationally. General Rasvan has never been a man I would consider acting within reason.

"That bastard has more children than anyone alive," I spat. "He can just pick another one of his brood to take over."

"Yeah, but he's trained the commander since he was a kid. Is it that easy to just switch him out?" Toma countered. "We all know his firstborn son ran away, which is when he started to mold Lucian into the perfect monster."

"Clearly something's changed, and if that's the case, then what he was telling Dani about killing his father might have been the truth," Cris said, giving each of us a challenging look. "I think it's time we start wrapping our heads around the idea that Commander Lucian is trying to end this war."

"Wouldn't that just be a miracle," I muttered. "Next, you're going to tell me we should help him do it." When no one said anything, I looked up at the others to find them staring at me like I'd just given them a brilliant idea. "Hey now, that wasn't supposed to be anything other than sarcasm. There's no way we could trust a man like him to keep his word about shit. We'd believe him and walk right into the lion's den. What better way to hurt the Southern army than to take out a group of their best people? This could be his plan to get revenge on us for destroying the outpost."

Petru stood and shouldered his rifle. "I suppose there's only one way to find out, and that would be to talk to the man."

"Oh, I want to do more than talk to him after stealing Dani like that," Sorin reminded. "However, I am going to order that no one is to kill Lucian, and if we can take him down without shooting him, I'd prefer it."

"Yes, sir," we all said in unison, acknowledging the order.

Cris tossed my pack at me, and I shouldered it nodding in appreciation. Knowing we weren't far behind them, I took off at a quick pace; the thrill of the hunt coursing through my veins. The others wouldn't care that I took off ahead since they knew I was one of the best trackers out of all of us. Petru and Sorin were stiff competition, but anytime we had a friendly challenge, I won. It's true I didn't get along with people well outside of this unit, and that's because they always felt the need to force me into compliance with the rules. That's not to say I didn't know and respect the laws of the Southern military. Nevertheless, many times in the heat of battle, those rules hindered me from being able to help my fellow soldiers.

Sorin knew that I wasn't that far off even if I split off from the group. If they needed me, I was within shouting or whistling distance. I had an easier time tracking when I didn't have them getting in my way. Halting, I dropped to a knee and spotted a footprint that could only be from my Little Spark. The other following after it was larger and told me I was on their trail. Cupping my hands around my mouth, I let out a bird call guiding them towards me. The sound could be heard all through the forest, but I changed the inflection at the end to ensure they knew it was me. I waited for a second and got an answering call back, giving me the freedom to keep moving.

It was then I decided I was going to break the agreement Sorin and I had about staying close enough to call. Dani was close, and I didn't plan on letting that woman slip further from me. Making sure the straps on my pack were tight, I shot off following the trail. Each step getting me closer to our Omega. Never in my fucking life did I think I'd be that Alpha who got his knot in a twist over a woman, although my Little Spark wasn't just *some* woman, she was the perfect woman. Petru had been right when he said the fates brought her to us, for I couldn't see another Omega crashing into our lives and showing us just what we'd been missing. The possessiveness and protectiveness I felt toward her were overwhelming, and I didn't know what to do about it except surrender. The moment I could, I'd be putting my mark on her so she'd never be lost to me again.

Sliding to a stop, I froze, ears straining, muscles tensing. I could feel eyes on me and the hairs on the back of my neck rising at the danger. "Lucian," I bellowed. "You made one big ass fucking mistake taking something that's mine to protect. If I don't see my Little Spark in three seconds, I'm going to hunt you down and make sure you understand just how fucked you truly are."

Silence filled the space. Not even the animals moved as I waited for his next move. The snap of a twig to my right had me squaring up, gun in hand, finger on the trigger and ready to act in a second. Not being as good as Petru when it came to shooting from a relaxed state, I kept my body alert.

"One," I called out while scanning the forest. "Two."

There was movement further to the right, almost putting them behind me, but there was another flash of someone to the left. *What game were they playing at? Why not come out?* Once the others got here, there would be no winning. Was this a test of some kind? Wait—what if Lucian gave her an order, and she's ignoring it but unwilling to show herself until the last second?

"Remember you chose this, *Commander*," I taunted, before shifting my grip and grabbing a smoke bomb from my belt. This one had a toxin in it that would make anyone who hadn't built up a tolerance start coughing and make their eyes water. It was a bitch and a half to master surviving the damn thing with no side effects, but I damn well did. Pulling the pin, I rolled the smoke bomb a little ways from me and waited for it to blast, sending the smoke everywhere.

Crouching as I reached the end of my silent countdown, not wanting to be an easily visible target if he started shooting. There was a sound that seemed to come from above, so I glanced up into the trees. Sure as shit, there was Dani, leaping like a monkey on her way over to me. Everything in me wanted to shout out, telling her to stay away from me so she didn't get hit with the smoke. It was too late, and the blast occurred, making the ground rattle and trees sway in the concussion of sound and energy. The blast helped spread the smoke and the second it started to fill the air, I was up and running for Dani.

She looked furious, but I wasn't sure what exactly she was mad about... Was it that I threatened her Alpha, or the fact that we showed up at all? Something caught her attention behind me, making her cry out and hurl herself out of the tree right at me. Her body slammed into mine, sending us both crashing to the ground. A second later, I heard the crack of gunfire and a bullet whizzed overhead, telling me I was lucky to be alive.

"Victor, you need to leave," Dani whispered, fear flickering in her eyes. "Please, Vicky, I need to know that you're all okay and alive if I'm going to accept never seeing you again."

That had my brow furrowing. "Why the fuck wouldn't you see me? Little Spark, I'm right fucking here with you sitting right on top of me."

"We...Lucian...I," she stumbled, unsure how or what to say. Growling, she shook her head as if clearing her mind and gave me a serious look. "Lucian marked me. We are bonded and now I'm the Omega to Commander Lucian of the Northern Army."

Ah. This explained her actions. "Little Spark, I don't give a flying fuck whose mark you carry. I vowed to look after you and keep you safe, which is what I'm trying to do right now."

"Danella!" a man called out, then started hacking up a lung as the smoke hit him.

That same smoke was just starting to waft around us, so I rolled us over, scooped Dani up, and took off the way I'd come. The effects of the smoke would stick with him for a solid ten to fifteen minutes giving me more than enough time to get her the hell out of the danger zone.

"Wait, Victor, we need to go back," Dani demanded, thrashing in my hold trying to kick and punch me. "Did you put poison in that smoke bomb?"

"There's a toxin, but it won't kill him," I admitted.

"It's burning him, his eyes," Dani choked out. "I can feel it, the pain he's in right now. We have to go back."

My steps faltered. "You can feel what he feels?"

"Yes, that's part of the bond, and right now, whatever toxin you used is making it so he can't breathe or even see," Dany explained. "Promise me that it won't kill him. I don't want to experience that."

Fuck, fuck, fuck, there goes the plan of just killing him to make the problem go away. I could never do something like that, knowing Dani would feel his pain as well as his death. That's not something anyone should have to live through. Quickly as I could so I didn't drop her, I slapped the comm button to speak to the others.

"Guys, I have Danella and heading back your way," I informed them. "One more thing...Dani can feel everything Lucian does."

That would be enough information to keep them from doing something stupid. I tapped the comm so I could hear.

"Petru, tell me you heard that," Sorin snapped.

"Yes, sir, I'm making an about-face and heading back to you," Petru answered, making me breathe a sigh of relief.

Crashing through a thicket of trees, I wrapped my body around her best I could to shield her from the branches. Once through, I spotted Cris, who I'm assuming was waiting on standby out of the fray, just in case she'd been hurt.

"Bring her here," Cris ordered.

Usually I'd be giving him shit about ordering a superior officer around, but I didn't even have the chance before he ripped Dani out of my arms. I watched as he hugged her to him so tightly she squirmed a little.

"Cris...can't....breathe," she croaked out.

He released his hold instantly to pull her away from him so he could scan a critical eye over her body. I couldn't see anything wrong, but I wasn't the medic, now was I?

"Are you hurt? We saw the other soldiers dead, and it made me so scared something happened to you," Cris blurted as he ran his hands down her arms then her legs.

She flinched and giggled when he got to her ribs. "Cris, I'm fine, I promise. No injuries at all, unless you count sore muscles."

I was about to rescue her from the Beta, except I caught the movement out of the corner of my eye, giving me a chance to brace myself before Lucian came barreling into me. A fist slammed into my face pissing me the fuck off. With a growl, I shoved him off me and got my feet, only to leap at him and slam him to the dirt. We wrestled, landing blows wherever we could land them. My fist connected with his shoulder which caused my hand to smart at the impact on bone. Swinging my elbow up, I clipped him in the jaw just as he wedged a knee between us and shoved me off him.

Rolling to my fell into a ready stance, I found Sorin was already in the thick of it. He had the man in a secure wrestling hold, locking his arms and legs while applying large amounts of force to his neck.

"Calm the fuck down so I don't need to beat your ass and put Dani through that pain."

Sorin's words had Lucian halting instantly. "What?"

"Do you know anything about what you've done?" Cris snarled. That shocked the shit out of me. "How could you choose to force something on her like that without even understanding what the hell you were doing?"

Anger, defiance, and hurt warred on Lucian's face at the accusations Cris was throwing his way. Sorin flipped the Northern Alpha over, face in the dirt, and used the cuffs to secure his hands. When he was contained, Toma helped Sorin sit the man up before removing all his weapons. The number they found on him was fucking impressive. There was more than I could manage to hide, making me curious as to how he did it. If he managed to live through this conversation then I'd ask. Until then I just planned to make sure he didn't cause more fucking trouble before we could get a handle on what was going on.

CHAPTER 37
Danella

Watching them tie Lucian up had my heart in my throat—but I kept silent. They didn't know what was truly happening and were acting on the fact that I'd been stolen from them. If I was going to have any chance to explain anything, they needed to feel I was safe. For the moment, at least. Sorin squatted in front of Lucian sizing the man up while Victor stood behind his leader, arms crossed, with a dark expression only amplified by the blood seeping from a wound on his cheek.

"Commander Lucian, seems we finally get the chance to meet one another," Sorin commented.

Lucian spat at the other Alpha landing a wad of spit on Sorin's upper cheek almost to the point it was in his eye. If it were me, I would have lost my shit and pummeled Lucian, but instead, he calmly wiped his face clean with the back of his sleeve.

"It's not nice to try and provoke me when we both know hurting you will hurt Dani," Sorin pointed out. "Truthfully, it's the only reason you're still alive. Trust and believe when I tell you none of us would lose any sleep over killing you right here, right now. However...it seems we're at an impasse since you marked an Omega that doesn't belong to you."

"She's always belonged to me," Lucian shot back. "I've been her Alpha since the day she stepped foot on Asturg soil."

"Errr, wrong answer, asshole," Victor retorted. "Just because you fucking branded her doesn't mean she was yours. We all know she ran away from you the second she saw the chance to make it happen. Now, why would she do that if she was yours as you so claim?"

This conversation was going nowhere if I didn't step in, but when I tried to walk over to them, Petru stepped in front of me. "No, Wildflower, you will stay right here."

"Tru, they're going to do nothing except fight and argue over the same things in a never-ending loop," I reasoned. "Let me help smooth things over. You all need to know what's really going on."

Petru's green eyes softened as he cupped my cheek. "Nothing else matters right now until we make it clear you're coming home with us. For that to happen, those three need to figure out where they stand in the pecking order, if you will."

"How can I go home with you if I'm bonded to him?" I questioned, brow furrowing. "You can't undo a bond once it's been made."

Petru pulled me into a hug resting his head on mine. "We aren't letting you go, Danella. The fates brought you into our lives, and that's where you belong, with us. Trust that we will find a way, Wildflower."

I had no idea how they could possibly find a way to make things work between us. Yet the soothing sound of Petru's steady heartbeat, combined with his sweet earthy scent of thyme and bergamot, had me relaxing into him. My body had taken a toll over the past two days and seemed to be sapping all the energy from me. Then again, I'd been running on adrenaline since Lucian abruptly woke me up. As it drained away, knowing I was safe here with them, I felt so tired and mentally exhausted. Another body came up behind me and joined in on this hug. The bright orange fragrance told me it was Toma as he nuzzled into my neck, the opposite side of Lucian's mark.

"Are you okay? To be clear, I'm not asking if you're hurt," Toma murmured.

How did I even begin to answer that question?

"I don't know," I whispered. "Part of me knew you'd come for me, though the other rational side knows it will be impossible for me to stay. I'm bonded to the heir of North Asturg, the son of General Rasvan, a tyrant by all accounts. The South would never allow me to be here if they knew."

"Did you forget that Sorin is the heir to South Asturg? We aren't without our own power and influence in the world," Toma countered. "As Tru said, trust in us, and we will find a way. Because if the past two days are any proof of how much we need you, losing you would cripple the unit for good."

Lifting my head, I stared back at Toma, seeing the truth in his eyes. "What happened?"

The men holding me pulled back to give me room as Toma pointed to Cristofor. "Ask him."

"Cris?" I ventured, worried that something awful had happened.

Cris dropped his gaze and shoved his hands in his pockets. "To be clear, I'm not proud of how I acted, but I would do it again." Pausing, he lifted his gaze to mine. "I lost my temper and bitched Sorin out for letting you get taken. In my defense, he didn't tell us what was happening when we noticed you weren't with Tru. He forced us to wait and ensure the plant was out of danger before admitting that you'd been taken. My fear and anger got the better of me. However, I couldn't just stand by when you were missing."

Pulling away from the other two, I wrapped my arms around Cris' neck and kissed him. He was a bit surprised. Yet, it only took him a moment before he kissed me back, tugging my body against his. I was enveloped in the essence that was Cristofor, earthy patchouli with the freshness of spruce. In the back of my mind, I realized I didn't hesitate to seek out this attention from Cris. As a bonded Omega, I shouldn't feel the way I do with all of them. Everything about this moment felt right, as if they'd always been with me. Was this realization hitting me because I was now bonded and understood what that felt like?

A snarling roar pulled me out of the moment and had me jerking away from Cris, even though he refused to let me go. "No, Dani, you have every right to kiss me if you want to, no matter what that bastard thinks."

I blinked at him for a moment. Surprised to hear him, of all people saying that.

"See what happens when you leave us," Victor pointed out. "The kid up and gets a mouth on him and a stubborn streak a mile wide. Kinda proud of him. However, he needed to put those balls of his to good use and speak his mind."

Twisting, so Cris' arms were wrapped around my waist, holding me to his chest as I took in the rest of my unit. Lucian was fighting against Sorin's hold to get to me, but Sorin wasn't a man you could push around. He was built like a boulder and knew how to put it to good use.

"Get your fucking hands off my Omega," Lucian barked out.

I flinched at the order. Even though it wasn't directed at me, I still got slapped with the energy of it.

"Shut your goddamn mouth before I break your jaw," Victor ordered, raising a fist in warning. "You do anything to hurt her, so help me God, I will bury you alive and let you suffocate slowly so you can think about what you did."

Lucian scoffed. "Yeah, I don't think so. You'd never put her through that. There's no way you could protect her from doing something like that to me."

"I wouldn't be so confident about that," Toma interjected. "It wouldn't be the first time we've had to help a bonded Omega when one of her unit members is dying on the battlefield. We can give her medication to block her ability to feel you suffer."

Fear flooded me at the mention of other Omegas having to experience that with their pack. I hadn't even considered what it would mean to be part of a unit that was sent to the heart of battle more often than not. Just the thought of being bonded to all of them and having to suffer a traumatic death or injury would be horrifying.

"Dani," Lucian called out to me. "My Heart, I need you to take a deep breath for me. You're starting to hyperventilate."

Pulling out of Cris' hold, I stumbled away shaking my head. Oh God, I couldn't do this. There's no way I could put myself in that kind of situation. I'd worked for so long to keep my feelings close to my chest, not giving my heart to anyone in this godforsaken country. Then suddenly, after two weeks, these men have wriggled their way past my defenses and made me hope again.

"Danella," Sorin barked as he appeared before me. "Look at me."

I shook my head, knowing if I gave in and did what he asked, I wouldn't be able to deny the truth.

His hand shot out and gripped my chin tightly sending a spark of pain through my body, clearing some of the panic. The second my eyes locked onto his chocolate-colored ones, I was trapped. His hold on me was no longer just physical, as I admitted that these men were important to me. Lucian, trying to take me away from them and questioning whether they would come for me, had already started the cracks in the fortress I'd built around my heart. Add in the mental shift of being bonded to an Alpha, understanding what that connection truly is and how precious it was—left me totally screwed.

"I...I can't," I whispered, my voice raw from holding back everything I was feeling. "I can't let myself feel that much, Sorin. If I let you in, we become a pack, and I lose one of you..." I had to swallow back the tears before they spilled out of me. "You should have just let me go. Then told everyone I died in the river and allowed us to disappear."

"Dani-girl, what did I tell you before we left on this mission?" Sorin asked, his voice so gentle and patient.

"To follow your orders," I answered.

Sorin stepped closer shifting his hand from my chin to rest around my neck, his thumb stroking my pulse point. "Yes, that is one of the things I said. More specifically, what did I promise you?"

A single tear rolled down my cheek as I cleared my throat. "That you would protect me, never betray me, and always find me when I needed you."

"Don't let me fail you now by making me turn my back on you," Sorin begged. "Give me, give *us*, a chance to figure this out. I refuse to believe there's no hope, because there will never be another Omega who could hold a candle to what you mean to us."

Now the tears refused to be held back. Sorin reached down and picked me up like I was a child, cradling me close to his chest as I buried my face in his neck. Here we were in the middle of the forest, secluded from the world and all that was happening around us. For just this moment, I was simply an Omega who desperately needed comfort from one of her Alphas. The others joined in the hug shortly after, wrapping me up in the warmth and security of a pack. Something I never realized how much I needed after spending so much time fighting alone. The security in knowing I could crumble and that others would protect me when I couldn't protect myself was priceless.

A trickle of understanding and resignation reached me from Lucian. Somehow in my panic, I'd blocked his emotions out of my mind. Yet now that it had subsided I reached out to our bond. The second he felt me reaching out to him, he sent waves of love and comfort my way. The feeling of him desperately wanting to hold, kiss, and comfort me but wasn't able to due to the restraints had me sitting up to look in his direction.

There he stood, hands cuffed behind his back, a fat lip, and clothes covered in dirt; but all that mattered to him right now was me. Slowly he approached but paused when Sorin turned his attention towards Lucian.

"Please, I just *need* to know she's alright," Lucian explained.

"Can't you feel that from where you are?" Petru questioned, eyeing him suspiciously.

Lucian gave the man a patronizing look. "Of course I can, but are you telling me you wouldn't want to hold her if you were in my place? There is a difference between mentally knowing she's okay and physically ensuring that's the truth. Dani is quite skilled at hiding her emotions when she wants to."

"Makes you wonder why she needed such a skill," Petru quipped but walked over to him. "Just so we're on the same page, I'm the best marksman in the whole Southern military. One step out of line, and I won't hesitate to drop you this time."

"Even if that will hurt her?" Lucian challenged.

"That pain would be momentary. Being ripped away from us would hurt for a lifetime. To me, it seems the odds are in my favor on that matter," Petru explained, cutting the cuffs off him. "Whether or not she will forgive me is another matter entirely, although I have faith we'd work through it."

Sorin nuzzled under my ear and purred, steering my attention to him. "Remember, you always have a choice, Dani-girl. Your life, your body, your decisions. Whatever those may be, we will always support you. Unless that choice puts you in danger, then we might need to talk about it."

That had me smiling as I pressed a kiss to his lips. "*Might* need to talk? Yeah, pretty sure I know how that's going to go, but I hear you."

Another quick kiss and a disgruntled sigh later, he set me down. I squeezed his hand in reassurance, but I got the feeling nothing would set him at ease while Lucian was around. To be honest, I felt like we were doing well on account that the two countries had been mortal enemies for at least three hundred years. That kind of baggage can genuinely weigh on a person, but they were both keeping their shit together—for the most part.

Lucian didn't hesitate to scoop me up and capture my lips with his. I could feel his insecurity in our bond, unsure if he was still welcome to show me this kind of affection in front of everyone. Cupping his face in my hands, I returned the kiss to convey to him he had nothing to worry about. The more I could put all of these men at ease, the better.

"I'm sorry; I didn't mean to say those things to upset you as I did. Everything within me was furious that they were touching what's mine," Lucian explained, resting his forehead against mine.

"It wasn't until I felt your panic and fear I realized what I'd done. Maybe I'm more like my father than I care to admit."

"You are nothing like your father. I know I only met the man once, but I'm pretty damn sure he'd never say he was sorry," I pointed out. "For the record, it wasn't just your words that sent me spiraling. It was the reality of what it means to have a pack who's in the military. The same thing applies to us, except it's much easier for me to keep up with you. When there are five or six people to worry about at once, there's no way I could keep track of all of you. That's what scares the shit out of me about all of this."

"What *exactly* do you mean by all of this?" Lucian pressed, setting me down without releasing his hold on me.

Looking up at him, seeing the harsh reality of his world so vividly in the scars that covered his skin. I wasn't the only one who'd been fighting their whole life for something others just couldn't see. No one was treating Omegas right, just as no one was caring for the Northern people the way they should. Each of us could see it so clearly but didn't know how to fix it. Right now, with all six of them standing here waiting for my answer, I could see the solution to both problems. Now I just had to get them to understand and agree.

"All," I answered, gesturing with a hand to everyone. "All of this, all of us, *all.*"

"What about us all?" Sorin inquired, coming to stand before me.

Groaning, I made a big show of waving my arms around. "How hard is this to figure out? Do I need to say it in Asturgian for you *all* to understand?"

Victor snorted at that, trying to cover up his laugh. "Little Spark, I think what both those men want is for you to spell it out for them like they're two. Make sure it's all small words. We don't want them getting hung up on the big fancy words."

Sorin flipped Victor off without taking his eyes off of me. "While I disagree with the delivery and the wise-ass remarks about my intelligence, he's somewhat right. Dani-girl, we can't afford to get this wrong, to make a choice that could get us killed or banished for treason, so you'll have to forgive us. We all need to know in plain words what you're asking us to do."

"Right, okay, fair point," I agreed, pulling out of Lucian's hold so I could pace. The tiredness I'd felt earlier vanished as my mind kicked into overdrive.

"Shit," Lucian swore.

The others snapped to attention and started to look and listen like they were expecting someone to come after us. "What, what did you hear?" Cris asked, his hand resting on the but of his gun, ready to grab it at a moment's notice.

"Sorry, I didn't mean to startle everyone. It's just I know that look on her face," Lucian explained.

Petru cocked his head as he looked at me. "What look? I see nothing unusual about her expression."

"Probably because I snapped her out of deep thought before you could see it. She gets this wrinkle between her brows, then she starts to pace, followed by chewing her nails or plucking at a loose thread in her clothes," Lucian explained.

Now it was Toma's turn to look confused as he crossed his arms. "What does that have to do with anything?"

Lucian faced Toma with a smug smile. "I think that's something I'm going to keep to myself for now. It's far more entertaining to see you figure out what it means."

"Bastard," Toma mumbled under his breath.

"Enough," Sorin snapped. "You were saying, Dani-girl?"

I watched Sorin for a moment, trying to figure out what exactly was bothering him. It wasn't obvious; this worry ran under his skin, where it was hidden until moments like this. Unable to pinpoint my spot of concern, I carried on, ready to tell these men the meaning of the word *all*.

"You want it simple, straight to the point, and small words. All right I can do that," I stated, then pointed a finger at myself. "Me Omega, you pack, we all one family, and we all end this war."

"That might have been too simple," Cris commented with a smirk, but then his face dropped onto a more serious expression. "Let's revisit the whole *one family* part first. Then we can move on to ending the war, which I'm sure more than myself has a few questions about."

"One family, a pack, a group of people who came from all walks of life but are choosing to remain with each other. Also known as the men I refuse to lose by being forced to pick," I elaborated. "Lucian and I are bonded, that's never going to change, and I won't let you kill him to make things easier. He's mine. Then that leads us to the five of you, the men who are my unit and have built a family they protect fiercely. Thankfully I feel lucky enough to be part of that family, even if I've rejected the reality of it countless times."

The guys all muttered to themselves about various things, and I knew I'd be hearing an ear full soon. However, Lucian intervened before the guys could start sharing their thoughts. "Danella, I don't know how to do that for you. I want to give you everything your heart desires, and I *know* how you feel about these men, even if you won't come out and say it. Yet I don't understand the first thing about family or packs. It was forbidden in the North for so many years. Once the ban was lifted, no one knew what to do with the option. Of course, we'd need an Omega to form the bond so there wasn't much chance of that ever happening. All that to say, I will do all that I can to give you what you need. Because you need them. However, everything will be against us."

"It's a good thing all of us are fighters then, isn't it?" I teased, trying to lighten the tension and heavy emotions I felt in the atmosphere around us. "I don't have the first clue how to make this all work, but I'd at least like to try. If it can't happen...then I'll accept that reality."

CHAPTER 38
Danella

Sorin cleared his throat and crossed his arms making his muscles more pronounced. "Let's start with this supposed plan to overthrow General Rasvan. If we can bring a peace treaty to the table, I feel we have a better shot of making them believe we're serious."

"Wait," I interjected, stepping back from Lucian and Sorin so I could see everyone. "You asked me what I wanted, to know what I was thinking. Now it's my turn to ask you, each and every one of you standing before me. What do you want? Ignore my needs and wants right now. Be honest and open about what you want for your life and future."

Unsurprising, Petru spoke first. "Wildflower, I thought we'd said it clearly already, but hearing you ask us that tells me differently. I will speak for myself now since you need our personal assurances." Taking a breath, he locked eyes with me, his look so intense I felt like he was seeing into my soul. "Danella, what I want for my future is to have a pack with you as our Omega. To wake up in the morning with you curled up in the arms of my brothers and lovers, safe and cherished. The love I feel for this family we are making will grow as we change the world around us. A world that starts with you as our center guiding us to be better men."

My throat tightened at his words as they speared me right in the heart making it swell ten times its normal size with his affection.

Toma took Petru's hand and raised it to his lips, pressing a kiss to it with an adoring smile. "Love, I couldn't have said it any better." Petru just smiled at his partner and squeezed his hand in return. It would seem I wasn't the only one caught up in my feels.

Pulling his gaze away from Petru, Toma blinded me with his sultry smolder making me feel the need to rub my legs together. Having his full attention was something I loved but always felt the weight of when it happened. "You and I got off to a bit of a rocky start didn't we?"

I nodded, remembering that day I chewed him out in the hospital, and his sister, the nurse taking care of me, kicked him out of the room. It had taken a little time for us to find our footing, but I think once we both got to see past the walls we both had we found our stride.

"Goes to show that you can't judge a person by their first impression," I reasoned. "Plus, once I got to know Cris and Petru better, I knew you could be the flirty playboy you pretend to be."

Toma snorted. "I do not flirt, nor am I a playboy. You know Petru was my first love, who I've always been loyal to until we added Cris to our relationship, together, mind you." He pointed out, wagging a finger at me playfully.

"Then you appeared like a tornado sweeping into our lives, throwing everything we thought we knew about Omegas out the window. All that sass poured out of you as you defended yourself, along with your friends, from a threat you had no hope of defeating. The more and more I learned about you, Danella, made it impossible for me not to see the truth. Petru told us from day one that you were ours. An Omega that the fates brought to us, the missing piece to the puzzle that our unit needed. So, after saying all that, what do I want for my future?" Toma pondered, repeating the question and shrugged. "Simple, one with you in it. Period. The end. However that needs to happen, I'm willing to try."

Cris started to speak, but Victor cut him off. "Hold up, kid, let me just say my peace before another long-winded speech. It will be fucking nightfall before we get this part over with." The man grumbled as he stomped his way up to me.

He stood towering over me, his sharp hazel eye pinning me to the ground. It was obvious why people were scared of him, though I'd never once felt anything but safe with him close by.

"Listen up, and listen good, Little Spark, because I'm not going to rehash this again," Victor growled as he held my chin in his hand. "You belong to us, plain and simple. I vowed to protect you, and seeing as there was no expiration date on that, I guess it means you're stuck with me for life."

Victor shifted his gaze from me to Lucian, making the other Alpha stiffen in readiness. "I'd keep in mind the fact I didn't put any limitations or rules on who or what I was going to protect her from... so don't make have to fucking protect her from you. That won't go well for either of us."

The two Alphas glared at each other for a moment, making me hold my breath and pray they wouldn't start fighting again. "I'd extend the same warning to you as well, don't give me a reason to take you out. There will be a truce between us. However, her needs and well-being will forever come first, no matter what."

"Good," Victor grunted. "Since we understand each other, there will be no surprises."

Lucian inclined his head in agreement, causing everyone to relax.

"Now, I feel like we can speed this along," Victor announced. "Cris, are you in or out?"

"What?" Cris said, then shook himself as if he'd been lost in thought. "Sorry, I'm in. Absolutely all in on doing whatever it takes to keep Dani in our pack forever. You both said pretty much all there is to say," he commented, glancing at Petru and Toma. "The only thing I'll add is that family is what you make of it. You have one you're born into, but in my opinion, the family you choose and chooses you in return is your true family. Sorin chose all of us when he made this unit, and now we're all choosing Dani. In addition, Dani chose Lucian, so now it's up to us if we will accept him into this family."

Sorin came up behind me and settled his hands on my shoulders. "For us to decide that, I believe it will take a little time, but we are all in agreement as a unit, family, and pack to try. Right now, I think it's best to find a place to set up camp. All of us are tired and hungry, and I'd very much like to have a conversation with Lucian about his plans."

Everyone seemed to agree as weapons were holstered and backpacks were shouldered. Every time I watched them work as a seamless unit, it amazed me. They were so in sync with each other, moving effortlessly from one task to another after years of working together. It made me think of the dream I'd had growing up of what my picture-perfect pack would look like. How they would swoop in and rescue me from my tragic Omega fate. What I didn't realize back then, was that I didn't want to be saved and protected from the world. The truth was I wanted to be part of the battle, helping to make changes for others like me. My need to fight for those who can't has always been seen as a problem. Not to these men; they supported that part of me with training and sharing their own dreams for this world.

This whole time I'd been fighting to be free of it all. To cast aside my designation and burn the entire system to the ground, only seeing the flaws. Yet these men were fighting daily to make a change and protect the country and the people who lived here. My view had been selfish, only seeing the world through my own experiences. If we could really pull this off, make lasting changes for the entire country of Asturg. Then I'd have to think of a new dream to strive for, now wouldn't I? Not sure anything could be as impactful as stopping a war and changing a whole country—but time would tell. I wasn't going to cut myself short.

Thankfully the pace Sorin set for us wasn't as fast as what Lucian had us doing, but then again, we weren't running from anyone this time. I could see the guys all watching for drones and other devices the South used to keep an eye on things, but none seemed too concerned. We were heading for a cabin that was stocked and ready to be used in such situations as ours. It was only a few hours' walk and the sun had just started hiding behind the trees when we arrived. This gave us enough light to enter the cabin, start a fire, and make sure all was good before it was too dark.

Toma set up communications and reached out to headquarters. "Marza command, do you copy? This is Sargent Toma reporting in."

"We hear you loud and clear, Sargent," a woman answered. "Hold one moment for Commandant Stoll."

My jaw dropped as I heard who Toma was reporting to. "Wait, isn't he *the* Commandant? Leader of the whole Southern military?" I whispered.

Toma held up a finger and hit a few buttons before answering. "Sorry, I just wanted to make sure we muted our side of the conversation. Yes, the Commandant oversees all the elite units, but he's always personally handled our team. He's as old school military as you can get, spent his whole life in the service, and my guess is he really hopes Sorin will refuse his father's position so he can take over the military one day."

"I didn't think it worked like that. Doesn't Sorin need a higher rank to even be in the running?" I questioned.

As part of my training, they'd been having me learn all about their military structure. That and all the top members of leadership, so if I ever ran into them on base, I knew who they were. The last thing any of us wanted was to cause waves, with me being from the North and originally from Oscad.

"Toma, tell me, my boy, did you find the bastards?" The suddenness and volume of the Commandant speaking had me jumping back from the computer.

Toma grimaced as he turned down the volume and answered. "Yes, sir, we were able to track down three northern soldiers. They gave us a good workout but aren't used to maneuvering through the woods."

"Good, good. Sorin, I'm assuming you're here as well?"

"You're correct, sir," Sorin confirmed. "I'd like to request we be given a few days to make damn sure we didn't miss any of them. The bastards made it too far past the border without anyone noticing, and I don't like it. Something tells me there's more to this than just fucking with the power plant and running away."

I frowned at Sorin's words, then realized they'd had to give a believable reason to come after me. They would have been expected to return to base after securing the power plant.

"Couldn't agree with you more," Commandant Stoll muttered. "I'll give you a week, not that I think you'll need it, but I don't want anyone in parliament coming back at us saying we didn't take this seriously. Your unit has the best trackers we've got, but if you need assistance, say the word and I'll have units Bravo and Charlie sent your way."

"We'll move faster with it being just us, but I appreciate the offer. We're making camp at location, charlie, alpha, bravo, india, november forty-two. It seems fully stocked for our needs but wanted command to know it will need to be serviced once we return," Sorin shared.

"Will do. Yasen is making a note of it as we speak. How is that little Omega of yours holding up? I was impressed with the feedback I got from others who'd been observing her training. Just wanted to make sure she wouldn't be a hindrance on this. Military life is vastly different from laying on your back all day," the commandant rambled.

Anger flickered through me at his words, causing my hands to ball into fists. On my fucking back—how dare he presume to know what my life had been like. I'd love nothing more than to see him survive a week with only one meager meal a day, no power, running water, or comforts I'm sure someone of his status is accustomed to. Hands reached out and gathered mine in theirs, forcing me to relax and open them. Small half-moon indents appeared on my palms, and a few of them even started to bleed. Toma let out a sigh as he signaled Cris to come over.

I tried to tug them back, not wanting to be looked after right now. Only then his grip tightened, and I got a disapproving look. Cris took a seat next to me at the table taking a hand from Toma and examining it with a little crease between his brows. Reaching down into his bag, he pulled out a few supplies and got to cleaning my hands.

"You really don't need to do that," I said in a quiet voice as Sorin and the Commandant continued to talk.

"Are you the medic?" Cris asked, to which I shook my head. "Then I would leave such calls to them. You've told me stories of people you'd seen yourself dying because they didn't look after simple wounds. Who knows when we will return to base or have the medical supplies we need if things worsen. So in my medical opinion, yes, I do think it's needed."

I wanted to argue with him but a hand wrapped around the back of my neck, stilling the words that were going to come out of my mouth. "Let him do his job, Dani," Lucian ordered, his tone brokering no argument.

It would seem that I wasn't going to win this fight, so I freed my other hand from Toma so I could offer both of them to Cris. Lucian bent down, pressed his lips to my head, and whispered. "Good girl."

A shiver of pleasure shot down my spine at his words, making me need to bite my lip, or a whine would leak out. That was the last thing we needed, especially with the leader of the Southern Military on the phone. Something told me the Commandant wouldn't take too kindly at getting hung up on so he wouldn't hear the sounds I'd be making as Lucian happily attended to my needs.

The sound of someone groaning caught my attention, and I turned to see Victor staring at me. His hands fisted, face strained, and the evident outline of a hard cock was pressing at his pants. What on earth would have caused that kind of reaction?

"Thank you, Commandant. I will ensure to keep you up to date on any and all information we have in two days' time. For now, my team and I are going to get some rest," Sorin informed his commander.

"Alright, we will speak again in two days," Commandant Stoll agreed. "Get your rest. We need your team in top shape as you investigate this situation. Who knows what could happen if they made it past the border and got this far into our territory. I wouldn't be surprised if Commander Lucian came and knocked on the president's door asking for sugar at this rate." With a laugh, the Commandant hung up the call.

"If I was going to show up at the president's door, I think I'd rather ask for some whiskey. Maybe a nice steak dinner, but it certainly wouldn't be sugar," Lucian commented before looking back down at me. "However, I think the more pressing matter is why does it smell like you're going into heat, Danella?"

"What?!" I blurted. "That's not possible, I've never gone into heat, and they gave me a suppressant that should last months."

"Little Spark, I can confirm with absolute certainty you are perfuming like crazy. Whatever he whispered in your ear flipped a goddamn switch," Victor said. "I have never in my life been this hard before, and all that happened is I caught your scent."

"No," I argued, shaking my head. "You don't understand, Victor. I don't go into heat, like ever. Not once in my whole life has it ever happened."

Lucian caught my chin and turned me to look at him. "He's not lying, My Heart. You have never perfumed like this before. I know you told me you couldn't go into heat, but the reaction of these Alphas would say otherwise."

"What are you talking about? I feel fine, there's no excessive need. I'm not begging anyone to fuck me right here on this table, there's no pain, and I'm completely clear-headed. I've seen other Omegas in heat, and I promise you, I'm not," I explained.

"Dani, you've never gone into heat, not once?" Cris asked.

Lucian let me pull out of his hold to look at the Beta. "Never, I've been examined for everything when I was back in Oscad, but they couldn't find anything wrong with me. They assumed I was just a late bloomer. I'm twenty-five now, and it still hasn't happened. I would call myself a lost cause at this point. Nevertheless, Beth gave me the shot a few days after I woke up and told me it should last at least two weeks."

"That's true, but it only works on those who've gone through a heat before. Any Omega who hasn't had their first heat must still take the daily pills. We don't understand why the shot isn't effective before that, but it's something we've learned over the years," Cris explained.

"Okay, that makes sense in its own odd way, but it doesn't explain why you all think I'm going into heat," I countered.

"I'm sorry, Dani. I wish I had an answer to that. While I'm a good field medic, I'm not a doctor who knows all the in's and out's of the Omega anatomy," Cris said, his regret apparent in his expression. "What I do know is that my mother always talked about how Omegas respond to the scent of Alphas they are attracted to. Alphas are the same way. It's the natural driving force to create a bond and pack to protect their Omega. I'm wondering if that doesn't have a large part to play in all this."

CHAPTER 39

Danella

This was making my brain hurt, and I wasn't really following his train of thought. "Wait, are you saying my body is going into heat because I'm with the right men? That I was waiting for Lucian to join the pack before my body decided it was time to start a family?"

"That's a rather crude way of putting it, although possible," Cris answered. "Dani, millions of mammals in the world refuse to allow their body to gestate if they're in danger, malnourished or stressed to the point it would be dangerous to carry a child. You could indeed have been an Omega who came into their heat late but think about where you've been since then. Compounding that with your core belief that you *can't* go into heat, it doesn't shock me at all that it hasn't happened. The other thing that changed is you're now bonded. That could have also been a trigger for your body, indicating it was safe."

Standing from the table, I grasped my head rubbing my temples as I paced the length of the cabin. "This can't be happening, not now. We need to make it stop. I'm not ready for this to happen with all of you. Fucking hell, how is it my life just can't be easy? Why, when I finally have a glimpse of the life I want, does something else need to complicate things?"

Petru stepped in my path and caught me by the shoulder, halting my movement. "Wildflower, you need to just take a deep breath. Come, do it with me." Petru then took in a long breath through his nose, held it for a second then let it out. "Dani, this wasn't a suggestion. I expect you to follow my lead this next breath."

Together Petru and I breathed in and out three times until my heart rate started to slow and my mind ceased to race. I'd accepted the fact I wasn't going to have heats, bear a child, and have a family in that sense. In a way, it had given me peace that I would never have to worry about my baby growing up in a world so full of hate and oppression. Now there was a possibility that might all change. If I did, in fact, go into heat, the only way to manage it was to drug myself into a stupor, so I didn't feel the pain of needing to be knotted. There was no way I would let any of them knot me at a time when a child could be born. Not until I knew we'd created a world my child could grow up in and be safe.

"Wildflower," Petru murmured, drawing my attention back to him. His eyes were so full of compassion and sorrow, as if he understood what I was thinking or feeling. "Did you know that I was left to raise my brother and two cousins on my own since I was thirteen?"

"I've heard bits and pieces from others, though I didn't know you were so young," I answered.

He hummed his understanding and wrapped an arm around me, guiding me over to the couch. Taking a seat, he placed his hands on my hips and gave me a questioning look before tugging me down to sit on his lap. Tucking my head under his chin, I took a deep calming breath as he wrapped his arms around me.

"My father was a contracted worker for the Southern Military in drone operations. He worked for the company that built the drones and would travel to various locations and services them. It was discovered that he was passing on information to the Northern Army on how to avoid detection. My father maintained his innocence till the day he died, saying it was someone else in the company, but no one would listen. You see, my grandmother had been an Omega who was rescued just after giving birth to my father. Even though he never knew anything but the Southern way of life, he'd always been labeled as a Northerner," Petru shared, letting his fingers run up and down my arm as he spoke, soothing himself as well as me.

"The trial they had for him was nothing but a sham. They'd already decided he was guilty long before then. Once he was killed, and our family was labeled traitors, my mother struggled to find work. No one would let her near anything they felt would be compromised because how could a wife not know what her husband was doing. After a time, it became too much for her so she took her own life, leaving me with my eight-year-old brother and my two cousins, ages ten and six, to look after. Thankfully our country has a system that allows us to stay together in a small apartment with a food ration allowance since I was thirteen. We all had to attend school and choose a trade to go into as part of the agreement for this care. So as soon as I was of age, I joined the military knowing they would give the best benefits to family members.

Now I'm sure you're wondering why the hell I'm telling you this story when our situations are entirely different. I just wanted you to understand that I fully comprehend what it means to be responsible for others' well-being. At thirteen, I didn't have a fucking clue how to look after anyone other than myself, but I had to learn. Three people were counting on me to ensure they were clothed, fed, warm, and safe in life which was a heavy burden. My brother didn't like that I joined the military since they were the ones to bring the claim about my father to the authorities. It wasn't my first choice either, but I knew I was doing what was best for my family in the long run. Rene, my little brother, still to this day won't forgive me, and he may never. I find comfort in that he now has a good job working as a teacher, has his own home with three others he loves, and has a family. Out of anyone here in this room, I understand the gravity of what it means for *you* to go into heat. It is the body's way of creating the best environment to conceive, which I get the feeling you do not want right now." Petru commented.

Pushing against his chest so I could sit up to see his face, I nodded. "I'd already accepted that I wouldn't have children. Now if that changes, I still don't know if I can do it. Who would want to raise a child in a world like this?"

"If you do not want children, then that is your right," Victor interjected. "It doesn't matter if you biologically have the ability to or not. It's your choice, Danella, one that I certainly won't make for you."

"He's right. If you truly don't want children, then there are things we can do to make sure it never happens. I know that doesn't help you right now, but once you have a heat the shot will work to prevent another occurrence until you've made a choice for the long term."

I looked at them all in shock. "Are you saying that if I choose to never have a child, you'd all be okay with that?"

Lucian shrugged. "Dani, I've already told you I never wanted to have a child. There was no way I'd ever force the fate of my people on my own offspring. I barely survived it. Why in the hell would I wish it on anyone else?"

"Truthfully, I wasn't sure we'd ever find an Omega for our pack, and the two people I love are men," Toma pointed out. "Also, having a military career doesn't create the best environment to have a child even if we adopted."

My gaze fell on Sorin, who'd remained quiet throughout this conversation. His face was unreadable as he stood there leaning against the living room wall, watching me. He shoved off the partition and walked over to me, squatting so he was at eye level with me. Resting a hand on my leg, he gave it a gentle squeeze.

"When I was a boy, I got incredibly sick. The illness wasn't something we'd ever encountered before. I was dying, and my father was desperate to do whatever was needed to help me live. They used an experimental drug that hadn't been fully tested, but in the end, it saved my life. What we didn't find out until later was the fact it left me sterilized. That's when building a unit of people I wanted to invest my life in became my sole focus. You and these men are my family, the people I choose to surround myself with and love. I knew that no matter what happened in the future when it came to an Omega within our pack, they wouldn't be able to have my child.

It took time to come to terms. A reality I didn't see for my life, yet there are so many other joys and other ways to have a child in my life if my family wanted that. The choice is yours, Danella, and we as your pack and people who love and care about you, will support that. None of us are blind to the challenges and dangers of our world. Just know that if it ever did happen, that baby would be the most protected living thing on this planet," Sorin said with a smirk. "Hell, you see how protective we are over you. Any child would be six times that with all of us together."

Flinging my arms around Sorin's neck, I hugged him tightly. Here was this proud exceptional leader, bearing his soul to me, sharing his weakness, and yet I don't think I knew anyone I respected more because of it. He'd flayed himself open, showing me his true self under any mask or title, allowing me to *see* him.

"Thank you," I whispered, then released him to look at the others. "You have all given me the greatest gift and I don't think you even realize it. All my life, I've been told I'm good for one thing and one thing only, made to feel inferior because of being unable to go into heat. In fact, without Lucian protecting me, I would have been killed for it. Yet here, all of you are telling me that I'm just as important to you even if I never can give you a child."

"People who believe that don't know what it means to truly love someone," Lucian pointed out. "My love for you, Danella, was born out of seeing you fight every day to be yourself, to never let the world change you into something you're not. Plus, how can I say that I love you if there are conditions to it? That isn't love, not real love."

Hearing Lucian tell me he loved me hit like a punch to the gut every time. It just shocked me to hear the rawness of it in his voice, the emotions that backed it up, and the knowledge that he'd turned his back on his country to get to me proved his words with actions. Our relationship might have started under the worst situation imaginable, with everything stacked against us, but nothing would break us if we could find a way to carve out a place in this world.

"So what do we do now?" I questioned.

"You've stopped perfuming," Toma informed me. "That makes

me wonder if your body is trying to go into heat but doesn't know how or if it's building until it reaches the tipping point."

"We have a week to remain here if we feel that is the right call," Sorin reminded us. "I think while we have that time, we need to discuss this plan to take out the General. As I said before, the only way I see us being able to stay together and not get marked as traitors are to bring General Rasvan's head and a peace treaty to my father and advisors."

Just as everyone agreed to this conversation, my stomach let out a loud gurgle. Slapping my hands over my belly, I laughed. "Maybe we can take a second to eat something? With all that's happened today, Lucian and I never got the chance to."

The guys all smiled as Cris and Victor headed into the kitchen.

"While those two are pulling something together, this should tide you over," Toma said, offering me a protein bar.

While I can't say I was super excited to eat a power bar I'd learned quickly you don't pass on food when it's offered. Sorin sat beside Petru and me on the couch while Lucian settled into the armchair.

"I'll admit my plan isn't the best I've come up with, but there hasn't been much time to plan," Lucian prefaced. "Before you caught up, Dani and I were going back to Northern territory, where we'd be heading for the mountains. That is where all those who've run from the army hide out. They are known to be violent and ruthless, killing anyone who supports the General. In my mind, I figured what better army to have than one who hates him as much as I do?"

"Once you have this army, then what? You just plan to storm the city and take him out in an all-out attack?" Sorin asked, his tone betraying how stupid he thought this idea was.

Lucian snorted. "Do you really think I'm that big of an idiot? I didn't manage to blow up one of your power plants, rushing into the situation and hoping for the best. Once I had the help I needed, I was going to devise a plan with them. If I plan to make changes in our country, I'm going to need their help to know I have people on my side. The citizens might be ready for a change, but those in power aren't going to like it at all. It isn't just the General that needs to be removed from his position, there are many others."

"At least you're aware of that," Petru said. "Many who have been trapped only have their eyes set on the captor, the one thing that will set them free. Their mistake is forgetting that most don't act alone and are caught by those hiding in the shadows."

"I've been watching the shadows my whole life," Lucian muttered. "We will need to take out my father. However, it won't be like cutting off the head of a snake; the body won't die. Ever since Savo's betrayal, my father's failing body, and my inability to produce an heir, he's put others in place to take over if needed. I might be heir to the country to my people and in name, but that's about it. There's one more layer to all this, though."

Sorin held up a hand, pausing Lucian. "Victor, Cris, I want you to hear this."

The main space of the cabin was fully open. Only the bunk room was sectioned off. So the two men pulling together a meal had been listening to all this, but I assume Sorin wanted them to give their full attention. They set aside what they were doing and joined us, Victor looming in the space with his arms crossed.

"You were saying?" Sorin said, gesturing for him to continue.

Lucian leaned forward, rubbing his face with his hands. "I don't know much, but the dying words of a woman who's been part of the army longer than any of us have been alive and then some. She believed the attacks on our border outposts somehow were calculated assaults working with someone in the south to make it happen. Furthermore, my father uses these attacks to motivate the people to continue this war. The hotter the Northern people's anger grows, the harder they will fight to defend it."

"What proof did this woman have to give?" Victor challenged. "She must know something if she's willing to waste her dying breath to tell you. Unless she was just that senile."

"Babaka was a decorated soldier put in charge of running all the breeding houses on our bases and outposts. Trust me when I say that woman didn't make false accusations, certainly not against my father," Lucian shot back. "There was another attack on a border outpost, one she fought in and survived. She said that killing a few would save many when creating a common enemy for our people. My assumption is that was the first one he tried, and when it worked so well, he did it again. The North is dying. My people are starving and wasting away under the rule of a man who wants power more than anything else. I don't doubt for a second that he would devise a plan like this."

"Who was the one to give you guys the order to attack the outpost?" I questioned.

"The same person who always gives us our marching orders," Sorin said. "We don't know who specifically decided on which missions to assign us. The higher-ups get their order, which trickles down to us pulling off the mission. If I had to guess, something of this level would have been brought to the Major General's notice and possibly even the Commandant's. Either way, intel of this importance would be known to almost everyone in the military."

That had me tapping my chin trying to figure out how the hell the two sides were working together without even knowing it. I honestly didn't think the Commandant or those leading the military would be the ones to sell out their own people. There had to be a middle person, someone who could be trusted to give information but not be involved with the actions taken.

"Where do you get this kind of intel? Toma said you don't have spies in the North, so how would anyone know that Lucian's outpost would be vulnerable? I'm assuming you all attacked because the fence was being worked on, and the landmines needed to be removed for the job," I reasoned, then turned to Lucian. "What had you leaving with so many as suddenly as you did? You'd told me before that you wouldn't be departing for a little while, then a week later you're off for who knows how long."

Lucian pulled his hair out of his ponytail and raked his fingers through it, a sure sign that he had a headache. I knew he got them fairly regularly, but I also knew he always took less of the rations and made sure I got more along with the vitamins and mineral supplements they gave us to counteract the poor diet.

Slipping off Petru's lap, I walked over to him, tugged his hands away, and started to massage his head and neck as he let his head rest on my stomach. "There was a runner who came to us from another camp further north along the border. He and a few others spotted a known elite task force that had been making their lives hell disappear from the fight. Without them, it gave the team a chance to get the upper hand and sent the Southerners running. What they were concerned about was the fact the whole attack had been odd, like they were testing the encampment and didn't truly intend to destroy them. There was one more outpost between them and us that was smaller, more of a training ground for newer recruits before being sent to resupply our two bases. They would need backup if the South sought a weak border point to attack."

"So you left without giving the word to anyone else what you were doing," I added, knowing he'd acted on his own.

Lucian nodded, rubbing his head against my stomach. Wrapping his arms around my waist, he hugged me tight. "They weren't testing the bases, they were looking for me," Lucian divulged. "Everyone was slaughtered because I wasn't there."

This was an emotion I understood well. So many times I felt like I'd failed Tori and Violet watching them survive the fate we'd all been dealt. If I'd been stronger, smarter, or figured out a way to free them, then I wouldn't feel this gnawing guilt. Even if I couldn't go with them knowing they were safe and free was all that mattered.

"Do you honestly think that would have changed anything?" I asked, tilting his face to look up at me. "Their orders were to wipe out the base and ensure you were dead. The attack happened so fast. By the time it was discovered we were under attack, it was too late."

"She's right," Victor interjected. "If you'd been there, nothing would have changed. Our number one mission was to hunt you down while the base was vulnerable. Once we realized we had the wrong outpost, we pulled back and headed to the second location indicated."

Lucian maneuvered me so I was standing between his legs so he could still hold onto me but see the others. "You were given two locations?" The guys all nodded. "That doesn't make any sense. I've been at the same outpost for roughly five years. It's not a secret that

I'm there, either. The General thought it was best to show his people he was willing to put his own son on the front lines so they should do the same."

"Could it be that they did that to throw off the scent of knowing too much?" Petru questions. "It would be suspicious for whoever brought this to our attention to know too much. This way, we hit two different camps, added to the tale that we're the boogie man, and hid the betrayal all in one swoop."

"I don't even know how to find out who the informant was," Sorin muttered, rubbing his chin. "If I asked questions about it, I know it would draw attention this long after the fact."

Toma cleared his throat and walked over to the table where his laptop sat. "There might be a way I can get to it, but I need to know if it's that crucial because I could tip our hand if they discover what I'm doing."

"That's good to know there's a chance, but I think we have plenty to deal with right now. We don't need to head down that path just yet," Sorin reasoned. "What we need to map out in explicit detail is how we're going to approach these people, get them on our side, and attack the main city. After that, we'll move into the actual attack and how that is best to be managed. Do you have any idea how many people are hiding out there?"

Lucian took a moment to consider the question. "People have been running from the war for at least the past fifty years my father's been in charge. I remember growing up hearing rumors about them and the rebellion they tried to lead against the country during my grandfather's time. Of course, they lost, and I'm assuming that took out a large chunk of their people. Each training we do, fifteen to twenty people make a run for the mountains, about five to ten survive those who hunt down traitors."

"All right, so let's say about a thousand people living in the mountains. Half would be able-bodied, maybe slightly less, depending on how they fair surviving isolated," Sorin rambled as he clearly was making mental notes for himself. "Toma, do we have any footage of those mountains?"

"I don't think so, but let me look," he answered, opening his computer. "They are closer to Oscad than they are to us, but you never know. It's possible that I might be able to see if I can get into the Oscad database. Would your friend be able to help us with that?"

Sorin's whole body went stiff as his gaze flicked over to Lucian so quickly I almost didn't notice. "Possibly, but I'm not sure I want to bring more people into this."

"Yeah, but what if we have Oscad's help on this?" Petru reasoned. "They have a military of their own, although it's rarely used. Ending the war between us is of value to them as well. Think of all the trade dynamics that would change if the South could work with them without having the North in the way."

"Plus, you can't tell me that Savo, of all people, wouldn't support this," Victor pointed out.

"What did you just say?" Lucian snapped, shooting to his feet as he plopped me in the chair. "The connection you have in Oscad is my *brother*?"

Ah hell, that wasn't going to go over well.

CHAPTER 40
Lucian

Savo.

They'd said Savo was their contact in Oscad. The man who abandoned his country and left me to take his spot. Clearly, he'd done well for himself if he had the ability to be of use to us in this fight on behalf of Oscad.

"How do you know Savo?" I demanded of Sorin.

"My mother and I were held prisoner in the North when I was a child for two years before they managed to free us," he said, shocking the hell out of me. "It was a secondary home of the General outside of the Stalhold City where, as you know, he kept his many breeders. One day, Savo was playing hide and seek with some other children and stumbled upon our cell in the basement. Since that time he came to visit and play with me until we escaped. Both of us kept in touch the best we could, but soon it became impossible once he was in the city. After his sister died and he left the country, I didn't hear from him again until about a week and a half ago looking for three Oscad Omegas that we managed to acquire from your outpost."

Mind reeling with the fact that Sorin had been held captive in my childhood home had my headache growing increasingly worse. "I don't understand," I whispered. "That is the house I lived in as well. Savo is only three years older than me, so I suppose I wouldn't remember any of this since I was never out of the caretaker's sight. Savo always defied our father, so I think he always planned on having me as a backup heir, even though Savo was his first choice."

"It's strange how the fates connect people together without us even realizing it," Petru mused. "Who would have ever thought we'd have a Southern heir friends with both Northern heirs?"

"Savo and I used to talk about changing the world when we were in charge, ending this war, and helping our people as friends," Sorin shared. "It would seem that dream might be fulfilled with your help. If you haven't decided that your anger toward your brother is greater than the goal at hand."

I let out a harsh laugh. "The anger I have is a mere candle flicker compared to how I feel about our father. Besides, there is more at stake now that is personally affecting us both. If you say that Savo can help us, then so be it. I won't stand in your way."

The promise that I made to Dani trumped everything else. No matter what it took, I was going to make this world a safe one for her to thrive in, even if it meant getting help from a traitor. A small gentle hand grasped mine and gave a squeeze. She didn't say anything, but I knew she could feel how chaotic my emotions were. I never thought I would have any contact with Savo once he left the country. Now here I was standing in a cabin on Southern territory, planning to overthrow my father with President Dragomire's son. Life certainly had a funny way of showing us how little control we had over anything. What's that saying—we make plans, and the universe just laughs.

"All right then, I'll reach out to him and see what he might have to offer. His people have had spies in the North tracking down all the Omegas that got sent over there against their will," Sorin said, his attention falling on one such Omega behind me.

"No matter what happens, you're still going to make sure Violet and Tori get back to Oscad, right?" Dani questioned.

Sorin nodded. "It might work out to make it all happen at once. If Savo feels that he can help us and already has his men coming out here to collect them, it's possible he could send more."

Through our bond, I could feel her relief. I knew how protective she was over those two, especially when the only times we would have heated arguments was when they revolved around them. When I told her there was nothing I could do for Tori when they came to take her baby, I thought I was going to need to sleep with one eye open. The rage written all over her face at my answer had me incredibly worried she would do something rash, so much so that I chained her to the fucking wall in my room. No matter how mad she got at me, I couldn't risk her attacking the guards or causing a scene that would force me to punish her publicly. Whipping a woman I was in love with wasn't something I had on my to-do list.

Thankfully when it came to Violet, she was still furious, but I didn't need to take any extra measures. She wanted to be by her side the moment they'd left, and last time I kept her in my room for a full day. The whispered fights we had over the past few years were far more intense than any screaming match I'd witnessed. Never in my life did I think such words could come out of a woman with such venom. To this day, I was thankful she was given to me so that I could protect her from the dangers of my world. The North didn't appreciate any sort of idealism, and she had it in spades.

"Do you plan on contacting him now?" I asked.

Sorin let out a heavy sigh. "I think we all need a day to sleep, eat a good meal, and regroup after everything that's happened the past two days. Once we've had our time, I'd like to go over some maps with you to see the locations you believe these rebels might be. Then we can give Savo more direction in what we're looking for."

The man was an intelligent leader, I had to give him that. Dani and I hadn't gotten much sleep. In fact, while she was resting, I was always keeping watch. The wave of fatigue creeping over me told me I wouldn't be much use to anyone soon. Since the day I left the outpost, I've been surviving off a few hours of sleep here and there. Even during our time in the cave, I had laid awake holding her and listening for any danger. I'd managed to get my Omega back, and I wasn't planning on letting anyone steal her again. Granted, now that I was bonded to her, I could track her down. Then again, there would be no need for that if she was safe in my arms, now was there?

Victor and Cris headed back to the kitchen to finish whatever they'd been making. Turning to face Dani, I noticed she'd curled up in the armchair and promptly fell asleep. Her brow was creased and her nose was crinkled, clearly upset about something. When I reached out through our bond, I realized the issue. Walking over to my pack, I pulled out a blanket and draped it over her tucking it tightly around her. It smelled like me and would hold her like she wanted but wasn't willing to admit to us. With a sigh, her expression eased, and she relaxed into the chair. The way her head was turned I could clearly see my brand on her neck and the shiny skin around it where I'd bitten her. I never understood why we needed to do that to create a bond, but the satisfaction of seeing that mark on her was bone-deep.

Sorin stood and caught my eye, gesturing with his head for me to follow him as he exited the cabin. Taking a moment, I put my hair back up in the nub of a ponytail and removed my gun and knife, setting them on the simple table before the couch. No matter what happened out there, I wasn't going to be the one to start the fight. They might not understand why I was adapting to all this so quickly, but they didn't have a direct line to Danella's mind and emotions. There was no way to describe to them just how much they meant to her. I still couldn't wrap my head around it, nor did I feel like I deserved it. One thing I knew with absolute certainty though, is if I dared to harm or, god forbid, kill any of these five Southern soldiers, I would lose Dani forever. That was one thing she'd never forgive any of us for.

Rolling my shoulders, I readied myself for the *conversation* I was about to have with Sorin. One or both of us would end up with some bruised, broken nose or a fat lip, but I understood why this needed to happen. We were both Alphas and leaders of our people, men who didn't take orders but gave them. If we couldn't figure out some system to work alongside each other, this would be hell. A hell we'd gladly suffer through for her, but fuck, it would be rough.

I could feel the other men watching me as I headed for the door. Pausing, I turned to look at Petru. "She doesn't step foot outside this cabin no matter what happens between the two of us. Understood?"

Toma stood from the table, his expression dark, clearly upset by my unspoken threat. Petru rose and walked over to his lover, resting a hand on his shoulder, holding him back. "While I do not take orders from you, Lucian, I will ensure that Dani is looked after."

Good enough for me. I spun on my heel and marched outside to see if there was hope for the North and South to come to an agreement. This is where it needed to start, if we were going to change the world, then the next generation of leaders needed to make peace. It wouldn't matter if I took out my father and called a cease-fire pulling back every single soldier. If the South didn't believe it was sincere, they'd just storm the border and take over, leaving us no choice but to defend ourselves. Putting us right back to square one.

The moment I stepped out of the cabin, Sorin grabbed me by the throat and slammed me into a tree. All the emotions he'd been holding under the surface were now in the forefront making his eyes blaze with fury.

"You fucking bastard, how can you say you love that woman when you did the one goddamn thing to her she wanted a choice in?" He snarled. "Do you know how hard it was to get her to let us in? To give us a chance to prove that not all Alphas are selfish pricks like *you*."

Well, this was starting off well...

CHAPTER 41

Sorin

The rage I'd been holding back this whole time we'd been looking for Dani came rushing out like a tidal wave. I wanted nothing more than to beat this motherfucker's face in for what he'd taken from her. The one thing Dani treasured most in life was the ability to make her own choices, to have her voice heard. Now this jackass went and bonded her to him without even bothering to warn her.

In my need as an Alpha to keep what was mine, I understood, except I wasn't just my designation and would not let that dictate what I did or how I acted. Dani and so many other Omegas have been oppressed, forced into lives and packs they never wanted. I had hoped to give her that chance to pick what she wanted, even if it was to walk away from us. Now she'd never know what that felt like because of this man.

"You don't have to tell me what I did was selfish. I'm fully aware," Lucian spat. "I showed up to rescue her from you and your men, but when I tried to get her to come with me, she said no. What was I supposed to do?"

"You can't seriously be asking me that," I answered, shaking my head and tossing him aside. "So your answer to a woman telling you no, she doesn't want to go with you, is to force her? Do you realize how fucked up that is?"

Lucian stumbled but remained on his feet as he glared at me. I could see the resemblance to his father in his eyes, but there wasn't the callousness I remember seeing in them. Anyone with eyes could see that he genuinely cared for Dani. What I took issue with was how he handled the situation. Granted, I don't know how else all of that would've gone down, because the second I showed up on the scene, I would have blown his head off. How in the hell had my unit ended up with the one woman who'd be tied to the Northern heir? Petru would tell us it was fate bringing us together so that we could end the war and live happily ever after, but it was a hard pill to swallow.

"Don't you fucking dare make this sound like I'm the only one crazy enough to do something like that. Are you telling me that if she looked you in the face and told you to leave, that you'd do it? It's obvious all of you feel as strongly for her as I do, but keep in mind she's been with me for three years. I know Dani. I've seen her at her lowest point hungry, homesick, and losing hope that she'd ever get the chance to make a run for it. What's worse is that I was powerless to do anything about it. I couldn't comfort her, offer the hope she desperately needed, or give the simple gesture of hugging her," Lucian raged. "Did she tell you she made rules for things between us? That first day we met with a backbone of steel and she told me if she was going to agree to the only thing that would keep her safe, I had to abide by *her* demands."

"What the fuck does that have to do with this? She should have rules for her own goddamn body," I argued.

Lucian growled and started to pace. "I'm trying to show you that I did the best for her from the very beginning. If I were any other Northerner, her demands would have been ignored. Worse yet, they'd have sold her out for being unable to reproduce. The moment she had that brand on her neck, she was mine to protect, which I've done to the best of my abilities. When she wouldn't leave with me, I had to make a choice, and that choice was to ensure no one could take her from me. Was it selfish? Yes, but what would have happened if she stayed with you and they figured out what that brand on her neck meant? They would have labeled her a danger to your people, tortured her for information, then killed her. With me, I could do whatever was needed to protect her from anyone and anything."

I scoffed at him in disgust. "Do you think I'm weak or don't have my own weight to throw around where it counts? I keep my head down and choose to keep my life separate from that of my father's. With one word, I could be pulled from the military and have a seat on the advisory board. That alone would be all the power I need to ensure Dani has the life she deserves." Rubbing my hands over my bald head, I groaned in frustration at knowing that none of this mattered now. What was done was done, and I needed to deal with it accordingly.

"That's what I'm trying to do now, give her the life she should have had all along. Once my father and those loyal to him are gone, I can rebuild. My country is dying, if not already past saving. If things continue as they are even for another two or three years, there will be nothing left for the South to take over," Lucian expressed, waving his hands furiously. "You and I both love that woman, as do your men. She needs me, needs us, together as a pack. However, if it's ever going to work, that starts with us. I wasn't lying when I said I'd do whatever it took to keep her safe and loved, so tell me what needs to happen. How can we start to build a bridge and meet in the middle?"

"Is this how you got her to forgive you? Pretty words and promises of a bright future?" I challenged.

His brows shot up, and a bark of laughter escaped him. "You think she's forgiven me?"

"We all have noses. I know you've fucked and knotted her in your time together," I retorted.

"Have you not been paying attention to our story? Sex is nothing new to us," Lucian said, crossing his arms as he squared up to me. "Dani didn't know if you would come for her, and life has taught her nothing but to expect the worst. She told me that because we're bonded, it left her no choice but to make the best of it. Me, forgiven? Absolutely not, but she's also come to terms with the fact she won't be rid of me until death. Dani is the queen of adapting, only to find a way to use it to her advantage. The advantage I bring to the table is ending the war."

I had to admit that sounded like something Dani would do, taking the good with the bad. What I couldn't wrap my head around, though, is how she let him touch her so intimately. It had taken such baby steps for us to get her comfortable with casual touches. Sexual advances were different as I thought about that time with her in the bathroom. I also know she'd stumbled upon more than one intimate moment between Toma, Petru, and Cris. They were about as subtle as an elephant in a small room when they got going. None of that seemed to bother her, but when one of us tried to cuddle up with her, that's when the walls went up. I'd been shocked when she let Petru hold her on the couch moments ago. Was it the fact she thought she'd lost us that got her to open up some more? Or possibly it was because she realized how wonderful affection could be now that she was bonded. None of that mattered when there was a sign of progress between us all.

Now I was left with the challenging task of figuring out how to blend our two worlds together.

"You want to build a bridge between us?" I asked, to which he nodded his agreement. "Then, while we are in Southern territory, you listen to my orders. Once we're in your stomping grounds, I'll do the same and defer to your calls. You don't know the in's and out's of this country, and I don't know yours. If we can agree to respect each other's knowledge of our own countries, it's a good place to start."

"So are you asking me to be one of your men here in the South, or are we equals?" Lucian countered.

That I had to mull over since he made a good point. It wasn't realistic to expect him to be a subordinate to me when we were of equal rank, per se. He was probably above me, but I wasn't going to be the one to point it out, not yet, at least.

"You and I will be considered equals, but you will defer to my judgment if I give an order. I'm open to hearing your suggestions, but if we're out on a mission, my orders will be listened to. As for my men, treat them like they are a unit under another commander who's assisting. They are not yours to boss around, yet they must also respect the rank," I explained. "Do you agree to these terms?"

Lucian extended a hand. "As long as the same rules apply once we get to the North, I'm in agreement."

Grasping his hand, I shook it. Then, in a last-second decision, I slammed my opposite hand into his jaw. Groaning at the impact, he stumbled back, clutching his cheek and swearing.

"Fuck," he snarled. "That is one hell of a left hook, asshole."

Grinning, I slapped him on the back a little harder than I needed to, but it certainly made me feel better. "You'll live even if there'll be one hell of a bruise. Let's be honest, though, you deserved it. I went easy on you because I didn't want to wake Dani from you getting your ass beat."

Lucian muttered something under his breath but followed me back into the cabin. Glancing at the chair, I noticed it was empty, although Petru was just stepping out of the bunk room. He caught my eye and gave me a nod letting me know he'd taken care of her. It was odd how having her part of our unit wasn't taking any adjusting at all. Each of us seemed to naturally step into any area that needed our attention, and that skill was being applied to our Dani-girl. The smells coming from the kitchen area had my stomach growling with excitement. None of us had eaten much today, and power bars only got you so far.

Victor looked past me at Lucian and gave an approving grunt. "Expected you to come back looking like you went through a meat grinder when he was done with you."

"He was too concerned about Dani to get in the damage he wanted to, though I'm sure you'll all find your ways to make me pay for what I did," Lucian sighed, dropping down to sit at the kitchen table.

"For a Northerner, you're giving into all this awfully easy," Victor commented, pointing a knife at him. "Just so you and I are on the same page. If you pull another kidnap-her-and-disappear bullshit, I'll kill you *dead*. Yeah, she might not forgive me, but I'll still know I kept my promise to keep her safe no matter what."

My brows rose at this declaration. Vic didn't make idle threats, and if he was laying down the law for Lucian, it would be the only warning he got. The two men glared at each other, almost as if it was some kind of mental pissing match to see who was stronger. If Toma hadn't walked between them to bring something to Cris, I'm not sure either of them would have given in. While everyone in this house, aside from Cris and Dani, were Alphas, we all exhibited that trait differently.

Toma and Petru didn't feel the need to posture or be in control of others. Those two were far more into the personal challenge of things. Each wanted to be the best in their chosen field, and they sure as fuck pulled that off. Victor was the Alpha who needed to control his environment and keep tabs on everyone. Having Dani stolen under his watch was what really pissed him off, but he was also an Alpha who needed to be in charge—without the red tape. On many occasions, they've tried to promote him to a high-ranking officer. Each time he refuses, doesn't want the paperwork nor the hassle of the higher-ups telling him what he can and can't do.

As for me, I would safely assume Lucian as well; we're natural-born leaders. The ones people follow. No matter our job or role, others will flock to us for help or guidance. While I would give anything not to be the next president, I know it's where this journey will end. Then again, if we really do end this war and find a way to create peace between our countries, my place in the world might change. I'll have to be in a leadership position without a doubt, but so will Lucian. Not having a clue what that will look like, I don't even want to speculate how that would work, but our people will need the reassurance of us reminding them that everyday things are changing.

My plan was to watch how Lucian interacted with the rest of my unit, trying not to step in but letting them resolve things for themselves. If we genuinely hoped to make this a blended pack, the first of its kind, with three different countries represented. What would Oscad say about the fact that one of their Omegas is choosing to stay and end this war? I'd heard whispers of their new leader, Head Speaker Marius, and how he tore the previous government down to keep his Omega safe. Surely a man like him will understand what we're trying to do here for Danella.

"Sorin," Cris called, with an edge to his tone making me think it wasn't the first time he called my name.

"Apologies, I was lost in thought," I offered. "Did you need something?"

"Food is ready, but I wasn't sure if we should wake Dani or not," Cris said, placing a large pot of stew on the table.

"No, I think it's best if we let her be. If the smell of food wakes her, then so be it. Although it's obvious she's wiped out. As strong as she is right now, we need to keep in mind her body still isn't back to a hundred percent," I reminded.

Lucian snapped to attention at this. "She was hurt? What happened? Fuck, did I push her too hard?"

I directed his attention to Cris, who could explain everything far better than I could. Meanwhile, the rest took their seats and started to dish up food, so I joined them. Cris was more than capable of dealing with Lucian on his own, plus I wasn't one to baby him. With everyone seated and food dished up, I dove in with gusto. The base always made sure we had decent meals that were nutritious and met the needs we had, but it could never beat Cris' cooking.

"From what I've gathered from Dani, her friends, and witnessing ourselves, the escape from the outpost went less than ideal. She stole a truck but then ran over a landmine which tossed her from the vehicle. Tori mentioned something about a second explosion as the truck blew up that Dani got hit with as well. Violet dislocated her shoulder, but Dani fixed it. Which, I have to say I'm rather impressed with her medical knowledge. It's limited to be sure, but still much of what she does know will come in handy on the battlefield," Cris praised with a bright smile as he caught sight of the woman herself coming to join us.

Lucian, with his back turned to her, slammed his spoon to the table. "Danella will never be anywhere near the battlefield if I have anything to say about it."

Cris started to point to Dani, who was now standing behind Lucian. How he couldn't feel her standing there, I'll never know. Maybe he did and chose to ignore her until he got his point across.

"She mentioned you were training her to be part of your unit. I didn't realize just how serious that training was until I saw the dead bodies. Dani isn't going to be in the thick of things no matter what she thinks or says." Twisting in his chair, he turned to face her. "Do we understand each other?"

"Do we understand each other..." Dani murmured, cocking her head. "...You know, I don't think we do because that is absolutely not going to fucking happen. This is as much my fight as it is yours. I deserve to be part of this, not hidden away someplace else while others put their lives on the line. You want to protect me, keep me safe. I get that, but there are other ways to do that where you're not taking my legs out from under me. Ask these guys. I've got what it takes to be a valuable asset to this team which is what I wanted for my life before you showed up and blew that all to hell."

When he'd told me she hadn't forgiven him, I wasn't sure I believed him. After this interaction, I've since changed my position to agree with him. Her words were like spitting venom as her eyes flashed with anger. Victor shifted in his seat next to me, trying to discreetly adjust himself. He'd confessed that he riled her up on purpose because he thought it was the sexiest thing to see her mad.

"Da—" Lucian tried, but Dani cut him off with the wave of a hand.

"Don't, you are my bonded Alpha, and I understand that drives you to be overprotective. Just take a second to think this through. We're not alone anymore, and we have all of them watching out for me too. By training me to be a fighter, you're gonna be protecting me. It's just gonna look a little different." Dani let out a sigh and spread her arms out before letting them fall in frustration. "Lucian, I'm never going to be the precious Omega who wants to be treasured and kept on a pedestal. What is it you tell me all the time? It's the fight, the passion that had you fall in love with me. So you can try to enforce keeping me off the battlefield, however I'll fight you every step of the way."

That's my Dani-girl. An Omega warrior fighting to free those who can't free themselves. Who wouldn't be in awe of her spirit? That's why, no matter what, she was going to need us all to keep her safe.

CHAPTER 42

Danella

When the smell of food woke me and I followed my nose out here, I hadn't planned on laying down a gauntlet between Lucian and me, but here we are. It didn't matter what I understood why he was telling me I couldn't fight, his intentions were loud and clear in our bond, but I wasn't going to let fear stop me.

"Look, I realized this is exactly what I freaked out about earlier, thinking of losing one of you for doing your job. The military is a dangerous life to live when you put yourself on the front lines to defend others. My panic was real. The mere thought of one of you dying makes me sick to my stomach," I shared, walking up to Lucian. "But there's another side of this for me. If I've been given the opportunity to make a difference in this world for Omegas, how can I just let it pass me by? I'd never be able to look at myself in the mirror, for all I'd see is the hundreds of Toris and Violets left to survive this on their own. They withstand being raped, bearing a child, and then having it taken away from them countless times if they don't die in childbirth. Heaven forbid they become an Omega who's never had a child. They get put to death because we can't spare the food for someone who can't give back to the army. What kind of life is that?"

Lucian reached out and took my hand, sadness welling up inside him even if he didn't show it. "I know," he whispered. "I know you won't let me hide you away, keep you safe, and protect you from the realities of war. You're too stubborn for that, not to mention the compassion you have for others would never allow you to walk away." Pressing his lips to the palm of my hand, he held my gaze, letting me see what I was feeling through our connection. "I had to try. Even if you never spoke to me again, I had to at least try."

"Then teach me how to protect myself," I urged. "You want to keep me safe, then use all that knowledge in your brain and teach me what I need to know. Work with Sorin and the others while we do what needs to be done to gather our army and get me as ready as possible for this fight."

He didn't answer immediately as he pulled me to sit on his other side. Victor got up, dished me a bowl, and handed it over like he's been doing for the past week. "Thanks, Vicky, but you know I can get my food myself. There's no one here you need to worry about messing with me. It's just us."

Victor just glared at me and pointed to the bowl. "Eat."

Rolling my eyes, I dug into the meal and moaned as the stew hit my taste buds. "Holy shit, how did you two make something so good out of the random stuff you found here?"

The guys all smiled, and Toma chuckled. "Cris won't tell us. He says it's a family secret from his mother."

"Vicky, wouldn't you know what it is since you help cook?" I pressed.

The big man smirked. "Little Spark, I just chop shit. Cris does the actual work, but I always help since we can't risk him cutting himself and I need to keep busy. It's a win-win if you ask me."

"Why does that not surprise me," I sighed, but the food was too good for me to get distracted from it.

"Cris, is your mother from the North?" Lucian asked.

"Yes, she was an Omega that was rescued from the North. She was found wandering the badlands after she escaped by my father," Cris shared. "They've been together ever since, but over the past few years, Father has been stationed at another base that he oversees. Mother didn't want to leave her work helping other refugee

Omegas, so she stayed close to the city and base. It's where they bring all rescued Northerners."

Lucian nodded as he took another spoonful of stew. "My mother used to make her stew like this as well. I'm surprised you can find the herb here in the South."

"I always collect some when we get close to the border," Cris said. "It grows untouched in the no-man's-land between the two countries. Mother loves it when I bring some back for her to cook with. She says it helps the girls feel like they're home."

A wistful expression crossed Lucian's face. "Your mother sounds like a rather amazing woman. I'm glad she's found a home and can live a life she's proud of."

Feeling that the emotions in the room were running high, I decided to change the subject slightly. "You should experience the couch she has. It's every Omegas dream. I got to sit in it once. I swear I didn't want to leave, it was that amazing."

"I know it's catnip for Omegas, but I have to say we all fight over who gets to sit on it when we visit," Petru added. "Maybe when things settle down, we can have one ordered for our own home?"

Everyone perked up at that. "A home, like an actual house that's ours to do with as we like? One where there's a kitchen, living room, and everyone can have their own room? A place to come back to after being gone and relax?"

The guys seemed surprised by my excitement. Granted, I didn't get excited about too much these days, but the prospect of having a place that was *mine,* well ours? That was a dream I'd let go of since being snatched out of my childhood home. Even if I found a pack, there was no guarantee things would work out the way you'd like. If they already had an established palace and designed the nest in anticipation of being matched with an Omega, it wouldn't be the same as a place I put together myself.

"I had no idea the thought of having a home would appeal to you so strongly," Sorin commented. "Honestly, now that I think about it from the viewpoint of an Omega, it makes sense. You've never had a nest, have you?"

Shaking my head slowly, I dropped my gaze and started to pick at the dry skin around my nails. There were things, dreams if you will, that I gave up thinking about roughly six months into living in Asturg. It was hard to see the possibility of something as stable as a home, let alone the luxury of a nest. I do believe that some Omegas suffered from not having these things, especially when they went into heat or were pregnant. The secluded room was nothing special or comforting; it was just as it sounded—secluded. We Omegas were wired a certain way, and just as Cris' mom explained that I was starved for physical comfort, we could be starved for the stability that a home and nest provided.

"All right then, when all of this is said and done, finding a home will be at the top of the list," Sorin told me. "Also, we are most definitely getting one of those couches. I can only imagine what it would be like to take a nap on it with you in my arms, Dani-girl."

The blush that heated my cheeks at his words surprised me. I honestly didn't think I could still blush, but Toma had managed to pull off the same thing a few days ago.

"See, I keep telling her she needs to do that more often. Look how adorable she is right now," Toma pointed out, making my blush even worse.

All the tension was gone from the room, and the conversation tapered off as we dug into our food. When we were done, Petru and I collected the dishes and washed up from dinner. The two of us worked in companionable silence, just enjoying each other's company. At one point, I leaned my head against his shoulder as I dried the dish I held.

"What is it, Wildflower?" Petru murmured. "Something wrong, or are you too tired? If you need to go back to bed, I can finish this."

"No, I'm fine," I sighed. "I just can't believe you came for me, and you're all still here."

Taking the dish out of my hand and setting it down, Petru grabbed my waist and hoisted me up on the counter so we were at eye level. He didn't speak, just rested his forehead against mine and focused entirely on being *here* with me. After a few moments, I pressed my lips to his kissing him deeply with all the feelings I didn't know how to say. For me, actions always spoke louder than words so that's what I tried to do when I was at a loss. Petru used a hip to widen my legs so he could stand between them and pull me against his body. He slipped a hand in my hair holding me in place as we indulged in deep, slow kisses enjoying the physical contact.

I felt a jolt of jealousy through my bond, and when I tried to pull back, Petru refused to allow it. "Wildflower, it will take time for him to adjust, but the only way to help him feel more at ease with situations like this isn't to run from them. We are doing nothing wrong, and we've all declared our intentions to build a pack with you. He was there for all those conversations and never once spoke out against them. Dynamics are changing for all of us. Some will adjust faster than others, but don't you dare feel guilty or like you're betraying any of us for moments like this."

Gnawing on my bottom lip, I just didn't know how to move past the guilt I was feeling. Petru shifted to the side slightly, and a hand gripped my chin tugging me to look up. Instead of it being Petru which I assumed, it was Lucian. He pulled me, so I leaned forward slightly, and he kissed me tentatively as if he wasn't sure I would want his affection. Grabbing the back of his neck, I deepened the kiss making him groan as I licked at his lips. As if that's all the permission he needed, he devoured me, pulling a whimper from me. Petru's lips started to caress my neck, tugging open one button so he could continue across my shoulder. My body roared to life with desperate need and heat. It was as if a fire had ignited within me, stoked even higher with every touch and caress.

Breaking the kiss, I let out a whine needier than I'd ever sounded. "Oh God, it's happening," I mumbled, clinging to both of them as a wave of *need* rolled over me. "My heat, it's here. I feel like I'm going to burn from the inside out."

"It's okay, Wildflower, we've got you," Petru assured me as he cupped my face gently between his hands. "You just need to tell us what you want. We can make it so it's just you and Lucian here in the cabin. None of us expect anything from you, but whatever will make you feel comfortable right now."

Like contractions I've seen in childbirth, the next wave of need slammed into me worse than the first one. My vision blurred, muscles in my lower region contracted, and slick poured from me, preparing me for what was to come. I cried out. The pain of not being filled clawed at me. We'd all been warned that the first heat would be the worst, our need the greatest out of all of them. A need so strong it could present in unimaginable agony making the Omega desperate enough to let anyone fuck them to gain relief. I knew Petru was trying to be a good man by asking me what I wanted, but it was too late for me to give an unbiased answer. Yet I knew in my heart that none of these men would lay a finger on me unless I agreed to it.

"I need you all," I managed to get out before my body contracted again.

"Please, help me," I whined, a tear rolling down my cheek. "If everyone really meant what they said about us being a family, a pack, then someone better fuck me right now."

That got a response from them, and in the haze of my heat, I became vaguely aware of them tugging off my clothes. Fingers slipped inside me, making me scream and arch into the glorious feeling of being filled with something. It wasn't enough, though. I wanted to be stuffed to the point I couldn't take anymore.

"Seriously, guys," I growled. "I'm an Omega in heat, pre-lubed, and desperate for cock. Just shove your goddamn cock up in me already."

Someone snorted, trying to cover up a laugh. "Is she always so vocal about her needs?" Victor asked.

If anyone answered, I didn't hear it as someone slammed their dick balls deep into my pussy. I would've fallen back on the counter if their arms hadn't wrapped around my waist catching me. Dragging me to the edge of the counter, they started to thrust their hips in deep, pounding rhythmic thrusts. My whole body shook with the impact and I don't think I've ever been happier.

"Fuck yes, just like that," I mumbled as my hands grasped the person and pulled myself to their chest. Chocolate and cinnamon flooded my nose, letting me know it was Lucian, whose cock was imprinting on my pussy walls. His mouth latched onto my neck where his mark was and he dragged his tongue over it. Nails digging into his scarred back I cried out as an orgasm swept over me. "Lucian!"

"God, I love to hear you scream my name," Lucian whispered in my ear. "There is nothing better than watching you shatter in my arms, crying out your pleasure and knowing my cock is what's giving it to you."

Picking me up off the counter, he held me in a tight hug as he rutted into me. My heels dug into his ass as I tried to force him deeper into me, knowing his knot felt best when it was deep inside me. I could feel it starting to swell, so I relaxed my grip on his neck, changing the angle as I leaned back, driving myself down on him.

"Give me all of it, Alpha, bury that knot until it can't get any deeper," I begged, swirling my hips in encouragement.

"What my Omega wants, she gets," Lucian bit out as my back landed on the table we'd all just eaten at.

Tilting my hips up, Lucian drove into me just as his knot snapped into place, locking him inside me. The feel of his cum filling me set off another orgasm exploding within me. "Holy shit," I gasped, chest heaving as I fell limp against the table.

Lucian chuckled. "You don't think we're done, do you, Dani?"

I glanced up at his smug face as his hands settled on my hips, holding me tight as he bent down, catching hold of my lips with his. As he tongue-fucked my mouth, he rocked against me causing his knot to hit all the fucking buttons to make me come so many times I lost count. Finally, when all I could do was whimper, and my body shook at the slightest touch, he relented. Scooping me up off the table, he cradled me against his body and walked over to the couch, where he laid down on his back with me draped over him. Someone covered me in a blanket, and I twisted my head so I could see the rest of the room.

Cris was squatting next to the couch with a warm smile on his face and a glass of water with a straw. "It's important we keep you hydrated during this."

A sleepy smile tugged at my lips. "Always the doctor," I teased but gulped down the water.

Lucian's hand stroked my back absently as the others joined us in the living room area. The second I saw their faces, the euphoric high I had was instantly gone as I shoved up to look at them. Lucian and I both groaned as I forgot that we were attached, so I settled for folding my arms on his chest to prop myself up.

"What's wrong," I demanded.

"Nothing's wrong, sweetheart," Cris assured me, letting his fingers brush along my jaw. "We just decided it was best to wait for the first wave to pass before joining in. For an Omega, they are incredibly vulnerable during their heat since their need makes them desperate, impairing their judgment."

I warred with fluctuating emotions of doubt that they even wanted me at all and loving that none would act without being certain I understood what I was agreeing to. Being an Omega in heat was turning out to be a roller coaster of emotions. Their tenderness made me want to weep, but the voice in my head told me they didn't want to be part of this mess.

"Cris," Lucian interjected. "She's panicking a little that you're asking her again."

The tenderness in Cris' gaze made my heart skip a beat as he cradled my face and kissed me like he was afraid I'd break. "Sweetheart, you've been through so much in your life, especially when it came to intimacy. No one wanted to take the chance. Each and every one of us wants this to work, even if we have no idea how to do that. The last thing you should be worried about is whether or not they want you. In fact, I'm the one talking to you because the others couldn't be trusted this close to you. Benefits of being a Beta, we're attracted to an Omega in heat, but don't lose our minds over it."

That got a smile out of me as I giggled, but it also reminded me to say something. "In Oscad, many people consider Omegas to be snotty brats who dislike sharing. You know I have zero issues with the three of you being together, right? In fact, the times I've stumbled upon your not-so-subtle hints at getting me to join in, it's been fucking hot. I just wasn't ready yet, for any of you, but I am now. I want all of us to take this to the next level."

"You figured that out, did you," Cris whispered and laughed. "It was all Toma's idea, but none of us minded since we instantly knew how much you enjoyed seeing it."

"What can I say seeing people who love each other fucking is a turn-on," I shared. "I thought I'd become numb to that sort of thing spending so much time around the breeding houses. That's when I realized there was a difference between fucking and lovemaking."

"Trust me, sweetheart, we have so much to teach you in that department. I was amazed to find out how many creative ways there were to fuck with three people, but adding you as our fourth will be an adventure. Especially since you can take more than one of them at a time," Cris shared, painting dirty pictures for me, making my pussy pulse with excitement.

Lucian hissed at the sudden way I was clenching around him. "Okay, enough dirty talk. You're gonna have to wait until I'm free and not so fucking sensitive. Does she being in heat turn everything up a notch?"

"Yup," Cris answered with a grin. "The other bonus is your knot will come down faster since your body will know she'll require more than one male to meet her needs."

Looking past Cris at the others, I cocked my head. "Are we good, because having you all standing over there watching like a bunch of creepers is killing the mood?"

Victor grinned and shook his head as he came to sit on the floor by the couch. "Damn, and we thought you had a mouth on you before. Yeah, Little Spark, that was good enough for me."

"It might be better if we move this to the bunk room," Toma suggested.

Sorin didn't look convinced. "There's only bunk beds. There's no way we'd manage with that kind of space."

"Clearly, you've never had multiple partners while in the military," Toma teased as he headed to the bunk room. "You take the mattresses off the beds and put them on the floor. With ten bunks, we can have as much room as you'd like to maneuver, Sorin."

CHAPTER 43

Danella

As if my body understood what it meant when Lucian's knot relaxed and let me free, my body blazed with heat again. Cris scooped me up as I started to shiver and couldn't get my limbs to work right for the life of me. We entered the bunk room, which was just like it sounded. All the bunk frames had been shoved out of the way, creating an open space in the middle that Toma and Petru worked furiously to cobble together. Blankets and sheets were spread out while pillows were tossed into the middle of the padded space. The bunk mattresses weren't luxurious by any means, but they were far better than any other alternative I could think of.

Cris laid me down on the pillows and brushed my hair out of my face. "Tell me what you need, sweetheart. How can I help?"

I just shook my head as I contorted with the wave of need curling into a little ball and letting out the most pathetic whine ever. Cris moved aside, and Victor appeared before me, naked, showing off all his muscles. Then my gaze traveled down his body, following the trail of hair that led right to his hard bobbing cock. A cock, mind you, that was pierced, not just once, either. He had a bar going straight through his shaft right after the head of his dick, then another further down the shaft before it got to his knot. Unable to help myself, I licked my lips wondering what it would feel like to run my tongue over them.

Getting to my hands and knees, I crawled over to him and peered up as I reached out to touch him. "Can I?"

"Little Spark, you can touch me wherever you like," Victor shared. "Just know that as much as I welcome your touch, you don't need to feel obligated to. I want you to *want* to touch me, if that makes sense."

Grasping the base of his shaft, I licked the underside of his cock, flicking the ball of the piercing. "Oh, I want to," I murmured, just before taking the tip into my mouth.

I don't know why I was so fascinated with this simple piece of jewelry, but I wanted to know what it felt like in every way possible —licking, sucking, stroking. I explored every fucking inch of his cock making him moan as I did so. The more pleasure I pulled from him, the needier I became, if that was even possible. Legs set wide, exposing myself to anyone who cared to look. I arched my back and wiggled my ass in invitation, hoping someone would accept the offer. Soon enough, hands glided over my ass, and a mouth descended upon my weeping pussy.

Whoever was back there feasted on me, lapping at my slick and purring, causing his mouth to vibrate. I moaned and fell forward as my hand slipped off Victor's thigh. Another set of hands curled around me, taking a breast in each hand, rolling my nipples between their fingers. This had me moaning even louder. My body was assaulted with sensations that made my brain explode with pleasure. Victor slid a hand into my hair and grasped a fist full, holding me still as he fucked my mouth. I let him take control, relaxing my mouth and throat as best I could to accommodate him.

"How does it feel to have so much attention showered on you, Wildflower?" Petru asked, whispering in my ear as he tugged my nipples gently. "Can you feel your body surrendering to us, begging for our knots and kisses?"

Holy hell, I did not think that Petru would be the one for dirty talk, but fuck, if it wasn't hot.

"Look at you arching so Toma can get the best taste of your

pussy, as Victor uses that sassy mouth of yours for his pleasure," Petru continued. "What do you think should happen next? Do you want Toma to fuck you as Victor finishes in your mouth? Or maybe..."

Petru paused to let a hand slide down my back and between my asscheeks. The feel of his finger massaging my asshole, had my eyes rolling into the back of my head.

"Did you know that Omegas are made to be fucked in each and every hole they have?" Petru asked as he gathered some slick from my pussy before slipping it in where no one had been before. "Unlike the rest of us who have to take some care in preparing to take our partners, you just need a little lubrication to get things started. You can even take a knot in this perfect ass of yours. Just think what it would be like to be filled with two Alpha cocks knotted and claiming what's theirs."

The combination of Petru's dirty talk and Toma shoving his tongue into my pussy had me exploding with an orgasm that was so strong I almost blacked out. Clinging to Victor as he shoved his cock deep down my throat as he came, knot swelling, cum shooting out, forcing me to swallow.

"Ah fuck," Victor groaned. "Yes, my beautiful Little Spark, take all I've got like the good girl you are." My nails dug into his thighs, but this only seemed to have him bucking into my mouth.

Mouth firmly locked around Victor's dick, I didn't know what to do and tried to pull back, only it was clear that wasn't an option. I gave a slightly panicked whimper then Victor stroked my hair and started to purr.

"It's okay, Dani, you're gonna be fine," Victor assured me. "Let me just lay down so we can both be more comfortable until my knot calms enough to get you free. Should've thought this through better, but I didn't think this was possible."

Petru and Toma helped as Victor laid on his side and a pillow was put under mine. While Toma eating me out had been amazing, it wasn't doing much for the need of my heat. I was beginning to think it was more related to being knotted than orgasms, which I didn't mind since I'd be getting orgasms either way. Trying not to move too much, I rubbed my thighs together trying to get some friction on my aching pussy. I really should have known better, thinking no one would notice my dilemma, when two fingers shoved into me making me groan at the pleasure.

"Is this what you're looking for, Dani-girl, something to wrap your pussy around?" Sorin asked as he stroked his fingers against my needy flesh.

My answer was to hitch my left leg up to my chest, giving him more room to work. He chuckled as he pumped his fingers lazily making me practically growl at him, but unable to speak, I couldn't make my demands known. I pushed on Victor's hip to have him roll onto his back, then I moved with him, so my ass was up in the air as I rested my head on his hip. If this didn't get the point across for our fearless leader, then I wasn't sure what else to do.

"Hmm, which spot should I use?" Sorin mused as he traced a finger over my asshole down to my pussy. "Has anyone taken you in your ass before?"

"Goo," I managed to say around Victor's cock. *When would this damn thing start to go down?*

Using the same slicked-up fingers, Sorin worked them into my ass testing my response—or so I assumed. Then two more fingers reentered my pussy so that he was finger fucking both holes making me lose my fucking mind. My eyes rolled back in my head as the euphoric pleasure washed over me. God, who knew the feeling of being *full* would be so amazing, however I needed more. It wasn't enough, even though it took off the edge so I didn't get frustrated enough to take it out on Victor's cock that was oh so conveniently located in my mouth.

"God, I fucking love the sounds coming out of her mouth right now," Victor shared as he massaged his fingers along my scalp. "So sexy, mewling as Sorin plays with you. Who knew we'd get so lucky when you crashed into our lives."

Lost in the feel of Victor and Sorin, I didn't realize I was free from Victor's knot until he was kissing me. His tongue explored my mouth as if to make sure he hadn't left behind any damage while thanking me profusely all at the same time. Grabbing the side of his face, I let him pull me up as Sorin held my hips and settled me hovering over his cock.

"Now you're going to be a good little Omega for Sorin," Victor ordered, pressing a searing final kiss before stepping back.

Gasping for air and feeling a little disoriented with so many people turning my mind into mush with their touches. Sorin nuzzled past my hair until he could find my neck trailing soft kisses from my shoulder to my ear. "Just relax, Dani-girl, I've got you."

Not understanding his warning, I sucked in a harsh breath as his cock pressed against my ass. My eyes snapped open and I searched for something, someone to hold onto. Cris didn't hesitate for a second once he saw my concern coming to kneel right in front of me. Instantly I grabbed his biceps as I took a deep breath and let myself sink onto Sorin's cock.

"That's it, sweetheart, just relax. Let your body turn into putty, allowing it to mold to Sorin's cock," Cris soothed.

It wasn't that I was scared, unwilling, or didn't trust Sorin that made this challenging. No, it was the fact this mother fucking Alpha had a *thick* cock, and it was just taking a little effort to achieve. My body was thrilled to be pushed to the max, to prove it could accommodate our Alpha's needs. Once I was seated in his lap, literally stuffed full of his cock, I leaned back against him. Letting my head fall back on his shoulder.

"Holy shit," I breathed. "It's huge. How have we been sharing a room, and I never noticed that?"

Sorin laughed, causing him to thrust against me, causing a cry of bliss to escape my mouth. He sat with his legs crossed while cradling me in his arms as his finger explored my body. "Seems to me that means we need to work on your observation skills a little more." Smacking my hand against his arm, I glared at him. "Okay, I won't tease you about it. Let's just say I worked incredibly fucking hard to make sure you didn't notice. Woman, I've been living with a cock of fucking stone since that night I got to taste you."

"Hmm, that was a good night," I murmured, remembering him hoisting me up against the wall and eating me out.

"Hold up," Toma cut in. "Are you saying the two of you were messing around, and we weren't invited?"

Lifting my head, I found Toma looking rather put out with his arms crossed. Reaching out a hand, I wiggled my fingers, telling him to come to me. He almost looked like he wasn't, then he let out a huff and crawled over. Brushing a hand up his arm, I curled my fingers around his neck and pulled him down into a kiss. It was clear that Toma was feeling just a little insecure after hearing that, yet there was no mistaking how much I wanted him. He tried to hold out, not giving in to me, but with a nip at his lower lip, he growled and took charge.

The kiss wasn't sweet and tender; it was far more intense than that. It was as if he had something to prove to me. All it did was make me want to soothe him, show him that I desired him. Letting my hands fall to his waist, I grabbed his cock and gently tugged him to me. Sorin seemed to realize what I was trying to do and sat back on his hands as he moved his legs out of the way.

Toma pulled back, panting, as he looked down at me. "Are you sure? You almost couldn't take Sorin."

"I'm absolutely sure," I answered, directing his cock to my entrance. "You're my pack, the one the fates brought me to. I'll be able to handle whatever you give me just fine because you're all mine as much as I'm yours."

Toma's mouth slammed against mine, kissing and nipping at me as he pressed me back onto Sorin's chest. Taking a second to maneuver himself into position, he then eased into me. I moaned long and loud as I felt him taking up what little room I had left in that part of my body. It was overwhelming in the best way, almost like my mind didn't know how to process it, so it just accepted what was happening. Sorin's hands cupped my breasts and played with my nipples as he slowly moved. Toma waited a few seconds, letting Sorin move more easily within me before rocking into me opposite him.

It was so much—too much. I was starting to see stars as the pressure built up, leaving me at the edge of the cliff. Once they decided to leave me dangling, as they refused to speed up.

"Faster," I pleaded. "Fuck me faster, harder, like the Omega I am."

"Dani-girl, you can't tell, but both of us can feel how tight you are," Sorin bit out. "You're squeezing the hell out of us which makes it risky to move faster. Neither of us wants to hurt you. This is about pleasure."

Tossing from side to side like I could wiggle my way further onto their cocks. "Trust me. This is torture to be left on edge. I promise I will not break. Please, just fuck me. Fill me with your come, mark me in every way possible that I'm yours. Make it so no one but my pack will ever be enough to satisfy me."

That had Sorin snarling and lifting me off of both of them. I wailed at the loss of them, my body shaking with need. The next thing I knew, I was lifted up in Toma's arms, wrapping mine around his neck. Before I could even say a thing, he shoved me down on his cock, hands gripping my ass hard enough that I was sure there would be marks. Something I was more than okay with. I wanted their claim displayed all over my body to make all other Omegas jealous about what I had.

"You want us to fuck you like we mean it?" Toma asked, to which I nodded vigorously. "All right then, you're gonna get your wish, Dani. Just remember, this is what you asked for."

I was about to ask him what he was talking about when Sorin slammed into my ass making me scream and shatter into a million pieces as I came instantly. Neither cared as they pistoned into me at the rhythm and pace that had me laughing, unable to express what I was feeling any other way. Hearing their grunts and heavy breathing surrounding me just made everything *more*. To know they were enjoying this as much as I was, was incredibly important to me. When a second orgasm crashed into me, I cried out as my body was overwhelmed with ecstasy making me unable to do anything but let them carry me through this.

The swell told me they were close. Only it didn't slow them down; if anything, it made them more erratic. Their thrusts fell out of sync, but they clung to me tighter as if worried they might drop me. Sandwiched between them like this, I believed nothing could ever harm me. I trusted them both to keep me safe, treasure me, and continue to see my worth as more than just a breeder. They were everything I needed, and I knew I wouldn't let them slip away no matter what happened in the world around us.

Leaning back, I wrapped an arm around Sorin's head and bared my neck to him. "Sorin," I called, my voice husky. "I want you to mark me. Put your claim on me so no matter what, they can never tear us apart."

Sorin faltered momentarily before yanking me away from Toma and dropping us to the floor. Pressing my head down as he kept my hips high, he rode me hard. The sound of my cries and slapping skin was all I could hear as my Alpha took what was his. With a roar, he came, his knot expanding. It burned, although the bite of pain kept my head clear as I climaxed.

"Do it," I pleaded, with a whine adding to my desperation, making it clear this was what I wanted.

Just when I thought he was going to ignore my request, I gasped at the shock of his teeth piercing the skin around my shoulder. Just as quickly as the pain registered, it was gone and replaced with bliss as I floated through the air. A tension I didn't know was knotted in the pit of my stomach unraveled as my bond with Sorin bloomed into existence. It was done. I was theirs, and no one could do a goddamn thing about it. A sob burst out as tears of relief and joy spilled out of me. I could feel Sorin's panic. Though when I showed him what I was feeling, he wrapped me up in his arms and curled around me.

"Shh, Dani-girl, it's going to be all right," Sorin whispered. "I got you, forever and always. We all do. Even without a bond connecting us, any one of these men would do whatever it takes to keep us together. We weren't going to let you go that easily."

Sniffling, I nodded, trying to brush away the tears. They just didn't seem to want to stop. A hand reached out and took mine, and I could feel Lucian's support and understanding, letting me know he was going to be okay with this. Petru and Victor joined us, creating a puppy pile of sorts of men trying to comfort me as I tried to rein in my emotions. It took a little while, but with their help, I was able to take a deep breath and settle things. I had no idea how much I'd locked away, deep inside, about this whole situation. Then the security of being bonded with Sorin released it all in one massive wave.

Relaxed and surrounded by my pack, I dozed until I heard someone enter the room. I tried to sit up to see who it was, but Sorin growled and put his mouth over his mark to hold me to him. Aftershocks of my orgasm shot through me, making me shiver and clench down on him. He rocked into me as if to remind me we were attached. Once I relaxed, he nuzzled my neck and started to purr which had me gasping at the vibrations I could feel through his *whole* body.

"Holy shit, that's a cool trick," I groaned.

Sorin nipped my ear as his purring stopped. "We have lots of things to teach you, Dani-girl."

I heard more moving around and saw Toma and Cris joining us. "Where have you two been?" I asked with a frown.

"Ah..." Cris said, rubbing the back of his neck. "Just needed to take care of something real quick before we could join you guys."

"Is everything okay? Did something happen?" I demanded, not appreciating the tiptoeing around.

Victor snorted. "I'll say something happened. Your Alpha there gave our man a serious case of the blue balls when he yanked you away. Poor man needed to get his happy ending, so Cris, the martyr he is, helped his partner out."

It took a second for my heat-addled brain to understand what he was saying, although when it finally hit I burst into laughter. The others snickered until Toma sat up. "Keep laughing, assholes. It will just make it easier to castrate you all. Then I'm the only one who can fuck Dani, and you all just get to watch."

That quickly shut everyone up and I drifted off, too tired to deal with their egos.

Danella

My nap didn't last as long as I would have liked it before the need arose in my body again. Wiggling against whoever was holding me, I whined, refusing to open my eyes and praying I could talk my body into getting more sleep. Sadly my heat would not be ignored, and as the desperation grew, so did my discomfort.

"All right, sweetheart, I've got you," Cris murmured as his cock slid inside me. "I have no idea if this will help since I don't have a knot. All I know is if I didn't get a chance to fuck you, my cock was going to explode."

"Wait," I said, twisting to look at him. "I want to do this face-to-face so I can kiss you."

Cris' smile was so bright and wide it made my heart flutter. How could such a simple request make him so happy? Rolling over, I let Cris pull my leg over his hip and thrust into me once more. Brushing the hair out of his face so I could pepper it with kisses, he started to rock into me. His arms wrapped around me, hands splayed wide on my back, holding me securely as he moved.

"God, you are so beautiful, Dani," Cris whispered, his lips bruising against mine. "Not to mention you're smart, loving, and when you choose to let someone become important to you, there's nothing you wouldn't do for them. No one in the world is as lucky as we are to have you."

My heart exploded with affection for this man in my arms, who was nuzzling soft kisses against my lips. To think there were men like Cris in this harsh, unforgiving world was a miracle. He was a pure soul, full of light and kindness that I wasn't sure I deserved but was too selfish to ever give up. Pushing back on me, Cris rolled us so I was looking up at him. Gathering my legs, he bent them so my knees were to my chest and hugged me tight as he started to move with a little more purpose. I was surrounded by him. He was all I could see, smell, and feel giving the illusion it was just the two of us for a change.

I loved having all of them around me, being the family I desperately was searching for. Yet every so often, I think it would be nice to have one of them all to myself for a bit. That might be something we need to discuss once we get our lives settled a little more. As if Cris could sense my mind wandering, he nipped at my bottom lip, making me smile.

"Dani, I'm going to make sure you smile ten times a day, no matter what. The way you look when you smile is radiant," Cris informed me.

Cupping his face, I pulled him into a long, slow kiss, showing him how much I liked the idea of that. "The person who's truly lucky here is me," I shared, letting my thumb caress his cheek. "I've done nothing to deserve such amazing men such as yourselves. All my life, I've been deemed the problem child with a smart mouth and a bad attitude. Yet, for some reason, none of you see that."

Cris chuckled. "Oh no, we see that. The difference is, we love that about you. If you didn't have the attitude or sharp comebacks, how would you keep all of us in our place? Someone needed to find a way to wrangle this group of hard-headed Alphas and Beta."

"No, you're perfect, Cris," I argued.

"Hey now," Petru interjected, appearing overhead. "No playing favorites."

I grinned at him. "Well, other than Lucian, Cris is the only one who's told me they love me. I think that's reason enough to make him my favorite... for now."

Petru glared at Cris, but there was no real feeling behind it. That man loved his Beta too much to ever be mad about something like this.

Cupping my cheek, he turned my head to look at him. "You make a good point, Wildflower. It seems our Beta beat the rest of us to the punch, but make no mistake, we all feel the same about you."

Cris paused in his movements to sit back and let me rest my feet on the floor, giving more room for Petru as he leaned down to kiss me. Hands on my thighs, Cris resumed his thrusting but kept it at a leisurely pace. My need for him to speed up and thrust harder had me rolling my hips to show him what I needed. When the man didn't give in to my coaxing, I let out a whine which had Petru pulling back to look down at me.

"Is he still your favorite? Can he do no wrong in your eyes?" Petru asked, teasing me, knowing exactly what was happening.

Wriggling closer to Cris in an attempt to fix the problem, he had the audacity to pull all the way out. "No," I cried, reaching out for him. "Please, Cris, I need you to fuck me, don't stop."

He leaned down and kissed along my inner thigh until his mouth latched onto my clit, and he sucked hard. A startled scream burst out of me as my hands gripped his hair, shoving him closer to me.

"Oh, did no one warn you that Cris' favorite game when he's allowed to be in charge is how long he can keep you on edge?" Petru commented, absently tracing a finger around my nipple as he watched with greedy eyes. "I suppose you're gonna need to rethink your definition of perfect now, aren't you."

With a frustrated growl, I batted his hand away as I slammed my legs closed around Cris' head. "Someone better fuck me right now, or no one's ever getting sex from me ever again."

Cris pried my legs open and lifted his head to look at me then Petru. "Shit, I think she's serious."

"Then it sounds like I should make sure you do your job well since you started this," Petru reasoned, moving to kneel behind

Cris. "Should we see how long you can hold out toying with her when it also sets the pace for you?"

I didn't understand what he was talking about until I felt two fingers scoop up some slick then heard Cris moan. "That's cheating," Cris panted as he arched into Petru's touch.

The Alpha chuckled and pressed a kiss to Cris' shoulder. "I call it proper motivation."

I watched as Petru loosened Cris up using my slick to lubricate him, which made it so much hotter. Cris' moans were so erotic I thought I was going to come just listening to them. Eyes hooded, cock pulsing with precum leaking out of it, I couldn't be a bystander anymore. Rolling onto my stomach, I crawled over to lick his cock from balls to tip.

"Holy fuck," Cris shouted. "Sweetheart, if you do that again, I'm going to come way too fast."

Catching Petru's gaze, I grinned before taking all of Cris in my mouth. The Beta released a string of swear words as I hummed in pleasure. I definitely needed to do this for them more often. Hearing them lose their composure at my efforts was such a power trip.

"Dani, wait," Cris begged, but I ignored him. Payback was a bitch, but at least I was going to let him come. His hands fisted my hair as he thrust deep into my mouth, shooting his cum down my throat. "Fuck, fuck, fuck!"

Not ready to release him yet, I kept him in my mouth, gently sucking and milking him as his body shook. A hand stroked down my back urging me to let Cris go as their fingers slipped between my legs then inside me. He thrusted a few times but pulled out to use those same fingers to prepare my ass.

Letting Cris slip from my mouth, I looked back to see Toma. "I think the two of us need a do-over, don't you?" he asked with a tender smile on his face.

Sitting up, I leaned against him as he teased my ass and made me moan. "Yes, a do-over sounds amazing."

Tenderly he pulled me back, so I was pushing myself down on him, relaxing into the feel. Letting out little mewling sounds of pleasure. It helped that he wasn't quite as thick as Sorin, making everything that much easier. Once I was filled to the brim with his cock he grabbed my legs and lifted them. Confused as to what the hell he was doing, I saw Petru stroking Cris' hard and ready cock as he eased himself in. Cris was breathing heavily as he gripped Petru's thighs, visibly overwhelmed with everything going on.

"Did you know slick from an Omega in heat can make any male hard again almost instantly?" Toma asked, his lips brushing my ear.

I shook my head and whispered a faint. "No."

"Handy trick when you have a needy Omega and not enough men to go around," Toma said as he settled me onto Cris' shaft.

Groaning at the delicious fullness I was absolutely addicted to, I took a few breaths before letting Toma urge me forward. Wrapping my arms around Cris, I hugged him and buried my face in his neck. Never in a million years would I have thought of this configuration, but I fucking loved it. Now all four of us got to experience love and pleasure together. The Alphas took control as Cris and I held onto each other unable to do more than that with the onslaught of sensation. Petru thrust Cris into me as Toma did the same from the other side, so Cris was deeper than any of them had gone so far. Knot or not, this Beta was hitting all the right places.

"So deep," I mewled. "You're both so deep it feels amazing."

Toma peppered my skin with kisses as he kept up a steady rhythm, not too fast but not too slow, either. All of this was so overwhelming I'm not sure I could handle more than this.

"I got you, Dani," Toma soothed. "Don't you worry, Petru and I would never let anything happen to either one of you."

Whimpering at the flood of emotions, I turned my head to kiss him. "You've been by my side since the beginning, and I never thanked you for it."

"There is no need to thank me," Toma assured. "It's what we do for the people we love, and you, our feisty little Omega, are loved indeed."

Tears pricked at my eyes at hearing him say that. "Will you make us a family? I want to feel all of you, to know exactly how you're doing and help when you need me."

"It would be my honor to claim you, Danella," Toma answered, a seriousness in his voice that I'd never heard before.

Turning to face Petru and Cris, I asked them the same question. "Will you be my family?"

Petru reached around Cris to draw me to him. "Yes, my perfect little Wildflower, whom I love. I will happily be your family." He kissed away the tears before giving me a searing kiss that I felt all the way to my toes.

Shifting the kiss, he bit my bottom lip between his teeth. I gasped in surprise, not thinking he would choose such a palace to mark me. Then I understood why he did it as he licked and sucked on the spot, making me instantly orgasm. Cris grunted as my pussy clenched around his cock, looking for the knot it craved. Petru released me but instantly went to Cris' neck and put his mark right where the neck and shoulder met. Toma did the same to me, placing his mark under Sorin's.

Both Cris and I screamed as we came again and again as our Alphas tortured us with the proof of their love for us. Just when I thought I would pass out, Toma came with a shout knotting himself deep in my ass, hugging me tight. My body twitched and shuddered, so overly sensitive to the slighted movement that had me spiraling into another climax. Gingerly, Toma pulled me away from Cris and laid us down on our sides. Petru did the same thing and pressed forward, so the four of us were in one big group hug.

"Toma," Cris croaked, tears shimmering in his eyes as he brushed his hand down the man's arm. "I did it. Petru was able to knot me."

Toma took his Beta's hand and kissed his palm tenderly. "I'm so happy for you, babe. I know how much that means to you and I look forward to that moment for us, too." Still holding Cris' hand, he bit down on the meaty part under the thumb, completing the circle between us. I sucked in a sharp breath as I felt them all at once. The tidal wave of love and devotion it hit me with was overwhelming and yet I didn't want to close the door on my end of our bond to give myself relief. This was exactly what I'd been waiting for my whole life, to have this connection to those who I chose, and chose me.

"Can you feel it?" I asked, needing to know if I was alone in experiencing this.

Toma tucked in closer to me and nodded. "It's amazing. I had no idea people could have so much love for each other."

"The fates have truly blessed us. What a gift to experience such a thing," Petru murmured, his voice full of awe.

"Dani, is this what it feels like to you all the time?" Cris inquired.

"Kind of," I answered, though it sounded more like a question. "I've only been bonded to Lucian for a few days, and there's a big difference between one bond and five."

Cris stroked my head lovingly as he kissed my forehead. "Do you have a way to turn it off if necessary? I don't want us clamoring in your head all the time. It would be too great a strain."

I snorted. "Once a medic, always a medic," I teased. "Yes, I believe I have a way to shut things off, although it would stop me from feeling you guys at all."

"Hmm, maybe that's something we'll need to explore as we all adjust to this. There must be some way for us not to come on so strong either," Petru mused aloud.

Nodding, I yawned at the same time my stomach growled rather loudly. "Seems like other things need some attention first."

The door to the bunk room opened, and Lucian entered carrying a large tray of food. "Seems we timed it just right. Are you hungry enough to eat in your current...situation, or do you want to wait?"

Giving my ass a little wiggle, Toma hissed and clamped his hand down on my hip. "Dani," he growled.

"It seems we're gonna have to wait," I concluded.

Everyone chuckled at that as Victor and Sorin joined us with drinks along with a bucket of warm water for us to clean up with. While I loved being connected to my Alphas, I was relieved when it didn't last too long so I could wolf down some food.

"I'm feeling way better for some reason," I shared, licking my fingers, not willing to pass up any trace of this amazing meat they cooked.

"There have been theories that the first heat can be managed better with bonding the Omega," Cris said, laying on his stomach, unable to sit just yet. "Everything about a heat is to create the perfect environment for an Omega to conceive. It's always been my personal belief that when Alphas and Omegas are compatible and drawn to each other by scent, they make the best scenario for that. So, in theory, if the body feels that it's done its job, the heat will be alleviated faster. Mind you, this is my conclusion. It hasn't been officially studied or anything here in Asturg."

"Sounds logical to me," Sorin commented. "Plus, heats can last from two to five days, so there's always the chance she just has a shorter heat. Nothing about her cycle has been what the statistics tell us."

Lucian nodded in agreement while chewing but held up a finger to give him a second until his mouth was empty. "Regardless of our theories on her heat, I believe it would be wise to stay for another day or so just to be sure it's safe."

Everyone seemed to agree on that, and I didn't mind either. While the *need* part of the heat seemed to be subsiding since I'd been able to go this long without begging to get knotted, I was still exhausted. My body felt like it was made out of lead and everything was a struggle to manage. Now full, it was becoming even harder to keep my eyes open, and I yawned.

Victor reached over and tugged me closer to lift me onto his lap and cradle me against his chest. Not complaining one bit about the arrangement, I curled up and tucked my head under his. With a hand on my hip, he held me securely, then started to purr as he nuzzled his cheek against my hair. This was pure Omega bliss, to have a full belly, just fucked soreness, and the warm body of one of my Alphas reminding me that I was safe and loved.

It was a heady realization of how much I'd been lacking when it came to having my Omega needs met. Now I was soaking up every opportunity to fill that empty bucket. I could feel a shift in me as well. Never before had I felt contentment such as I was right this second. We had no idea what the future held, how things would turn out, or if we'd ever be able to return to the life Sorin and his men once had. None of that mattered, in any case. As long as we had each other, we could make anything work. Lucian was proving that to us all with every passing moment and I didn't know how to thank him.

His gaze met mine as if he could tell that I was thinking of him. I focused on our bond, letting the others fall to the back of my mind as I gave him my full attention. He needed to know and understand just how much I appreciated all the sacrifices he was making on my behalf. Mouthing the words—*thank you* he smiled tenderly at me. Everyone believed he was a cold, callus man like his father, but he was quite the opposite. Even if he hid it well. Now nothing was hidden between us, and while I valued that for moments like this. I also knew it would lead to a fair amount of arguments as we grew together as a pack.

"What's the plan going forward?" Victor asked, his deep voice rumbling under my ear. "Once we know it's safe to travel with Little Spark's heat over, then what?"

CHAPTER 45

Danella

Sorin shifted, so he was now leaning against the wall and tucked a leg up by his chest, the most relaxed I'd ever seen him. "I planned to reach out to Savo, see if he could be of any help and what he had in mind to get Dani's friends out of Asturg. That will help me know if we need to hide Lucian for a few days and report back to base or not."

I could tell Lucian wasn't thrilled about that choice, and Sorin glanced over at him. "Look, it's not my first choice. The simple fact is we need to maintain any and all pretenses that things are fine. That nothing went wrong with the manhunt, and the North is not an issue. If there was a way I could keep us all together, I would."

"What about having him hide out with my mother?" Cris offered. "He would be closer, protected, and no one would dare to enter that home without permission."

That had me tensing, not at all liking the idea of endangering his mother. Even though she hadn't told me her whole story, it was clear her life hadn't been easy.

"I will keep that as an option, but I would prefer to try something that won't have any backlash on an innocent," Sorin said, helping me to relax a little.

"Don't worry about me," Lucian cut in. "I was hiding out near the base for a week, and no one ever noticed. My specialty is sneaking into places and not getting caught, but first, it might be smart to see what my dearest brother has to say."

Sorin sat silently for a while, stroking the scruff on his chin. I could feel how intensely he was considering everything, and I remember Toma once mentioned this was a typical occurrence with Sorin in tough situations. Our leader wasn't one to make quick, snap decisions if he had the time to think it through.

"Truthfully, I should just call him now and see what he has to say. Regardless of the answer to helping us, he'll still need time to pull off the rescue," Sorin announced as he rose to his feet and headed out of the bunk room.

I wasn't sure if he would come back, but no one else seemed to feel the need to follow after him, so I stayed where I was. Victor's fingers stroked along my hip, sending tendrils of heat spreading from my leg right to my pussy. A moan, almost more like a hum, escaped me as I nuzzled against him. This feeling wasn't as strong as the bone-deep need I'd been experiencing. It was more like intense desire. I wanted to feel him, to be connected to him in the most intimate way possible. Although, if I'm being honest with myself, I wanted to feel what those piercings were like rubbing inside me.

Reaching down, I freed his cock from his boxers and directed him to my entrance. Shifting around until he glided into me, giving me that sense of fullness as the jewelry added a new enticing sensation. Wrapping both arms around my body, he hugged me to his chest burying his head in the crook of my neck and *purred*. Gasping as his deep rumbling purr turned those damn piercings into vibrating pressure points that hit *all* the right spots. Lazily I rolled my hips, not really trying to ride him, more to feel all of him in every way possible. He seemed to be on the same wave link as me, understanding that this was more than just sex as he rocked slowly in and out of me. This bear of a man was always trying to protect me and keep me safe, treasuring me above all others but this pack. I got the pleasure of seeing this vulnerable part of him. Not every time would it be like this if the way he fucked my mouth was any indication. Still, it was nice to have this moment.

Sorin rejoined us with the satellite phone, then paused at seeing Victor and me. "Ah..."

"Make your call," Victor said, practically ordered. "My Little Spark will be able to keep nice and quiet like the good girl she is. I'll just have her keep my cock nice and warm until the conversation ends, and I can make her come."

My mouth suddenly went dry with how shocked and turned on I was. Would Sorin actually do it? Everything in me knew Vicky wouldn't just let me sit here while Sorin was on the phone. He was going to test just how quiet I could be while another Alpha was on the phone, who was also Lucian's half-brother. Sorin's gaze flicked to me letting his eyes drink their fill of my naked body and Victor's cock buried balls deep inside me.

"This should be interesting," Sorin muttered, then shifted his attention to Lucian. "Are you okay with this?"

My admiration for Sorin increased tenfold at the fact that he would take the time to ask Lucian that. How the fuck had I found myself such good men who were willing to put in the effort to make our dynamic work.

"Don't worry, the second I think she's getting too loud I'll have something that I think will manage to keep her quiet," Lucian answered, and the smoldering look he gave me told me exactly what he was planning.

Getting the answer he needed, Sorin entered the number and put the phone on speaker so we could all hear it ringing. "Interesting how no one asked me how I felt about this little stunt," I muttered.

"Little Spark, if you didn't want to play my game, you'd be out of my lap faster than a lit fuse. We all know good and well that if you don't want to do something, you give zero fucks in letting us know," Victor chuckled.

I was going to share a few more choice words, but then a man answered the phone. "Hello?"

"Hello, my name is Sorin. I'm a friend of Savo's. Is he there?" Sorin asked.

"He's here...somewhere. Let me go find him. Things have been a little crazy around here since our son was born. No one is getting much sleep, and things are falling through the cracks. So if you had a meeting set up with him, I'm sorry he didn't reach out," the man rambled, the tiredness in his voice adding to his words.

"Congratulations on a healthy birth of a child. I'm sure the lack of sleep is worth it," Sorin said with a small smile on his lips.

"Spencer, why are you talking on my encrypted cell phone?" another man demanded.

"Huh? Oh... well, he said his name is Sor—"

"Stop," Savo ordered. "Please take Dalton back to Cambrie. I just finished changing him so she could get a shower."

"Oookkaaayy," Spencer responded, clearly not pleased with being cut off. "Come here, little man, we'll let grumpy Daddy-S take his important phone call, keeping all the secrets to himself. Don't worry. I'm sure mommy can get it out of him later."

"I told you Daddy-S isn't gonna be a thing. It's Otec," Savo yelled, then sighed heavily. "Hello?"

"It seems I called at a bad time," Sorin commented.

There was a deep grunt on the other end. "With that little wonder now out in the world and not in the safety of her womb, I'm not sure anytime will be good. Fuck, man, I had no idea how becoming a father was going to fuck with my head so much. I nearly shot a delivery driver when he walked up to me as I was working in the garage, thinking he was coming to take my kid."

"While I've never experienced it, I have seen a drastic change in those blessed with children. It does indeed change everything," Sorin agreed. "Speaking of someone stealing children, I was calling to find out your plan to return these Omegas to their families. Also, to ask a favor."

"I figured as much. Let me head to my office where we can talk a little more freely. I try to keep Marius and Nixon out of this part of things as much as possible. Marius especially feels responsible for the Omegas getting shipped off in the first place even though we're slowly getting back all that we can," Savo explained.

A lull in the call occurred as I could hear a door opening then closing, a chair being drawn out, papers shuffling, and a clunk like he'd set the phone down. This was the moment Vicky decided to make his move. The bastard pretended to adjust me so he could stretch his legs out and lean back against one of the bunks making his cock thrust up into me. I stifled a gasp leaning forward, bracing my hands on his thighs as I now straddled the man.

"Hold on, I'm grabbing my file on this real quick. Cambrie will have my head if I don't make sure my information is correct. She likes to make sure we can track down the families, so they're prepared for their homecoming," Savo said absently as papers shuffled.

This had my head snapping up to stare at Sorin. He knew all too well I desperately wanted information on whether my mother was alive. To save myself the pain, I just accepted she was gone, but to get confirmation would just put the wondering to rest.

"All right, I have Victoria Bombardo, also known as Tori, age nineteen. Both parents are still living and have great-paying jobs. Seems they sent her to the Care Center the moment she presented as an Omega since they both lost their jobs," Savo shared, surprising me with how much information he had on us. "Violet Antonal, age twenty-three, her mother is still living, but her father passed two years ago of a terminal illness he'd had most of his life. Danella Holstad, age twenty-five, has both parents still living, but her mother is not well. They're a prominent family, so she is getting excellent medical care. However, it doesn't look good. The sooner we can get her home, the better if she hopes to say goodbye."

Hearing the news about my mother, I covered my face and burst into tears. Someone approached me and pulled me into their arms. The sweet chocolate scent told me it was Lucian. He was the only other person who knew I'd longed to find out about my mother. Clinging to him, I sobbed, shocked to hear my mother was alive and tortured with the knowledge I still might not get to see her. Lucian carried me out of the room and settled on the couch, rocking me as I processed all this.

"My Heart, if there is a way we can get you home to see your mother, then I vow to you it will happen," Lucian whispered, pressing his lips to my forehead. "If she is your mother, then clearly your strength came from her. If Savo tells her you're alive, I have to believe she will hold on until she can see you."

I tried to talk, but I could only manage hiccupping gasps of air as I fought back the tears. Giving up, I just surrendered to the feelings but tried not to overwhelm the guys with them.

"Don't do that, Wildflower," Petru scolded as a blanket was tucked around me. "Don't hide your pain from us. In fact, do the opposite. Give it all to us so we can carry that burden for you, at least for a little while. You've been holding onto this for so long. Being so strong and brave. It's time to allow your family to support you in freeing yourself to be weak, just for now. When you're ready, we will help you back up, dust you off, and stand right beside you."

Blinking away tears, I looked at him, wondering if he really meant what he was saying. Petru took a tissue then wiped the tears and snot from my face making me realize I must look terrible.

"I don't want to be weak," I croaked out.

"Dani, you are hardly weak. Even now, you're fighting to pull yourself together so you can charge ahead," Lucian chided. "All he's asking is that you don't shut us out, hiding the parts of you that *you* think are weak. We all heard the same thing you did, and it doesn't take a genius to know how important your parents are to you. Hell, we've seen the lengths you'll go to for your friends. How could a parent hold less importance to you than them?"

Sniffling, I wiped at my nose and brushed my hair out of my face, trying to ground myself in something. Then I realized what he was saying, what they both were saying. The thing I needed was right here, in front of me, ready to slog through this emotional baggage with me. Why did it have to be so hard for me to let them help me? I trusted them to protect me physically, but why didn't that extend to emotionally?

"How... How can I be strong but let you help? I don't know how to do that," I sobbed.

Petru gave me a sad smile before he pressed a soft kiss to my lips. "It's okay. We will figure it out together, but I need you to answer one question. If we can get you back to see your mother, do you want us to make that happen, however necessary? Meaning, we can send you back with Tori and Violet while we deal with things here, so you have time with your mother."

My eyes grew wide. "Are you asking me to leave?"

"No, my sweet little wildflower, I am telling you that if this is important and you need to do this. Your pack will support you one hundred percent no matter what," Petru explained. "What I don't want is for you to assume it's impossible for you to go home right away."

"What if something happens and you get put in jail or killed? I won't know if anything's wrong since I'll be back in Oscad." I shook my head furiously. "No, we either go together to see her, or we don't go at all. Besides, how can I see my mother, tell her I have a pack and you're not with me? She will want to meet all of you."

"Okay, then that's what we'll do. No matter what, when this is over we'll visit your family and you can introduce us," Lucian decided. Petru gave him a disapproving look but sighed as he stroked my cheek with his thumb. "I love you, Danella, and I want to fix this for you, but if this is your choice I will support you as promised."

"That's my choice. We all go, or we don't go at all," I announced, knowing it might mean never seeing my mother alive. Even still, I wouldn't do that without them by my side. We were a pack, and packs do things together, as a team, end of story.

"I'll tell Sorin," Petru murmured, kissing me quickly before heading back to the bunk room.

CHAPTER 46

Toma

Feeling Dani's heartache first hand wasn't something I wanted to experience often. It was as if my own heart was breaking at the thought of losing my mother, who was still alive and well. Never did I imagine all that would be involved in being bonded to an Omega. We'd gone from one extreme of overwhelming love and joy to not only hearing our girl sobbing in the other room but experiencing it with her. I rubbed a hand over my chest like that would relieve some of the pain, but it wasn't mine to manage. Petru, unable to hold back any longer, headed for the living room.

"Hold on one sec, Savo," Sorin said abruptly, cutting off what the other man was saying to whisper something to Petru as he passed by. With a nod and a reassuring squeeze on Sorin's arm, Petru went to look after our Omega.

Sorin closed his eyes and softly cleared his throat, before resuming the call. It was the only sign he was aware of what Dani was dealing with right now. "The situation since we last spoke is a little different. Tori and Violet are both safe, awaiting whatever plan we have to get them out of Asturg. Danella, well...She's now my pack's bonded Omega."

Silence fell on the other end of the line.

"There's more," Sorin added. "A rather unexpected occurrence that I think will literally change the world as we know it. I'm not talking out of my ass on this, either. Because of Dani, I've been placed in a situation where we might be able to end this war."

"I believe you, man, hell I have firsthand experience with that. Our Omega, Cambrie, is the reason we took a stand and changed things here in Oscad. It's fucking nuts the lengths you will go for someone you want to protect with every ounce of your body," Savo said, his words full of emotions I could now understand.

It's only been an hour since I bonded with Dani and Cris, but there is no doubt in my mind that I would destroy anyone or anything that dared to harm or take them from me. As an Alpha, I've always been more laid back, but I had a feeling that was about to change.

"Seeing as you've gone through this already, I feel more confident in sharing the rest of this with you. My team found Dani and her friends after we attacked an outpost on the border. The outpost your half-brother Lucian was commander of. In a series of events I'm not going to go into, Lucian is also bonded to Dani," Sorin shared, letting that bomb drop and now awaiting to hear the reaction.

"Lu... Lucian? Is that who my father picked to take my place when I left?" Savo asked.

My brows shot up, utterly surprised he had no idea. Had the man not kept tabs on what was going on in Asturg? Could it be that he'd turned his back on everything so completely he didn't want to know?

"You didn't know?" Sorin asked skeptically. "How could you not know who was next in line when your packmate is the fucking Head Speaker?"

"Hey, I don't do the politics side of things. My job is to protect our Omega and ensure she stays out of trouble as she tries to rescue the world. The second I crossed the border, Asturg was dead to me. I wanted nothing to do with it, ever. Then I had to go and pick myself a woman to love more than life itself, who got the bright idea to send black market smugglers in after the stolen Omegas. Now here I am, waist-deep, in the shit that's my home country," Savo growled. "So no,

I didn't have a fucking clue about Lucian. Father liked to keep his sons separated once they were old enough for him to train individually."

Sorin grunted at this as if he was willing to accept that answer. "Regardless of your personal view of Asturg, Lucian and I are uniquely positioned to change things. We are formulating a plan to kill your father and his men and take over the country. Once we do that, we'll approach my father about a peace treaty and end this godforsaken war once and for all."

"Oh, is that all?" Savo drawled.

"No, we want to build an army of people who've hidden from the camps in the mountains and possibly ask Oscad for assistance as well," Sorin continued. "As you said yourself, our Omega is from a prominent family. I'm the president's heir to the South, as Lucian is to the North. Now tell me a better scenario for making real, lasting change happen in your home country?"

A heavy sigh could be heard through the phone. "Let me talk to a few people and see their reactions to this situation. I can't promise anything, but I know for a fact that if Cambrie finds out about this, you'll end up with more than you bargained for."

"Sounds like our Omegas would get along well," Sorin chuckled. "Dani is never one to underestimate."

"Ha, well, I'm sure a disciplined man such as yourself has a handle on things," Savo teased.

Sorin laughed softly. "Just as I'm sure you keep your pack in line, following all the rules I remember you loving to enforce."

"Fuck, who are we kidding? That woman rules this home, as I'm sure yours will soon," Savo groaned. "Although I think she's going to have competition with Dalton now in the picture. That baby can make the burliest of men turn to putty with a single coo."

"I'm truly happy for you and your pack, my friend. It sounds like leaving here was the right choice for you, and I'm glad you found peace and love after all you've endured," Sorin said, his words ringing honest and true. "If I could ask one more small favor on behalf of Dani."

With timing that couldn't be more perfect, Petru walked back into the room and shook his head before telling Sorin something in a low voice. Our leader's face fell into a scowl, not liking the answer he'd been giving.

"Tell me what it is, and I'll see what I can do," Savo answered. "I'm guessing it will be easier to accomplish than overthrowing the government and stopping a war that's been going on for generations."

"Dani heard you say her mother isn't doing well. I tried to have one of the others convince her to go back with the other two so she can see her. Danella was living this whole time under the impression that her mother didn't survive Dani being taken from their home. My request is for you to tell her mother that she is alive, safe, happy, and part of a pack that loves her. It's my hope that knowing her daughter is alive and well will help her to hold on until we can get Dani back to see her," Sorin explained.

"Consider it done. Cambrie will meet with her parents immediately to tell them that if I let her. Family is incredibly important to her, so it will be no trouble at all to make it happen," Savo assured us. "Also, I'm sorry. If I'd known she was there and could hear me, I wouldn't have put it so callously."

"There was no way for you to know, and it's been something that's weighed heavily on her for an incredibly long time. Now she has answers, and the sooner we stabilize things here, the better," Sorin reasoned.

"Do I have a day or two to gather the information and see how willing they'll be to help?" Savo inquired.

Sorin scratched his chin, then nodded to himself. "Two is the most I can give you before we need to make a move. If the other two Omegas need to sit tight while we try to end this war, they are in the safest place we can provide them. Just so you have all the facts when you talk to your people."

"Then I'm going to hang up and get to work. Stay safe, Sorin," Savo said before hanging up.

The four of us waited in silence to see what our leader would decide to do as we waited. We'd already agreed to stay here for a few days to make sure Dani was well and truly out of her heat, but that didn't mean we couldn't use the time wisely.

"Toma, I need you to work on a route that will get us through Southern territory avoiding towns and military stations that will get us as close to the mountain range as you can. I know Lucian was going to head North then cross over, but I think it might be smarter to do it this way. I also need to see if you can dig up whatever maps we have of the Northern territory. For I'm not so worried about where towns and outposts are. I want to know more about the land-scape," Sorin instructed.

I nodded my understanding and got up to pull some clothes on. As he continued to give orders to the others, I headed for my laptop in the kitchen. Lucian was lying propped up on the couch with Dani curled up on his chest, fast asleep. Quietly I walked over to them crouching to brush a kiss on her lips. She gave a contented little hum and snuggled in closer to Lucian. I was glad to see she was able to rest, but it gutted me to see her puffy tear-stained face.

"Why didn't she want to go home?" I murmured. "I could feel her pain and desperation to see her mother again."

Lucian lovingly stroked a hand down her back as he gazed down at her. "She didn't want to go without us. Silly woman said her mother would be upset if she showed up alone without her pack."

My eyes grew wide as I met his gaze. "What?"

"Why are you surprised? You've seen the way she is with those two girls. She's like a mother hen to them, protecting her little chicks from the world as best she can. There is no way she'd leave us to fight a war while she's safe in Oscad with her parents. To her, it would be a betrayal, and that's not something she can stomach," Lucian reasoned.

Sitting on the floor beside them, I just stared at her. Etching her features into my memory, so no matter what, I would remember the face of a woman who was stronger than anyone I'd ever known. I tried to put myself in her shoes, to get the news that my mother was dying while on a mission and knowing there wasn't much time to say goodbye. Of course, I'd know that Beth would be with her. The two of them were incredibly close.

My mother was also a nurse; it's what made Beth want to become one herself. Our father was a teacher who once taught at one of the city's largest schools. He'd worked there until his failing mind prevented him from continuing. Our medical practices were top-notch. Even still, there wasn't a way to repair the nerve damage that caused his memory to fade. That and he'd signed a document long ago that prevented us from using experimental or extraordinary measures on him. He believed that when it was a person's time to go, they should do so with grace, knowing not many got the luxury of dying from old age.

Since my father couldn't look after himself, my mother retired from the Med Center to look after him full-time. Both Beth and I gave them half our salary on top of the retirement pay they lived off of, so they had nothing to worry about. Neither of my parents loved that I joined the military, even if right now it was providing for them as my family. A perk of the job since our government understood the risk we faced every day and the toll it took on our families.

I couldn't wait for Dani to meet them simply because I knew they'd take to her right away. They'd always been supportive of my relationship with Petru and Cris, although I knew they hoped one day I'd find an Omega to add to the family. There have been many dinners with the whole unit at my parents' since I was one of the only members of the team to have both parents alive. Victor's father was alive, though they didn't have a relationship. Sorin's parents were alive, but obviously, they weren't the type to have cookouts in the backyard. Cris' mother would join us if she felt comfortable leaving her current house guest alone.

All in all, I was lucky to have a sister I saw often, parents who loved and supported me, and a pack who was my family. It was silly to get all emotional like this when there was so much pain and hurt in the world. Yet experiencing that feeling of loss through Dani put things sharply in perspective. We could head off to the North, rally the troops and storm the castle saving the day. Then on the flip side of that, we could fail and die, no one ever having a clue what happened to us. This was the dark side of being part of the military.

You fought for your country even at the risk of possibly not coming home.

So was it worth it?

That was the question each and every one of us needed to answer for ourselves. Today Dani had decided that being with us, trying to stop this war, and knowing we could fail was worth it. So much so, she was willing to chance never being able to see her mother again. Did I have that kind of courage? Feeling eyes on me, I pulled myself back to the present and saw her gorgeous green eyes flecked with gold looking at me. When she saw I noticed her awake, she reached out a hand to me, which I took and kissed.

"What's wrong?" she whispered. "You feel so anxious and conflicted. Did they say they wouldn't help us?"

Shaking my head, I just held her hand pressed to my lips for a moment before answering. "I'm just amazed by you, Dani. I don't think I could pass up the chance to see my mother if I knew she was dying. Greater good be damned. I want to be able to say goodbye to her."

"Toma, I've been living the past nine years thinking my mother was already dead. The part that's more painful for me is to know she's been alive all this time and didn't know if I was okay. Would I love to see her, tell her I'm safe, loved, and looked after so she can rest easy? Yes, but what would I tell her when she asks me where you are?" Dani pressed. "I'd have to tell her you're fighting to end a war that would change the lives of everyone in your country. How can I look her in the eye knowing full well I should be right here with all of you? Oscad is where I'm from, it's the country I grew up in, but Asturg is now my home. It's where all of you and your families are."

"Just like that?" I asked.

"What do you mean, just like that?" she teased, smirking at me. "I've been in Asturg for three years. I know the language, signed on with the Southern Military, and found myself a pack. What more is there to convince me that this is where I belong?"

"When you put it that way," I muttered, running a hand through my hair before smiling at her. "I'm sorry my worrying woke you up. Go back to sleep, I've got some work to do and you're far too distracting."

She lifted her head for a kiss which I gave her gladly, deepening it for a moment, letting her feel how incredible I thought she was. Pulling back, I gave her a wink and tucked the blanket around her again as she settled against Lucian.

"You good?" I asked, feeling the need to check in with him like I would any of the others.

He nodded as he stroked her hair. "I've got everything I need right here."

Fuck, if that wasn't the truth of it. Now we just needed to make sure we deserved her.

CHAPTER 47

Danella

Two days passed, and there was no word from Savo, but that didn't stop Sorin from preparing. It was rather remarkable to watch him and Lucian working side by side. Toma had found some old maps of the Northern territory, so Lucian was helping them update them with current information. Knowing the current locations of outposts and small towns helped plot out the course we wanted to take to get to the mountains. Once we got there, though, we were going to be blind. No one knew anything about those that hid among them other than they would kill to stay out of the war.

My heat was well and truly over, even though my sex drive was now kicked into high gear. This turned out to be a problem for sparring with the guys. More than once, it had devolved into quick, gritty sex with all our clothes mostly on and no knotting. Never did I think that the mere sight of one of the guys without a shirt on would have my panties soaked. We all did our best to keep it together and get training done. There wasn't much time left before I was going to need every skill they were trying to teach me.

It had been decided that if we didn't hear from Sorin by the morning, we would head out on our journey North. We'd stop at one of the smaller bases along the way to gather the supplies we needed that wouldn't attract attention. Sorin's team was well known for going on missions that they couldn't disclose and expected the base to keep their presence on a need-to-know basis. It was risky, but we had little choice. If we went back to main headquarters trying to ask for approval of a mission that we didn't have any evidence of, it would be more suspicious.

Our ace that Sorin wanted to wait to use until there was no option, was to locate a Northern incursion and hunt them down. No matter what we did, there would be a point our presence would be missed, and they'd try to recall the unit. What happens when they can't reach us is anyone's guess. They would know our last known location, but we'd be long gone by then, without clues about where we'd gone. Although I'm betting their first thought wouldn't be that we were on a mission to end the war.

"Wouldn't it be wiser to leave the laptop here?" Lucian asked as we sat down for dinner. "I'm aware we don't have much tech in the North, but I'm guessing they could track us if you use it."

"While we are in the South, that is a possibility," Toma agreed. "However, I think I found a workaround to mask our exact location by making the area so large they'd have no way of pinpointing us. Downside is I won't know if the program has worked until I check it on another one of our computers. Which is why I vote to gather supplies close by since they're aware we are, in fact, here."

Reaching for a slice of bread, I was scooped up and plopped on Cris' lap. "Hold her until I get her plate settled," Victor instructed.

"We seriously need to figure out how to deal with this overwhelming need to prepare my plate for me," I grumbled. "What will you do when we're on the go and we have no plates?"

"Oh, we have plates. They're part of your mess kit in your pack," Cris pointed out.

Shifting, I glared at him over my shoulder. "Not helping," I muttered through my teeth. "Seriously, there has to be a limit to this. What if we agreed you got to handle breakfast or just dinner, something so I don't feel like a helpless Omega that needs to be catered to by her pack."

All the guys paused to look at me as if I'd said something ridiculous. "What?" I asked, tossing my arms up.

"Wildflower, you are an Omega who absolutely should be catered to where we can. There are so many things that we can't offer you in a military life, so we will take advantage of what we can do," Petru reasoned.

"Also, no one thinks you're helpless, so don't even try to pull that crap," Lucian added.

Crossing my arms, I pouted at them like the petulant Omega I tried *not* to be. Victor set down two plates then removed me from Cris' lap to place me on his own. This had been his newest obsession. Not only was I unable to get my own food, but I was also now expected to sit on his lap so he could make sure I was eating enough. God forbid your stomach growled a few hours after dinner, only to get the third degree of questioning from my dear Vicky. So here I sat, in his lap where I couldn't leave until half the plate was empty.

"Little Spark, you're finally getting to the point your cheeks don't look so hollow. This mission will be grueling, and I won't let you backslide. Protection means—"

"Protecting me from myself and others," I said, cutting Victor off, having heard this argument at every meal for the past two days. "Just you wait, I'm going to find something I can lovingly make as irritating as possible in return."

Victor kissed my cheek, his beard tickling my skin. "I look forward to seeing you try, Little Spark."

This had the others laughing, knowing Victor was almost as rigid in his routines and taking care of himself as Sorin. If I could find something to exploit, it would be a rather impressive feat.

"Might I suggest that whatever food supplies we gather from the base everyone holds onto until we're in Northern territory," Lucian commented, keeping his voice calm and neutral. "Here in the South, you have the ability to hunt and forage, which will be lacking once we cross the border."

Whatever agreement the two men figured out between them was working. Lucian didn't try to order or command anyone, while Sorin kept Lucian in the loop on everything. Sharing information freely with no judgment or suspicion when the commander asked questions. Much to my surprise, the person who was having the biggest trouble warming up to Lucian was Cris. It made me wonder if it had to do with his mother or all the horrible things he's heard about what happens in the North. Everyone else was making an effort to bridge the gap. I had a feeling it would just take Cris a little more time.

"That is a rather brilliant idea," Petru said. "The rations we get at the base will keep until we need them. No sense in needing to use them up too quickly. Plus, once we get a uniform for Lucian, there's no reason we can't stop in a few towns along the way to get food."

Sorin nodded his head in agreement. "I think that's one thing we'll be able to learn from you, Lucian, is how to make the most of what we have and what's around us."

"Yeah, well, if they didn't starve their people, it wouldn't be a skill we'd need so desperately," Cris muttered before shoving food into his mouth.

My brows shot up at his words. When I tried to reach out to our connection through Petru and Toma, I found he'd cut himself off from us. He knew he was in the wrong for saying that and didn't want any of us harping on him, I suppose. My gaze caught Toma's as he had a crinkle of concern on his forehead as well as feeling his anxiety. For now, I was going to leave things as they were. It wasn't my place to tell someone to get over something just so it would make it easier for all of us. Cris needed to sort out his feelings. Although if he pushed this hateful attitude any further, the two of us were having a heart-to-heart, that's for damn sure.

"I agree," Lucian stated, then returned to his meal, seemingly unaffected by the comment.

Too bad for him that I could see just how much guilt and shame he was feeling. It tore him up inside to know his country and people were dying. If it wasn't starvation that did them in, it was the lack of basic medical supplies. Getting an infection of any kind was basically a death sentence, one I'd seen firsthand. The North desperately needed us to pull this off so innocent people would stop dying, and people could start to live full and happy lives.

The strained silence that fell over the table was interrupted by the phone ringing. Sorin quickly rose from his chair, grabbed the phone, looked at who was calling, and frowned. "It's not Savo's number."

"Answer the damn thing. What if he's calling from another line," Victor urged, waving a hand to make him respond faster.

I could feel the war going on inside our leader right this very second. He wanted to answer but was also afraid it could be something else, something worse. Letting out a frustrated growl, he answers the phone. "Major Sorin speaking."

He didn't put it on speaker, so I couldn't hear who it was. They certainly had him surprised, in any case. After my meltdown, he's been careful not to have phone or video conversations where I could hear them. I didn't blame him the last few times; those we spoke to were less than kind regarding topics about Omegas. It was the nature of the country and one area that I hoped to encourage change. There was no reason to see Omegas in such a black-and-white view. We were just as diverse as every other kind of designation.

"Head Speaker, it's an unexpected honor to talk to you directly," Sorin said, filling us in on who precisely he was speaking to. "Yes, I can do that one moment."

Dropping the phone from his ear, he turned the speakerphone on and looked directly at me. "She's sitting across the table from me, sir, but just to make you aware that my whole pack is also present."

"Thank you for your honesty, Major Sorin, but I would assume whatever I said would be relayed back to them once we hung up. It seems to me this would be a more efficient approach to get the information from the source, so there's no questioning what I meant," Head Speaker Marius replied. His voice was calm, even, and gave off an aristocratic air that fit his status.

It had taken a moment for my brain to catch up and realize what Sorin had said. Pointing to myself, I mouthed, *'he wants to talk to me?'* Sorin nodded, and a grin was tugging at his lips as if my amazement was funny to him. What the hell would the Head Speaker of Oscad want to say to me?

"Danella," Speaker Marius called.

I gulped down my nerves and answered. "Yes."

It came out more like a squeak than an actual word, so I cleared my throat and tried again as I felt Victor laughing silently. "Yes, Head Speaker?"

"Please call me Marius. While I might be the leader of Oscad during the day, right now I'm at home and making a personal call. In fact, I'm sitting here with my Omega Cambrie, who wants a chance to speak with you as well, if you don't mind," Marius requested.

"Hello, Danella," a sweet voice chimed in. "I'm sorry to spring this interaction on you so suddenly. I just wasn't sure how else to make it happen. You see Savo, one of my other Alphas you spoke to the other day, and I run the Omega Recovery Project. Our goal is to find as many of the Omegas that got sent to Asturg and Shearia as possible to offer them the chance to come home. Savo shared that you and the other two girls are friends. Is that right?"

"Yes, we've been close friends since we met in the Care Center," I answered.

"How fortunate to have had them with you this whole time. I know what it feels like to be all alone in the world and believe if you disappeared, no one would notice," Cambrie shared, her voice full of the sadness of that time in her life. "Thankfully, I was blessed to be rescued more than once by people who care greatly about me. Lord, I'm pretty sure if I stepped off the sidewalk when I wasn't supposed to, I'd have them all swarming around me."

"Don't act like you don't love that about us," Marius scolded, laughing. "Danella, what we would genuinely like to understand from you is: are your friends in the same situation as you, now bonded to a pack, or are they indeed seeking to return home?"

"No, they are not attached to anyone. The North doesn't believe in having a pack structure," I shared. "Tori and Violet both desperately want to go home to Oscad. They've suffered enough, and I think they'll only begin to heal if they are somewhere they believe to be safe. I'm not sure there's any place in the world truly safe for Omegas, but Oscad is the best choice."

"You might be right, but in the past three years, a lot has changed here for the better. We still have a long way to go, but I see so much improvement from where we started. There are no more Care Centers. Omegas may now live at home with their families. That being said, all Omegas that we bring back do stay at a halfway house of sorts. Just to ensure they get the best help we can provide the way each individual Omega needs it. I know what's going on in Northern Asturg. How Omegas are being treated like cattle, and if your pack is going to try and put an end to this, we want in," Cambrie announced.

"*Keski*," Savo said with a warning tone I knew all too well and sounded so much like Lucian.

My gaze drifted to him, and he sat up a little straighter at hearing his half-brother's voice. I knew he blamed Savo for leaving and forcing him into this position. Yet, if the two of them were similar at all, I could understand why Savo left, unable to handle the horror of it all. The difference was Lucian felt so strongly for his people that he could never abandon them.

"What?" Cambrie challenged. "Was I wrong?"

"Princess, we agreed that would be the conversation Savo, Sorin, his pack, and myself would have. You requested to have a moment to speak with Danella. Let's not get distracted trying to help overthrow another government. They seem to have a pretty good handle on that part," Marius reasoned.

There was a sigh that filtered through the phone before she agreed. "All right, I'll stick to the matter I wanted to speak to her about in the first place. Dani, can I call you Dani?"

"Sure," I offered, smiling at the interaction with her men that reminded me a fair amount of mine.

"Lovely. I think Danella is a beautiful name. I'm working on making female friends, which is harder to do than you think. Dani sounds more like something a friend would call you, and after speaking with your mother, I'm confident that we'll be friends," Cambrie shared.

My heart leapt to my throat at hearing her talk about my mother. Cris reached out and took my hand, lacing our fingers together before reassuringly squeezing it. Victor wrapped his arms around my middle and hugged me tight, kissing the back of my neck.

"You spoke to my mother?" I ventured, proud that my voice didn't waver.

"She is a sweet, loving woman, who was elated to hear about you," Cambrie answered. "I kept things as vague as possible since I don't truly know your story or how you ended up with your pack, but I tried to give her as much hope as possible. After meeting Edith and seeing her with my own eyes, I don't think your mother is as terminal as we were led to believe. To be sure, she is not well. However, your father ensures me she is getting the best care. Now having gotten word about you, she has even more reason to keep fighting and hold on. It's my opinion that she will be here waiting for you when you've settled things there."

I couldn't stop the sob that erupted out of me at this news. My mother was holding on. She would be there waiting for me when I finished what I set out to do. There was no greater gift that anyone could have given me, and I had no idea who to thank.

"I...I don't even know what to say," I stammered, furiously wiping away the tears, determined not to fall apart. "What in the world had you going to such lengths to speak to my mother?"

"Well, your pack asked us to on your behalf since you couldn't make it back at this time," Cambrie said. "Did you not know?"

Covering my mouth, I shook my head then realized she couldn't see me. Pulling myself together enough to answer was more challenging than I expected. "No, they did that all on their own."

"Sounds to me like your pack really loves you, and wow can that be overwhelming sometimes, am I right?" Cambrie teased, laughter ringing in her voice. "Answer me this one thing honestly, Dani. Do you love them? Are you happy being their Omega?"

"That's two questions," Lucian pointed out as he stood and walked over to me to let his fingers brush along my jaw. "Two questions I know we all want to hear the answer to."

While our pack hadn't been built in the conventional way, nor did they all like and trust each other—yet. I didn't have to think twice about my answer. "Yes, I love each and every one of them..." I shared, taking a moment to look at each of them. "... and I'm proud to be their Omega. We still have to learn a lot about being a family, but I know we'll figure it out together."

Sniffling could be heard from the other end of the phone, breaking the tender moment we were sharing. "I'm sorry, my hormones still haven't returned to normal yet, and that was just such a perfect answer. Seeing and hearing about other Omegas finding a pack that loves and appreciates them is what keeps me fighting to make this a better world. It's a concept that has been lost over the years."

"I couldn't agree more," I blurted. "We dream about having a life like this but don't expect it to ever happen. If we can stop this war and help the people and country heal, I think we can start showing everyone a better way of life. One that's not pain and suffering, one that can have love or a promise of a future."

"Yes," Cambrie shouted into the phone. "See, I knew we'd be friends. So many people don't see why we need to change and grow. They don't want to risk the unknown. Yet if people stop growing, learning, and dreaming, then what is the point of living?"

"I hate to interrupt your Omega rally meeting, Cambi, but Dalton is in a mood and none of us will do. Not even Oscar's piano playing will do the trick," a new voice interjected.

"It's about time for him to eat again, so I'm not surprised. I'll be there in just a moment. Dani, I'm sorry I have to cut our conversation short, but I guess this means we'll need to meet in person soon," Cambrie suggested. "Don't let these men do something stupid. They're brilliant but sometimes reckless."

"No promises, though I'll see what I can do," I offered. "It was nice to meet you, and I'll make sure we meet when I come to visit my mother."

CHAPTER 48

Danella

There were murmured words and the sound of people entering or leaving the room. Then the line fell quiet for a few moments before Marius rejoined us.

"Thank you for allowing the two of them to talk. I wasn't going to stop getting puppy dog eyes until it happened," Marius shared with a chuckle. "Now, as far as matters concerning your request for our help. In the room with me, I have Savo and Nixon, who are part of my pack and people I trust. Nixon is also a voting member regarding important decisions like offering up our troops for a war that isn't ours."

While his words were direct and to the point, they lacked the bite of someone who would instantly reject your proposal.

"On this end, it's just my pack," Sorin informed them. "We can't return home with Lucian unless we have a peace treaty in hand for the president to look over. We planned to head out in the morning if we hadn't heard from you."

"Sorin, this is Nixon speaking. Can you tell us if we offer you the help you're looking for, what are the expectations? Is it that you need more men to fight or the proof that Oscad is siding with you? I guess I'm asking if things go well, you now have control over the North. Where does that leave us?" Nixon asked.

To my surprise, Sorin deferred to Lucian for the answer, handing him the phone. Lucian took it hesitantly, like he expected the man to change his mind. Now with the phone in hand, out came the commander side of Lucian. It was like I could see a shift in his posture and expression, but this time, he didn't hide behind the mask his father forced him to wear.

"I hope you don't mind if I, Lucian Bakal, answer the question since I'll be the new leader of Northern Asturg when this is over."

"No, not at all. The question should have been directed to you in the first place. My apologies," Nixon offered, his tone sincere.

Not at all surprised, Lucian stood so he could pace. Whenever he was strategizing or working on one problem or another, he couldn't sit still. Many days, I found him walking laps around the couch in the living room, hand cupping his chin deep in thought.

"My first and primary reason for doing this at all is to save my people. Our land is dying, and the only way I can stop it from getting worse is to remove the man and his followers who don't give a fuck. The secondary reason is that Danella deserves to live in a world that respects her. She doesn't need to fear for her safety every waking moment. To do one or the other, they both must happen. If I don't feel my own Omega and the woman I love is safe even when she's right by my side, how can anyone else?" Lucian took a breath rubbing a hand down his face.

"You asked what I'm looking for and where it leaves Oscad when this is over. I would love nothing more than to be a bridge between us. The South has much to offer the world, but the North has cut them off. That and as silly as it might seem to anyone else, I need there to be good relations between us because that is Danella's home. Where her parents live. I never want to be the reason she can't see them whenever she likes. Plus, I believe that with our three countries working harmoniously together, it can only be to everyone's benefit," Lucian concluded.

These men were trying to kill me with all these amazingly romantic gestures. Not to mention just how sexy it was to hear Lucian allow himself to dream. To finally get to share his ideas for his people all along. I could only imagine what kind of leader he would become once allowed to do it his way. He's seen all the wrong ways to run a country; it was time to let the man off his father's leash and see him thrive.

"I believe that is something we can work with," Marius said after a moment of silence. "Allow me to be frank. I didn't actually think this was how our conversation would go. If I'm understanding you correctly, Lucian, you're looking for an alliance. One not just for this fight but to have it continue after so that we might build a friendship between our countries."

"Correct. That is exactly what I'm hoping for," Lucian confirmed. "If I'm going to have a hope of rebuilding, my country is going to need friends and support to pull it off. We're out of resources and won't be able to create more right away. Of course, I'm not looking for favors by telling you this. It's just the reality of my country."

"Luc," Savo cut in. "Do you honestly intend to go to the deserters?"

Biting my lip, I waited to see if Lucian would react to his brother calling him by a childhood nickname. "Who else would I go to when I need someone to hate the General as much as we do? They clearly know how to defend themselves since we've all heard stories of the skirmishes in the foothills. Many run off part-way or just after completing training. I doubt they just forgot it all."

"Those are fair points," Savo agreed. "Do you have a plan to get close to them?"

"Once we cross the border into Northern territory, we'll change into civilian clothes. We'll still have our packs, but what person runs without supplies? All I need is to get to one of the hidden villages and lay out the plan. Once they understand what I'm trying to do, they'll see the benefit in helping." Lucian outlined for his brother. "Where I feel Oscad will be most beneficial is after I've gotten the deserters on our side and we devise a plan. I want to make sure the army has no idea what we're up to, so it won't be a direct attack."

"Oh?" Marius commented in surprise.

Lucian handed the phone back to Sorin, who'd come up with the idea. "If we don't have a clue how many people we have to fight with, we need the best strategy to thin out the number of soldiers that will be in the main city. If we send out troops to different locations run by major supporters of the General, it will not only deal with them directly but remove reinforcements. This will also cause the General to send help to squash what he believes is a simple uprising. If we can focus their attention on somewhere else, they won't see the actual attack coming."

"I must say this is a rather clever plan," Nixon shared. "So you would have our people to wait and assist you with the attack on the main city?"

"As far as plans go now, yes," Sorin answered. "However, we won't know the specifics until we figure out just how many people we have at our disposal."

"That's understandable. Nevertheless, knowing your vision of how you want this to play out helps us," Marius pointed out. "I believe we have more than enough information to bring before the voting board of our governing body. As soon as I have an answer, I'll have Savo contact you. I assume you'll keep him in the loop of how to do that?"

"Of course," Sorin confirmed. "We'll be venturing to the mountains in the morning, so we will be on the move. I only bring that up in case you can't connect to the satellite phone. It would be worth trying again. This alliance is of the utmost importance to us, and fate willing, we will see this through."

"Godspeed and good luck on your journey. We will be in touch," Marius said before hanging up.

We all sat in silence around the table for a moment taking in the fact that the phone call was a massive step in the right direction. Not only had we been given a chance to share our plans, but we also got to say them to the Head Speaker himself. Having Oscad as an ally would be massive in the long-term scheme of things. Now we just needed to make the rest of it happen.

"I want everyone to turn in early tonight," Sorin instructed. "We will be up and out of here before dawn. Something in my gut tells me we don't have much time to make it out of the South. I want to get over the border before anyone realizes that we're not doing what we're supposed to. So make sure your packs are stocked with what you can gather from here, and we'll stop at the base we normally top off at two days from now."

We all dug into our dinner that had been interrupted before starting on the rest of the tasks that needed to be completed before the morning. While the guys gathered things around the cabin, I worked with Cris to distribute the supplies. Taking what we needed was a tricky balance to ensure we didn't make it too heavy and slow down. I wasn't thrilled they made my pack the lightest when we needed to make the most out of the space we had.

"Sweetheart, if we make your pack too heavy, it will be harder for you to keep up. This would mean everyone slowing down to make sure you weren't left behind. We can get more supplies, but we don't have much time to get where we need to go. Of the two choices, a lighter pack is the more beneficial," Cris pointed out.

Hearing him explain it like that got me to stop arguing with him. I still wasn't happy about it, however. When everyone turned in for the night, I was settled in the middle of the makeshift bed while the others had puppy-piled around me. Since my heat, this was how we'd been sleeping, and I adored it. To know I had them all with me and I didn't need to worry who was getting more of my time than another. I noticed the guys rotated without anyone saying anything about it, so whoever had been closest to me shifted back for others to get a prime cuddle spot. Tonight Victor was my pillow as Toma and Cris curled around my body to keep me warm and safe. I thought I'd struggle to sleep, but Victor was already prepared for that as he started to massage my scalp right away with a soft rumbling purr to lull me to sleep.

CHAPTER 49

Danella

All too soon, it was time to wake up and head out. Silently we dressed and put on our gear before heading out. The air was cool, but now that spring was heading into summer, I knew it would be hotter and hotter as the days went on. Weather like this made traveling easier as we worked up a sweat with the pace that Sorin had set for us. It wasn't as fast as Lucian pushed for when we were on the run, but it left no room for talking.

The sun came up a few hours later, casting its warm glow over the forest. We would have one full day in its shade before entering a wide section of prairie land that would make up most of our travels. The closer we got to the North, the more vegetation would fall away before reaching the badlands. I didn't remember much about that area except they'd described it as barren land with hills and valleys attached to the mountain range we aimed for. If all went to plan, it would take us two or three days to get to the badlands. Once there, no one was entirely sure since we'd need to find a river crossing. Using the main crossing was out of the question since it was heavily guarded on the Southern side due to it being a weak point. That and it was much farther south than we wanted to be. Our hope was that we'd find a suitable place to cross as the river narrows in the mountains.

We walked until the sun was high in the sky, making the air around us more humid, warning that rain could be a possibility. Finding a place with some cover, we rested for a bit munching the leftovers from last night. Tonight we'd stop early enough for the guys to do some hunting and cook it up in the likelihood it would last us for the next few days. As Lucian suggested, saving the rations would be smart for when we entered the North.

Stretched out on the grass, staring up at the sky, I saw something glint, like metal reflecting the light. "Guys..." I called, pointing upward. "Is that a drone?"

"Fuck," Toma swore. "Quick, get the thermal blankets out."

I hadn't understood why exactly we'd packed these thin silver sheets they swore were blankets. Now it made sense. It was to block the ability of the drone to pick up on our body heat. Victor grabbed me by the waist and yanked me over to him, pulling the material over us. My breath came in short pants as adrenalin roared through my veins. Clutching Victor's shirt in my hands, I strained to listen, trying to hear if the damn thing was past us or not. Toma had checked the routes planned for the drones two days ago when they'd been changed, but it seems we'd missed one. That or they sent out more we didn't know about due to the North slipping past their patrols.

"Little Spark, you need to slow your breathing. The harder you make your heart work, the higher your body temperature goes up," Victor whispered.

Nodding, I closed my eyes and tried to do the breathing exercises Petru had taught me to use during shooting practice. Breathe in for a count of five, then breathe out for the same while visualizing the calm body and mind I wanted. Fortunately, it worked, and I relaxed against him, letting my head rest on his arm. I looked up into his hazel eyes, using them to ground myself at this moment. Reminding myself that he would never let anything happen to me. Loosening my grip on his shirt, I lifted a hand to trace along his beard. It had gotten longer and wilder without him looking after it. Somehow this suited him better than the cleaner look the Military enforced. Twisting his head, he kissed my hand before catching it and pressing it over his heart. This gesture had me once more aware of the fact he was the only one of the pack who hadn't marked me.

"Vi—"

"All clear," Sorin shouted.

With the moment gone, it was impossible to ask my question now as Victor cast off the blanket. He got to his feet first then pulled me up, giving me a quick once-over to ensure I was fine.

"Nice use of the breathing exercise, Little Spark," Victor praised, then pressed a kiss to my forehead as he grabbed his pack. "You have no idea how many other soldiers would have pissed themselves in panic or frozen up entirely. Knowing how to control your response to a situation is one of the most valuable skills you can learn."

"Yeah, but you had to tell me to do it," I pointed out. "If you hadn't been there with me, I'm not sure how I would have reacted."

Gripping my chin with a hand, Victor leveled me with an intense gaze. "Dani, I'll always be right there by your side, keeping you safe no matter what. I made you that promise when you first arrived, and my dedication to that has only strengthened since then."

Dropping his head, he gave me a searing kiss so full of intense emotions. I ached to understand him like I could the others, but that was not something to deal with now.

"Let's move, double time. We need to get well away from this section if they're sending out extra drone scouts," Sorin ordered as he snapped the chest buckle and tightened the straps on his pack.

Petru helped me back into mine and also clicked the chest strap. It was amazing how much more secure it felt on my back, and when Sorin started to jog away, I understood why it was needed. Taking a deep breath and getting my head back in the game, I picked up the pace and headed after them. Petru took up the rear, his sniper rifle in hand, ready to shoot a drone if we needed to.

We kept up that pace until the sun had lowered to the point it was casting shadows through the trees, making it harder to see. There wasn't much in the way of coverage as the rain that had been threatening all day started. We managed to make do using tarps to create a tent of sorts. It was cramped, although it kept us dry for the most part. The plan to hunt went out the window, so we settled for using the power bars as our dinner. I slept fitfully. The sound of the rain beating down on the tarp was deafening. At some point, it stopped, and I was able to get at least an hour or two of good sleep —I think. Only to have Sorin waking us up to move out.

The rain made the ground muddy and slippery, forcing us to slow down and travel at a more moderate pace. Thankfully we broke out of the forest and into the open prairie lands, which weren't as affected by the rain. It was crazy to see rolling hills of grasslands as far as the eye could see. Now I understood why our route must be carefully plotted to avoid towns and military bases. People would see us coming a mile away, and there would go our anonymity. Luckily this day went without incident, and Petru even managed to shoot some rabbits and a few ducks flying overhead. We even found a small grouping of trees to give us a little coverage. Taking the risk, we started a fire and cooked the meat early before the sun was completely gone to hide the light of the fire.

"Where did you learn to do that?" I asked Victor as he skinned the rabbits with ease after he'd plucked the ducks.

Without looking up from his work, his knife paused a second before resuming. "My family owned a farm. Well, I guess I should say they still do since my uncle runs it now. Growing up, I was taught how to live off what we could grow or raise with our own two hands."

"I don't think I've ever heard you talk about your family before," I pointed out.

"Not much to talk about, same sad story as anyone's in this country," Victor answered with a shrug.

It took everything in me not to keep pressing, but it was clear that he didn't want to talk about it. He was right, in any case. I'd learned quickly that people didn't have many cheerful stories about growing up, myself included. The world we lived in forced us to grow up fast if we wanted to survive and make something of ourselves. People either learned to deal and adjust, or they were dragged along, kicking and screaming.

"It must be nice having been taught those skills. I can see how they'd come in handy with this life," I mused aloud, tossing another stick into the fire. "Nothing growing up prepared me to be anything but dependent on others. It's kind of cruel if you ask me. Everyone wants to have a purpose in life."

"You did have a purpose, just not one you wanted," Victor corrected.

Tilting my head, I contemplated him. That statement sounded like it was one he learned from personal experience. "Is that what happened to you?"

He stopped and met my gaze, unveiling the rage behind them. "Yes, and that's all I will say on that subject. Just because you're born to a certain set of people doesn't make them your family. The people I consider family are right here. You and the others are all the family I need. If you want to ask about life with them, I'll tell you whatever you want to know. Everything, before I joined the military, is irrelevant and dead to me."

Reaching out, I took the half-skinned rabbit out of his hand and set it aside on a tarp with the other two. Crawling into his lap, I hugged him tightly, nuzzling my face into his neck. "If they couldn't see the person you are and how unflinchingly loyal, kind, and loving you are, then fuck them. There is nothing I would change about you... well, I might like to get my own food once in a while, but it's not a deal breaker. So it looks like I'm keeping you, Vicky."

Victor set aside the knife before crushing me to his chest, resting his head on my shoulder, and taking deep breaths of my scent. I loved how it felt to be wrapped up in his spicy ginger and clove scent that somehow mingled perfectly with mine.

"You do not know how much that means to me, Little Spark," he murmured. "I need you to understand that I love you more than I've loved anyone or anything in my entire life. You have filled a hole in my life that I didn't know I had and seamlessly completed this family of ours. Now I need you to promise me you'll believe that I mean it before I tell you something."

"Vic—"

"Promise me," he growled.

"I promise to trust and believe you love me with everything you are," I answered, a trickle of fear running down my spine as I pulled back to look at him. "Vicky, you're not leaving me, are you?"

"No, never. I'm not going anywhere," he assured me, but I still wasn't convinced. "Fuck, I just don't know how to say this. It's not like I thought I'd ever have an Omega I'd need to have this conversation with."

"Talk to me, trust my love for you, and say what's been bothering you. I've noticed that there was something off since my heat was over," I commented.

Victor rested his forehead against mine and took a deep breath. "No matter what, I can never bond with you. My mark will never be left on your beautiful body in the traditional display between an Alpha and Omega. However, I plan to find another way to have something marking you as mine once things settle down, I promise."

That had not been at all what I thought he was going to say, and a mixture of emotions filtered through me as I absorbed what he was saying. "Can I ask why?"

"This will stay between you and me because you deserve the right to know why I'm asking this of you. My father was an Alpha, and my mother an Omega. A bonded pair. Just after I was born, my father was drafted and sent to war, having never wanted to be a soldier. When he came back three years later, he was so fucked in the head from all that he'd seen and done it caused my mother to kill herself. She had a direct line into his thoughts, emotions, and the nightmare he was living through every time he closed his eyes.

I don't know if my father knew how to shut off his thoughts or if they were so bad that it didn't matter. It pushed my mother over the edge to the point she couldn't take it anymore. She tried to leave him, or so I was told. Which is why my father locked her up, refusing to let her abandon him. My uncle told me she lasted a week before ending her life and turned my father into a crazy bastard who took his anger out on me. So when I was old enough to enter the military, I ran away and haven't looked back since," Victor shared in a neutral, almost distant tone.

"So you think what happened to your mother might happen to me?" I asked.

Hugging me tightly against his chest, he nodded. "You have no idea the horrors I've seen, experienced, and done to others. I vowed to protect you, and that's exactly what this is. You have five others you're bonded to who can support you that way, but I won't risk it. Danella, you're too important to me to ever allow the chance something like that could happen to you."

I nuzzled into his neck and squeezed him as hard as I could, needing him to know that nothing had changed between us. "I love you, Vicky," I whispered. "Bonded or not, mark or no mark, you are still part of my pack and one of my alphas."

"I love you so much, Little Spark," Victor said, his voice muffled from where it was pressed to my shoulder. "Thank you for loving me back even though I'm far from deserving it."

"Oh shut up, self-deprecation is not a good look on you," I grumbled, punching him in the arm. "Where is my Vicky? You know, the man people are too afraid of to look in the eye for fear he might kill them with a single thought."

Lifting his head to look at me, he frowned. "What?"

"You haven't heard that rumor? Oh man, it's one of my favorites," I teased.

Muttering something under his breath about me being trouble, he lifted me off his lap to sit beside him and resumed skinning the rabbit. I leaned against him and watched the flames as he worked. A small smile on my lips I couldn't hide as I enjoyed the warm glow of being in love and loved in return.

Sleep came much easier that night with a full belly and my pack nestled together. Sorin also had everyone taking hour-long shifts as lookouts, excluding me. I wasn't bothered by it. I knew I didn't have the training, and with how out in the open we were, it was best to have those who knew what they were doing be on watch. I think it was also because the guys knew this sort of travel and pace was harder on me. I didn't have the level of conditioning and experience they did, but it would be a different story by the time this was over.

Thankfully the night passed without any issues, and we were

back at it before the sun was peeking over the horizon. The day so far went as planned, so we should be stopping at the small base they frequented on most missions. Sorin had wanted us to arrive at dusk then leave first thing. Apparently, that was their regular routine, and it seemed that we'd be following it this time as well.

Back at the cabin, Lucian had found a stash of all-black Southern uniforms left in a trunk. He'd switched out his Northern uniform and burned it last to make sure there wasn't evidence in his pack on the odd chance they'd want to search it. It was so strange to think we were going to bring the heir to the Northern territory right into a Southern Military base. If people figured it out, there was no doubt in my mind they'd shoot us no questions asked. Now I just had to pray the fates were on our side through this.

"When we get there, if anyone asks who you are, tell them you're an engineer on loan from another unit," Sorin instructed as we spotted the base ahead. "No one knows every soldier or unit on sight, plus some of the more specialty soldiers never leave head-quarters."

"Anything I should or shouldn't do that will help not give me away?" Lucian asked as he tugged his cap lower trying to hide as much of his scar as possible.

"Don't use any words tied to Asturgian. No one uses the old language around here," Petru mentioned.

"If you don't know something, just don't answer and give them a good stony glare," Victor suggested with a shrug. "They leave me alone when I do that and it keeps you from saying something you shouldn't."

Sorin stopped and faced Lucian, grabbing his shoulder compan-ionably. "People here aren't nosy, they all know we're just stopping in to top off before heading in to fight. No one wants to be the last person to talk to someone before they die. Bases like this are remote and don't get rotated back to the main base often. They'll be as clueless as you about current matters and information."

Lucian nodded his thanks but didn't say much, apparently taking Victor's advice about just staying silent. I couldn't blame him for his nerves when I had them too. This would be my first time being around others as an Omega bound to a pack and under their protection. I had enough visible marks that my status should not be questioned. Feeling my trepidation, Lucian caught my hand and held it tight in his as we got closer to the base. The simple gesture helped more than I expected and I was immensely grateful for it.

"*Halt*," a soldier called out from the top of a metal wall surrounding the base. "State your rank, name, and business."

We halted and gathered behind Sorin since he would take the lead. "My name is Major Sorin Dragomire. I'm here with my unit to top up supplies before we head into the badlands."

"Wait there," the soldier ordered and disappeared from the wall.

"Nothing to worry about. They always check their list of approved unit leaders," Sorin told us. "This close to the North, our power is spotty so they do everything by paper."

Moments later, there was a blaring alarm and a flashing red light as the metal door slid open.

"Subtle," Lucian muttered. "Let's just hope we don't need to sneak out in the middle of the night."

"Oh, don't worry, I know how to get around all of that," Toma informed us. "I'm part of the team who helped set it up, and for various reasons I always leave myself a back door into programs if I can."

Lucian looked at the man. "Impressive. I'm sure that's come in handy."

"More than you know," Toma muttered as we entered the base.

CHAPTER 50

Petru

It had been only three weeks since we were last at this base, but I felt like a lifetime of changes had happened in that period. As always, nothing here changed. It was the same small station with two buildings for barracks, a training area, a mess hall, and an ample supply depot. There were only about two hundred or so soldiers stationed here. The primary purpose of this base was to be an emergency backup if there was trouble on the border and a response was needed immediately.

"Major Sorin," Captain Furlan greeted us as the gate closed behind us. "Sending you back to the front lines so soon?"

"What can I say, an elite unit's job is never done," Sorin answered, shaking the man's hand. "Until the war is over, I have a feeling this is where we'll always be."

"Curse of being too damn good at your job, I suppose," Captain Furlan grunted. "Looks like you've added to your team, and I see congratulations are in order. It's been a long time since an Omega has decided to take a military unit as their pack."

Sorin smiled as he turned to look at Dani. "The fates have blessed us indeed. We will just stay the night and need to take advantage of your supplies. Our unit ran into some Northerners who'd managed to get farther into our territory than we'd like."

"Of course, I'll have Sargent Kolar take you over there now. Take what you need. Just make sure Kolar marks it all down so headquarters will restock us," Captain Furlan instructed.

Both men saluted each other before Furlan headed off, barking out an order for someone to find Kolar. Sliding an arm around Dani's waist, I leaned down to kiss the top of her head. "Come on, let's find a room to put our packs in since it will be dinner time soon."

"Don't we need to help get supplies?" she questioned.

"Sorin and Victor will handle that. There's no need for all of us to go. Cris might if he feels there're medical supplies needed, but normally we just let those two deal with Kolar," I explained, trying to give her a reasonable explanation without telling her the real reason.

She nodded and allowed me to guide her away toward the barracks with the others, leaving Sorin to handle the bastard. If Kolar dared to speak to Dani the way he did to most women, Victor would snap and we couldn't afford that to happen.

Toma led the way to the second building and climbed the stairs to the third level that was left open for traveling units like ours. There were four rooms for smaller units like ourselves then the rest of the floor was rows of bunks for the larger platoons. It would seem we'd arrived at the base at the same time reinforcements for the front lines had. The sound of soldiers talking, laughing, and kidding around made me worry. Thankfully the unit rooms were before that section, so we didn't need to deal with them. Nevertheless, the more people around, the larger the chance someone might recognize us.

"Why are you so nervous?" Cris whispered. "This helps us. They won't pay attention to what we're doing with all of them around. All those soldiers will want to drink, talk, and gamble, enjoying life before they are in the thick of it. No one will even remember we're here."

He made a good point, it would help to keep us from being the new people who arrived. I know Sorin said they wouldn't press for information, except that wasn't always the case. They might speak to *him* about it, but many times at meals, others would sit with us and beg for some news of the outside world. Maybe there's a possibility that we have our meal up here instead of in the mess hall?

"Who wants top?" Toma asked, a smirk on his face telling me he knew exactly how everyone would take that question.

"Tell me...what's that like?" Dani asked, tapping her chin as humor danced in her eyes.

"Don't ask him. He wouldn't know either," I interjected. Everyone turned to look at me with stunned faces. "What?"

"You just said a dirty joke," Dani said with a giggle. "I know the three of you all take turns, although I would never have guessed Toma being the pillow prince."

"I am not," Toma blurted, crossing his arms. "In fact, Petru's favorite thing is to be in the middle."

"Yeah, with you at the bottom," Cris added, trying not to laugh. "Let's be honest, the only one of us who doesn't bite the pillow on a regular basis is Tru."

Lucian cleared his throat as he rubbed the back of his neck awkwardly. "So..."

"You heard right," Cris snapped. "Got a problem with Alphas who like to be topped? Or is it the fact that two Alphas like to fuck each other?"

Lucian reared back at the venom in Cris' words. I couldn't blame him, for they were harsh and uncalled for. The anger I felt coming off Cris was so out of character for my sweet, gentle Beta. I'd known he was struggling with this change, but I never imagined he would use such a tactic.

"Enough, Cris!" I barked. "I realize you're trying to stand up for Toma and me, though Lucian gave you no reason to act like that. Everyone realizes that it's going to take work for this pack to mend centuries worth of conditioning that made us view each other in a certain light. Will we butt heads and say things that can be hurtful to one another? Yes, but you outright attacked him with no provocation using me and Toma as an excuse. I strongly take offense to that."

The room fell into a tense silence as Cris and I squared off at one another. For a large portion of my life, I've had to not only stand up for myself in the wake of my father's execution but for being an Alpha who loved another Alpha. It wasn't forbidden but deemed unusual and not widely accepted. None of that mattered to me, I loved who I loved, and Toma had been by my side through hell and back many times. Cris was young and had grown up in a house where his wonderful mother raised him, but I believe she might have sheltered him from the reality of the world just a little too much. He'd come a long way, learning that things were not as black and white as we'd like them to be.

"You take offense to me protecting our relationship? For standing up for myself and my lovers?" Cris asked, his voice full of hurt and betrayal.

"Yes I do, especially when it really isn't about Toma or me," I answered. "What you just did, that wasn't out of love. It was an excuse so you could justify it to yourself by picking a fight with Lucian."

Cris stepped up, closing the space between us with a scowl on his face. "You're defending him?"

"The man said nothing, Cris, nothing," I said with a frustrated sigh. "What exactly do you believe he's done against any of us? I've not heard him say one single thing that would lead me to believe he has any issues with who fucks who in this pack."

"It's the way he looks at us, the judgment in his eyes. Northerners don't do packs, they don't take lovers of the same sex, and they certainly don't know how to actually love anyone. They make all the promises in the world to get what they want. Then use it against you, forcing you into a life you never wanted," Cris raged. "We think we can change them, give them a second chance, but it's a lie."

Toma reached out, turning Cris to face him. "Where is this coming from? None of this is making any sense, babe. I'm gonna need you to help me out here."

"I was never supposed to tell. No one was to know the truth," Cris muttered, his jaw clenched with anger. "Hell, I wasn't ever supposed to learn the truth, but what can you do when you're caught red-handed by your own son."

This was about his father? Now I was even more confused because I couldn't figure out any connection between what was happening and Cris' reaction to things.

"Are you talking about your father?" Toma asked, having come to the same conclusion.

"Yes, if I dare call the bastard that," Cris spat. "Do you know why he marked my mother? The real reason?"

"No..." Toma hedged.

"Well, we all know she's a rescued Omega from the North, and supposedly my parents fell in love on the way back to headquarters. In fact, they were so in love they couldn't wait until they were back. Father marked her the moment she admitted her feelings to him," Cris shared. "At least, this is the story I was told growing up. Yet how do you explain away the fact that this man who was supposed to be a doting lover and father is never the fuck around? A strong sense of duty and the need to protect this country and our people. Well then, imagine when I arrive at a base where my father has no reason to be at fucking the brains out of some Beta bitch behind a building."

While it did not surprise me to hear this, it still hurt my heart knowing how Cris had looked up to his father.

"When I interrupted their tryst, I told him I would tell Mother about it. The bastard just laughed at me and told me to feel free since she knew all about his vulgar habits. Then I found out he bonded with my mother because she knew the truth, that he was a Northerner. They had stationed him at a base that was attacked, then he assumed the identity of a fallen Southern soldier and returned with the battalion. I have no idea how he pulled it off or who he manipulated to keep his secret, but it was almost ruined when my mother remembered him. He'd been one of the Alphas to frequent the breeding house on base. So to keep her quiet, he marked her so if she ever went to the Southern Military and told them the truth, they'd kill her too.

That's why he's never around. He doesn't give two fucks about my mother. All that bastard cares about is living a comfortable life and ordering people around. He manipulated his way to the rank he's at now, digging up dirt for blackmail, using his knowledge of the North to get ahead, and I'm sure doing whatever favors needed to be done, no questions asked. I think the only reason he got my mother pregnant was just to add another accomplishment to his life he could brag about. Too bad for him I ended up being a Beta, not an Alpha like him, so I ruined his entire plan," Cris finished bitterly.

I could feel his pain, the tears he was fighting back, and the rage that blazed within him. How Toma and I never realized our third had been dealt such a blow, I don't know, but it killed me to know he'd been carrying this around for some time. Wrapping my arms around Toma, I sandwiched Cris between us, trying to help him hold it all together.

"I'm so sorry," I whispered, resting my cheek on his shoulder. "I'm so sorry you've had to deal with this alone. We should have noticed. There's no excuse for you to shoulder this all alone."

That's when the soft sobs started and I heard the other two leave. I didn't love the idea of them wandering around the base without one of us. However, dealing with this was crucial. Hopefully, they would try to find Sorin and Victor soon, and everything would be fine. Right now, I needed to be here for Cris, and a soft echo in my bond with Dani told me she understood. I let her use me as a conduit to share her feelings with Cris since she couldn't do it directly.

"Cris, when did you find this out?" Toma asked.

"Right before we attacked the Northern outpost," he croaked. "So much has happened since then. I simply kept ignoring that anything was wrong. Then *he* showed up and took Dani from us, forced his mark on her, and now he's just using us to get what he wants."

"What do you think that is?" I inquired, trying to understand his mindset.

"Power," he stated. "He's using Dani as leverage against us to manipulate the situation. Lucian is the Northern heir with a father who's batshit crazy and refuses to give up power, so now he's using us to kill him and take over. Now he's even got Oscad on his side with those fancy lies he keeps telling everyone."

Lifting my head, I looked at Toma, who seemed to have the same concerned expression I did. His anger and hurt towards his father were clearly being put on Lucian as a surrogate. I was at a loss to know how to help in this situation, but it needed to be settled before we entered into the last part of this journey. If our pack divided, there was no hope of saving the rest of the country. Especially when everyone would be thinking like Cris, assuming the worst and being blinded from the possibility of change.

"What would he have to do to prove himself to you? Is there even a chance of that happening?" I asked, praying he would have some sort of answer for me.

Cris pushed away from Toma and I stepped back, giving him the room he wanted. Rubbing his face with both hands in an effort to wipe away his tears as he took a deep, shaky breath. "I honestly don't know. How can you trust someone you've been taught all your life to hate?"

"Are you saying what we're trying to do is pointless, then?" Toma challenged, as he leaned against the bunk, trying to keep this conversation as relaxed as possible.

The room fell silent as we waited, hoping Cris would have an answer for us. I watched as he sank onto the bunk, hanging his head as he clutched his hands tightly. "I don't want it to be pointless," he rasped.

There were a few moments in my life when I didn't know how to move forward. With all that I'd suffered growing up, along with the loss of my parents, there wasn't an option of getting stuck. It wasn't just myself I was looking after. Three other people depended on me, forcing me to find a way through whatever difficulty we faced. Cris had never been faced with a dilemma that didn't have a clear-cut answer, and I believe that's what he was struggling with the most right now. If he couldn't trust his own father, how could anyone else in the North be?

Heavy footsteps approaching alerted me that Dani had found Sorin. Our leader charged into the room and squared up to Cris, hands on his hips, Alpha energy crackling around him. Cris' head snapped up to look at the man, unable to ignore his presence.

"Do we have a problem, corporal?" Sorin demanded.

Cris started to say something, then slowly shook his head.

"Good answer," Sorin commented. "Whatever issue you seem to be dealing with right now must stop. Put it on the back burner to deal with when we're not in a Southern Military base surrounded by people who would shoot us on sight if they knew who we'd brought in. My first priority is to keep my unit safe and alive. To do that, I'm gonna need you to keep your thoughts and emotions to yourself until we leave. That's an order, understand?"

"Yes, sir," Cris answered, getting to his feet and offering a salute.

"I fucking hope so," Sorin muttered. "Everyone down to the mess hall. It's dinner time, and I don't plan on wasting the chance to eat my fill."

Turning on his heel, Sorin left as swiftly as he arrived, having accomplished what he needed to do. I watched Cris cautiously out of the corner of my eye, although it seemed the Major had snapped him out of whatever melancholy he'd fallen into.

"You heard him, let's go," Cris said before heading out.

I glanced at Toma, but he just shrugged his shoulders and followed. Double checking we didn't leave anything in the room that might tip anyone off about our unusual situation. I closed the door behind me as I left, then jogged down the steps to catch up with the others. Lucian, Dani, and Victor were waiting, but both Sorin and Cris marched right past them to the mess hall. I could feel Dani's unease and she looked at me with a questioning gaze, only I just shook my head. Sorin was right, this was not the time or the place to deal with this particular problem.

Dinner was a silent affair since no one really knew what to say to one another. That and Sorin forced Cris and Lucian to sit next to each other as if to prove a point, to whom I wasn't sure. Once dinner was done, Cris vanished, but I suspected he headed back to the room while the rest of us hung out in the rec room. There was a bar set up, and many of the men started to play cards or other various ways to gamble. I'd never felt the urge to gamble, but I liked to watch. It was fascinating to see how people acted. To my surprise, Lucian joined a game and was damn good at it too.

"There's no way you can keep winning," one soldier accused. "Maybe we should check your sleeves to see if you have anything hidden up there?"

"Shut up, Nado. You're just too fucking easy to read," one of the other men said, shoving Nado with his elbow. "That man right here, has the best poker face I've ever seen, not even a flicker of emotion or a twitch as a tell."

"Yeah, well, there should be a limit to how much money he can take from us," Nado grumbled.

Lucian leaned forward and tapped the table. "You could stop putting money in the pot. Then you're guaranteed not to lose it."

The whole table erupted with laughter as the guys hassled their teammates, and Lucian gave them all an easy smile. This was the world he knew and felt comfortable with. It was the most relaxed I'd seen him other than when he was with Dani. Who happened to be approaching him right now.

"Luke," Dani called, grabbing his attention. "Sorin's looking for you."

"Well, boys, it seems you get to blame someone else for the money you're losing the rest of the night," Lucian taunted as he rose from the table, wrapping an arm around Dani's shoulders.

"Your leader ain't lookin' for ya. I bet you twenty marks she's just looking to get some Alpha cock in her." One of the more intoxicated soldiers slurred.

Lucian froze and half turned around, his face like a thundercloud looming overhead. "What did you just say?"

"I said, your bitch wants to get boned," the idiot shouted.

Before Lucian could even take a step in the man's direction, Victor was slamming his fist into the drunken man's face. Instantly he flew out of his chair and fell to the floor in a heap, groaning.

"Fucking bastard, you'll pay for that," yelled another soldier coming to his friend's defense.

Victor made quick work of him too, as well as the five others that rushed him. It wasn't until one of them smashed through a table that things had gone too far. Now everyone was on their feet looking to get in on the action.

"What the fuck is going on here?" a booming voice demanded.

When the soldiers parted for the man, I realized it was none other than Cris' father, Lieutenant Colonel Lino Nems. *What the fuck was he doing here?* Then the realization hit that he was the one leading this battalion of soldiers. He can't see Lucian or Dani with her brand since I'm betting he would recognize what it means even if he didn't know it was for Lucian specifically.

Quickly, I stepped in front of them both and whispered harshly. "Get the fuck out of here *now*. Tell Sorin we need to leave immediately. It's not safe to stay here even a moment longer."

Thankfully, Lucian took me at my word, snatched up Dani, and hurried out of the mess hall. I just had to pray to the fates that the bastard didn't see them, but Lino Nems wasn't one to be underestimated.

"Petru?" Lino questioned. "What are you doing here? Aren't you supposed to be hunting down those Northerners who were trying to destroy the power plant?"

Gritting my teeth, I ensured my face was calm and neutral before I faced the commanding officer. "Lieutenant Colonel, I wasn't expecting to see you here, either."

"Yes, well, it seems the North has gotten bold with this recent attack, so my men and I are going to pay them a little visit," he answered. "You didn't answer my question, however. Why are *you* here?"

Victor stepped up next to me and fielded the question for me. "We caught up with a small group of Northern soldiers, but they never work in teams that small, so we've been tracking the rest of them. Since we didn't plan to be away this long, we needed to stop for supplies."

Lino narrowed his gaze on Victor, as if he looked hard enough he could tell if the man was lying or not. "I see... and what happened here?"

"Nothing but soldiers blowing off steam, sir," Victor answered with a shrug. "Seems some can't handle their spirits as well as others, but since we're to head out well before dawn, we were just walking back to get some shut-eye."

Crossing my fingers, I hoped he would believe our story and let us leave. The last thing we needed right now was Lino Nems butting into our situation.

"That's not what happened," blurted the drunken man, who stumbled forward. "He and that other guy with the fucked up face didn't like what I said about their little bitch of an Omega."

Before I could even process my actions, my hand shot out to grab Victor's arm, keeping him from doing anything stupid. To his credit, he hadn't so much as tried to take a step toward the man but clenched his hands into fists.

"You have an Omega?" Lino demanded, his brows snapping together in anger. "I don't remember any teams getting approval to establish a pack."

"This has happened all rather suddenly. She was assigned to our unit about two weeks ago," I offered. "She also happens to be a refugee, so there wouldn't be the same type of paperwork had she been a Southern citizen."

"Are you saying the son of the Southern president is bonded to a *Northern* Omega?" Lino spat.

His disgust was almost laughable for a man who was born and raised as a Northerner and is bonded to an Omega who was rescued from the North.

"I thought President Dragomire already had a female selected for your pack, Mora Korda?" Lino questioned. "She's the daughter of Prvos Korda, an advisor to the president."

"There was no such arrangement shared with me," Sorin interjected as he joined the discussion. "You two may go. I'll handle any questions the Lieutenant Colonel still has."

After years of working with the man, I knew an order to get everyone else the hell out of here while he distracted the bastard when I heard it. I gave a sharp nod and a salute before turning on my heel and marching out with Victor right behind me.

How the fuck had this night gone so wrong.

CHAPTER 51

Danella

After being whisked out of the mess hall, Lucian ran all the way back to the barracks until we reached the room we were supposed to be staying in. Kicking the door in, not caring at all that Sorin and Cris were sleeping, or trying to, Lucian entered the room but refused to set me down.

"Pack everything up. We need to get the fuck out of here," he ordered.

Toma set aside his computer, looking confused. "What's going on?"

"Look, I get that I'm not allowed to give orders around here, but if we want to get out of this base without blowing the whole mission up, we need to go *now*," Lucian explained.

Sorin tossed back the covers and stood wearing only his boxers. Biting my lip, I stared up at the ceiling knowing now was not the time to be getting all hot and bothered.

"You're gonna need to give me something, Lucian," Sorin challenged. "Help me understand the problem so I can make sure our next action doesn't put us in more trouble."

I could feel Lucian's uncertainty as he set me down. He then glanced over at Cris, who was sitting up in his bunk watching us. "Can you please tell me your last name?"

"What?" Cris asked, his face scrunching up. "Why do you need to know that?"

"It's Nems," Toma answered over top of Cris' protests. "His last name is Nems."

"Then it would seem your father is the commanding officer of the battalion of men who are staying in this building with us. Petru recognized him right away, then made sure Dani and I got out of there before being spotted," Lucian informed them.

"Fucking hell," Sorin growled as he snatched up his clothes and yanked them on. "Get our shit together and meet me at the far entrance near the end of the training yard. Toma, do you have what you need to make this happen?"

"Yeah, I can get us out quick and silent," Toma assured, hoping off the top bunk. "Did we get everything we needed supplies wise?"

"We have enough to make due. I was going to grab a few more packs of rations to be safe, but it's not worth it now," Sorin shared with a sigh. "Where are the other two?"

"Petru and Victor are still in the mess hall. The reason he even showed up is because of me," I said, hugging myself feeling it was all my fault.

Sorin had made me promise that when it turned ten o'clock, I'd get Lucian back up to the room to sleep. I hadn't even considered the fact that other soldiers might cause an issue, but I was used to the respect my unit got back at headquarters. Here people didn't give a shit what rank you had, they were all going to war and could possibly die the next day.

A hand gripped my chin, and Sorin forced me to meet his gaze. "Dani-girl, you did exactly as I asked. You are not responsible for how other people act, only for yourself. I'm also betting that you weren't the one to start the fight."

I blinked at him. "How did you know there was a fight?"

Sorin chuckled. "Do you think Victor would let you step foot out of this room without him being close by? If he saw someone doing anything disrespectful, then a fight was bound to happen no matter what anyone said. That being said, I really should head down there to make sure Victor doesn't do something he'll regret one day."

A quick peck on the lips and Sorin was out of the room, leaving us to manage.

"Okay, everyone grab two packs and follow me," Toma instructed. "The supplies we got today will be in a locked locker waiting for us. We always used the same combinations, so any one of us can access it for situations like this."

It appeared that Cris didn't change out of his uniform so we only had to wait for him to lace up his boots before we left the room. Toma led us over to the supply depot and a row of large metal lockers. He quickly imputed the combination and yanked open the door.

"Pack fast. We'll sort it all out once we get far enough away from here," Toma said as he started to shove things into his pack.

Having no clue what I was grabbing from the dark locker, I froze as I stared down at the package wrapped with a label marking it as C-4 explosives. "Ah..."

"It's fine, Dani," Cris assured me. "Trust me, after living with Victor for as long as we have, we've all gotten used to explosive stuff lying around. That won't explode without the right detonator, so just keep it all together and there will be nothing to worry about."

I gulped but trusted he wouldn't put me in danger, and if Victor brought it into the house, then it couldn't be that dangerous...right?

Packing things up took longer than I expected, but I don't think I realized just how much they wanted to bring with us. There were even another two duffle bags that were filled with supplies, mainly food. Just as we finished, I heard footsteps approaching and whirled with my gun at the ready.

"Whoa there, Little Spark," Victor called out. "It's just Tru and me. No need to shoot."

Letting out the breath I'd been holding, I relaxed and lowered the gun. "Where's Sorin?"

"Keeping the dear lieutenant colonel busy while we get out of here," Petru answered.

"What? Wait, we can't leave him behind," I panicked.

"Shh, Wildflower, he will be right behind us as soon as he gets the chance," Petru assured me.

"Yeah, he just needs to keep the asshole from looking for us or investigating the fact we now have an Omega, thanks to that drunken shithead. I should have hit him harder, then his ass would be knocked out and no one would have been the wiser," Victor muttered as he pulled on a duffle, then shouldered a pack.

"That's everything, let's head over to the back door," Toma urged. "Once we get there, I'll need you guys to hang back just a little so it doesn't look weird that I'm messing with the controls."

Moving in as silently as we could in the shadow of the night since the sky was conveniently lacking a moon. We waited behind a supply shed as Toma darted forward to a large metal door. I watched as he pulled a small handheld computer and plugged in some wires into something I couldn't see very well from this far away. Waiting for him to give us the signal to join him was torture. It felt like it took hours when I'm sure it was only minutes. Yet knowing that everything we wanted to accomplish could be destroyed in one single moment had my anxiety clawing at my throat.

Is this what missions are really like for them, or is this a unique situation?

A sharp whistle had the guys moving before my brain even registered the sound. Shaking my head to focus on the here and now, I kept low as we followed along the wall until we reached Toma. He motioned for us to wait and carefully turned the large wheel that seemed to lock the door. A loud *thunk* echoed around us, sounding like a bomb had gone off. Even though I'm reasonably sure it wasn't that loud in reality. We all waited to see if anyone was going to sound the alarm or come running, but nothing happened. Slowly, Toma pulled the two-foot thick metal door open, revealing the wide-open field that surrounded the base.

"Head to the east. There is a grove of trees that should keep us hidden until Sorin meets up with us," Toma instructed. "I'll be right behind you guys. I just need to make sure it won't lock when I close it."

I didn't like this. I didn't like it at all, but I dutifully followed the others as they slipped out into the night. There was no time to question anything as Petru led the way with Victor and Lucian corralling Cris and me in the middle. Each of them had a gun at the ready, and I was surprised to see they were willing to shoot one of their fellow men. I suppose this was a moment where you saw a line drawn in the sand. You're either part of the pack or not—those outside the pack were considered the enemy.

Ducking behind a clump of bushes, we waited.

I swear I could hear my heart beating in my ears, and it was pounding like a fucking drum. *What if something happened to Sorin? Did the door stay unlocked? Could we really pull this off? Why in the world did it have to be Cris' father leading those men?* The torrent of questions that whirled around in my brain kept spinning faster and faster, like a whirlpool trying to suck me under.

Then there was the sound of a twig snapping close by, followed up by a bird call that had me letting out the breath I'd been holding. Shooting to my feet, I flung myself at Sorin burying my nose in his wintergreen and eucalyptus scent.

He held me tightly, nuzzling my head. "I'm here, Dani-girl. We all made it out just fine." Sorin soothed.

Lifting my head, I pressed a kiss to his lips *needing* to know he was alive and here. He kissed me back but didn't deepen it before setting me down and taking a pack from Victor. "We need to move, I don't know how long we have before that asshole reaches out to the Commandant. For some reason, he was unjustly pissed that we bonded with Dani. He didn't give a shit that we were out here chasing Northerners, but fuck if we did something impulsive like falling in love."

"I agree his reaction was quite odd when he learned about Dani," Petru agreed. "At least the stop was worth it and we have the majority of supplies we need. It would be worse if we left empty-handed."

"Agreed," Sorin said with a nod. "Let's get a few miles away from here at least, it would be better still if we could make it to the edge of the badlands. That would be pushing it, but it's the opposite direction than they'd be looking for us since it's not close to the bridge at all."

"Lead the way, boss, we'll follow," Victor stated.

Sorin took one last toward the base as if he wasn't sure he trusted to put his back to it. Unfortunately, that was a feeling I was well acquainted with, especially knowing there was a threat we'd left behind. His face fell into a determined expression and he marched forward knowing this was the point we couldn't turn back from. We either pulled off this mission, or we'd be killed for treason by one country or the other. Yet off we went with a dream and a heart full of hope. If we could pull this off it would all be worth it.

WE MANAGED to make it to the badlands that night and found a cave to sleep in and get ourselves organized. While we had an idea of where we were going the maps we'd been basing this off of were old and certain landmarks had changed or been altered over the course of time. It took us two days before we found a place to cross the river and even then it was a terrifying situation.

"You are not fucking throwing me across that," I snapped, pointing at the gap between two mountain outcroppings.

It looked as if once upon a time, they had been connected, but the middle of it crumbled away. The test to see if we could make the gap was for Victor to literally hurl Toma across. The scream that came out of me shocked everyone and almost made Victor stumble at a crucial point. That's when Lucian slapped a hand over my mouth until Toma had safely landed on the other side.

"Little Spark, do you think I would even be considering this if I didn't think I'd get you across just fine? Why do you think we started with Toma?" Victor questioned.

"Because he's fucking crazy," I shot back, hands on my hips. "How is the last person, aka you, going to manage, Vicky?"

He shrugged and grabbed a coil of rope. "I'll have one of the others hold one end, carry it over, then find a place to anchor it so if I fall short, I'm not splattered on the ground below."

"I think I'm going to be sick," I muttered, rubbing my forehead. "You know I'm all for the daring option, but that's when there's no other choice. How do we know this is the place to do this? What if the river gets smaller further upstream?"

"Dani-girl," Sorin interjected, grabbing my shoulders to look at him. "We can't keep heading in the wrong direction. If we keep going, we'll head west as the river curves and head into the opposite mountain range than we need. I realize this isn't anyone's first choice but we need to make a choice and this is where it's going to happen."

"You guys coming?" Toma yelled from the other side. "If you leave me over here, I'm gonna be pissed. He didn't even ask me if I wanted to go first."

Victor chuckled at that and flipped Toma off. "You weren't going to just leave him over there, were you, Little Spark?"

I let out a groan as my head fell to Sorin's chest. "Okay, I get it. This is how it has to be."

"Would it help if you saw the others make it over?" Sorin asked as he stroked a hand over my head trying to calm my fears I knew he could still feel.

"It might," I admitted.

"I'll go next," Lucian announced, causing me to turn my head to look at him. "Then I'll be there waiting to catch you."

God, that man could be so sweet sometimes. How the hell did he survive his father all these years?

"Promise?" I asked.

Pulling me out of Sorin's arm, he cupped my face and kissed the hell out of me to the point I was breathless. "Yes, My Heart, I promise."

Nodding, I moved out of the way when he released me and Victor stepped up. "All right, so the plan is you come running full tilt towards the gap. Then I'll grab your arm and fling you as you jump. You're the largest of us, so that means no hesitation, no second-guessing, you fucking run straight ahead."

Rolling his shoulders and shaking out his limbs, Lucian prepared. Sorin was already throwing over the heaviest packs so they didn't weigh us down or cause us to become unbalanced. Toma managed to catch most of them before they hit the ground, but one pack was heavier than he expected and almost fell headlong off the outcropping.

"*Toma*," I screamed, darting forward.

The man sat back and landed on his ass, clutching the pack for dear life. "Hoollyy shiiit."

"Are you all right?" I demanded, my heart pounding in my chest as I refused to look down. The last thing I needed was the mental image of where he would have splattered on the ground.

"Y...yeah," he stammered, then cleared his throat and stood. "Maybe a warning that it's heavier than the others might be a good call."

"Sorry, man, I should have said something," Sorin admitted. "That was the worst of them, but I might suggest backing up a little since Lucian's coming over."

Toma took a few steps back, setting the pack out of the way but keeping close enough to help if something happened. Lucian jogged in place for a second then I could feel the shift in him as he charged off to the end of the stone shelf we were standing on. His footsteps pounded like the beating of my heart as he flew over the gap as Victor swung him forward, adding to his momentum. For a full three seconds, my heart stopped beating as Lucian arced through the air. He crash-landed but rolled into it and Toma was there to make sure he didn't end up going off the side of the damn mountain.

"He's good," Toma called.

Before I even had time to recover, Petru was flying through the air and landed on the other side with slightly more grace. With a forward somersault, he popped back up on his feet and jogged a few steps to slow himself down.

Three down, four to go.

"I'll go next," Cris decided. "This way, she can see someone lighter like herself making it over this thing with ease."

How I envied his confidence right now. Cris kept a pack on since he was lighter it shouldn't cause a problem and some things we'd picked up at the base, really shouldn't be thrown around. Starting as far back as he could, Cris darted forward. Just as Victor grabbed Cris' arm, he stumbled over a rock, but he was going too fast and was too close to the edge for him to stop. To my horror, I realized he wasn't going to make it. There wasn't enough speed anymore to carry him far enough.

My throat seized up, making it impossible for me to scream, and just when I thought I was going to watch Cris die, Lucian was there. With a rope around his waist, the Alpha reached out to Cris and managed to grab the pack. Toma and Petru held tight as the eight of both men hit the end of the slack pulling them forward. Rushing to the edge, I dropped to my knees, looking down to see Lucian with a dangling Cris clinging to the straps of the pack below.

"Cris, grab my leg," Lucian instructed. "You need to help me get some weight off this pack, or the straps are going to break. Grab my leg and see if you can climb up on me."

I wasn't sure if Cris heard him or not since the man didn't move. He just hung there, stunned.

"Corporal Cristofor Nems, look at me," Lucian barked. The command was so strong I flinched just hearing it.

However, it did the trick and Cris' head snapped up to look at Lucian, fear and panic in his gaze. "Don't drop me. Please don't let go."

CHAPTER 52

Danella

With my heart in my throat at Cris' words, I prayed to the fates that the pack would be strong enough to hold on a little longer. Not to mention I'm fairly certain it's also the one with the C-4 in it. None of the guys had liked me being so close to it, so they rotated it between them all, and Cris had just been given it.

"Grab my leg," Lucian instructed, speaking slowly and clearly.

Cris finally responded and twisted to get at a better angle to grab Lucian's leg. Once Cris was able to grab tight around his calf, he reached out to Lucian's other leg and grabbed that one too. Now that he wasn't dangling just by the pack's straps, I felt marginally better.

"Now, you're gonna need to work your way up until you can wrap your arms around my waist. Toma and Petru are on the other end of this rope, but I don't want them pulling us up until I know you're secure," Lucian informed him.

The Beta nodded and reached up a hand to Lucian's belt, gripping it tightly as he tried to drag himself up. Lucian had one hand still holding the pack, but his other hand was clasped around Cris' bicep trying to lift him as the other pulled. I didn't think they would be able to do it on pure upper body strength alone, but Lucian pulled through. With a roar of desperation, the Alpha made a snap judgment and released his hold on the pack. Cris started to slip with the sudden change in weight, but Lucian already had his hand under Cris' armpits and hauled the man up.

My mouth fell open as I could see the muscles bulging in Lucian's arms and veins popping out on the side of his neck. There was no question if that man was giving it his all and then some. It did the trick, though, and Cris not only could wrap his legs around Lucian's waist but also managed to grab the rope that was between them.

"*Pull*," Sorin bellowed.

Instantly Toma and Petru got to work slowly pulling the two men up until Cris could grab the edge and pull himself up with Lucian shoving from below. Free of the double weight, it was much easier for Lucian to get dragged over the trim back on solid ground. Tears streamed down my face as both men were safe.

"I don't know how many times my heart can take something like that," I sobbed as Victor wrapped me up in a hug. "But I know I can't ask you not to do your job or be who you are, and I don't want to. That was just so scary. I almost lost them both."

"Shh, Little Spark, everything is going to be okay," Victor reassured me, rubbing my back.

Gripping his shirt tightly, I shook my head. "How can you say that? We have no idea what we're getting into once we cross this river. Everything from this point is unknown."

He pulled me back and searched my face. "You're absolutely right. Past this point, we don't know what's going to happen or what dangers we might face. Though, you could say that about every day you open your eyes. There's no way to tell what a day will hold, but one thing I do know for certain is that I have all of you right by my side. As long as we face life head-on with each other, then it doesn't matter what happens."

I let out a sound that was somewhere between a sob and a laugh. "Who are you, and what have you done with my cynical Vicky?"

"What can I say, this sassy little Omega showed up one day and made me realize that giving a shit might not be all that bad," Victor said with a grin and a shrug. "Now, I'm going to kiss you, tell you I love you, and throw your ass across this gap, okay?"

My eyes grew wide, and I started to shake my head but his lips fused to mine with so much need and promise. He nuzzled his nose against mine in an unusually adorable moment, then pulled back. "I love you more than I've loved anything or anyone ever in my life. If anything ever happened to you, I'm pretty sure I'd either kill myself or run headfirst into battle hoping someone would put me out of my misery. Now knowing that, I need you to trust me and not fight against what I'm about to do."

I was scooped up, spun, and launched across the gap with no time to have any feelings on the matter. My mind didn't even catch up in time to scream before another set of arms snatched me out of the air. Lucian's chocolate and cinnamon scent swirled around me and that was all I needed before I grabbed his face to kiss the fuck out of him. Meeting my need with his own as he started to purr, I wanted nothing more than to cling to him forever, but he wasn't the only one I needed. Ripping my lips away from his, I looked around for Cris and spotted him nearby.

Reaching out a hand to him as I pleaded with my eyes for him to take it. He did, much faster than I thought, and soon my lips were being devoured by Cris'. The two men sandwiched me between them, pressing kisses anywhere they could, desperate to know that we were all still alive and in one piece. When we finally calmed down, Lucian set me on my feet letting his hand linger on my ass. Cris held my hand tightly, interlocking our fingers as if afraid he'd lose his grip on me.

"Thank fuck you're both all right," I blurted. "Don't you ever fucking scare me like that again, or you're not sleeping in the puppy pile."

"I'm sorry... the what?" Cris asked, a smile tugging at his lips.

"The puppy pile, you know, when we all sleep together at night," I explained, confused as to why they were puzzled.

Lucian chuckled and pressed a kiss to my head. "You've always had your cute moments, My Heart, but since you've been marked they happen far more often, and I love it."

"I see, well, keep teasing me and see just how cute I am once you've pissed me off," I shot back. "Alphas, you certainly know how to take a moment and ruin the sentimentality of it."

Cris gripped my jaw and turned me to face him, placing a sweet kiss on my lips. "Be nice, he saved my life, you know. I think that earns him some slack."

I melted at the emotions I could feel from him and realized that he's been shutting me out. Since I didn't have a direct bond with him I assumed it wouldn't be as strong, but if what I was feeling now was any indication, he'd been definitely holding out on me.

"Hey, any chance we can come join the party?" Victor yelled, breaking us apart. "I think it might be best if we get a rope attached to Sorin before I chuck him over."

This got the guys moving, and in mere moments they were ready to get the last two of our pack across. Sorin was able to make it easily enough with them pulling along with Victor's added momentum. Using the same method, Victor ran full out as Sorin and Lucian pulled him with Toma and Petru standing at the edge to grab him when he got close enough. Thank fuck they were there too as Victor's boot slipped on the edge, the rock crumbling under his weight. Swiftly they latched onto his arms yanking him forward. Sagging against Cris, I was relieved to have this over and know all my men were safe and sound.

As much as I wanted us to take a moment, Sorin was adamant that we kept going. "We're too out in the open here. I would feel better if we kept pushing and found a good spot to rest early tonight."

The promise of this day being over sooner than later had me grabbing my pack. "You heard the Alpha. Let's go."

The guys all chuckled at my imitation of Victor but gathered their packs all the same. Forging on deeper into the mountain's foothills, our pace slowed with the unsteady footing. There was no established path, so we made it up as we went. I trusted Sorin to make the best call, however. Eventually, I heard the sound of running water and tried to pinpoint where it was coming from. None of us could see the source, but after we made it over the crest of the hill we'd been climbing, we found ourselves in a pretty grotto with a small waterfall flowing. The pool of water looked clear, fresh, and inviting.

"How is this possible?" Toma questioned. "I thought the main river was the only water source for the North."

"I would seem that isn't the case," Lucian muttered. "No one ever ventures into these mountains knowing the rebels live here. My guess is there are some peaks high enough to get snow and this is what's melting off them."

"Damn, that means these rebels had the right idea," Victor commented.

"The chances of there being a town or some kind of civilization is much higher, seeing as this environment is viable," Petru added.

"What?" Cris questioned, his brow furrowed.

"We're going to find the people we're looking for if we follow the water," Sorin translated. "Here seems as good as any to rest, and we can even wash up before the sun sets."

Falling into the routine, we'd developed since traveling, we set up our basic camp. Tarps were strung to create a shelter, a fire was started, and we refilled all the water. Having completed all the essential matters, we could finally relax and enjoy this little oasis we had discovered. I stripped out of my uniform until I was down to my underwear before dipping my toe in the water.

"Brr, that's freezing," I announced, snapping my foot back.

The temperature had been rising every day the closer we got to the North. Now that we were here, I was reminded just how hot the days could get. We were still on the edge of the cooler season, but it would be blazing hot in a few weeks, and a pool like this would be more than welcome.

At the sound of pounding feet, I darted out of the way as Victor charged into the water, leaping the rest of the way once it was up to his knees. Seconds later, he came shooting out of the water with a gasp. "Holy balls, that's fucking cold. I think my balls just curled up inside me to keep warm."

I tried to fight it. Nevertheless, I burst into laughter at his reaction, which was cut short as he grabbed my arm and dragged me in with him. Then he picked me up and tossed me into the deepest part that was fortunately shallow enough to stand. Even if the water came up to my chin, it made me panic that I might drown.

"What the actual fuck, Vicky, I can't swim," I berated him.

His smile fell from his face as he waded out to pluck me from the water. I wrapped my limbs around him as my teeth chattered. "Why didn't you tell me you can't swim?" Victor demanded. "What would you have done if we needed to swim across the river?"

"Held onto someone," I ventured, my words choppy, unable to stop my shivering.

"Damn it, woman," he muttered, slogging out of the water to sit near the fire. "How the hell am I supposed to look after you when I don't know something as important as that?"

I understood his irritation, but I couldn't think of anything other than getting warm at this moment. Curling up into a tight ball against his chest, my teeth clattering together, telling everyone how cold I was. Sorin came over and draped a blanket over me, which Victor tucked in around me for good measure.

"Dani-girl, Vic makes a good point. It truly is important for us to know things like you can't swim. That way we can make accommodations or avoid the situation altogether," Sorin reasoned, as he sat in front of Victor taking my leg and rubbing his warm hands against my skin. "Is there anything else that we need to know like that? What about allergies?"

"A... allergies?" I stammered.

"Yes, such as foods, animals, plants, anything that might affect your ability to fight or run from a situation," he explained.

I shook my head, not thinking of anything except I'd never really spent much time around animals or even plants. Foods were fairly limited most of my life, controlled by others, yet I didn't think that was going to be a problem for me.

"Well, if you think of anything, be sure to let us know," Sorin instructed, pinning me with a look like he didn't believe I would.

"I will, promise," I said, giving him a small smile, something that was harder to do than is should be as I was still shivering.

Victor rose and walked over to the spot we'd laid out our beds.

"Sorin, can you put these closer together? She's not warming up fast enough, so I'm gonna need your help since you didn't swim."

That had me looking to see where the others had gone. Petru, Toma, and Cris were in the shallows of the water washing up, but I couldn't find Lucian. When I reached out to him through our bond, I could tell he was close by but a little further up near the top of the waterfall. Reassurance washed over me as Lucian tried to tell me he was fine and not to worry. He must be scouting the area to ensure we would be safe here.

"First, we need to get her out of these wet things, or she'll never warm up," Sorin stated as he popped the clasp of my bra.

Victor set me on my feet then knelt, hooking his thumbs in my underwear and sliding them off me. Almost instantly, I felt better. Still cold as hell, but I didn't feel like a block of ice was seeping the heat out of me. Moments later, I was sighing in relief as Victor pulled me against him and Sorin's naked body pressed against my back, sandwiching me between them as we lay on our sleeping bags.

"This is much better," I moaned, as the tingling feeling of blood circulating more freely told me I'd be just fine.

Sorin reached around and cupped one of my breasts in his hand. "I don't know this area still seems to be rather cold..."

"Wait, let me check," Victor offered, dipping his head to suck on my nipple sharply. "Yeah, it's still pretty chilly. I think I might be able to warm it up, though."

The feel of his lips closing around my nipple and his hot tongue flicking the raised nub had me arching into Sorin. "Oh God," I whimpered.

"Looks like it's working. Keep it up, we'll have her warm in no time," Sorin pointed out.

Victor's eyes flicked up to meet my gaze. "With pleasure, yet I feel like we can turn up the heat a little together."

Both of them started to purr, sending vibrations all over my body that made my heart speed up and my breath quicken. As Victor purred, he continued to suck, nip, and lick my breasts which turned me into a puddle of need, my slick coating both legs in the hope this would lead where I hoped it would. Sorin let his hand glide down my leg until he reached my knee and lifted it to hook it over Victor's thigh. Now there was room for him to slide two fingers into me making me mewl in pleasure, tossing my head back.

"Does that feel good, Dani-girl?" Sorin asked, his lips brushing the shell of my ear.

I couldn't speak but managed to nod until he nipped at his mark on my neck and an orgasm sliced through me out of nowhere. The scream that erupted from me was cut off when Victor slammed his lips to mine, stifling the sound.

"If we're going to do this, my sweet Dani-girl, then you need to keep your voice down. What would we do if the rebels attacked, and here you are soaking wet and needy? It's not going to help our cause if we kill them all for seeing you in such a state," Sorin chided.

Once Victor was sure I wasn't going to be too loud, he pulled back, licking his lips as if he loved the way I tasted. "Little Spark, I have a question for you."

"Yes," I said, my voice barely audible.

He leaned in, letting his nose caress mine. "Which hole do you want my cock to fill?"

My whole body shuddered at his words, nails digging into his skin as I tried to keep myself grounded. "Don't care, you choose."

"What about Sorin? Do you want him to fill whichever one I leave empty?"

"Fuck yes, I want you both to fill me. I don't care how or where, all I need are your cocks thrusting into me," I begged, as my scent perfumed through the air in hopes it would draw them closer and fulfill my request.

"You heard her, Sorin. Which door would you like to use?" Victor asked.

Fingers glided from clit to asshole, gathering my slick then using it to massage the tight ring of my ass. "I'm happy with either, but since her pert little ass is rubbing all over my cock. I think that's where it wants me to be."

"Now that we have that decided," Victor said right before he lined his cock to the entrance of my pussy and thrust all the way into it. "Fuuuccckkk," he groaned. "You feel so damn good, Little

Spark, the way your pussy wraps itself around my dick like it never wants to let me go."

Once more, my body was trembling but this time it had nothing to do with being cold. Panting, I let my head fall to his shoulder as I wrapped my arms around his neck. When Sorin let his finger sink into my ass, I groaned at the overwhelming feeling. I wanted to push into him, to feel him deeper inside me, but I was already speared by Victor's thick, pierced cock. As an Omega, it didn't take long at all until Sorin could get two, then three fingers into my ass before he nudged the entrance with the blunt head of his cock.

"Moan for me, Dani-girl. I'm going to give you exactly what you've been looking for," Sorin promised. "We'll always be here to take care of your needs no matter what."

With gentle kisses along my shoulder and neck, I felt his cock fill me up in the most amazing way possible. The feeling of them inside me had me wriggling trying to fit every damn inch of them inside me. Never in a million years would I have said the sensation of fullness was one of pure bliss. There was nothing else quite like it, and knowing the cause was two men who loved me unconditionally made it all the better.

When they finally began to move in slow, drawn-out thrusts, it took everything within me not to demand they pick up the speed. I knew both of them needed to make sure my body was ready for them to fuck me how I wanted in order for them to feel comfortable —overprotective worrywarts. As their movements sped up, the cries coming out of my mouth became louder. Sorin gripped my jaw and turned me to him so he could muffle my sounds with his kisses.

Here I was, pressed between two formidable bodies of my Alphas as they literally thrust their love into me. All my mind could focus on was the euphoric devotion I received through our bond. They wanted to show me physically as well as emotionally how much I meant to them. The faster and harder they thrust, the more pressure built until I was ready to explode. Victor caught my breast with his mouth sucking sharply at the nipple just as Sorin pinched my clit. Instantly my body detonated, but when I tried to cling to them, to hold their knots hostage, it couldn't find them. At the last second, they pulled out enough to ensure I wouldn't be stuck to them. In my mind, I understood why. It wasn't safe, and neither of my Alphas would allow harm to come to me if they could prevent it.

I tried to fight it, but the whine wouldn't be held back.

"Shh, Little Spark," Victor crooned, stroking my cheek as he rested his forehead against mine. "I know, and I'm sorry. God, I fucking want to knot you so bad. To fill your pussy, so we're connected in the most intimate way possible. Even so, this is how it has to be when we're not somewhere safe."

Sorin nuzzled his mark before letting his tongue run over it, making me shudder with aftershocks. "We might not be able to knot you, but I think we can come up with something to make your body feel like it didn't miss out."

They both eased out of me, and Sorin slid me further up and rolled so I was laying on his stomach. Taking my legs, he pulled them to my chest and spread them wide, giving Victor the perfect view of my pussy dripping with slick and cum. I really didn't know what was going to happen next. Then Victor latched his mouth over my pussy and shoved two fingers in my ass. He fucked me with his tongue and fingers, not giving two shits about the mess between my legs. Sorin played with my nipples as his fellow Alpha gave me orgasm after orgasm until I blacked out from the stimulation.

CHAPTER 53

Danella

When I opened my eyes once more, I found it was dark. The moon was starting to grow but was still a sliver in the night sky. I'd clearly been out for quite some time if it was this late already. The fire crackled, and I saw Toma on watch sitting beside it. Shifting, I found myself in one of the guy's shirts, and the spicy clove and ginger scent told me it was Victor.

Getting up, I realized Lucian had been at my back while Sorin was still on my other side. Victor must have had to take his turn relieving Lucian from watch. It made me smile to think how well things were going when it came to sharing time with me. Each of them seemed to instinctively understand that they would need to respect each other's time together. I'd been worried they would try to keep Lucian out of the mix or Victor would keep me to himself in the name of protection. Yet other than Cris having a hard time because of more personal issues, things had been great.

Keeping the blanket wrapped around me, I joined Toma. He instantly wrapped an arm around me, pressing a kiss to my lips as I cuddled close. "They really wore you out, didn't they?"

"You could say that," I giggled. "I had no idea how badly I needed that. It's like all the tension I had in my body is now gone, I'm able to relax a little more."

"Cris warned us that we'd need to make sure you got some extra lovin' even when we were on a mission," Toma commented, which had my mouth falling open. "Easy there, love. He didn't mean anything by it other than the fact that Omegas need certain things to feel stable and secure in their packs. We don't have a nest or a home for you to retreat to when things get overwhelming. What you have is us, and one way to help you not having these other things is to do so physically."

I didn't really feel like that made things any better but I could see some logic in it.

"Did we happen to find anything fresh for dinner tonight?" I asked, as my stomach gurgled in reminder that I hadn't eaten dinner.

To my delight, Toma handed me a plate with cooked fish on it. "Lucian found a spot further upstream where a whole school of fish was trying to run upriver, so he caught a few for dinner."

"Bless that man," I mumbled as I peeled off the outer layer of skin to the flaky goodness inside. It had been *years* since I'd had fish of any kind so I didn't care that I had to pick it off the bone with an eye staring at me as I ate.

I picked that damn thing clean, feeling the perfect amount of fullness as I relaxed against Toma. The nights were cooler than the day, making it comfortable to easily sleep. One year it got so hot it was just unbearable to try and sleep at night with no breeze. The breeding house would get so stuffy and the thick scent of sex always hung in the air making me gag. It was strange to think that was my life for a time as I now sat with one of my Alphas, staring up at the stars in the sky.

"How long do you think it will be until we find any sign of civilization?" I asked.

Toma didn't answer right away as he considered my question, twirling a lock of my hair around his finger. "If it were me, I wouldn't want to be too close to the border. You never know who or what might be coming from that direction. Then again, being higher in the mountains would make things harder too. So my guess is we stick to the foothills, follow the river, and we'll find signs of life sooner than later."

"Out of all the things we have to accomplish to make this happen, getting these rebels on our side is the most important, isn't it?" I mused aloud.

"That would be a safe bet," he agreed, glancing down at his watch. "It's about time to wake up Tru. Do you want to come back to bed with me, or are you going to stay up?"

With my now full belly, I let out a yawn. "Curling up with you sounds nice," I murmured.

Scooping me up, he headed over to where Petru and Cris were sprawled out. He set me down before kneeling next to Petru, stroking his face lightly before kissing him. It took a moment, but Petru's hand lifted to curl around Toma's neck, keeping him right where he was. The two made out for a moment, causing me to blush as I rubbed my legs together. The three lovers didn't really ever make a big deal about their relationship, nor did they feel the need to prove to others they were together. It was a beautiful blend of people who cared deeply about each other, first and foremost. The benefits that came with being intimate were a significant bonus.

"You're the only one who wakes me up like that," Petru shared as he looked lovingly up at Toma.

Toma snorted. "Do you really want Sorin and Victor making out with you?"

"Hmm... I suppose not, but it is rather lovely to experience," Petru said, then yawned while sitting up and stretching. He then spotted me and his smile grew wider. "Would you wake me up like that, Wildflower?"

I returned his smile and nodded. "I would be happy to, but I'm not sure I'd have as much self-control at Toma."

He reached out to gently tug on a lock of my hair and winked. "Give it time. You'll find balance once the newness of us all together is worn off a little."

"I don't want that to happen," I argued. "No matter what, I

always want to feel like this about you guys. The moment you get lazy in a relationship is when you take people for granted."

Petru took my hand and tugged me over to sit in his lap as he wrapped his arms around me and kissed my temple. "You, my Wild-flower, have the biggest heart I've ever seen. How you strive to ensure every person feels valued and seen is beyond amazing. While I agree with you that it should never get to the point where we don't find joy, love, and lust in our partners. I was simply pointing out that with time you will trust that none of us are going anywhere, so controlling your desires for us will become easier."

Heat bloomed in my cheeks as he pointed out I'd probably over-reacted just a little. Everything was new to me, and I was so afraid that I'd mess something up, when having a pack was the biggest dream I'd had for my life.

"Sorry," I muttered.

"Don't be sorry. It's important to communicate, speak your mind, and say what you're really feeling about things. How else is anyone going to know what you're thinking? We can check in to see how you're feeling about things, but that gives us rather limited information," Petru reassured me. "Now I'm going on watch. You stay here with Toma and Cris."

With a kiss goodnight for both Toma and me, Petru got up, collected his rifle and started his perimeter check. I watched him until he couldn't be seen, then let Toma pull me to sleep on his chest as Cris snuggled into his side, our own little puppy pile for the night.

WE TRAVELED for two more days following the river before finding the first indication that anyone other than us could be around. A stone ring that had once had scorching on it to show a fire had burned, with a small little lean-to made from wood, rocks, and a sun-bleached tarp. The place didn't show signs of anyone having been there recently, but it gave us hope we were heading in the right direction.

It was odd to think this mountain rage was all that divided us from the North that was overrun by war. Almost like they'd forgotten there was still more land past that region and this side had far more life. There was grass, small trees, the river with fish, and at the bottom of the foothills, there was prairie like the South. I suppose I shouldn't be all that shocked, for at one point, this whole place was one country. Why wouldn't they have attributes that are the same.

From what Lucian told us, no one ventured past the mountains. It was believed to be wild and ruthless since the rebels claimed it. Now I am starting to think that was a lie someone generations ago told people to keep them from venturing out and building their own kingdom, leaving the North with yet another person to fight over land with. What was odd to me is there was no way of knowing what lay beyond that. Oscad was at the end of this mountain range, although what was further west?

"It would be cool one day to explore this part of the North," I commented as we took a break to eat and drink something. "There's all that land out there, but no one knows anything about it. What if we are just a small section of this world we live in?"

"Wouldn't it be crazy if there were other cities and countries that knew about us, even though we don't have a clue about them?" Cris voiced. "I mean, we know there's another civilization further south past that mountain range, so why can't there be more?"

Victor gave the Beta a friendly shove. "You're making my brain hurt just talking about it. Don't we have enough to deal with here? I say we leave the explorer talk for when there's even a chance we can do something like that."

"Yeah, yeah," Cris said amicably. "I suppose we should deal with one life-altering event at a time."

Packing up, we traveled until it was dusk and set up camp. We didn't find a place where we could set up a shelter so we slept under the stars. Sorin and Lucian thought it was best we didn't make a fire, so it was rations for dinner and water from the canteen. We'd been lucky enough getting fish and other small animals to help with the variety of food since we needed to make sure the rations lasted as long as we needed them to. Not having a destination or timeline made things rather tricky in that department.

The guys stayed up late chatting and talking strategies. I ended up falling asleep in Sorin's lap since I wanted to be part of the conversation but had little to add. The cold bite of metal on my throat had my eyes snapping open, and I came face to face with a man I didn't know. He lifted a hand to his lips, telling me to keep quiet as he pulled me out of Sorin's arms. Everything in me wanted to scream, but I kept my mouth shut when I saw how many we were up against. So far, they had done nothing but wake me. Before I could even ask a question, the man pinched me, making me gasp, only to have him shove something in my mouth and pull a hood over my head.

It was pitch black with this thing on, making me incredibly disorientated, and I stumbled when I was jerked forward. My hands were tied, then my feet, and moments later, a shoulder shoved into my stomach as I was tossed over it and carried off. Thumping the man with my wrists, I thrashed, trying to knock the man off his feet, anything to give me the chance to warn the others.

There was supposed to be a watch. Someone at night was always awake, monitoring things. How the fuck had this happened? Then I realized the weight of Sorin's arm over me was truly dead weight. Normally, he held me close to his arm curved all the way around my stomach. Did they kill everyone? Why save me? That was a stupid question. I was an Omega. I'll always be desired and fought over in this country.

I don't know how long we walked. It could be minutes, an hour, or more since I had nothing to gauge with. At one point I tried to count how many steps the person was taking but I lost count around six hundred when I was handed over to someone else. With the whole exchange, I lost count of my exact number as this person walked with a much longer stride. I kept fighting, trying to find a way to get this fucking hood off, but it was no use. Then I was dumped on the ground forcing a yelp from me as my shoulder landed at a funny angle.

"Are you trying to fucking break her?" a man demanded. Up until now, not one had spoken.

"What does it matter, she's a fucking bed warmer for the soldiers. They didn't even have to tie her up because she's been so brainwashed. We aren't going to get anything out of her, so what does it matter if she's a little battered and bruised?" a nasally voice responded.

The sound of a fist hitting flesh was one I'd become familiar with during all the training. The guys took one hour out of the day before we got walking to spar or do various exercises to help keep up their endurance. One of them took a day off and worked with me on my sparing. Fat lot of good that's doing me now. What's the point of all this training when I'm unable to even use it?

"She's a fucking human being, you asswipe. I told them it was a mistake to bring you in on this development. You're not the only one the North fucked over, so take the stick out of your ass and use your brain for once," the first man snarled back.

There was no answer, only the sound of retreating footsteps. Seems I was going to live through the day after all.

When hands grabbed me, I lashed out, my tied hands balled together packing a wallop as I hit the person. He grunted then secured my hands before removing the hood. I looked into a familiar pair of eyes and could have wept for joy when I realized it was Branko, the Beta guard I'd become friends with at the breeder house.

A small smile was on his face as he realized I had recognized him. "Hey, Dani, long time no see."

"How?" I blurted, my brain feeling like it was short-circuiting.

"That's a bit of a long story, but let's just say I'm back where I belong," Branko answered cryptically. "Enough about me. Let's talk about how you ended up here in the Forbidden Mountains?"

"We were looking for the rebels," I answered, not willing to give too much information until I knew what was happening. "Why did you take just me?"

"One of our scouts warned us there was military in the foothills so we've been observing you for about a day now. What we couldn't figure out is why you were with them and how the hell Lucian is here with a group of Southern soldiers. Since I knew you and we'd been friends of a sort, I figured it would be best to have a chat. Besides, if you were with them against your will, then getting you out of their clutches was the best thing to do," Branko explained. "So, I'll ask again, what are you doing here?"

I heaved a sigh and tried to brush some hair out of my face except my hands were still tied together. "Is this truly needed?"

"You forget I know how much of a fighter you are," he chuckled. "Damn near gave me a bloody nose trying to get the hood off you. Not to mention you left some serious bruises on my man who was carrying you here. For now, I think we'll keep them on until we get things sorted."

Branko reached out to help me get the hair out of my face, but I flinched back. The simple thought of someone other than my pack touching me had my skin crawling. I knew Branko wasn't a bad man—or so I thought. Right now, I just had no way of knowing if the Branko I had known for the past three years was the real version or simply the part he needed to play.

"Dani, I'm not like those men," he said fiercely, his lip curling in disgust. "I would never force myself on you or anyone who didn't welcome my touch. The way you and all other Omegas have been treated is downright disgusting. You have no idea how hard it was to stand in that house day after day seeing the vile filth who came and went."

"If you found it so disgusting, why did you let it happen? You could have done something, gotten us out of there, or hell, even kept the violent bastards from hitting them. Don't fucking tell me how hard it was for you," I snarled, then spat at the ground next to him, furious he would even dare to say something like that.

Shoulders sagging, he hung his head and nodded. "You're right, there was so much I could have done, but I wasn't willing to risk the major mission. I just couldn't stand the thought of you thinking I was anything like those bastards. When the attack happened, I knew the mission was a bust and it was time to get out of there. I brought all the girls I could along with me, but when I tried to find you, Tori, and Violet, there were no signs of you."

"Damn right, I grabbed my girls and we got the fuck out of there," I shared, leaning back against the rock wall of the giant cave we were in.

The space could easily fit twenty or thirty people seeing as it felt so roomy even with fifteen people inside. Two fires burned, each with a group of men sitting around eating as if they didn't have a care in the world. Only one man was watching my interaction with Branko with undivided attention. Everything about him told me he was dangerous, but what sold it was the dead, emotionless eyes that tracked my every move.

Was he the one who carried me the second half of the walk back here? He seems the type to think I'm good for nothing other than a hole to be fucked. I'd seen his type time and time again coming to the breeder house. If he was so in alignment with the Northern thinking on that subject, why be part of the rebels?

"Dani," Branko said as he nudged my leg.

Looking away from the biggest threat in this space wasn't my favorite idea, however I needed to find out what they planned to do with me. Letting my gaze meet Branko's, I waited to see what he had to say. One thing I'd learned in the month or so I'd had with my guys is silence makes people uncomfortable. It would get them to speak first, keeping you from saying too much.

"I would advise against giving him an excuse to come over here," he warned. "Cyril isn't someone I can trust to follow an order when given. The chip on his shoulder when it comes to the North is larger than most, but he's one hell of a tracker. It's one of the only things keeping him alive on my team for the time being."

"This is your team?" I questioned.

"Nah-ah, we aren't going to play this game," Branko warned with a chuckle. "You've always been a sly little thing, haven't you? Which is why I find it so hard to believe you would be traveling with such an odd bunch of Alphas."

"They are an odd bunch, aren't they," I agreed.

"Be honest with me, are you with them voluntarily, or do they have some sort of hold on you to keep you from running away? I can offer you sanctuary here in the mountains. As you've already seen, it's able to sustain us far better than anywhere else in the North," Branko offered, his tone almost beseeching.

Using my bound hands, I pulled my hair away from my neck and tilted it so the firelight would show. "They aren't just a bunch of Alphas, they're my pack. A pack I love and who loves me back. A group of men who set aside their differences, so I didn't have to choose between them. Tell me, is that an act of selfless love?"

Branko's face looked horrified at the sight of my marks, though I didn't expect him to understand. How could he? No one in the North was ever taught what love or a family should look like. They'd only been taught one thing—how to be the perfect soldier.

CHAPTER 54

Cristofor

My head was pounding.

It felt like someone was taking a rock and smashing it against my skull, it throbbed so badly. Rolling over onto my back, I groaned when the sunlight smacked me right in the face.

Wait. Why was the sun up high enough to be this bright? Why hadn't anyone woken me up? I was supposed to be on the last shift to take over watch. It shouldn't be sunny at all.

Shifting back to my side so the sun wouldn't spear into my eyes and worsen the pain. Tossing my arm over my head as well just to be safe before cracking an eye to look around. Sure enough, we were all lying in the circle we'd been sitting in as we talked last night. I spotted Victor across from me, Lucian, and Toma as well. Slowly, I sat up as a wave of nausea hit me.

Fuck, it's as if I drank myself into a stupor, but I know that isn't possible since we have nothing but water to drink.

Rubbing the back of my neck, trying to get my body to calm down and realize that we were going to be fine. I hissed as something pricked deeper into my skin. Grabbing it with two fingers, I yanked to find a small dart in my grasp.

"What the fuck?" I muttered as I took a look around again.

Everyone was asleep, not just resting or dozing off. They were passed the fuck out. Petru was closest to me, and he was the one who'd been supposed to wake me up. Yet it didn't seem like he'd been on watch before whatever happened. Crawling over to get a better look at him sleeping on his side, I spotted a dart in his back near the shoulder blade. Removing it, I then felt around the puncture wound to make sure it wasn't poison and it was killing us slowly. Thankfully, there was no heat at the site, and Petru's breathing seemed normal. Checking his heart rate to be sure, I found it a steady fifty beats per minute, which was typical for someone in a deep sleep.

Still feeling too groggy and sick to my stomach, I didn't try to stand. Instead, I just crawled over to Toma. He was half sprawled over Lucian and looked almost like he'd been reaching for his gun. His dart was on the side of his neck, but there was a second on his chest. *Did whoever shot us miss the first time? Or maybe it was a case of Toma didn't go down fast enough, and he was the only one awake.* None of this was making any sense at all.

Checking on the others, I found nothing amiss other than they were still asleep. Then I looked around for Dani. There was no empty bedding to mark where she'd been sleeping, so had she gotten up and looked for help when she couldn't wake us? No, that wasn't like her at all. She'd never wander off, leaving us vulnerable like this. In fact, I'm pretty sure she'd be standing guard over us with a gun at the ready to fend off anyone who dared to mess with us. So where the fuck had our Omega gone?

Glancing over at Sorin again, I noticed the second blanket beside him and realized, to my horror, she'd been sleeping with her head in his lap. Rubbing my eyes with the palms of my hands, I tried to pull myself together. With the pain in my head, it was making my vision slightly blurry and my brain work way too fucking slow. Forcing myself to my feet, I looked around the space and spotted footprints in the dirt, a lot of them. We'd been attacked by who the hell knows and they mother fucking stole our Dani.

Stumbling over to my pack, I grabbed my med kit and a canteen. Flipping open the lid of my medicine stash, I popped three pain relievers into my mouth and chugged some water. I *needed* my head to stop hurting so I could get a grip. I had to find a way to wake everyone up and deal with the side effects of whatever drug they'd dosed us with. Going letter by letter in the alphabet order I tried to jog my brain to remember all the medication or herbal concoctions that could be used to create something like this.

Then I thought of it—*sleeping nightshade.* They might never wake up if even the slightest amount of it was given to a person. Digging through my pack, I found what I needed and crushed the pills up knowing I didn't have enough to treat them all, but it might be enough to get them alert. Once awake, dealing with matters would be so much easier and would mean no one had died. Putting the crushed pills in the canteen, I shook it gently to get everything to dissolve.

I decided to start with Sorin since we needed a leader to keep our shit together once they realized Dani had been taken from us once again. Tilting the Alpha's head back, I opened his mouth and poured some of the medication into his mouth. Closing it, I pinched his nose forcing him to swallow before I released him. Doing this three more times, I moved on to Victor repeating the same steps. Once I had Petru and Toma dealt with as well, that just left Lucian. A battle raged inside me, the view of Northern men I'd been taught to have all my life only made worse by the discovery about my father or doing the right thing for a pack mate.

Over the past week of traveling together, seeing how loving he was with Dani, and then saving my life without even second-guessing the choice to jump off a cliff to get to me. If nothing else, I owed this man a life for a life, but I was also willing to admit there was a chance I could have been incredibly wrong about him. I wasn't willing to say that about the North as a whole, but for Lucian as an individual... yeah, I might have been wrong about him.

"Come on, man, try not to spill. There isn't a whole lot left," I mumbled to myself as I worked.

Just as I got the last of the medicine into Lucian, Sorin let out a groan and rolled on his side. "Holy fuck, what did we drink?"

Making sure Lucian was good, I hurried over to our leader pressing a hand to his shoulder to keep him from getting up. "Easy, don't get up. You were poisoned with sleeping nightshade, but I gave you an antidote, so it should help with some of the side effects."

"What do you mean I was poisoned? How the hell could that happen, we didn't drink anything but from our own canteens," Sorin argued.

Shaking my head, I sat next to him. "I don't have a clue what happened. Only when I woke up a little while ago feeling like death, I discovered a dart on my neck. Each of us had one knocking our asses out cold, but I don't have a fucking idea who did it or why."

Sorin groaned as he sat up and nearly fell back, but I caught him helping to get him upright. The stubborn Alpha wouldn't settle until he didn't feel quite so vulnerable. Giving him a moment to deal with the nausea, I noticed Victor stirring. The others should come around soon, although Toma might take a little longer since he was shot twice. I just begged the fates that I'd gotten enough of the antidote into him before it was too late. *No*, I couldn't let myself think that way. We would all be fine. Then we'd rescue Dani and destroy those who dared to take her from us.

It was really unfortunate for whoever they were, because we were nowhere close to recovering from when Lucian ran off with her. I might not be the violent one in the group. However, the second Sorin, Victor, and Lucian figure out she's missing... we might not have a country to save when they're done with it. All I needed was enough time for the others to recover before explaining that part. Right now, no one would be of much use to her if they couldn't even stand.

"Where's Dani?" Sorin questioned. "She was right here with me all night."

"Sorin—"

The man lunged forward grabbing my t-shirt. "Where is she?"

"I don't know," I stated calmly, my training the only thing keeping me from losing my mind at this moment. "She wasn't here when I woke up, and the second I realized we were attacked I needed to get you guys the antidote. There's no way I would have been able to get her back on my own, so I did the next best thing."

Sorin released me and sat back, dropping his head in his hands. "How the *fuck* did we let this happen, again? Why didn't whoever was on watch alert us?" Sorin growled.

"They shot Toma twice with darts. My guess is he was the one on watch and they took him out first. We have no idea how many of them there were either. They could have gotten us all at the same time for all I know," I reasoned. "Once we have everyone on their feet, we will find her. Between Victor and Petru, no one will be able to hide their tracks well enough from them."

"Lucian's a damn good tracker, too," Sorin admitted. "You made the right call, Cris. It's clear this was a calculated attack."

"Thank you for saying that," I admitted. "I'm not a soldier. I'm a medic, and the way I respond to certain situations might not always be the best course of action. When under stress, my main focus is to deal with the problem and people right in front of me, not to chase down the bad guys."

"Oh god..." Lucian groaned, throwing an arm over his eyes. "Tell me I'm not dead. No, this is too much pain to be dead. How the fuck did we get dosed with nightshade? Goddamn, that is the worst feeling ever to wake up from."

Shocked that it was his first guess I didn't know how to respond. "How did you guess it was, nightshade? Also, why does it sound like you've experienced this before?"

"Because I have," Lucian muttered, slowly sitting up. "Dear old dad thought it would be smart to work on making me immune to poisons once I took Savo's place. Nightshade is one of the few poisonous plants growing well enough here in the North."

"Why did it affect you then if you've been building up a tolerance?" I demanded, my previous suspicions of him betraying us at some point throughout his journey rearing its head.

He turned to look at me as if I was an idiot. "Would you keep poisoning yourself if you were given the option not to? When I was given my own base to command far, far away from that bastard, I discontinued the practice. If you don't keep it up then your body resets to react normally to things."

That actually made perfect sense.

Realizing that, the guilt I was feeling washed over me, but a hand gripped my shoulder, and reassurance from Petru kept the guilt from downing me. "Give it time, Cris. You can't change what you've been taught overnight, but you're trying and that's what counts."

Taking a deep breath, I covered his hand with my own in thanks. Knowing he could see into my heart and understood I was working on it helped. "How are you feeling?"

"Like I got run over by a Humvee," he muttered. "What happened?"

"Let's wait for the other two to wake up before we go over that. It will be faster to catch everyone up at once. For now, drink as much water as you can to help flush out the poison. I used all the meds between the five of you," I explained as I stood to grab all the water I could find for them.

As I passed Victor, I realized he was awake but hadn't said a word or moved at all. He just laid there on his back, staring up at the sky. Kneeling next to him, I checked his pulse, and it was fine, but he didn't react to my touch.

"Vic?" I said, shaking his shoulder. "Hey, you okay?"

"You should have let me die," he rasped. "I failed her again after I vowed to never let anything else happen to her. How can I dare to call myself her Alpha?"

The shock of hearing those words and that mindset coming from him had me reeling. "Victor, what are you talking about? Each and every one of us made the same promise to her. We all failed in this."

"That's not it," he mumbled, then looked at me. "I took the meds you gave me last night. If I'd been awake, then this never would have happened."

Realization clicked as I understood what he was talking about. "Victor, you've been awake for five days surviving on short naps. You needed to sleep, truly sleep, or else you'd have burned out."

"I was too weak. If I hadn't given in and used the sleeping pills, I would have noticed something was wrong," he argued.

"Stop being a fucking idiot and pull your shit together," Lucian snapped. "If you want to be useful, then maybe you'd better help me figure out where the fuck those bastards ran off to. Otherwise, if you're serious about giving up, then make sure you do it quickly and only use one bullet. We need to preserve our reserves."

Horrified at what Lucian was saying, I gawked at him. "What the *fuck*?"

"No, you don't get to look at me like I'm the monster, Cris," Lucian growled, pointing a finger at me, then shifting it towards Victor. "If he wants to believe he's the only one to blame, then let him. No one can change his mind once he's decided. We all know that. Besides, Dani deserves an Alpha that will stop at nothing to get her back and the fearsome Victor is telling us that he's not that man."

Victor dove across the space and tackled Lucian, fists flying as they grappled and fought. Seeing them feeling well enough to pull this off made me feel better about the others. Toma was the one we needed to keep an eye on, as he'd yet to wake.

"Fucking Northern bastard," Victor raged. "How dare you say those kinds of fucking lies. You think I won't get her back? She is *mine*, and I'm not letting her end up some fucking breeder to the rebels or sold like a piece of meat on the black market. I'll fucking kill you!"

The two men fought with everything they had, the thud of fist meeting flesh made me sick to my stomach, but no one dared to stop them. Besides Sorin, Victor was our best hand-to-hand combat specialist, and Lucian was going toe-to-toe with him. It all ended when Lucian landed an uppercut to Victor's stomach forcing the man to puke up everything in his stomach. Dropping to his knees, he heaved over and over until nothing was left.

"Drink some fucking water, and you'll start to feel better now that you've gotten that out of your system," Lucian ordered as he snatched up a canteen and offered it to the man. "Sleeping pills mixed with nightshade can mess with your head. I had to provoke you so I could get you to fight me. Otherwise, the longer the two interacted with each other it would have made matters worse."

"What?" I blurted. "You did all that on purpose?"

Lucian nodded, wiping away a trail of blood leaking from his nose. "Told you, I've had my fair share of experience with nightshade. If I wasn't willing to take the poison, they'd knock me out then dose me."

"Fuck, man," Victor grumbled as he picked himself off the ground. "That is some twisted shit right there, but I suppose for my own sake, I'm glad you know what was going on."

Lucian grinned at Victor then shrugged. "Can't say it didn't feel good to beat your ass for a change."

Laughter erupted out of Victor as he spat water everywhere. "Fucker."

"Cris," Sorin called, pulling my attention from the others. "It's Toma."

Panic speared through me, but I darted over when I saw him trying to sit up. "Slowly, you're not going to feel very good."

"That is the understatement of a lifetime," he muttered. "Oh god, I think I'm going to puke."

Grabbing his head, I turned it away as he did indeed throw up. Holding him steady as his body purged itself, I tried to think of what I had in my pack that might help. From this point on, I was going to make some adjustments to my stock and suggest that everyone else did too. No matter what the outcome of this might be, it was wise for any military to be prepared for poisoning. It was a sound tactical move.

"Sorin, can you grab one of the licorice roots out of my pack," I requested. "If anyone else is still feeling sick to their stomach, take one too. It will help."

Toma groaned. "You know I hate those things."

"Do you want to keep throwing up?" I challenged him.

He shook his head and leaned back against me, closing his eyes. Sorin brought over a canteen as well which he offered to Toma.

"Slow sips," I warned.

"Yes, mother," Toma teased, just as he would with Bethany when she got overprotective of him.

Hearing him act so normal made the tension between my shoulders relax as I held him. While my medical brain kicked in and took over once I realized the situation, now that it was over, I was getting hit with the awareness that I could have lost them all today. We *did* lose one—Dani was taken from us, and no one knew what happened. How the fuck could we call ourselves her pack if we left shit like this keep happening?

Resting my head on Toma's shoulder, I breathed in his orange and basil scent, grounding me as it always had. Petru came to sit behind me, wrapping us both in his arms. "I love you," I whispered. "I love you both so much."

Toma shifted his head to rub his cheek against mine. "I love you too, Cris, and I'm sorry we gave you such a bad fright."

"You saved us all," Petru murmured, kissing my temple. "We are beyond lucky to have you and blessed to have your love as well."

"Now we need to do the same for Dani," I reminded. "There's no telling what could be happening with her or who even has her."

"Rebels," Toma growled. "It was the rebels we've been looking for. They were hiding in the upper part of the ridge. I didn't notice anything amiss until the first dart hit me, and then it was too late. There had to be a dozen or more of them half-armed with fucking blowdarts. It's how they got the drop on us so fast."

"They took Dani," Sorin informed him. "Did you hear them say anything before you passed out? It doesn't make sense why they let us live and took her."

"I'm sorry, I didn't. It all happened so fast, and the drug was taking effect well before they hit me with the second dose," Toma answered, then froze in my arms. "Wait, did you just say they took Dani?"

"Yes."

"Then what the fuck are we doing sitting here like we have all the fucking time in the world?" Toma yelled, pulling out of my hold, and stumbled to his feet. "We need to go after them."

"That's the plan, but we needed you to wake up before we could do that," Sorin countered. "It might help for you to be able to walk on your own too. Right now, you're more likely to fall off a cliff and slow us down saving your ass. So take a seat, chew the damn root, and drink some water. I just sent Lucian and Victor to scout out the surrounding area to see if we can figure out what direction they went."

Toma looked ready to argue but didn't as he sat on a rock and started to chew on the licorice, grimacing at the taste. I took the time to repack my things and double-check what I still had and what we might need if we found Dani in rough condition. While I didn't want to think about it that way, I knew it was better to plan for the worst-case scenario than not. By the time the two got back, the rest of us were as ready as we were going to be for this. Toma could manage on his own, even if he was moving a little slow.

"We've got a pretty clear trail," Victor informed us. "It's almost like they either didn't expect us to come after them, or they wanted us to."

"It is a high probability some of them also recognized who I am. So if they saw my brand on Dani's neck, they could be trying to use her for negotiation or leverage of some kind," Lucian pointed out. "Either way, we can find them, but we must leave now. They've got quite the jump on us, and the thought of leaving Dani in their care for any longer than fucking needed is motivation enough to push hard."

"All right," Sorin agreed, shouldering his pack. "Let's go get our Omega back."

CHAPTER 55

Danella

Since I showed Branko my marks, he refused to speak to me and left me in the back of the cave while he spoke with his men. Frustration at how he'd responded outweighed the fear I might have had trapped in a cave with men I didn't know or trust. If they'd wanted to kill me, then they wouldn't have carried me all the way here. Unless that changed now that Branko knew I wasn't a victim.

Even though it was dark in the cave, I could tell from the entrance that it was light outside. We couldn't have gone that far from where we'd camped for the night—right? Either way, I knew the moment my pack found out I wasn't there, they'd be hot on our trail. Closing my eyes, I reached through my bonds, trying to see if I could reach them, let them know I was okay. While I could feel them there I didn't get much of a response. Not really knowing the limitations of this kind of thing, maybe we were too far apart for them to know anything more than I was still alive.

"Here," Branko said, causing me to open my eyes as he threw a canteen my way.

"Why bother?" I asked, not moving. "Obviously, your opinion of me has changed now that you know I'm bonded with them, so why keep me alive?"

He studied me for a moment, then crossed his arms. "What I

can't come to terms with is the Danella I knew back at the outpost wanted nothing more than to return home with her friends. Now here you are, bonded to Lucian, who you hated, and a bunch of Southern soldiers. How can you not be in this against your will? Fuck, how can Lucian share you? That man is a possessive bastard."

That brought a smile to my lips. "Yes, yes, he is. Funny enough, so are the others, and that didn't go so great in the beginning. There were a few fist fights they tried to hide from me, but it's not that hard to notice when fat lips and black eyes appear out of nowhere. What essentially changed things though, is Lucian marked me first. He could feel how I felt about the others. When my heat came upon me, and I craved them as much as him, he realized I needed more than just him."

"Nah, that's some sort of brainwashing going on. It has to be," Branko argued. "My bet is Lucian knows he's being hunted by his father and decided to team up with others who would help him take out his old man."

"In a manner of speaking, yes, that's true," I shared.

Now that threw Branko for a loop. "Excuse me?"

"Lucian is working with the others of my pack to take down the General," I explained.

"So you think the seven of you can overthrow a man like General Rasvan?" he said with a laugh.

I shrugged. "We will probably have a better chance after we convince the rebels to join us."

The laughter cut off as he heard what I'd just said. "Wait one goddamn minute. Is that why you're here?"

"Whoops, looks like the cat's out of the bag," I drawled.

If I could get Branko on board with this idea, then it would only help us get the powers that be to listen. They trusted him enough to send him on a critical mission as well as lead this team of men. Plus, it would help me gauge the reaction of people.

"Start at the beginning," Branko ordered as he sat cross-legged in front of me.

"You know the beginning, we were attacked, so I grabbed my girls and ran. Unfortunately, we didn't get very far before the South spotted us and were hot on our trail. Of course, they had no idea we were Omegas and not soldiers, so when we ended up getting cornered we jumped off a cliff and down into the badlands. I thought we could have lost them there, but I didn't account for the fact that I'd gotten a concussion or slammed into a boulder on the way down.

We hid in a small cave since I was in no shape to run off into the darkness, beaten to hell. That's where the Southern soldiers found us and where I first met the men of my now pack. They brought us back to the main Southern Military base at the capitol, and I received medical attention," I shared. "Is this what you wanted to know, or should I skip to a different part?"

"No, I want to know everything. If you expect me to believe a fucking word out of your mouth about this, I need to know how it's even possible," Branko muttered, motioning for me to continue.

"You know, for a Beta, you're acting an awful lot like an asshole Alpha right now," I shot back. "All you had to do was say please, continue. No need to be a prick about it."

He gritted his teeth then nodded his head. "Dani, please continue. I'd like to hear the whole story."

"No problem. I have a feeling I'm gonna need to explain this to more than just you by the time this is all said and done," I sighed. "Where was I? Oh, right, medical attention. That's where I woke up, in the Med Center, and let me just say that is where you want to be when you are in the condition I was in. I'm not sure I would have survived even if I'd made it back to Oscad. The South is incredibly advanced in their medical treatment."

Branko gave me a look that told me I better move on to more important things.

"Once I was healed enough to move around and work on building up my strength as well as gaining some weight, that's when my pack came to me with a deal. See, the girls had told them what the brand on my neck meant, and they decided it would be smart to take advantage of the knowledge I had. The terms were if I helped them learn about the North and shared all the information I knew, they would get Tori and Violet back to Oscad. It would appear that

Oscad has been sending covert teams to collect all the Omegas that had been sent away against their will. Somehow they were made aware that we were in the South and, interestingly enough, there was a connection between the Alpha who leads our unit and someone in the Oscad government. Well, he's not *in* the government. However, his pack mates are, and they all share an Omega. Whatever, you get the point. All I was trying to prove is that the deal I made was legit. So here I was, given a chance to stick it to the North and get my friends back home safely. How could I turn it down?" I asked.

"What about you? Did that mean you were theirs? Is that how you ended up bonding with them because of this deal?" Branko pressed.

"I was promised that once I'd given them all the information I knew and completed their military training, if I didn't want to stay, I would be allowed to return to Oscad as well. In hindsight, I don't think that's what they wanted to do, and the whole thing was a ploy to make me give them a chance. They'd set their sights on me the moment we met as the perfect Omega for them. However, the challenge was them convincing me of that, so I became a member of their unit. We lived, trained, and ate together for a little over a week before something happened and we got sent on our first mission. That's where all the carefully laid plans blew up in our faces and how we ended up here," I said.

Branko studied me for a moment, scratching his chin. "That doesn't explain how Lucian ended up in all this with them."

"He was the one who blew up their plans," I pointed out. "There was a perceived attack on a main power plant in an area of the South that the North shouldn't have been able to get to or know about. When we arrived on the scene, Lucian was lying in wait, assuming like yourself that I was with this group of men against my will. He snatched me, marked me, and we journeyed down the river and through the woods to get back to the North. Only thing was, my pack was made of one of the top elite units in the Southern Military. They tracked his ass down in three-ish days and ta-da, here we are."

"Yeah... I'm going to need more specifics than ta-da," Branko countered. "Lucian marked you against your will, stole you from this team who you claim have feelings for you, and now you're one happy family?"

"Well, when you put it that way, it sounds rather unbelievable," I muttered, hooking my bound arms over my knees to rest my head on them. "As I mentioned before, there were lots of fights. More with words than fists because they knew I was connected to him. Seriously though, it doesn't make sense. Even to me. And I'm the one they're doing this for. When my first heat hit me like a fuck ton of bricks, I wouldn't have been able to manage with only Lucian. I'm sure we would have figured it out, although after that time we spent together training, it showed me there was a different way for Alphas and Omegas to co-exist. Each and every one of those men respects me, listens to what I have to say, and finds my smart-ass personality endearing. Which, as you know, not many people say that, like ever."

"That still doesn't tell me how they allowed the heir of the North to live when they could have killed him and been done with it," he grumbled. "Why the hell would they let that chance slip through their fingers."

"Evidently you've never been in love before," I quipped.

Branko's face scrunched up in a mix of confusion and disgust. "What does love have to do with it?"

"Do you love Jan?" I asked, changing tactics.

He jerked away from me as if I'd just slapped him. "What the fuck does that have to do with anything?"

My brows shot up at his anger. "Ah... did I miss something? He told me you two were together, together. Was that not correct?"

"He never would have told you that," Branko snapped.

"Whoa, you need to take a deep breath before you draw everyone's attention, and I'm guessing that isn't what you want to be doing right now," I said, keeping my voice low. "I'm sorry, I didn't realize that would be such a major question. The only reason Jan said anything is because I made a comment that you two were a cute couple and it was nice to see people actually caring about each other in the North. He didn't confirm it immediately, but when he did, he asked me to keep it to myself. Well, then, a day later all hell broke loose. So trust me when I say I've not spoken to anyone about this."

The man before me lost control of the mask he was hiding behind and I saw the tortured expression on his face. "It was never supposed to happen, he and I. There was too much at stake to risk getting close to someone, but I couldn't help it. Jan was so easy to fall in love with, no matter how hard I tried to fight my feelings."

"Branko, did Jan die?" I whispered for fear of saying it out loud would make it true.

Jan was unlike any Northerner I'd ever come across. He treated people equally and with kindness. He was a healer through and through, making him invaluable to the outpost, which is why Lucian never let him come on missions.

"No, Jan is alive and thriving as a doctor for the rebels. Believe it or not, we have far more medical supplies than you'd think since we steal all that we can heading to various bases in the area," he replied, but the tone of his voice was so sad.

"Then what happened?" I pressed.

"I have a wife." Branko divulged, the self-loathing thick in his words. "I fell for Jan when I had a woman waiting for me to come home to her. A woman that I've loved since I was a teen and managed to convince to marry me. You think I don't know what it means to love someone? Well, being raised in the rebel city, we fight against all ideologies the North forces on their people. Summit Stronghold is a place for people to be free of the oppression of war and have a fulfilling life. Ester is my life. I can't picture a future without her, so how could I betray her like that?"

While I suppose I should've felt bad for his wife and Branko, I couldn't help but see this as the fates providing me with someone who would truly understand my situation.

"Let me ask you that question again. Do you love Jan?" I asked, holding my breath, hoping he would be honest with me as well as himself.

The man looked up from his hands, and I could see the answer in his eyes before the words came out of his mouth. "Yes," he whispered. "I love him deeply, and it's not a love that replaces how I feel about Ester. She still means everything to me. I was overjoyed to be back home with her, but it killed me to tell Jan we couldn't be together anymore."

"When I say this next thing, I need you to understand I'm not trying to put salt in the wound or make you feel bad. I think you're just missing something important," I explained, as he gave me a quizzical look. "If you are truly a rebel, and you're bucking the system and going against all that the North has taken from people, then why the fuck did you break it off with Jan? How is it that you seem to have forgotten one fundamental thing about who we are as a species? Bran, we are wired to love more than one person, have packs, have family units, and share love and responsibility with those we want to create a life with. How dare you make Jan feel like the other woman in your life. Also, give your wife a little credit here, Jan is the most loveable person in the fucking world. Maybe, just maybe, you were all meant to be together. Only you thought you knew best and fucked it up."

We both just sat there for a moment staring at each other. It was clear I'd blown his little rebel brain, and now I just needed to give him a minute to get his head wrapped around the concept.

"Dani—" Branko started to speak, when suddenly the sound of a car horn being blasted through the cave had everyone jumping into action.

What I wouldn't give to cover my ears as the sound echoed off the walls and made it so much worse. I assumed it was some kind of alarm that an intruder tripped, but the confused and panicked faces of the men told me that might not be the case. Everyone had guns at the ready and was falling into formation, telling me that this group of rebels made it through training or were taught by those who had.

Branko grabbed my arm and hauled me up to stand, with me acting as his shield. "What the fuck, Bran?" I yelled over the sound of the horn.

"Look, you want me to believe you're everything to them, right? What better way to find out than to see how they react when I have a gun to your head." The lunatic explained just as the deafening noise stopped.

I tried to yank myself out of his hold, but with my legs and feet still tied up, I wasn't able to do much. "All you're going to do is get yourself killed. You don't understand how seriously skilled these men are. All they need is enough space for a bullet to fit, and you're dead."

"Then I suggest you make sure they don't do that if you want me to take you to the stronghold," Branko countered.

I let out a growl of frustration, pissed that I was once again stuck in a position to use none of the skills I was given. When was I going to catch a mother fucking *break*? There had to be something I could do to minimize the damage. The last thing we needed was for my guys to kill all these men and fuck us over with the rebels.

"What about your men?" I blurted. "If you keep me hidden back here, they will kill everyone else. Take me to the front entrance, let them see you have me, and ask to negotiate. Be smart, Bran. You want to go home to Ester and Jan, right? I can help you do that, but you can't hide back here to cover your own ass, be a fucking leader and protect your men."

I thought he would ignore what I'd just said for a moment, but instead, he dropped to his knees, cut the ropes around my ankles, and dragged me to the front. His men scattered out of the way, all shocked to see me coming along with him. When we got to the entrance, Branko grabbed me with an arm around my waist and lifted me so I was covering the important parts of his body.

"You fucking coward," I spat. "How the hell did I think you were a good man all this time? You know what, you don't deserve Jan. Let the man be so he can find a better man to love him."

"Shut up," Branko snapped. "Everyone has to do what they must to survive. Well, this is me surviving."

He took two more steps, so we were *just* outside the cave entrance and I could be seen in the glow of the setting sun. Clearly, it was far later than I'd first guessed, but no matter, they were here now. All I had to do was make sure no one died unnecessarily.

"Don't shoot," Branko yelled. "This little birdie tells me you want to make a deal. If you want your Omega to remain alive, come out where I can see you and drop your weapons."

I groaned internally. How stupid did he think my men were? There is no way they would agree to do something that stupid, being up against twice as many men.

"If you want your men to stay alive, I suggest you put her down and show yourself like a man," Sorin called back. "What kind of leader uses a defenseless woman to hide behind?"

Branko let out a bark of laughter. "We both know Dani is far from defenseless. If I didn't have her tied up this whole time, I have no doubt a fair amount of my men would have black eyes and fat lips."

"Lucian, it's Branko, one of the guards from the breeder house," I shouted.

"What the fuck do you think you're doing?" he hissed into my ear.

"Seriously, do you think it makes a difference if he knows or not? Besides, I'm just leveling the playing field," I reasoned.

There was the sound of rocks shifting and Lucian appeared to the left on the ridge above, gun aimed in our direction. "You'd think someone who'd been a soldier under my command would know how foolish this was."

"What makes it foolish? I have your precious Omega and more men than you. From where I'm standing, it seems I have the advantage," Branko boasted.

"Look, we don't want to kill anyone. We came to talk, to ask for your help, as a matter of fact. However, that won't happen if you put so much as a scratch on Dani," Lucian warned. "Just so we're clear on the stakes before we set off the alarm, we planted C-4 in the entrance and on top of the cave. With one word, your men will be crushed under a pile of rock and then where will you be?"

"You wouldn't dare. Dani's too close to the entrance. It will hurt her, too."

"Not if I shoot you in the leg and give her the chance to run away before your men can even act," Lucian threatened. "Tell me, are you willing to call my bluff?"

CHAPTER 56

Danella

Even though I knew Lucian would never let anything happen to me, that didn't make the anxiety any less real as we all waited for Branko's answer. Were we going to have to kill everyone, or could we possibly find a way to make this all end peacefully?

"I will let her go only after the rest of your pack shows themselves," Branko countered. "That's right, I know you're all bonded to Dani. What I want to see right now is just how much she means to you. Will you sacrifice yourself to make sure she's safe?"

Not more than two seconds later, the rest of my guys appeared out of their various hiding places all over the cliffside. Mind you, they still had their guns aimed right at us, but that hadn't been part of the terms. He'd demanded they show themselves, and that's what they did. I happened to notice that Victor had a detonator in his hand, almost as a way to prove that they really did set the entrance to blow. *Damn, these guys were sneaky.*

"Here we are," Sorin said, as if it had been a magic trick. "Now you're going to unhand our Omega, and no one has to get hurt. We came to talk. That's the whole point of us being here."

"I'm well aware of that fact. Dani's been telling me all about the adventures she's been on since she ran from the outpost. What I can't seem to figure out is why the fuck would you Southern bastards give two shits about helping the heir to the North take over? It seems like killing him would be the better option," Branko reasoned.

Sorin nodded along as if he agreed with everything the man was saying. "You're right, it might be the smarter thing to just kill him and be done with it. The problem with that logic, though, is that it does nothing long-term. Sure, we've taken out the person who's going to be in power, but what of the bastard that sits on the throne now? Killing Lucian doesn't weaken the General. He's been so careful in building his power structure that no one person could topple him off his pedestal. Wouldn't it make sense then to have someone with insight into all the inner workings of the North if I'm going to destroy it once and for all?"

"Destroy it..." Branko repeated. "What do you mean, destroy it?"

"Exactly that. I want to take out the General, his underlings, and then stop this goddamn war once and for all," Sorin announced. "Thing is, the seven of us can't do that on our own. We need people who want this change as much as we do. The average citizen of the North is beaten down to the point they have no will to hope or believe that a change can be made. So who better than the rebels who are already fighting against the system?"

Branko's grip started to loosen as he listened, so I decided to take advantage of it. Lifting my leg, I slammed my foot back hitting him right under the knee, where doctors always check reflexes. Branko buckled and tried to steady himself, but my thrashing caused him to stumble and hit the ground on his side. Free from his hold, I rolled away from him and popped up on my feet the best I could, but Victor was already there, hooking me with his arm under my ass. I tossed my arms around his neck so I could hold on as he darted off. Toma and Petru were hot on our heels, leaving Lucian and Sorin to deal with things. It was then I realized Cris hadn't been with them, which honestly shouldn't be a surprise since they didn't like to put him in harm's way. We ducked under a ledge that took us down a narrow path with rock walls on either side. When we came out the other side, it opened up into a grotto of sorts. There was another way out that looked like a similar path, although you could also climb up.

Had this been how Lucian got behind them without being noticed?

All thoughts ceased as Victor slammed his lips to mine and kissed me until I was breathless. A blade glided along the skin of my inner arm as someone cut the bindings off of me. The second I was free, someone pulled me from Victor and crushed me in a hug.

"Wildflower, I thought we told you never to scare us like that again," Petru mumbled against my neck.

I hugged him back just as tightly. "I'm so sorry, I tried to get away, but they tied me up and kept my head covered the whole time we were walking to the cave."

Another body pressed up against my back hugging Petru and me. Toma buried his face on the other side of my neck, so I was wrapped up in them both, cloaked in their scents. It was soothing, yet I knew we didn't have time for this. "Guys, I know we're all really happy to be together again, but we need to talk about what's happening. Lucian and Sorin better leave them alive, or they'll fuck this up for us."

The two Alphas separated and set me down, only for Cris to grab my face and kiss me roughly. I slid my arms around him knowing he needed to make sure I was okay before we could move on. Breaking the kiss, he leaned his forehead against mine as we both caught our breath.

"Sorry, I just had to," Cris apologized, pressing one more quick kiss on my lips.

Twisting in his arms when he didn't seem like he was going to let go, I faced the others. "What happened? How did they get the drop on us?"

Toma hung his head, which told me he'd been the one on watch when it happened. "I went to wake Lucian up for his turn and before I could, a dart hit me right in the chest, quickly followed by another. They took out everyone simultaneously and I managed to stay alert long enough to realize what was happening, but that's it."

"They used a sleeping nightshade. It's a toxic plant that, if too much is used, could kill a person. Thankfully whoever made the darts knew what they were doing and just knocked everyone out. I woke up first and was able to get meds into them before things got too bad. Once everyone was recovered, we came after you," Cris explained.

Toxic darts? Who would have ever thought of such a thing? Branko did say they were stealing supplies, but what if they didn't have enough weapons or ammo? It would make sense that they'd need to devise a different plan to fight.

"Tell me, Little Spark, did they do anything to you?" Victor asked as his hands balled into fists.

"No," I answered and shook my head. "They tied me up, tossed me over someone's shoulder, and then I ended up in the cave. I have to ask...were you really going to blow up the cave?"

Victor grinned. "Why on earth would I do that? I could have hurt you."

"I knew it," I blurted, pointing a finger. "I mean, I didn't know it but I guessed you might have been bluffing. But damn, you guys put on a good show."

"There was no other way we could think of to get you outside the cave except you managed to convince that asshole to do it all on your own," Toma muttered. "Was that man special to you, back at the outpost?"

I burst out laughing from seeing Toma's jealous expression, looking like he'd just eaten a lemon. "No, he was one of the guards at the breeder house. Not to mention he was in a relationship with the doctor and, as I've come to learn, also married. Those two kept an eye on me when Lucian was sent off on missions. They were friends of a sort."

"Ah, so that's how he knew you were a fighter," Petru determined. "I couldn't figure out why he would know something like that about you."

"That's because he had to break up most of my fights regarding the other women in the breeder house. There's a chance once or twice he might have stepped in when I was about to start a fight with another soldier as well," I shared. "You have nothing to worry about in that regard. I have zero interest in anyone but you six."

A collective sigh of relief could be heard from each of them at this news, making me smile.

"So, did you guys have a plan once you got me out of their clutches?" I questioned. "Take that also as what the hell are Lucian and Sorin still doing back there?"

Each of them looked at the other, but no one seemed to genuinely have an answer for me. "Look, we didn't necessarily have a plan for after we got you. It was more of a play it by ear," Victor finally admitted. "I know for a fact they're staying behind to make sure no one follows us. They'll join up when it's safe."

"Good, then we need to figure out a way to meet with them on neutral ground so I can finish the conversation I was having with Branko," I shared.

"The fuck you are," Victor snapped.

"Why would such a thing be crucial?" Petru questioned.

"Not a chance," Toma added at the same time as the others.

I held my hands up as if to defend myself from the onslaught of emotions from them. "Wow. Do you think you guys could dial it down just a smidge? If you'd give me a chance to explain, I'll tell you why this is important."

Cris nuzzled against my cheek and pressed a kiss to it. "I think you should wait to have the conversation once the other two are back. Something tells me you'll need everyone's approval for this idea of yours."

He made a fair point, which I agreed with. "All right then, I'll wait, but we will discuss this. I'm not gonna let you get all Alpha on this and force me to take a back seat. You keep telling me I'm part of this unit and pack. Well, it's time to prove it by hearing me out."

"When the others arrive, I'm sure we can all manage to let you explain without getting too upset... right, Victor?" Petru asked pointedly at the man.

Arms crossed and a fierce scowl on his face I didn't think he'd agree, but he shocked the hell out of me with a sharp nod.

"Very well, then I'll wait," I agreed. "Unless you think that is going to take all night. We really need to make sure they don't leave in the middle of the night, putting us back at square one."

"It will take however long it takes," Victor stated, clearly unhappy with me.

While I respected the man's wishes not to bond, it seriously was hard not knowing what he was thinking or feeling. *Was he mad at me or just the situation? Could it be tied more to the fact they didn't want me to be in danger? Or have I somehow found a way to piss him off without even realizing it?* So many choices, and any of them could be correct.

Tapping gently on Cris' hands clasped around my waist, he released me, albeit reluctantly, so I could go to Victor. Reaching up, I placed my hands on his arms that were still crossed over his chest and peered up into his eyes. "Vicky, I know protecting me is your main priority. However, you need to realize that ending this war is mine. If I have the chance to do something, then I damn well need to do it."

The big man gave a heavy sigh. "I know, Little Spark, I know. That doesn't mean I have to like it."

"No, you're right. You don't have to like it, you just need to respect it," I countered. "Branko knows me. We already have a connection from living through the same hell at that outpost. In fact, we also have a connection, loving two people from completely different lifestyles. He's our ticket into this. I *know* if I can get him on our side, we can pull this off and get their help."

Victor unfolded his arms to rest his hands on my shoulders. "How did you become the center of all this? If you hadn't shown up in Lucian's life, then ours, none of this would have ever been a thing."

"Guess Petru's been right all along, and the fates have been calling the shots the whole time," I offered. "Either way, I have to try. If I win out, then really, it's a win for us all."

"What are we winning?" Sorin asked as he entered the grotto. "Because it's certainly not friends after Lucian had to shoot one of that guy's men who almost shot you guys."

I cringed hearing this. That was the last thing I wanted, but if it was between us being dead and someone else, I'd pick us every time.

"You make it sound like I killed the guy," Lucian interjected as he dropped down from the rock wall. "It was a simple leg wound that will heal just fine, but it definitely stopped him from chasing after you guys."

"Oh, thank god," I muttered, trying to comb my hair out of my face, but it had gotten so tangled I just gave up.

Toma took my hand and had me sit on a boulder while he grabbed a few things out of his bag. Surprisingly, he started to brush and style my hair for me.

"Where did you learn how to do this?" I asked, peering up at him.

Frowning, he adjusted my head to where he wanted it and resumed. "Beth, she wanted to make sure if I ever ended up with a woman, I would know how to spoil her."

"Huh... remind me to thank her when we get back because I could get used to this," I teased.

He just snorted and continued doing quick work out of managing my curls enough to get them in a bun and tied down. "Not the best I've ever done, but it's out of your face, off your neck, and contained for the time being."

"What more could I hope for at this point, because seriously we've been washing in rivers and buckets with a bar of soap," I reminded, reaching out to catch his hand. "Thank you, I really appreciate it."

He dropped a kiss on my head. "For you, anytime."

I have no clue why that made me blush, but everything about that made me feel so cherished.

"Dani-girl, why were you so relieved that Lucian didn't kill the man? Does this have to do with whatever we're winning at?" Sorin asked, redirecting us back to the topic at hand.

"I'm so glad you asked. They made me wait until everyone was back to be able to broach this topic," I informed him and shifted so I could see the others better. "We need to go back and talk to them."

"Ha," Lucian laughed. "Oh, you are funny, My Heart."

"I'm not joking. I'm being dead serious here. We need to go back so I can convince Branko to take us to the rebel city and plead our situation. He is a person they will listen to. Lucian, he isn't one of your men. He was born and raised at Summit Stronghold and was a spy who had infiltrated the army. What exactly he was doing, I don't know, but that was his group of men to lead. A rebellion doesn't just hand over their men to anyone off the street. He earned that right," I explained. "That's why we need him on our side."

Lucian didn't look convinced, but at least Sorin didn't seem as closed off by the idea.

"How well do you know this man?" Sorin inquired.

I shrugged. "As well as you ever know your jailer." Sorin gave me a look, and I continued, "He is a kind of friend. He and his partner Jan, who's the doctor at the outpost. Branko always looked out for me, ensuring I didn't get into too much trouble. Did I have a clue he was a spy? Not one bit. Then again, if I did, he wouldn't be very good at it, would he?"

"Then what makes you think he's the person we need to convince?" Lucian challenged.

"Because he's the only one who's going to believe that the heir to the North and the heir to the South would give up everything for a woman," I justified. "Granted, he has no idea who Sorin is. I didn't feel like that was the time to share it. Which, yet again, is why I think we need to have another chat. I don't know how we do it, but it needs to happen."

Lucian groaned and muttered something to himself before turning to Victor. "You willing to help me do this?"

"Thought you'd never ask," Victor said with a smile.

"What? What are you doing? He didn't ask anything," I yelled as the two men climbed the wall out of the grotto. "It's rude to ignore someone when they're talking to you, assholes."

"Let them go, Wildflower. They have a plan in mind. I'm sure it will all make sense when they come back," Petru assured me. "Now, have you eaten at all?"

"Trying to distract me with food?" I grumbled.

He paused and cocked his head. "Would you rather I try sex? I didn't get the feeling you were in the mood, although I'm sure none of us would have a problem fixing that."

My jaw dropped. I would have expected this from Toma or

Victor, but to have Petru be the one to make such a dirty comment stunned me. Ignoring my reaction, the Alpha just kept looking for whatever he needed in his pack. Finally, he pulled out a wrapped bar of something and offered it to me. Looking down, I noticed it wasn't a meal bar as I'd thought, but a candy bar.

"Where in the world did you get that?" I gasped, snatching it out of his hand.

Petru smiled at my excitement. "Happy birthday, Danella."

Since leaving my parents' home, I hadn't celebrated my birthday. The Care Center always mentioned it at the morning meal, and I got a special breakfast and a cupcake at dinner, except it didn't *mean* anything. With this simple gesture in the oddest of places, I never thought I'd find myself feeling loved.

"Thank you," I whispered, trying to fight back tears as I just clutched the candy, staring at him in disbelief. "How?"

"Bethany mentioned it to Toma about two weeks back that it was almost your birthday and told him the date," Petru showed me his watch, which also listed the date on the screen. "See, it's the twenty-third, meaning it's your birthday. I'm sorry we couldn't do much more for you besides the candy, but when I saw it back at the base, I knew I had to bring it along. No one should have a birthday that's ignored. It's an incredibly special day because it's the day you entered the world."

Now there was no chance of me holding back my emotions. Throwing myself at Petru, he snatched me up and swung me around before showering my face in kisses. "You deserve so much more, my beautiful Wildflower, and we will make up for it next year."

"This is perfect. The fact that you even knew, remembered, and found this for me is more than I could ever ask for," I mumbled into his neck as tears seeped from my eyes.

Petru knelt and held my face in his hands, wiping away my tears with a gentle smile on his face. "Oh, my sweet Danella, how much we have to teach you about realizing how special and important you are to us. Thankfully we have plenty of time to work on that after all this is done."

"You're talking like there's no doubt in your mind that we'll end the war," I pointed out. "We haven't even gotten the rebels on our side."

"Just a matter of time," Sorin interjected. "Dani-girl, if there is one thing we learned fast about you, it is never to tell you that you can't do something. It's like you have a mission to prove us wrong. So I'm trusting in that stubborn streak of yours, and if you tell me that you've got a way through with this Branko, that's what will happen."

"We told you from the beginning that you would be part of this team, an equal," Cris reminded. "If you truly think this is the best course, I'm behind you one hundred percent."

Toma grabbed a shirt from his pack and started wiping the tears and snots off my face, making me laugh. "You better hope there's time to wash that before you need to use it again," I teased.

"What a little snot when the other shirt has been worn for three days?" Toma challenged. "Come on, let's just relax for a bit. Eat your candy bar, and we'll wait for those two to return. Who knows, they might have found something tasty for dinner."

I highly doubted that since the river we'd been following got smaller and smaller with less water flowing. There were no fish, and even the rodents and birds were becoming scarce. This was the true nature of the North, though I was glad it held off for so long since we were definitely searching longer than we thought we would for the rebels.

When the other two finally returned, I was dozing in Cris' arms with my legs in Toma's lap as he massaged my feet and legs. The second Sorin noticed the shifting of rock he was on his feet, gun at the ready, only relaxing when he heard the bird whistle. When the two stepped into the firelight, I realized they weren't alone— Branko was also with them.

CHAPTER 57

Danella

There the Beta stood, mouth gagged and hands bound, looking a little worse for wear. Other than a bloody nose, he looked fine in any case. When he spotted me, he started talking and gesturing wildly with his hands, yet I couldn't understand a word of it. Getting up, I snatched the gag, a rolled-up sock, out of his mouth.

"Oh, thank god, Dani, tell them they can't kill me. If you want any hope of us working together, my death isn't going to help things. They came out of nowhere and grabbed me, not saying a word about why," Branko rushed, trying to get all his words out before anyone could stop him.

Looking at the two men who seemed rather pleased with themselves, I quirked a brow. "Would you care to explain why Branko is joining us against his will?"

"Happy Birthday, Little Spark. You said you needed to find a way to talk to him on neutral ground," Victor answered. "This might not be exactly what you meant, but this way you can have your chat and not be disturbed."

That had me frowning. "What did you do to the others?"

"We might have found one of their dart guns and put it to good use," Lucian shared. "I feel like it's only fair play since they used it on us and should know what it's like."

Dropping my head into my hands, I groaned. "Remind me the next time we need to save the country that I'm a little more specific in how I want situations like this handled. Can you please untie the man? He's not going anywhere with all six of you around."

Lucian pulled out his knife and cut off the bindings. Branko flinched but was smart and didn't try to run away. "Please take a seat by the fire. Make yourself comfortable. I promise that no one will try to kill you... as long as you don't provoke them," I added, just to be safe.

Victor and Lucian sat on either side of him as if to reinforce the don't be stupid part of this situation. Once everyone relaxed, I briefly watched Branko as he studied the guys individually. Sorin looked like he was about to say something, but I shook my head wanting Branko to be the one who initiated things.

"They truly do get along," Branko murmured as he met my gaze. "When you told me they chose you over their loyalty to their country and were willing to have him part of this I didn't believe a single word of it," he shared, jerking his thumb over at Lucian. "Then here I am as a result of those two working together in a coordinated attack that took down my whole team with just two people."

Victor shrugged. "We could have done it earlier, but since we didn't know where Dani was, it seemed smarter to get her out in the open."

"The cave wasn't rigged to blow. I had my men check since you left with her and the detonator. I couldn't risk you returning and completing the job," Branko commented.

"All that matters is you believed us and we got our girl back," Sorin pointed out. "We aren't here to talk about that, though. Dani tells us that she's mentioned what we're trying to do but that you weren't quite convinced. Tell me what would have you understand beyond a shadow of a doubt, that we were serious about working with the rebels to take out the General and end the war?"

Branko sat there staring into the fire as he thought while the rest of us waited for his answer. When he looked back up, I saw a determined set to his jaw that told me he'd made a decision.

"Who else is backing this?" he questioned. "If all you have is the seven of you, then there is no chance, even with the rebels assisting you."

Two days ago, we'd gotten the call from Savo with two words making it through the awful connection we had on the satellite phone—*we're in.* This was the last part we needed to show the rebels that we weren't just a group of dreamers using wishes and rainbows to make this happen. If Oscad was willing to lend its military power to make this happen, there was more hope than ever before.

"If you're given that information, how do we know you won't sell us out?" Lucian challenged. "You were a spy before in my own ranks, how do I know you didn't flip to the other side, and you're reporting back to my father what the rebels are doing?"

Branko laughed. "What could the General possibly have on the likes of me? He'd need to know who I was and the fact I was an agent for the rebels at all. Besides, how fucked in the head would I have to be to believe anything that the North promises would come true? They have done fuck all for anyone but themselves."

"Gotta agree with the man there," Lucian muttered. "What about the rest of you? Do you feel it's all right to share with him, or do we keep it to ourselves until we reach the stronghold?"

"See, that's the thing, if you don't tell me then I'm not going to take you there. No one can find it without a guide. It's a refugee camp hidden away from the prying eyes of the North and the flying eyes of the South," Branko shared.

Toma leaned forward, seemingly confused. "Wait, there have been drones flying around here?"

"Not so much the past year, but yeah, there have been drones," he assured. "We shoot them the second we spot them, although everyone knows the North doesn't have technology like that."

"That can't be. A person needs to be within six miles since it needs to be operated by control. None of my people would ever be able to get this close to the mountains without us noticing missing equipment or missing people," Toma countered.

"Look, all I can tell you is what I've experienced myself. And with my own two eyes, I've seen those damn things flying around. If we ever make it to the stronghold, I'll show them to you. We keep whatever we can find on the off chance there's something we can do with it or make from it. The fact that you evidently feel like you should have knowledge about this and don't has me interested, though," Branko mused aloud.

"Speaking of the South, I feel like it might help the situation if I introduced myself," Sorin said, holding out a hand. "I'm Sorin Dragomire, son of President Dragomire, and heir to the South."

Branko took the offered hand and shook it slowly, his eyes wide. "I'm sorry, did you say..."

"Dragomire, yes, that's correct," Sorin finished for him. "Unlike my father, I don't particularly want to make my mark on the world in politics, but there are some duties you can't avoid. I feel my place in the military is protecting our people and helping them that way. If we can end this war, that means everything changes for both sides. Our hope is for the best. Things won't be easy and we need to know there are people in our corner who can show others a better way. Clearly, you rebels are doing that all on your own, fighting for freedom and living the life you've wanted. Now, we need your people to stand with ours to show it's possible."

A laugh escaped Branko. "I thought you said you didn't want to be in the world of politics?"

Sorin grinned. "Can't help how you were raised, but I won't argue that learning how to be persuasive has been rather helpful."

"So does this mean your father and the Southern people are behind you on this?" Branko inquired.

There was an awkward pause as we waited to see how Sorin would handle that question.

"You're looking for honesty from us, to put all our cards on the table, right?" Sorin pressed, resting his elbows on his knees as he leaned forward. "My father does not know I'm here or that I've bonded with Danella. No one but the people around this fire knows Lucian is part of our pack or that we've come up with this fucking crazy ass idea. However, if I come back with a signed peace treaty with Lucian's name and mine once the General is gone, he one thousand percent will support it."

This had our guest frowning as he crossed his arms. "You're doing this without approval?"

"Oh my god, you can't be serious right now," I said with a burst of laughter. "The rebel is upset that the heir to the South didn't ask his dad if he could end a pointless war that was killing thousands of people a day? Bran, what the hell?"

"Hey, rebels understand what it means to be labeled a traitor for doing what you think is right. We also know there is a time and place to make that happen. Throwing it in the president's face that his son turned his back on his people and fled to the North is not a good look," he reasoned.

"That's not what happened at all," I argued, my irritation turning to anger at his purposeful manipulation of the facts.

Arms reached out and circled my waist before I was pulled onto Lucian's lap. "Settle down, My Heart. Anger is not going to help get us anywhere in this problem. Bran is making a valid point. The South's first response isn't going to be one of joy but of fear. It's how everyone seems to take in change. They fear it and lash out at those who created it. Right or wrong, it's the way of the world."

Everything in me wanted to deny that, to think people wouldn't be so closed-minded. Then I thought of all the times people looked at us Omegas, and the moment we tried to show them we could be more, they locked us away in Care Centers or breeder houses. As long as they could control us, then all was right with the world.

"So, how do we make sure that doesn't happen?" I bite out.

Bran motioned for me to slow down. "Whoa, let's not get ahead of ourselves. I still haven't agreed to shit, but no matter how you go about this, you will need to be aware of that backlash. Who knows, it might be worth bringing the south in on this to prevent all that from being an issue."

"Won't make a fucking difference. We got our backing else-where," Victor announced. "Sorin here is buddies with a certain exiled prince, if you will. Savo. He's now in with the leadership of

Oscad, and they are going to lend us a hand taking out the General."

"Savo... the son who abandoned the North?" Bran scoffed. "I wouldn't trust a traitor's word for shit."

"It's not his word we're trusting," Petru said calmly as he tossed more wood on the fire. "We spoke to the Head Speaker himself along with another government advisor when we pleaded our case. This is not an under-the-table transaction. We gave our request, it was voted on, and then confirmed they would offer their assistance. On top of that, once the new leader of the North is in place, they will happily develop trade agreements with both the North and South countries of Asturg."

Victor shoved Bran with his arm and smirked. "That enough backing for you?"

"H...how is that possible?" Bran gasped.

"You ask that a lot, you know," I mentioned. "How is it so hard for you to believe that there are people out there sick and fucking tired of living this life? I wasn't born here, Bran, but I've decided this is where my home will be with these men, and I want the best life we can live. My dream is to see everyone have the chance to find their pack, a family to love them. Isn't that worth taking a risk and reaching way farther than you thought possible just to see if you can?"

He held my gaze as if searching for the lie, yet couldn't find one. This wasn't a joke to my men or me. What we dreamed of is so simple, but if this war didn't come to an end then we'd never be able to be together peacefully. Unless we hid away in the Forbidden Mountains with the rebels, that's not real life either.

"If, and I mean *if*, I bring you to the stronghold, you'll need to surrender your weapons," Bran explained. "It's the same rule we have for every person coming to seek asylum with us. Many are soldiers, and we can't risk danger to families and children we can prevent. Once you've surrendered your weapons, you'll be placed in holding until the council can speak with you. Normally they do it one at a time, however I might be able to convince them they are better speaking to you as a bonded pack."

All of us were nodding in agreement before he even finished speaking. Whatever it took, within reason, we would do it. We didn't have a purpose or need for our weapons, so giving them up would be simple. The necessity to keep us contained until they were ready was also logical. Anyone would do the same thing. What all of us were waiting for was the catch we knew had to be coming. All of this was far too sensible to be the whole deal.

"Finally, if they say no to your request to help you with this war... you're not permitted to leave the stronghold. Our biggest advantage is no one having knowledge of where it is. Even if we blindfold you to get there, you'll know where to look once you've seen it. You would remain with us until we felt you were loyal to the cause and then given some small freedoms. There is the ability to become free-moving citizens once more, but that's after you've proven without a doubt you'll never speak of the stronghold to anyone."

And there it was.

"So what makes the difference if they say yes?" Victor questioned. "We still know where they are."

"True, but you would be an ally against a common cause," Bran reasoned. "You wouldn't be able to bring anyone from Oscad to our stronghold. We'd need to meet them in a neutral location. The stronghold must be protected at all costs, so know that if they feel like you'll be a threat, they will either kill you or imprison you to ensure that happens."

Lucian and Sorin looked at each other momentarily as if having an entire conversation in just one look. Sorin nodded as they'd come to an agreement and addressed Bran. "We agree to the terms. There's no way to win this without the rebels' support, so either we try and fail, or we just give up the idea altogether."

"All right, then I will return to my men to make sure they're okay, and we'll leave at first light," Bran decided and rose.

"Yeah, not so fast," Lucian cut in. "We agreed to go with *you* to the stronghold and meet these leaders of yours. None of that involved having a group of fifteen armed men escorting us to this meeting."

Branko frowned. "You expect me to just leave my men with no clue as to where I've gone and take you to the stronghold?"

"I mean if you want to write them a note. We can drop it off," Lucian offered. "What would you do in our shoes? We only have the smallest amount of trust in you because Dani said you were the right person to make this happen for us. Other than that, there is no mutual trust."

Branko seemed to ponder this a moment. "Now that you put it that way I can see how having my men along would be perceived. What if we came to a meeting in the middle of sorts? You can keep all your weapons until we get to the entrance of the stronghold. At that point, you will have to give them up. If I plan to double-cross you, it won't matter if I have my men with me or not the second we enter. There are more than enough people in the stronghold to take you in an instant."

The guys all looked at each other. There were a few shrugs and a nod from Cris in this strange nonverbal communication.

"We accept that, but you will remain here with us tonight," Sorin determined. "Your men will be out for quite some time. There's no need for you to return right away."

Opening his mouth to argue, Sorin just narrowed his eyes, which caused Branko to sigh and sit down. "Do you at least have some food? I was kidnapped before I had a chance to eat anything."

Cris grabbed a rations packet and tossed it over. "That's supposed to be beef stew. They aren't the best tasting thing in the world, but they do the trick."

"This is what all your soldiers get for rations?" Branko asked, looking the whole thing over as if it was a miracle. "How can it be safe having traveled around in your pack? Do I need to heat it?"

"I mean, you could heat it if we had boiling water for you to put it in. Otherwise, most of us just rip off the corner and squeeze," Toma explained. "As for how it stays good... I try not to ask too many questions. The old timers tell us about the powder meals they had to mix with water then drink. I'll take mystery meat any day over that."

Doing as Toma suggested, he ripped off the corner and sniffed, only to gag a little.

"Sorry, forgot to warn you not to look all that closely at it. Just slurp it down, my man," Toma said with a grin. "When there is no other option for food, these things are amazing, but you never forget your first one."

"Ask Dani about her first experience," Petru commented and had to dodge out of the way as I chucked a canteen at him. "Now, now, Wildflower, I'm just trying to make him feel better about the situation. He needs to know we're not poisoning him with the thing."

I turned to Branko with a serious expression as I explained. "Don't question what it is or how it smells. Just close your eyes and swallow, knowing it will keep you alive for another day. If you don't, you'll end up with a mouth full of something vile and throwing up all over yourself."

Toma started to snicker, Only when I glared at him did he stop, appearing a little guilty. "To be fair to her, we didn't give her any warning whatsoever about them. She also ended up with the one that most people hate as it is."

"As she said, it will keep you alive," Sorin agreed. "Over the years, there have been many alternatives, and this seems to be working the best even if it leaves plenty to be desired."

Still not seeming convinced, Branko closed his eyes and did just what I told him.

"Oh god," he gagged. "How the fuck is that food?"

"See, that's the one thing we never called it," Victor pointed out. "It's not *food*, but it is full of life-giving nutrition."

"I think I'm going to be sick," Branko murmured, his head between his knees.

Victor slapped him on the back a few times. "Hang it there. Your stomach will settle, just give it a minute."

With a thumbs up, Branko just sat there silently for a little while as the rest of the guys told stories about the worst things they'd ever had to eat. I was eternally grateful that I got to enjoy my candy bar before this all occurred, otherwise, I'm not sure I could have stomached it. Once Bran recovered, he joined in the conversation, sharing his own experiences in and out of the Northern Army. I couldn't help but smile as everyone relaxed, and the evening felt like a gathering of friends. This would only help us when we got to the stronghold because if Bran was indeed on our side, it would make all the difference in the world.

This was it, the final step we needed to make this possible. Hopefully, by this time tomorrow, we'd know what the fates had in store for us. Would we change the world, or would our world be changed, locked away with the rebels? Truthfully, in either situation, I was winning out since both scenarios left me with the ability to stay with my men. There wasn't much I couldn't adjust to as long as we were all together.

CHAPTER 58

Danella

The reception of the soldiers when they woke up to find us there with them was as welcoming as we expected. Which is why we made sure to take all their weapons and put them outside the cave for our safety. Once Branko explained what would happen and everyone took a minute to recover from the nightshade, which they had an antidote for, a tense truce was reached. By the time we were ready to head out for the stronghold, the sun was high in the sky making us all sweat as we walked.

"How far is it to the stronghold?" I questioned after a few hours of walking.

He looked over his shoulder at me and shook his head. "You'll know when we get there and not a second before. As I said, the location of the stronghold is the one thing we've kept hidden all these years, and I don't plan on being the one to fuck it up."

That was hard to argue with, even though I didn't relish the idea of being led aimlessly around. Too much of my life had been choices made for me with the expectation I wouldn't question things, but that phase of my life was over. Now I was questioning everything until I was satisfied with the answer. The hard part was that in a situation like this, I knew it was wiser to leave things alone, yet my past had me rioting against that plan.

"Can you tell us if we will make it there tonight?" I tried, hoping if it was less specific if he would give me something.

"We'll get there when we get there." Was his response. "Keep pushing this, Dani, and I'll change my mind entirely."

With that statement, it was clear he wasn't willing to appear weak in front of his men. We were the supposed enemy and Branko was their leader. It didn't matter if we knew each other from before; now was a whole different situation. A thing I did take note of is that we were moving higher into the mountains, away from the water source. The bonus was the higher we got, the cooler the weather was with the breeze that picked up not blocked by the mountain itself.

As the path grew steeper, it was tricky to navigate. However, Branko knew where he was going and the trail was clear of anything hindering our climb. While I'd been growing stronger daily, this incline was killing my legs. It was getting harder to breathe as Branko didn't offer any breaks for us to adjust to the altitude change. I couldn't tell if his drive was to get us there before dark or some other reason I hadn't considered.

Things started to level out as the sky turned a stunning shade of orange mixed with bright pink creating a vibrant sunset. I was so enamored by it that I almost crashed into Petru, not realizing we'd come to a halt. Sorin grabbed my arm and pulled me to a stop a hair's breadth away from Petru's back. Peering around my Alpha, I noticed the cave entrance before us. It was so craggy looking that it was hard to tell at first that it was anything but a depression in the mountainside.

"When we enter, you need to follow the person in front of you closely. The path through here is narrow. It will also be pitch black except for the light we provide, so don't think you can wander off. Trust me, you'll never find your way out because there are quite a few split-offs to mislead those who might stumble upon the entrance," Branko informed us.

As we entered the cave, Branko and his men flipped on small lights attached to their packs that illuminated their feet so they could see clearly. It gave off enough light that with us staggered among the others we could move with no issue. The further we went from the entrance, the darker it got. I'd never been one to be afraid of the dark, but this wasn't dark; it was pure void. There was nothing. Merely the sounds of dripping water, the twittering of bats as they flitted around irritated at our intrusion, and the soft shuffle of our feet. I had no idea if one step to the right would have me falling into the abyss or if the roof of the cave was mere inches from my head. Add on the awareness that if these men wanted to, they could leave us here to die with no light and no sense of direction. It was a fear unlike anything I'd ever experienced.

Just as I thought I might start to actually panic, a wash of reassurance came over me through my bond with Petru. It felt like drinking a cold glass of water on a hot day the way it seemed to soothe my fraying nerves. Then Sorin added his steadiness to the mix, so I straightened my back and stopped hunching for fear of something coming to get me. Soon, each of my bonds was grounding me, reminding me that I wasn't doing this alone. I might not have them next to me at the moment, but they had my back no matter what.

The thing about walking in total darkness is your mind has nothing to gauge the passing of time. We could have been in there for an hour, three hours, or ten minutes and I'd have no idea. Finally, off in the distance, there was a faint glow, the promise that we were almost to the end of this hellish journey. The closer we got, the brighter the light became, and then we were out in the open air. I took a long deep breath, letting my head fall back to stare at the sky. It was a beautiful sight to see.

"You okay?" Cris asked, running a hand down my back. "Felt like you got a little nervous there."

"I don't think I've ever experienced something that ever made me feel quite so small and powerless," I shared, turning to look at him. "My mind kept racing with all the worst things that could happen in the blink of an eye that I couldn't do a damn thing about."

He nodded as he pulled me into a hug. "Not many people know what true darkness feels or looks like. It makes everyone equal in the challenges they face and the dangers that lurk in the dark. Now that you've experienced the sensation, you'll know how to handle it the next time."

"I suppose if we came in that way, we'll have to leave through there as well," I mumbled.

Cris didn't actually need to answer that, and he didn't. Just pressed a kiss to my head before letting me go. In a gesture that made me smile at him, he laced our fingers together and gave them a comforting squeeze before we started forward again.

We were out in the open, not at our destination but at the bottom of a ravine. Our path was wide enough for three people to walk side by side, which was a welcome thing after the cave. Just as the sun shared the last of its light with us, we arrived at the stronghold. The town laid out before us in a lush green valley that looked so much like the South had me speechless. There was even a small lake that animals were peacefully drinking from. If someone asked me to picture a fairy tale land hidden away in the mountains, *this* is exactly what I would picture. Full towering trees were scattered throughout the space, explaining where the wood for the houses came from. Smoke plumed out of chimneys attached to simple houses with flickering light coming from the inside making it all seem so warm and inviting.

"Welcome to Summit Stronghold, the city of rebels," Branko announced, gesturing to the sight before us. "Follow me. I'll show you where you'll be staying the night. Although, first, I need you to surrender all your weapons to my men."

I snorted as Victor took off his pack and handed it to the man who'd stepped in front of him. "Be careful. That's loaded with different types of explosives and detonators. You come here and take these other things from me." He directed to another soldier.

The number of weapons on that man shouldn't surprise me, but I honestly didn't know where he hid them. I only had my knife and gun to hand over, but it took a second for anyone to realize I even had any for them to take.

"Seriously, guys? You should know better than to assume that I wouldn't have a weapon just because I'm a female and Omega.

What if they figured you wouldn't check me, so they gave me their spares to hold on to? If you really want to keep this place the best-kept secret, then treat everyone like they plan to sell you out," I warned.

Branko's man seemed less than thrilled to be chewed out by the likes of me, yet I didn't care. For me, it wasn't about keeping the stronghold safe. It was the fact he immediately assumed I wasn't a threat. When were people going to learn? Not to mention they'd heard Branko say I was trouble and a fighter. Taking a deep breath, I shook off the irritation. End the war—then change people's minds about Omegas. It's better to solve the world's problems one at a time.

Relieved of our weapons, Branko motioned for us to follow him toward the town. We walked down the center street, which had various supply shops that had been shut down for the night, until we came across the bar. Seems every town had to have one of those. At the back of the town, a large building two-stories high loomed before us.

"This is the town hall. The council meets here to do business during the day in the top half. It also serves as our school on the lower portion," Branko shared.

We walked around the hall and found ourselves standing before a simple wooden building with barred windows and two men stationed outside the door.

"You're going to be staying in our holding rooms. As I mentioned previously, this is the same process every person who comes here goes through. We have an area specifically set up for this," he explained. "Granted, it's not meant for packs since it's set up more like a barracks, but I'm sure you'll manage for the night."

"Won't be the first time we've stayed in a place like this. We'll be just fine," Sorin agreed. "Is there anything we should know about tomorrow? What or who to expect? I don't want to cause any trouble if something unexpected occurs."

"I'll come back in a bit with some food, real food, I might add. After that, no one should be bothering you until I've spoken to the council and explained what's going on. If they agree to meet with you tomorrow, I'll be sure to accompany whoever they send to escort you to the town hall. It is possible they'll want a little time to talk amongst themselves about the matter, so it could be that they'll wait until the following day to meet with you," Branko informed us. "Other than someone bringing meals, it should be pretty quiet. There is a bathroom attached with a shower, toilet, and sink. Pump the handle to get the water to flow to start, but once it's going, you're good to use as much as you like. Oh, it's not heated, but it will get you clean if that's what you're looking for."

"Hey, that sounds like heaven to me. We haven't seen a real bed or shower in over a week," Victor muttered.

"I'll be back with food. Let me know if there's anything else you need at that point," Branko said as he opened the door to the building and motioned us inside. "I'll be locking the door, but it's for everyone's safety. Please understand."

"You've been incredibly clear that this is the normal way of things. We will follow the rules your people have put in place," Sorin assured him.

With that, we were left to our own devices. The building was set up exactly as he said, with rows of neatly prepared bunks waiting for whoever might need them. Each bed also had a large and small towel stacked at the foot of the bed. There was nothing fancy about the place, but it was absolutely well-maintained. These rebels weren't a ragtag group of people but a whole other world hidden within the North. This is what things could be like once we put an end to the war and pooled resources.

"How are they so well supplied?" Cris asked as he picked up a towel. "None of this is what I expected at all."

"Branko told me they raid supply trains to the various bases around the area," I shared. "Although I've never seen things so nice get sent before."

"It's possible they could have gone after one of the supply runs that Oscad sent. There was a time before they considered sending us Omegas that goods like this would be more than what we needed. They were right, but my bastard of a father thought it was a waste.

It could be why he didn't feel the need to go after them for it," Lucian offered.

I picked up a towel and looked at the label. Sure enough, it was branded by a company from Oscad. "Oddly enough, that makes perfect sense. Oscad wouldn't know to look out for rebels, and they could have simply posed as soldiers and handed things over to them without a second thought. If the General didn't make a scene over it, then there's no reason for Oscad to have known."

"Either way, I'm taking a shower," Victor announced, grabbing a bar of soap out of his pack along with the towels.

Curious, I followed after him to see what the bathroom looked like. The space was simple with three sinks, two shower stalls, and three toilets also in individual stalls. There was a large hand pump in the middle of the bathroom, which Victor immediately started to work.

"Little Spark, can you turn on one of the showers? I'm not sure there's another way to see if I've got it working," Victor requested.

Sliding open a curtain and standing to the side, I turned on the knob. I yelped as the water instantly shot out. The spray was wider than I expected, drenching me before I could get out of the way.

Darting out of the stall, I crashed into a naked Victor who just laughed. "You need a shower too, might as well commit now that you're already wet."

There wasn't much point in arguing with him. So I allowed him to help me out of my soggy clothes. They needed a good washing as well. With only one other change of clothes, they got pretty grimy rather quickly. Shivering, I looked at the shower dreading how chilly it was. While it was nowhere close to being as cold as that pond was, it was still nippley.

"The faster you get in and start scrubbing, the faster you'll be done," Victor pointed out as he scrubbed away at his body.

Watching the suds float over the ripples of his muscles had my pussy clenching with need. It was as if I was mesmerized by watching his hands run over his body, as if he was teasing me with the sight just to get me in the shower. With his hand clasped around his cock, he started to stroke it. I knew he'd done this for my benefit.

With the glide of the soap, he was easily working over his piercings, making me shiver for a whole other reason as I remembered what that sensation felt like.

Before I knew it, I was removing his hand so I could do it for him. A pleased rumble echoed deep in his chest at my touch, making me smile up at him. He knew how much I loved to be able to draw those sounds out of my guys, to hear just how much they enjoyed my attention. Working the soap into a lather, he started to wash me as I stroked his cock, letting my thumb swirl around the tip as it jumped in my hand.

"God that feels so good," Victor moaned, needing to brace himself on the stall of the shower.

Using both hands, I started a gentle wringing motion to switch up the movement. "What about this?"

"Little Spark, anything you do is amazing. It's more the fact you want to give me pleasure that makes this all so incredible," Victor whispered into my ear as he cupped my breasts and flicked my erect nipples.

Shuddering, I whimpered at the touch arching into his hands. So went the rest of our shower as he washed every inch of my body and I kept him on the edge of coming the entire time. I would speed up my movements, see the way his jaw clenched as the build grew more intense only to switch up the rhythm and slow it down. The heated look I got the third time I did it told me that I was walking on thin ice.

Grabbing the back of my legs he hoisted me up against the stall of the shower and pressed himself against me. To my surprise he didn't thrust into me, just against me, letting his cock thrust over top of my pussy, the tip of his cock hitting my clit in the most perfect way. His face buried in my neck he rutted against me, grunts of pleasure escaping his lips as he bucked moments before he came. Hot cum splashed on my stomach as he ground against me, sending me over the cliff into my own climax.

"Yes, fuck, fuck, fuck," I mumbled as Victor slid a hand between my legs to rub out every last drop of that orgasm. As my nails dug into his shoulders I was hit with a second orgasm stronger than the first one making me bare down wishing there was a cock inside me.

"So beautiful," Victor said in a soft voice, the heat of his words drifting across the skin of my neck. "My stunning Little Spark coming undone in my arms, there will never be a more precious sight to see."

Love and warmth suffused me as he carefully placed me back on my feet, making sure I was steady. I thought there might be a moment where my legs wouldn't hold me but they did. Then in the most loving gesture, he rinsed the soap from my body with small handfuls of water so I wasn't assaulted with the cold spray. It didn't work for my hair but he held me in his arms keeping me as warm as possible. People always talk about the grand gesture of love, but for me, simple moments like this were what spoke volumes.

CHAPTER 59

Danella

The cleanest we'd been since leaving the cabin, Victor carried me out of the shower, set me on the counter between two sinks, and wrapped the towel around my shoulders. Having boxed me in with his arms, he used that opportunity to kiss me until my toes curled and my pussy begged for more orgasms. With a final searing kiss, he stepped back with a pleased smirk on his face.

"There is nothing better than to see the look of bliss written on your Omega face. Don't you agree, Cris?" Victor asked, staring in the mirror behind me.

Realizing what he'd just said, I peered around Victor's body to find Cris watching us from another shower stall cock in hand. I'd been so distracted by Victor that I hadn't even realized someone was in the stall next to us.

"Indeed, but I think our girl has been a little neglected since we've needed to be so vigilant while on this mission," Cris commented, as he approached. "Here we are, stuck in this building for the foreseeable future. What could we possibly do to pass the time?"

Victor smiled, stepped aside, and clapped Cris on the back. "I'm sure you two will think of something. I'll let the others know the showers are open."

Taking Victor's place between my legs, Cris let his hands slide up my legs until he stopped at my hips. "Tell me, sweetheart, was that enough for you?"

Not waiting for me to answer, he slipped two fingers between my legs and ran them over the outside of my pussy, stealing a sharp intake of breath from me. Lifting those fingers to show me, I could feel my body clench as they glistened in the light with my slick.

"This tells me it's possible that you might need more, yet there's no way to tell without you telling me," Cris pressed, slipping the two fingers in his mouth and sucking them clean. He moaned like it was the best thing he'd ever tasted. "Hurry, sweetheart, tell me what you need, or I'm going to lose control and come right where I stand."

Snapping my hand out, I grabbed his wrist and yanked him closer to me. "I want you to fuck me. Bend me over this counter, take whichever hole you want, and ride me as only a Beta can."

Cris' smile grew so wide it made his eyes crinkle to the point you almost couldn't see them. "I fucking love you, Danella," he whispered, leaning in as his lips brushed mine. "You truly are perfect for us in ways you probably don't even realize. Betas are often seen as less than by Omegas because we can't fulfill your need to be knotted. Yet here you are, begging me to fuck you like I'm the only one who can fulfill this need."

"Because you are," I stated simply. "You don't have to hold back for fear of knotting me. I love the tender moments I have with all of you with the cuddles and kisses. Yet sometimes a woman just wants her partner to lose themselves in the moment and take what's freely given to them."

His lips slammed to mine, a need and power I'd never felt from him before sparking through our bond. This was a moment he'd waited and yearned for between us but had been too nervous to ask with my history.

"Promise me one thing," Cris said, our foreheads resting against each other. "If it's too much or you're not enjoying it, then you *have* to tell me."

"If it's with you, I know I'll enjoy it. However, yes, I promise if something needs to change, I'll tell you," I assured him, pressing a soft kiss on his lips as I shrugged off the towel and wrapped my arms around his neck.

The sweetness of the kiss turned hungrier as he pulled me flush to his body. I could feel his hard cock pulsing with need on my stomach sandwiched between us. Breaking the kiss, he moved to nip and lick down my neck, slowly leaning me back until my breasts were presented to him. Shifting so he could get a better angle, Cris latched onto a nipple biting down with his teeth making me gasp with the shock of pain that he licked away, soothing the area. The blend of rough moments followed by a showering of affection was intoxicating. It's almost like he was working me up to more, seeing what I reacted to and what I might not like. So far, everything he'd done had me panting and begging for more.

"Are you ready for me to fuck you now, sweetheart?" Cris asked, pulling me up so we were nose to nose.

"Yes, I want you," I whined.

"Did you know you're perfuming so much it's making this whole room smell like the purest flower waiting to be plucked, with an edge of spice, telling me you can handle what I'm about to do," Cris murmured as he gripped my hips lifting me from the counter and turning me so I could see him standing behind me in the mirror. "It's making it incredibly hard not to slam into you and come right away with knowing how badly you want me."

This was a side to Cris I'd never seen, and I was enjoying it. Now I understood a little better how two Alphas and a Beta could be such an even match. They were comfortable changing power dynamics when it came to each other, allowing them to experience all sides of the relationship. Cris placed a hand between my shoulder blades and pressed, urging me to give in to his touch.

This was exactly what I wanted, to throw caution to the wind and explore sides of sex that I'd never felt comfortable with until now. While I didn't want to be controlled, an intimate moment like this was different. I'd craved the feeling of safety with a person to trust they would take care of me if I gave over control. Who better to experience it the first time than with Cris, the member of my pack with the sweetest spirit who would always keep my best in mind?

Stretched out flat on the counter, I rested my head to the side so I could see if anyone had entered the room. I wouldn't have any issue with my guys watching or participating. It was just so ingrained in me to keep a watch of my surroundings. Cris brushed his hands down my whole back, pressing kisses along my spine, easing me into the situation. I giggled when he kissed both my ass cheeks and gave them a squeeze for good measure. Nudging my legs wider with a foot, I sensed him squatting, his hands still on my ass spreading me open.

He wasted no time in burying his face in my pussy, thrusting his tongue into me, making me moan and arch back into him. "God, I love when you use your tongue on me."

There was a crack on my ass that made me yelp and shy away, but he held me firm as he continued feasting on my pussy making my eyes fall shut. Hearing someone enter the bathroom, I forced them open, only to find Toma and Petru frozen as they took in what the two of us were up to.

"That sneaky bastard," Toma muttered. "He didn't give us a warning or anything."

"Really, we should be thanking him for ensuring it was the two of us who showered next so we could enjoy the show," Petru countered, as he started to undress. "Who knows, maybe they'll let us join, but I know that look on Cris' face. He's in Alpha mode."

Toma smiled and wrapped his arms around Petru's waist. "Or you could Alpha me, and I get to have you all to myself."

"Did you see the way her eyes just dilated? I think she likes the idea of me bending you over next to her and making you scream along with her," Petru shared, reaching back and grabbing the back of Toma's neck in a sexy yet wildly possessive gesture.

"Good thing we have plenty of time to kill. There are so many options," Toma added, unbuckling Petru's pants and letting them drop to the floor.

He grabbed Petru's shirt next and pulled it up and over his head, leaving him only in tight boxers that showed how turned-on he was.

Cris must have noticed I was a little distracted, and instead of his tongue, three fingers shoved into my pussy as he shifted his mouth to my ass. Finger fucking me as he worked to relax my asshole turned me into a puddle of overwhelming sensation. My legs started to shake as my orgasm came barreling up and slammed into me, pulling a scream from my lungs.

I would have crumpled to the floor if Cris hadn't been there to keep me pressed to the counter's edge. Slowly he removed his fingers and stood kissing whatever bare skin he could get to. "You come so beautifully, sweetheart, and fuck if you don't taste as sweet and spicy as your scent. I could spend all day eating you out."

I let out a shaky laugh. "Maybe we should try that sometime, see how long either of us can last."

"Oh, I'd be careful offering things like that, sweetheart. You never know when it could happen or if I plan to let you come as I take my time feasting on you," Cris warned.

Fuck, why did that sound even more amazing now that he said that?

"We will leave that for another time. Right now I want to shove my cock into that perfect pussy and rut into you until I fill you with my cum. The others get to leave their mark on your skin, but I'd much rather leave mine deep inside you, where only those who are your pack can be," Cris whispered in my ear, nipping the shell of it as he straightened.

Well, if it wasn't clear to me before, it was glaringly apparent that I was a major fan of dirty talk. Especially when it came from sweet, gentle Cris who you never expected it from. Before I could even prepare myself, Cris was balls deep in my pussy, with his cock pressing me into the counter. There was no name for the sound that came out of my mouth at that point, but it was a mix between a moan, a scream, and a begging for him to do it again. Which he did over and over and over until my eyes rolled back in my head with these long deep strokes. It hit places so deep inside me I didn't know were even there, but I damn well did now.

"That's my girl, taking my cock so well. Do you have any idea how sexy it is to watch your body take every single inch of me so fucking deep?" Cris growled as he fisted my hair toward the base of my skull. "Now that I've gotten you right where I want you, it's time to rut myself into you."

Grabbing my right leg, he lifted it so it rested on the counter and changed the angle to where he was even deeper than before. Keeping his grip in my hair and another on my hip, he stayed true to his promise and fucked me with abandon. The sound of slapping skin echoed in my ears so impossibly loud. It wasn't until I heard Toma cry out that I realized it wasn't just Cris and I but their moans added to ours.

"Do you want to see?" Cris asked as if sensing what caught my attention. "Would you like to watch our Alphas we love in the throes of passion?"

"Please," I managed to get out.

In a move I never expected, Cris had me stand up, then hooked his arms under my legs and lifted, never once letting his cock slip from me. Turning, we faced the two Alphas still in the shower stall. Toma's face was pressed up against the wall with Petru's hand on the back of his neck keeping him there. His other hand was on Toma's hip, keeping pulled back as Petru pounded into him, head tossed back in ecstasy. It had to be one of the most erotic sights I'd ever seen.

Cris leaned back against the counter as he rolled his hips fucking up into me. I let out a cry as this new angle hit that delicious spot deep inside that was going to shatter me in mere moments. This caught Petru's attention, and he turned to look, faltering in his movement at the sight of me.

"Jesus fuck," Petru swore, releasing his hold on the other's neck. "Toma, look at them."

With Petru's order, he swiveled his head to face us and groaned. "That's not fucking fair, putting her pussy on display as he fucks her. God, I want in on that so bad."

"Yeah?" Cris asked. "If that's true, then come over here and suck on her clit. I'm about ready to cum, and she needs a serious fucking orgasm so she'll squeeze the shit out of my Beta cock."

Petru pulled out of Toma and slapped him on the ass. "You heard him. Get over there."

This is how I came to die of pleasure with Cris' cock hitting that magic button, Toma's mouth on my pussy licking and sucking away, as Petru fucked him mercilessly. The feel of Petru's eyes on me as he devoured the sight of us all together was my undoing. When I came, not only did I come harder than ever before, but I sprayed Toma in the face with my cum. Then my pussy became a vice grip around Cris' cock milking every last drop out of the Beta, not giving a shit there wasn't a knot. Toma gave one good last suck on my slightly abused clit and I was a goner. Blacking out as another climax hit, I screamed long and loud until the world became black as I floated on a sea of euphoric feelings.

~

"DO WE LET HER KEEP SLEEPING?" I heard Victor ask.

"Is there a reason she needs to be awake?" Lucian questioned.

"What if they come and tell us the council wants to meet with us right now?" Victor argued. "It would put her in an unfair position to have just woken up, hurried to get dressed, and then be expected to answer high-pressure questions."

"Guys, it doesn't matter, she's already awake," Cris muttered from behind me, then pressed a kiss to my temple. "Aren't you, sleepyhead?"

Burrowing deeper into the pillow, I groaned, not willing to admit I was awake just yet. It had been *years* since I'd had the chance to just lay in bed for as long as I wanted. "No," I mumbled.

Fingers played over the bare skin of my leg until it reached my foot. Shooting up, I tackled the only person who knew my feet were ticklish. Lucian caught me effortlessly as we tumbled to the floor, laughing the whole time.

"You bastard," I snapped, glaring down at him. "Didn't we agree you were never going to do that after the last time?"

"My Heart, I was never going to actually do it. The threat alone was all I needed," Lucian pointed out with a cocky smile.

Gripping his shirt, I loomed over him. "You want another black eye?"

This sobered him up enough that I felt a little proud it was a decent threat.

"Wait, hold on, back the truck up," Victor cut in, grabbing me off Lucian and setting me down with him serving as a wall between us. "*You* gave *him* a black eye?"

"Damn straight, I did. He had to lie about it to everyone too, which was rather enjoyable to watch," I added. "You see—"

Victor placed a finger over my lips, stopping me. "Little Spark, if you expect me to hear a word that comes out of your mouth, I'm going to need you to put clothes on. I have only so much willpower with you standing there, naked and ripe for eating, with your hair wild and cheeks flush."

"Here," Sorin said, stepping up and offering me a bundle. "It's clean clothes from Branko."

It was then I noticed all of them dressed in normal civilian clothes or jeans and t-shirts. Looking down at what I'd been given, I frowned, seeing it was shorts and a tank top. While it wouldn't be my first choice, it would be nice not to have to wear my uniform. With my time in the Northern outpost, I'd learned not to wear anything that was too tight or revealing without drawing attention. Once I lost weight and my curves, it wasn't as bad, but in the beginning, it was awful. I use my own undergarments even though the new clothes fit well enough, and I was even given a pair of sneakers.

"This better?" I asked, hands on my hips, looking at the others.

Toma shook his head as Petru looked at me critically. Lucian had seen me in outfits like this previously, since it was one of the only ways to make it through the summer heat.

"Nope, I'm definitely going to kill someone if I catch them looking at her," Victor muttered, rubbing a hand over his face.

I looked down at the clothes and didn't see the issue. The shorts covered my ass even if the cut left them low on my hips. The tank top fit perfectly, yet it wasn't exactly baggy. So it showed off the slight curves I'd started to gain back, only to lose with the training.

"I'm not seeing it, guys, nothing is too tight or too low, and the shorts fit well too. What am I missing?" I questioned.

Sorin walked up to me and caught my chin in his grip, forcing me to meet his gaze. "You're missing the fact that you're *our* Omega. One that happens to be incredibly attractive, especially in clothes like this that show off all the definition you've gained through training. You might not have put on all the weight you need to, but you do have curves in all the right places. This outfit shows off everything sexy about you, and we'd rather greedily keep that to ourselves."

"Oh..." I commented, not having even thought to consider things from their point of view. "I don't have anything to wear, though. The spare uniform desperately needs to be washed, and the clothes I was wearing yesterday are probably still in a heap on the floor in the bathroom."

"Actually you don't have either of those. They took our clothes to wash when giving us these to wear," Cris explained. "So there is no other option but for you to wear that because naked is not an option. We'll just have to keep our fingers crossed that no one does something to make Victor kill anyone."

"Yeah... that is not a great plan, but it's the best we can do," Toma muttered, then held out his hand to me. "Come over here, Dani, we saved food for you since you slept through dinner and breakfast. Guess Cris really wore you out."

My cheeks flushed as I remembered what had happened in the bathroom between the four of us. It was fucking hot and just thinking about it had me needing to rub my legs together. While I would be all for another round of playtime with my guys, now wasn't the time since we could get called to speak with the council at any moment. Toma guided me to a space at the far end of the building where a table with ten chairs was set up. A tray of food, or at least I believe that's what it was since it'd been covered and left on the table.

Tugging the cloth off the top, I found a sandwich and roasted vegetables waiting for me. My stomach growled with excitement as I sat down. The sandwich was huge with lots of filling that made my mouth water uncontrollably. While I stuffed my face like a heathen, the guys sat at the table, keeping me company as they talked strategy. Weighing the pros and cons of what would go down if the rebels were willing to help us or not.

"We need to at least talk about it if they tell us no," Petru reasoned. "It would be foolish of us to assume just because we have a great plan and the next generation of leaders on our side that we'll get their help."

"True, but if we don't stop the war, no one else will," Victor countered. "Once we regain our privileges, we'll leave and do just what we planned."

"What if it takes years for them to do that? Who knows what will become of the agreement with Oscad. If they think we're dead or decided against the whole thing, convincing them to give us a second chance will be even harder," Petru pressed.

This caused Victor to stand and slam his hands on the table. "So what? Do you just expect us to accept the fact that we failed and live a peaceful life here in the mountains hiding away from the real problem?"

"Sit the hell down," Sorin cut in, motioning to Victor, who returned to his seat. "He's not saying anything we haven't all thought of already. If the council says no to us, then, yeah, we're going to have to accept the fact that this place will be our home for the foreseeable future. However, in the time we're forced to spend here, we could convince them to work with us and Oscad. Don't be so black-and-white about this. There are always two ways to tackle a situation. Right now, you're choosing to see it as an all-or-nothing when that isn't the case."

Victor brushed a hand over his beard, which had gotten longer and thicker since we've been gone. "I know we knew the risks when doing this, but being faced with the reality of it is a whole other matter. I'm sorry, Tru. I lost my temper and you didn't deserve that."

Before Petru could respond, there was a knock at the door. A moment later, the door was unlocked and Branko entered. "The council would only like to speak with Lucian, Sorin, and Danella.

The rest of you will need to wait here until I come back for you, or these three return."

"Why?" I demanded.

"I'm sorry, Dani, but this is how they would like to move forward with the meeting," Branko apologized, his tone sounding slightly defeated. "I did try, but they felt it would be best to speak with those that will have the answers they need, and that was you three."

Slowly I pushed my chair back and stood with the other two following suit. Taking a second, I impulsively kissed the four staying behind. "I love you all. We'll be back soon."

Taking Lucian and Sorin's hands, needing them to ground me, we left the building and headed across the way to the town hall. This was it, the one chance we got to convince them we could do this and change the world for the better.

CHAPTER 60

Lucian

Through the bond, I could feel how nervous Dani was even though she had her shoulders back and head held high. This woman never ceased to amaze me, and even more so at seeing her soften under the attention of the other guys. At the same time, I'd never planned on having an Omega in my life, bonded or otherwise. The bigger thing I wasn't prepared for was having a pack—now I suddenly had both.

Our start was less than desired, and we were far from being a family, although we were working on it. Now that matters between Cris and I had come to light, giving me a better understanding of where he was coming from, I didn't hold it against him. Fathers could really fuck shit up in your life; I knew that from *years* of personal experience. Where he was struggling though, was the fact he'd idolized his father only to see the curtain lifted and see the man for who he truly was. I had more suspicions about the man, but I wouldn't voice them until I was certain. No need to cause more emotional damage for the Beta if I didn't need to.

Branko led us into the town hall and up a flight of wide stairs to the second floor. The building had a vaulted ceiling, providing a roomier feel as well as adding more grandeur to the space. We headed down a hall past doors leading to what I might guess to be offices. When we reached the end, there was a set of double doors that a guard was standing in front of.

"I'm here with the pack members they requested," Branko informed the guard, then stepped to the side. "This is where I leave you. I'm not allowed to be part of this discussion. Just know that I spent most of last night and all this morning talking with them, so I've had the chance to share my peace."

Reaching out, I offered the man my hand. "Thank you for doing this, Branko. I know we didn't give you much choice initially, but you've gone above and beyond on this."

The Beta seemed shocked by the gesture but shook my hand all the same. "I'll take your thanks, but just know that Dani is why I'm doing all this. She made a lot of good points and showed me some truths about myself I didn't want to acknowledge. If it had just been you guys, we'd have killed you right then and there at your camp."

I couldn't help but smirk, as I knew exactly what he was talking about. "Trust me, I wouldn't be here myself rubbing elbows with the Southern heir if it wasn't for her either. The woman has a gift for throwing your biggest character flaws in your face and making you take stock of your life."

"Yeah, it's a little brutal, isn't it?" Branko chuckled, rubbing the back of his neck.

"The council will see you now," a woman said, interrupting our conversation to scowl at us. "Bran, you know better than to keep your mother waiting."

"Of course, Ida, I'll be going now," Branko told the woman, giving us all a parting nod before heading back the way we came.

"Follow me," Ida ordered, turning sharply on her heel like a practiced drill sergeant.

The room we were led into was nothing special, just rows of chairs set up before a long table with three people sitting behind it dressed in red robes. It would seem one thing never changes no matter what kind of civilization you create—those in power want to be noticed. A woman sat in the middle with two men on either side of her. They all had graying hair and harsh wrinkles on their faces showing the hardships they'd endured. They reminded me of

Babaka and her commanding energy even in her old age. That woman had been one of the fiercest women I'd ever known.

"Greetings to you, I'm Councilwoman Nadeja. To my right is Councilman Filip and our final member Councilman Libor." She introduced, gesturing to each man. "It has been brought to our attention that your reason for coming to us is to make a rather bold request."

Last night, while the others were sleeping, Sorin and I agreed that I would take the lead. Out of the two of us, it was going to take more convincing that *I* was serious about making changes. These people had been living under the tyranny of my father and his predecessors for decades. It would stand to reason they'd need some reassurances from the horse's mouth.

"That is correct," I answered, taking half a step forward. "Allow me to introduce myself. I'm Lucian Bakal, son of General Rasvan and heir to the Northern territory. With me is Sorin Dragomire, son of President Dragomire, heir to the Southern territory. Between the other four members of our pack as well as the two of us, we have the honor of being bonded to our Omega Danella Holstad. She is originally from Oscad but was brought into Northern Asturg three years ago as part of the treaty agreement that has since changed."

Pausing a moment, I allowed everyone to exchange greetings and the room to fall into a natural silence before I continued.

"Councilwoman, you mentioned our request being rather bold and I would agree with you. I believe that Branko has shared a bit about what we hope to accomplish, but he wasn't given much time to fill us in on what he covered. If you could tell me what he shared with you or what questions you have, we'd be happy to answer what we can," I said.

It had been trickier than I thought to word things, so they would have to tell us what *exactly* Branko told them. Now knowing that this woman was his mother, he would know the best way to approach this matter, and I hoped to do the same.

"He is under the impression you wish to remove your father from power, end the war, and create peace among our people,"

Councilman Libor divulged, his callus manner of speaking telling me he thought it was all bullshit.

"All of that is true, and we plan to nurture an alliance between us and Oscad as well. It would benefit all involved to partner with them since their strongest asset is their skill with infrastructure. The North will need to be rebuilt, and it would be rather impossible without their assistance," I added.

The three of them just stared silently at us for a moment, completely caught off guard. It would seem that while they trusted Branko to do his job and perform as a soldier, they didn't take his word seriously regarding political matters.

"I'm sorry, but I find it hard to believe that something like this is even possible," Councilman Filip said, breaking the silence. "We have been working for years to figure out how to remove the General and his men. The bastard is so paranoid he's got himself surrounded by his own militia, who are all blindly loyal to him. There's no possible way to get close. We've tried just about everything we can think of." The councilman finished waving his hand as if to brush the whole idea off, as Councilman Libor nodded in agreement.

However, Councilwoman Nadeja leaned forward. "When you say, *plan to work with Oscad*, is there even a possibility of that? Would they add bodies to this fight, or are we left on our own to take all the risk for them only to come in, pick up the pieces, and claim to be our savior?"

"The last time I spoke to the Head Speaker himself, that wasn't the agreement we were working on," I answered, making her eyes widen as she picked up on the point I was trying to make.

"Are you saying that you've spoken to Head Speaker Marius himself?" Councilman Libor blurted, half rising out of his chair.

"It would seem that my half-brother Savo is part of Marius's pack. Like Sorin and myself, they found themselves in love and bonded to the same Omega. Through Savo, we were able to make our request known and, to our complete surprise, he wanted to speak to us directly on the matter. We haven't had the chance to check in with them. However, our last contact with them made clear they agreed to the terms and would help us," I explained. "So the final piece to the master plan we have is you and your people. We need those who want this change as much as we do to help pull it off."

The two men leaned forward, muttering something to each other as Councilwoman Nadeja studied the three of us. "Mr. Dragomire, you've remained rather silent through all this."

Sorin shifted to clasp his hand behind his back, falling comfortably into his military stance. "Is there something you wish me to add to the information being provided?"

A smile tugged at the corner of the woman's mouth. "Merely an observation, is all. Do you typically defer to Lucian's leadership in matters such as these?"

Dani stiffened next to me, and I could feel a zing of irritation coming from her. Our feisty Omega noticed, just as we all did the veiled barb in that question, and Dani wasn't one to let that shit slide.

"Lucian and I discussed the best way to handle this conversation last night," Sorin responded. "Both of us know the same information and collaborate on almost everything. Although I felt that out of the two of us, Lucian needed to convince you that he was sincere. It's expected that I would welcome the chance to take out General Rasvan and end the war. What isn't as believable is his heir, who's been trained since a young age to believe that the North must win at all costs, is willing to throw that aside and work alongside my men."

"Your men," The councilwoman quipped. "Are you referring to the other men within your pack?"

"Yes, I am the commanding officer of our unit in the eyes of the Southern Military," Sorin answered.

I applauded his skill in sharing only what she asked for and nothing else. So many people felt they needed to prove themselves every chance they could, but all they did was overshare and give people more ammunition with which they could shoot us. It was clear he was a politician's son in the way he could word things and turn the tide on the other person without them seeing it.

"Fascinating," Councilman Filip murmured. "So the only thing connecting you two is this lovely lady you've carefully placed between yourselves?"

"That is how our pack was created, but it's not the *only* thing that brings us together," I answered. "All of us do what we do in an effort to make the world safer for the people we protect. Once the dream of ending the war came into existence, we found another link in that. From there, as I've gotten to know the fellow men of my pack, we share much in common. Yet if you ask any of us, we will happily admit our love for this woman is the most important part of what we share."

The man actually smiled at that and turned to Nadeja with an expression I knew well. They were profoundly in love with each other even as she tried to ignore his look. Still, she gave in and finally reached for his hand.

"I would say the same is true for us, wouldn't you agree?" Councilman Filip questioned.

"Flip," she warned him. "This is not the time or place."

"Oh, relax, Naddie," Councilman Libor said as he leaned back in his seat. "It's obvious these three aren't going to judge us from the way they freely talk about their own partner."

"Hold on," Dani blurted as she charged forward. I immediately grabbed her around the waist and pulled her back. That got me a glare, but over the years, I'd gotten used to them and now I found them rather adorable on her. "Really? I wasn't going to do anything stupid."

"I didn't think you were, but the guards in the room might not have felt the same way," I reasoned, gesturing with my chin in the direction of the two men with guns at the ready who paused in their approach.

She swore under her breath, although instead of fighting against me, she resigned herself and relaxed. But if I thought she'd given up on whatever mission she'd been on, I was mistaken.

"It was mentioned that you were Branko's mother. Is that true?" Dani asked rather bluntly.

I cringed internally, but then I remembered that this is who she was. A ball buster in the best way and one of the reasons I fell head over heels for her.

"That is true..." Nadeja answered hesitantly. "I'm not sure how this pertains to anything, though."

"Both of those men are your partners...husbands... lovers? Whatever you want to call them, they're both in love with you, and you're in love with them, correct?" Dani pressed, utterly ignoring that this woman did not want to have this conversation with us.

"Ms. Holstad," Filip said, drawing Dani's attention. "Would you mind sharing with us what information you're trying to gather with these questions? It's not that we are by any means trying to be evasive. However, these are rather personal inquiries that don't have anything to do with why you're here."

Dani took a deep breath and centered herself before she spoke again. Through our bond, I could feel something about all this was upsetting her, yet I couldn't figure out what it could be.

"Forgive me. I was getting ahead of myself, and I'm sure that came across as me being rude," Dani expressed. "Branko and I were friends back at the outpost where you placed him. During that time, I noticed that he and our medic developed an intimate relationship. No, that's not the right term. They were and still are in love with each other, but when Branko came back here, he broke things off with Jan because he is married to a woman here. With the nature of his mission, I understand why he couldn't tell Jan about his wife, but he didn't need to cut the man out of his life, either. We, as a society, are wired to have more than one partner. It's those who only end up having one I feel are the odd ones out, not the other way around."

The look on Nadeja's face told me she had no clue about any of this. Even I could attest to the fact that while the two of them kept things discreet, it was no secret they were a couple. It wasn't something as a commander that I should have let carry on. However, personally, I felt there was no need. They both performed their duties and never let their connection impede what needed to be done.

"Bran, my son, has another partner?" Nadeja questioned.

"Sort of," Dani answered, teetering her hand from side to side. "Bran told me when they left the outpost to return here, and he brought the Omegas, he broke things off with Jan telling him about his wife. What I don't understand is why would he see it as such a betrayal if he sees you happy and in love with more than one person?"

Nadeja's shoulders sagged, and immediately her partners reached out to reassure her. "That's my fault, I suppose. You see, neither of these men is Branko's father. I met them both after my late husband died protecting a group on a supply run. Here I was, the first woman to be on the council, with a wonderful husband and a smart, caring son, and in the blink of an eye it was gone. Then one day, things didn't go as planned, and the Northern soldiers retaliated. They managed to kill two others, including my husband. Branko was at the impressionable age of sixteen and idolized his father above all else. Losing Matej was so much harder on Bran than I ever dreamed it would be. Overwhelmed by my own grief, I didn't handle things as well as I should have when Libor and Filip started making their interest known a year later. I acted selfishly trying to find happiness again in my life, and soon the three of us were in love and became a family. Branko saw this as a betrayal of his father. That's when he began to do everything in his ability to distance himself from us, not wanting to have any part in my new life."

Hearing this story made me think of my own feelings regarding my parents. Never had my father shown much loyalty to my mother. She was one of many Omegas he kept for himself. However, I could completely understand the feelings Branko was experiencing in this situation. If his mother truly loved his father, how could she turn her back on him and create a whole new life with these two men?

"Dearest, you can't keep beating yourself up for this," Filip urged, grasping her one hand in both of his. "As Ms. Holstad keenly pointed out, we're meant to foster more than single relationships. If it's true that Bran has come to realize this by unexpectedly falling for another, then this might be the perfect time to try reaching out.

He's returned from his mission alive after three years, now would be the perfect time to offer an olive branch."

Clearing my throat intentionally to catch their attention, I added my thoughts. "I, of course, can't speak on your family's particular situation but I can share from my own. Having grown up in the heart of the North, spoon-fed the ideology that my father wants everyone to believe, I understand where your son is coming from. While I can clearly see with my own eyes and hear that you view relationships as essential, there is still an undercurrent of what the North has forced you to believe. Many who join you don't know how to have a healthy relationship or even comprehend the possibility that you can genuinely care for more than one person and not have those feelings taken away from someone else.

The love you have from one person to another is different, not less, not more, just different. Yet how long have we been told that feelings and attachments to others are worthless? It will only lead to pain and heartache, so why bother at all? Just use each other, take what you need, and move on. It makes things so much more straightforward. Now here is Branko, a man who believes in loyalty above all else, doing what's right by his wife since he committed to her first. Only then did he meet Jan, and those perceived lines blurred until they were gone and new connections were built. I will bet you everything in the world he still loves Jan, and it's killing him to know he's hurt him so badly," I shared, no longer looking at them but at the woman in my arms.

"Interestingly enough, this was the dynamic that occurred between Danella and me. While our stories are distinctly different in many ways, I understand his feelings. I was forced to find the best way to be loyal to my father and protect the woman I love. The only thing I could come up with was to keep her at a distance and stay silent about my feelings. As much as I wanted to show her the real me, it was too dangerous to be that vulnerable. Except no matter how hard I tried, my love only grew. Then she found Sorin and his pack sending me into a tailspin," I admitted. "There was a desperation to get her back and selfishly keep her to myself after seeing how happy she was and it was as if Sorin and his team had the skill to get

Danella to bloom where I was stunting her growth. This feeling had me doing irrational things that were so impulsive and unlike me. Never had I wanted to take choices away from her, especially after all she'd been through. Then I did the one thing that honestly I should never be forgiven for," I murmured, tracing a finger over both my marks on her neck, causing a slight hitch in her breath at the touch.

Tilting her head back, she looked at me with those stunning golden-flecked green eyes. Caught off-guard by the surge of emotion I felt for her as she looked at me with such trust and love. That was something I never thought I'd witness in my life, especially from her. Each time I saw that expression, it served as a reminder that I owed her everything.

Pressing a kiss to her forehead, I looked up at the council. "Your son needs someone outside of his own relationships to guide him. I truly wish I'd had someone stepping in to make me think about the choices I was planning to make. Trust me when I say right now, he's drowning but is too prideful to say anything about it to a person he pushed away for doing the same thing he did. Don't take no for an answer when you talk to him. Make him listen. Then when he starts to talk, because he's going to, just listen and allow him to own what he's been feeling yet ignoring. You're the only one he can talk to, Councilwoman. You knew his father, the life you had with him, and have experienced the same pain he did. No one can relate more to a person than their mother."

The tears welling up in Nadeja's eyes told me I'd gotten through to her in a way that others couldn't have.

"Thank you," Nadeja whispered, her voice rough with emotion. She paused to clear it and took a sip of water from a metal cup on the table. "While this topic was unexpected and not at all the direction we planned to take this interview, I believe it answered our questions. More profoundly than I could've anticipated, if I'm being honest."

Libor surreptitiously wiped at his eye as he nodded. "I would agree with that statement. You see, Branko was very adamant that we needed to help you in this cause, because you were probably the only people who could pull it off. Now I can see why he believed that and have to agree with his assessment. That being said, we'd like to offer you our assistance with the understanding that we would like input or representation in whatever new leadership you decide to implement."

I left that for Sorin to answer, knowing he'd handle a question like that better than I would.

"Currently, we have not addressed those details. We felt it was best to deal with tasks one step at a time," Sorin admitted. "That being said, I don't have a problem being open to the idea of representation. Summit Stronghold should be treated as an autonomous group in all this."

"Well then," Filip said with a clap of his hands as he stood. "I believe the next step should be to see what plans you have in mind and share with you what we already have in place. Things are the worst they've ever been, and it's time to end this era. Follow me, and I will take you to the map room, otherwise known as the strategy room. With your combined knowledge of not only the military procedure but of the country itself, we'll finally be able to fill in some of the gaps."

"We've wanted to bring the fight to General Rasvan's doorstep for some time. The problem was without better knowledge of the bases and Stalhold City as a whole, we lost every time. Then we stopped making frontal attacks and tried other ways to get our shots in, but nothing seemed to faze the bastard," Libor grumbled as he shoved open a door, revealing the room.

Calling it the map room was a literal name for the space, but in the middle was a massive table inset with a relatively comprehensive map of the North. The rest pinned to the wall were detailed drawings of all the major bases. I had a feeling that's what men like Branko were doing while pretending to be Northern soldiers.

"Now begins the real work, men," Nadeja announced as she joined us. "I just asked one of my guards to gather the rest of your unit so we might get their input on this as well. It seems you have a rather specialized group of men under your command, Major Sorin."

"When I started out, I wanted to be the best. So I recruited the best my military had to offer, even if they didn't see it in themselves," Sorin shared with a shrug. "I will admit though, we truly became the best when we bonded as a family. Those men are my brothers and I would do anything for them, which they would do in return for me. It's easy to become the best when you trust those watching your back."

Surprising me, Sorin slapped me on the back and grabbed my shoulder companionably. "Lucian has some catching up to do, but he's finding his way just as they all did when I brought them into the unit. No family is without arguments or getting on each other's nerves. It's how the matter is resolved that's the most important."

The compliment hit me harder than I thought it would, but over the past two weeks, Sorin and I had been working to build trust and respect with each other. We both knew if we could figure it out and lead by example then the others would follow. Now getting ready to gear up for war, that trust was going to be put to the test. Even still, I had confidence we'd come out of this a stronger pack that no one could come between, giving us the honor of showing our people it could be done.

CHAPTER 61

Danella

The following week flew by as we worked with the council to train their men, strategize with their military leaders, and coordinate Oscad's involvement. It was like watching them assemble a massive puzzle of people, placing each piece where they would be most effective.

During the day, I trained with all the other soldiers building on the foundation my guys had started. This was it, and I needed to absorb everything I could to ensure I would be an asset. Hand-to-hand training was the hardest, not because I couldn't pick up the moves, but because I wasn't allowed to spar with anyone that wasn't part of my pack. The first day I ended up with a black eye, not moving fast enough to dodge the hit, and I thought Lucian and Victor were going to kill the poor man. After some incredibly heated words between the instructor and my guys, it was determined I could do everything that didn't involve another person.

That didn't mean I was off the hook. Victor and Sorin made sure I had early morning training with them before I met up with the rest. In a way, getting such one-on-one time with an instructor was an advantage, and I progressed quickly enough. Shooting became easy as I gained more confidence with my gun, moving through an obstacle course to give more real-situation experience.

With the guys focusing on strategy and plotting, I didn't get to see them as much, so I was thankful for the purpose training gave me.

Every night we always made sure to have dinner together as we did back on base. The council provided us with a house to use during our time here, giving us a space to call our own for the time being. It was the first time since we bonded that I felt like a real family living under the same roof. I rotated which room and guys I slept with at night since we couldn't all be together. It's not that I didn't love how we spent time as a pack, but it was nice to get some time to focus on one or two of them at a time. For all we've experienced together, we were still learning about each other on a deeper level. This was something we genuinely needed before the battle began. For once it started, there wouldn't be time for relaxed, intimate moments. So we indulged while we could.

"Dani-girl," Sorin whispered as he ran his fingers over the naked skin of my back. "It's time. We head out in an hour."

Groaning, I turned to look at him. "You have to be kidding me. I feel like I just fell asleep two seconds ago."

"I waited as long as I could so you could get a full five hours of sleep," he said with a smirk. "I'll admit I might have gotten a little carried away last night."

"A *little*?" I squeaked.

Leaning down, he caught my pouting lips in a fierce kiss. "What can I say, you're just irresistible, and who knows when any of us will have enough time to get that many orgasms out of you."

"No one should get ten orgasms on a regular basis. It would fry their brain," I muttered, tossing back the covers. "If I'm too fucking sore to walk all day, I'm going to tell everyone it's your fault."

"Sorry to be the one to tell you this, but a threat like that isn't a deterrent," Victor commented from the doorway. "In fact, I would fucking love for you to tell everyone what we managed to get out of you last night."

"We know the neighbors are well aware of what happened in this room last night," Lucian chuckled. "Gotta say, those were some rather inventive moves."

"Right, I read about them in a book once and thought it would be interesting to see if you could really pull it off," Victor shared with a giant grin on his face. "Let's go, Little Spark. We have coffee and breakfast waiting for you. If you don't eat it in the next ten minutes, you're gonna be waiting until lunch."

"What? Sorin said I had an hour?" I argued, grabbing clothes and yanking them on.

"Oh, that's till we leave. There's still a shit ton to do, Dani-girl," Sorin corrected.

Tugging my shirt over my head, I glared at them. "I hate you all."

"Not what you said last night," Victor tossed over his shoulder as he left the room.

Finished getting dressed, I wandered into the kitchen where Cris was sitting at the table looking over various lists of supplies he was coordinating. The council appointed him the head medic for this whole thing since he was the best-trained person and had the skills. As I walked by, his arm shot out, pulling me to sit on his lap.

"You're not even going to say good morning?" he asked, giving me puppy dog eyes.

Smiling, I pressed a quick kiss to his lips. "You looked busy, I didn't want to disturb you."

"Sweetheart, I'm never too busy for you," he countered. "You need something from me, or you just want a hug, kiss, or my attention. You have it. All you need to do is ask, understand?"

I nodded, but he caught my chin and frowned.

"I'm gonna need you to say it, so I know you believe me," Cris instructed.

"If I need you for any reason, I will make sure to ask," I said, grinning at him. "This whole putting you in charge thing brings out the Alpha side of you. I'm not sure I'm convinced you're truly a Beta when you get all broody."

He leaned down and brushed his nose along mine. "Trust me, if I were really an Alpha, you'd know the second I knotted that perfect pussy of yours. Besides, just because I'm a Beta doesn't mean I need to be a passive person all the time. In fact, there is this Omega I know who can be incredibly bossy. It's so unlike any other sweet, demure Omega I've ever met," he teased, giving me a searing kiss that left me breathless.

"Hey now, she needs to eat. So you're gonna need to let her come up for air," Victor interjected. "Come on, Little Spark, I'm gonna have you sit over here so you don't get distracted."

Sliding off Cris' lap, I sat where Victor dragged out the chair and wasted no time in digging in. Today was going to be a long, hard day, and we all knew it. We needed to get out of the mountains and to the meeting point further West, where the Oscadians would await us. We'd stay the night there and head out before first light to the first Northern military base run by a heavy-hitting supporter of General Rasvan.

The impact of this first attack needed to be enough to draw the general's attention, forcing him to send his personal military out of Stalhold City. Once we got word from the spies already in place there that the majority of the soldiers were gone, our unit would break off and meet a second group of Oscadians who would help us take the city. The battle between the rebels and the bases that supported the General needed to continue as we made our way to the city keeping all the attention on them. It was not easy to hide hundreds of soldiers when there was no cover from nature or buildings. General Rasvan had it all removed to ensure that if there was an attack, he would immediately know about it. However, we planned to use that in hopes we could turn the citizens against their leader to protect themselves.

"Don't forget to chew, Wildflower," Petru reminded me as he dropped a kiss on my head.

Shooting him a thumbs up, I gulped down the last of my coffee, washing down the final bite of eggs. "No worries, I'm finished. Let me wash these things up, and we can head to whatever's next. Wait, do we need to do anything with the house? I know we've been on top of keeping everything tidy, although if all goes to plan, we won't be coming back here for a long, long time."

"It's fine, Dani," Lucian assured me. "I talked to Nadeja, and she already was planning on having someone come in and clean up after us. It would seem this house is one they use for guests like us that are only here for a time or between missions and things like that."

"Huh...well, that comes in handy," I commented as I pumped the handle for the water.

Once my dishes were clean and put away, we grabbed our packs with everything we owned and then headed out. It was kind of surreal to have planned and hoped for this day, and in the blink of an eye, we were off to end a war. First, we needed to start another war to make it happen, yet in the end it would be worth it.

Life was peaceful within the stronghold. People lived average lives gardening, tending to the animals, woodworking, and many other things most people took for granted. Even in the North, they had factories that put things together and spit them out to be sent off to war. Given those same factories also stole all the power from everyone else, but hey guns and bullets were still being made. There had been much speculation on why there was no power to the rest of the country and that was one of the main things Toma was going to work on when this was all over.

It was rather exciting now that we'd planned for the future and made our dreams a reality. The Summit council had brilliant ideas as well to help bridge the gap and repair things between the people and their leadership. No matter what we did, it would take time to gain any kind of trust with the people here in the North, let alone figure out what to do with the South. Sorin was confident that when he brought his father the ceasefire request to broker an end to the war, it would happen, no question. Everything in me wanted to believe that, yet the reality of what was ahead of us would be a long, slow road. The first time I heard that this could all take *months* to see the results we needed, I choked on my drink. Granted, I hadn't assumed it would be days, but months just made it seem impossible.

Shaking my head to clear the negative thought, I broke off from the guys to my training team. We'd all agreed that it would be best for me to be in the mix of soldiers for safety. We knew everyone, all eight hundred soldiers by name and sight, so no one could try to sneak into our ranks once we got this siege underway. The rebels used that tactic more times than any of them could count, though it also meant we knew what to look out for. My pack, alongside the three military leaders of the rebels, were coordinating this whole thing and they needed one less thing to worry about.

So I broached the idea of me staying with the soldiers during the day and joining them at night. Today was a trial run to see if everyone could handle it. My money was on either Lucian or Victor cracking under the fact they couldn't keep their eyes on me at all times. Even Petru had gotten more protective lately and didn't enjoy it when my team asked me to have a drink with them or hang out. Overall, it would be an interesting experiment I wasn't sure would work for long.

"COMPANY, *HALT*!" our section leader called. "You have thirty minutes to eat, piss, and rest before we continue on."

There was a collective sigh of relief through my whole unit as people sat right where they stood and grabbed food out of their packs. This was when my guys swooped in and plucked me from the group.

"Sorry, guys, but she's coming with us," Toma said when a few of the soldiers protested, blocking them from following. "I would kindly remind you that she's our bonded Omega, so don't get any ideas. If you'd like to fuck around and find out, then anyone of us would be happy to show you how terrible that idea is. Any takers?"

With some grumbling, those that stood returned to their spot and grabbed their food.

"Wildflower, what trouble could you possibly have gotten into to cause that reaction?" Petru asked as he carried me off to wherever the rest of our pack was.

"Nothing," I said adamantly. "Seriously, all we've done is talk and get to know one another. A few of them needed to get some stuff off their chest, not having anyone to listen to them. I suppose the fact that I can relate to them might have fostered an emotional connection, but it wasn't intentional."

Petru just cocked a brow at me. "Dani, haven't you realized the natural ability to bring people to your side? Trust me, if we could be born based on our personality and abilities, you would have most certainly been an Alpha. Every time I turn around, you're off recruiting people to the cause without even realizing it. At the beginning of the week, we had half as many men and women willing to fight with us. Then you were let loose to spend time training with them, and more came flooding in to be added to the list."

"Bullshit," I blurted. "There is no way that's true. If that were the case, then I would have had people all over that outpost backing me in how to treat Omegas fairly."

"That was before you opened yourself up to others," Toma pointed out. "When we first met you, there was a ten-foot wall of 'fuck off' wrapped around you. It's totally understandable. You had to do what was best to protect yourself. Now though, that wall is gone so you're letting people see your true self. The 'you' who is full of passion and hope, which everyone desperately needs."

I chewed on that thought as Petru set me down and took my hand in his. Toma took my other hand, lacing our fingers so he could stroke the back of my hand with his thumb. These two were acting like they hadn't seen me in days when it had been hours. Something told me the chances of me going back to my group were slim to none once lunch was over.

"What took you so long?" Victor demanded when he spotted us.

"Care to share what's got your dick in a knot there, Vicky?" I asked, pulling my hands free to cross my arms. I'd learned that when Victor got in these moods I needed to stand my ground and not let him get into caveman mode.

"My problem is that we now only have twenty minutes for you to eat," Victor informed me.

I frowned. "No, that's not it."

"Stop, don't you do that thing you do," he grumbled, wagging a finger at me.

Confused, I cocked my head in question, wondering if he would fill me in on what exactly it is he *thinks* I do.

Marching up to me, he grabbed my chin and forced me to gaze

up at him. "Little Spark, there are times when I don't want to have my emotions analyzed the way you have a habit of doing. However, you're, you so I'll be honest. I'm feeling insecure about meeting up with the Oscadians tonight. Out of all of us, I'm not bonded to you in any way, so they could take you from me."

"What are you talking about?" I shot back. "Why the fuck would they take me from you? I'm bonded to the rest of the men in this pack and you're a part of it. In Oscad, many packs from older generations have members not bonded to the pack's Omega. Some people don't fit together. It would be like saying if Cris and I never ended up lovers, does that make him any less part of the pack?"

This seemed to throw Victor off. "I thought it was a rule in Oscad that all members of the pack had to bond with the Omega?"

"That is the hope. It certainly makes family dynamics easier as well as increases the chances of having children. However, it's not something they can dictate by law," I explained. "Who told you that?"

"Councilman Filip mentioned I should be aware of the chance that there could be a problem," Victor muttered, rubbing the back of his neck.

"Why would you believe him about something like that when you could have just asked me?" I challenged him. "Did you think I wouldn't be honest with you?"

"No," he blurted, grabbing my shoulders. "Never that, Little Spark. It was more about the fact that I made you agree to the fact I wouldn't mark you, and then that very request might be the thing that makes me lose you."

"Then ask me to marry you," I threw out there, tossing my hands up in frustration. "If you want a bond between us that is recognized as an official union, that's your answer."

Never in my life did I think I would see Victor shocked to the point of being unable to move, let alone respond, but here it was before my eyes. Reaching up, I grabbed his face and pulled him down to me so I could kiss the life back into him. Instantly he responded by pulling me up to where I wrapped my legs around him. He kissed me breathless as if trying to steal the very breath from my body.

"Little Spark, have I told you how much I love you yet today?" Victor murmured against my lips.

I paused to think about it. "No, not today, I don't think..."

He playfully nipped my nose before kissing me again, then setting me down. "I love you and that idea, Little Spark, but I won't ask you now. Something like that deserves to be given some thought and planning because you deserve that from me."

"I wasn't expecting you to do it right here and now," I commented with a smile. "Do you feel better now?"

"Yes, and I promise that if I ever have a question or concern like that again, I'll address it right away with you. It was fucking stupid of me to believe someone who isn't even from Oscad. There isn't much I find myself insecure about, but you mean everything to me and I never expected to have such a person in my life," Victor shared, brushing the back of his fingers along my cheek. "Now let's get you food since there's only fifteen minutes left and I won't be able to relax at all if I don't see you eat enough."

"Such a worrywart," I teased but settled down between Lucian and Sorin, as Victor handed me my rations.

Lucian wrapped an arm around my waist and nuzzled into my hair as I ate. "Just in case you thought you'd be returning to your group after this, I'm telling you now that's not happening. You'll be with Cris or one of us if he's busy. However, none of us like this plan you came up with, My Heart."

I couldn't hide the grin at his words. "I fucking knew it. Damn, I seriously wish I had someone to bet against because I would have won so much money."

"If you knew we wouldn't like it, why suggest it?" Sorin inquired.

"Each of you has about ten different things to deal with at any given time, and I thought it would help if you didn't need to worry about what I was doing," I admitted. "Plus, it keeps me hidden in the crowd of people."

Sorin snorted at my answer and shook his head. "Dani-girl, if you think we'll ever stop worrying about you, then you don't understand Alphas at all. It doesn't matter if you're by my side or in my sights I'll always worry about your safety. I do appreciate the thought behind it, however. It was sweet of you, misguided, yet sweet."

"Then how the hell are we going to handle when the real fighting starts?" I questioned. "Each of you needs to be in a different spot to lead the people they put you in charge of."

"Right now, we feel the best choice to have you with Petru and the sniper team. You're an excellent shot and getting better, so you'll be able to help, but we'll know you're safe," Lucian answered.

Swallowing the final bite of my food, I frowned. "Doesn't it seem unfair that I'm getting placed out of harm's way, yet we're asking everyone else to put their lives on the line?"

"The truth of it all is that war is not fair," Lucian admitted. "Everything about war is getting the advantage over the person you're going up against. While we plan to do everything in our power to minimize the death toll in this, there will be losses on both sides. In the end, some people will choose to die for the belief that General Rasvan is right and we must wipe out the South. People who have taken that truth to heart will never change, no matter what we do to prove them wrong. They become blinded by hate, prejudice, and the lies they've been told at such a young age. Those will be the people who choose to die rather than ever let us change things."

"On the other hand, there will be those who know what's happening is wrong and will be willing to surrender," Petru pointed out. "There are always two groups—those who believe and fight for that truth. Then there is the other, those who had no choice in the matter and fight to live, knowing the alternative is to die as a traitor. It's for those people we will always offer the option to lay down their weapon and surrender. Anyone who does will be spared, and fate willing, they will give us a chance to prove there is another way."

That made me feel mildly better, yet I didn't know how to accept that I would be sheltered from this battle I asked them to fight in. It was a problem that I mulled over for the rest of the day as we marched to the meeting point and one I didn't know if there was a solution to. Maybe I was trying to find fairness in something that, at its core, was genuinely unfair. However, I wouldn't be able to live with myself if I didn't at least try.

WE ARRIVED at the meeting point before the Oscadians. This provided a little time to set up camp for the night while the sun was setting and we had light to see by. The handy part of having such a large group is we had wagons that carried the larger supplies such as tents, extra supplies, and larger rations for making evening meals. Part of our training had been making this whole process efficient and we had the whole camp set up in no time with a fire burning for the cooks to start the meal.

It was easy to tell when the Oscadians arrived since they had vehicles to transport some of their men and all the supplies. A fleet of military vehicles arrived first, with soldiers spilling out of them who immediately started to set up camp. The difference between our two camps was drastic since they had a government funding their efforts, providing the best for their military. It was one of the things Lucian, Sorin, and the council haggled over with Marius and his military leaders. While the rebels had done remarkably well with what they had to work with, they lacked equipment and supplies that would be standard to any established military.

After countless rounds of negotiations, Oscad agreed to help even out the differences between the two groups. They would send updated communication equipment along with additional vehicles to help with our supplies. We needed to be able to move from base to base more efficiently to keep up the pressure and prove we would be a real threat to the General. Of course, there would still be tons of soldiers walking, but having a team that could go ahead to get things in place would make this more efficient. Then those who've walked all day can get a hot meal and rest right away keeping everyone at peak performance level.

When my guys noticed a group of men dressed in tan camouflage military uniforms heading our way, they rose to meet them. Tired as I was, I shot to my feet and headed after them, not willing to miss out on talking to someone face-to-face from Oscad.

Cris motioned for me to stick with him when I caught up and leaned down to whisper. "Let them feel each other out and don't intervene no matter what happens. This is one of those moments that make us roll our eyes at Alphas, but once this is out of the way everything will go much smoother."

"So, in other words, a pissing contest," I muttered. Cris just smiled and gave an affirmative wink as we reached the other group.

"Damn, I'm not even going to question that you're Lucian because you look an awful lot like your brother." The leader of the group said with an easy smile and relaxed posture as he extended a hand to Lucian. "Names Rick, we've spoken a few times on the phone, but it's nice to finally meet you face-to-face."

"You guessed correctly," Lucian said as he took the man's hand. "It's been ages since I've seen Savo so I'll have to take your word for it but can't say I'm surprised."

"Well, you'll get the chance to see him again with the second team. He asked to be part of this. Said he owed it to you and his people to make up for abandoning them," Rick shared, then turned to the side so we could see the other men more clearly. "Anyway, let me introduce you to my pack and fellow leaders of this battalion: Senior Officers Anson, Emmett, Quade, and Karston. If there are any issues or you need something, you can come to us, and we'll deal with the matter. I don't tolerate any bullshit from my men, and I expect them to act right no matter what setting we're in."

"We'll make sure to do that," Sorin assured, then introduced us all to Rick and his pack. After an exchange of handshakes, things seemed to be smooth sailing between the two groups.

"I'd really like it if we could meet with all the leaders tonight to go over the plan once more. There is always a difference in things when it happens in person, and it's my goal that there will be zero tension between all of us. That shit trickles downhill and none of us can afford to have that," Rick requested.

"Couldn't agree more," Victor said with a nod of approval. "Come on, dinner is about to be done, and we can all talk over a meal. Nothing says manly bonding than planning war over food."

Everyone chuckled at that as Victor led the way back to our camp. The rest of the night was spent rehashing every detail of this plan three times over in monotonous detail that it put me to sleep. I woke up cradled in Sorin's arms as he carried me back to our tent. We'd been given one large enough for all of us to fit so we didn't have to split up.

"Go back to sleep, love. This will be the last night of peaceful sleep until this is over," Sorin whispered, pressing a kiss to my forehead.

Taking him at his word, I snuggled closer to him and let my eyes fall shut to dream of what the world would be like after we won.

CHAPTER 62

Danella

No one warned me about the solemn tone the entire army would have when we arrived at camp. It had taken the whole day to get to our destination. Things happened rather quickly as we ate and were sent right to bed. It worked out since we couldn't risk any fires alerting the base to our presence, so there wasn't much reason to stay up. The attack would commence before dawn, hitting them when they least expected it. Everyone believed it would be a fairly straightforward attack, since there was no reason for them to even consider they were at risk.

This particular base was a training facility that was in the middle of Northern Asturg. Once we took this base, it would allow us to fan out in both directions and hit the smaller bases nearby. With the addition of the Oscadian soldiers, we had roughly three thousand men at our disposal. While it was still a small group compared to the Northern Army, it was far more than we ever thought we'd find on our own. The hope was that those who surrendered at each fight would be willing to join the cause, adding to our numbers as we went along. If this was achieved, we'd be able to split off and attack more aggressively and swiftly. After this battle, we'd know if the plan was effective or not.

As we geared up, the whole camp was silent as everyone focused on the task ahead of us. I tugged my cap down over my hair, ensuring it fit snuggly as I stepped out of the tent. The air was crisp, but we all knew it would get hotter as the sun came up. Dressed in my Southern uniform with my newly assigned rifle slung over my shoulder, I headed for where the sniper team was to meet up. We'd be heading out in advance of the rest to place ourselves in the best position to offer support.

This base had high metal walls that had been constructed many years ago. According to Lucian, this used to be the main base the Northern Army operated out of. Two generals ago, things were shifted to Stalhold City as the hub of army operations. Now it was the most extensive training camp, and taking this first would cripple General Rasvan's ability to send out new troops. There were two other training camps, but they were half the size and didn't have veteran instructors like this one. Making this our first target would get the attention we needed instantly.

Thanks to Lucian's insight and having been trained at this camp, he knew the layout and the weak points. There was a section of the wall that looked solid from the outside, but on the inside, you could see the damage done by an attack long ago that's only gotten worse over time. If we blasted it right, we'd be able to gain entry with no problem. We just had to get our men close enough to set the charges. Which was where we snipers came into play. We'd be positioned in the best places to pick off anyone who might try to shoot them from the top of the wall or the watch posts.

Aiding us was that this part of Northern Asturg was hilly and still managed to keep scruffy tall grasses that we could use for cover. The other advantage of doing this before the sun even touched the horizon was that with everyone wearing all black for this operation, no one would spot us since they didn't have stable enough power to run the floodlights. Lucian explained they had a generator but wouldn't use it until they realized they were under attack, giving us enough time to set the charges. I tried not to think about the fact that Victor would be leading that team, but it gave me all the more reason to be watching his back through my scope.

"Attention," Petru ordered, as he walked up.

Instantly everyone stood straight and turned to face where he stood with Karston next to him.

"If you haven't already been introduced, this is Senior Officer Karston of the Oscadian Military. He will be adding ten other men to this group, and I expect you to treat them with the same respect you do each other. We are fighting for freedom, peace, and the end of this pointless war. Oscad has stepped up to be an ally, assisting us in this effort when they have no reason to. To me, that is a show of true friendship and standing behind their desire to be an ally. I hope this doesn't need to be said, but I will make it perfectly clear anyway. If Senior Officer Karston or any of the other four leaders of the Oscadian Military give you an order, you listen. The same applies to their people, so I don't want to hear any bullshit about fair play," Petru informed, his tone brokering no questions. "Have I made myself clear?"

"Yes, sir," everyone said in unison.

"Do you have any questions for either of us?" Karston asked, hands clasped behind his back and a commanding energy coming off of him. When everyone stayed silent, the Alpha nodded and whistled over his shoulder.

The ten men Petru mentioned jogged over to join us and fell in line standing at attention. One thing I noticed about the Oscadian Military is they ran a tight ship, and their soldiers could move seamlessly as a unit. I thought the Southern Military had a good grip on this type of thing, but seeing them made me glad I wasn't forced to be at their level. There was no question if these men would listen to orders or not. While they were on personal time, it was like a switch was flipped and they became ordinary people. They weren't robots, interacting without emotion, but there was such a dramatic shift in attitude and demeanor when they were called to attention. It was impressive and terrifying at the same time.

"Unit Sigma, you are now under the direct order of Staff Sergeant Petru. He is your commanding officer and what he says is law," Karston stated, then turned to Petru. "Good luck, and may your bullets shoot true."

"Same to you and your men. May the fates be on our side,"

Petru responded. Both men saluted each other before Karston turned and left, heading back to the men he'd be leading. "All right, let's move out."

The Oscad soldiers fell into their formation of three across stacked one after the other. Since we didn't really have a specific formation, we fell into theirs. When we got close enough to see the looming metal walls in the moonlight, Petru signaled for us to spread out. Each of us was to split off into groups of two or three and cover half the base, with a heavier concentration on the area we'd be blasting. As was agreed upon with my guys, I headed off with Petru and one of the Oscadian soldiers. Not taking the time for introductions, I glanced at the patch on his uniform. His name was Byres. However, I was unsure if that was a first or last name. Scouting out the perfect location was a much more challenging task than I would have imagined. We would stop to check the wind, temperature, and line of sight, ensuring that when we were on our stomachs, nothing wouldn't be blocking our target. It took a few tries, but we found the optimal spot and hunkered down. A click came over the comms, sporadically followed by nine more, letting us know everyone had found their mark and were ready to go.

Raising a hand to his neck, Petru activated his comms. "Base camp, this is eagle eye. We are in position and ready for infiltration."

"Copy that, eagle eye. Any unusual movement from the base?"

Petru took a moment to scan the area with a set of night-vision binoculars. "That's a negative. I see what we expected, one person at each lookout and no one walking the wall."

"Understood. We are sending in the blast unit now. Your orders are to take out the watch and provide cover if needed to the blast team."

"Roger that, base camp, eagle eye out," Petru said before switching channels and giving a double click as a warning before speaking. "Sniper team, they are sending in the blast team and we've been given a go on removing the night watch. Provide cover where needed. Click to confirm only." Once more, nine clicks could be heard in response.

To my surprise, the Oscadian soldier wasn't a sniper but a spotter as he pulled out this odd-looking scope set on a tripod.

"Target spotted, northwest corner of watch platform," Byres informed Petru.

Fascinated, I watched as Petru adjusted. Curious, I followed along and spotted the man right away.

"Range five hundred yards and slight right to left wind," Byres said as he looked from his scope to a handheld device that apparently was tracking the wind. Petru made a few adjustments to the dials on his rifle that I still was learning to use and gave a grunt of approval.

"Spotters up," Byres called.

"Ready," Petru answered.

"Send it."

With those two words, I heard the crack of the rifle and watched as Petru's bullet hit the mark. The surprised look on the soldier's face before he dropped made me a little sick to my stomach, but I knew this was part of the deal. War was awful, but a necessary evil to stop the tyranny that would only continue if we did nothing.

"Target one down," Petru said into the comms.

"Target three down."

"Target two down."

"Final target down. Night watch is removed."

Just like that, in a matter of two minutes, we'd officially waged war on the Northern Army.

"Ground leaders, this is eagle eye, you're clear," Petru updated Rick and Lucian, who were in charge of coordinating the leading group of soldiers.

There were two clicks in response followed by three more, signaling everyone to go radio silent. This was the part that I knew I was going to struggle with. Victor and his crew of five men would sneak up to the wall, plant the explosives, set the timer, and book it out of there before it blasted. At this point, the base would be flooded with our people, who would then search every single building for two men—Colonel Papez and Colonel Shaban. These two men had been loyal to General Rasvan throughout his whole time leading the Army. As thanks, they were given the cushy job of running the training camp. This made them doubly essential to remove from the board of players the General could use against us. Like pulling teeth out of the lion's mouth to make him less lethal. It would be dangerous work, but it would be worth it at the end when General Rasvan realized he had no more bite to threaten us with.

Keeping my eyes fixated on the spot Victor and his team were aiming for was the only reason I spotted them. They moved low and quick, getting to the wall with no one the wiser. Shifting my attention away from them, I scanned the wall, ensuring no one went up to check on one of the watchmen to find them dead. Even though I knew it was coming, the blast from the explosives had me flinching. Directing my scope to the spot, I saw a gaping hole large enough for three people to walk through. I hadn't expected it to be so large, but something smaller would have made it easier for them to pick us off as we entered.

A shrill alarm sounded through the early morning stillness alerting everyone within the base that they were under attack. Soldiers appeared on the wall. Only I didn't shoot. They weren't threatening our people yet, and we'd been instructed to keep casualties to a minimum where we could. Someone shouted and pointed, then raised their gun to shoot. Taking a deep breath, I let it out slowly and pulled the trigger. My shot went a little high and hit him in the shoulder, but another bullet struck him in the chest.

"West section of the wall looks like they have a machine gun they're setting up." Byres alerted us.

Rotating to the spot he was talking about, I saw five men gathered around a large weapon. I took out one hitting him in the back and as the fates would have it, he'd been holding the gun. He dropped like a sack of potatoes freeing up the line of sight to the man beside him. Once I took that man out, Petru had already dealt with the other three.

"Eagle eye, once we're in, pack it up and bring your team in," Lucian ordered.

That translated to, keep covering us until we have all our troops in the base, then join the fight. As much as they wanted to keep me out of the fray, there was no way that could be accomplished the entire time. What they could do was make sure I was part of the team who went in last. The thinking was they'd have things well in hand by the time we made it to the base.

"Copy that, ground leader," Petru responded, as he continued to sweep his gun back and forth keeping an eye on things.

I pushed up on my arms to better see our people rushing the entrance we made. Shouts rose as the alarm was shut off, with the sound of gunfire reverberating through the air. Suddenly light flooded the surrounding area outside the wall exposing our men hidden in the grasses waiting to enter the hole.

"Take out the lights," Petru ordered.

Dropping to my stomach, I zeroed in on one of the spotlights and pulled the trigger. The thing exploded in a flurry of sparks and shouting. Shifting my sight down, I took out two more men struggling to get the second light to work. I paused, knowing I was out of ammo and switched out magazines for a full one. Back in the game, I scanned the wall now that it was dark on the outside. The buildings within the base were lit up, but we couldn't do much with that.

"Sniper team, regroup. We're going in," Petru instructed as he sat back on his heels, packing away the items he'd been using. "Come on, Wildflower. It's time for us to make sure the General hears us loud and clear."

Slinging my rifle over my shoulder, I followed after the two men as we jogged to the meeting point. It took a few minutes once we reached it for the other teams to join us, then we were off. Handguns at the ready, we weaved our way over the rocky terrain to the opening. The sound of panicked screaming was the first thing that hit me, followed by people shouting orders and gunfire.

Petru grabbed my arm and spun me to look at him. "You stay right by my side, do you hear me? No wandering off or needlessly putting yourself in a situation. I want to feel you right at my back the whole time, otherwise, you'll get one of us hurt or killed."

"I understand. I'll be your perfect shadow," I answered.

We hadn't even stepped foot inside the base yet, and I could feel the chaotic energy flowing out of the place. Nothing could prepare anyone for this because there was no way to recreate the feeling of sheer panic and desperation. This was war, and it was kill or be killed, and I wasn't looking to die today. Petru studied my face a second longer then nodded, and away we went.

~

THE WHOLE EXPERIENCE was a blur that had me relying on my training and instinct. People were everywhere, running, screaming, crashing into you; only to shove you out of the way so they could keep going. Others dropped to their knees, tossed their guns away, and begged for mercy. They were grabbed, tied up, and brought to the large open training area. I couldn't tell you how long the whole thing took. It felt like hours, yet it seemed to be over in a flash. The sweat on my brow and the empty gun in my hands told me another story. Quickly I switched out for a fresh round of ammo and used my sleeve to wipe the sweat from my face.

Slightly bewildered, I almost tripped over a body on the ground, but Petru caught me. "Careful, Wildflower. I know this is a lot. It's almost over, so just hang in there."

Everything seemed to slow down as I saw a woman step out from behind a building, gun raised and aimed right at Petru, whose back was turned. With a strength and speed I didn't know I had, I stuck my leg out and shoved Petru backwards, sending him crashing to the ground. The moment he was in motion, falling backwards, I let off two shots as I saw the muzzle flash from her gun. My aim was true; both hit her right in the chest, making her jerk back with wide, frightened eyes. She tried to shoot again, but I fired another bullet that nailed her right between the eyes.

With that hit, she collapsed and the world seemed to speed up again. Suddenly Victor was in my face grabbing my shoulders and yelling at me. My adrenaline was still coursing through my body, making it hard to focus on his words. It felt like I was still in slow motion as everything else moved normally. Then everything came flooding back, and I screamed as Victor's grip on my arm tightened.

"Dani, what's wrong?" Victor demanded, releasing his hold on me. Then we both noticed the blood on his right hand. Yanking off the outer layer of my uniform revealed a gash on the outside of my biceps. "You were fucking *shot.*"

Hearing his words kicked my brain back into gear. "Petru," I blurted.

Twisting out of the hold, I found the man in question picking himself up off the ground. He looked unharmed, but the pissed-off expression had me questioning that. "Are you okay?"

"Am I okay?" Petru scoffed, running his hands through his hair. "Goddamn it, Danella, didn't I specifically tell you not to do anything that would put you in danger?"

"She was going to shoot you," I shot back. "Your back was turned. There was no way you'd have gotten out of the way in time."

"Guys, we need to move," Victor cut in. "I promise I'll spank her properly only after we're not sitting ducks. This section hasn't been cleared yet."

Before I could protest, Victor scooped me up and charged off towards the training field I could see in the distance. When we arrived, Rick and Emmett were dumping two bodies where all the captured soldiers could see them. My guess was they were the two colonels we'd been looking for, based on their uniforms and how much older they were.

"Listen up!" Rick bellowed. "We have an offer to make all of you, one that includes you being able to see the rest of this day."

"Why the fuck should we listen to rebel scum like you," a man shouted.

The crowd of soldiers all started yelling in agreement, hurling insults and threats. Just when I thought they might try to rise up against us, even with their hands tied behind their backs, Lucian arrived. He looked regal, wearing all black with blood splatter on his face, scars in full view, and his hair pulled back. He stepped over the two dead bodies of his father's supporters, and silence fell over the base.

"Do you all know who I am?" Lucian questioned. A majority nodded or murmured their answer, while a few looked confused at the response of the others. "For those of you who might not know me, I'm Lucian Bakal, heir to the Northern territory. I'm also the one who coordinated and executed this attack. That being said, if you're still unsure as to why you should listen the fuck up, then there isn't much hope for you surviving long in this world."

Lucian took a moment to scan the crowd before him. I didn't have a clue what he was looking for, although whatever it was he seemed satisfied.

"Now that I have your full attention, I'd like to offer you an alternative to becoming a casualty of war. It's been brought to my attention that my father is trying to kill me, removing me from being his heir. My answer to that is I will systematically destroy his foundation and, ultimately, him as well. Once I'm in power, I aim to end this war with the South. It's gone on long enough and all it's doing is killing us as a nation. Soon there will be nothing left to fight over but the dust under our feet," Lucian said as he grabbed a handful of dirt and let it slide through his fingers. "What if I told you there was another way? Would you be willing to fight for the chance to be free?"

No one spoke up for a moment then a man shot to his feet and spat. "You're nothing but a traitor, turning your back on your people by aligning yourself with the rebels."

"So you would rather starve to save your pride?" Lucian shot back. "Soon, there will be no food, no medicine, no supplies to keep fighting this war. Already we've been sent to the dark ages as they pull all the power we have to run the factories to make the weapons. Women are raped, children taken from their mothers and raised in group homes by people who fill their minds with lies. We have no hope of winning this war, but I can save you all if you let me."

"What do you want from us?" a woman shouted.

Lucian swept out his hands in a pleading gesture. "Stand up for yourselves. Stop fighting to profit someone who doesn't give a shit about you. Instead, join me in taking back our country, breathing life back into it, and finding a real life worth living. No more war, bloodshed, or death looming all around us. There can be hope once more in this place, the chance to dream of a better life where you can die from old age instead of on the battlefield. If you are sick to fucking death of clawing your way through life, join me in making a change."

Slowly one by one, people stood and walked forward. Then more popped up until there were only about a hundred people left still kneeling. Those who refused the offer would be locked away for the day, and if they still held their allegiance to the General, they would be put to death. It was brutal and something I wished didn't have to happen, but if we left them alive, they would only become enemies we'd have to kill later on. Better to deal with things now than to let the disease fester and spread.

As for those who chose to take a stand, they would be placed in one of the dorms under surveillance and processed by Rick and his fellow pack members. We all agreed it was best for those outside of the situation to give an honest judgment of the person. If they agreed the person was sincere and would be willing to fight, they'd be added to the mix of other units. That way, we could keep an eye on them and they would be the minority, for now at least.

"Time to face the music, Little Spark. We're gonna have you looked at by Cris," Victor said as we headed into the infirmary.

It took two seconds for Cris to spot us, then dropped what he was doing. "Why is she bleeding?"

"Seems our girl got herself shot, fucking shot, Cris," Victor explained.

Cris took my arm and examined the wound, turning it this way and that without touching the wound, for which I was grateful. The thing throbbed with a dull ache and was getting worse the more I thought about it.

"Bring her over here," Cris directed. "Fortunately, it's just a graze. Still, it will need to be cleaned and stitched up."

"Shot is shot, Cris," Victor muttered, setting me down on an exam table.

Ignoring the man, Cris gathered what he needed and cleaned up the wound. I hissed as he poured something over it that fizzed like crazy. Once he was sure it was clean, he put a topical numbing cream over it and had me wait a few minutes while he tended to other patients. It wasn't long before the other three stormed into the infirmary, fuming.

"Danella," Lucian said through clenched teeth. "What the hell happened?"

"Guys, this really isn't that big of a deal," I argued. "I'm not in any real danger, it just needs a few stitches and I'm good to return to helping."

"The fuck you are," Sorin snapped. "How did you get shot, and don't you even think about downplaying this because Tru will tell me the whole story."

I blew out a frustrated breath and explained the whole situation in enough detail to make them happy. None of them said anything right away as Cris returned to stitch me up. Ten stitches later, I was bandaged up and out the door so they could make room for those more severely injured. The guys didn't lock me away in some room, but I was always glued to one of their sides, unable to lift even a finger to help.

Thankfully overall, our injured soldiers were few, and casualties had been minor. It was also determined that we would be staying at this base for the next two or three days, allowing us to get things under control with the new additions. Not every battle would go this smoothly, but this one was the most important because it would send a message loud and clear to the General. The war for the North had just begun, but in essence it had been a success. Now it was down to a battle of wills. How long would it take for General Rasvan to view us as a big enough threat that he would send his personal militia to deal with us? Only time would tell, and we were in this for the long haul—was he?

ONE MONTH

LATER....

CHAPTER 63
Danella

War was exhausting.

It forces you to give a hundred percent every day all day long. Since that first battle, we've taken out four other bases and one more training camp, leaving the General with one left. Our plan to recruit along the way has been the most miraculous part of all this. As we took over bases with established soldiers, convincing them to join us was easier. They were so sick and tired of starving, day in and day out, and fearing a simple scratch might get infected and they die a horrible death. We didn't have to convince them how shit their life was— they were *well* aware of it.

The influx of soldiers took some to adjust, since we now had more mouths to feed. We took all the supplies from the bases, meager as they were, and that helped to balance things slightly. Oscad willingly supplied rations and other supplies we needed, but Lucian and Sorin wanted to do that as minimally as possible. They were thankful for the assistance but didn't want to abuse the newly forged alliance when we didn't have much to offer in return. Marius explained it was an investment in the future and had no problem helping however he could. Even still, the pride of Asturg men was something that couldn't be changed and I believe that with Savo's help, everyone agreed it would be food assistance only for the time being.

Out of the twenty bases and outposts that covered Northern Asturg, we now controlled five at the country's center. Lucian had plotted this on purpose since it would force the General to send his men, but they would have to travel for two or three days to get from Stalhold City to us. That way when we took the secondary group of soldiers Oscad was sending, they couldn't return to fight in time, leaving the city defenseless. There's been no word yet if the General has deployed them, but I believe once word of the second training camp we took yesterday will seal the deal.

"Dani-girl, take a break and come eat something," Sorin urged from the doorway to the infirmary.

I shifted in my chair, which was placed next to the bed where a very pregnant Omega was resting. This training camp had a breeding house, and two of the women were pregnant. Except this poor girl had gotten sick. No one knew what caused it, but she had an extremely high fever and was spotting. Cris and I worked all night long to get the fever to break and now she was finally resting peacefully. We'd needed someone to watch over her, so I volunteered knowing if she woke she'd feel better seeing a woman by her side.

"I can't leave, not until she wakes up," I whispered.

Sorin's gaze softened at my words. "I figured you'd say that, so I asked Tiffany if she would sit with her while you took a break." He stepped to the side, revealing the woman behind him.

Tiffany was a Beta that we'd rescued from a breeder house on one of the other bases. She wanted nothing more than to learn to fight and protect herself. So she stayed with us instead of heading to the refuge camp Oscad set up for women such as herself. To see a woman like her bound and determined to take back her life was inspiring and it became something we bonded over.

"Go on, girl, I got this," Tiffany assured me as she rested a hand on my shoulder. "I know right where to find you or Cris if anything happens. You won't be of any help to anyone if you don't get some sleep or eat something."

Letting out a sigh, I gave in. Tiffany pulled me to my feet proving just how tired I actually was. Glancing back at the woman whose name no one knew, since she didn't speak a word, or so the other girls told us. Her heart-shaped face was finally relaxed as she rested. I'd instantly become attached to her because of how young she was, reminding me of Tori when she first arrived at the Care Center. Everything in me wanted to protect and keep her safe from the world that saw her as nothing but a breeder. People like her drove me to keep fighting this war even if I was bone-deep tired and pushing myself to the max. It would be worth it when I knew places like breeding houses would never exist again.

Sorin took my hand and led me down the hall and out into the midday sunshine. The hot season was officially upon us and it was brutal for everyone as we marched from location to location. Thankfully Oscad provided special additives to help combat dehydration and heat stroke. I turned to head for the mess hall, only Sorin just shook his head and tugged me to follow him into another building up a flight of stairs. Eventually, we ended up in what looked like an officer's quarters that reminded me a lot of Lucian's apartment above the supply depot. The rest of the guys were also there with a huge wooden basin that had steaming water in it.

"Is that a bath?" I questioned.

"Damn, it's been so long she doesn't even remember what a bath is," Victor teased, for which I flipped him off, making him smile. "Ah, so she's not tired enough to have lost her sass. Good to know. Now get naked and hop in."

Too tired to argue, I stripped off my uniform, cursing that it was all black and with Toma's help climbed into the bath. I let out a little whine of pleasure as I sank into the water. "Oh god, this is amazing."

"We figured you could use a little pampering," Toma mentioned as he soaped up a cloth and started to wash my arm. "War doesn't give many opportunities for us to dote on you like Omegas need, although we're trying our best to find ways to make that happen. So lay back, relax, and leave this to us."

They didn't have to tell me twice. Within minutes I was happily dozing as Victor washed my hair and Toma scrubbed every inch of my sore, tired body. When they were both done, Cris massaged a balm with a wonderful cooling effect that helped my sore muscles ache a little less. It would come as no surprise that I fell asleep in the middle of that. When I woke up, Lucian and Sorin were wrapped around me and the sky was dark. My stomach growled, letting me know that was the reason I'd awoken.

Crawling out from between the two, they didn't ever stir, indicating they were just as tired as I was. I pulled on a clean uniform and stepped out of the bedroom into the living room kitchen area. Searching through the cabinets, not seeing any food, I knew the mess hall would have some for those who were on watch duty. Jotting down a note, I left it on the counter and headed downstairs. As I crossed the open space between the officers building to the mess hall, a hand clamped over my mouth and I was dragged into the shadows.

The acrid scent of musky cologne told me it wasn't one of my guys playing a joke on me. Once this realization occurred I reacted, thrashing around, kicking, and even nailing the man in the gut with my elbow. There was a grunt of pain from my attacker before I was slammed into a wall and pinned there with his body. Then he shoved a cloth in my mouth to keep me quiet and free his hands.

"You fucking whore, how dare you attack me," the man snarled.

There was something familiar about his voice, but I couldn't quite place how I knew it.

"Do you have any idea what you've done? How you've ruined my life, you fucking bitch," he spat, his stench coating my mouth and nose making me want to gag. Never had I experienced an Alpha who affected me in such a way, yet it was a visceral disgust that had every hair on my body standing on end. "Since you've fucked me over so badly, I think I'm going to do the same to you. I should get something out of this, right?"

Terror shot through me, and I reached out desperately to any of my guys through our bond. As the man started to pull at my clothes, I tried to scream and fight, never allowing myself to give up. I wouldn't be a victim again. I'd become a soldier, a damn good one who was almost as good a shot as Petru.

"What the fuck do you think you're doing to my woman," Cris roared, followed by the sound of fist hitting flesh, and I was freed.

Yanking out the cloth, I turned to see who'd attacked me to find Cris' father sprawled out on the ground. Confusion had me faltering in my plan to beat the shit out of the person who dared lay a hand on me.

"Dad?" Cris said in disbelief, his gun still trained on the man. "What the fuck are you doing here, and what the hell are you attacking Dani for?"

"It's your fault. I should have killed you the moment you found out what I really was. Then none of this would have happened because you never would have saved her," his father spluttered, eyes wild.

Cris lowered his gun, brows creased. "What nonsense are you saying? What does Dani have to do with me finding out you're from the North?"

"You truly are an idiot, aren't you?" He laughed, tossing back his head. "God, I should never have let your mother raise you. Maybe you would have been more useful to me rather than destroying everything. The General thinks I'm to blame for letting all this happen. That I should have known my own son would band together with that bastard son of his and start a war within their own country. I got those men passed the border to kill that son of a bitch, and then I find out you're the ones who took them out, leaving me a mess to clean up."

"Actually," I cut in. "I'm the one who shot those Northern soldiers."

He turned his attention to me, snarling as he got to his feet, charging at me. However, Colonel Nems didn't get very far as the sound of a gun going off next to me splintered through the night. The pathetic man before me jerked and fell to his knees, clutching his chest. Blood began to seep through his fingers and then out of his mouth as he turned to stare at his son.

"What have you done?" he wheezed.

"What I should've done the moment I found out you didn't give a shit about me or my mother. This is what it looks like to protect those you love," Cris answered as he stepped up to pull me behind him. "She is my lover and my family, who I promised to protect with my life. Obviously a concept you'd never understand since you only think about yourself."

"You have no idea who you're going up against. General Rasvan won't forgive this, and he'll do everything in his power to crush you like the bugs you are," his father said, spitting a wad of blood at Cris' feet.

Unfazed, Cris squatted down and locked eyes with his father. "Good, that's exactly what we wanted. Let the coward hiding in his city come find us. Maybe then he'll fight us like a man." Finished with what he wanted to say, Cris rose and took my hand. "Let's go. He doesn't deserve to have anyone around to see him die."

"Wait," I said, digging my heels in. "I have a question for him."

Cris nodded but didn't let go of my hand as I faced his father. "Tell me, are you the one who gave the order to attack the outpost?"

"My first failure in twenty years," he admitted. "Then I tried to fix it, except some fucking breeder had to keep getting in my way, always slipping through my fingers. I knew if I could get a hold of you, I'd have Lucian by the balls. Let me guess, that old hag tipped you off about me, didn't she? I knew I should have killed her, but I didn't think she'd survive those wounds at her age long enough to say shit."

Anger surged through me, and I yanked out of Cris' hold and slammed my fist as hard as I could into the bastard's face. Once, twice, three times until he fell to the ground. "That old hag was more of a man than you could ever be. In fact, you're not even worth insulting like a man, you fucking cunt."

Finished, I grabbed Cris' hand and marched back out into the main section of the base just as two night watchmen ran up to us.

"We heard shots fired?" one asked, panting.

"False alarm. It was just a big fucking rat that scared me," I explained.

"Did you kill it? I fucking hate rats," the other soldier muttered.

"Yeah, it's dead," Cris assured him. "We'll be heading to the mess hall just so you know someone's there now that we startled you."

They gave their thanks and continued on their patrol, leaving Cris and me alone. I turned to look at him reaching out through our bond to see how he felt, but the connection was blocked. He pulled me into a hug and buried his face in my neck. "I can't face this right now. Let me have tonight to myself, and we'll talk about it with everyone in the morning, okay? Right now I just want to make sure you get something to eat, then head back and curl you up in my arms, so I know the images playing in my head aren't true."

"Okay," I answered, hugging him as tightly as I could. "Thank you for saving me and know that I love you so fucking much."

"I love you too, with all my heart."

SLEEP CAME FITFULLY EVEN though I knew I was safe and tucked into bed with Cris, Petru, and Toma. My mind raced with everything we'd discovered and confirmation that Colonel Nems had been the person behind the attack on the outpost that set this whole ordeal into motion. In a twisted way, I should be grateful. If there hadn't been an attack, I never would have run. Without running, I wouldn't have met my pack and found the happiness I lived each day. Yet no matter how I looked at it, he'd been the cause of so much death and perpetuation of this war.

Why the General used him to remove Lucian didn't make sense. While he was the heir, it wasn't like he'd been the poster child of the future who'd turned their back on him or their manifesto. For my own peace of mind, I settled on the fact that, like Cris' father, General Rasvan had lost his mind. His fear of someone trying to take his place and kill him had rotted his brain to the point that he was seeing things that weren't truly there. Of course, now he'd made his worst fear a reality by pushing Lucian to the decision where he had no other choice but to kill his father.

I must have fallen asleep at some point because I was jerked awake by someone pounding on the door to our apartment. They continued beating on the door until I heard someone open it, and low tones of someone talking drifted through the partially closed bedroom door. Moments later, Sorin walked into the room with an expression that told me they had found Cris' father; only there was something more.

"Cris," Sorin said brusquely. "Do you know anything about a dead body being found this morning behind the supply building?"

He rolled on his back and tossed an arm over his eyes. "It's my father."

This admission had Toma and Petru sitting up in bed to look over at their Beta.

"Why the fuck am I hearing about this from the morning watch and not you?" Sorin demanded.

"Because I didn't want to face the reality that my father is a traitor who attempted to rape Dani before he tried killed to her," Cris stated, his tone detached, clearly trying to distance himself from the whole thing. "He left me no choice but to shoot him."

"I'm going to need you to explain this in a little more detail for the rest of us," Sorin warned. "Everyone needs to get up and get ready anyways. I received word that the militia left the city in the middle of the night." With that announcement, he turned on his heel and left the room.

Cris groaned and rolled out of bed, not looking at any of us as he got dressed.

"Cris..." Petru started but stopped when Cris held up a hand.

"I'm only talking about this once, so please just wait until then to say anything," Cris pleaded, grabbing his boots and leaving the room.

The two men turned to me with questions written all over their faces. "He saved my life doing what he did. Nonetheless, having to carry the weight of a parent's death, whether they deserved it or not, isn't easy. We saw how well he took finding out his father was a cheater and a liar. This is going to be even harder for him."

"How could he not say anything last night?" Toma questioned, hurt shadowing his eyes.

Pressing a hand to his chest, I shook my head. "You can't think like that. It has nothing to do with you and your relationship. The moment he talks about it and other people know, it becomes real. Who knows how people will judge him? Think about it, he knows what Tru went through when people believed his father was a traitor. What Cris' father admitted to last night is so much worse than I would have ever thought."

"She's right. He's protecting himself right now from the perceived backlash he thinks is coming," Petru agreed. "Let's do as he's asked and hear the whole story before we press him for more information. There might be nothing left to deal with now that he's dead. However, if there is, we will help him navigate that with our full support."

As we got ready for the day, we packed up the few things we'd used knowing we'd be leaving soon now that the militia was on the move. Dumping our packs by the front door, we gathered in the small common space where Cris was pacing, chewing on this thumbnail absently. Even without our bond, it was clear that he was in massive turmoil, but I had faith that once he told the others what happened, there would be no question about his actions.

"We're ready when you are," Petru commented once we were all seated.

"Maybe Dani should start since I assume this note has something to do with what happened last night," Victor said, waving the piece of paper.

I agreed it was best for me to start. Then it would be crystal clear that he'd made the right choice other than not saying anything to them. I got so many looks of disapproval after explaining my trip to the mess hall, then getting snatched by an unknown assailant, and Cris coming to the rescue.

"Why didn't you wake one of us?" Lucian snapped. "These bases are not as safe as we'd like to believe with the intermixing of the Northern converts."

"I got up and dressed without you or Sorin moving a muscle. Do you realize how tired you must have been for that to happen? Most nights I shift in my sleep, and you're awake making sure I'm okay," I justified.

Sorin's frown deepened. "Not good enough, Dani-girl. You know we agreed you wouldn't wander off."

"Can we put a pin in that topic? If the militia has been mobilized finally, it means this is almost over," I reasoned.

Victor snorted. "You think that once this is over that we're going to worry less about your safety? Little Spark, you're smarter than that. Just because we have the power and stopped the war doesn't mean this place will change overnight. It's going to be incredibly dangerous for you, especially since you're Lucian's Omega."

"It already is," Cris bit out. "My father went after her because he believed she was the reason he kept failing to kill Lucian. He thought if he could kill her or hold her hostage that he'd have the upper hand. He's also the one who pushed the attack on your outpost Lucian since your father wanted you dead. That failed, so he helped those Northern soldiers across the border to hunt you down, failing yet again. This was his final attempt to do what he'd been ordered to, and it got him killed by his own son."

The guys didn't say anything for a moment as they digested what Cris had just told them. This went way deeper than just trying to kill Lucian. Colonel Nems was a respected officer, giving him access to many things he could use against the South. His desperation not to get caught and to continue living the cushy life kept him from doing anything too drastic. Yet it made me wonder if someone like him is the reason Petru's father got accused of being a spy. Especially if other Northern soldiers had infiltrated the same way, blaming innocent people for their actions. Once we managed things here, we'd have to address this with Sorin's father to ensure nothing crucial had been altered or manipulated. The list of wrongs we'd need to right was ever-growing, and I wasn't sure it could ever be completed. However, that was a worry for another day. Right now we needed to regroup and focus on meeting up with the Oscadian strike team so we could start making changes.

"Cris, I'm sorry about your father," Lucian said, breaking the silence. "To be clear, I'm not talking about him dying. That undoubtedly needed to happen, just as my father's death is inevitable. What I am sorry about is the fact you believed he was a good man who had some flaws but cared for you and your mother. To have those blinders removed and see the real person underneath it all makes you question everything about yourself. I will tell you the same thing an important person in my life always told me. You probably aren't ready to accept it right now, but I'll keep telling you either way."

Pausing, Lucian stood and grabbed Cris by the shoulders so he could look the man in the eyes. "Sharing blood and DNA with someone doesn't mean you *are* that person, or will even become like them. It just means they aided in your creation, nothing more. The person you become in life is a choice *you* make. So choose to be better."

Tears burned in my eyes as I held them back, not wanting to upset everyone. Hearing Lucian be so vulnerable and honest with Cris had my heart swelling with pride and love for all these men. Roughly three months ago, we were seven people living our lives in such different ways you'd never believe we could be a family. Now when I saw interactions like these, it showed me just how far we'd come together. The two men hugged, which for Lucian was a big deal. Other than with me, he wasn't one to accept or enjoy physical contact, but he clearly knew Cris needed it. Which is what I've learned from my guys, that this is what family does for each other.

CHAPTER 64
Danella

With the matter of Cris' father settled, we grabbed food in the mess hall and met up with Rick. Who'd already been in contact with Savo.

"In anticipation of this moment, we have a team already camped out near the Asturg border the past week. We all agreed that taking this second training camp would most likely be the tipping point and turns out we were right," Rick explained, pulling out a map and spreading it over the table. "Now, this is where the team is currently, and this is the meetup spot we agreed upon weeks ago. It will take them five hours to get there, but it will take you eight, even with the vehicle. Leaving in the next thirty minutes will get you there before dark. There isn't anything around, so using the headlights shouldn't be a problem. What can I say, I'm more on the cautious side."

Lucian looked over the location critically as if he wasn't sure it would work anymore. Then he grabbed a tool to double-check the distance from that spot to Stalhold City. "Another seven hours to the main city where there is no chance to sneak up on them. Damn the bastard for leveling out the whole area and giving us no coverage. The second we get within a few miles of the place, they'll know we're coming."

"Well, then it's a good thing you have a day to sit tight and figure out the best solution while we wait for the militia to attack here," Rick pointed out. "Besides, Savo is leading that team. While he might have been gone for a long time, he knows the area too. It's better to have two minds figure this out than one."

Lucian didn't respond. He just kept staring at the map as if it would give him the answer.

"All right then, grab your shit and let's move out," Sorin ordered, then reached out to shake Rick's hand. "Thank you for everything. I know we've kept you away from your family to make this happen. Hopefully, once this is over they'll be able to switch other people in to take your place so you can see your wife and kids."

"That's what's keeping me going, and the fact that we can video call twice a week. At least I know our kids don't forget their fathers' faces," Rick shared with a wistful smile that fell away into a more serious expression. "Give 'em hell and the best of luck to you all."

We stopped by the supply station to gather what we needed for the trip knowing the strike team would be set to accommodate us once we got there. Lucian drove since he knew the terrain the best, with Victor as co-pilot, leaving the rest of us in the covered back of the truck. It was decided to take one of these versus the Humvee so we could conceal how many people were in the back. It did, however, mean it was one hell of a bumpy ride reminding me of that first trip to the outpost three years ago. Now here I was, coming full circle. Only this time when we arrived at Stalhold City, I wouldn't be a captive, I would be a liberator and that was an amazing feeling.

Rick had been spot on with his prediction that we'd arrive at sunset, meaning we didn't need to use the headlights. Although, I'm sure that even without them, someone would quickly notice a random covered military truck driving through the Northern wasteland. The real question was would they do anything about it?

The strike team was already there with the camp set up in the structure that Rick had us adapting to since it made sense and offered more protection. Hopping out of the truck, I almost fell over with how numb my legs were from sitting on the hard wooden bench in the back. I pitched forward, but a pair of hands caught me in time to steady myself then took a step back.

Looking up, I found a massive man with striking green eyes and familiar features towering above me. I knew instantly that this was Savo. The family traits were evident to me, even if he was taller than Lucian. They had the same jawline and nose, but they must have gotten their eye color from their mothers because neither had the muddy brown of the General.

"You must be Danella," he greeted with a gentle smile that contradicted his appearance. "I'm Savo. It's nice to finally meet you in person."

"Likewise," I answered as a pair of hands settled on my hips.

I knew from the touch and the smooth, spicy scent that it was Lucian. "Hello, brother, it's been a while."

"Lucian, you've filled out since I last saw you," Savo commented with a grin tugging at his lips.

A snort came from behind me. "Yeah, that happens when you haven't seen someone since they were a teen."

"I suppose you're right," Savo laughed. "I hope after this it won't need to be long between visits. I have a feeling that once Cambrie and Danella meet, they will instantly become friends."

The others joined us and ran through quick introductions since it was more about putting a face to a name after all our phone conversations. With that matter settled, he showed us to the tent we'd be staying in and gave us time to settle in.

"Dinner should be ready soon. There will be a meal call so you'll know when it's ready," Savo mentioned before waving a farewell as he ducked out of the tent.

There was a moment of silence before Victor blurted what we were all thinking. "Holy shit, that man is massive. I'm not a small guy by any means, but fuck, he's a giant. Tell me he doesn't get that from your father because that changes the whole ass game."

I didn't even try to hold back the laughter that bubbled up from his outburst. Seeing Victor so impressed and slightly intimidated by someone was strange, though I didn't blame him—Savo was indeed a giant.

"Our father is that tall, but he isn't nearly as muscular. Pretty sure it's why he picked Savo in the first place. He was intimidating without even having to say a word. Fact of the matter is that under the bulky exterior is a rather sensitive guy," Lucian shared. "His sister died in one of the breeding houses, and that I think was the final straw. With not having any siblings and father already having used my emotions against me when it came to my mother, I didn't understand why that broke him. Now having a family, I can see how hard that must have been to deal with."

I was happy to see that he was willing to put himself in his brother's shoes. When I'd first heard him talk about his brother who abandoned him and their country Lucian had so much anger he couldn't see past it. Now they've had to work together, moving towards a common goal of freeing their people. He's never said it outright, but I think having Savo here fighting alongside the rest of us meant a lot to Lucian. I also got the feeling that Savo was right about Cambrie and I becoming friends, which meant spending time around her pack. Working through their issues now would only help in the future.

A long shrill whistle could be heard through the camp, and I would bet anything that it was letting us know dinner was ready. We'd just finished laying out our beds for the night so that way we could pass out after dinner. After not sleeping well and all that's happened today, I knew a full belly would knock me right out. Filing out of the tent, we spotted where everyone was gathering and headed over.

Savo noticed us and motioned us to join him where he was standing. "Listen up, soldiers," he bellowed, grabbing everyone's attention followed by instant silence. "I'm going to introduce you to some important people you will treat with the utmost respect. Is that understood?"

"Yes, sir," all the soldiers shouted.

With a nod, Savo clapped a hand on Lucian's shoulder with a wide grin on his face and started the introductions. "This is my brother, Lucian, and his pack mates Sorin, Victor, Petru, Toma, Cris, and their bonded Omega Danella. They are why we're here and able to be part of history. We have the honor of assisting them in ending this feud between North and South Asturg. They are also fellow military men and outrank everyone of your sorry asses, so if they give you an order, do it. We will have a rest day tomorrow as we finalize our strategy for the following day as we prepare to strike Stalhold City, the capital of Northern Asturg. Eat up and enjoy your rest while you have it."

Having released them to their evening meal, all the men lined up and to be served their meals. It looked like they'd made some kind of hearty stew, and my mouth was watering. Unable to wait any longer, I headed for the back of the line when a mountain of a human cut in front of me.

"Hold up, little sister," Savo said with a chuckle. "Didn't you hear me tell them that all of you outranked them? That included you. Grab a bowl and walk right up to the front of the line, and no one will say a damn word."

"No one but me," Victor interjected. "Little Spark, you know the rules regarding food and people."

Rolling my eyes, I let out a groan. "We were doing so well this past week. I got my own lunch four times and nothing bad happened. Couldn't we negotiate this?"

"Nope," Victor stated, then jabbed his finger, pointing at the ground under my feet. "Stay right the fuck there, woman. I mean it."

Having given his warning, he headed towards where dinner was being served, ignoring the daggers I was staring into his back.

"You'll have to be patient with those of us who are gifted with a little *extra* Alpha in our makeup. I promise we mean well when we do things like this that drive you crazy. My *keksik* normally isn't allowed to go anywhere without me as her shadow. I hired a bodyguard in my stead because I can't stand the thought of something happening to her," Savo shared. "She was kidnapped out of our own house once before we were bonded. Thank fuck whatever higher power you believe in that I was placed to be her bodyguard by her kidnapper of all things. Knowing that it's happened once, I can't get past the fear it could happen again. It drives my protective instinct into overdrive and I have a feeling that's what's happening to him."

I glanced up at him, intrigued by the tidbit of the story he'd dropped, but it was clear he wasn't going to continue. "Tell me, does Cambrie mind how overprotective you are?"

"It drives her mad," he admitted. "Nonetheless, she also loves me enough to let me do it so I have peace of mind. When we're home and the others are there too, I give her the space she needs if she wants it. That woman has seven of us to deal with, and now our son, so she's got her hands pretty full. You pick your battles and fight for those truly important to you. Then even assholes like myself and your man Victor, will realize how important it is to you."

I was surprised by that advice, yet I had to agree it made perfect sense. There wasn't a chance in hell that I would win this battle with Victor, but there were others I might, if I saved my energy to do it. "Thank you, Savo. I'll keep that in mind."

"You're welcome, little sis. We're family, after all... right?" he said but almost made it sound slightly like a question.

"Yeah, we're family," I agreed with a smile. "You know it means a lot to him you're here, even if he never says it."

"A wise and loving woman told me that when an opportunity presents itself to fix a mistake in the past, I would be a fool not to take it. Like always, she was right," Savo explained. "I refuse to let our father take more from us than he has already. He's not worth it. The power he once had over either of us is gone, and now it's time to remove his hold on our country."

On that stance, I don't think we could have agreed more and it showed me that the brothers were far more similar than they realized.

"Dani-girl, come eat," Sorin called from where they were all sitting around a fire.

Savo let out a huff of laughter. "Woman, you've found yourself a pack full of top-tier Alphas, didn't you?"

Smiling at that, I nodded. "They were the only ones who would have been able to handle me. Anyone else and I would have walked all over them or gotten myself in serious trouble. As Petru says, the fates put us together knowing we were destined for one another." With a tiny wave, unsure how else to end our conversation, I headed over to my guys.

Victor pulled me onto his lap, offering me a bowl of steaming stew he'd procured for me, and kissed my temple. "Eat what you want..."

"... and you'll finish off what's left," I finished knowing the routine by heart. "There might not be anything left, I'm damn hungry and this smells amazing."

It was strange to think we were on the eve of the most important fight of our lives, but there was a sense of peace around us. I had total faith we could accomplish anything as long as we did it together. Each hurdle we've made it over has proved that time and time again. One more to go, and we could start to make the dream we've been fighting for a reality.

True to my premonition of being unable to stay awake with a full stomach, I walked back to the tent with Cris. Neither of us was up for hanging out with the soldiers. In fact, all I wanted to do was curl up in a pile of pillows and blankets with my guys curled around me and nap all day tomorrow, but that wasn't going to happen— yet. It didn't take more than ten minutes before Cris was snoring softly against the back of my neck. On the other hand, I couldn't fall asleep until all the guys were back and settled into our puppy pile formation. The only thing I could connect my weird mood to was that I desperately wanted a central home with a nest and the knowledge we wouldn't be moving from location to location. Seems my Omega side was wearing a little thin and needed some recharging.

Soon, I reminded myself. Soon we would be able to have all of that once we removed the General from power and damn if that couldn't come fast enough.

∽

THE FOLLOWING day was spent huddled around a table with various maps and images of the city. Since I'd been there last, a concrete wall had been built around the place. I could only imagine how many people it took to pull that off with how large the city was. The tall, crumbling buildings still stood—kind of. Many of them had crumbled further making them shorter, but what was left of them still stood.

"They made the wall extend so it would include the power plant and weapons factory as well," Savo explained, sliding over a photo for proof.

While we had spies in the city giving us information on the movement and activities of the General and his militia, no images were sent along. Oscad used a crewless aircraft to fly over the city and take pictures. It could fly high enough that no one would notice it, keeping our plans to attack secret. This had been the most useful thing out of all this, because we knew there was a wall. Except seeing how tall and thick it was, gave a whole new meaning to the problem.

"That bastard has seriously lost his mind if he thinks he needs a wall like that to keep people out," Lucian muttered.

Shuffling through the photos, I paid close attention to the people I could see in them. When I first arrived, I thought they looked haggard and thin, but now the expressions on their faces were devoid of any life. There was no hope. They looked like walking skeletons, clothes hanging off their bodies and sunken cheeks.

"What if it's not to keep people out," I said, pausing at an image of the militia beating a man in the street. Flipping it around, I showed it to them. "What if it's to keep them from leaving? This is where the children are raised, right? How would it work if all the people in the city left and abandoned everything there? There might even be a possibility they are taking children with them too."

Sorin reached out and took the image from my hand, his eyes flashing with anger. "How could this man call himself a leader if this is how he's treating his people?"

"He doesn't," Lucian pointed out. "Never has he called himself a leader of the people. That's why he goes by general. He leads an army, not a country. Everything he's founded his life on is about war, strategy, and winning at all costs."

That took a moment for my Southern men to wrestle with. It's hard when you're faced with a reality you'd never expect and realize this is the life people have lived for *generations*. The South isn't perfect, but it's always had the ability to feed its people. Starvation brings out a different side to humanity and forces you to do whatever is necessary to survive. Which gave me an idea.

"So if the militia is gone, what kind of enforcement does our dear General have to deal with his people?" I inquired.

"He would keep a small group back to protect at least him. However, from what the spies told us, he pretty much sent them all to crush us," Lucian answered.

I nodded as I flipped through the photos once more. "This is a crazy ass idea and I have no idea if it will even work, but it might be worth a try..."

The guys all looked at me curiously, but Savo motioned for me to continue. Setting down the photos, I pulled the map of the city and started to share my idea. Instantly Petru was excited about it, while the others had questions that we worked through. While my idea didn't pan out in its origin, it did spark the others to come up with similar options that we broke down and hashed out. By the time the dinner whistle was blown, we'd devised three different plans, each leveling up in intensity. All of us agreed this wasn't a fight with the people of the city, and we would do all that we could to protect them. Our battle was with General Rasvan and his military, who were trapping these people in a life that will only kill them in the end.

This would be a battle unlike any we've tried to pull off, but if it worked, it would be a massive step for the people of the North.

CHAPTER 65

Danella

The sun was particularly scorching as we traversed over the barren wasteland on our way to Stalhold City. We'd left early knowing the sun would be brutal, but this seemed to channel the General's energy as it beat down on the trucks. Thank god for the coverings, or all of us would be fried to death before we could even fight. The energy of the soldiers was different from what I'd experienced in the previous battles. These men were focused, determined, and full of energy prepared to do whatever it took to make this happen.

Granted, the soldiers I'd been with over the past month weren't really actual soldiers but men and women who'd had little choice in the matter. If they wanted to survive and keep their existence alive, then fighting is what needed to happen. So on battle days, they would be more reserved, almost as if they felt guilty about what we were doing. Not being citizens, these men didn't have the same tie to this place, but oddly, I felt like it helped. If a hard choice was needed to be made, they'd do it without question, without feeling the sense of betrayal Northern soldiers would.

"Cities in sight," Savo's voice called over the comms. "Twenty minutes out, weapons at the ready. We don't know what our reception will be."

Taking a deep breath, I double-checked my handgun and rifle to ensure everything was in order. Touching a hand to my hip, I felt the pouch with extra ammunition for both guns next to the sheath for my knife. Closing my eyes, I worked through the meditation Petru had been working with me on to slow my heartbeat, keeping my mind clear from the rush and panic of adrenalin. A sniper couldn't be accurate if they weren't able to focus on their target.

"Dani," Toma murmured, resting a hand on my thigh trying not to startle me. Opening my eyes, I met his gaze. "I need you to know how much I truly love and admire you. Spending time in the North and seeing what it's like here, the life you had to endure, it makes me sick to think what would have happened if we hadn't found you."

Reaching out, I cupped his cheek, my thumb brushing across his skin. "I love you too, and I thank the fates every day you all were brought into my life. I've always needed a purpose, a mission, something to make me feel like I'm making a difference in the world. You gave me that, along with learning what it means to truly love someone. I'd been so resistant to allowing anyone to help or care for me, fearing it would make me weak. What actually made me weak was thinking I could do it all on my own."

"We've only begun our life together," he pointed out. "I hope you don't think this is what it will always be like. Since the day you brought up wanting a home and a nest, we've all been working toward that goal. It was a dream we didn't know we wanted, though maybe it was because our family wasn't complete yet. Anyway, I just wanted to make sure there was no doubt between us about how I feel about you. That way, no matter what might happen today, nothing is left unsaid."

Everything in me wanted to tell him not to talk like that, we'd be fine and make it through this with no problem, but I didn't. The past month has taught me that there is no warning when a loss might hit you. One moment things are fine. The next, the world can come crashing down around you. I was eternally grateful that other than a few grazes, bruises, and a broken finger, we'd made it through together.

When the truck came to a halt, nothing was said. I had to hold back from getting up and peeking. We were to remain right where we were until the order to get out of the truck was given. There were twenty trucks full of soldiers that were surrounding the city as we sat here. Being the first truck in the line, we had to wait for the others to fall into position. The plan was for the people behind the wall to have no idea how many soldiers were in each of the trucks. This way, we could use their fear to end this with as little to no bloodshed as possible.

"Stalhold City, we have you surrounded," Lucian said through a megaphone, alerting the people within just in case they didn't notice the trucks. "I am Lucian Bakal, heir to the current General, and I demand to speak to him or one of his advisors, or we will attack this city."

"Sniper team, at the ready," Sorin ordered. "Explosives team, you are a go."

Much like our plan for the first training camp, charges were set at various intervals along the wall that would collapse the whole thing. Concrete, while effective in many ways as a deterrent, wouldn't be keeping us out. My guess was they did it this way because there were no other materials for them to use, so they did with what they had.

Staying in the back, I moved forward and flipped back the cloth covering the front just over the cab of the truck. Setting my rifle on a beanbag to keep it steady on the metal since there was no room for a tripod. Getting into position, I swept the top of the wall, ensuring no soldiers were in my designated section. There was no movement at all. I couldn't even be sure if anyone was on the other side of the wall. Then a person appeared, though it was clear they were a civilian and therefore protected from us. Two more joined the first, and then the wall was flooded with people. Could it be the bastard was putting innocents up on the wall to keep up from blowing it up?

"Explosives team, you are not to detonate anything without my direct order. Civilians are flooding the top of the wall. I repeat do *not* detonate without a clear, direct order," Sorin snapped.

It would seem he had the same thought I did.

"People of Stalhold, we know the militia is no longer in your city to protect you. Our fight is not with you but with General Rasvan. So again, I ask for him or a representative to make themselves known," Lucian informed them.

A gap was made, and a person stepped up to the edge of the wall. He was dressed in a military uniform and didn't show the same signs of malnourishment. After a moment's hesitation, this man produced his own megaphone and responded.

"We do not recognize you as the heir to the North. The North has no heir and needs no heir while the great General Rasvan lives," he announced. "If you truly mean to attack this city, you will have to take down the wall. And as you see, doing so would kill all these people."

"What?" Toma snarled as he shot to his feet. "You can't be serious. Did they really just do what he said, Dani?"

I glanced over my shoulder at him. "He absolutely one hundred percent did."

"Bastard," one of the other soldiers cursed.

"Then I no longer need to speak with you. Instead, I will speak to the people," Lucian stated. "Did you all hear that? The great General Rasvan is happy to sacrifice each of your lives to save his own. Hasn't he killed enough of us with this damn never-ending war? This wall isn't to keep you safe. It's there to make sure you don't abandon him and run to the mountains seeking a better life for yourself. I'm standing here today because I want to offer you that chance, a chance for all this to be over and free yourself."

As Lucian spoke, I'd been watching our military friend and saw him draw his weapon aiming it at Lucian. I decided to give the people around him a few seconds to see what was going on and react before shooting him. A woman screamed and dove out of the way, crashing into others, and one man fell over the wall crashing to the ground below. Wasting no more time, I pulled the trigger, nailing him right in the heart I wasn't sure he even had. It was confirmed, though, as he also fell forward off the wall.

"Medic team, grab the civilian and see if we can save him," Savo ordered.

Lucian gave everyone a few minutes to calm down before he started speaking again. "We have a medic team on the way to help the man who fell due to the actions of the General's representative. I apologize for needing to shoot him, but as you can see, he didn't give a shit if anything happened to you. He just wanted to shut me up. Tell me, have you had enough? Are you willing to stand up and make a change, fight for your freedom, and stop the war that's been bleeding our country dry?"

There was hesitation, but then a man climbed on the back of another, thrust his arm into the air, then yelled long and loud. "Enough is enough."

With his battle cry, the others cheered, clapped, and whistled their agreement. Then slowly, a chant began that built louder and louder as more people joined. "Enough is enough, enough is enough, enough is enough."

"Holy shit, Dani, your plan is totally working," Toma said in awe as he stood next to me, observing through a pair of binoculars.

Indeed it was. I'd firmly believed that the people of Stalhold City would be our greatest asset in this fight. Not only would it work in our favor to have them choose to be on our side, but it helps them make a stand for themselves. This was only the first part of the plan, the second wasn't going to be so easy.

"If you believe that and want things to change, then come down from the wall. Open the gate to the city, and allow us to deal with the General," Lucian instructed.

This had the people quieting some, until a woman snatched up the megaphone that had been dropped. "What assurances do we have that you won't kill everyone in this city the moment we open the gate?"

"Nothing you will be able to hold or see tangibly. Nevertheless, I understand not wanting to take me at my word. However, that's all I have to offer you. My fight isn't with you, it's with my father, who created all this and is destroying the home we've been spilling blood over for generations. It needs to stop, and it won't while he's alive," Lucian responded, and I prayed it would be enough.

This was the part of the plan we couldn't anticipate. They would either let us in, or we'd be forced to do something so fucking awful it would give me nightmares for life. Then in a miracle I wasn't sure would happen, people started filing off the wall. There was a lull in movement. Once we couldn't see anyone, gunshots were heard accompanied by screams. My stomach clenched as I prayed there wasn't some mass shooting that had just happened to keep them from opening the gate.

With a screech of metal against metal, the gate was pulled open and a flood of people rushed out as if their lives depended on it. Shifting my angle, I aimed for the entrance to see a group of soldiers being swarmed by people as others ran by. Being as careful as I could, I picked off two soldiers trying to enter the fray. The others were so close to innocents that I didn't dare risk it. While I was a good shot, I'm pretty sure only Petru could make it safely and he was stationed in the truck to our right.

Once the volume of people died down, Savo gave the order. "Move out. Protect the civilians, but remember that our goal is to take the building the General is in."

Soldiers spilled out of the trucks, guns ready as they jogged across the open space to the city. Three blasts echoed through the air as the explosives team donated their charges. We needed more than one entrance to infiltrate the city fast enough, and now that the people were gone, it was safe. Toma was right by my side as we moved down the main street, past the dilapidated buildings at the front of the city to the area that was actually used. These buildings weren't in much better condition, but they showed signs of effort and use.

The General had taken up residence in a single-story bunker-type dwelling. Diving out of the way as soldiers started shooting from windows and shielded positions on the roof. Looking around, I spotted a ladder that I could climb to get up to what used to be a fire escape balcony.

"Toma, cover me," I yelled, then darted across the street and leapt for the lowest rung.

"Goddamn it, Dani," Toma shouted as he started shooting.

I climbed as fast as possible and crawled forward on the grated platform, taking aim. None of them had noticed me since more soldiers flooded the area, but all the more reason why I had to take advantage of it. I picked off the first man on the roof and went for the second. He was harder since my angle wasn't right, but I clipped him in the shoulder. It got him to move, allowing me to take him out with the second shot. Now that those two were dealt with, the rest of our people could get in close enough to deal with those in the windows. Dropping down to the street, I was instantly grabbed by the back of my neck making me lash out.

"Little Spark," Victor growled. "What the fuck do you think you're doing putting yourself out in the open like that?"

The fight left me hearing it was him, and I let him escort me safely behind another building. Toma and Sorin were there as well, expressions darker than a thundercloud.

"Don't speak," Sorin snapped. "Nothing you have to say right now will make us any less upset. I understand what you did, but twenty other snipers could have done that same thing. I'm so fucking glad this is almost over because you're taking years off my life I don't have to spare, Dani-girl."

I knew they were scared more than mad about what I did, but I wouldn't let them keep me in a bubble when everyone else was putting their lives on the line. A few moments later, the other guys joined us, along with Savo, who had a cut above his brow.

"Are you okay?" I asked.

"Yeah, bastard missed his shot. Shrapnel from the building got me instead," he explained.

Cris quickly cleaned it up and put a bandage over it so the blood wouldn't get in his eye. Lucian was at the edge of the building watching as our soldiers were picking off the remaining men, one by one, then the gunfire stopped.

"Ready?" Lucian asked, looking at Savo.

"Hell yeah, I'm ready. Time to pay dear old dad one last visit," he muttered as he finished loading a new magazine with a full round of bullets.

We all stepped back into the main street and headed for the bunker. Just as we arrived, the front door opened and out rolled General Rasvan himself in a crisp uniform that looked like it had never been worn before. The shocking part was seeing him in a wheelchair looking like a frail old man. That is, until you looked into his eyes which were bright with life and intelligence even if his body was failing him.

"Well, if it isn't my two biggest disappointments coming to visit me," Rasvan said, his voice gravelly and full of disdain.

"Father," Savo bit out as if it pained him to call him that. "Seems the evil you've been spreading in the world has finally infected you."

"Ha, evil you say," he laughed bitterly, then pointed a finger at Savo. "How am I more evil than the government you chose to side with that supplied me with all I needed to keep this war going? Don't you come here and look down your fucking nose at me when you ran the hell away. What kind of man abandons his people to hide under the skirts of another country just as corrupt as I am."

"You're right, I did desert my country and people who needed me to fight for them. Which is why I'm here now supporting Lucian, who's managed to do what I failed at," Savo pointed out. "I'm well aware of my sins and make atonement for them daily. There's nothing you can say that I'm not already well aware of."

Rasvan sniffed and turned his attention to Lucian. "Who knew you'd be the one to cause me so much trouble? The boy who used to cry himself to sleep and wander around like a kicked puppy. How many years of beatings did you have to endure before you found that goddamn spine of yours? Fucking waste of space and energy, the lot of you. Had to pick the best of the rotten fruit those breeders managed to produce, and that was you. Now here you are with a traitor at your side using his men from a different fucking country to best me. Fucking pathetic, couldn't even die when I needed you to."

"Then you should be grateful that we're here to put you out of your misery, so you no longer have to see the world as it crumbles around you," Lucian said, crossing his arms. "Look at you, the man everyone feared for so many years is now nothing more than a dying old guy. No wonder you couldn't come out to the wall and face me like the man you believe you are. I bet you can't even wipe your own ass anymore and have to get someone to do it for you."

Rasvan snarled and lunged forward but made sure to grip his chair so he didn't fall out. "How dare you fucking speak to me like that, you fucking waste. I should have killed you with your mother. That cunt filled your head with lies, making you soft. Fucking pussy of a man can't even fuck a woman properly to get her pregnant. Does she fuck you? Is that what your prefer? Or maybe she's just been your cover-up for getting dick shoved up your ass, wasting the chance for a real soldier to be born."

The venom in his words had me taking a step back into Victor, who wrapped an arm around my waist as if preparing to pull me out of the way.

"You want to know the truth? I made goddamn sure I could never have a kid because I would never allow them to be raised by the likes of you. The vile way you think, stepping over everyone and everything just to make sure you get to stay on top. The mighty General leading his fucking army, yet that's not what you are. Look at you, a fucking old man sitting there in that chair, unable to scare a mouse."

The rage that burned in General Rasvan's eyes would have burned this whole city down with how intense his anger was. Baring his teeth like a rabid dog, he lifted a device as if he was going to throw himself at Lucian. "Can't scare a mouse? We'll see about that. Tell me how scared you were when we meet in hell."

"*It's a bomb. Run,*" Victor bellowed as he turned, got five steps, and dropped to the ground with me half underneath him.

CHAPTER 66
Danella

The blast was deafening, and the heat seared along any part of my skin that was remotely exposed. My head was ringing and the weight of Victor's body over mine had me panicking when he didn't move as I wriggled out from under him. Dust and debris were everywhere making me cough and my eyes water. Rolling Victor over, I saw a mark where he must have hit his head when he fell, creating a dark bruise and bleeding as head wounds do. Pressing my ear to his chest, I could hear his heart beating steadily, putting me a little more at ease.

"Help!" a man screamed.

Sitting up, I scanned the area trying to figure out where the call was coming from. I spotted Lucian and Savo, who'd managed to get behind a crumbling wall saving them from the worst of it. Cris dropped next to me, grabbing my face and looking me over.

"I'm fine. Victor shielded me with his body, but I think he knocked himself unconscious," I said, realizing that I was shouting at him with my ear still ringing.

He said something to me, but I couldn't understand. I tried to shake my head, except he was holding me firmly. Then I realized the look on his face told me something was wrong.

"What's wrong?" I begged, grabbing his wrists.

Petru stumbled over with one sleeve missing from his jacket and his arm exposed showing a terrible burn. Horrified at the sight of it, I started to hyperventilate.

"Sweetheart, you need to calm down," Cris soothed. "The faster your heart beats, the more blood you're going to lose."

"What?" I gasped. "I'm not hurt, Cris. Where am I bleeding from?"

"You can't feel it? There is no pain at all?"

"Tell. Me," I pleaded.

Licking his lips, he moved one hand down my neck just above my clavicle. "You feel nothing right here?"

I was going to shake my head but clearly, he didn't want me to do that. "No, I'm in no pain other than my head pounding. I'm pretty sure everyone is going to feel that way, however."

"Lodged in this spot here is a chunk of metal. It looks pretty deep, so I don't want to remove it when I don't know what damage it's done," Cris explained.

"Danella," Lucian called, as he and Savo reached us. "Oh fuck," he gasped at seeing my neck.

"Cris, what do you need to deal with this?" Savo asked.

Looking over at the Alpha, he let out a huff of laughter. "Any chance you got a way to fly us back to the South so I can get her to our medical facility there?"

"Done," Savo stated.

That shocked us all.

"You have working helicopters?" Sorin demanded. "Why are you telling us this now? Do you know how much that would have changed the game if we'd been able to use those?"

"Yeah, which is why we never offered them," Savo stated as he pulled out a satellite phone. "Marius, we need the fleet of medevac helicopters to Stalhold City now. The fucking bastard set off a bomb he hid in his wheelchair. I'll need to take one so we can get Danella to the Med Center in the South, and the rest can go back to our hospitals." There was a pause and a few exchanges of yes and no answers then he hung up. "They should be here soon enough. Do you have what you need to at least make her stable enough until they arrive?"

Cris nodded and started to pull things out of his pack. "Once I get her situated, then I'll start checking on others. Can one of you coordinate an area to put everyone?"

"On it," Petru said and started to walk off.

Lucian grabbed his uninjured arm. "Whoa, you stay with Dani once he's done with whatever he needs to do for her. That arm of yours isn't going to allow you to be much help to anyone. I'll coordinate a triage area."

Petru accepted the reality and stayed with me. Once Cris wrapped the piece of metal to make sure it was secure, he was off to help others. Savo had brought five other medics along, but none had the experience that Cris did, so he needed to give them a fair amount of guidance. I was carefully moved to the triage area near one of the blasted holes along with Victor, who'd woken up with a pounding headache. Petru joined the efforts to search the site under the condition he wouldn't lift anything. Toma and Sorin were relatively unharmed, just battered and bruised with some cuts on any exposed skin. Out of all of us, I was the one who'd been hurt the worst.

They'd managed to get everyone accounted for by the time the helicopters arrived and landed outside the city. Men with stretchers started to carry everyone out with instructions from Cris. Some had started IV bags and pain meds given for transport now that we had the supplies. Then it was my turn.

"All of you go. I will stay here until you guys get back," Savo promised. "Just worry about your family, Lucian. No one will be taking this city from me. Rick will be on his way with the rest of your troops."

The two clasped arms in a manly hug and Lucian jogged to catch up with us. Getting strapped in and flown out of the city was a wild experience. One I'm not sure I'd like to do again. I preferred my feet on the ground, but the guys seemed to enjoy it. My bigger fear though was what would happen when we landed outside the Mraz Command outpost.

Here we are in an Oscadian helicopter, something no one has seen in their lifetime, with the new leader of the North and their bonded Omega no one knew about. Oh, and then there was the fact that Sorin and his unit had disappeared for over two months without communication. This wasn't going to go well. The second we touched down, the helicopter was surrounded with shouts for them to turn the engine off and put their hands up.

Sorin yanked open the door and hopped out. "You better put your goddamn weapons down right now and get the hell out of our way."

The two Oscadian medics were already undoing the restraints as Toma and Lucian took the stretcher to carry me to the Med Center.

"You guys take off. I don't want there to be any trouble for you. I'll make sure they don't shoot you out of the sky," Sorin assured them.

Once we were all clear, the helicopter started up and took off, leaving us at the mercy of the South. That is, I would have been if I was bonded to anyone other than Sorin Dragomire. While we had an armed escort, no one stopped us as we walked through the entrance to the base and right over to the Med Center.

Bethany was there waiting for us with a worried look on her face. "What the hell happened to all of you? God, it's like you got blown up or something."

"You would be correct on that one," Toma muttered. "Thankfully, Dani and Petru are the worst of it for us."

"That's what you think," Bethany sniffed. "I want all of you to have a full examination. What if you have internal bleeding from the concussive force of the blast? Nope, we're not taking any chances." She paused to face the staff who were waiting for direction. "Listen up, I want all these men looked over. They were in a blast, so look for the signs of any internal damage even if the outside looks fine. Chop-chop, people. Let's go."

With that, I was transferred to a gurney and rushed into surgery. They had to knock me out so I never heard how bad the damage was. To be honest, I wasn't worried. I knew I was in the most capable hands, with Bethany watching over me. Besides, we were family now, even if she didn't know it yet. Oh god, now I was going to have to meet their parents... I supposed it couldn't be any worse than getting blown up by a tyrannical dictator.

EVERYTHING with the surgery went well and there was minimal damage. The fear, I found out, was that if it had gone a few millimeters deeper it would have hit my carotid artery and I would have bled to death. Information I feel like I could have lived without knowing, but it all worked out fine in the end. I had to stay in the hospital for a few days, but that was just a precaution. Petru and I shared a room since they had to do treatments on his arm to help with the burn. It was amazing to me the medical advancement they had here in the south. They believed the scaring would be minimal with the regiment they were doing and he'd have full function of his arm. The others checked out fine, although Victor did have a concussion. Yet it could have been so much worse.

Toma, Cris, and Victor took turns coming to hang out with Petru and me while we were stuck on bed rest. Lucian and Sorin, however, were trapped in Couver City going over every single detail about what happened over the past two months. The guys would fill us in on the happenings as they went back and forth to share their part of the story. Apparently, Bethany was the roadblock from them talking to me, which they desperately wanted to. We needed this to work, so I made them take me to the city the day I was released from the Med Center. I'd never been to Couver, and it was amazing to see a city so much like Oscad after spending so much time in the North. I was beginning to think there weren't real cities anymore.

"Don't worry, Little Spark, I'm sure we'll be back here often enough for you to get sick of it," Victor teased as I gawked at all the stores and the things they held.

I just rolled my eyes and continued window shopping. When we finally got to the Presidential Hall, I got a little nervous, but then I reminded myself of everything we'd done and survived already so then I felt better. Sorin was there waiting to greet us and scooped me up in his arms, kissing me until I moaned.

"Stop. I can't meet your father for the first time all turned on and perfuming, that's embarrassing." I hissed.

He just smiled and twisted around to walk down a hall, refusing to put me down.

"Seriously, I'm in enough trouble as it is. Do you think it's wise that this is how I'm introduced?" I pleaded.

"Dani-girl, I'm gonna need you to take a deep breath and relax. No one is in trouble. It's quite the opposite, actually," Sorin informed me.

A security guard at the door opened it for us, and I found myself in a large conference room. At the table were Lucian, Councilwoman Nadeja, Councilman Libor, and two other men I didn't recognize. At the head of the table was a man who was clearly Sorin's father. They couldn't argue the fact they were related to anyone. The only difference was President Dragomire had hair and Sorin shaved his bald. Everyone rose and smiled a greeting, making it clear Sorin hadn't been lying to get me to calm down.

Setting me down and positioning me in front of him, I was introduced. "Father, I would like you to meet my bonded Omega Danella Holstad."

President Dragomire walked over, beaming at me and instead of reaching out for a handshake, he hugged me. I let out a startled squeak but recovered quickly enough to return the hug with my one arm. For the other arm Bethany insisted I keep it in a sling for a week to prevent the stitches from pulling.

"It is so wonderful to meet you, Danella," he said once he stepped back.

"Likewise, but I'll be honest, this wasn't the reaction I was expecting to receive walking in here," I admitted.

He just smiled and motioned for me to take a seat. "Please sit, there are some questions I would like to ask and I believe the others do as well. Oh, where are my manners? Let me introduce you to Head Speaker Marius and Advisor Nixon from Oscad."

"It's lovely to finally meet you, Danella," Marius greeted.

"Yes, it's great to finally have a face to put with a voice," Nixon added.

Feeling more comfortable knowing pretty much everyone, I took a seat. For the next few hours, I was asked question after question until I thought there was nothing left they could learn about me. Sorin finally cut in and requested a break for dinner. Thinking we were finally going to leave, I started to get up, but then a waiter entered the room to take orders. I realized that wasn't going to happen.

This carried on for another three days, sitting, talking, planning, and negotiating the rebirth of a country. An official announcement had been made that a ceasefire was in place as peace talks were being negotiated. When I was told that, I burst into tears, unable to believe we'd done it. Our pack of misfits, that never should have worked, managed to end a war between two countries that had been fighting for generations. Of course, this was only the first step in mending the damage that had been done, but damn, if it wasn't one of the happiest moments of my life.

We stayed in Couver for a week, hashing out the plan to restructure between the North, South, and the rebels. It would take time, and we'd probably change things more than once as we learned what was truly needed. Yet all of this was so exciting I couldn't wait to get to the North and implement everything we wanted to do now and in the future. The dream we had that seemed so unattainable now sat in the palm of my hands. All that was left to do was hold on tight and watch it grow.

Epilogue

DANELLA

Four months later...

If there was another time I'd been more excited I couldn't think of one. After months of hard work, we'd shut down all the bases save one since it wasn't smart not to have a military at all. The rebels moved out of their mountain oasis and joined us in the valley, using all they learned to help us turn this country around. With the weapons factory shut down, Toma and a group of people from the South have been working nonstop on the power plant. Yesterday they finished the final repair, and now a quarter of the country has consistent, reliable power.

It might not seem like much, but this allowed us to start changing the infrastructure bit by bit. We'd be building more and using the knowledge that the South has to benefit both sides. Power was only one of the significant hurdles to cross. Next was agriculture. The North needed to start producing its own food, but thankfully the South was more than willing to help out in the meantime.

I honestly thought the greatest struggle we'd have to face was the people. Don't get me wrong, it's been hell and there is lots of predisposed prejudice. However, they saw the leadership working together and so many of the people at their wit's end having hope again. The more they saw the benefit of working together with power, food, water, and clothing. We needed it, and the South was willing to give it. Oscad was instrumental in supplies for building since we decided to create a new capital city near the river on the border of the two countries. Our reasoning for that was when Sorin's father passes, the duty will fall to his son. This plays into our next dream, a dream where there was no north or south, just Asturg as it was always meant to be.

Today we were taking a much-needed break, and the guys woke me up crazy early this morning and dragged me out of my newly created nest for this. Each of them promised that I would love this surprise, but I wasn't so sure about that as they forced me to get in a helicopter once more. However, when I realized we were headed to Oscad my attitude changed. I had no idea what they had up their sleeve, but this would be the first time I'd be back in my home country in four years.

We landed in the city on the roof of the Oscad Capitol Building, and when I hopped out, I was instantly wrapped up in a double hug with squealing, shrieking girls. The last time I'd seen Tori and Violet, I sent them home with their children. We'd set up a program to help match children with their mothers if the mothers wanted to be reunited. The joy of giving children real homes and parents fulfilled all the needs I had for that part of my life. I wasn't cut out to be a mother. I was a soldier who would spend the rest of her life fighting for everyone's freedom. If I felt the need for a baby fix or to be around children, I would just go to the group home and love on the little ones there who were still looking for families.

"Can you believe it? Here we are in Oscad together again," Violet gushed as she stepped back, clutching her hands to her chest like she was worried her heart would pop out. "You told us we'd see our home again and I never should have doubted you." She grabbed for another hug, rocking me from side to side in her excitement.

"Let her go, you're gonna squeeze her to death," Tori scolded with a laugh. "There's someone else who wants to meet her too."

That made me curious as my two best friends freed me at last, stepping to the side to reveal a woman standing next to Savo. She was stunning, with a heart-shaped face and warm, bright blue eyes with shiny blond hair that had a thick streak of teal right up in front. Her smile made me feel like I'd known her forever, even though I knew we'd never met. Slowly she walked up to me and reached out a hand, yet I already knew who she was so I wrapped her up in a hug.

"Hi, Cambrie," I whispered as she returned my hug just as fiercely. "It's really, really, nice to finally meet you."

"I just knew we'd be best friends the moment we met," she said with a chuckle and pulled back still holding onto my shoulders. "Come on, we have somewhere important to be."

Frowning, I looked from her back to my guys, who all had stupid happy smiles on their faces.

"Let's go, girl. You don't want to be late for this, trust me," Cambrie urged, grabbing my hand and hauling me after her. "Now tell me, did my suggestions for the nest work?"

The house we were now living in was the first one to be built in the new capital city that didn't have a name yet. My guys wanted to surprise me with it and only filled it with the most basic of things so I could design the whole place to my liking. Problem was, I had no idea what I wanted or liked. Stressing out about the situation, Cris brought his mother over, and then we called Cambrie. After that, the three of us planned it out.

"It's so amazing. I think I spent the last two days just napping in my nest. I was so pissed when the guys pulled me out this morning but this is one hundred percent worth it," I shared.

"While you're here, I wanted to show you some things I think you might like. Spencer is brilliant with this stuff too, so I thought we could do a shopping day tomorrow," Cambrie rattled on as we walked through the maze that is the capitol building.

"Um, no one told me how long we were going to be here," I said, trying to keep up with everything she was talking about.

Cambrie stopped in her tracks and faced the guys. "You dragged her out of her nest and all the way here without telling her a *thing*? Shame on you. Did you even pack a bag for her?"

"I did," Cris spoke up as he showed the duffle. "Three days' worth, but I figured you would probably get more while we're here."

My jaw dropped. "How long are we staying?"

"The answer I will give you now is a week," Sorin said. "I will be more specific once we get through tonight."

"What does that mean?" I demanded. "You can't just go around being all cryptic like that."

He chuckled and caught my chin in his grip. "Do you trust me, Dani-girl?"

"Yes..."

"Good, then there's no issue, right?" he teased.

Batting away his hand, I scowled. "Just so you know, you're not sleeping next to me tonight."

"Something tells me you'll think differently later, but I'll take my punishment as long as you take yours," Sorin warned.

Cambrie tried to cover up her laughter, but she was failing miserably. "Oh man, you guys remind me of how my pack must look to people. Now no more interruptions. We have things to do."

The things to do included going to a spa, getting my hair cut, a facial, getting a massage, and getting my makeup done. During this time, the guys went to hang out with the rest of Cambrie's men as Savo watched over us. When my nails were dry, I was escorted to a dressing room where a beautiful silver cocktail dress was waiting for me to change into. Never in my life did I feel more pampered than I did right now. The dress showed off all my marks from my Alphas making it even more special to me.

Leaving the spa, we climbed into a limo where all our guys were already there. Cambrie introduced me to her three men that I hadn't met Oscar, Bodie, and Spencer. It was clear to see just how in love all of them were with her and a few with other members of the pack. It created this warmth that I understood and experienced daily with my pack.

We were so engrossed in conversation that I didn't even look to see where we were until I got out. Taking Petru's hand as he helped me out of the limo, I stood and looked up to find myself in front of my home. Tears instantly burst into my eyes as I took in the familiar features of a place I never thought I'd see again. I tried to pull myself together, covering my mouth with a hand, but then the front door opened and my parents stepped out. Dropping Petru's hand, I ran up the steps to the front door and threw my arms around my mother.

Now we were both sobbing as she clung to me as tightly as I did to her. My father wrapped his arms around us, kissing me on the head as he always did when I was little. "Welcome home, Danella. We've missed you so much."

When I finally stopped crying and got myself together enough, we made it into the house. They escorted us to our front sitting room and I got the chance to introduce my parents to my guys. Seeing the joy on my mother's face as they hugged her and shook hands with my father was priceless. They had tea brought in, and I spent the next hour or so giving the short version of what my life had been like since I left at seventeen.

"Oh, my sweet girl," mother said with a sniff dabbing at her eyes with a hanky. "I hate hearing how hard your life has been and then thinking I died that day. Just makes my heart break hearing about it."

I stood and sat next to my mother on the small couch, grasping her hands. "It was tough, but you raised a daughter who didn't know how to be anything but tough. You showed me every day of my life what true strength was every day you got up and fought to make the most of it. How could I not do the same?"

She burst into tears and pulled me into another hug holding me tightly. "My sweet, sweet girl, so strong and kind, just like I always knew you'd grow up to be."

"You sure you boys are up for the job?" Father asked, making me laugh.

"It's a little late for that, don't you think?" I pointed out.

Father frowned as he looked the guys over. "It's a father's duty to ensure his daughter is given the best life with the best partners. I just want to be sure they are the right ones for the task."

"You're absolutely right, sir," Victor said as he stood. "Which is why I've waited until now to ask this question, but I would like your blessing to marry your daughter."

My jaw dropped as Victor got on one knee. He wasn't looking at me, however. He was waiting for my father's answer. "Son, if you think I actually have a say in who she spends her life with, maybe you aren't the right person for her."

"Honestly, I just wanted to see her reaction to me asking," Victor said with a smirk, turning to me holding up a ring. "Danella Holstad, will you marry me?"

Fighting back tears, I nodded trying to get words out of my mouth and when they did, I couldn't believe what they were. "Fucking took your time, didn't you, Vicky."

He laughed, taking my left hand and kissing the back of it before sliding on the ring. "I wanted this to be a moment that would live in your memory forever. Plus, how could we not have your mother at our wedding?"

"Wait, what?" I blurted, feeling like I had missed something. "We're coming back here to get married?"

"No, Little Spark, we're getting married right now," Victor clarified. "I waited long enough to put my mark on you. Now that I have, there is no more wasting time to make you mine forever."

He tugged me to my feet and opened the outside door to the garden. It was beautifully decorated with twinkle lights and an arch with white, flowing gauze. Out there waiting for us was Rick with his wife Sasha and the rest of their family. Tori and Violet were there too, with the kids grinning like fools. With Cambrie and her men along with my parents, it made up all the people who had impacted my life and the future I would now have. Victor walked me right up to the arch and Marius came to stand before us under the arch facing the rest of the guests.

"Are you ready?" he asked softly. I couldn't speak so I nodded.

Then he proceeded to lead us in one of the most beautiful ceremonies I've ever heard. Full of wisdom, hope, and dreams for the future. It was all I could do not to cry through the whole thing.

"Do you, Danella Holstad, take this man to be your husband?"

"I do," I proclaimed with a confident voice.

"Do you, Victor Hosdeu, take this woman to be your wife?"

"You bet the fuck I do," Victor stated, then pulled me in for a kiss that I felt all the way down to my soul.

Everyone cheered, clapped, and whistled around us, making the moment more special. Victor scooped me up and let out a battle cry as he spun us around making me laugh so hard my stomach hurt. My life had been hell at times, reaching moments where I didn't know how I could go on and still see the good in the world. Then the fates blessed me with these men who healed my heart and made me proud to be an Omega. No longer was I a breeder, a slab of meat for someone to use. I was an equal, my opinion was valued, and I protected those who couldn't protect themselves.

This was the gift I wanted to give back to the world, and we would do it, one dream at a time together as a pack.

The End

About the Author

International Best Seller Elizabeth Knight, has been writing and telling stories as a hobby for years, but wasn't sure it would make a living. After her other job was shut down due to the pandemic she was encouraged to take her writing more seriously. So she published her first reverse harem Discovering Synergy April 2020. Since then Elizabeth has written prolifically and is constantly exploring new genres and ideas, putting her own twist on things. It's incredibly hard work, but she's never been happier than when she sits down at her desk with new imaginary best friends to share with us all.

If you'd like to stay in the know, then sign up for her newsletter:

Sign Up Here
https://geni.us/EKLinks

Also By

Sunshine & Rainbows Omegaverse

<u>Bailey-Rose Duet</u>:

Clouds & Daydreams + Petals & Promises

<u>Lyra Duet</u>

Knot Now Knot Ever + Yes Now Yes Forever

Caprioni Queen - Complete Series

Glitter & Guns

Blood & Heartache

Revenge & Truth

Love & Power

Gun Runner Princess

(Caprioni Queen Spin off)

One For The Money

Two For The Show

Omega Assassin - Complete series

Dual Nature

Hidden Nature

Perfect Nature

Knot All Omegaverse

Knot All Is Lost: Part 1 & Part 2 (Complete)

Knot All Is Ruined: Part 1 & Part 2 (Complete)

Hidden Empire Series - Complete series

Two Tricks

Three Tricks

Four Tricks

More Tricks

Our Tricks

Hidden Empire Novel

(Suggested to be read after Four Tricks)

Harper's Renegades

Standalone Books

Nicolette: Ladies of the MC

Lying Lainey: Underground Omega Syndicate